D1588136

Field of Blood
Harry's Game
Red Fox

Gerald Seymour

Diamond Books
an imprint of HarperCollins*Publishers*,
77–85 Fulham Palace Road,
Hammersmith, London W6 8JB

This Diamond Books Omnibus edition first published 1993
9 8 7 6 5 4 3 2 1
Field of Blood © Gerald Seymour 1985
Harry's Game © Gerald Seymour 1975
Red Fox © Gerald Seymour 1979

ISBN 1 85813 209 6 (UK)
ISBN Diamond Books 0 261 66157 4 (international edition)

Photoset in Linotron Times by Rowland Phototypesetting Ltd,
Bury St Edmunds, Suffolk

Printed in Great Britain by MacKays of Chatham Ltd

Contents

Field of Blood

The author gratefully acknowledges help from many sources in the researching of this novel. For all that it depicts some of the recognisable horrors of life in Belfast, every character in *Field of Blood* is purely fictional.

To Gillian, Nicholas and James

PROLOGUE

It was a good plan. The Chief and his Brigade Officers had worked at it for five weeks.

They knew in which car the target would travel, and which routes his escorts could take between the detached suburban house and the Crown Court. They had the timings on the car, and they knew that all the routes used the same final half mile to the Court buildings.

The weapon was in the city. The weapon and its single projectile were available and waiting. The marksmen were available and waiting. The strike was fixed by the Chief for the Thursday of the following week.

It was a good plan, too good to fail. That it seemed to have failed was a matter of dismal luck, the luck that had haunted the Organization in the last months.

Eammon Dalton and Fran Forde were stopped on the Glen Road at a randomly placed police road block. On another evening the two Volunteers might have carried off the Person Check with indifference, given their names and addresses quietly and calmly, spilled the fictitious every-night story of where they were going, and been cleared and sent on their way. They were heading, when they were waved down, to a final briefing from Brigade. They were nervous and strung taut and they aroused the interest of the heavily armed constables peering down at the two young Catholics' torch-lit faces. Dalton wouldn't speak, and Forde gave, in the heat of the moment, an alias which was found a minute later to differ from the name on his driving licence. Dalton swore as soon as Forde had opened his idiot mouth. At first, of course, the policemen didn't know what they had, but they guessed they had something. Dalton and Forde were pulled out of the car and their hands were spread on the roof and their legs were kicked apart, and they could hear the sergeant feeding the registration of the car into his radio's microphone – and that was bad luck because the car was a Datsun and the plates had been lifted off a Sierra. They were covered by an M1 carbine and a Sterling SMG, and they stayed very still because they knew the policemen would dearly love to have them break and run, and they knew the fingers were stroking the triggers. The report on the plates came back to the sergeant's earpiece and the handcuffs clicked on Eammon Dalton and Fran Forde's wrists. They were hustled to the dark interior of the police landrover.

For these two Volunteers the war was over, for some years at least.

The Chief and his Brigade Operations officer were brought the news of the arrest by courier.

The Chief reflected. The plan was too good to fail just because a piss-arse Volunteer couldn't remember the bloody name on his driving licence. The weapon was good, but bloody damn useless in the fists of a man who hadn't been trained for it. He'd learned how useless this prize weapon was in untrained hands when a projectile had overshot an Army Pig vehicle and blasted a Primary classroom, and when a projectile had missed a Pig and hit the front axle of a coal delivery lorry. Dalton and Forde had been trained to use the weapon. They had had the luxury of test firings in a remote Donegal quarry over the border, into the South.

The plan was too good to waste. He had the weapon, but only one projectile. No bastard could make it work on a live first time firing.

The Brigade Operations officer read his mind.

'I'd do it myself, but . . .'

''Course you would, 'course I would and we'd be lucky to hit a bloody wall, let alone a bloody car.'

'In this city you had two boys only who could use it, both gone . . .'

The frown cut into the Chief's forehead. 'What of the old teams, the old boys who used to be trained on it?'

'One's shot, one's in the Kesh, one's buried for blowing himself away with his own bomb. And one went down South, way back.'

'Could he still fire it?'

'Too right, but he went over the border, quit.'

'Get him,' the Chief said.

'He walked out on us – he was good with it, but he quit on us.'

'Get the fucker back.'

'He could fire it, if we could get him here.'

'It's too good to waste. Get him back.'

1

He rubbed at the condensation on the window and peered out at the slow-moving car.

It was the second time it had cruised past the caravan.

A grey, misted morning. The cloud fog softened the greens of the grass on the canal's bank and brightened the yellows of the collapsing weed beds and darkened the tarmac of the roadway running beside the straight line of the canal. He had first seen the car when the bird had flapped fast away from the perch he had placed for it in the grass. He always fed the bird at that time.

He moved quickly from the end window to the side window and stretched across the small formica-topped table and his stomach wobbled the sauce bottles he had left out for his tea. His fist smeared against the window so that he could better see the car as it went on up the narrow road towards Vicarstown. His vision was obscured by a wild hedgerow but he made out the red flash of the brake lights, and he knew that the car had stopped. He darted back across the caravan and switched off his radio and strained his ears in the new-found quiet. Very faintly he could hear the drive of the car's engine as it turned in the roadway and skidded on the verge beside the canal. He saw the bird, apprehensive in a tree across the water, watching.

Then silence. Only the wheeze of his own breathing. His eyes were against the window. He saw no movement from between the hedgerow branches where the brake lights had shone.

He cursed and hurried the three strides back to the end window of the caravan from which he had first seen the car. He looked both ways up the road and he saw nothing.

He went to the door at the back of the caravan, the end away from the road, and opened the door carefully and looked out over the fields to the squat farmhouse two hundred yards away. Smoke from the chimney climbed straight to the cloud ceiling. No sign of life. Again he strained his ears and heard nothing. He closed the door behind him.

For two years the caravan had been his home. It had a single bunk, a table, a chair, a gas ring, a sink. Behind a curtain near the door was a chemical bucket lavatory. On the wall above the table was a photograph of his wife and one of two of his children. The photographs were fastened to the wall with old, dried out sellotape. His breakfast plate and mug lay in the small sink. Across the width of the caravan, at eye

11

level, hung a string carrying two pairs of pants and some socks and a shirt. Because a cable reached from the farmhouse to the caravan he had the electricity to burn a single-bar fire. The caravan was his home.

He had made out the blurred outline of two men in the front seats each time that the car had passed. He wondered why they waited. Perhaps they worked to a schedule and waited on their watches; perhaps they allowed themselves a cigarette before coming to him.

It was more than a year since he had been visited at the caravan. It had been two detectives then. They'd said they were Crime and he'd known they were Special Branch, and they'd come down from the station at Monasterevan, and they'd looked around and talked gently with him, and said it was only routine, and that if he stayed clean then he'd be left to himself, and that if he went dirty that they'd fucking smash him. The one had looked quietly around the caravan, and the other had spoken with a twinkling eye and a soft Cork brogue. Alright for a Belfast man to live down south, but Jesus had he better be clean . . . Because if he was dirty, if he was Provo dirty, then he was in a heap of shit. And they'd shaken his hand, and called him by his first name and closed the door behind them and gone on their way. He had been clean before they came to the caravan, and clean ever since.

That was the last time that the young kestrel bird had been frightened away at feeding time.

He rubbed again at the window, and tried to see the car and could not.

It was two years since he had taken up the offer of the caravan on the farm of his mother's cousin. The cousin lived on his own, and didn't look for a stranger's company. There was the caravan at the end of the lane, beside the roadway, and it was available for a distant relative who was a refugee from the north. In the summer if there was hay to be cut then he helped, or if there was repair work to be done on a roof of an out-house then he would do it. Mostly weeks went by and he only saw the old man at a distance across the fields. It was a lonely life and Christ for all that it was better than the life he had lived before two years back. Only on a Saturday evening would he take the bicycle into Vicarstown and drink some stout in a bar. He knew that his accent betrayed his origins and wondered what the local men said of him. He was lonely because he did not seek the locals' company, nor was he given it. When he drank he'd have a plastic carrier bag beside his knee that was filled with sliced loaves and packets of margarine and a pound of rashers and a pound of sausages. He took his milk from the farm, he took his money from a Thursday morning ride to Monasterevan and the 'brew' from the Post Office.

The bird was his only companion. The farmer had taken the fledgeling kestrel from an abandoned nest a month after he had come to the caravan, and fed it on bread and milk and meat scraps to maturity. The bird wasn't tame, not so it could be touched, but it nested within sight of the farmhouse and the caravan, and it came most days for food. He

12

talked to the bird, softly so as not to frighten it, and it had his bacon rind and slices of raw sausage. The bird wasn't a prisoner, no clipped wings, no thongs. The bird was free, as he was free since he had come to the new life two years back.

He loved the bird.

Before he had come south he couldn't have imagined himself as pansy enough to love a pink-tailed kestrel bird. He loved his wife, too, but she was in Belfast. The kestrel bird was with him, and was all the company he had.

Through the window of the caravan he heard the dulled bang and knew it was the slamming of a car door.

If his wife had travelled south with him then he might possibly have wriggled a lasting escape from the life of before two years back, but she said there was no way she was going to exist in a soddin' field. She said Belfast was bad but it's where it's familiar. He'd told her it was a mobile home they could live in, she said it was a soddin' caravan, and no place for the wee ones. She said she'd prefer to be with her Ma and her Da, and his mates and her friends, and not hidin' in a soddin' bog down south. She said she knew why he'd gone, because he had to go, she don't think the less of him for going. He went back three times the first year, four times the second year. Back to Belfast to be with her, to be with the kids. He hadn't been for two months, but he'd be back up with her and the kids for Christmas. He often had the radio on inside the caravan, and when the reporters broadcast of house searches and lifts and aggro and shootings in the area where his wife lived, where his kids were, where his Ma and Da were, where her Ma and Da were, then he would suffer a little in his helplessness. But she always said that she understood why he had gone away. She never blamed him. Christ, it would have been easier if she had.

He wiped once more at the window glass. There were two men walking up the centre of the road towards the caravan.

He saw their pale town faces. The taller man wore a cap and the shorter man's hair was long to his shoulders and his beard covered his throat. The taller man bent and picked a stone off the side of the road and threw it hard and high into the tree where the bird perched and watched the bird fly swiftly away. He grinned as if it pleased him that he had disturbed a picture that had been at peace. The kestrel flew frightened away down the length of the canal. The shorter man retched and coughed and spat and dropped a half-used cigarette into the road where it burned on after he had walked past. They came to the hole that was cut in the hedgerow.

He saw them cock their ears, he saw them turn their heads and swivel their eyes down the road in front of them and behind them.

There was no weapon in the caravan. Weapons were Belfast. He had no need of a weapon to keep him safe in a caravan beside the canal near Vicarstown. The taller man's jaw was cartwheeling as he chewed

13

at a mouthful of gum. When they were satisfied they came fast through the hole in the hedge. They crossed the long grass that bordered the vegetable patch square that he had dug out in the summer. He saw the grimace of annoyance from the taller man as the wet grass splayed over his shoes. He grew the vegetables for the old man in the farm to sell to the store in Vicarstown, lettuce in the spring, carrots and parsnips now that it was winter. He saw that they said not a word to each other, and nor did they look up at his face in the caravan window.

He knew it would come and yet he was jolted upright by the rap at the caravan door. His eyes closed. His teeth bit on his lip, and he felt a moment of pain. He dragged a gulp of air down into his chest. He stared at the door, and he saw the inexact outline of the two heads beyond the glaze glass.

The shorter man was standing on the step and was lighting a cigarette and smiled as the door was opened. The taller man showed no visible expression.

'Yes?' He tucked the thumb of one hand into his belt, and the other hand was in his trouser pocket. The strangers should not see the tremble in his fingers.

'McAnally?' The shorter man spoke with the raw accent of West Belfast. 'Are you McAnally?'

'Yes.'

'Sean Pius McAnally?'

'Yes.'

And your home, up there, is 63 The Drive in Turf Lodge . . . ?'

'What have you come for?' He snarled the question because that way his nerves were hidden from them. He disliked them because they had frightened him. He was not a man who should easily have been frightened. No man who had led an Active Service Unit in Turf Lodge, Ballymurphy and Whiterock would admit to fear.

'Easy, boy.' The taller man spoke.

'Come to take you back,' the shorter man said.

'Better talked about inside, pissing cold out here,' the taller man said.

'Nobody tells me where I'm going.'

'Like he said, easy . . .' The shorter man smiled a second time.

McAnally stood aside from the door, made way for the two men to climb up into the caravan. Suddenly the inside of the caravan was crowded, bursting. It was his place of refuge, and it was invaded. They looked around them, they stripped the privacy from the walls. In turn they bent to look at the photographs, at the sink, at the curtain that hid the chemical lavatory seat. The taller man leaned his bottom against the table-edge. The shorter man sat on the chair and stretched out his legs. McAnally closed the door.

'What do you want?'

'What I said . . .' The shorter man dragged far down on his cigarette,

14

went to the door, threw the stub outside, coughed and spat, shut the door, went back to the chair. 'What I said, come to take you back.'

'Who says?'

'It's what we've been told, take you back.'

McAnally thought they might as well have crapped on his floor, on the linoleum, or they might have pissed on his walls, on the photographs. Between the two of them they suffocated the privacy of his refuge, the privacy of the caravan.

'What's your name?' McAnally asked the shorter man.

There was a smile without amusement, without pity. 'You've been away too long . . . we don't like names.'

McAnally laughed, shrill, excited. 'Because you're all riddled with touts. Weren't any touts in my time.'

'Your time's not done, Gingy,' the taller man said.

McAnally rocked slightly on the balls of his feet. That was his name when he was in the war. He was always called 'Gingy'. All the men liked a name that was short and sharp and familiar. All the men had their nicknames. Ducksy and Cruncher and Puffer and Bronco and Buster and Bluey and Fitzy and . . . He was Gingy because the moustache that was now shaved away had once been redder than his hair. He was Gingy in the Turf Lodge, and Gingy in the A.S.U. He had been Gingy for five years in the Long Kesh prison camp, and Gingy in the Remand Wing of the Crumlin Road gaol. Gingy was his name before two years back.

'Who wants me back?'

'The Chief wants you back.' The shorter man grinned. There was a gap in his front upper teeth. Now that the shorter man wasn't smoking, McAnally could smell his breath and his armpits. 'You won't be asking his name?'

McAnally said softly, 'And what it's for . . . ?'

'We wouldn't know, would we? Cop on, Gingy. You'll be told when you've come back.'

'I'm out, I quit.'

'You took an oath, you swore your oath,' the taller man said.

Eleven years before Sean Pius McAnally had made his oath to the Organization. He had made it in his own home. They couldn't use the front room because his Da was watching telly, couldn't use the kitchen because his Ma was dishing the supper. He had made his oath on the upstairs landing, and they'd all had to whisper because his sister was trying to get her baby to sleep in the back bedroom. He had made his oath, he had offered his allegiance to the Provisional wing of the Irish Republican Army.

'An oath's an oath. An oath's a lifetime,' the smaller man said.

'An oath doesn't get torn up just because a boy wants to sit on his arse in the south . . . and let others do what the boy swore to do himself,' the taller man said, and McAnally had to lean forward and strain to hear the words.

An oath whispered on the landing of a three-bedroomed Housing Executive semi-detached. An oath made while a sister crooned to a baby, while the telly blared a comedy, while Ma crashed the saucepans.

'We're wasting time, Gingy,' the smaller man said.

McAnally wondered if they were armed. Didn't matter, because there were two of them. And two of them could wreck him, and wreck the caravan. As he stared into their faces his thoughts were totally lucid. If he expelled them from the caravan, if he damaged them, then they'd be back, and others would be back. The smaller man lit another cigarette and looked into McAnally's face and then down at the dead match in his fingers and dropped it onto the linoleum. They were squatting over him, crapping on him, pissing on him. He shrugged.

'I'm not promising anything.'

'You're not being asked to promise anything,' the taller man said. 'You're being told to obey an order from Belfast Brigade.'

McAnally crossed to the bunk, stepping over the outstretched legs of the shorter man, insinuating himself past the taller man. He crouched down and reached into the space underneath the mattress for a canvas grip bag. There was always a pain in his right knee when he bent low where the rubber bullet had ricocheted up from the pavement in the Motorman fight. He winced, and stood up. He collected the clothes from the drying line and folded them into his bag.

'If they want me, then it's something special,' McAnally said to the taller man. He looked him in the face, eye to eye. 'If they want me then it's for a job that's too big for the likes of you fuckers.'

He thought the man would have liked to belt him. He watched his fingers tighten on the seams of his jeans. The shorter man was making a play of grinding his cigarette out on the linoleum as McAnally zipped up the bag.

'All I hear on the radio down here is about the touts up there . . . Am I safe from touts if I go back with you?'

The taller man shouted, 'You call me a tout, McAnally, and I'll break your neck. You can be a fucking Battalion Officer, a fucking Brigade Officer, you call me a tout, I'll break your fucking neck.'

McAnally saw the sweat on his forehead. 'No one ever informed in my day. You could beat the shit out of a man, and he never told. Whatever the 'tecs did in Castlereagh and Gough and Strand, a man never touted . . .'

'Touting isn't something you make a crack about,' the shorter man said, and the smile was gone from the white chubbiness of his cheeks.

'I want to go up to the farm.'

'What for?'

'To see the old man.'

'To tell him you're going back to Belfast, to tell him the boys came to fetch you back to Belfast?' The sneer of the shorter man.

The taller man asked, 'What have you to tell him?'

16

McAnally hesitated. He would have told his Ma's cousin that he'd be away for a few days, that the kestrel needed feeding. He couldn't tell them that, not these bastards. He shrugged.

'Doesn't matter,' he muttered.

From the hook behind the door McAnally lifted down his anorak, slid his arms into the sleeves.

'Will I see my wife?'

'You'll be dropped there tonight,' the taller man hissed.

McAnally unplugged the electric fire, and then the connection to the single bulb that hung down from the ceiling. He took what remained of a loaf and a packet of margarine and the bacon and the sausages from the one cupboard and handed them to the shorter man to hold.

When they were out of the caravan he busied himself fastening the padlock on the door, and then they walked together through the gap in the hedge and onto the road. They let McAnally walk in front, as if they were an escort to him. From the roadway he threw the margarine and the bread into the grass by the canal, and the bacon and the short string of sausages to the place where the kestrel fed. He reckoned the bird could peck into the margarine carton.

It was mild and there was a fleck of rain in the air and already the light was sliding over the bare-branched elm trees that were mirrored in the canal.

They went up the road, towards the rusted Cortina that was parked flush to the hedge.

McAnally looked around him, into the still canal and into the thin stretching roadway and into the small fields and into the deep blanket of cloud. He saw the kestrel a long way off, watching from a diseased elm branch. He stared back one last time at the roof of the caravan. He remembered when he had decided to quit the Organization and go south. He climbed into the back of the car and slumped against the seat and closed his eyes and heard the gunning of the engine.

The taller man drove. Going north and three hours to Belfast. Three hours for Sean Pius McAnally to reflect that two years of escape was gone.

He was born into the Falls, screamed his first baby shouts in the front bedroom of a brick terraced house that was without a bathroom, without a flushing lavatory. His eldest sister helped the mid-wife with the delivery.

The early memories were of the van that came to move the cheap furniture from the old decay of the Falls to the new decay of Turf Lodge. Turf Lodge was a sprawl of a housing estate out to the west of the city of Belfast, and well away from any comparable Protestant housing estate. The memory of the loaded van competed with the memory of his father coming back to the new house in Turf Lodge within a week of the move, and his father's lip was bleeding and his front lower teeth were missing

17

or chipped, and the scurrying words between mother and father were of intimidation and that the buggers said they wouldn't have a Taig working in a Prot butchers. The memories slid easily into the groove of a father who sat the days away in front of a fireplace that burnt scavenged wood, a father who no longer believed in the possibility of work. The memories drifted through a three-bedroomed house that was home for a family of Ma and Da and five sisters and Sean Pius McAnally. The memories eddied into the wearing of a cast-off blazer carrying the badge of St Peter's Secondary School, Whiterock Road, a good walk from Turf Lodge but Ma liked the priests there, and of the misery of homework in the quiet of the box bathroom that was the pride of a Turf Lodge house; a bloody waste of time, that homework, because there wasn't work after school for half of the St Peter's leavers. Gone from school at sixteen, and no exams passed – exams were for the Protestants in their Academies and Institutions, exams weren't for kids from Turf Lodge.

Those were the distant memories. Sharper were the memories of the times since the war began.

He was recruited when he left school. The second year of the war.

At first the stoning and the petrol bombing of the Pig armoured cars that patrolled Turf Lodge, the night watch at the end of the Drive and the Avenue and the Parade with the whistle in his hand and ready to blow the warning if the foot patrols came through. Aged seventeen he had seen his first soldier die. A file of soldiers, spaced and on both sides of the Drive, patrolling in Turf Lodge. One echoing crack of the Armalite, one belt from the widow maker. The teenage boy had joined the other teenage boys and the teenage girls of the Drive as they chanted at the tops of their voices 'If you see a Brit soldier die, clap your hands, clap your hands, if you see a Brit soldier die . . .', and he had hated the boy whose blood was spilling in the road's gutter, and he had loathed the bitter-faced troops who bent over the boy and who trained their rifles on the crowd. And he had worshipped the unknown man who had fired the single shot.

When things in Turf Lodge were hot then Sean Pius McAnally, the teenager, was on the streets. When they were cold he was lounging on the street corner, or flopped in the chair by the fire at home, always bored when it was cold, always restless.

Two days after his twentieth birthday, ten long years ago now, when he was combing his hair in the bedroom that he shared with two of his sisters, when he was thinking about his supper, when he was wondering how far he would get with Roisin O'Rourke behind the garages when it was dark, two men came to offer Sean Pius McAnally membership of the Organization and the rank of Volunteer in the movement. The oath on the upstairs landing. A binding oath, an oath of a lifetime. Onto an A.S.U., a member of the new cell system. Into action against the Brits and the pig police. Quick learner, wasn't he? No bloody exams at school, but good with the American M16 rifle. His eyes were quality,

18

and his hands were steady, and he was told that if he kept going well they'd give him a job with the sniper gun, with the Remington Woodmaster M742. He had money now from rolled banks and held-up Post Offices and a twenty-first birthday wedding to Roisin O'Rourke, and a week's screwing, and back to Belfast and her Ma's small bedroom, and the first time out with the Remington Woodmaster. She was a great girl, his Roisin, a great kid, and the crack in the Drive was that he was one hell of a lucky bugger to have had her.

Crystal-clear memories now. Memories of a road block manned by the fucking Fusiliers with the fairy pom-poms on their berets, of the driver spinning the wheel, of the rifle shots impacting into the driver, of the North of England voices yelling commands, of crawling out of the car with his hands held high. Memories of the Castlereagh Interrogation Centre, and of the beatings. Memories of not touting, of enduring the pain. Memories of the trial at the Crumlin Road Court House, and of a judge in red robes who looked down on him as if he were a bad smell. Memories of the H blocks, and of the stink of the shit protest, and of the weapons classes in Long Kesh. Memories of mastering the theory of the R.P.G.-7 rocket launcher that was armour-piercing and death to the Pigs and the Saracens and the reinforced landrovers. Memories of crying his frustration at the cell walls because he would have to wait to use the rocket against the bastards.

Memories that were fresh as yesterday, of release, of handling the R.P.G.-7, of firing it three times in fourteen months, of seeing the devastation on the telly news, of watching a funeral on the evening round-up. Two more kids conceived in the trembling aftermath of a firing. Targets getting harder, police Intelligence getting better. The R.P.G. wasn't fired from behind a wall, the R.P.G. had to be lined up, aimed, held firm. The risk getting worse, the chance of success getting poorer.

Memories of the day that was a sledgehammer, the day that a Volunteer in the Turf Lodge was turned, became a grass, touted on the rest of his A.S.U. Shit, that day was sharp in his memories. Not Sean Pius McAnally's A.S.U. . . . If it had been his A.S.U. then he would have been away to the Kesh as a lifer. No fucking way, not him doing a life stretch. He hadn't asked their permission, he had told them he was going. He didn't reckon a man who was expert in the use of an R.P.G. needed to get bloody permission.

Memories of the first week in the caravan. Memories of lying in the narrow bunk bed and knowing that he was safe, knowing that the life sentence in the Kesh was another bugger's and not his own, and of the day when he had first coaxed the bird onto the grass beside the caravan door, and it had plucked at the bacon strip.

All the memories of the times before he quit.

*

19

They had come across country to join the main road north of Drogheda, then through Dundalk and over the border where the Customs men of both the Republic and the North were warm in their huts, and up the fast drag to Belfast.

Off the motorway at Stockman's Lane, up Kennedy Way, over the roundabout and onto the Glen Road. He felt pleasure coursing in him as the car took him closer to Roisin, and to Young Gerard and Little Patty and Baby Sean. He sat hunched forward with his arms tight across his chest, and he was smiling. The sight of a soldier crouched with his rifle at his shoulder in a garden gateway was momentary.

They were past the church, towering in the darkness, short of the Andersonstown R.U.C. station, almost onto their turn-off left into Turf Lodge, when they came to the road block.

McAnally shivered. He always shivered and sweated at a road block, and would do to his dying day after what had happened at the block eight years before. The soldier he had seen in the gateway was positioned to pick up those who spun to make an escape. The taller man, the driver, would have heard the spurts of McAnally's breathing, he gave McAnally a single sharp glance, then was changing down through his gears, feeling the brake pedal.

'Easy, Gingy, nothing to fret on, the plates are clean,' the shorter man said quietly.

They had stopped. They waited their turn in the short queue of cars. The soldiers were as young as the one spitting towards death while McAnally had sung his triumph thirteen years before, as young as the constable who had been killed in the flame-flash of the R.P.G. missile three years before, as young as the soldier blinded by a missile's shrapnel two years before. The soldiers were young and cold and bored.

He watched their faces. He saw the roving of their eyes. He saw the rainwater dribbling on their cheeks. He knew the wicked hitting power of their rifles.

A corporal bent down to shine his torch on the number plate of the car, and then he straightened and spoke into his radio. He was feeding the computer at headquarters. McAnally sat very still. He peered at the corporal who walked a slow circle with the radio held against his ear, waiting on the computer.

From the corner of his eye, McAnally saw the face that was now close against the rear door window. A different face, firmer and stronger than the faces of the young soldiers. He saw the embroidered pips of a first lieutenant on the shoulder flaps. He saw a quick brittle smile that the lieutenant aimed at him. He responded without thinking. Meaningless, short smiles. The lieutenant's face was daubed in dark cream. McAnally saw the flash of ordered white teeth, he saw the dark hair that lay underneath the beret, he saw the eyes that beaded on him and stripped him.

20

'Clear, Mr Ferris . . .' the shout from the corporal.

The lieutenant stepped back from the car. He nodded to the driver. 'Have a good evening, gentlemen.'

The car surged forward, then went left into Norfolk Parade. McAnally was twisted round, staring through the back window of the car.

'Smug shits . . .'

The shorter man laughed. 'You'll get your chance, Gingy. That's what we brought you back for, so you'll have the chance to damage the smug shits.'

The taller man spoke softly. 'You'll hear when you're wanted.'

The car had stopped. He had come home. The lights were on upstairs at Number 63. He could hear a baby crying. He walked towards the front door and did not look back as the car drove away.

2

He was on his back and he was asleep and again he screamed his protest.

'I won't do it . . . you can't tell me . . . I'm outside, you can't make me . . .'

Roisin lay awake on her side, her back to him. After the first and the second time she had cuddled him and tried to comfort his torture and had lulled him back to a calmer sleep. She could see the clock beside her head and knew that she had another hour before she must get up and begin preparing Young Gerard for school.

'You've no fucking right to tell me what I have to do . . . I'm not having my fucking arse shot off just on your say-so . . .'

The bed heaved as he bellowed his dreaming fear around the small front bedroom. She could smell the sweat scent that his stomach had spread on her belly when he had loved her earlier in the night; when he had loved her before sleeping, before dreaming, before screaming.

'Find some other bugger, I've done my time, let another bugger share what I've done . . .'

To Roisin her marriage to Sean Pius McAnally was a miracle of survival. When he was over her, covering her, pounding her, then she could play at a fantasy that her life was a kingdom, that she was a queen. To her Ma the fantasy was a lie, to his Ma the marriage was catastrophe. Her husband, the king in her realm, had never worked in his life and now lived in a dirty caravan box away from her. He was a stranger who came back in a guilty blurt of excuses to share her bed in the leaking house provided by the Housing Executive. He could be no

21

support to her, not now that he had run, nor before when he had been active, nor before that when he had been locked away in the Kesh. The support for her existence and the life of her children came from the Green Cross donations for prisoners' dependents, from the occasional charity of the Organization if she showed a favour to a big man, from the Social Security and the Supplementary Benefit and the Children's Allowances. Only a dribble of Republic bank notes came in the post from the letters marked Monasterevan. From the start the marriage had been a disaster to her Ma and his Ma . . . A week on the seafront at Bray in the south's County Wicklow in a guest house where they reckoned they were doing you a favour if they made the room up before lunch, and where it had rained on each and every one of the six days, and where he had humped her so frequently that he had run out of the Johnnies by the fourth night and not known how to replace his stock in good old Catholic Twenty-six County Ireland, and got her in the family way on the fifth or the sixth night. And on the seventh morning in the hotel, the morning they were leaving, the dawn they were going back to Belfast, that morning and that dawn the bastard Special Branch had paid a call. In the first early morning light, three SB men had crowded into the tiny bedroom that was a double and a wardrobe and two chairs and hardly more room for a cat to stand upright. The SB men had taught her that they were of the same breed as the Northern peelers, that a fighter for the unity of Ireland was as much a piece of dirt to a Republic policeman as he was to a Six County policeman. There had been a brusque, thorough, intimidating search of their two bags, the spilling out of her new underwear, and her in tears and him never opening his mouth. A marriage that started with the stamp of disaster, and gone on as a disaster when he was lifted at the road block one week after their return, and yet she loved him.

She had loved him through the months of taking the prison bus through the morning sickness, and through the bulging pregnancy . . .

'You can't fucking order me to do it, that's fucking suicide what you're saying . . .'

She had loved him through five years of taking the prison bus with a pram, with a push chair, with a toddler, with a growing boy who did not understand why his father was always on the far side of a heavy wood table, why a man in uniform and a shined peak cap stood at the side with his arms folded and contempt smirking his lips. A small boy going to his first Infant school, and coming home and chorusing in a tinkling parrot voice, 'Is my Da a Provo? The priest says the Provos have spat on Jesus, has my Da done that?' To Roisin McAnally, née O'Rourke, there was no disaster, only a strengthening love, and his Ma told her she was bloody mad.

She did not turn her head. She hissed into the pillow. 'Don't bloody tell me you're not going to do it, tell whoever's bloody asking you. If you're outside, then you're outside, don't tell me, tell them. If you didn't want to do it then why did you bloody come back?'

She felt him heave, and the bed shook, as if he convulsed in waking. She heard the new panting speed of his breath. He would be lying on his back, he would be staring up at the dark ceiling. Perhaps the bugger could make out the damp patch in the right-hand far corner. The day he had come home she had spent four hours with her children in tow trying to interest the Housing Executive in the damp patch in the ceiling. Some bastard manager with a house in Dunmurry and a salary and a pension scheme who didn't give a shit that a front bedroom in Turf Lodge had water running from the ceiling of the front bedroom.

'Did I wake you?' He spoke gently.

'Me and half the bloody street.'

'I'm sorry, love . . . must have been dreaming.'

'Bloody nightmaring, more likely.'

He took her shoulder and pulled her down onto her back and his hands were warm on the flesh of her thighs and the skin of her small slack breasts.

He hadn't used anything the night before, he'd said the machine down in the Bar's jacks was broken. The bloody priests who said you shouldn't use anything, they didn't know what it was like to be dropping kids. A bit of labour pain wouldn't be lost on *them* . . . She laughed out loud. She saw in her mind a flash picture of Father Mulvaney lying on a bed on his back with his spindle legs up round his ears, groaning in delivery agony.

He'd stopped.

'Not at you, Sean, wasn't laughing at you . . .'

She put her hand over his hand, the hand was down at her thighs. She usually guided him. He was always a bit fumbling when he came back from the bloody caravan, so she knew he hadn't a woman down there . . . If he would only cut his nails . . . He loved her, she knew that. What ever he'd done, why ever he'd gone south, when ever he came back, she knew that he loved her. She had other men, not often, not out of habit, only occasionally when the loneliness was too great to bear. Just sometimes she needed a man, just needed a body with no strings and no one beside her when she woke in the morning afterwards. The children were hers, more than they were his. His kids wouldn't tell their Da that sometimes a man stayed late. She hoped he didn't know.

'What did they want you to do?'

His second day back two men had come to the house. She had been doing the kids' tea, beans and toast and a mug of Bovril. They'd gone upstairs with Sean. They'd have sat on her bed, and after they'd gone, when she went up to bed there was the smell of cigarettes in her bedroom and ash on the floor. She'd heard the raised voices.

'Something big . . . Shit, that's lovely . . . I said I wouldn't.'

23

'Because of me, that wasn't why you said you wouldn't?'

She blamed him for nothing. If the house leaked then that was the fault of the Brits who refused to come and repair it. If her man hadn't work then that was the fault of the Brits who wouldn't provide employment for the work force in the Nationalist housing estates. If Sean Pius McAnally was in the Provos then that was the fault of the Brits for putting their fucking soldiers on the streets of Turf Lodge and the 'Murph and Andy'town, and Whiterock. She would have thought the less of her man if he had not been in the Organization. She had nagged him once into going for a job at the De Lorean, and he'd been taken on, just after coming out of the Kesh, and the day he should have started he'd chucked it and gone with the A.S.U. – that was somebody's fault, not her man's fault.

'It wouldn't be because of me that you said you wouldn't?'

She was glowing, she was wet. His hand was strong, good, brilliant. She had never argued when he'd said that he was going south. He'd sat that night, more than two years before, on the end of the bed and he had said that if he stayed he was either dead or he was in for a 'lifer'. He'd said that after a time any man had the right to quit. He'd said that staying alive and staying free was luck, that a man in an A.S.U. used up his store of luck. The bloody Brits with their army and their police and terror gangs of SAS murderers would take him. He'd said he wasn't a coward, he'd said he was just being smart. He'd said that some other bugger should do his turn. She hadn't blamed him.

His chin was on her shoulder, the nipple of her breast was swollen hard between his fingers, his lips were beside her ear.

'Not because of you. Perhaps it should be, but it's not.'

'Why won't you do what they ask?'

'Shit, I don't mind helping . . . What they want isn't helping, it's fucking kamikaze . . . Fuck, you're lovely . . .'

The bed sang as he climbed onto her, spread her, wriggled inside her.

Baby Sean had begun to cry, a clear sharp wail through the thin partition wall. Young Gerard was shouting at Baby Sean to shut his face. Young Gerard was the son of the night's loving in the hours before the southern SB came to the honeymoon room in Bray. Little Patty and Baby Sean were both conceived after he had run the risk of standing clear on a street corner to aim the R.P.G. at a Pig or at an armoured landrover. After that the risk of getting Roisin in family had seemed pathetic, unimportant. Baby Sean crying and Young Gerard shouting at him.

She pushed him off her. She swung out of the bed and he saw the gleam of damp on her legs. He lay on his back. He thought he saw tears in her eyes. She went out of the bedroom and through the wall he heard her speak to Young Gerard and croon to Baby Sean. She

24

came back into the bedroom and laid the baby in the crook of her husband's arm. She started to dress.

'So you've said you won't do it, so what's going to happen?'

'I'm to be taken to see a man.'

'What man?'

'The Chief.'

'And when he asks you to do it, what'll you say?'

'I don't know,' he said.

'I'll make some tea.'

She wore jeans and a sweater and she was shivering in the chilled room as she pulled on her socks. She combed her hair perfunctorily, rich and lovely black hair that fell to her shoulders. She was tall, as tall as him, and he thought she was beautiful. He was blind to the worry bags under her eyes and the pallor of her cheeks. She kissed him on the forehead and went out of the bedroom and down the stairs. He heard her stumbling in the darkness of the downstairs front room for the packet and her first cigarette of the day. Beside him Baby Sean gurgled in delight and tugged at his Da's hair.

He had had bread and jam for breakfast and more tea, and he had cleared his pockets of Republic currency that his wife would change at the bank in the Andersonstown parade, and he was listening to the radio news, when the knock came at the door.

Not much on the radio, a quiet night it had been in the war. Three aimed shots at an army patrol in the Derry Bogside, all missed. An R.U.C. constable cops on that there's a bomb under his car when he does his morning check, defused. Waste of fucking effort . . . The boy at the door was straight out of school. Roisin stood at the bottom of the stairs and watched.

'In thirty minutes, Mister, you're to be on the corner of Westrock Gardens and the Parade. You'll be told then where to go.'

The boy didn't wait for an answer.

'Is you going out, Da? Can I come?' Young Gerard stood behind his mother, and two stair steps higher.

'It's a school day, 'course you can't go with your Da.'

McAnally took his anorak from the hook behind the door.

'You won't be knowing when you'll be back?' his wife asked.

'No.'

McAnally went out through the door, pulled it noisily shut behind him. The wind caught his face and he felt the light rain on his cheeks. He should never have come back, but he had not known how to refuse. His hands were buried deep in his anorak pockets, chin down on his chest.

His home might be a caravan in a soddin' field down south, but it was better than Turf Lodge. He saw the decay of the pavement and the roadway of the Drive; he saw damp rotted windowframes of the houses, he saw the neglect in the overgrown front gardens. The house in the Drive in Turf Lodge was a prison when set against the freedom of his caravan in a field beside the canal at Vicarstown. There were no trees here for his companion the kestrel. At the far end of the Drive he saw the foot patrol approaching, four on each pavement, moving warily. He saw the hackles on their berets, and thought it an act of insolence by the soldiers to wear the red and white feathers that would make a splash of colour for a sniper to aim at. He had never wondered where the soldiers hailed from, whether they had been kids in another faraway rotting estate that was no different to Turf Lodge. He had never imagined the soldiers as being anything other than cold bastards in uniform with a Self Loading Rifle tight in their khaki-gloved fists. He knew that sometimes the soldiers were frightened, that sometimes they were arrogant; he knew that always the soldiers were his enemy. A woman came out of Number 11, and was pushing a pram and had three more kids with her. She set off towards the patrol and when she came to the lead soldier she walked straight on as if he didn't exist. The soldier hesitated and made room for her. The woman didn't see the soldier, nor the other three behind him, and she walked straight ahead, and the last soldier in the stick gave her a sign that wasn't for victory, but he stepped out of her way.

As McAnally walked down the slope of the Drive, he closed on the approaching patrol. The soldiers had a stuttering movement. Jogging, crouching, lying flat and splayed in the aim position, up again and sprinting. Trying to create an absence of a pattern. Sniping wasn't McAnally's job, never had been, so he reckoned it wouldn't have been easy to take one of them out, difficult to bead on the ducking, bobbing, weaving figures. He took his cue from the woman with the pram. He passed the first soldier without a glance. He stared straight in front of him. He smelled the stale damp sweat of the soldier play at his nose.

'You, here . . .'

McAnally heard the officer's command. Bastard Brit officers always had the same voice, always bloody shouted. He thrust his hands deeper into his pockets and walked on. The second soldier in the line was bent low against a lamp post. His face never turned to McAnally as he covered the roof-tops and the upper windows of the street. The soldier spoke from the side of his mouth. North country England, and a snarl from the side of his mouth.

'You. Fart face. My officer's calling you.'

McAnally stopped, looked around him. The officer was on the other side of the Drive, standing with his arms folded, waiting for him. The soldiers in the patrol had scattered and taken cover. The officer carried a rifle. He was distantly familiar to McAnally.

'Here, please . . .' A voice of authority. McAnally bit at his lip, and started across the roadway.

The officer looked at him. Not hostile, just careful. Examined him.

'My name's Ferris, Bravo Company 2 R.R.F. My platoon works Turf Lodge . . . I don't know you.'

'Sean McAnally.'

'Roisin McAnally, of 63 . . .'

'That's my wife.'

'And where are you when you're not at home, Mr McAnally?'

'Down south.'

He remembered the name and he remembered the face. The road block of two nights before. McAnally shivered, his breath was spewing in front of his face. Under his tunic and his flak jacket Ferris wore a heavy knit sweater. Bastard would be warm enough. Bastard wouldn't be hurrying.

'Work down south?'

'Kind of.'

'I hope you'll be able to stay with us till Christmas, be nice for the lady and the children.'

'Suppose it would.'

'It's a cold morning, Mr McAnally. You should have wrapped up better. Nice to have met you . . .'

The officer, Ferris, walked on. The patrol materialized from their hiding places. McAnally set off again for the end of the Drive. He loathed himself for his fear, and the bastard officer had seen it and had cracked his little private joke about a cold morning. When he turned round the patrol had almost reached the bend in the Drive.

On his way to his rendezvous he went past the barricade at the Andersonstown R.U.C. station. Shit, the place had been well drubbed since he had been active. Smashed up and patched. Dirty, shitty place behind the screens and the wire netting and the concrete sentry boxes and the high tin gates. The wire netting was for him. The wire netting was to explode the armour-piercing charge of a rocket propelled grenade.

But he had said no to the men who had come to his house to get him back into the Organization. And because he had said no, he was on his way to meet with the Chief, with the Commander of the Belfast Brigade.

He walked past the sentry box. He wondered if it was a rifle or a stub-barrelled carbine that covered him from behind the aiming slits. It was one thing to turn down a messenger. It was a different thing to spit in the face of the Chief.

The gates of the Milltown cemetery on his right were open wide. Inside were the stones, and far away on the reverse slope and hidden by the stones of crosses and Jesuses and Marys was the Republican plot. That's where they all were, in that plot, all the Volunteers and the Company Officers and the Battalion Officers and the Brigade Officers, all the martyrs of the Organization. He knew what the Brit squaddies called it, they called Milltown the 'home for retired gunmen'. Fucking

27

young, weren't they, all the boys in the Republican plot. Sean Pius McAnally hadn't wanted to join them, so he'd run down south. He still didn't want to keep them company, but he was going to see the Chief. Hands deep in his pockets, chin hard on his chest, cold, and shivering.

Half way up the Whiterock Drive he saw ahead of him the boy who smoked and sat on the bonnet of a car. He reckoned the boy was twelve or thirteen years old, and he was wearing the local uniform of close-cut hair, a windcheater and jeans and high laced 'Docs'. He reckoned the boy four or five years older than Young Gerard. The bugger was playing truant. He wondered whether his Gerard would be running messages for the Organization in four or five years. And if in four or five years his son was out of class and on a street corner for the Provos, then would his Da be shouting? Like father, like son. And if his son grew up and shot a Brit, or smashed a peeler, then would his Da be shaking his head and telling him 'Fucking well done, boy'? He wondered what future his son had that was beyond the walls of the Kesh and the stones of the Milltown cemetery. He didn't think like that often, only when he was down. But a man who had blinded a Brit and taken out a constable could hardly cuff his son on the ear if the kid wanted to follow his father into the Organization.

McAnally saw the frank admiration in the boy's eyes. He felt better, stronger.

'Into Westrock Gardens, take the left, on the left-hand side the second from the end.'

'Thanks.'

The boy grinned, pleased, and ran. McAnally saw that he had a school bag with him. Shit, couriering for the Provos before playground time. He saw Young Gerard's face and bit the flesh of his thumb to shift the pain.

The door of the small red-brick house was opened for him by a grandmother. She was old enough to be a grandmother, and in the hall was a playpen with a baby trapped in it. The woman had curlers in her thin hair and a Sweet Afton blowing a cloud from the side of her mouth, and she wore fluffy slippers that had once been pink, and she shouted over the noise of her vacuum cleaner. 'In the back room. You'll take a cuppa?'

He sat in the back room for half an hour. He cleaned his nails, he pinched hairs from his nostrils. Over and over again he planned his refusal to the Chief.

Through the thin walls of the house he heard the front door's bell.

He was standing when they came in with his hands held across his crotch, and he felt he was a bloody felon.

'Morning, Gingy. Good to see you. Long time.'

McAnally knew him, not well but he knew him. A cold, hard fucker, those that knew him well said he was. They'd met in the bars after

28

McAnally had come out of the Kesh. They'd known each other when McAnally was a big man who was on the R.P.G.-7 A.S.U. This was the Chief. There were three men behind him. None of them kids, none of them the prison fodder that were the Volunteers. Brigade men. Men that the *Mirror* called the Godfathers. The Chief wore a black donkey jacket with the collar up and round his cheeks, and he had a flat cap down over his eyes. His fingers were fidgeting, couldn't help himself. McAnally smiled. He had on the end of his tongue the name that the Chief was called. He was called 'Windsy'. Not to his face, but behind his back. It was said that he lived off Chinese takeaway, noodles and rice and spare ribs, and that was why 'Windsy'. Be a brave bugger, or a daft bugger, who would call him that to his face. A fierce face, power and authority jutting from the little that McAnally could see of it.

'Yes, it's been a long time.'

'When was it you went away, Gingy, how long?' A grating nasal voice.

'Two years.'

'They all need a rest . . . those that can get it. You'll be well rested now.'

McAnally put his hands on his hips. He stood at his full height, and he was three inches shorter than the Chief. He smelled the soya.

'I quit . . .' McAnally said.

'No, Gingy, you rested.'

'I said that I'd quit . . . that's what I meant, you know how it is.'

'I don't fucking know how it is. You rested. There's boys here, brilliant boys, who'd give a lot for two weeks resting, not two years but two weeks. It's *tiring* fighting the war, Gingy, more tiring than resting for two years.'

The Chief smiled. What showed of his face was pale except for the ruddy scar across his nose. A soldier's baton had done that back in '71. The story had it that seven soldiers had been needed to hold him down, and all swinging the batons, and him alone with his fists. A bit of myth was needed by a man if he was to make C.O. of Belfast Brigade.

'The boys came to see you, Gingy, you told them to piss themselves. They spelled out the plan. They tell me that you said it was a crazy suicide plan . . .'

McAnally blurted, 'To stand in the Crumlin, daylight, with the R.P.G., too right that's suicide.'

'My plan, Gingy, you farted on my plan,' the Chief said, and his voice was little more than a whisper.

Christ . . . McAnally saw the cold smile on the Chief's mouth. A little joke between the two of them, not shared by the three men behind the Chief. Bitter, pinched faces, hard, killing faces . . . Christ.

'Perhaps the plan wasn't explained that well, Gingy.'

'Perhaps it wasn't,' McAnally said bleakly.

29

'Missus . . . Missus . . .' The Chief's voice bellowed in the room, and his face never turned away from McAnally. 'Tea for five would be nice.'

There was a muffled reply. 'I'll leave the tray at the door.'

The Chief lit a cigarette, and belched with the first drag.

'You're going to do it, Gingy, because I'm going to ask you to do it.'

'Why me?'

'Gingy, there was a time when we had ten R.P.Gs up here, five in Belfast. When you went for your rest two years ago there were three R.P.Gs here. Now we have one. One for Belfast, Derry and South Armagh. You know how many projectiles we have now? Right now I've got one projectile in Belfast. I've got Chief of Staff and Army Council breathing on me. If I don't use it, then I'll be ordered to ship it out, send it where it can be used. It's not like your day any more, the R.P.G. isn't for police wagons and Brit pigs, the R.P.G.'s too precious for that. Are you listening to me, Gingy?'

'I'm listening.'

'My plan, the plan you said was a bad plan, is to use the R.P.G. so's the bang's heard across the Six Counties, and across the Twenty-six Counties, and right across the bloody waters to the States. My plan says that the biggest bang comes in the Crumlin Road tomorrow morning. My plan says that you, Gingy, you make that bang.'

McAnally saw the bright diamonds of the Chief's eyes under the shadow of his cap. He saw the spittle at the sides of the mouth that was close to his.

'Why me?'

'That's what you said when the boys came to see you. You said, why did it have to be you, why couldn't it be some other bugger, that's what you said. I tell you. You were the firer on the R.P.G. You were the Belfast R.P.G. team. You had four shots of practice across the border in Donegal before you took the army Pig, before you took the police landrover. You had the training, and you delivered. Bloody good you were, Gingy. Two firings, two hits.

'There were four on your team that had the training. Now I've got one warhead, one firing chance, and no chance of training a team like you had. My last two got lifted, you were told that . . . What happened to the four on your team, Gingy, the team you had when you quit? Tell me what happened to them?'

McAnally said, 'Shay got himself shot, peelers had him. Chicko's in the Kesh on a tenner. Gerry blew his face off, mixing . . .'

'And you were the fourth, Gingy, and you were the best.'

'I quit,' McAnally said.

'And you changed your mind,' the Chief grinned.

There was a light knock at the door.

'Thank you, Missus.'

One of the men who stood behind the Chief opened the door and

30

lifted in the tray and kicked the door shut behind him. He set the tray on the table, and began to pour. The baby was shouting happily in the hallway.

The Chief took from his jacket a folded Ordnance Survey map of Greater Belfast, spread it out on the floor and knelt beside it.

'Come on down, Gingy, inch to 300 yards. When I've talked you through it, tell me then if it's still a crazy plan.'

McAnally sank down on his haunches. The Soya smell was foul. He swallowed hard.

'You're the only one who can do it for me, Gingy. That's why it's you.'

The Chief slapped his fist across McAnally's shoulders and one of the others put a mug of tea in his hand.

'Come.'

The Intelligence Officer was sitting in his usual posture, chair tilted on the back two legs, shoes on his desk. He nearly always managed to spend his day in shoes, as if it were a perk of the job along with staying in his office with the gas stove on while the likes of Ferris were out tramping the streets of West Belfast. Battalion Headquarters worked out of the back of the Springfield Road R.U.C. station. Captain Jason Perceval had done well for himself. Intelligence Officer was a good number. He had an office big enough for his desk and chair, plus an easy chair, plus his VDU, plus a table for his portable television set. His walls were papered with the photographs of escaped prisoners and activists gone underground, what he called the OTRs, those On The Run.

He had been reading, and he placed the papers upside down on his desk as if Ferris represented a security risk.

'What can do, David?'

The telephone rang. The Intelligence Officer grimaced as if to explain the pressure of work, picked up the receiver.

'Wait one, David . . . Yes, yes . . . There's someone with me. Call me back, please. Five minutes . . . Now, what can do, David?'

Ferris often wondered where Jason Perceval had learned his language, and where he had learned that toothy smile that was meant to charm.

'Just came across a new face today, thought you might like to have it.'

'Very conscientious . . . What new face and where?'

The majority of the Battalion officers were Grammar School or Comprehensive, different to ten years back, sign of new times. The minority had been privately educated. Ferris thought the minority were bloody anxious to point up the difference.

31

'Gave his name as Sean McAnally, address as 63 The Drive, Turf Lodge . . .'

'Doesn't ring with me.'

'If you're not interested . . .'

'I didn't hear myself say I wasn't interested. No need to scratch. Tell.'

'Sean McAnally, aged about thirty, fair hair, ginger really, says he works down in the Republic. Wife is Roisin, she's full time up here with the kids. My platoon hadn't come across him before. He was in a car we stopped at a VCP two nights ago, the car was cleared. That's all.'

'Kind of you, squire.'

The Intelligence Officer lifted his chair across the room to the table and the Visual Display Unit. He flicked the switch, animated the screen, and started to type.

Ferris watched as the Intelligence Officer eased his chair back, waited for the Headquarters computer to throw them some information, and lit himself a black papered Sobranie.

'I'm all for HumInt,' the Intelligence Officer said easily. 'ElInt's got a place in things, but HumInt's what scores . . .'

The screen began to fill. Ferris disliked the military's jargon. Human Intelligence in Ferris's book was simply observation, and Electronic Intelligence was mechanical surveillance.

'Bit of a bullseye, David. Very good. McAnally, Sean Pius. Born 1955. Fianna Youth cadre. Aggro brat. Thought to be A.S.U. member in Turf Lodge and Ballymurphy through to mid-seventies. Done on possession of firearms in '76. No statement, written or verbal. Five years in the Lazy Kay. Wasn't on the dirty protest, didn't wipe his shit on the walls. Wasn't on the list of those wanting to slim for Ireland, not a Hunger Striker. Came out and went back to his old ways, but sharp enough never to have been incriminated, never found in flagrante, and never informed against either. Two years ago he went south. The law have checked him out down there, the word came back that he'd cut his links. Probably just back to give his lady a touch of the tickler . . .'

'Are they able to cut their links, do you think?'

'Perhaps, perhaps not . . . That's why it's useful to hear your news.'

'He looked as if he could have messed his pants when I had him over.'

'You're not starting to feel sorry for the vermin, David?'

'He was pretty pathetic.'

Jason Perceval looked keenly at David Ferris. 'Your job's soldiering, laddie, not feeling sorry for them.'

'I only said that he looked pathetic.'

'Have you ever seen an armed terrorist, David?'

Ferris hesitated. 'No . . . well, I've seen prisoners.'

'Have you ever seen a terrorist with an Armalite or a nail bomb or an M60 machine gun?'

'No.'

'Well, I fancy that if you had then you wouldn't be talking about him looking pathetic . . . '

'That's twisting what I said.'

'I'm telling you, once you feel sorry for them, then the next step is saying that if you'd been brought up in Turf Lodge that you'd be a terrorist, that sort of drivel.'

'I don't have to take that.'

'What I'm telling you is this, you muttering about known terrorists looking pathetic doesn't exactly move along our war effort. They're vicious psychopaths, and recognizing that is the first step towards grinding them down.'

'You know what . . . ?' Ferris flared. 'That's precisely the attitude that has kept us here fifteen years, not winning . . .'

'They're vermin.'

'They're human beings, and when we start realizing that we might stop losing.'

'What utter shit . . . If you weren't a damned good officer I'd see this conversation went further.'

Ferris spun on his heel and slammed the door behind him on his way out.

It was dark when he came home, and he had no front door key for his own house. He pressed the bell, he heard the shouts of the children inside, he heard the slither of his wife's slippers. The smell of soap was still on the palms of his hands from when he had sluiced away the traces of weapons oil.

They had worked on the plan, they had taken him to a lock-up garage where the R.P.G. was stored and he handled it and cradled it and checked the projectile, and after that they had taken him to a bar. He had been told to wash his hands. Two years ago it would have been second nature. He had flushed because he had had to be reminded.

Roisin opened the door. He hurried past her. He was bursting. She followed him to the half-closed door of the lavatory off the landing.

'You just missed your Ma, she waited all afternoon for you. She says for you to go round tomorrow morning.'

'I'm out early tomorrow morning,' McAnally called over his shoulder, and pulled the chain.

There was a flatness in her voice, not approval and not criticism. 'They talked you into doing what they want.'

He was at the top of the stairs. He nodded. 'They talked me.'

33

'You want me to wish you luck?'

'I want you to love me.'

'You're jarred.' But she was smiling.

'Love me.'

'You'll get your love when the kids have had their tea, and washed, and are in their beds . . . You'll get your love then.'

He came down the stairs, loud and clumsy. He held his woman in his arms, and the strength with which he clung to her squeezed the grin from her cheeks.

She kissed him under the ear and she whispered, 'You'll go careful.'

'I told them it was a suicide plan. They didn't listen to me.'

Her eyes were closed. Her face was hard against her man's.

'Go careful, Gingy.'

3

There were three men with him, and the car was behind them against the wall of the backyards of the flats, its engine throbbing quietly and the exhaust fumes pouting from its tail. He didn't know the names of the men. He knew that one would drive and that two would ride shotgun with Armalite rifles. He knew that the mission was controlled by a Citizens' Band radio.

It was raining. A dreary soft Belfast morning . . . The rifles were on the back seat of the car, covered by a coat, loaded and cocked. The R.P.G. was in the boot of the car, laid diagonally because the projectile was attached and it had to be laid that way to fit inside.

The CB radio would give him two minutes' warning. Two minutes to extract the launcher from the car, to drape the coat over it, to walk across Regent Street, to take up a position alongside the dark, derelict walls of the Methodist church, to look down busy Clifton Street at the cars approaching the Carlisle Circus.

He knew the target car would be a black Rover.

The car would not be difficult to identify; the armour-plating in the doors would weigh it down low on its wheels; sometimes, he had been told, they made it easier, the driver and the car's escort, by flashing the headlights of the Rover and the back-up as they approached the roundabout.

Shit . . . blasting the car wasn't the aggro bit, the bad bit was the clearing out afterwards.

He knew how to use the optical sight on the R.P.G. He'd studied a

34

translation of the Soviet manual, provided years back by a Russian language student down in Dublin. He'd used the optical sight on the police landrover. He wouldn't use the optical sight that morning. From the edge of the church wall to a car manoeuvring left on the roundabout was point blank range, so he'd use the iron sights, aim up on the forward leaf on the tube and the rear V above the grip stock. The three men talked occasionally in low voices behind him. They ignored him, as if he were separate from them.

The Chief had told why the target had been chosen, why the firing had to be in the shadow of the Crown Court House, why it had to be within earshot of the gaol that was across the road from the yellow and honeysuckle of the Court's façade. The Chief had said it had to be a one-off because he had only one fucking projectile.

He stamped his feet. The driven rain was on his face. He badly needed to piss.

He heard the click of the boot being opened. He spun. He saw one man thrusting the earpiece cable for the CB into his anorak pocket. He saw the launcher being lifted out of the boot, a crude, heavy shape under a raincoat. He saw the driver slip behind the wheel of the car.

'On his way . . . Two minutes, boyo.'

David Ferris was in a rare good humour. A patrol from his platoon was accused of shoplifting from a Sweets and Fags lock-up on the Falls. Bravo's Company Commander had advised a hard, defensive line. Take it on the chin and give them a blunt denial. Ferris was to attend Hastings Street R.U.C. station and there make a statement denying all knowledge and gilding the character of his Fusiliers. Actually he didn't believe the charge. They were tough little buggers, his Fusiliers, from the work-less zones of the north-east of England. If they had gone in for shop-lifting they would have stripped the lock-up bare, and probably lifted the knickers off the proprietor's wife for good measure.

He travelled by landrover. The Battalion's Sunray didn't believe in closed landrovers. Sunray had taken his style from the commandos and the paratroopers. Open landrovers offered more visibility to the riflemen. Great way to travel when it was raining, marvellous when you were stuck on the traffic lights. Ferris sat beside his driver, his rifle on his thigh, watching the front. There were two Fusiliers behind him covering the side and rear.

So Ferris was getting wet, but that was a damn sight better than footing it around Turf Lodge.

With a bit of luck, if the policeman wasn't too quick with a longhand statement, he would spin this into coffee and biscuits time.

They were out into the traffic. The gates of Springfield Road were squealing shut behind them. Ferris smiled at the banter around him.

'I hear, Nobby, they've got women Old Bill down where we're going.'

'Bollocks, it's chaps, you have a grope, see what you find.'

'Had to be women there, that's why a good-looking fucker like me's on the escort.'

'What's a woman look like, Nobby?'

'Not like anything you'll see here, fucked if I can remember . . .'

'Eyes peeled, lads, and concentrate,' Ferris said.

'You ever seen an actual Provo, Mr Ferris?' the driver asked.

'Provos are to me what women are to you, Fusilier Jones,' Ferris said. 'All photographs . . .'

'Good one, Mr Ferris.' Laughter from the back.

'That's enough, lads.'

Ferris's eyes raked the taxi stopped in front of him at the red light, and the van in front of the taxi that had a dark interior because the rear doors were off, and he switched his attention to the pavements and the early morning drifting crowds. Divis Street in the Falls. All wire-meshed windows and cement-blocked doorways and daubed slogans of sometime's victory and petrol bomb scars and blast scrapes. Famous throughout the Western world for its hatred and its killers . . . and so damned ordinary.

His thumb was close to the safety catch of his rifle, and his fingers rested hard against the trigger guard.

They stood beside the church wall. His legs were tight, stiff muscled, as if the walls across the deserted narrow Regent Street had been a bloody marathon. He hadn't seen the dog mess that he'd walked through, smeared. Shit, and he was naked. One of the men stood in front of him and was able to see down Clifton Street to the place where the slip road came off the Westlink. The other man was behind McAnally, sheltering the loaded launcher against his legs. Five past nine in the morning, bloody daylight, out in the open for any shit to see. Out in the open and squeezing his bladder back into his bloody stomach. The Court House with all its armed peelers was a quarter of a mile up the Crumlin from the roundabout. The gaol with all its armed squaddy Brits was a quarter of a mile up the road. The North Queen Street R.U.C. station was three hundred yards to the north. It was still suicide . . .

The man in front of him raised his hand, hesitated for a moment, dropped it smacking against his thigh.

McAnally's hand snaked behind him. He gripped the launcher. He pressed it against his leg and stomach. He took the pace forward.

'Make it fucking count . . .'

'Fuck off behind me.'

He stood at the corner.

He saw the black Rover eighty yards from him. He saw the face of the driver, and of the front passenger. He saw the pale blur of a head against the back seat. He saw the headlights of the back-up car. His mouth was set, his face was contorted as if in rage. He thought, just the right bloody weather, peeing rain, and the 'tecs in the back-up have the windows up . . . can't shoot out . . . because the 'tecs would see him, see him as soon as he took the last step forward and heaved the launcher onto his shoulder.

The Rover was up to the roundabout, slewing left. Thirty yards. He saw the red flash of the brake lights. He didn't look any more for the back-up car. He drew air down into his lungs. The launcher was on his shoulder. The V of the rear sight and the leaf of the forward sight were locked onto the back window of the Rover. Twenty yards. His finger found the chill metal of the trigger. He thought he might piss himself. He squeezed the trigger.

Fucking judge, fucking bastard. He saw the bald crown of the target's head silhouetted in the back window.

He felt the shuddering jolt that tore at his shoulder bones. He felt the hot air blast that flared back from the church wall. He felt the bitter smoke smell at his nose. He felt the thunder of the impact of the projectile with its armour-piercing high explosive warhead against the window of the Rover.

A catastrophe of noise burned in McAnally's ears.

He turned. He was running for his life along the side of the church wall. An arm tugged at his, half-halted him. The launcher was snatched from his grasp. Momentarily he saw the face of a boy he had never seen before. As he reached the car he saw the boy and the launcher disappear in a headlong scramble over the wall and into the backyards of the Unity flats.

The car doors were open. The driver was nudging forward. The man who had given the signal dived for the front passenger seat. The man who had held the launcher for McAnally now shoved him hard into the back, across the seat.

The car was skidding, spinning, ripping at the waste-ground earth, before the tyres gripped.

They went the wrong way round the circus. McAnally lay face down on the seat. They went down Clifton Street and surged hard and screamed right for the slip road and the Westlink.

*

37

They were half way along Divis Street, past the Library and the Baths when they had heard the explosion. If it had been a closed landrover they might not have heard the distant, thudding report. All ears were cocked. The smoke-grimed pigeons wheeled squawking to the north.

'About a mile, Mr Ferris, like an anti-tank, sounded like a Milan,' the driver said confidently.

'Or an R.P.G.,' Ferris said grimly. The driver had slowed. They were waiting on his decision. He felt very cold. He felt totally alone.

'VCP procedure, coming towards us,' Ferris snapped.

With a mirthless grin on his face the driver heaved the landrover across the centre of the road. He straddled the spaced white line. Ferris's men in the back jumped clear and split. One forward of the landrover as a block to a vehicle that spotted them and turned back. One behind the landrover to take out a vehicle that crashed them. The driver took a firing position low beside the front wheel. Ferris stood behind the landrover peering down the length of Divis Street.

Cars, taxis, lorries wafted past them. They were ignored by Ferris. A getaway car would be different.

There was no pursuit from the roundabout.

The detectives from the back-up had first spilled out of their seats and sprinted to the wreckage of the Rover. The one in the back was young, new to plain clothes. He held a Sterling sub-machine gun in his right hand and aimed it at pedestrians who sought to come forward towards the raging inferno that was the Rover, and was shrieking obscenities and weeping. The front seat observer of the back-up sprayed the flames with an extinguisher.

Hopeless, bloody waste of time. When the extinguisher was virtually empty he realized that all his efforts to damp the fire had been at the front of the car, where his friends had been. He carried on with the foam, spraying until the black seat-belted shapes were doused in a white shroud, until there were no more flames in the charred interior of the Rover. He dropped the extinguisher into the roadway. He walked over to the new boy, still yelling.

'Do us a bloody favour and shut your face.'

There were more sirens in the air, converging on them. He had lost his colleagues, he had lost his charge.

He went to his transport.

'What have you put over?'

The back-up driver said, 'Just a Contact. That it was an R.P.G., that it was a hit . . .'

He took the microphone, stretching the length of its cable away from the window. In front of him the Rover was smouldering dark smoke.

He could see the police and the troops who had sprinted down from the Court House.

'This is Foxtrot Zulu 24. Timed zero nine zero seven. We have lost Jupiter. R.P.G. direct hit. Jupiter is dead . . . so are my bloody mates . . . out.'

He walked away from the car and was sick on the raised stonework of the roundabout.

Each man in the car had a critical role in the execution of the plan.

All the previous week the lookout man who had given the signal had tracked and tailed the judge's transport. The man who had stayed with McAnally was regarded as an expert in the use of a folded stock M16, he was responsible for the safe escape. McAnally was the marksman, and he had scored. Crucial now to the escape from the hit scene was the driver.

The driver of the getaway had first come down Clifton Street, then taken the sunken dual carriageway of the Westlink under the bridges that led to the Shankill Road and Divis Street. When the Westlink surfaced to ground level at the Grosvenor Road he had gone hard right and right again to insert himself amongst the modern terraces of Cullingtree. He was doubling back as he swept past the kids playing outside the crumbling escarpment of the Divis flats. The description of the car would by now have been broadcast over the police and army nets, and the car would have been identified as heading south-west along the fast road that hooked onto the motorway.

His only participation in the Organization was as a driver. He reckoned he was the best, and there weren't many who told him otherwise. Always the need to shift the first car at speed away from the scene. The car wheels screeched as they curved and bounced over the rough broken ground in front of the flats. There was a sharp confident smile at the driver's face. It was what he was good at. The car lurched onto Divis Street. The plan called for him to drive most of the length of Divis Street, as far as the Library, go right into Sebastapol, left into Odessa, right into Clonard, right into Kashmir, left into Bombay. In Bombay Street there would be two cars waiting for the break-up of the team.

They were in the traffic stream. The smile wiped from the driver's mouth. They were slowing. Fucking lorry in front winking its back brake lights. Not the time for the driver to settle back in his seat and pick his bloody nose, not before the first car switch, not before the split. He swung the wheel, he jerked the car out into the on-coming lanes. His foot stamped down on the accelerator. No power in a bleeding Ford. He ground past the lorry.

'There's a fucking block . . .' McAnally screamed.

McAnally had seen the Fusilier who was positioned furthest down Divis Street. The red and white feathers of the hackle had caught his eye.

All together the four men in the car saw the landrover parked across the centre of the road.

'Shit . . . Christ . . . Fucking Jesus . . . Bust the bastards . . .' Curses swimming in the ears of the driver.

The driver saw the tall upper body of the soldier behind the landrover. He felt the frightened pants of McAnally's breathing on his neck. The man beside him was dragging the rifle from under his knees. He heard the unison clatter of two rifles being armed.

The driver saw for a fleeting moment the staring young face of the soldier who was low at the front of the landrover.

There was a hospital outpatients' van heading towards him. Fuck it, let it look after itself. He was back into the on-coming lanes. With all the impetus he could kick out of the clapped-out Ford he swerved past the tail of the landrover. The rifles in the car were on automatic. A stink of cordite in the car, and the hammer sounds of the firing. McAnally was shouting behind him, the driver couldn't understand the words. The driver saw the soldier who had been behind the landrover hurl himself down onto the road.

'Down . . . down . . .' the driver yelled. He saw the solitary soldier who had been placed in a doorway behind the landrover. He was the wrong side for his riflemen. The driver took the car straight towards the soldier and when he cowered away, then the driver wrenched his car back onto the track of the road. He heard the scream of the van's horn . . . Fuck you, mate . . . he heard the single report of a rifle shot that had missed.

They swept on up Divis Street, and took the right into Sebastapol. They were all yelling, laughing in the car, and slapping the driver's back.

Ferris climbed to his feet, spared a moment to wipe the wet dirt from his camouflage trousers. He looked in front of him and behind him. He saw his Fusiliers sprinting back to his position. His driver stood by the bonnet of the landrover and his face was creased as if he had been presented with a puzzle to which he could not fathom the answer. Already a crowd had gathered on the two pavements to watch him.

A child with a shrill, cutting voice called out, 'Heh, Mister, the Provies wiped you on the ground. The Provies made an arsehole of you, Mister.'

Ferris depressed the Speak button on his radio. His hand was shaking. He could barely hold the button down.

*

The Secretary of State for Northern Ireland had once been considered an ambitious member of Cabinet. Too ambitious, had been the verdict of certain colleagues in government. They were highly placed, these colleagues, high enough on the ladder of influence to speak into the Prime Minister's ear when they stood on tiptoe. So this ambitious man had been given responsibility for the United Kingdom's warring province some eighteen months earlier. It was a pretty damned awful job. He gained very little credit when the violence diminished, the laurels went to the Generals and the Chief Constable. When the wheel turned, the media splashed gory headlines and the Secretary of State took the brickbats. He was no longer ambitious.

He had flown into Aldergrove that morning and then been lifted by RAF helicopter to his residence and office at Stormont Castle. Questions in the House of Commons and a dinner for American industrialists had taken him to London. A barrage of accusations of incompetence from the Protestant M.P.s, and vague promises of economic commitment had been the order of the previous day. Now, back to the treadmill. Back to the misery.

On the castle lawns he smilingly shook hands with the helicopter's pilot. His face was masked in a fraud of confidence. It was part of his work to seem unmoved by catastrophe, to appear saturated in optimism. His bodyguards flanked him as he walked briskly towards the Castle's side door. He always walked briskly, not because he was an athletic man, but because that was the instruction of the Detective Inspector from Scotland Yard who headed his security detail.

Waiting on the steps at the Castle's side door was an Ulster-born civil servant, a gaunt and cheerless man.

When the civil servant was on the steps it only added to bad news. The Secretary of State was without an overcoat, the rain was flapping on his jacket, staining his tie.

'Morning, Fred.' The Secretary of State liked to call his advisors by their first names, to create a team atmosphere.

'Morning, Secretary of State.'

The civil servant had fallen into step beside him, taking precedence over the two secretaries who had come over from London.

The Secretary of State smiled loosely. 'I've had a good night's sleep, I've had a good flight, I'm as ready as I'll ever be. Give me the gloom.'

'It's been a bad morning for the Province.'

'My memory doesn't stretch back to a good one.' The flippancy was a disguise.

They went into the Secretary of State's office, palatial and yet comfortable. A warm and friendly room, subdued lighting, new-cut flowers on the table by the window that was screened with blast-proof glass.

The Secretary of State said abruptly, 'Well, don't hang around, Fred.'

'They've murdered a judge.'

The Secretary of State looked at the floor. He saw the blades of wet grass at the side of his shoes. His lips pursed. A judge . . .

'Details.'

'Half an hour ago. P.I.R.A. have already claimed it, that's in the last five minutes. Mr Justice Simpson, Billy Simpson. Always gave ten years for conspiracy or firearms possession . . . You know, "Tenner" Simpson.'

'Wasn't there any damned protection?' the Secretary of State flared.

'He had five with him, three in the escort, two in his own car. His car took a direct hit from an R.P.G.-7 rocket. There were two detectives with him, and they died with him.'

'And no arrests.' The Secretary of State tried to be angry. 'Of course, no arrests.'

'No arrests.'

The Secretary of State stared into the lined, fleshless face of his civil servant. 'So what do I do?'

'I suggest you speak to the Prime Minister . . . sorry, but that's what you ought to do first. Then a statement to camera for the lunchtime bulletins. Then a meeting with the Chief Constable . . .'

'I'm turning into a bloody parrot, you know that? I haven't the faintest idea of what I'll say that I haven't said before. I detest this place, Fred. I detest it because it has rubbed all sense of shock and outrage from my mind.'

The Secretary of State sagged into an easy chair. He heard his civil servant let himself out of the room. When he was alone, when he had calmed his thoughts, he was able to remember Billy 'Tenner' Simpson. One of a golfing four at Shandon Park, a pretty good player and near to scratch. A small, round, unsmiling man with a detective to caddy for him, who had not had much that was nice to say about the Secretary of State's game. All the usual phrases cavorted in the Secretary of State's mind . . . Senseless murder . . . bestial cowards . . . determination of our government . . . all decent-minded people . . . personal loss . . . never be deflected . . .

He reached for the telephone. He asked the switchboard for Downing Street.

'I thought you should know, Prime Minister, it's been a bad morning for the Province . . .'

Ferment in Springfield Road barracks. Always the same after a major incident. Local commanders always saturated their areas after a nasty one. Road blocks, foot patrols, and mobiles. No local commander would have it said that his response was lacking. Saturation in the Falls and

Clonard and Springfield and Beechmount and Ballymurphy. Kick the backside of a platoon lieutenant or a uniformed R.U.C. sergeant who ventured to ask what they were searching for. Good reaction time was what mattered.

The Ford had been found, and collected from Bombay Street. It had been towed into the yard at the back of the barracks. It was surrounded by traffic warning signs and a scrawled notice that read DON'T TOUCH – WAITING ON F-PRINTING.

Fusilier Jones stared at the car. Nobby's bullet hole was there to see, side of the boot entry, not too far from the back passenger seat, but just too far, worst fucking luck. He could see into the back seat through the open window.

'Bugger me . . .'

Fusilier Jones spun away from the car and doubled towards the Ops Room to find his lieutenant.

'He's sure?' asked Sunray.

The coded radio callsign of the Commanding Officer was Sunray. He enjoyed it, he encouraged its use. He had been heard to remark that it emphasized the Battalion's active service and operational role. He would be the Commanding Officer again when they left the Province, but in Belfast he could be Sunray.

'He's positive,' Ferris said firmly.

'Has to be watertight.' Sunray sat at his desk.

'Can't afford a mistake, on a thing like this.' The 2 i/c was by the door.

'If it's a Roger it's something of a coup.' The Intelligence Officer held in his folded hands the VDU print-out concerning Sean Pius McAnally.

'He's absolutely positive,' Ferris said again.

'He'd have to be.'

'He'd have to swear to it in court.'

'S.O.P. would be to bring in our friends in bottle-green . . . but we just might lift him ourselves.'

'Fusilier Jones will swear that the man I questioned yesterday in the Drive, Turf Lodge, and gave his name as Sean Pius McAnally, was the same man that he saw in the back seat of the car that we failed to stop in Divis Street this morning,' Ferris said. 'That's the beginning and the end of Fusilier Jones's statement.'

'Steady, David, you did damn well this morning. Fast professional thinking, damn well done.' Sunray's accolade.

'It's identified from the R.P.G. attack location as the getaway car . . . It would be a hell of a thing for the Battalion, sir, if we nailed a

Johnny for murder. Could be the high spot of the tour . . .' The Intelligence Officer's enthusiasm.

'Not a lot of thanks we get from R.U.C. these days, they'd be on their bended knees for this one.' The 2 i/c's cunning.

Ferris thought of the moment when he had seen the Armalite barrel spitting from the window of the Ford, the moment of terror, and the moment he thought he would die. He could feel the scrapes on his knees and elbows. He hadn't seen the face in the back seat of the car, he had only seen the black barrel of the Armalite.

'Right, Standard Operating Procedure's that we inform R.U.C. of our suspicions concerning McAnally . . .' Sunray was lighting his pipe.

'Police presence isn't essential for the arrest.'

'We can do it under Section 14. There's no problem.'

The face of the man burgeoned into Ferris's mind. The scrappy ginger hair, the nervy eyes, the slack chin, the mouth in the half-smile that tried to please.

'Your platoon'll do it, David, 0200 hours tomorrow morning. It'll be an excellent show for your platoon . . . and bloody well done.'

'Are we going to have a surveillance detail on the house, sir?' Ferris asked.

'What for?'

Ferris blinked, seemed so obvious. 'So we know he's there, sir, when we go in.'

'No surveillance. We don't have that capability, not in Turf Lodge. Stand a damn sight better chance of lousing it if I put men into the Drive, kicking dustbins over. We go in cold because that's best.'

'Yes, sir.'

'And bloody well done, David.'

They had left their transport, two Pigs and a landrover, at the junction of the Drive and the Parade. They would leg it to Number 63. Blackened faces and hands. Rifles cocked, one up. Quiet padding feet. The glow of the image intensifier night sights carried by the marksmen. Twenty men briefed on their positions in the outer perimeter and the inner perimeter, four more with Ferris for the snatch. Always bloody raining, and the haze of mist cloud sneaking in from the fields at the foot of the mountain to blanket Turf Lodge. No street lights; the street lights had been knocked out in '71, Internment, and replaced; knocked out again in the Queen's visit rioting, and replaced; knocked out again in the Hunger Strike fighting of '81, and abandoned.

A pace behind Ferris was Fusilier Jones, loping along like he was heading for Wembley, like he had a Cup bloody Final goal on the end of his boot.

Only it wasn't a game in Ferris's book. It was going to snatch a man out of his house in the dark of the night, strip him from his bed, tear him away from his wife and kids. It was going to put a murderer into a cell for a life sentence. Some bloody game. If it was a game then it was a dirty bloody game.

Number 63. His platoon sergeant was beside Ferris.

Ferris heard the whisper. 'All ready . . . let's get the shit out of his wanker.'

He had woken the moment before the explosion of the front door caving in. He had sat up, straight up, the moment before the screech of the front door's lock being smashed clear of the door post. He felt Roisin stir beside him. She'd four Bacardi cokes in her to his six Stouts, she moved drowsily.

McAnally heard the oaths from the foot of the stairs. Baby Sean's pram was always outside the door in the day, brought into the hall at night, no other place for it . . . Mother of Christ, fucking English oath.

He wore a Marks vest, nothing else. He heaved himself out of the bed, dragging the sheet and blankets with him. He saw the white blur of Roisin's thighs, and her stomach. He crashed into Baby Sean's cot and was out of the door before the baby had screamed. From the landing he saw the torch at the bottom of the stairs, and a dark shadow figure wrestling with the pram. He saw the torch beam dive forward towards the stairs.

'Freeze, McAnally . . .'

The yell blasted at his ears. He charged into the back bedroom, jumped on Young Gerard's bed, stumbled on Little Patty's body, reached the window, ripped at the cotton curtains. He had no thought but flight, to run and to survive. He heard the thunder of boots on the staircase, sounds amplified and magnified by the tininess of the back bedroom.

His fingers found the window catch, he heaved it up, pushed the window open. Night air closed on his gut and his privates. Light flooded into the room. He saw the terror shape of the soldier charging into the room. He saw Young Gerard rise up from his bed and grapple with the soldier. He saw the soldier cuff the boy away. As the soldier lunged for him, McAnally jumped.

He was dazed, stunned.

He hit the small flat roof of the kitchen, bounced, scraped his shins and thighs and stomach on the roof guttering. He toppled down onto the concrete slabs beside the kitchen door. A leg was caught between the frame of Young Gerard's bicycle. He could see the bicycle, see its colours. The light from the back bedroom lit the small square backyard. He was clear of the bicycle when he saw the soldiers materializing from the shadows, from behind the coal bunker, from behind the kids' swing, from the shadow by the back fence.

McAnally kicked the first soldier who reached him. The bare instep of his foot hacked into the soldier's groin. Above him he saw Roisin dark-framed in the back bedroom window and flailing at a squaddie with Baby Sean's yellow plastic pot. The soldier bent double in front of him. Scream, cunt . . . but the soldier only moaned. He lashed with his fist at the soldier who came from the side and his knuckles caught the rim of a helmet. A rifle stock hammered into the back of his skull. A boot cracked into his shin. A soldier dived on him as he fell, and McAnally groped and found the man's cheeks and eyes and raked them with his nails. He fought with his hands and with his teeth and with his feet as the blows fell on him, clubbed down on his body. He heard the pain shouts of the soldiers, and further off the screams of Young Gerard and the anger of his Roisin. He fought only for survival. He lost the feel of pain. He lost the sight of the soldiers. He lost the sounds of the voices of Young Gerard and his Roisin.

A numbness in his body and a mist in his eyes and wads in his ears. He saw the indistinct shapes of the legs that stood over him.

'For Christ's sake, pack it in . . .'

He felt the blood on his head and running from his lip.

'That's a prisoner, for Christ's sake.'

The officer stood over him.

'He is a prisoner and he will be treated as a prisoner . . .'

The soldiers were in a ring beyond his reach. And he now was beyond theirs.

'You're soldiers, you're on active service not in a bloody pub brawl. Sergeant, this man is not to be touched. Come here, Jones.'

The officer had taken hold of McAnally's wrist, held it securely. He shone a torch into McAnally's face, blinding him.

'That's him, Mr Ferris, that's the one I saw.'

The torch was switched off.

The officer said, 'Sean Pius McAnally, I am arresting you under Section 14 of the Northern Ireland (Emergency Provisions) Act, 1978. You are not obliged to answer any questions other than those relating to your identity . . . You'd better get some clothes on, Mr McAnally. You won't be hurt, you're in my custody.'

After what he had done the morning before, they could have beaten the life out of him. He had seen the car on the telly before he had taken Roisin to the bar, seen the car wreck and the photographs of 'Tenner' Simpson and two detectives. He had heard the tributes . . . they could have battered him to death for what he had done.

The officer led him back into the kitchen. McAnally covered his groin.

4

A little before three Ferris was back in the Mess.

He had been on the go for close on twenty-one hours, but he'd had to tell his story, laconically in the style of the Regiment, to the I.O. and the Bravo Company Commander and separately to Armstrong and Wilkins with whom he shared his room. He could have done without the accolade treatment after he had checked his prisoner into police custody and the Springfield Road cells.

There was a handwritten note from Sunray. 'Excellently done, a most creditable night for the Battalion, fast professional soldiering. Congratulations, Townsend.' He'd have to go through it all again in the morning for Sunray.

He had two glasses of orange juice, and then the I.O. told him that there was a detective coming up from Castlereagh, a chap called Rennie, and would he wait up for him.

He was left to wait in the Mess, stretched out on the sofa, able to doze.

The Company Commander had been gushing, the I.O. had been cool, Armstrong and Wilkins had been jealous as tom-cats. He hadn't spoken of the sledgehammer attack on a wet rotten front door, nor of being snagged in the hall by a pram that stank of nappy urine, nor of pounding up the carpetless stairs, nor of a kiddie of seven or eight years who had taken on the soldiers to help his father, nor of a proud woman who had spat her hatred at his men. He didn't think they'd want to know.

Sam might want to know. When he'd finished with the detective, and had a hell of a sleep, and a bath if he could find any hot water, he'd write to her. He was thinking of Sam, drowsily and happily, when the ceiling light billowed across the Mess.

'Are you Mr Ferris?' The scrape of the Belfast accent.

Ferris sat up. 'That's me.'

It was a huge man that towered over him, his size accentuated by Ferris's position on the sofa.

'I'm Rennie . . . Detective Chief Inspector Rennie . . .'

He spoke the words slowly, as if the rank gave him pride. Ferris sat up, rubbed his eyes.

'Howard Rennie, Castlereagh . . . I hear you buggers have been fart-arsing with us . . .'

47

'I beg your pardon . . . ?' Ferris yawned. The Mess was bloody arctic. He stood, and tucked his shirt down into his trouser waist.

'The police lift men in Belfast these days, if you didn't know. The military provide support, if requested. I can do without clever buggers.'

'You've no right to come in here, into our Mess, with that sort of language on your face.'

'I like a man out of his bed, into the landrover, down to Castlereagh, while he's still asleep. I like him stripped and weighed and checked and in his cell before he's had time to think. I have to work on him, young fellow, and I've shit all time to do it, as you'd know if you took the trouble to read the P. of T. Act, and what doesn't help me is him sitting in a cell here getting used to the fact he's in the cage. As I see it, young fellow, getting my friend into the Interrogation Room in the right frame of mind is more important than your fucking Colonel getting a back slap from his General. Got it?'

Ferris thought he liked the man. He was laughing quietly. 'Got it . . . round here, Mr Rennie, you might believe that the capture of old McAnally added up to the final victory.'

It was a big weathered face that confronted Ferris. There was no crack of a smile. The hairs of the moustache were splayed out. There was a nick from a fast shave on the throat. The breath was of cigarettes and gin. The ceiling light glowed on the high forehead. 'Tomorrow, if I can take the time off from "old McAnally", I'll have two funerals to go to, good friends, so I'm not in the mood for a laugh in your Mess. I want McAnally now, I want you and the lad who identified him down at Castlereagh in the afternoon for statements.'

'He's already in police custody, why don't you just bloody take him?'

'There's a form for these things. He's going to appear in court, long after you've been ferried out and back to war games in Germany. Long after you've gone some smart lawyer will be putting the arrest procedure under a 'scope. You won't be here but I will, so I say that everything has to be right, and I'm taking him from *your* charge. Got it?'

Ferris led the way. Out into the night air and across to the police cells, down the corridor, escorted by a constable. The crash of the keys, the swish of the door. McAnally sat on the iron bedframe. His knees were clamped close together, his arms were hard against his chest. His lip was swollen. Ferris was behind the shoulder of the detective, but he could see McAnally stiffen, straighten, at the sight of Howard Rennie. Ferris reckoned it the defiance of a trapped rat.

'Morning, Gingy . . .'

McAnally stood up. He tried to lift his chin. He walked to Rennie and then turned his back, reached his wrists to the base of his spine, and was handcuffed. He turned back to face Rennie.

'The injury to the prisoner's mouth, Mr Ferris, that happened during his arrest?'

'Correct.'

'Just getting it right, Mr Ferris, like I said. Come on, Gingy.'

Detective Chief Inspector Howard Rennie strode away down the corridor. His shoes were iron-tipped, reverberating. His quilted, open anorak seemed to fill the corridor. Ferris followed, walking alongside McAnally. The constable was behind them. Rennie was hurrying, as if the whole visit to Springfield Road had been a bloody liberty taken at his expense. Ferris felt the light kick at his heel. McAnally was close to him. The prisoner looked up once into Ferris's face. He spoke quietly, almost a whisper, out of the side of his mouth.

'I know what you did.'

'What I'm paid to do.'

'You stopped them kicking the shit out of me.'

'Safe journey, Mr McAnally.'

McAnally was bundled into a police landrover. The engine was already running, spewing smoke across the yard. Rennie was unlocking the door of his car. Ferris saw him take off his anorak and sling it into the back seat, and then produce his pistol from a shoulder holster under his jacket, and cock it and place it in his waist. The convoy of the landrover and Rennie's car swept out through the gates, out into the early morning darkness.

Ferris headed off in search of a cup of tea and then bed.

'You go easy with it, I'll fix it proper later.'

The neighbour stepped back to let Roisin McAnally out through the front door of Number 63. All the neighbours had called on Number 63 in the hours since the military raid. The first had come in their sleeping clothes, in their dressing gowns and slippers. As the light had come up, they had come dressed for the day. Some came to comfort, some to help, some to witness the scene. This neighbour had come with his tool kit to repair the front door.

'That's a terrible bloody way to be coming into a family's wee home . . .' The neighbour shrugged. He had come with his drills and screwdrivers because his own woman had told him that he must. He wouldn't have said that he liked Roisin McAnally. With drink taken he would have called her a stuck-up cow. But his wife had told him to come and so he had made a job of mending the hinge fastening on the door. And the bitch hadn't even thanked him, just looked through him, and stamped off down the pathway to the front gate that was already hanging slack from a long time before. He was buggered if he'd fix the front gate . . . To himself the neighbour reckoned that all the Provo widows were the same, stuck-up cows. Not that he would have ventured that opinion in public, wouldn't have said that down at the bar on a

Saturday evening. They were always called 'the widows', whether their man was dead or running or walled up in the Kesh, and he reckoned they all wore their widowhood with a sort of bloody arrogance. So, she hadn't thanked him for fixing her door, and he simpered a smile behind her back as she stalked away. In a right paddy temper, the neighbour thought. Could see it in her chin and in her mouth and in her eyes, like she's going to kick the arse off the first man that crosses her.

'You go carefully with it, Missus,' the neighbour called at her back . . . and more quietly . . . 'or you'll be doing the fucking thing yourself, if you bust it.'

The neighbour had read Roisin McAnally right.

She smouldered in a ferocious anger as she set off down the broken pavement of the Drive. She walked with her back straight, and her head up, and knew that the curtains all the way down the slope of the Drive would be flickering back. They would all be watching her, all of them in 61 and 59 and 57 and 55 . . . and all the curtains on the other side of the road would be twitching, and those that couldn't see her because there was a car parked in the way would hustle up their bloody stairs to get a grandstand view . . . They'd been there in the night, whining their sympathy, and asking the sly bloody questions. 'What had he been at, Missus McAnally? . . . He's not one for stepping into trouble, is he, Mrs McAnally? . . . Doing well down in the Free State, isn't that him, Missus McAnally? . . .' Her mother was now in the house, and fretting, and minding the kids, and the kids were all quiet as if they'd been thrashed. Young Gerard hadn't opened his mouth since the soldiers and his father had gone, and Little Patty had cried in her bed and wet the sheets which she hadn't done for a year, and Baby Sean had screamed because his mother was cold and numbed and couldn't offer him love.

And the coldness had changed to fury.

She knew where to go. She knew in which house she could let rip her temper. A quarter of an hour's fast walking on a chilled damp morning.

She knew her man's speciality was the R.P.G. launcher.

She knew what he had done the previous day. She had known he was on a hit from the time he had crept out of the house before dawn, and from the time when he had come back home and made a joke and laughed and his chin had shaken as if the muscle-wires were loose and uncontrolled. She had known from the way that he had paced the little front room and picked up the kids and made too much noise and not been able to settle. From the way he had smoked half a packet of cigarettes and stubbed each butt down. From the way he had loved her in their bed . . . He had been silent only once the previous day, when the telly news was on, when he had seen a blackened car and a chorus of politicians and churchmen keening a litany of condemnation. And

50

she had never referred to it. She hadn't pretended that she knew. That wasn't the way of the widows. The widows did not expect to be told. The widows expected to serve up the food on the table and the comfort between their legs. Deep down, hard down, she supported her husband's involvement in the Organization. Down in her guts she saw herself as a prop to her man. She had a brother and a first cousin in the Kesh. She accepted that her husband was involved. She had not cared to understand why her man had gone south, and turned his back on the war. She knew the strain of fighting the war. She carried the same strain. Roisin McAnally was no quitter. She believed in the war, she was committed to the armed struggle. She wept no tears for the enemy's fallen. If she could have killed one of the soldiers who came into her house in the small hours of that morning, she would happily have done so.

Her raven black hair streamed out from her head as she walked into the teeth of the wind. She wore jeans and a sweater and a bright red nylon shower-proof jogging jacket. Her clothes, and her children's, she gathered from jumbles and from relatives' cast-offs. And with her head up, and her chin jutting, and with her eyes burning in her anger, Roisin McAnally was beautiful.

The man opened the door to her knock. He was Battalion staff. He had not shaved. She knew him because in the old days he'd brought her money. He wore his socks and his trousers and a vest. He had his kids round his legs, jam and crumbs at their mouths. He had once tried to bed her, but he'd been pissed and she hadn't counted it against him. He would have seen her anger, and he made way for her and hurriedly opened the door of his front room that reeked of old smoke and smelt of cold damp, and he cuffed the kids out of the door and closed it on their protests.

'They took my Sean, the army came this morning and took him.'

She saw the shock spreading on his face and the shadows forming in his frown.

'They took Gingy . . . ?'

She roared at him. 'They took Sean. He's back two days, and they came for him. First job in two years, and he's lifted. How did they know to come for him? He's been informed on . . . he's been fingered by a bloody tout . . .'

The man ducked, as if attempting to deflect the accusation. 'Informer' and 'tout', they were the obscenity words of the Organization. His teeth were biting on his bottom lip. Nicotined teeth on the pale pink of his lips.

'You can't say that, woman.' Said as if he hardly believed his denial.

'I can say what's the truth . . . He comes back, and he goes out, and he's lifted. It wasn't a routine lift. My house was half filled with bloody soldiers. Who touted on my Sean?'

51

The man squeezed his eyes closed and shook his head. 'How can I answer . . . ?'

'You find the bloody answer. You find who touted on Sean.'

'You best go home . . . You're better at home.'

'Don't you want to talk to me? Won't you face me?'

'If Gingy's been touted on then I've work at hand.'

'Kill the bastard. Kill him for me.' The blaze in her eyes was misted.

'If there's a tout, we'll find him.'

'And kill him . . . What sort of bloody army is it when a man doesn't know whether the boy with him is a friend or a bloody tout?'

She was sobbing, and the man took her in his arms. He thought she was a great girl, he thought she was one of the best. He held her against him and felt the ripple movements of her crying.

'If there's a tout then we'll find him. That's a promise, Missus.'

'Bloody good for me,' a small voice, choking. 'My Sean's on a lifer . . .'

She went out onto the street still crying. She stumbled once on the broken pavement where the slabs had been lifted to be smashed into missiles. As far as she looked there were narrow roofs and spirals of smoke and grime-laden façades. In that moment she hated Turf Lodge. In Turf Lodge a man had touted on her Sean. She saw the graffiti . . . 'Provos Rule' and 'Brit Bastards Out' and 'Smash the H Blocks' and 'Touts Will be Shot'. Shooting was too good for a tout.

It did not enter her mind that there could be any other reason for the arrest of her husband. He was in the cage because a tout had put him there. She saw a lifetime ahead of her, from youth through to middle age and through to old age, of traipsing to the stop for the prison bus . . . because of a bastard tout.

All around her was the emptiness of the early morning. A lifetime of waiting for the fucking prison bus. A lifetime without a man. A lifetime of scrimping and saving her pounds.

She began to run, and her tears hastened her. She ran back to the Drive and her home, back to her children.

The word would spread, like the scent of foul air, like the drift of a winter wind off Divis Mountain. The word said that Roisin McAnally had claimed to a Battalion Staff Officer that her husband had been touted. The Organization cringed at the word. More than all the soldiers and all the policemen ranked against them, the Organization feared the tout. The tout was a dark shadow swimming as a germ in the blood-stream. The tout struck at the core of the Organization. The tout was to be tortured, hooded, executed, dumped.

Within an hour of Roisin McAnally's reaching home, the news of

Gingy's arrest had reached the Housing Executive maisonette in Andersonstown that was the current refuge of the Chief. He called for a conference in the early afternoon. He summoned to the meeting those who were closest to him, those that he trusted absolutely. But the doubt gnawed in his gut. The men who were closest to him were the same men who had known of the arrival of McAnally in Belfast.

The Chief had a way with touts. Cigarettes on the balls and the stomach, for the confession. Then the hooding. Then the noisy cocking of the pistol against the ear of the tout. Then the shot into the ground beside the tout's foot, so that he pissed himself and messed himself. Then the barrel against the back of the neck. Then the killing.

It had to be a tout, and a tout who knew only of McAnally's role in the Crumlin Road hit. A tout who didn't know the names of the man who had driven the car, of the men who had ridden shotgun, of the youth who had fled with the used launcher.

The girl he lived with, Mary, stayed in the bedroom, abandoned him to his angry pacing of the living room.

'You stay in your bed when they come.' He shouted at her as if she was just something to be kept in a cupboard, put away when there was business. He felt a flicker of regret . . . There had been a man once who had told him earnestly and sincerely that his Mary was a risk to his security, and he had smashed the man's chin. Now he had shouted at her as if she was danger to him and his closest lieutenants.

'You are not obliged to say anything, unless you wish to do so, but what you say may be put into writing and given in evidence . . . You are Sean Pius McAnally?'

'You know my name.'

There were two detectives with him in the Interrogation Room. He knew there was a father-mother of a row over his arrest. He knew that if they had been expecting him then the detectives would have gone straight to work.

'63 The Drive, Turf Lodge?'

High on the wall and facing him in the bare room was the camera. In the old days they would have beaten him, half knocked hell out of him. He knew that the camera ensured that the detectives wouldn't touch him. He knew all the rules under which the detectives operated.

'You know where I live.'

'We'll call you Gingy, right?'

'You call me what you like.' McAnally sat on a chair at a table. The detective who asked the questions was behind him, standing. Across the table from him was the detective with the notepad.

'Would you like to tell us where you were yesterday morning, Gingy?'

Don't reply. That's what the big men said. Think of your woman, think of your kids, don't ever listen to what they say to you.

'Yesterday morning, Gingy. Tell us where you were.'

He looked at his finger nails. He saw the wrinkles in his hands, and the little cuts that came from the farm work down by the canal in the south.

'Prefer it if we told you where you were?'

Before the new rules were enforced in the Interrogation Rooms, he would have been on the end of their boots and their fists, straight up, no messing. That's what they'd done to him way back, when he was married a week.

'Prefer it if I said you were in Crumlin Road yesterday morning, how about that, Gingy?'

He hadn't broken the last time, not for all the slapping and the punching and the kicking. The bastards knew how to do it, so there weren't bruises. Just so there was the bloody pain.

'Gingy, you're in bad shape. You're identified. You're placed at Crumlin Road on the R.P.G. team. That's murder three times. You're placed in Divis Street in the getaway. That's attempted murder. That's a life sentence, Gingy. There isn't a way round that. Sitting on your bum and saying nothing, that's not a way out of it. It'll be a life sentence with the judge's recommendation that you serve a minimum of twenty-five years. That's a bad scene, Gingy.'

He knew their trick. The trick was always to pretend they knew more than they did.

'Twenty-five years, Gingy, that's a hell of a bloody stretch. Is that what you came back from the south for, to serve twenty-five years?'

He thought of Young Gerard twenty-five years from now, and Little Patty, and Baby Sean. In twenty-five years Roisin would be a grey-haired widow. In twenty-five years the kids would be grown up, left and married.

'Gingy, my book says that the man in the back of the getaway is the jewel. The man beside him and the front passenger, they're the back-up, and there's the driver. My book says that the jewel is the laddie who was on the R.P.G. My book says that you're the jewel, Gingy McAnally . . . and my book says that a big precious jewel like you goes down for twenty-five years.'

Difficult for him to imagine Young Gerard as a grown man. A grown man who might travel to the Kesh to see his father, aging in an H Block. Young Gerard had fought the bloody soldiers, bloody child and he had the loyalty to his father to fight the soldiers.

'Great future, isn't it, Gingy? You inside for twenty-five years. What's the old woman going to do, Gingy? Good girl, is she? Keep herself good and clean and wait for you? What do you reckon, Gingy?'

He clamped his teeth together. He could smell the aftershave of the

54

detectives, and he could see their laundered and ironed shirts. They wore well cut jackets and slacks with creases and shoes that were polished. He thought that when they had finished with him then they'd go and take a cup of coffee and a sandwich, and at the end of the day they'd have a few beers, and they'd be pissing themselves laughing about Gingy McAnally.

'Please yourself, Gingy. This is just getting to know you, and you getting to know us. This is just for you to know where you stand . . . you'll be standing for twenty-five years, Gingy. That's all . . . for now.'

They went to the door. They didn't bother to look back at him. The detective who had asked the questions whispered something that McAnally couldn't hear to the detective with the notebook, and they were chuckling as they went out.

A uniformed constable was framed in the open doorway. His face was expressionless, cold. He nodded curtly for McAnally to come to the door.

From Rennie's office the information was fed to the Press Office at Police Headquarters on the Knock Road. From the Press Office the information was dispersed on the Not Attributable basis.

Lunchtime's local television news and the Belfast evening newspaper first editions carried the report that 'according to senior police sources a man is in custody following an anonymous tip-off, and is being questioned in connection with inquiries into the murders yesterday of Judge William Simpson and his two police bodyguards'.

Roisin McAnally watched the lunchtime news and felt vindicated.

The Secretary of State was handed a transcript of a radio broadcast, and was seen by an aide to sigh with relief.

David Ferris was given a digest of the news story carried in the evening newspaper. He had slept, he was rested, but he shook his head as if in confusion when the Intelligence Officer drily explained the sophistications of 'psywar'. And he hadn't time to stand around when he and Fusilier Jones were already late for their Castlereagh appointment.

The Chief heard the radio, and was convinced, and waited for the men he had summoned to gather at the maisonette.

And Belfast went about its business. The shops were full in Royal Avenue, and the bus stops were crowded by the City Hall. The city breathed and continued with its life. And the disgust at a triple murder waned with the daylight.

*

'It wasn't the boys who brought him back from the South. I'd stake my life on them,' said the Brigade's Adjutant.

'It's not any of those who were with Gingy at the Crumlin Road, or it wouldn't have been just Gingy who was lifted,' said the Brigade's Quartermaster.

'And all of us, we knew that Gingy was up from the South, and we knew what he did.' The Chief spoke with a mock lightness, an ice tinkle in his voice.

'That's fucking ridiculous . . . if one of us is a tout, then the whole fucking war's finished . . .' The hoarse response from the Brigade's Intelligence Officer. 'If that's meant as a crack . . .'

'I tell you what I'm thinking, this is what I'm thinking . . .' The Brigade Quartermaster was tugging at the Chief's sleeve for his attention. 'I'm thinking, is Gingy McAnally one of us?'

'What's that mean?'

'It means that he quit. He walked out over the border.'

'You've not told me what you mean.'

'How's he going to be in there, that's putting it flat.'

'What's you saying?'

'Shit, do I have to spell it?'

The Chief stared him out. 'You have to spell it.'

The Brigade Quartermaster looked for the support of Intelligence and Operations, didn't win their encouragement. 'I just wondered how Gingy would stand up in Castlereagh, because he'd run once . . .'

The accusation dried on his lips.

'I brought Gingy McAnally up from the south, that's down to me,' the Chief said. 'If I brought him up then he's not a man to tout. And you're talking out of turn. It's a liberty, diabolical, for you to be talking about Gingy McAnally, whether he'll turn, when some shit's just dropped him.'

'It was worth saying.'

'And I've answered it . . . There was the boy that couriered him to the meeting with us.' The Chief's voice was a wind whisper.

'That's Mattie Blaney's . . .'

'I know who he is.' The face of the Chief was settled, as if everything before had been preamble.

'Mattie Blaney's as true a Republican . . .'

'I was at Mattie's wedding.'

'It would kill Mattie, to think his kid touted.'

'The boy who brought Gingy, when Gingy wasn't so keen, he saw only Gingy.' The Chief smiled, a sad crisp smile. 'Only Gingy's been lifted.'

'Mattie's boy's only fourteen fucking years old.'

'A tout's a tout.' The Chief slapped his hands together for effect. 'Touts destroy us. People have to learn that there's no future in touting.'

They went their way in silence. They went their way to hand out the order to those whom they could trust. They left their Chief to cross the landing to Mary and his bed. They left to find the men who would pick up Mattie Blaney's boy, the boy who had been sitting on a car smoking and waiting to direct Sean Pius McAnally to a rendezvous before going to school.

Rennie walked with David Ferris and Fusilier Jones down the corridor that ran the length of the ground floor Interrogation Rooms.

A far door opened. Two detectives spilled out. Hard on their heels came the prisoner and his escort.

The prisoner saw Rennie. His head had been down, his face was strain-torn. He saw Rennie and managed to snarl at him. A captured man with no chance of fighting to freedom.

The prisoner saw Ferris. The moment had been created by Rennie for a formal identification of the prisoner by Fusilier Jones. The prisoner saw Ferris and for an instant his defiance dissolved. Perhaps his mouth moved as if to speak, Ferris could not be certain, and he heard nothing, and Ferris couldn't help himself and he smiled quickly.

Rennie saw this silent exchange. They flattened against the corridor wall to let the prisoner and escort pass.

Rennie was pondering.

'Well?'

'That's him, sir. That's Sean Pius McAnally, who I positively identify as being in the car in Divis Street,' Jones replied.

'Very good. We'll get you onto paper. Sorry for the performance, but it's necessary.' Rennie's voice died. He was watching Ferris's face, and he was watching Ferris's eyes that followed the prisoner away down the corridor.

5

In the old days of the Troubles, the days of Army supremacy, a military intelligence officer had once remarked of Howard Rennie, 'Get blood out of granite, that one.' The remark had been thought amusing by a more junior officer, and over a glass in the Lisburn H.Q. Mess, it had been passed to the major who acted as R.U.C. Liaison. Through the major's daily contacts it had travelled to Police H.Q. The title of Granite

Rennie was now embedded in the lore of the police force. There were some senior officers who flitted in and out of the front line of the war. There were some who served two years in Criminal Investigation in Andersonstown or Crossmaglen, before a transfer to the safer Protestant recesses of County Antrim or County Down. Howard Rennie had never left the sharp end. He was now serving his ninth year in Criminal Investigation, and before that he had endured six years of Special Branch work.

He was now forty-nine. He had enough years behind him for a reasonable pension, and there were many commercial groups in the Province who would have paid him handsomely to come onto their staffs as a security consultant. He had never entertained the thought. Nor had he considered requesting a posting to a desk job. Howard Rennie was a front-line fighter.

His size and the intimidating cragginess of his face had fashioned for him a formidable reputation as an interrogator. Amongst the P.I.R.A. ranks, amongst men locked up and at liberty, he was a man marked down for killing.

His strength lay in the force of his belief in an ultimate victory. Not a victory tomorrow, or next week, or next year, but a sometime victory. He believed in the day when the opposition would be drowned in their own filth, the day when their ability to retaliate would finally have been destroyed. It was not a view shared in high places, either in Police H.Q., or amongst the politicians from London who administered the Province. The opinion of Howard Rennie was reckoned to be out of step with upper echelon thinking, and so he had stayed as a Detective Chief Inspector and been many times passed over for promotion to the rank of superintendent. His war was that of attrition. He could not contemplate an end to the war that involved appeasement to his enemy. If there was to be a sometime victory then it would have to come on Howard Rennie's terms.

The puffiness at the jowls was evidence of his fierce off-duty drinking. He would have denied angrily that he was an alcoholic, he would have said that he drank as much as the next man, and no more. Because of that high profile police work he was under perpetual strain, and some comfort from the strain came from the gin bottle. To the Organization he represented a considerable threat, a threat they had attempted twice to eliminate. The living room of his cul-de-sac house in the quiet Dunmurry suburb of the city was replastered and repapered but still showed the indentations of a burst of Armalite on automatic when the animals had made it inside his house to wait for his return home. More recently they had tried to car bomb him. A Ford Fiesta loaded with fertilizer mix and parked on the main road at the junction past which he must drive on his way to work, and the remote controlled detonation a split-second late, and the force of the blast taken by a young housewife out

58

shopping. The housewife had died, and Rennie had survived untouched and drunk a half-bottle before lunchtime. He was supported by his wife, who had spent one ever-to-be-remembered Sunday evening cuddling her children and facing the Armalite barrel and the pinched, hating face of a Provisional marksman. She never questioned her husband nor urged him against his prosecution of the war. She accepted that on the table beside their marriage bed there would always be, at night, a loaded P.P.K. pistol. She was Gloria. She lived behind blast-proof windows, she lived in a house that was bathed in light at night. She helped with the outings for the R.U.C. Widows and Dependents, and with the tombolas that paid for them. Her husband left the house most mornings before eight, and returned fourteen or fifteen hours later . . . and through the day she listened to each and every one of the local radio news broadcasts. She thought Howard Rennie was a grand man, and she knew she had no chance of changing him.

In the war, the Interrogation Rooms were his chosen battleground. In the twenty-one Interrogation Rooms at Castlereagh he was a familiar figure. He could be hunched and confidential and kindly, his elbows splayed on the table, his face close to that of his prisoner. He could be angry and pacing and shouting and threatening. The camera watched him, but there was no microphone in a Castlereagh Interrogation Room.

It was the middle of the evening.

Rennie had eaten his tea in the canteen. Sausages and chips and a smear of brown sauce, and a mug of tea with two sugars. From the canteen he stamped his way over to the Interrogation Block. He rarely strolled. It was his habit to hurry. McAnally was up for the third time. And the third team of detectives was working on him. Rennie knew they had been brief and cursory the first time. That was often the tactic. Let the implications of capture swim in the prisoner's mind. The second session was always tougher, more direct, attempting to exploit those implications . . . but, of course, since the bloody Amnesty fellow travellers and the European Court creatures had had their pennyworth, then the likes of Howard Rennie were no longer permitted to slap and tickle a prisoner – that was the camera's job, to make certain the likes of Howard Rennie didn't take a fist to the chin of a horrible little bastard whose only talent in life was sniping with a Remington Woodmaster rifle, or mixing fertilizer for a beer keg bomb . . . Shit, and if you couldn't belt the bastards, then there was sod all hope of getting them to talk.

Rennie knew that in the second session, McAnally had not opened his mouth. Not one bloody word from the little beast that was useful.

He shouldered past the uniformed policeman patrolling the corridor, into the fifth room from the end on the right. He nodded for the younger of the detectives to get himself up from his chair and out. Bloody regulations, regulations said that no more than two detectives should be

59

present at any one time for interrogation . . . bloody regulations tying the hands of the men who tried to keep the Province safe for decent people, that was Howard Rennie's anthem.

McAnally was looking up at Rennie.

'I'm obliged to give you my name. I'm Rennie, D.C.I. . . . ' Rennie spun the chair back to front. He sat heavily down, elbows resting on the chair's back. He belched, all the bloody chips. He was leaning forward.

'Being helpful are we, Gingy?'

Behind McAnally's head the detective shook his head.

'Are we going to be sensible, or are we going to be difficult? Are we going to have a life sentence without a minimum recommendation, or a life sentence with twenty-five years written in?'

McAnally flopped his head down onto his fists.

A cold grin from Rennie. 'I'm not allowed to offer you an inducement, McAnally, but all the big boys know the form. Help us, and there's a life sentence without a recommendation, that's a bloody sight easier than a Twenty-five . . .'

McAnally closed his eyes.

'McAnally, if you're not daft you'll examine your position. You were informed on . . . that's how rotten your organization is, it's rotten from floor to ceiling. Your own people grassed on you.'

McAnally opened his eyes, glowered at Rennie. His lips trembled, but he said nothing. Fighting to say nothing.

'Couldn't have been many who knew you were coming up from down South. Well, one of them that knew was friendly enough with us to grass on you. Are you going to spend a bit of time working out in your head which one it was? 'Course you'll spend a bit of time, you'll have twenty-five years of time to think which one it was . . . if you're not sensible. You've been inside, Gingy. You know how long twenty-five years takes inside.'

McAnally rolled off his chair.

He lay on the floor of the Interrogation Room.

He was face down on the floor, and he covered his ears with his hands.

'Getting the message, Gingy?'

Rennie was now off his chair and dropping to his hands and knees, and then straightening his legs as if about to make a press-up, and he lowered himself down, down onto the floor, down beside McAnally.

'You should be getting the message by now, Gingy. They grassed on you. They brought you up for a one-shot, and that was the end of their use for you.'

Little Gingy McAnally and big Howard Rennie both stomach-down on the floor, and McAnally squeezing the palms of his hands against his ears, and Rennie whispering into the cracks between his fingers.

'Nasty cut that one on your lip, Gingy.'

McAnally's tongue slipped between his teeth, rolled over the swollen lip.

'Don't you like a beating, Gingy? You're good at handing it out. You gave a bit of a beating to Billy Simpson. There's plenty in here would like to kick your stomach through your arse.'

Rennie saw McAnally try to bury his head down against his chest, as if that way he could better shut out the tap-drip of the voice in his ear.

'I would have thought the soldiers would have half killed you, Gingy . . .'

He saw McAnally's head move in the barest and quickest acknowledgement. Rennie crouched over McAnally and his hands were either side of McAnally's head, and his mouth brushed against the nape of McAnally's neck.

'The officer saved you, didn't he, Gingy, saved you from a bloody thrashing, didn't he?'

McAnally nodded.

'The officer stopped them from belting the shit out of you, Gingy?'

'Yes.'

'That officer showed you a bit of kindness?'

'Yes.' A tiny, reedy voice.

'A bit of kindness where you didn't expect any kindness?'

'Yes.'

'You'd trust that man, that officer, would you, Gingy?'

'Yes.'

'You'd trust him because he was a good young man, because he wasn't a bastard like me, because he saved you from a beating. Right, Gingy?'

'Yes.'

'And that officer's name is Lieutenant Ferris?'

'Yes.'

All of interrogation was a chance. Each day when he went into the Interrogation Rooms it was without a clear idea of how he would respond to his suspect. He played his hunch, sometimes he won, many times he lost. Rennie's head dipped, his forehead was against the floor. His mouth was close to McAnally's ear.

'I reckon that officer feels sorry for you.'

Rennie reached up. His fingers found the table's edge, and he levered himself to his feet. 'I must be about my business now, Gingy. I'll be back. And in the meantime you just have a wee thought on your friends,' Rennie said. 'No great urgency, of course,' he added, as the door closed behind him.

*

61

Past nine in the evening and the inside lights glowing through the thin curtains of the Turf Lodge streets. Wet streets, glistening in the land-rovers' headlights. Empty streets, because the Social Security was not paid till the next morning, and there was no money left for the bars. The landrovers cruised slowly, engines whining. Ferris and his driver and two squaddies, in the lead vehicle.

Ferris was thinking of Sam. He hadn't had a letter from her that week, but then he hadn't tried to ring, so it was quits. When he did write to her, or telephone, he never had much to say about Turf Lodge, about night patrolling. If he didn't write often and he didn't ring often, it was because there was nothing to say that he thought she ought to know, not because he didn't miss her. A girl who lived with her parents in a six-bedroomed stone house with a paddock and an orchard in rolling Somerset wouldn't have too much in common with patrolling the Turf Lodge estate – so he didn't tell her about it. He'd tell her about Sean Pius McAnally, but only enough for her to know that his platoon was getting the Glorygrams from Sunray. She'd like that, and she'd tell her father. Sam's father was a retired half Colonel. Effectively he had made Major and Company Command in the old Somerset Light Infantry, but he'd been upped to half Colonel to oversee the local schools' Cadet units. Not a bad chap, Sam's father, and he didn't stand in the way of what Sam did when David Ferris was down on leave. Trouble was he'd forgotten he hadn't made General, forgotten it clean out of the window when he'd had the Falklands map pinned up in the study during the South Atlantic affair.

She was lovely, his Sam, but thinking of Sam on a cold, wet night in Turf Lodge was enough to get himself sniped. Safer to be thinking that there might be a marksman in a snipe hide between the Drive and the Parade. She had bloody good thighs because she jogged three times a week, and bloody good breasts because she drank a pint of milk each morning and she was a bloody good girl because she kept herself for David Ferris all the time he was cruising through the Turf Lodge estate. If a chap had to be sniped then so much the better if he had a clear picture of Sam's very beautiful body in his head when the bead was on him.

'What are you thinking of, Jones?'

'Fanny, sir. What are you thinking of, sir?'

'Military tactics, Jones, what else?'

In the faint light Ferris could see Jones holding a straight face. He smiled. He heard the snigger of the squaddies behind him.

'. . . DELTA FOXTROT COME IN OVER . . .'

His head spun with the cry in his earpiece. He found the button on his radio, twisted the volume down.

'. . . Delta Foxtrot receiving over . . .'

'. . . DELTA FOXTROT THIS IS 49 . . . S.A.P. PARADE STROKE AVENUE R.V. . . . OUT . . .'

Ferris said quietly to Jones: 'Soon as possible to the junction of the Parade and Avenue.' He turned to his squaddies behind him. 'Sharp look-out, lads . . .'

Fusilier Jones knew the Turf Lodge like a local. Three right turns and a left.

The headlights swung along the street and caught a squaddie crouched against an overgrown hedge, and then the corporal who was bent down against the wall of a lock-up garage. Ferris saw what seemed to be a bundle of rags, perhaps a sack, beside the corporal before Jones killed the lights. Ferris swung his legs out of the landrover and scurried to his corporal.

The corporal's masked torch shone down into a small white face. Ferris saw the terrified, staring eyes and the blood-drained cheeks that were smeared with tears.

Ferris's thoughts were racing. Bloody hit and run driver, no bloody lights in the street . . . But the corporal's torch was moving down the short length of the boy's jersey . . . Ferris saw the hole at the elbow, worn through . . . and the torch moved on down the boy's thigh. He saw the blood-soaked knee of the boy, and the dark bullet hole set in the spread of crimson.

'But it's a bloody child . . .'

'It's a child, Mr Ferris, and he's been knee-capped,' the corporal said grimly.

'God Almighty . . . I don't believe it . . .'

'He's Liam Blaney, he's thirteen years old. Father's in the Kesh . . . Want to see his stomach?'

The corporal didn't wait for Ferris's reply. He pulled back the boy's shirt, lifted his jersey. Ferris saw the burns and the bruises.

'Must reckon him an informer, sir,' the corporal added.

Ferris knew the corporal's own children from back at the depot in England. He knew the dry, flat answers to be a sham.

'I'll run him down to the barracks, have an ambulance rendezvous there. Snap them up on the radio . . . Come on, son.'

He lifted the boy up in his arms. He felt him struggle, and then wince from the pain. He heard him cry out. He could sense what it would mean to the child, to be held in the arms of a British officer, and he thought he could sense the agony that would follow a bullet fired at point blank range through the bone and muscle and tissue of a knee-cap, and that was after the cigarettes, and after the beating. He held the child against his chest, tight so that he couldn't fight him. He walked to the landrover and climbed in, and the boy was cradled in his lap.

'They wouldn't do this to each other if they lived in a bloody zoo,

63

Mr Ferris,' Fusilier Jones observed, and slapped his hand onto the gear stick.

'Just get the thing moving, Jones . . .'

He didn't know what to say to the boy. He did not know how to comfort a child who had a shattered knee-cap and whose stomach was burned. He wedged his rifle between the seats and held the boy closely and tried to protect him from the lurching journey of the landrover.

'So what sort of a lad is your Ferris?'

Rennie, thank God for it, had been given a gin by the Commanding Officer.

Sunray had a Scotch, and the Intelligence Officer had a half-pint silver beer tankard cupped in his hands.

'A very professional young officer, proved that by his actions yesterday.' Sunray sat at the desk of his office, his fingers played with a paper knife.

'I'm not interested in his professional abilities, sir. What's his personality. Frankly, please.'

'Pretty much the same as everyone else,' the Intelligence Officer said cautiously.

'If he was pretty much the same as everyone else I wouldn't have bothered to come. If he wasn't *different* I'd be at home now in front of my bloody fire. If you can't be straight with me then I'm wasting my time, and I'll leave you in peace . . .' Rennie drained his glass, slapped it down on the polished table at his elbow. 'If you are able to be straight with me then . . . then Mr Ferris might just be very useful to me . . . Colonel, if it wasn't important, then I wouldn't be here.'

Sunray had little time usually for policemen in the Province. This man he could respect. A rough-cut stone, and a hard, tired face.

'Tell him, Jason.'

'There's no family tradition in the army, he's not the sort we usually get. He tried for a University commission, but he didn't get the college marks so he went to the Royal Military Academy, came to us that way. He's in our Regiment, but I wouldn't say he's part of us. Tried to leave us last year when we'd finished in Crossmaglen. He went for the Special Air Service selection course. Understand me, it's not against him, but S.A.S. evaluation of him was that he lacked the necessary cutting edge for that outfit . . .'

Sunray cut in. 'If the army was confined to graduates and S.A.S. qualifiers it would be a pretty small army. Wouldn't have me for a start.'

'He's a quiet man, Inspector Rennie, doesn't put himself about. If we have a Mess thrash, then he won't be there, not his scene. He'd regard the likes of me as a black and white merchant, therefore a bit stupid.'

Sunray said, 'His men are quite obviously fond of him. Which may not always be a good thing.'

'He has a pig-obstinate streak. If something's stuck in his head then it's time wasted to try and talk him out of it. And he's a doubter, if you know what I mean.'

'What does he doubt?' Rennie asked.

'What we're doing here, what else? . . . Example, he bawled me out the other day after he'd P.-checked this McAnally creature, before the R.P.G. hit. I said he should wake up to the fact that we were fighting psychopaths, he was jabbering about human beings. We had a bit of a stand-up.'

'It's what I hoped to hear,' Rennie said. 'I'd like to borrow Mr Ferris from you, Colonel.' Rennie smiled. He held out his glass. 'And I'd be obliged for the other half.'

The ambulance was already waiting inside the barracks yard when Ferris brought in Mattie Blaney's boy. The tears had stopped. Ferris thought it must be the shock setting in.

His squaddies hadn't talked on the drive back to the barracks. It was as if a message had sunk through to all of the soldiers in the landrover; if the enemy would do this to a child, to one of their own, then what would they do to a soldier if they were ever able to lay their hands on him, what would they do to a plain clothes soldier of S.A.S. or Mobile Reconnaissance Force or Intelligence Corps . . . ? And the thought was enough to make Ferris shiver.

The priest had arrived at Springfield Road. The squaddies called him 'F Two' or the Fucking Friar. He was Father Francis . . . It was said that he spoke the Gaelic language as a first choice, and was more fluent there than in English. Whenever there was an incident he was always fast down to the barracks from Turf Lodge. He was young, not out of his twenties and wore short-cut hair and heavy pebble glasses over pink cheeks that were hardly ready for the razor. The officers in the Mess all reckoned that he prayed on bare knees each night for the ground to open up and swallow all of the British army in Northern Ireland and then close over and suffocate them. The priest made a point of brushing against one of Ferris's soldiers as he went forward to watch the boy being lifted into the rear of the ambulance, and he could have walked round the soldier. He seemed to whisper in the ear of the boy before the doors were closed.

Ferris felt the anger rising in him. They were told always to be polite to priests. Headquarters laid down that the priests were a moderating influence on the community and were a necessary vehicle by which to detach the population from the clutches of the Provisionals. Headquarters only talked to the bishops.

'Quite a nice class of parishioner you have, Father Francis . . .' Ferris said.

'Mr Ferris, isn't it? I presume it's what you wanted, Mr Ferris, a boy knee-capped, or a man executed.'

'What I wanted? . . . Absolute bullshit.'

The priest glared at Ferris. 'Obscenity is usually the hallmark of a second-rate vocabulary. You lifted Sean McAnally, a good family man, a man living in the South and trying to renounce violence, you lift him when he comes home to see his wife, and then you make your vicious insinuation in the media . . .'

'What the hell are you talking about?'

'You let it be known that an informer had led you to Sean McAnally. You know what happens to informers, Mr Ferris. That's why I say with confidence that the mutilation of this child is what you wanted.'

The priest turned to walk away.

'That's just not bloody true,' Ferris called after him.

The priest swung to face Ferris. 'I haven't the time to stand around, Mr Ferris. I have to go to the Royal Victoria Hospital to offer consolation to a small hurt child while the surgeons rebuild his knee-cap. They do a good job, but he'll never run again. Then I have to go to his mother. Someone has to try to sweep up the filth left by your dirty tricks.'

The priest was gone, out from under the arc lights, out into the night. The high iron gates closed behind him.

Ferris shook his head, as if there was a bad taste in his mouth and a pain in his forehead. He had heard the phrase 'anonymous tip-off' on the radio, and he'd wondered, and he'd had a laugh to himself about it when the Intelligence Officer had explained the ploy. Christ, what a bloody awful place. He had used his sleeve to wipe the tears off the child's cheeks.

The Intelligence Officer was standing in a doorway, watching. He would have heard the exchange.

'Sunray's office, David.'

Ferris went to the Weapons Pit, aimed at the sand, cleared his rifle, and headed for the Intelligence Officer. He felt betrayed. There was a sort of a truth in the accusation of F Two. 'Psychological Warfare' the Intelligence Officer called it. 'Dirty Tricks' the priest called it. And both *knew* they were right . . .

He followed the Intelligence Officer to Sunray's office.

He saw Rennie sitting in an easy chair, with a glass in his hand, and comfortable. Sunray didn't offer Ferris a drink. He went straight to the point. Detective Chief Inspector Rennie had made an unusual request that Ferris be from time to time available at Castlereagh. There was nothing frivolous about the request, and he had been convinced of the urgency of the matter and so had waived the normal etiquette of consulting with Lisburn Headquarters. Ferris should put himself at Detective Chief Inspector Rennie's disposal. Ferris looked at his watch. Near to ten o'clock.

'Let's shift ourselves, young man.' Rennie acknowledged the drink with a nod to the Commanding Officer, and led the way out.

Ferris travelled in Rennie's car. Hell of a job holding a Self Loading Rifle in some state of readiness while sitting in the passenger seat of a saloon. There was a police landrover behind them. Rennie drove fast, eyes alert and scanning the road ahead and the pavements. There were occasional bar crawlers meandering on the streets' sides. Generally the pavements were deserted.

The silence was broken by Ferris as they came off the Grosvenor Road to cross the centre of the city. He wouldn't have spoken while they were in 'hostile' territory, wouldn't have distracted the driver.

'It wasn't true that we were acting on a tip-off for McAnally . . . whoever put that out should be bloody well ashamed of himself.'

'I put it out,' Rennie said. 'And, Mr Ferris, it'll take a lot more than that to shame me.'

'It was a kid.'

Rennie looked away from the road, looked into Ferris's face.

'I've been fighting this war for more than fifteen years. In that time a few things may have happened that I regret having happened. But I don't need a lecture on mistakes from someone who's been here eight weeks . . . there's a war going on here, Mr Ferris. You want some victims of the war? Try the Pentecostalists hymn-singing when they're shot down, try the nurses who're going to bed when the hostel's bombed, try the folks having a meal out at the La Mon when they're incinerated. I care about those victims, worshippers, nurses, folks having their dinner. I care about them more than I care about a Provo kid getting his knee blown.'

'And the kid isn't what I've been dragged out for?' Ferris said brusquely.

'Don't tell me you're knackered, lad, we're all knackered. And don't tell me it's unfair, because everything that happens in this God-forsaken place is unfair. Listen, my mates are buried here. That's why I care about winning this war. That's why mistakes don't keep me awake.'

'I'm listening.'

'So listen, and don't interrupt.'

Ferris grinned. 'Let's have it, Mr Rennie.'

'First the logistics. We're allowed four interviews with a prisoner in any one day, and the day finishes at midnight. We'll be at Castlereagh at eleven, and we've had three sessions with our laddie . . .'

'With McAnally?'

'Do us a favour, young man, shut up . . . I have one more hour with McAnally before I have to tuck him up for the night, and I don't get back to him until he's had his cooked breakfast in the morning. That's the logistics. Now the history . . . In the old days, when the police role was upgraded to primacy over the army, we were given the job of criminalizing the paramilitaries. We had to get them into court and win a conviction on a criminal basis – murder, attempted murder, possession of firearms, membership of a proscribed organization. No witness'll dare to come forward, can't blame them, so we used to be a bit physical in persuading the "freedom fighters" to sign away their liberty. They confessed and the courts locked them up, and the politicians across the water got faint-hearted and started screaming. We were filling the Kesh up, putting the bastards away . . . That's history. Castlereagh's wired for cameras now. There are uniforms crawling up the bloody corridors. Confessions don't come easily any more. Got the picture?'

They were out into the south-east suburbs. Tree-lined roads, solid family houses. Homes for the Protestants to sleep safe in while the war was fought in their name away in the ghettos, away to the west of the city.

'Got it.'

'So, we had to find another way. We have one thing going for us here, it's the only bloody thing. We have money, we have as much money as we can spend. We had to stop thumping the confessions out of them, and we started to buy the information we required. We bought informers . . . Twenty-five a week in old notes, or fifty, or up to a couple of tons if the leak was good and sharp. P.I.R.A. doesn't like informers, so the bodies started showing up on the wasteground. Our informers were getting the message that it wasn't a pensionable job. We moved on, we started to work on those we already had safe in custody, those that were safe from a kangaroo court and a bullet. We called it the Converted Terrorist policy . . .'

'Supergrass.'

Rennie was bent over his wheel, talking quietly into his dashboard.

'The Brits have to anglicize every bloody thing. "Supergrass" is your word, from the East End of London. "Converted Terrorist" is mine. To the Provos, he's a "tout" . . . Even the bloody man in Stormont Castle calls them "supergrasses" . . . if that's what you want, David, we'll call them that, we'll keep it British. It's a genius trick . . .'

'When it works.'

'It's genius because they don't know where the risk comes from next. They have to spend half their bloody time wondering whether they're going to be shopped by their own crowd.'

'I read the papers, I'm not a damned idiot, you've had some that have worked, you've had more that have reneged on the deal.'

Rennie ignored the interruption. He had a cigarette in his mouth and was lighting it with a match and turning left and changing up through his gears. Expert hand and eye.

'We've found something of a pattern for the man who might go supergrass. He's in the twenty-five plus age group. He's beyond the aggro corner stuff, petrol bombs and stones, he's too old for that. He's got a woman, probably he's got kids. He's got a fixed address. He's done a stretch inside, knows what the Kesh is like. He's come back out and returned to his old ways, and he's been lifted, and this time he's going away for a lifer, or as near as makes no difference. He's on a treadmill because with his record and his new offences he's going away until he's an old man. That's the one we convert.'

'That's McAnally,' Ferris said softly. He saw ahead of them the high brilliant lights of the Castlereagh perimeter. He felt the trembling of his hands on the stock of his rifle.

'When you lifted him he was still wearing his vest, silly bugger, and very considerate. They don't learn. Forensic's done the work on the vest. Forensic puts McAnally on the R.P.G. Your Fusilier puts McAnally into the getaway car. McAnally's away for twenty-five years, that's what I've told him.'

'Why me?' Ferris knew the answer.

'For a man to turn, he has to make a hell of a decision. He's chucking over his shoulder everything that he knows, every single bloody thing except, perhaps, his family.'

They had come to the gate. Rennie held up his I/D for the police sentry to see from the gatehouse window.

'Why me?'

'He's turning his back on everything he's ever relied on before, and he has to have a hell of a trust of us.'

'And he trusts me, is that why it's me?'

'Something like that.'

Rennie accelerated into the Castlereagh car park. He stopped, switched off the engine.

'Once they start there's no stopping them. It's getting them started that's the hard bit. Get Gingy McAnally started tonight, and I'll kiss you on both bloody cheeks of your arse.'

Rennie climbed out of the car; when he looked back he saw that Ferris was still sitting in his seat, staring ahead through the windscreen, expressionless.

'I told you. I haven't all night.'

'I don't know whether I want to do it.'

Rennie climbed back into the car, his knee was on his seat. He lowered over Ferris. 'Don't fucking tell me what you *want* to do. You can't choose what you *want* to do . . . you just bloody get on with it.'

Ferris slammed the car door shut behind him. He went to the

gatehouse and accepted a chitty for his rifle. He followed Rennie through the inner gates and into the cell block.

He had been briefed in the canteen over a tired cheese sandwich and a beaker of coffee. He knew what he had to say. He knew the time that had been given to him.

McAnally was sitting cross-legged at the head of the bed. He wore his trousers and was bare from the waist up because he had taken off his shirt, and they had taken away his vest.

Ferris sat on the floor, his back to the wall. The cell was dimly lit from the ceiling. The cell was warm. McAnally said nothing.

Ferris talked, and sometimes McAnally seemed to listen, and sometimes he was a year away, and sometimes a mood away, and sometimes he reacted and squirmed, and sometimes he screwed down his face as if the emotion was too great to bear. Ferris could see that McAnally was exhausted, twenty-two hours since he had been lifted, desperate for sleep. Ferris thought that if McAnally had not been so tired he would have to have seen through the clumsiness of the subterfuge.

Ferris said that he happened to be at Castlereagh at that time because he had been out on patrol and this was the first opportunity for him to make a formal statement, hadn't had the time when he was down before. He had drifted on, a rambling monologue.

'. . . we were patrolling Turf Lodge, round your home. The lights were on upstairs, I suppose they'd gone to bed, didn't see anyone, we didn't knock the door. It's three kids, isn't it? I'd have liked to have spoken to your wife. If the lights were on upstairs, I suppose she was putting the little ones into bed. That's a hell of a boy you've got . . .'

Drifting on, just as he had been told.

'I'm a bit upset tonight, actually. We saw a pretty horrible thing in Turf Lodge. I had a call-up from one of my foot patrols that was out in tandem with us. They found a boy who'd been knee-capped. I'd never seen a knee-capping before. I think he's thirteen, the boy they knee-capped, and they'd burned his stomach with cigarettes. I took him down to the barracks and packed him off in an ambulance. He couldn't really talk. Shock, I imagine. He was really brave . . . God, I can't imagine what the pain would be like. It seems that your friends reckoned he'd informed on you. His name's Liam Blaney . . . I suppose you know him. I was told they can fix these things up pretty well in the Royal Victoria. He was really gutsy . . .'

Ferris could not take his eyes from McAnally's face. He saw when he scored, and he saw when McAnally was able to deflect him. But the face was more rested, not in such turmoil. The eyes were less haunted.

'The policeman who took you away from us, I was talking to him this

70

evening. He told me that you'd made it out of the Organization. From my side of things I shouldn't say it, but that must have taken a damn great effort. He said you were down south, that you'd gone down there to live. It must be really difficult to break out . . . Well, it must be difficult, but I suppose it's wonderful that you can go to bed at night and know that you'll sleep through to the morning, that you won't have the likes of my platoon heifering in on you . . .'

There was a weak, poor smile on McAnally's face.

'You were the first Provisional I'd ever seen, you know. I'd seen guys up for screening, that sort of thing, guys that the I.O. said were in the Organization, but you were the first real live one . . . They've told me now that you're implicated in the Crumlin Road thing. That's bloody dreadful . . . I mean, you made the effort and went down south. I suppose they brought you back for this, for the R.P.G. job . . . sorry, don't say anything, I'm not a detective. When I say that's bloody dreadful, what I mean is that it's dreadful that the buggers couldn't leave you alone. There's you, building a new life, and then this happens . . . To me, not leaving you alone down there is worse – yes, I reckon it's worse – than what was done to the Blaney boy . . . God, I can't get that kid out of my mind, can't get away from knowing that after what was done to him he'll never run again, never kick a football . . . I know my squaddies turned you over a bit, you got one of them in the goolies, but what they did to you, that's nothing like what was done to Liam Blaney . . .'

Ferris looked at his watch. McAnally's eyes seemed to plead with him as he stood up.

'Sorry, I have to be off, look at the bloody time. They took your watch, of course . . . it's close to midnight. If I see the wife about I'll speak to her, tell her you're in good shape.'

He went to the cell door. He rapped his knuckles on it. When he looked around he saw that McAnally faced the wall.

'Goodnight, Mr McAnally . . . Try to find a way to help yourself . . . after what the bastards have done to you, after the shit they've dropped you into, see if you can help yourself, and your wife, and your kids . . . God knows what's possible now. If anything's possible, hang onto it . . . Goodnight, Mr McAnally.'

Ferris looked for a last time at the face in profile against the wall. He felt soiled. Rennie had decided that a serving officer of 2 R.R.F. was soft enough to strike a chord with an R.P.G. marksman of the P.I.R.A. who faced a triple life sentence. And the shit had decided right. McAnally bit at his lip and muttered at the white-painted bricks of his cell wall. Rennie had known his chemistry.

'Do you know anything about kestrels, Mr Ferris?'

'No, sorry. I don't,' Ferris said.

71

The constable had opened the door, made way for Ferris to step out of the cell.

Standing by the protected door at the end of the cell block, Rennie watched Ferris come towards him. He saw Ferris pass under a bright ceiling light. He looked for the mood. His cheeks broke into a smile. He sighed deeply in relief. He saw the trouble in Ferris's face.

'Well done, David . . . and if you didn't know it, the war's bigger than that little rat.'

'Your little rat asked me if I knew anything about kestrels.'

'What did you say?'

'That I didn't know anything.'

'Then find out.'

'Why?'

'Because a kestrel's freedom, that's what I want him talking about, thinking about.'

6

When he was active, before he had gone south, in the time that he was on the R.P.G. team, the Volunteers and Battalion men were briefed on the tactics employed by the interrogators, and on the counter-measures to confound those tactics. The men who gave the briefings were those who had been with some frequency in the solitary cells and the Interrogation Rooms of Castlereagh in Belfast, or Gough in Armagh, or Strand away in Derry. The first twenty-four hours weren't the hardest, the briefers said, because the prisoner was still close to his home and his family and his muckers, but the isolation was clawing at the prisoner by the second twenty-four hours, and was worst for the third twenty-four hours. After three days, the briefers said, then the isolation slipped. They could only hold you for seven days. After seven days they had to charge you, or release you. After seven days the prisoner was either turfed out to make his way back to his family, or he was booked and shipped off to the crowded Remand Wing of the Crumlin Road. Seven days was the length and breadth of the isolation. For seven days the prisoner saw only the escorting policemen and the interrogating detectives. And the second and third days were worst, because after the third day the prisoner was on the downhill road and heading for the company of his family or the Remand Wing. The briefers said that if a man was to implicate himself or himself and his friends then he would do so on the second day of solitary or on the third day.

The briefers said that it was the easiest for the man who could stay silent . . . Shit, McAnally had tried to stay silent, he'd even laid down on the floor to get away from the water-drip of their voices, and the bastard Rennie had followed him down to the floor. The briefers said that it was the worst for the man who tried to argue the facts put before him. The briefers said that it was good if you could get a small stone or a sliver of glass into your shoe and under your toes, if you could squeeze your toes down and hurt yourself and turn your mind from the questions. The briefers said that the detectives would always pretend they knew everything. The briefers said that the detectives would try to turn you, and they'd offer money, money and immunity, money and immunity from prosecution and safety for a lifetime in return for a statement that betrayed the Organization.

Sean Pius McAnally had six more days of resistance.

And after the six days? After the six days there was a year of remand. And after the year of remand? After the year in the Crumlin Road there would be a sentence with the recommendation that the prisoner serve a minimum of twenty-five years.

He thought he could remember each day of his five years served in H Block 7 . . . Shit, this was a five years' sentence times five. This was every day of five years times five. Every day in a two bunk cell times five, every strip search and cell search times five, every visit from Roisin and her mother and his mother and Young Gerard times five, every sneer from the screws times five . . . and every year when the victory wasn't closer times five. After five years times five his mother and her mother would be dead, and Roisin would be age lined and – shit – Young Gerard might be in another cell in the block.

Day after day in the caravan near Vicarstown he had sworn to himself that he would never go back, never reinvolve himself in the Organization . . . because he would disintegrate under the weight of another five years times five.

He had told the bird about the Kesh. When the bird had the freedom to fly, and when it perched in the branches over the caravan door for the bacon rinds, he had told it about the compounds and walls and cell blocks and keys and bars and watch towers of the Kesh. The bird knew what the hell it was about. The bird could fly from the trees by the caravan and soar in the winter winds high above the canal. He had once gone into the library in Monasterevan and he had found a book on Falconry on the shelves – first time in God knew how long that he had taken a book from a shelf – and he had read about the equipment used by people who kept tamed birds of prey. He reckoned it was all shit. He reckoned the hoods and jesses and the leash and the bells were the same words as compound, wall, cell block, key, bar. To trap that bird and tame it would be to sentence his kestrel to the Kesh. In his mind he could see the bird, and he wondered if the farmer, his mother's cousin, had come to the caravan to feed it. He wondered if the bird waited for him, or if the bird had flown.

The cells were sound proofed. He was alone and stifled in his own silence.

They wouldn't hurt him, not like they had the last time. Who needed to be slapped and kicked and punched when they had six more days of him in Castlereagh, and a year on remand, and twenty-five more years in H Block 7? Jesus Christ . . . and he had sworn an oath, an oath of loyalty on the landing above the stairs of his Da's house, and never had a doubt that he could handle the bloody oath.

The cell door opened. McAnally hadn't heard the footsteps approach down the outer corridor.

The policeman looked at the prisoner curiously, like he was a bloody freak.

'You alright, McAnally?'

Why shouldn't he be alright? Only got six more days and then a year on remand and then twenty-five years in H Block 7.

McAnally nodded his head. So bloody tired, and a pain behind his eyes, and the figure of the policeman in the doorway was blurred. The policeman spoke with an English accent, one of the bastards who had come across the water to do a dirty job. They were always the worst, the English ones. They had a bolt to run to, back home.

'Bring your tray here, McAnally.'

Without thinking he picked the tray off the cell floor and carried it to the policeman. There was a trolley in the corridor, and another policeman who eyed him with distrust and dislike.

'What time have you, sir?' McAnally asked.

'What time? Breakfast time, of course.' And the policeman was laughing with his mate as he closed the door, locked it.

He hated them, because they were the enemy. And when he had the R.P.G. in his hands, then the bastards wouldn't be laughing at him. He tried to remember the feel of the R.P.G. So bloody long ago . . . Two days ago.

'What happened last night?'

Armstrong passed the marmalade to Ferris. He had been on Ops Room duty when Ferris had returned from Castlereagh.

'Not a lot.'

Wilkins slid the butter dish across the table. 'You slunk in last night like the world was on your shoulders.' From the Chaplain's room, enjoying a coffee, he had seen Ferris returning to their room.

Armstrong persisted. 'Something must have happened for them to want you down at Castlereagh.'

'I was put in with McAnally.'

'What on earth for?'

'To turn him,' Ferris snapped. 'What else could it be for?'

'Shirt on, old chap, just asking.'

'And now you know.'

Wilkins said, 'Hope of a supergrass, eh? That's big time for a platoon commander.'

Armstrong said, 'I suppose he's all wet round the privates now he's in the cage.'

'I'm trying to eat my bloody breakfast.'

'Is this going to happen often?' Armstrong was filling his coffee cup.

'What's it to you?'

'If you're going to be swanning off to Castlereagh then George and I are the buggers who're going to be covering your rosters, that's what it's to do with us.'

'My advice, David,' Wilkins said deliberately, 'don't get involved.'

Ferris clattered his chair back. A triangle of toast was buttered on his plate, untouched. He stormed to his feet.

'I didn't bloody ask to be involved. I was told it didn't matter a toss what I wanted.'

'Supergrass is police work.'

'Pity nobody said that last night, when I was hijacked.'

'Not a chance, not if he's like he was when I had him yesterday.' The detective, McDonough, had done five years in Criminal Investigation, was reckoned a good interrogator.

'You weren't there for the last session, I was,' Rennie said harshly. 'And he had his soldier friend for Horlicks before we tucked him up . . . There's a good chance.'

'He's going down for triple murder. What's on offer for him?' Astley was younger than McDonough, more obviously keen.

'Nothing specific's on offer, but McAnally's a shaky boy right now, and needs to be kept shaking.' Rennie closed the file.

'You're on hand this morning, Mr Rennie?' McDonough asked.

Rennie hesitated. 'Not this morning, got some business. After lunch I'm here.'

'Nothing on offer then?' Astley was polishing his spectacles. More of a schoolmaster than an interrogator.

'For a few names, for jumping up in the witness box, there might just be no recommended minimum,' Rennie said.

'Out in seven years, fifty bloody per cent remission.' McDonough's lips twitched in disgust.

'Like I said, for a few names.'

*

The Secretary of State stood bareheaded in the light rain. This once he had contradicted the Detective Inspector who was responsible for his personal safety. The Detective Inspector would have had him stay in the church after the service, and avoid the graveside because there was a crowd gathered at the church gate, and they had jeered the Secretary of State on his way in, and when the body was down and covered their inhibitions would be slight. He had insisted that he should go to the graveside whether or not the threat existed of kicks and fists and stones.

William 'Tenner' Simpson was being buried in a village churchyard north of Ardmillan, within sight of the dark islands littering the inshore waters of Strangford Lough. It was Protestant country. It was the country of people loyal to the Crown.

'Yet, O Lord God most holy, O Lord most mighty, O holy and most merciful Saviour, deliver us not into the bitter pains of eternal death.'

Not a wet eye in sight, the Secretary of State thought. These were not whining folk. They stood straight-backed, straight-faced. They ignored the Secretary of State as an unwelcome interloper. He would not be ignored at the church gate. When he left the consecrated ground the crowd would angrily show their gut feelings for the security policy over which he presided.

'Forasmuch as it hath pleased Almighty God of his great mercy to take unto himself the soul of our dear brother here departed, we therefore commit his body to the ground.'

The Prime Minister had been on the telephone before he left Stormont. Prime Minister's Questions in the House that afternoon, and a question down calling yet again for the Secretary of State's resignation and demanding to know what action was being taken against the Republican gangs who could assassinate a judge in broad daylight . . . He would dearly like to have told the Prime Minister that a Sean Pius McAnally was to be charged with Billy Simpson's killing. He had only replied that a man was helping police with their inquiries, and heard the whistle of impatience on the scrambled line.

'Earth to earth; ashes to ashes; dust to dust.'

The soil scratched the coffin wood.

The Secretary of State felt the light tap on his shoulder, and turned to his civil servant.

'Bit soon, Fred,' the Secretary of State mouthed.

'No one here will miss shaking your hand,' the civil servant said. 'You've been photographed here, that's good enough.'

He flushed. He walked away from the mourners. The civil servant was at his side. There were eight detectives in a wall around him. They went out through the gardener's gate of the churchyard to where his car and the back-up were parked alongside the grass cuttings and the compost heap. Uniformed policemen were holding back a knot of sullen-faced men and women. The widow was still at the graveside. He

76

might get away without an incident. The detectives were hurrying him, almost forcing him to run. The crowd loathed him because they held the man from Westminster responsible for the atrocities of the Provisionals . . . The back door of the car was open for him. The civil servant nudged him forward, pitched him down into his seat. The cars surged forward. For a moment a woman's face was pressed against the armour-plated window by the Secretary of State's head. He heard her howling at him, couldn't understand what she told him. A constable heaved her back, and the car and the back-up were away.

'What did she say, Fred?'

'She said, "You'll be making him a supergrass, the rat that killed our Billy, and giving him immunity", that's toned down a bit.'

'The man who killed a judge get immunity for grassing? Over my dead body.'

McDonough smoked a pipe. Astley lit a cigarette. McDonough was pacing. Astley lounged against the wall.

McAnally sat at the table.

'So you haven't an offer to make to me?'

Astley shook his head.

McDonough said, 'What's on offer, Gingy, is three life sentences . . .'

'What about a bloody offer?'

'With a recommendation of a minimum number of years to be served.'

'We reckon the judge'll recommend twenty-five, Gingy,' Astley said. 'He's hardly going to go easy when it was one of his own.'

The breath sighed in McAnally's mouth. Sometimes he could see Astley's watch. He had been in for an hour. There had been long, aching silences. They didn't seem to be interested in talking to him, they seemed prepared to let him sit at the table and brood on twenty-five years.

'You've got a problem, Gingy,' McDonough said earnestly.

'Twenty-five fucking problems.'

'That's quite witty, Gingy.' Astley chuckled.

McAnally scratched his forehead. He thought of his oath. He thought of Roisin and Young Gerard and Little Patty and Baby Sean. He thought of the men who had been on the hit with him, and the men who had brought him up to Belfast from the caravan. He thought of a life sentence in H Block 7. He had no stone in his shoe, no splinter of glass to press against his toe. They always called him 'Gingy'. Whether they shouted at him, whether they whispered at him, he was always 'Gingy'. His friends called him 'Gingy', his friends on the R.P.G. team, and the men he had known in the Kesh who were still in the cells there, behind the wire there. Who were these bastards to call him 'Gingy'?

The quiet was broken by Astley's hacking cough, a smoker's cough. Then, after he had cleared his throat and snorted into his handkerchief, the quiet was back again and simmering through the room.

'What's the best that could happen?' He heard his own voice booming back from the walls.

'That "Tenner" and his two 'tecs could walk through the old door, that's about the best that could happen . . . but they won't come through the door.' McDonough was beating his pipe bowl into the tinfoil ashtray on the table. 'So I don't know what's the best that could happen.'

'Don't piss on me.' McAnally's eyes raced between the two men who watched him without passion. 'What are you offering me?'

'We're not in the offering business, Gingy,' Astley said.

'We don't have to offer you anything, Gingy,' McDonough said.

'We've got three life sentences on you,' Astley said.

'With a minimum recommendation,' McDonough said.

'What I'd suggest, Gingy . . .'

'Listen carefully, lad.'

'. . . is that you have a little think, on your own . . .'

'Try and think what we might be grateful for.'

'There's just a possibility, Gingy . . .'

'No more than a possibility.'

'. . . that we might get a judge to forget the minimum recommendation,' Astley said.

'If we were to say that we were really grateful,' McDonough said.

'Why don't you have a little think, Gingy?' Astley's hand was on McAnally's shoulder. He jerked him upright, and frog-marched him to the door.

'Some quiet thinking, Gingy,' McDonough said.

Middle morning in Turf Lodge. The patrol moved circumspectly through the estate. Upstairs curtains were drawn in 31 and 35 and 39 and 47 and 53 of the Drive. Ferris noted the drawn curtains. He knew the men in those houses had no work. The wife would have been up early to see the children to school with their sandwich boxes, the man would have stayed in his bed. The man would get up before lunchtime, and in the afternoon he would take his place on the corner of the Drive and the Avenue if it wasn't raining and gossip with his cronies, or stand in silence beside them to watch the slow-moving life of Turf Lodge. Ferris knew that there was fifty per cent plus unemployment amongst the men of Turf Lodge. He supposed there were estates on the fringes of English towns where the workless rate was as high. What he did know was that there were no estates in English towns through which soldiers walked with so great a caution.

David Ferris's father was a bank manager living on the outskirts of the Lancastrian town of Preston. He firmly believed in the advice offered by an English politician, that the unemployed should get on their bicycles and set off in search of work. David Ferris's father knew nothing of the life of Turf Lodge, and less than nothing about what his son did in the Turf Lodge estate.

The middle of the morning was a bad time for the patrols . . . Earlier, there would be the children and their mothers going to school, and at lunchtime there would be the mothers collecting the smallest children, and in the afternoon there would be the older children coming home. The soldiers were always more relaxed when the pavements and roads were filled with children. The risk of bombs was always greatest when the streets were empty; the car bomb, the bicycle bomb, the culvert bomb, the pipe bomb, the booby trap bomb. The bomb could be resting in the boot of the rust-damaged Ford Cortina parked half on the pavement and half on the gutter, it could be laid in the strapped-down bag on the back of the bicycle seat, it could be placed under the man-hole cover in the pavement, it could be stuffed into a length of builder's plastic piping, it could be under the wood stairboard of a derelict house. The bomb could be detonated by remote command, by wire control, by contact.

David Ferris thought that his father, sitting in the manager's office in his bank, would not have been able to comprehend what it was like for his son to walk through Turf Lodge mid-morning in early December. He knew his mother and his father went to church now, he knew that they prayed each week for his safe return from that barbarian place, and would do until his sixteen weeks were done.

He saw Mrs McAnally, with her push chair and with the little girl beside her legs, come out through the broken gate of 63. She was on the same side of the road as Ferris, coming towards him.

The soldier in front of Ferris made way for her to squeeze between him and a front garden hedge. She had her eyes down when she passed the soldier. When she looked up, Ferris was in front of her. For a moment she stared at him, recognizing him.

'Mrs McAnally . . .'

He saw her lip curl in dislike, the tired prettiness of her was wiped away.

'I saw your husband last night.'

For a moment her chin quivered, as if she were about to reply to him, then she thrust the push chair forward and the wheel bounced on his boot and a wing bolt caught at his trouser legs, and she was past him.

He felt a sense of despair. For a few seconds, the time it took him to move a dozen yards, his mind was clouded by the disgust in her mouth and eyes.

And she would have seen him dead, he knew that, and if he had been dead in the Drive it was a good bet that she would have clapped.

Sean Pius McAnally lay face down on the mattress of his cell bed.

His hands covered his eyes. His wrists protected his face from the bedding material.

The thoughts bellowed in his head, and tortured him. The thoughts were of opting out, of going south again and turning his back on the Organization, the thoughts were of a lonely life in the caravan beside the canal. He hadn't asked to be brought back. He hadn't asked to have the bloody R.P.G. put into his hands . . . and he hadn't asked to be dumped in a cell in the Castlereagh Holding Centre, staring twenty-five years in the Kesh in the face.

In his agonies, lying on his stomach, Sean Pius McAnally resolved to fight to win his freedom. He didn't concern himself with the morality of the decision, nor with the consequences. His thoughts were simple and immediate. They were of the echoing cold wings of the H Block, and of his children crawling over him, and of the warmth of Roisin against him in the night, and of the bird in the tree above the caravan, and of the clean night mists rising from the canal.

Abruptly he sat up and faced the door of the cell and waited for the policeman to lead him back to the Interrogation Room.

The police band was far to the front, crying out the death march. Howard Rennie walked in the tenth row of mourners behind the hearse. In the first rows of mourners were the family of the Detective Sergeant who had died in the Crumlin Road, and behind the family were the Security Forces' public faces – Chief Constable, Deputy Chief Constable, G.O.C. N.I., G.O.C. Land Forces who had helicoptered in from Billy Simpson's burying. Rennie was back amongst the 'tecs, with the men who had worked with the Detective Sergeant and who faced the fair old risk of following on the same trek into the Roselawn cemetery.

She was a great girl, the widow. She'd not let herself down, not in the church, not at the graveside.

Rennie knew the Presbyterian Minister who was burying his friend. He'd heard him at the last police funeral for a parishioner, heard what he'd said about the killers of a policeman. If the Minister came down to the Interrogation Rooms at Castlereagh, and sat in on the questioning of murder suspects, then he'd wipe the waffle about conscience from his funeral addresses. Rennie had yet to discover remorse in the Interrogation Rooms. Regret at being caught, yes. Conscience, never.

He would be going straight back from Roselawn, with the grave earth on his shoes, to Castlereagh, to the murderer of his friend.

'Don't go biting my head off, I'm just telling you there's a powerful anger at what happened to Blaney's boy. That's all I'm saying.'

'Who's angry?' The Chief sat in the snug of the bar on the Falls down at Beechmount. There was a man on the door of the snug. The drinkers in the main bar could not see in. That morning the Chief was holding court for two members of his Brigade staff and the Falls Provie Battalion Commander. It was a dark recess of a room, with the small window's light diminished by the heavy protective mesh outside the glass. 'Who's bloody angry?'

'People are angry, people from the Blaney boy's street.' It was rare for the Provie Battalion Commander to take on the Chief.

'Gone soft on touting, have they, in the Blaney brat's street?'

'They're angry because they say he's not a tout, they say no boy of Mattie Blaney would be a tout.'

'There was a court martial . . .'

'He didn't admit to nothing.'

''Course he wouldn't bloody admit it. It was legit . . . I'll not have fucking touts, who's ever son they are.'

'That's my place up there, Turf Lodge, that's my swim . . .'

The Chief leaned forward across the table. He hiccupped sweet and sour breath. 'Touts kill us . . . got it? Touts kill us, so we kill touts. The Blaney boy was lucky he wasn't killed . . . got it?'

'What if he wasn't a tout?'

The Chief's fist darted across the table, caught at the collar of the Provie Battalion Commander and twisted so that the collar bit into his throat. 'I don't want to hear about the Blaney boy. I don't give a shit for Mattie Blaney's boy. I care for Gingy more than Mattie Blaney's boy . . . and Gingy's in fucking Castlereagh . . .'

The fist loosened its hold.

'I was just telling you, that's all . . .' The Provie Battalion Commander was a window cleaner. He was good with a rifle, and poor with words. He wished that he had kept his mouth shut. In the subterranean areas of his mind he cut off the thoughts of Mattie Blaney's boy and the cigarette burns on the kid's stomach, and the screaming, and the blood from the smashed knee-cap. He cut off the thoughts because he was aware in all his waking moments of the Chief's principal fear, the fear of touts.

There was a knock at the outside of the door to the snug. The door was opened a few inches. A paper bag was passed in. The Provie

Battalion Commander thought he might be sick at the stench of the Chinese cooking.

'I'll be away.'

The Chief was dragging the tinfoil caps from the food bowls and the plastic fork from the bottom of the bag.

'If we don't hit at touts, then the touts will destroy us,' and the Chief was busy with his food.

He was brought into the Interrogation Room, he sat down, and he heard the door close behind him, and he said, 'If I make a statement, what'll you do for me?'

Behind him Astley smirked. In front of him McDonough sucked at his pipe.

'What's for me if I talk?'

McDonough's expression was a mask. 'I am Detective Sergeant McDonough, this is Detective Constable Astley. Sean Pius McAnally, you are not obliged to say anything unless you wish to do so, but what you say may be put into writing and given in evidence . . . Can we have that again, Gingy?'

'If I make a statement, what do I get for it?'

McDonough played indifference. 'If you make a statement implicating yourself, a little bit. It might count for a bit, not a lot. If you make a statement that implicates others, then a little bit more . . . but this is the wrong way round, Gingy. The way it happens is that you make the statement, and then the Director of Public Prosecutions has the say in what happens to you. I don't make deals . . .'

'That's not done at our level, Gingy,' Astley said.

'It has to be a matter of trust, Gingy,' McDonough said. 'You have to trust us, because there's no other bugger for you to trust. I'll put it frankly, Gingy, we'd need an awful lot from you to count in the smallest way against what you've done. What I'm really saying, lad, is that I can't see that you could give us enough to do yourself any good . . . I said I'd be frank.'

McAnally was trembling. His body shook and the legs of the chair on which he sat tapped out a beat on the floor as he rocked the chair backwards and forwards.

'Can't I say anything that'll help me?'

'Have to be a terrible lot said to help you, Gingy.' Astley's voice was quiet, soothing. 'And we don't make the offer, we don't give any inducements. You have to ask, Gingy.'

His fingers were pattering on the table. He was breathing heavily. There was a sweat sheen at his throat.

Smoke clouded from McDonough's pipe between them.

McAnally looked into McDonough's face. He saw the hard, uncaring mouth of his enemy. He saw the pitiless eyes of his enemy. The words seemed to croak from his throat.

'I want immunity.'

'Immunity, Gingy?' McDonough whistled his surprise. 'Two 'tecs blown away, and a judge, and you want immunity?'

'Immunity from prosecution.'

McDonough shook his head, theatrically slowly. 'I can't see it . . . Can you see it, Detective Constable Astley? I mean, how do you get immunity from three murder charges?'

'That's all I'll talk for, for immunity.'

'Going supergrass, Gingy, is that what you're saying?'

' 'Course it's what I'm saying . . .' The words rattled from McAnally.

'Are you talking about going the whole hog?' McDonough spoke as if to a child.

'Into the box, Gingy? Into the witness box to give evidence?' Astley asked quietly from behind.

'Into the box, if I get immunity . . .'

The words hung in the air, hung with the smoke of McDonough's pipe. McAnally glared at McDonough.

Why did everything have to be repeated again and again? And why didn't the bastard smile and look pleased?

McDonough sighed. 'Wouldn't it be lovely, Gingy, if it were so simple. Two 'tecs killed, and a judge, but Gingy McAnally's going to go supergrass and inform on a few of his horrible mates, and we're going to pull in a handful of P.I.R.A. Volunteers, and he's going to get immunity. Wouldn't it be lovely, Gingy?'

'What do you mean?'

'Cop on, Gingy . . . What have you got to offer that's equal to two 'tecs and a judge . . . ? Sorry, wrong, not equal . . . What have you got to offer that's bigger than a conviction of an R.P.G. man for three murders?'

'There's another matter, Detective Sergeant McDonough,' Astley said.

'What's the other matter, Detective Constable Astley?' McDonough asked.

Astley said easily, 'Why did they bring Gingy back from the south? They brought him back because they knew he was good on the R.P.G. Where did he get to be good on the R.P.G.? Got to be good when he was using it, stands to reason. Stands to reason that Gingy's so damn good on the R.P.G. that he's the man they have to have . . . Stands to reason he's used it before. Stands to reason there are other charges of a very serious nature that we haven't even come round to thinking about yet.'

'Gingy, I'm corrected by Detective Constable Astley. I should have said . . . What have you got to offer that's bigger than a conviction of an R.P.G. man for three murders, and for crimes that we haven't even come round to thinking about yet . . . It really isn't going to be easy. You do see that, don't you, Gingy?'

McAnally felt the sweat drip from his neck to the small of his back. He felt the damp in the fold of his stomach, and running to his groin. He seemed to hear the clanging of the cell doors in the H Blocks, and the laughter of Young Gerard. He seemed to feel the wet cold of the Kesh exercise cages, and the fire heat of Roisin. He seemed to know the loneliness of the prison wings, and the peace and freedom of the caravan beside the canal. The hysteria was rising in Sean Pius McAnally.

'The guys who were with me in the Crumlin Road . . .'

'Volunteers in an A.S.U. . . . ? Not enough,' McDonough said.

'The ones who brought me back.'

'Couriers, nothing . . . they're rubbish.'

'The guys who briefed me.'

'Battalion Ops, Battalion Intelligence, can't see that being enough, Gingy.' McDonough's voice fell to a whisper.

'The fucking Chief briefed me,' Gingy screamed at him.

McDonough smacked the bowl of his pipe into his hand, dropped the remnants into the ash tray. He was reaching in his pocket for his tobacco pouch.

'Come again, Gingy?'

'The Chief briefed me.'

'Belfast Brigade Commander?'

'He briefed me.'

'Who was with him when he briefed you, Gingy?'

'Brigade staff – Quartermaster, Intelligence, and Operations.'

McDonough was filling his pipe, filling it like a blind man, by touch. His eyes never left McAnally's. 'When you were briefed it was by the Belfast P.I.R.A. Brigade Commander, and Quartermaster and Intelligence and Operations of Brigade, that's right?'

'That's what I bloody said.'

'And that's what you're offering us?'

'For immunity.'

'And you'd make a statement, and you'd go into the witness box?'

'For immunity.'

McDonough struck a match. It was a moment before his flame found the filled bowl of his pipe. 'Would you get Rennie in here?'

The door closed behind Astley.

'Is that enough, for immunity?'

'I don't know,' McDonough said, and stood up, and stretched himself. 'I don't make the decision, thank God.'

*

84

Astley followed his knock, strode into Rennie's office. He was beaming with excitement.

'McAnally's going to cough . . . He's going to give us the Brigade staff . . .'

Astley saw the black tie pulled loose on Rennie's throat below the unfastened top button.

'For immunity, he'll give us the Brigade staff in Belfast.'

Rennie clasped his hands, rested his chin on his fingers. 'Little bastard,' he said.

'It's what you hate, isn't it, Mr Rennie, seeing them go free after what they've done?'

'The comfort I get, young man, is in the knowledge that it's a rough sort of freedom.'

He closed the file on his desk. He thought of the widow who had stood tall and proud at the graveside. He leaked a quick half-smile at Astley. Rennie walked out of his office, and towards the Interrogation Block, to begin the process of turning the man who had made that girl a widow.

7

The uniformed policemen who patrolled the corridors of the cell block and the Interrogation Block at Castlereagh knew the signs. There had been enough of them in the previous two years for them to read the signals that heralded the turning of a prisoner.

On that afternoon the uniformed policemen saw Howard Rennie and Astley stamping down the corridor on the ground floor of the Interrogation Block . . . Another little shit had changed sides to save his neck.

The uniformed constables always saw the plain clothes detectives as the cowboys, the mavericks. They liked to smile behind their hands when the 'tecs came pounding out of the Interrogation Rooms in search of a senior man. They shared something of the excitement now when they heard that Blackbush bottles were being opened up in the Administration offices, but they liked to smirk with each other when the deflation set in, when a convert turned the rest of the circle and retracted.

It was one thing, the uniformed policemen would have said, to get a Provie to make a statement implicating his former friends, and quite another thing to build into the bastard the courage to go, weeks and months later, into the witness box to testify. The uniformed policemen had seen and heard the celebrations. Also they had seen and heard the wakes of the detectives when word slipped through that another supergrass had retracted.

Astley closed the door of the Interrogation Room behind himself and Rennie, shut out the interested eye of the uniformed policeman who hovered in the corridor.

'Let's get the formalities through,' Rennie said. 'I am Detective Chief Inspector Howard Rennie. You have already been cautioned by Mr McDonough and Mr Astley. Now let's hear what you've got to say.'

McAnally sat limp in his chair. The presence of Rennie seemed to crowd the room around the prisoner. McAnally slowly straightened, as if the movement exhausted him.

'I want immunity. If you give me immunity I'll make a statement . . .'

'What's the statement going to tell me?'

'Who was with me, when I was on the hits . . .'

'That's not good enough.'

'Who briefed me. I was briefed for Simpson by Brigade.'

'Names?'

'Yes.'

'You're offering that for immunity?'

'That's a hell of a lot, that's more than you've ever had.'

'And you'll go into the witness box, into court?'

'I've said I will.'

'And you're asking for immunity?'

'And I want my wife out, and my kids. I want to be shipped out.'

'I don't know that I can deliver, Gingy,' Rennie said.

'You've got to deliver,' McAnally's voice was rising. Big eyes, staring eyes, beading onto Rennie. 'I can't go back in there, not into the Kesh, not for twenty-five . . . I can't . . .'

Rennie's hand snaked out. He patted McAnally's shoulder gently.

'Easy, lad.'

'Everything I can bloody give you, I'll give you, but don't put me back in there.'

'Easy, lad, because it's not that straight.'

'I've said I'll go into the bloody court, I'll finger them, the whole of Brigade . . . What more do you bloody want?'

'Gingy, listen . . .' Rennie was bending over McAnally, and his hand had secured a father's grip on McAnally's jersey. 'Listen . . . last year, and the year before we were into chucking immunity about in return for a promise of going into court and giving evidence. We got to look a bit silly, Gingy. Too many chickened out, too many retracted . . .'

'I'll go the whole bloody way, I swear I will.'

'All the ones who retracted, they all swore they wouldn't.'

'What does that mean?'

'It means that it's a bad time for me to promise immunity, and for you to promise to deliver.'

McAnally's head lurched forward onto his hands. Rennie wondered whether he was about to weep. He reckoned that he had seen them all, all the marksmen and the bomb-makers and the executioners. Bloody awful figure they cut when they were alone, without an Armalite to cradle.

'You won't do it?'

'Did I say that, Gingy? Listen to me. What it comes down to is a matter of trust. We both have to trust each other. You have to trust me, and I have to trust you. Trust is a two-way thing. Are you listening, Gingy?'

McDonough watched, and shook his head slowly. Jesus, and you had to hand it to the old man. Winding the bugger up, wasn't he?

'Trust, Gingy . . . You have to trust me, as I'm going to trust you. You have to talk to me and trust that I'll do the best I can for you. It might be no minimum recommendation, it might be immunity, you have to trust me. That's one side. There's another side. I have to trust you. A statement from you, naming names, naming dates and places, that's no use to me unless I get you into court, unless I have you under oath and standing up to cross-examination. Two sides to the coin, Gingy. The trouble is, Gingy, can I trust you?'

'Trust, you and me, you're fucking joking, Rennie,' McAnally snorted. 'Forget it. It's immunity or it's nothing.'

McDonough choked. Astley had stiffened straight, no longer leaned against the wall. Rennie was flushed, angered.

'I'm one man,' McAnally said, spitting. 'I'm sod all use to you in the Kesh. The Brigade staff, that's useful to you, that's more bloody useful than me. I want an answer.'

Rennie bit at his lip. His fingernails were driven into the soft part of his hand. He controlled himself. 'I'll get you an answer, Gingy.'

Rennie spun on his heel, strode out of the Interrogation Room.

'If it's a joke, Fred, it's a joke in the poorest taste.'

'The Chief Constable isn't given to jokes.'

The Secretary of State pushed back the tray on his desk. The civil servant helped himself to a sandwich, and wiped his lips carefully with his handkerchief.

'I can't make a decision on immunity.'

'The Director of Public Prosecutions makes the decision. The Director is answerable to the Attorney General in government. The Attorney General is in Cabinet, as you are. If you were to recommend to a political colleague that he should take a certain course of action . . .'

'The Prime Minister would have to sanction it.'

'The Prime Minister would, you are quite correct.'

'Can you imagine . . .'

'What the Prime Minister would say? I've a fair idea. The Chief Constable's taking an unusual course. He's bringing with him the Detective Chief Inspector handling McAnally.'

'To confuse me with security jargon?'

'To put you in the picture.'

'When's he coming?'

'Half an hour.' The civil servant reached again for a sandwich. They were potted shrimp. He fancied the Secretary of State's wife had made them up in the flat. They were quite excellent.

'I've got the Moderator then, to hector me about the security of his flock on the Border.'

'He's on ice, you're fine to see the Chief Constable.'

'Damn you, Fred. I detest letting a beast like this McAnally go free, whatever he does for us.'

The civil servant smiled. 'Principles are a luxury, sir, in wartime . . . I'll sit in on the Chief Constable and his hatchet fellow.'

Ferris's landrover arrived at the supermarket with the first of the ambulances. The street in front of the supermarket windows that were festooned with the cut-price advertisements suitable for dole customers was filling with Pigs and police wagons. The shoppers who had been inside at the moment of the raid and the shooting were spilling out onto the wide forecourt of the supermarket. He saw the shock and white numbness on the faces of the housewives. Bloody amazing, wasn't it, that fifteen years into the Troubles these folk could still manage a snatch of shock? Bloody daily occurrence, wasn't it, a hold-up that went wrong?

He saw the Company Sergeant Major. Ferris went to him.

'You want a Sit. Rep., Mr Ferris?'

'Just what's happening will do.' Ferris saw the C.S.M. pucker his mouth in amusement. All the Battalion N.C.O.s knew they couldn't lure Ferris into the army shit talk.

'A couple of heroes went in after the Christmas Savings fund box. There's a pay-out this afternoon. Assistant Manager said it was in the safe and he hadn't the key, got himself shot as encouragement to fish in his pocket. An R.U.C. mobile trotted past as the heroes were bunking. The Old Bill put down a barrage like it was Port Stanley, they've managed a grannie, the heroes managed to leg it. They're off into Andy'town now.'

'Descriptions?'

'Good laugh, Mr Ferris . . . Deaf and dumb brigade here.'

Ferris watched as the first stretcher was carried out. There was a young man, on his back, with his mouth wide open and his breath coming in short bursts. His shirt was blood-soaked . . . What a vile place, what a bloody awful place to spend a bloody awful afternoon. He saw the old lady who lay at the far end of the forecourt. They'd covered her head with a blanket from the back of the ambulance, a warm scarlet blanket. Her ankles protruded from the blanket and Ferris saw that she wore thick stockings and sensible shoes, and the blood seeped from under the blanket by the bulge that was her head. She'd be there until the police photographer arrived.

He walked away from the C.S.M. He'd go through the routines. He went to a crowd that had gathered to watch the casualties and the ambulance men and the milling police and the crouched soldiers in their fire positions. Jones, his driver, was close behind him.

'Anyone see what happened?' Ferris managed a good, authoritative voice.

'The peelers shot Mrs Murphy.'

'Only just out of hospital, and the fucking bastards shot her down.'

'She'd a hernia, murdering pigs.'

'Mrs Murphy wasn't thieving, didn't stop her getting shot.'

Perhaps he should have laughed in their faces. Perhaps he should have laughed until his stomach sides hurt.

'There was a robbery . . .' Ferris said.

'And the peelers came and killed Mrs Murphy, out for her week's shop.'

'Did anyone here see the robbers?' Ferris tried to be deliberate and spelled out his question as if talking to backward children. 'Did anyone here see the two men who carried out the robbery on the supermarket?'

'I's seen Mrs Murphy shot . . .'

'Bloody murdered, more like.'

'I's seen the peelers do that.'

'But you didn't see the thieves . . . ?' Ferris stared at the faces of the crowd. 'You didn't see the Freedom Fighters . . . ? You didn't see the bloody freedom fighting A.S.U. attacking the legitimate target of your own bloody Christmas box . . . ?'

'Don't you fucking swear at us, you fucking Brit cunt face.'

Ferris turned to his right, sought out the voice. She was quite a pretty girl. She was about seventeen, and she wore a tight sweater under her open anorak and tight jeans, and her mouth was twisted in a savage arc.

'Pithily put, Miss.'

He went back to the landrover. Ferris and his escorts and Jones mounted up. He told Jones that they would tour round the Andersonstown sidestreets, away behind the supermarket. It was a case of finding something to do.

They drove off the main road, into the maze of small streets flanked by red-brick houses.

'She needed a good fuck, that cow . . .' Jones observed. 'Ever get the feeling you're wasting your time here, Mr Ferris?'

'That's not the kind of thought permitted to an officer, Fusilier Jones.'

They drove through Andersonstown for half an hour. Since they had no idea of what their fugitives looked like or were wearing, it was a wasted effort.

When their radio called them back to barracks they drove past the supermarket. A smaller force of police and soldiers were still in position and white ribbons marked the area of the incident. The shoppers were streaming round the ribbons, in and out of the supermarket. Ferris couldn't see the bloodstain from the old lady's wounds, washed by the rain.

'Fusilier Jones, if we weren't here then it would be even worse than it is,' Ferris said. 'That's why it's worth us being here.'

Fusilier Jones kept his eyes on the traffic in front of him. 'If you say so, Mr Ferris.'

McAnally had eaten his lunch in his cell. The uniformed policeman had given him a cigarette when the tray was taken away. The uniformed policeman knew McAnally was special, and had given him one of his own Bensons. He sat on his bed. McAnally was an oasis in the cell block. All the cells were occupied. He was the one who had turned, who had asked for immunity. In the other cells were men from the Provos and from the I.N.L.A. and from the U.V.F. and from the Ulster Defence Association. Castlereagh was not sectarian. The Prod paramilitaries had the cells beside the Taig paramilitaries. He drew on his cigarette. He rarely smoked. Roisin always had a fag in her mouth, even when the baby was on her knee . . . It might have been the strength of the cigarette, it might have been the fact of his asking for immunity, but he felt light-headed, like he'd sniffed glue. All the cells were taken, but his was different. In his cell was a man who had turned, a man who had offered to break the oath of the Organization. And it had all been so easy . . . Sean Pius McAnally was not a man to examine his own navel, but he chuckled to himself when he considered how easy it had been. And he had the bastard Rennie running every bloody whichway, had him sprinting up his arse. He'd make a statement. He'd give evidence. What was the big deal about giving evidence? No big bloody deal . . . He'd give evidence. Then there was the new life. There was a life outside Belfast, a life outside Ireland . . . All so bloody easy, all so bloody simple.

He would be living a new life with Roisin and Young Gerard and

90

Little Patty and Baby Sean, while the H Blocks were full, while the courts were full, while the bloody cemeteries were filling.

They'd reckoned Gingy McAnally was a pushover when they'd come down to the caravan beside the canal, they'd bloody learn what it could cost them.

Supergrass . . . Super Gingy . . . Super McAnally . . . Super hit man on the R.P.G. . . . . Supertout.

He was laughing. His laughter cracked back at him from the cell walls. He felt no remorse at the treachery. He felt no guilt at the betrayal. He felt an ecstasy because he believed he had avoided three life sentences with a recommended minimum of twenty-five years to be served.

Super Gingy McAnally, and no bloody pushover for any bastard.

'Every instinct, Chief Constable, every instinct I possess points to the moral and political dangers of granting this man immunity.'

The Secretary of State was fighting his corner, and losing.

The Chief Constable was a brusque short man, glorying in his reputation of direct aggression when confronted with politicians.

'Your instincts are wrong, Secretary of State.'

'It's a dirty business, the supergrass business, and shown to be fallible.'

'The policy of the Converted Terrorist has provided us with a greater fund of intelligence than we've ever had on the P.I.R.A.'

'Every retraction after the granting of immunity makes us a laughing stock.'

'That's the worst, Secretary of State, the retractions. Even if there's a retraction we have still gained valuable information.'

The Secretary of State believed the Chief Constable to be a non-drinker. He never took a drink when they met socially. He believed there to be a direct link between monumental pomposity and alcoholic abstinence.

'I've been in this job three years, for the first time in that three years I believe I am close to dealing a very considerable blow to the mainstream effectiveness of P.I.R.A. . . . . political dangers are not my concern. As to moral dangers, I would regard myself as being as aware of those as any other man. I want to hit the Godfathers. I want immunity for McAnally.'

The Secretary of State fidgeted on the settee. That had been his first error, sinking down into the soft cushions while the Chief Constable sat on a high-backed chair, on the raised ground where he could dominate. And Fred was no damned help, kept his mouth shut. And all the time there was the towering figure of the detective that the Chief Constable had wheeled in, and who stood behind his master's chair as if he was struck dumb.

'McAnally's a murderer.'

'We'll have a dozen men charged with murder, and we'll have the Brigade staff for conspiracy.'

'Cabinet won't agree to it.'

'You have to make them agree to it, otherwise there are many people alive and well at this moment who will lose their lives, if those Brigade staff men go free.'

'That's rhetoric, Chief Constable.'

The Secretary of State heaved himself up from the sofa. The room was too hot, he was perspiring. He went to the window. He felt as if his room was invaded.

'What do you want of me?'

The Chief Constable's voice softened with the fruits of victory. 'I want you to speak with the Attorney General, and I want you to listen to Mr Rennie. Mr Rennie is one of two officers based at Castlereagh who head the Converted Terrorist programme. He is a formidable opponent of the Provisionals, who have twice tried to murder him. I want him to tell you at first hand of the importance of the Brigade staff of P.I.R.A.'

'Tell me, Mr Rennie.'

'I went to a funeral this morning, Secretary of State, as you did. I carried the coffin some of the way. He was an old friend, a good friend. He was killed by Sean Pius McAnally . . .'

Such a stern, strong face, the Secretary of State thought. God, would he ever be rid of these suffering, intense faces. He was an intimidating man, this Rennie. The Secretary of State rarely met the men who fought the war in the middle echelons. He met the Generals and the Chief Constables at conference, and he met the private soldiers and the constables for fast casual conversation.

'I spend my time locking away Volunteers. I never get my hands on the men who control those Volunteers. Brigade staff don't carry weapons, they don't carry target maps, they don't carry my photograph. The rubbish kids carry the weapons and the maps and the photographs. Brigade stays above incriminating evidence. If I can get a man into court to give evidence against the Brigade staff then I will have severely damaged their movement. I need McAnally to have immunity, I need McAnally to know that he's not going down. I have to win his trust, perhaps even his affection . . . and he killed my friend. The Brigade men believe they're safe from us. I don't want them to feel that any more.'

The next weekend the Secretary of State would be at his English home, on his Yorkshire acres, and while he was out on the moors with his dog, this man would be in the Interrogation Rooms at Castlereagh.

He saw Rennie hesitate, question to himself the wisdom of speaking again.

'No, Mr Rennie, I want to hear everything.'

'The ghettoes in this Province, sir, are maintained by two factors, fear and loyalty. By breaking with his people McAnally has cut his loyalties. They'll work the fear on him. It's a fear that it's difficult for an outsider to comprehend, because it's the fear of a bad death at the hand of your own people . . . What I'm getting to is this. If we're to use McAnally against the Brigade then we have to show trust in him. If we try and kick him into the witness box, or trick him in, then we'll fall on our faces . . . Sir, he's gone further down the road than I'd dare go. Myself, I'd rather do the twenty-five years.'

'And for us to win his trust you want immunity?'

'Yes, sir, I want immunity for McAnally.'

The Secretary of State said, very quietly, 'So be it.'

'Thank you, sir.'

Rennie's eyes roved over the room, as if hunting down a whisky decanter. Not a drop in sight. The Chief Constable stood with his brief-case, and looked ostentatiously at his watch. The civil servant showed relief, because the Moderator could still be fitted into the schedule.

The Secretary of State smiled, the public smile. 'What sort of fellow is this McAnally?'

'A disgusting little wretch, sir,' Rennie said.

Disappointment clouded the Secretary of State's face. 'If I'm to argue for his immunity I'd like to have heard him spoken better of . . . You won't fail me?'

'You'll have my best effort, sir.'

Ferris was tumbled off his bunk by the shout of the adjutant. He was led to the Commanding Officer's room.

A telexed order from Lisburn HQ was handed him. The G.O.C.'s office instructed Sunray to make Lieutenant David Ferris available at all times possible for liaison with Detective Chief Inspector Howard Rennie, R.U.C. Castlereagh.

'It's not of your doing?'

'No, sir.'

'What's being cooked?'

'I don't know, sir.'

'I don't like clever games that get in the way of professional soldiering.'

'It seems I don't have much choice, sir.'

'You've no choice, and neither have I, which is why I don't like it. What's so special about you and this McAnally man?'

'Nothing that I know of, sir,' Ferris said.

Sunray looked curiously at Ferris. 'The battalion's an open family, David. The battalion doesn't have secrets.'

'I'm as much in the dark as yourself, sir.'

A police landrover was standing ready to take Ferris away from the Springfield Road barracks.

The identity of the Chief, who had taken over responsibility for the running of Belfast Brigade two and a half years previously was known to only a small handful of men in the city. As a figure in the background of public events, the Chief had seen off the threat of informers that had threatened to strike at the very intestines of the Provisionals' Organization. One after the other, the supergrasses had copped out, backed down, retracted. The Organization had survived, but was now warier. He reckoned the Organization was tighter than at any time since he had grasped the rank of Belfast Brigade Commander. He operated on the need to know philosophy. Through a labyrinthine chain of command he controlled the activities of the A.S.U.s, their weapons' systems supplies, their financial support through the robbing of banks and Post Offices and businesses, and the discipline of the movement. This chain was well disguised. No Volunteer could finger him, nor a Company officer, nor the men who ran the skeleton staffs of the Battalions. Those who formed his Brigade companions were friends from the beginning of the war. He liked to read of the frustration of the Prime Minister, expressed in British newspapers, at the inability of the Brit forces to trap and capture him.

The Chief was a militarist. He had studied the history of the freedom wars. He fought a battle of attrition. It was the attrition of his own comrades that had brought him to the command of the Belfast Brigade. He believed in no sudden stroke that would collapse the British administration and the Protestant resistance. He rarely made speeches, but when he talked late at night to his cronies, and they sat around him in a respectful silence, then he talked of striking at the defenceless base of the powers of occupation – hitting the policeman overseeing the school road-crossing, the headmaster who was a part-timer in the Ulster Defence Regiment Reserve, the unarmed prison officer coming off duty. The Chief would have preached to his faithful that if the ordinary man walks alone in the shadow of death while the big men of the community are cluttered with bodyguards, then the ordinary man will lose confidence in the Brits' ability to protect him. 'Tenner' Simpson was an exception. 'Tenner' Simpson was a good target, a popular target with the boys, good for the boys in the Kesh doing their tenner handed down by Simpson. The Chief would fight until he was captured or shot dead by the Army's S.A.S. or M.R.F. squads or the police Support Units. He had a deep contempt for the former fighters who had discarded the Armalite and taken to electioneering as candidates for Provisional Sinn Fein. He despised them because he reckoned they'd sold out of the only game that mattered, the fighting game. He was contemptuous of them because he reckoned that campaigning for housing conditions and drains and bus routes was the poorest substitute to beating the Brits where it mattered, on the street battlefield. What was relevant was sending Brit soldiers home in boxes, and having the police band play the death dirge into Roselawn.

He was a lonely man. When he had been a street aggro organizer he had been able to swim with the crowds. When he had been rated as a marksman, one shot only and that a killing shot, he had moved with the companionship of the Volunteers. When he had led the First Battalion, he had still moved with a kind of freedom. He was lonely because the commander of the Belfast Brigade had to be. And lonely, too, since the death of his wife. Mary was an indifferent replica of his wife, younger and prettier but nothing in comparison. The Brits killed his wife, that was what he said . . . On the afternoon after a dawn army raid on his home, she had taken an overdose. He had been away, down south, negotiating with the Army Council for a shipment of weapons. The army had come and wrecked his house, they had torn up the floorboards, ripped open the thin Housing Executive walls. She had emptied a bottle of Nembutal down her throat. The Brits had killed her . . . It had never crossed his mind that any responsibility for her death lay with him, that the O.C. of the First Battalion had in fact brought the soldiers into his home.

A lonely and desperate man sought by thousands of troops. A ruthless and skilled man hunted by thousands of policemen.

Because the Chief had dedicated his life to the campaign to drive the Brits at barrel point from the Province, he was a man of rare calibre in the Organization.

Beyond the windows of the maisonette in which he stayed the afternoon was going and the evening closing down on the street outside. The downtown radio headlines had told him of the unsuccessful raid on the supermarket in Andy'town. The headlines in the morning would tell whether there had been success for the sniper A.S.U. in Clonard. The war went on, in failure and success, the war of attrition.

Rennie had met Ferris at the entrance to the Interrogation Block, taken him from the escorting constable.

'What am I here for?' Ferris said aggressively.

'You're here because I said I wanted you here.'

'That's not a reason.'

'You're here because what you can do in Castlereagh is a damn sight more important than anything you'll do traipsing the streets,' Rennie said.

'Are you going to tell me?'

They went into the Interrogation Room. Bare walls, no decoration. A table and two chairs. Ferris faced the two detectives already there.

'This is DS McDonough . . . this is DC Astley . . . David Ferris, Lieutenant.'

They shook hands, Ferris and McDonough and Astley, with caution.

'Sit down, David.'

Ferris sat at the table. The policemen all stood. He felt the damp in his clothes from the day's rain, he felt the twelve-hour stubble on his chin.

'You have a line into McAnally, and that's a line we're going to hang onto. Trust is the name of the exercise, and McAnally trusts you. You're going to believe me when I tell you that we are doing our damnedest to get McAnally immunity . . . in return for the full works . . .'

'How full's that?'

'P.I.R.A. Belfast Brigade, and going into court to give evidence. It's a hell of a chance that we're taking, David. What I'd say to you is that without your co-operation the chance isn't worth taking.'

And the damned Intelligence Officer had advised that he shouldn't get involved . . . Jesus.

Ferris remembered the faces of McAnally. The face in the back of the car, nervous. The face in the P.-check on the Drive in Turf Lodge, frightened. The face in the yard at the back of 63, broken. The face in the cell block the previous night, despairing. He wondered what the face would have been at the moment of firing the R.P.G., at the killing of a judge and two policemen.

'You'd better bring him in,' Ferris said grimly.

McAnally was at the table. He knew it was different. More than two 'tecs in the Interrogation Room told him the rule book was out of the barred window.

Ferris was opposite him, sitting as well. The big 'tec, Rennie, was behind Ferris. The other 'tecs were behind him.

It was hard for McAnally to concentrate. All the good news was spilling out of Ferris's mouth and into his ears. All the bloody good incredible news.

'You're *going* to get immunity, Mr McAnally . . . the problem is that we can't say that for definite, not now, not at this moment, but we know you're going to get it. It's got to go to the D.P.P., and then to the Attorney General, and he'll have to clear it in London. Because of who you are, and what's involved, you're going to get immunity but the nobs in London have to give the green light. That's going to take a few days . . . Before we get it for definite you've to trust us, Mr McAnally. We've five days left, and then the police have got to lift the men you've named. You see, under the Prevention of Terrorism Act after seven days you're either to be charged or released. After seven days you go into protective care, and the lifts are on. If you're not released and you're not charged then everyone'll know that you've turned, and they'll run. They'll vanish. And your evidence will be of no use. You've got to start talking to Mr Rennie and his colleagues *now* . . . I know that you're going to get immunity. I really believe that, Mr McAnally . . .'

'And a new life?'

'A new life for you and Mrs McAnally and for your children.'

'Out of here?'

'Right away from here . . . It's going to happen, Mr McAnally. You believe me, Mr McAnally?'

'I believe you.'

'And they're going to trust you, Mr McAnally, that you'll go through with it.'

'I'm going to do it, Mr Ferris. I bloody swear I'll do it.'

'Stand up in court, Mr McAnally.'

'You can trust me, Mr Ferris, as I trust you.'

There was no weight on his soul. He arced his neck back as if that was the way to prove to himself that the weight was gone from his back. He thrust out his hand. He saw the officer hesitate, and then respond. Their hands met. He felt only the sense of the freedom.

And McAnally was laughing, laughing back at the officer, and gripping his hand. He didn't see the slow satisfied smile on Rennie's face. He was laughing fit to bust, he was laughing so that his shoulders quivered, and his hand and the officer's hand banged on the table as he laughed.

He was still laughing when he heard the rasp of Rennie's voice.

'Very good, Gingy, now let's start earning that immunity.'

No one had been to visit her, not through the whole day.

But then Roisin McAnally had been out and away from the Drive until the late afternoon. Her Ma had been in the house, her Ma didn't always hear the door knock. Her Ma had been there from lunchtime looking after Little Patty and Baby Sean, and Young Gerard had been at school. She had been into the city. She had sat for more than an hour in the waiting room of the offices of Mr Pronsias Reilly. She had spent a black taxi fare both ways because she couldn't wait for the buses. Most times Mr Pronsias Reilly acted as defending solicitor for men from Turf Lodge. She hadn't an appointment, hadn't found a telephone in Turf Lodge that was coin box and working . . . and over her dead body would she have gone crawling to a neighbour to use a phone and know they were listening from the front room to what she said in the hall . . . she'd sat for seventy minutes in the waiting room outside Mr Pronsias Reilly's office, and been told first that he was in court and expected back, and then that he'd gone across to Crumlin Road Remand Wing for a prisoner interview . . . He wouldn't be back. She had never before met Mr Pronsias Reilly. He was just a name that she'd heard of until she had seen his photograph on the wall of the waiting room – fat and sleek and doing well from the Legal Aid, doing bloody well from the boys who were behind the wire. She had to have a solicitor. She had to have a solicitor to bang on the gate at Castlereagh and demand access to Gingy. He was her man . . . She'd packed her Ma off and protesting that she'd help with the tea . . . What bloody tea? Sausages and spaghetti hoops . . . She couldn't stand Ma fussing her, and fussing the kids, not when Gingy was in Castlereagh . . . There was a sale of clothes at the church in the morning, she had to go for the sale, had to find shoes for Little Patty, had to get the shoes before she could think of going back to the city on another day in search of an interview with Mr Pronsias Reilly.

'Ma . . . Ma . . .'

She was in the kitchen. She was frying the sausages slowly. If she fried them too fast they burned and the goodness was wasted. She heard the piercing voice of Young Gerard.

'You come here, Ma.'

She was in time to see on the television the familiar flashback pictures of Judge Simpson's car. She stood in the doorway. She could hear the sizzling of the sausages on the ring. Young Gerard turned to her.

'They showed two peelers getting buried . . . did our Da blow the fuckers out?'

She turned, and went back to the kitchen.

'Bring Patty, Gerard,' she called. 'Your tea's ready.'

Rennie paced the Interrogation Room, never speaking.

McAnally talked.

McDonough sometimes prompted, mostly sat quiet at the table facing him, nodding encouragement.

Astley sat at the table that had been brought in and placed behind McAnally and filled the pages of a notebook.

Always begin at the beginning, Rennie taught his interrogators. They had started with Sean Pius McAnally's release from Long Kesh four years before. There were no time limits set against them now, they would talk deep into the night. The bastards always amazed Rennie. The matter-of-fact description of a killing with an R.P.G. A constable's life swept away, and told like it was the scoring of a goal on a Corporation soccer pitch, and names named like they were the other boys in the team. Later, he would slip out of the room to telephone his wife and warn her that he would be late home, again.

He had sent Ferris back to his barracks before the note-taking started.

'. . . Shay was on lookout, Shay saw the landrover turn into Whiterock. There was this gap between the garages. I couldn't see the landrover, not till after Shay shouted . . . Eug passed me the R.P.G. when Shay shouted. We'd been there three times before in two weeks. I fired. Dommy took the R.P.G. off me. We didn't stop about, we just pissed off. I knew I'd hit it . . . We ran to Flaherty's place. He'd got some cans in the fridge. We had a few cans, then we went home. It was really good, the R.P.G., went a dream. Eug drove me home from Flaherty's . . .'

Stroke of luck, latching onto the Ferris boy, Rennie thought.

8

While Sean Pius McAnally gushed his recollections to his interrogators, Belfast spluttered and coughed and existed through the winter days.

Every morning and every afternoon and every evening the rain dripped down onto the streets outside the high fences and the tin walls and the locked doors of Castlereagh. Alone with McDonough and Astley, in oil-fired warmth, lit by bright fluorescent strips, McAnally talked. He wore clean socks that they had brought him, and new underwear, and he was allowed a razor for his personal use, and he was cocooned from the breathing and dying of the city.

A comedian from cross-Channel played at the Opera House, and told the B.B.C. Northern Ireland interviewer that he always liked to play in the Province because the audiences were the best in the United Kingdom, and the interviewer gave him a tired grin and wondered why the star needed to be so patronizing.

An industrialist from Germany came and looked at the dead De Lorean car factory and talked to the Chamber of Commerce of a thousand chemical plant jobs, and the businessmen clapped him and wondered why he had lied.

A Royal cousin-in-law journeyed to the Province and planted a tree and opened a children's wing at a hospital, and spoke from a prepared text of the courage of the civilian population, and the nurses wondered what option anyone had but to show courage.

As the Secretary of State flew to Heathrow he mused to his civil servant whether back-bench oblivion might not be preferable to the running of Northern Ireland.

The flowers were dying on William 'Tenner' Simpson's grave.

A young part-timer in the Ulster Defence Regiment was outside his mother's house in Finaghy cleaning his car when the assassins came for him, travelling by motorcycle, and sprayed at him with a Mauser and missed and decapitated his mother's cat, which was probably why the incident rated space in the English newspapers.

A man was shot dead in his house in Newtonabbey, but the police press desk told the journalists not to concern themselves because it was only family, which was why the killing didn't go cross-Channel.

A boy of sixteen years, five months out of school, appeared before the city Magistrates charged with writing down police car number plates as they left Andersonstown R.U.C. station.

The Chief Constable issued a warning that men prominent in public life should take especial precautions against Republican gunmen . . . A Guards battalion completed their tour and sailed home on the Liverpool boat, and more than a hundred were sick with relief and alcohol before they docked . . . A priest issued a statement to the *Irish News* complaining of army brutality in Ballymurphy . . . A Protestant politician called a news conference to denounce the Security Forces softly softly approach to terrorism.

Outside of the perimeter of Castlereagh, the days slipped by, unmemorable and unremarkable.

Each in his differing way, McDonough and Astley were good at their work.

They were trained to show no animosity to the informer. They listened to the catalogue of hits and attempted hits and aborted hits without ever revealing their disgust. They had both been on the course with the English psychiatrist who had talked of body language communication with the informer. Nothing that they heard appeared to shock or horrify them. Not the death of a constable, not the blinding of a soldier. McDonough always probed for the information. Astley always wrote the verbatim at the second table. Through the passing days they saw the growing cockiness of McAnally, as if he revelled in the attention given him. They let it ride, they made no attempt to deflate that cockiness . . . Soon enough Gingy McAnally would be put to the test, and then the louse would need all his cockiness.

'. . . I wanted to get the Pig in the middle. I reckoned if I got it in the middle that I'd do the squaddies inside. If there's a Pig out then there'll always be half a dozen squaddies in the back. A Pig's a sitting duck arse for an R.P.G. We were down in Beechmount, there's plenty of Pigs come up the Falls through Beechmount. We took over this house . . . There was just an old gasser in the house, Fatsy watched him, I went upstairs with a young lad . . . didn't have a name, not to me. It didn't bloody work like it should have done. We had the window open, of the front bedroom . . . Shit, it stank in the old gasser's bedroom, he slept on bloody newspapers . . . It didn't work because the Pig braked just as I was on the trigger. Once you start on the trigger you can't help yourself, it's like pissing. The squaddie braked just as I was firing, when I was still on the engine. The engine went up, only did a bit of damage to the driver, didn't even kill him. I went down the bloody stairs, like I got the claps. You know what Fatsy was doing? I'm hitting a Pig with a bloody R.P.G., and Fatsy's supposed to be minding this gasser, and Fatsy's got the back off his telly and he's fixing the line hold for him. You know what, Fatsy went back and finished the job three days later. That's rich . . . The lad and I and Fatsy, we got out the back of the house, and belted . . .'

'Fatsy was who?'

'Fatsy Rawe . . . we belted down Iveagh Parade to where the motor was. Bugsy was on the motor. We went down Broadway. I reckoned we got out just before the blocks went in. It was a real bad one because the kid didn't show who was to take the R.P.G. We had to keep it with us. Couldn't hang about, could we? . . .'

'Who's Bugsy?'

'We call him Bugsy, he's Eamonn Malone . . . You know what . . . ? I pissed myself in the car. I pissed myself down my leg. I went home to my woman and I had to go straight upstairs and change my pants, so she wouldn't see. I got a load of stick for that one, they said I should have held the fire, or got the Pig in the middle. Those bastards, they don't know what it's like on the R.P.G. You have to line the R.P.G. up, and if you fire it in a room you're dazed afterwards, I know. You try telling the bastards . . .'

'Who were they, Gingy, who gave you stick?'

'Jimmy Flanagan, Noel Connelly, Brennie Toibin, they were Battalion . . . They gave me some stick because they said the R.P.G. warheads were gold dust, they said I only wounded the squaddie and didn't get all the rest with him. But they split their heads when they heard the kiddie hadn't turned up to take the R.P.G. At least he got a beating. It was gold dust, the R.P.G. Because we hadn't dropped it, Bugsy took the R.P.G. home. It was behind his sofa for a week . . . That's a bloody

101

laugh, his missus was screaming blue about it, so he told her to fuck off and cracked her. The whole thing was a shambles . . . I mean, we got one squaddie, but one squaddie isn't worth an R.P.G. round. Well, it isn't, is it? It was just bloody cowboys . . .'

The Secretary of State was rarely invited to Downing Street other than for Cabinet. He was in London every week of the year, whether the Commons were sitting or whether in recess, but he seldom received the summons.

Inflation was down, the pound sterling was steady, unemployment was at last bottoming. Central government's posture was buoyant and aggressive. It was trumpeted that the nation's health was improving. Only Northern Ireland cracked the mould of success.

The Secretary of State had not raised the matter of immunity for McAnally at Cabinet. On the aircraft over he had decided to broach the issue in private to the Attorney General. And callow fellow that he was, the Attorney General had slipped the word to the Prime Minister. Sometimes the Secretary of State, from the distance of his pro-consulship in Belfast, believed that his colleagues in Cabinet only broke wind if they had first received the Prime Minister's permission. An hour after his conversation with the Attorney General, and barely back at his desk in the Northern Ireland Office, the Secretary of State had received the call.

They met in the Prime Minister's personal office, with a Principal Private Secretary taking notes. The walled garden outside took his attention for a moment before he was waved to a chair. It was well cut down for the winter. Because it was warm and damp the songbirds were in force on the lawn. Nice little things . . .

'The Attorney General, quite rightly, brought this matter to my attention. You are asking for immunity for a man who slaughtered a courageous judge and two dedicated police officers. You are suggesting that the man who took three fine lives should be allowed to walk free, and given the chance to begin a new life at the expense of our taxpayers.'

'Putting McAnally away, Prime Minister, would win us a skirmish. Giving him immunity provides the opportunity for us to win a battle . . .' The Secretary of State quite liked that. Fred had fed it to him in the drive across Whitehall.

'The idea of this man having immunity is one I find repellent.'

'The reality of Northern Ireland is often repellent, Prime Minister, as I'm sure you've found from your visits.' Good one . . . the Prime Minister came at Christmas to be photographed with the troops, particularly enjoyed being photographed while wearing a Marine beret or a flak jacket.

102

'I don't think public opinion would stand it, and I for one . . .'

'We can handle the public opinion side. There's enough chaps at Army and Police Headquarters to handle that.'

'And what if you don't deliver?'

'That's the gamble.'

'What's to stop him accepting our immunity, and then retracting, and going free?'

'There's nothing to stop him.'

'That's a dreadful answer.'

'It's the truth.'

'If that's your final word then my mind's made up, no immunity.'

The Secretary of State stood up. His arms were folded easily across his chest. 'Very good. Thank you for the decision. Let's hope there are no leaks . . .'

He knew the Prime Minister. He knew the neurosis on the leakage of confidential information. He saw the angry frown settling on the forehead.

'. . . Let's hope there are no leaks from Castlereagh or from Headquarters. I'd hate to have it thrown back at me that by sending one man down for a life sentence we had passed over the chance to put away the nucleus of the Provisional Brigade staff along with elements of Battalion command and a bus full of Volunteers. I'll do my damnedest to see that doesn't leak, and to see that it doesn't come back to your door, Prime Minister. Thank you for your time.'

He turned. He wondered if he would have reached the door before he was called back.

'Your job depends on it, on him not retracting.'

'People's lives depend on him not retracting. Thank you for the decision. To give this creature immunity hurts me as much as it does you, but you've made the right decision. Good day, Prime Minister.'

'There were too many getting lifted. I says, I says Gingy McAnally's not going to be one of them. It was just after I'd done the Pig. There was guys getting lifted every bloody morning round West Belfast. I'd had one go in the Kesh, and I wasn't going back inside, not just for hanging about and waiting to see who was going to tout next. If it hadn't been for the problem with the R.P.G. then I might have stayed. I went to see Joey – that's Joey Mulvaney. Joey says to me that I'd used the last of the warheads they had for the R.P.G. He said they'd get some more, that they were down south. He said they had a stack of them down south, but he said that South Armagh wanted them, and Derry had chipped in for them. He was pretty good to me, Joey Mulvaney, he didn't bullshit me. He said it would be weeks before Army Council's

Quartermaster let them go. He said that I'd had two firings and that the boys down in Armagh and Derry were bleating for a bloody go at it. He said they'd need warheads to train with. He said we were bottom of the list . . .'

'Joey Mulvaney was . . . ?'

'Two Battalion, O.C. . . . I wasn't a marksman . . . well, I'd been out with an M16, but I don't reckon I hit the wall behind the squaddie. Marksman's a different thing . . .'

'Date, place, who you were with?'

'Christ . . . September, must have been the eighth, 'cos it was the day before Roisin's birthday . . . I didn't want to go, I said I had to buy her something, I went and then had to leg it down to the Avenue to get her something. I didn't get to Royal Avenue, I went to Smithfield, I bought her a new iron . . . well, it wasn't new, it was seconds . . . We had three rifles. We were behind the wall at Milltown boneyard, waiting for the squaddies to come out of the Andersonstown barracks. That's when it was, where it was . . . Joey was one of the rifles, Dusty was the other . . .'

'Dusty?'

'O'Hara . . . Damien O'Hara. Billy Clinch took the shooters off us at the bottom of the graveyard. Dusty nearly shot him, he fell over a stone and he hadn't gone to Safety. Fierce bloody language Billy used on him. I was no marksman . . . I wasn't anything on the explosives. All our bombs came up in kits from Monaghan. The feller down there made them up, and they came in pieces to be assembled up in Belfast. I wasn't going to touch no bloody bomb. He was a watch mender, the man that made the bombs, so he always used old watches for the timing that had been left with him and not collected. The lads always used to say that the Jap digitals would put him out of business. I never heard his name, but he was somewhere behind the market in Monaghan city. So, I didn't do sniping and I didn't do bombs. I was R.P.G. and they'd no warheads. And the lads were being lifted, every bloody day . . . So, I went south. Roisin didn't fight me. She didn't say I was yellow, nothing like that. She didn't say I shouldn't. She's wonderful, my Roisin. She never gave out, just packed my bag. I went down south . . . Shit, I didn't know life could be so bloody perfect as it was down south.'

'We have to know everything. Every single thing.'

'There was a Post Office. There was two cars I hijacked. There was a punishment shooting, I didn't actually shoot him . . .'

'One at a time, in order, and the names.'

'Am I doing alright?'

'You're alright so far. We'll start with the Post Office . . .'

'It is indeed a lovely thought, Mrs McAnally. It's a beautiful thought but it just doesn't work that way. In theory I can drive down to

Castlereagh and announce at the gate that you have instructed me to take your husband's case and that therefore I have come to seek a visit to him. And if they let me in, and they gave me access to your husband then that would indeed be lovely and beautiful. As I say, it doesn't work that way.'

Mr Pronsias Reilly's desk was deep with briefs. He had the briefs on his desk of four men who had been up before the Magistrates in the morning, and more briefs for two more who would be up the following morning. He had the briefs of six more clients who had been on all day in the Lord Chief Justice's court room on the Crumlin Road, and that was a counsel trial with a chance of acquittals. He had his preparation reading to do that night before the morning sitting.

'If I had all the hours of the day to devote to your husband, Mrs McAnally, then I just might get into Castlereagh, and they might just have to produce him. They know my work schedule, they know what time I have available, so they'll keep me kicking my heels while the clock goes round. That's the way it works.'

He thought she was quite a good-looking girl. He thought that if she wasn't running a house in Turf Lodge on Social Security then she could have made herself into a really good-looking girl. Bony round the hips, and a little slack on the chest, but a smashing face on her. Hell of a sight better than half of the slags that came and parked in his office looking for help in keeping the husband out of the Kesh.

'With your husband's, er, antecedents, he'll know to keep his mouth quite shut for seven days . . . after that he's home, or he's in court and charged. If he's charged I'll be in court to take his brief . . . It's Mr Justice Simpson, isn't it? I hear, round the corner information, that his clothes didn't do too well at Forensic. Believe me, Mrs McAnally, even if I were to camp at Castlereagh and finally get access, I don't think that I could keep him out of court.'

He saw her chin quiver, and her lips were thin and pale and tight, and her fingers clasped a small handkerchief. She was a tough one, she'd screw like a steam engine . . . He smiled, held out his hand to be shaken, and to indicate that the interview was terminated. He often thought that if the P.I.R.A. men were as tough as the women they left behind then the war would have been won many years before.

'Thank you for dropping by, Mrs McAnally. You should look on the best side of things . . . I'm sure Mr McAnally is much too sensible to incriminate himself.'

Dropping by. He knew the poor wretch would now have a fight on her hands in the black taxi queue, and then the trudge from the Glen Road back into the depths of Turf Lodge.

*

105

'. . . I used to come up from the South every three, four months, but only for a few days, and to see Roisin and the kids. You get a bit hungry for the woman, you know it's like that. You have to have a woman, if you're not a bloody monk, and you have to see the children. The boys left me alone when I came up . . . They must have known that I was up, you don't bloody cough in Turf Lodge without the boys knowing, so they'd have known that I was up and with Roisin, but they let me be. I reckoned they left me alone because they hadn't a launcher, or if they had a launcher they hadn't any warheads for it. I'd go down the bar sometimes when I was with Roisin, and I might see someone that I knew, and I'd wave, and they'd wave, but they left me to myself. I guess it was kind of understood . . .'

The confidence of Sean Pius McAnally was full grown. And in front of him McDonough was nodding earnest encouragement, and behind him Astley was writing furiously. The fifth day was slipping by, and McAnally was now a favoured creature, part of another man's army. He told himself that what he did was for Roisin, and for Young Gerard and Little Patty and Baby Sean.

'. . . Then these two came to the caravan.'

'Names, Gingy.'

'Never had any names, and I'd never seen them before. They didn't give me their names. They brought me back. They didn't ask me to come, they just brought me back, like I'd bloody deserted. They didn't have the right to treat me like I was some sort of filth.'

'We'll work you through the snapshot book.'

'They'd no call to treat me like I was rotten. They brought me back, they seemed to think I'd just cut and run when I went to the Free State . . . Bastards.'

'When you've finished with them, Gingy, they'll wish they hadn't treated you like filth.'

'I was a good man, I was one of the best men in the Organization. When I was with them I never let any bugger down. I did what was bloody asked of me, I did it good and well . . .'

'We got the message, Gingy. They'll get the message.'

'Too bloody right they will.'

Each evening the typists took dictation from Astley, and the statement file of Sean Pius McAnally grew fatter. And the statement file bred other files, and the cross-indexing and the computer searches splayed outwards. There was a cross-index and a new file for every name mentioned by the new tout. And each night, after the typists had finished, the new files and read-outs from the P.-Band computer ended on Rennie's desk.

It was brilliant, magic.

He knew it was just for starters. Turning them was one thing, keeping them turned was the devil's own work. Howard Rennie was a

106

methodical man. By the fifth evening he had started to plan the lifts and swoops that would follow the seventh day of McAnally's incarceration at Castlereagh, and he let it be known that he would require the entire cell block to be cleared and waiting empty for a new intake. And a message had come down from on high, from the Castle at Stormont. The message said that he, Howard Rennie, was responsible, that his career depended on McAnally's statement.

The platoon had been on 'Immediate', so they were scrambled first from Springfield Road.

Two landrovers and two Pigs, and bursting out of the barracks with the headlights on and the horns blasting and the traffic scattering, and bellowing off down the Falls.

The report that had tumbled the platoon out of the quiet of Springfield Road was as vague as all of the initial call-outs. The reports said there was a crowd on Divis, gathered outside a chipper, that shots had been fired. There would be nothing clearer until Ferris and his platoon were on location, and back on the radio. Not much talk in the landrover. All tensed because they were off and riding into the unknown. Tensed and hushed because no man in the platoon could wipe from his mind the thought of a come-on, the ruse to lure the Security Forces into the field of a sniper's fire, or within range of a hidden mine.

They came across the junction of Falls and Springfield.

Ferris saw the crowd, half way down Divis, spilling from the pavement onto the street. He heard the baying of angered voices.

There were three single shots, and for a fraction the crowd was silent and scurried back, and then surged forward again, as if the shots were insufficient to frighten it. Behind Ferris there was the metal scrape of the escorts arming their rifles. If there was any slight reassurance it was in the heavy engine whine of the Pigs behind Ferris. Nearer to the crowd now and the voices were sharper and belting out hostility.

The platoon had a drill for such an occasion. Nothing for Ferris to say, the drill would be automatic. His landrover and the rear landrover came right to the edge of the crowd before scratching to a stop. The first Pig swerved past them and then slewed across the road fifty yards ahead to block the oncoming traffic. The second Pig would do the same behind them. The cordon was immediate.

Hate filled the faces wherever Ferris looked. The women were at the back of the half-moon crowd, their voices braying at the upper windows of the brick building, screaming and finger pointing at the twin windows above Fiori's chipper. It was a silly thought, but Ferris briefly entertained it . . . World's worst urban guerrilla battlefield, and the place was chosen by Signor Fiori to open a chipper and flog hamburgers and

107

sausages and rock salmon . . . Christ, it must have been bad in Naples to get Signor Fiori to try his luck in the Falls of Belfast . . . A bloody daft thought . . . The women were at the back, and in front of them were their menfolk. Ferris saw what they called in the Mess the aggro yobs who threw themselves against the closed street door like there was no tomorrow. It was the door at the side of the chipper that was their target. The door would lead to a staircase and a self-contained flat above the chipper. Ferris could see the upper windows were broken, and were curtainless . . . a derelict flat.

The voices were a cacophony around him as Ferris and his escort and Fusilier Jones came out of the landrover. The noise was ringing in his ears, but in those first moments he seemed to hear no single and distinguishable voice, only a reeking babble of alien accents. The soldiers prised their way through the crowd and to the front of Fiori's chipper, and used their rifle butts to chop the crowd back from the door. When Ferris looked up he fancied that he saw a shadow pass close to the window. His nose puckered at a sharp, acrid, smarting smell.

'Rear's secure, Mr Ferris . . .' The shout of Ferris's platoon sergeant. 'But there's no back exit.'

Ferris was close to the side door. There was deep grey smoke filtering from underneath the door and through the old post slit. He felt the irritation at his eyes. Bloody gas . . . C.S. gas . . . The faces of the crowd were close to him, twisted in their anger as if a prize was escaping them. At last he understood the venom of the words.

'Fucking S.A.S. bastards . . .' 'Come to keep your fucking spies safe, have you? . . .' 'Bloody killer squads . . .' 'Found out, you bastards, because you're not as fucking clever as you think you are . . .'

Ferris understood.

The derelict flat was a covert observation post occupied by the Special Air Service, and not covert any longer. And the mob had gathered for them, and the S.A.S. troopers had fired warning shots and tipped C.S. grenades down the stairs to hold the crowd back. Not bloody laughing gas, but Ferris was grinning. He'd heard once, down in the country on his first tour, of a shop owner who'd reckoned he'd rats in the rafters, and who'd called in the Pest man, and that fellow had crawled through a ceiling hole with his tin of poison paste and confronted a long-stay surveillance squad . . . some rats. The S.A.S. getting themselves rumbled was enough to bring a grin to any soldier, especially to Ferris, passed over by that Regiment.

'Back the Pig up, right up to the door . . . Don't take all bloody day.' A whining Brummie accent squeaking through the post slit.

Ferris gave his orders. His Fusiliers patiently worked the crowd back, but the fury was gone because the chance of success was lost. The Pig was driven close to the door, and its back doors opened to make a shield, to separate the crowd from the doorway.

The gas had now caught at Ferris's eyes. You weren't supposed to wipe your eyes with your sleeve, you weren't supposed to blink and try and squeeze the irritation out. He did both.

He bent to the post slit.

Ferris shouted. 'You can come out now, it's safe . . .'

Ferris felt himself reeling. And his balance was frayed at the hands of the men from the Regiment that had turned him down. He could hear voices raised in laughter against him as he struggled to stand straight.

The door was wrenched open.

'Took your time, cocko . . .' The Brummie came out through the door. He was short, squat, like a well fed spider. He wore a navy boiler suit, and a week of beard growth and a wool stretch hat. He carried a rifle, a pair of bulbous night-sight binoculars and a rucksack. He came through the door fast and jumped easily into the Pig. There were two more following, laden down with surveillance equipment and personal weapons.

Ferris stared into the Pig.

'What blew you?'

The last man out replied. He was Glasgow. 'I got leg cramp, swung my leg straight, kicked our shit bucket . . . Get us out.'

He didn't expect politeness, not from the clandestine heroes. Ferris went to the front of the Pig, gave the driver his instructions.

He watched the Pig drive away. He thought to himself that he was enjoying a soft war in comparison with men who squatted in the damp cold roofing above Fiori's chipper for days on end.

He heard the jeering of the crowd as he gave the order for the pull out.

'. . . The morning after I came back there were two men who called up at the house. They just came in, like it was public . . .'

'Names, Gingy.'

'There was Phonsie McGurr and another fellow, Devitt, I don't know his first name, big fellow with a tricolour tattoo on his wrist. They didn't give their names, but I knew them before I went away. They seemed to reckon they just had to snap their fingers and Gingy McAnally was jumping. They said I was on a job in the morning, I said I wasn't. They said there was a job in the Crumlin all set for me, I said it was for someone else. They said that everyone had sweated to set it up, and it was going to happen at early morning tomorrow, I said they could bloody think again . . . I said I wasn't standing out in the middle of the Crumlin in daylight firing an R.P.G. . . . We'd gone up to the bedroom, we were sitting on Roisin's bed . . . They said it was going to be the

109

biggest belt in Belfast that year, they said it was going to have the Brits screaming all the way to London. They said it was a one-off, that I'd go home after it, and that the next day I could be away down south again like nothing had happened . . . I said I wouldn't do it. Every time I said that I'd quit, they just kept talking like they weren't hearing me. They were right pigs, they just wouldn't hear me. They said there was no one else that could use the R.P.G. 'cept me. They said it had been a hell of a business to get the R.P.G. into town and to get a warhead for it . . . They said it had to be me. We were all shouting together . . . I'd come back to see my wife and my small ones, and I'm ending up in the bedroom shouting whether I'm going on a hit. They said that I'd see the Chief . . .'

Astley's eyes flickered up from his concentration on his notepad. McDonough bit hard on the end of his pencil.

'The Chief . . . ?' McDonough was a good experienced detective. He had the commendations from the Chief Constable, but there was a hoarseness in his echoing of the words.

McAnally smiled, cheeky now. 'The Chief . . . Belfast Brigade's big shot.'

'And you saw him?'

The grin was spreading on McAnally's face. 'You said we were working from the beginning, you said we wasn't to jump . . . I didn't see the Chief till the morning.'

'Sorry . . .' McDonough tried to match McAnally's fun. 'Fair cop, Gingy. My fault . . . when we come to the morning we'll come to the Chief.'

For a moment McDonough's hand rested on McAnally's tight fist, on the table. Astley watched them.

Astley felt a slight, fast chill of fear. If the Provos identified the detectives who had successfully twisted a man into the supergrass system, then they shot those detectives. Done it in Londonderry, done it in Belfast. They slaughtered the detectives, if they could name them, who had converted a man to touting. And the man sitting at the table with McDonough and Astley was the best 'grass, the biggest tout, the most considerable informer yet to have been through Castlereagh. If they ever identified the 'tecs who had turned McAnally, they'd put them top of the list. He could have worked in a bank, he could have sold insurance, he could have gone across the water to England. Astley breathed deeply, concentrated again on the written page.

McDonough was still grinning. 'Right, Gingy, so they said to you that you'd better see the Chief . . . ?'

*

110

'What's with Gingy McAnally?'

The Chief and Frankie Conroy walked a wet evening pavement. The Chief liked Frankie. It was rare for the Chief to form friendships inside the Organization, few friendships since he had muscled his way to commander of Belfast Brigade. Frankie was loyal and subservient, and he did what he was told, didn't question what he was told. Frankie had a good record, for the Organization . . . and he had a good record with the Director of Public Prosecutions.

They walked in Andersonstown. Coat collars up, flat hats on their heads, duffle bags on their shoulders. To a passing mobile patrol they would have seemed like two workmen returning home in the dusk.

'You feel bad about Gingy?' There was a sibilant whistle in Frankie's voice. Way back he had been shot in the throat by a Brit undercover man, and he'd done half of a twelve stretch for attempted murder, possession and membership.

Each time the Chief saw the puckered hole in Frankie's throat, then he reckoned the man was lucky to be alive.

'I feel bad about any bugger that's lifted.'

'He was special, didn't want to be in, that's what I heard.'

'You met the joker who wants to get lifted, Frankie? What's the word on him?'

'The word is that he's playing stone statues in there.'

'Where did you get that?'

'My cousin's boy, he's a scribbler on the *News*. He meets the big 'tec, Rennie, at a club, a bloody rugby club. My cousin's boy's a good player or they wouldn't let him in the bloody place, it's a Prod's club. Rennie told him that Gingy hasn't opened his mouth since he's been there. He's like a fucking dumb man, that's what my cousin's boy said Rennie told him.'

'Have they enough on Gingy to charge him?'

'They charge him tomorrow, or he's out. My cousin's boy didn't say about a charge.'

Frankie heard the wind breaking from the Chief, the scent was at his nostrils. He was too long in the Chief's company to react.

'There's a nice one coming up, Frankie. The Brit battalion at Springfield use open landrovers, always open. When they're at the lights on the Falls, when they're stopped, there's a hell of a chance of getting some petrol out of a top window onto them . . . like it, Frankie?'

'Like it . . .' Frankie looked into the Chief's face. 'That kiddie, Mattie Blaney's boy, the kiddie that was 'capped for informing on Gingy, that was right, was it?'

He saw the distant glint in the Chief's eyes. He was over the line. He was always frightened of the Chief when he was over the line.

'I was asking you, Frankie, how you'd like it, warming up some Brit squaddies in an open landrover.'

'Yeah, I'd like it,' Frankie said, and looked away from the Chief's face.

'So, who was in the room?'

'The Chief . . . and Brigade Q.M., and Intelligence, and Operations.'

'Names, Gingy.'

'The Chief, that's Kevin Muldoon . . . Q.M. is Ollie O'Brien . . . Intelligence is Joe McGilivarry . . . Operations is Tom McCreevy . . . They were all in the room when the Chief told me his plan.'

'No second thoughts, Gingy.'

'I told you I'd do it.'

'When the going gets rough, Gingy . . .'

'I said I'd bloody do it.'

'It'll get really rough, Gingy.'

Sean Pius McAnally stabbed his ferret glance at McDonough. 'But I'm getting immunity, aren't I? And you're going to keep me safe, me and the missus and the kids, aren't you?'

It would be a frantic evening for Howard Rennie.

Into Central Belfast as the offices were closing for a session with the Director of Public Prosecutions, to confirm the issuing of immunity to a self-confessed killer, and to drop off a seventy-eight page statement of confession and implication.

Afterwards to Police Headquarters for the briefings on the lifts of twenty-eight men and three women.

And later, very late, five minutes of the Chief Constable's time.

'You'll get him into court, Rennie?'

'If I have to carry him there, sir.'

9

He sat in the back of an armour-reinforced police landrover.

Over the shoulders of the driver and the forward seat observer he could see the nightlights of the deserted city.

Rennie was on one side of him. Hemming him in on the other side was a police sergeant, uniformed and huge in his bullet-proof vest.

It had been explained to Sean Pius McAnally that he was no longer a prisoner, that he was no longer in custody. Rennie had told him that he was a free agent, that he was in police care. If he had been in custody he would have been handcuffed as the convoy swept out of the gates of Castlereagh. Because he was in care he was merely sandwiched between Rennie and the sergeant. There was a difference between custody and care . . .

And Sean Pius McAnally needed care because he had become a traitor to his own.

There was no talking in the back of the landrover. McAnally and Rennie and the sergeant and two constables sat in deep silence. There were the flashes of their matches and their lighters, and the glow of their cigarettes. When they dragged on their cigarettes, McAnally could see the faces around him. They were the faces of the men who had been his enemies. There wasn't much thinking in him. He had been up late, and woken early in his cell. They had come for him, at four. They'd given him a mug of tea and a Penguin biscuit, and he'd felt the beard on his face and the dirty cold in his crutch. They had taken him to Rennie and the car park. Rennie had said, 'I've taken a chance with you, Gingy. I've taken one hell of a risk. I've chanced that you've the bottle to see this through. I've chanced getting immunity for you. You're now a free man. You can turn your back on us and walk out on us. But you won't do that, Gingy, because you know that after today you're dead if you do that. Don't get me wrong, Gingy, I'm not making threats. What I'm saying is this: after your statements, after our lifts, you're dead without us looking after you. That's facts.' They had stood, Rennie and McAnally, in the car park, out of earshot of the uniformed men. They had been wrapped in the cold in their own shadows. When Rennie had said his fill he had cuffed McAnally hard on the shoulder, as if that were the end of the private talk for all time, and McAnally had known the force of Rennie's fist, and they had gone to the landrover.

Too early in the city even for the Corporation's cleaning carts. Wide, wet streets. A convoy of three landrovers. McAnally crammed between two men, and his landrover between two others.

The landrovers swung past the roundabout at the bottom of the Grosvenor Road. He was coming to his own territory, and coming in protective police care. He felt against him the warmth of Rennie and the angles of the sergeant's armoured vest. He was coming back to collect his wife, and to gather up his kids. He was shivering and not cold. He tried to remember what he would say to Roisin, and his mind was vague, and the words were lost.

They passed the Royal Victoria Hospital. The soldier he had blinded long ago with the R.P.G. had gone to the casualty at the R.V.H. The policeman he had injured when he had killed another had been rushed to the same rear entrance of the old hospital. No traffic on the Grosvenor, and the landrovers went over the junction traffic lights on red.

Not hanging about, were they, the landrovers traversing Provoland, not when they were carrying a traitor? The convoy slowed on the approach to the Springfield Road barracks. McAnally sensed the tension of the men around him. Eyes on the upper windows, a pair of hands tight on the wheel, other hands on cocked Stirlings. Christ . . . and he had to find the words for Roisin.

They turned into the gates.

The barracks was a staging post. When the rear doors opened McAnally was gestured out, and he saw the scores of men and their vehicles in the barracks yard. Soldiers in combat gear, uniformed police, and Saracen armoured cars with their engines whining and the fumes coughing out of their exhausts. He stayed close to Rennie. He was a dog in a strange street and he kept himself close to his master. He couldn't help himself. He saw the eyes on him. The sharp eyes of the young uniformed policemen, and the eyes of the soldiers set as bright jewels in the camouflage cream on their faces. Every bugger in the yard knew he was on duty at five in the morning because Gingy McAnally had gone supergrass. The eyes followed him, tracked him.

There was a hand on McAnally's sleeve. He spun. He saw Ferris, the officer. And in the moment of recognition Rennie had abandoned him. Pass the bloody parcel, Rennie off to talk to the big shots, and Gingy left with Ferris, the officer.

'Well done, Gingy . . .' Ferris's quiet voice close to McAnally's ear, private.

'What's you mean?' The snapped question. McAnally searching for his answer and looking up at Ferris's blackened cheeks.

'For doing the right thing.'

'I'm not doing this because . . .'

'Doesn't matter why you're doing it.'

'It's for my missus, and the kids, you got that?'

'Got it, Gingy. And good luck.'

Ferris walked away. Rennie was striding back to McAnally, testing a personal radio against his ear. McAnally lost Ferris amongst the mess of uniforms as the soldiers made for their vehicles. There was the shouting of orders, and the Saracens and the landrovers were filling fast.

The police sergeant was behind McAnally and holding his Sterling readied, as if safety was from now on a dubious matter. Rennie took McAnally's arm and led him back to the landrover.

The long column of vehicles spilled out into the Springfield Road.

Going fast, going for surprise. Through the road blocks that were already in position to seal off West Belfast.

The column was splitting, dividing, hiving off its parts.

He couldn't remember the bloody words. It had been easy enough to remember the bloody words when he was in his cell. He wouldn't have long. They'd told him that. Just long enough to get the missus dressed and the kids into their clothes and the cases packed. Not long enough for a bloody debate.

Hammering up the Springfield Road, heading for Turf Lodge. A traitor coming under the cloak of darkness with the soldiers and the policemen, coming back to his home.

Bravo Company and Charlie Company of 2 R.F.F. and some two hundred policemen were on the move, out on the streets.

Thirty-one names shared out amongst the soldiers and the police for lifting.

Ferris rode in the front of his open landrover, behind him was a Saracen and two police landrovers.

In the breast pocket of his tunic was a 4″ × 2″ photograph of a middle-aged man, features indistinct from magnification, with the over-stamped name across the base of the picture of Kevin Muldoon. In the pocket, against the photograph, was his notepad and the pencil-written address on the top sheet where Kevin Muldoon was thought to be sleeping.

'What have we got, Mr Ferris?' Fusilier Jones asked cheerfully. 'A good fat cat?'

'Do you think they'd tell the Poor Bloody Infantry, Fusilier Jones, if we were going for a fat cat or a bottle washer?'

He could see and hear again the evening when he had been in McAnally's cell at Castlereagh. He had willingly joined the conspiracy to turn a fighter . . . Bugger what the fighter had done. He had upset the flywheel of a man's soul. He shook his head, to Fusilier Jones he seemed dazed, because he wondered how Gingy McAnally would be when he had to stand face to face with what he had done.

'You alright, Mr Ferris?'

When he reached Number 63 The Drive in Turf Lodge then Gingy McAnally would know what he'd done.

'I'm fine, thank you.'

The landrover stopped at the cordon that was half way up the Drive. Beside McAnally, Rennie leaned forward and talked urgently through the driver's window to a uniformed Inspector. There were voices, urgent and hushed sweeping into the back of the landrover, Protestant voices of the Province and faraway English voices. Rennie was satisfied. He tapped the driver's shoulder.

He saw his own home in the landrover's lights. He felt sick. He saw his own curtains and his own door and his own front gate. The headlights were cut. There were the shapes of men running as shadows past the windscreen of the landrover. His eyes were closed as Rennie pushed him firmly towards the back doors. He opened his eyes. Rennie was pressed against him, crouched under the low roof of the landrover. There was the smell of Rennie's breath and of old cigarettes and of the exhaust fumes. The doors opened.

Rennie led McAnally up to the front door. Only the two of them going up the path.

'Knock her up.'

Rennie had taken his place behind McAnally.

Almost diffidently McAnally rapped on the door. Behind the door was the quiet of a sleeping home. He tugged savagely at the short crop of his hair. He heard Rennie breathing impatience behind him. He hit the door with his fist, then craned forward to lift the letter box flap and listen. An upper room light fell onto the front garden. There were policemen cursing softly and scurrying to new shadows when before they had been hidden. A noise upstairs, an opening door. He pressed his mouth to the letter box flap.

'Roisin, it's me, Gingy.'

More lights, and a fast footfall on the stairs, the drumming on the boards, the squeak of the pram's wheels, the growl of the bolt being drawn.

She wore a nightdress of pink flannel. There was a dressing gown slung over her shoulders that she held secure at her throat. She looked full into his face, and her chin was loose and her mouth was wide and her eyes were staring in astonishment. There were a hundred questions on her lips, and each one stifled. Her arms were rising up, to take her man against her, and then she saw the hulking shape of Howard Rennie, and the beam from the opened door caught the policeman crouching with a rifle at the front gate. There was a small choke in her throat, a waking from a dream. Her arms fell to her side, and the dressing gown slid to the floor.

Rennie shoved McAnally inside the door.

'Get on with it, Gingy.'

She backed into the pram, winced. She was going for the stairs. McAnally surged forward, caught her with his hands. She was looking back past him as Rennie led the stream of uniforms and weapons into the hallway. There was no part of it that she understood. McAnally's hands were on her hips, feeling the bones of her body through the nightdress. He forced her onto the first steps of the stairs and held her when she stumbled, and drove her up, and all the time she was gazing, dumbstruck, back at the police in her hall.

They reached the top of the stairs. He led her to their bedroom. He heard the catarrh cough of Little Patty. He saw their bed, and Baby Sean asleep under the ceiling light and half covered by the bedclothes.

'I've done it for you.' A desperation in McAnally's voice.

Her lips were apart, she was shivering as if in shock.

116

'I've done it all for you.'

There were low, muffled voices rising from the hallway, and the static scream of a radio set.

'It's all for you, and for the kids . . . That's why I've done it.'

Through the thin wall, Young Gerard's bed sang as he turned in it, and again the hacking throat of Little Patty.

'We're going to be alright. It's going to be a new life. We're going to have a new life . . . that's what they're going to give us.'

Now she understood. Her hair was across her face, ignored. She pushed him harshly from her. He could see the shapes of her body. He could see the anger settling on her forehead.

'It's what's best for us,' he said aloud.

'You've touted?' she accused.

'For all of us, for you and me and for the kids . . .'

'You've gone supergrass, you've gone tout . . . ? Jesus . . . Sean, tell me that's not true.'

He might as well have smacked his fist across her face.

'Get yourself dressed, get the kids dressed, get your clothes in a case.'

'Have you gone tout, Sean, not really . . . ?' And no more doubt on her face, only a world collapsing.

'I was going down for twenty fucking five years,' McAnally shouted. 'Is that what you fucking wanted? Did you want me away for twenty-five years? Did you want me away till I was old, you were old, till the kids were gone. It's us first, it's no other bastard first in front of us.'

His words blasted at her. She seemed to sag as if her strength had gone from her.

'You bloody damn fool, Sean.'

'Get the kids dressed. Get yourself dressed.'

'What did you do it for?' Her voice was a murmur. She slipped down onto the bed. Her fingers were at her mouth. Her nightdress had tumbled from her shoulder.

McAnally caught his wife's chin, pulled it up from her hands. 'I did it for twenty-five years of my life, and that should be good enough for you.'

Her head fell back onto her fists, the tears began.

'Mrs McAnally . . .'

Rennie was framed in the doorway.

He spoke brusquely. His words cracked through the room. 'Mrs McAnally, there are certain facts about your husband's situation that you should understand. Your husband has made a full statement concerning his criminal activities while a member of the Provisional I.R.A. Your husband has implicated many of the senior members of the Organization. In return for your husband going into the witness box and giving sworn evidence against close to thirty men, he has been guaranteed personal immunity from prosecution. He has also been promised the

117

chance of making a new life for himself with you and your children at a place where you will be safe from the Provisional I.R.A. You should do as you're asked, Mrs McAnally. You should get yourself and your children dressed.'

She sobbed, 'You've turned my man into a bleeding tout.'

'Converted terrorist, we call it.'

'I hope you're proud, of what you've done to us.'

'He's more than lucky to have had the chance to turn. You've got less than ten minutes to shift yourselves.'

'And if I won't . . . ?'

'Then you never see your husband again, as long as you live, Mrs McAnally,' Rennie said. 'And your children will never see their father again . . . I can't see the point of argument.'

Her glance, loaded with anger, slashed past McAnally and rested on Howard Rennie. He stared her out. She heaved the nightdress over her head, and tossed it behind her. For a moment she was still on the bed, naked, white, defiant. Then she shook with her crying. She took her underclothes from the chair and dragged them on automatically and without thought, and her jeans and her sweater and her socks and her sneakers.

'It'll seem better later on, Mrs McAnally, and it'll seem a hell of a lot better than you staying on.'

'We've never had a tout in our families before.'

'Probably because there's never been any one before with the guts.' Rennie closed the bedroom door silently behind him.

'Roisin, a life elsewhere for all of us has to be better than you here and me in the Kesh on twenty-five.' McAnally's hands were fidgeting uselessly in front of his stomach. She tossed back her head, fastened her hair ponytail with an elastic band. He turned for the door.

'Where are you going?'

'To get the kids up.'

'Don't you bloody go near my children.'

He stalked to the wardrobe. He remembered the door was always stuck because the wood was warped from the damp. He wrenched it open. Baby Sean had started to cry. There was only one suitcase in the wardrobe. It was the suitcase in which she had packed her sparse trousseau for the honeymoon in Bray. He pulled out the suitcase and unzipped it. There was pale green mould inside. He was wiping it furiously away with the sleeve of his anorak.

Six minutes later they were gone from Number 63.

Two white-faced, button-lipped children and a baby who was crying fervently and Roisin McAnally, and Sean Pius McAnally who had turned supergrass, were hurried through an avenue of armed policemen down their front path, through their front gate, across the rough pavement and into the back of the landrover.

All along the Drive the upstairs lights were on, and the upstairs curtains were heaving. The neighbours saw a policeman lift Little Patty up into the landrover, and saw a suitcase passed in after her. The neighbours would like to have seen the faces of McAnally and his missus, that would have been gilt on the ginger, but the early morning darkness denied them that pleasure.

Over his radio Rennie broadcast to the Ops Room at Springfield that the trawling in of the McAnally family was complete.

The landrovers revved their engines. The street was bathed in moving headlights, and then the night quiet fell again on the Drive in Turf Lodge.

Roisin McAnally allowed her husband to hold her hand in the back of the landrover. Her ankles were against a police constable's boots, and Little Patty was on her knee and Baby Sean was gurgling on her shoulder and Young Gerard was clinging to her elbow. He held her hand. She made no attempt to hold his. She was dead to the comfort of his hand. She was not crying any more. She would not let the constable sitting opposite her, with the Stirling on his knees, see her crying.

Over the radio came the coded message to announce that the lifts were in progress.

The squaddie in the centre of the three hung by his arms from the shoulders of the other two men. His legs swung free as they stampeded across the inner hallway of the maisonette block. He jack-knifed his knees up and thrust the soles of his boots into the lightweight door. The door caved in. Ferris was behind the squaddies with a uniformed Inspector. The light from the landing half lit the hallway, showed them the closed doors leading from it. The first door they tried was the kitchen, the second door was the living room, the third door was the bedroom.

It took them a moment to find the light switch by the door. It was a tiny room, big enough only for a double bed and a small wardrobe and two wooden chairs. The bed was lengthwise against the far wall. They had come in at a rush and now they were leaden in their tracks because there was only a girl in the bed. She was a pretty little thing, young-faced as if she were just out of school, and she had tousled, curling, auburn hair. She was sitting up in the bed, the straps of her nightdress on her shoulders and the sheet held vice-like over her chest.

Ferris saw the grin on Fusilier Jones's mouth.

'Sorry for the intrusion, Miss, but I have a warrant,' the Inspector intoned. 'I'm here for Kevin Muldoon.'

For Fusilier Jones and his mates, tipping a bare-arsed girl out of bed at 05.35 on a wet December morning made soldiering worthwhile.

'He's not here,' she was defiant, lovely, blazing eyes.

A squaddie opened the wardrobe, touched the Inspector's arm for attention and shone a torch onto a crumpled heap of a pair of trousers and a shirt and a jersey and a man's shoes.

The Inspector's smile was mirthless, not matching Fusilier Jones's happiness. The Inspector pushed past Ferris and the squaddies, he went to the bed, and heaved the bedclothes down onto the floor. All the soldiers in the room saw her legs and the gold below her stomach, and one sniggered, and they all saw the pyjama bottoms abandoned by her feet. The Inspector caught at the girl's arm and pulled her off the bed. Ferris and his Fusiliers took the cue and slid the bed back.

The man lay on his side against the wall. He was naked, he was shivering, his face was livid red. He held one hand over his privates, the other was raised to protect his head.

Ferris stared down at him, fascinated.

Rifle barrels and Sterling barrels were turned on him. Ferris saw the scar across the bridge of his nose. He thought that if the man had worn trousers he would have hurled himself at his captors. A man can't fight without trousers.

'Hands above your head, Muldoon,' the Inspector said dispassionately.

The hands were raised, then snatched by a constable, and the handcuffs clicked into place.

Kevin Muldoon was dressed in the clothes that had been thrown in haste onto the cupboard floor, the shirt and jersey pulled over his handcuffed wrists. The Inspector recited the terms of the Emergency Provisions powers as the trousers were drawn up over the knees of the man.

The crowd of armed men in the room eased back to allow Muldoon and his escort to be run out of the bedroom, away across the hallway and out to the landrovers.

'What is he?' Ferris quietly asked the Inspector. 'What is Kevin Muldoon?'

The Inspector turned on him a supercilious glare. 'What's that to an infantry lieutenant?'

'I helped pull in McAnally.'

Now the interest sparkled on the Inspector's face. 'He's the top boy. He runs Brigade.'

Ferris looked back and through the open door of the bedroom, and the open front door. He looked out into the night where the street was alive with the sounds of the soldiers and police and their vehicles. He understood why McAnally was a diamond in Rennie's scheme. He understood why McAnally had squeezed his hand tight to confirm the trust. He thought that he had achieved something after all in the weeks in Belfast, and the achievement was the arrest of a naked man who hid on the floor under his bed.

Ferris said, 'That's a great man to put away.'

'If we put him away . . .' The Inspector shouted from the hallway, 'Are you dressed yet, lady, I've not all day.'

'McAnally will put him away.'

'If you think P.I.R.A.'s going to lie down under this one then you're a green young soldier, Lieutenant. There's going to be all hell over this one . . . Lifting Kevin Muldoon's the easy bit, putting him away is going to be bloody, bloody hard, whatever that creature McAnally says now . . . or didn't they tell you that? Didn't they tell you that going supergrass is no picnic? I tell you this. If McAnally sees this through when it gets hot, then it'll be a bloody miracle.'

The girl stood in the doorway of the bedroom. She was dressed. There was a constable in front of her and one behind her, and still she showed no submission. She looked as though she would spit in the faces of the soldiers and police.

The Inspector said evenly, 'We'll be on our way, lady . . .' He turned to Ferris. 'In my job I don't see much sign of miracles.'

The door of the maisonette was too damaged to fasten shut after them, and they left it open, with the lights on in the hallway and the bedroom, and with a guard outside to await the arrival of Forensic.

The police landrovers were pulling away as Ferris came out onto the street. There was the first grey smear of the daylight hovering over the roofs and chimneys of the street. He had seen the man who ran Brigade, and the bastard was in no way different to the hundreds of men of middle age that he saw on the Falls every day that he was out footslogging on patrol.

Roisin McAnally sat in the police canteen at Springfield Road.

Her back was to her husband who stood with a powerfully built detective and whispered the names and peered through the small slit he held open in the venetian blind.

She thought she was being smothered with capable attention by the two policewomen who tripped around her and her children. They had found a portable high chair for Baby Sean; they had brought chips and sausages for Little Patty and cut the sausages for her; they had discovered some Space War comics for Young Gerard. She was proud of Young Gerard. Her son turned the pages automatically and showed no sign of pleasure. She was proud of her boy because he gave nothing to the bitches who fussed around him. She could have kicked Little Patty who ate as though this were the first food she had taken in a week. And Baby Sean didn't give a shit, because Baby Sean smiled in wide-faced happiness at the policewoman who made contorted grimaces across the high chair tray, Baby Sean didn't give a shit that his father was a tout.

There were the sounds of the landrovers arriving in the yard below the canteen window. Though he whispered, she could clearly hear her husband.

'That's Ollie O'Brien.'

'Brigade Quartermaster, Gingy.'

'That's right, Mr Rennie.'

She had heard many names spoken. She had heard the names of Joey McGilivarry and of Tom McCreevy and Joey Mulvaney and Billy Clinch and Dusty O'Hara . . . She knew them all. She used to neck with Dusty when she was seventeen, used to let his hand into her blouse but not down her jeans. And Billy used to bring her money when her man was in the Kesh. And there had been a night the year before when Joey had called and if it hadn't been curse time she'd known that she'd have taken him upstairs because the kids were asleep in bed. And Tom sang a dream in the bar on a Saturday night, sang of bloody victory. And Joey had gone serious with her sister, till he'd got nicked and she'd gone to Canada.

And more names . . . A policewoman had her hand on Young Gerard's arm and asked him if he'd like some food now, and smiled sweetly at him when he dumbly shook his head. It was a dream she couldn't wake from. There were policemen coming into the canteen and making a noise and laughing too loud, because a few minutes before they had been out on the streets and afraid and so they had to crack a big laugh now to show how brave they were. They carried their trays past Roisin McAnally and the two policewomen and the kids, and they all dropped their voices then, and they all looked the other bloody way, and they all pretended there was nothing that was special about the family at the table.

'That's Kevin Muldoon, Mr Rennie.'

'Tell me who he is, Gingy.'

'You know who he is.'

'You tell me, Gingy.'

'He's the Commander of Belfast Brigade, Mr Rennie.'

With both her hands she clasped Young Gerard's head, and she pulled it close to her mouth and she kissed his hair. When she let his head go free he said nothing, and went back to turning the pages of the comic books. Little Patty had tipped the brown sauce on the table and the policewoman said it was nothing and was wiping it with a tissue.

She couldn't cry. If she hadn't cried in the landrover, she couldn't cry in the police canteen.

*

122

There was a splash of thin sunshine as the rain cleared briefly over the Belfast dawn, and the landrovers carried the haul of prisoners from Springfield Road to the Castlereagh Holding Centre. All but two of the men and women named by Sean Pius McAnally had been successfully lifted. Only one of those held had tried to resist arrest and he would have a technicolour eye by lunchtime and two constables would wear facial sticking plaster for the rest of the week.

Mr Pronsias Reilly was woken by the clock radio beside his bed. He always started the day with the downtown headlines. The first news bulletin of the day usually let him know whether he was required early at the Magistrates, whether he could go straight to the Crumlin Court House. It was only after the headlines and the weather that he realized the omission. No announcement of a charge against Sean Pius McAnally. If a man had been charged with 'Tenner' Simpson's murder, and with the murder of two 'tecs, then the Press Office would have been crowing the news like an early morning cockerel to the News Rooms. And he had heard on the vine that the chemical tests on McAnally's clothing would stitch the case tight against him.

For Mr Pronsias Reilly, dabbing on the pre-shave lotion, groping for his battery razor, there was only one conclusion to be drawn from the downtown headlines . . . Sean Pius McAnally had made a deal.

Alone, in his bath, walking on the Sperrins, sailing on Carlingford, alone in his private and most honest thoughts, he would not have regarded himself as a fellow traveller with the P.I.R.A. But he was a Republican, he was a believer in a United Ireland, and he hated the Protestant ascendancy. He had lived too long inside the Catholic minority ever to abandon his roots. He was a self-taught lawyer before gaining his exam passes at Queen's University.

He remembered the woman who had come to his office. He remembered what he had thought of her. He remembered the fierce loyalty of the woman to her imprisoned man, and her faith was in a fucking tout.

He had been, the previous year, calling on a client in Whiterock and his car had been hijacked by some kids. He had shouted and screamed on the pavement and a big man had come to him, a man with a bullet wound in the throat. The man had calmed him and walked away, and twenty minutes later the man had come back at the wheel of his car and not a scratch on it. He had tried to pay the man, and the man had refused. Mr Pronsias Reilly didn't know what ranking Frankie Conroy held in the Organization and didn't ask. Three times since Frankie Conroy had escorted women to see him and consult with him when their man was inside.

One turn deserved another turn.

He rang the number of Frankie Conroy.

He heard the sleep-filled voice repeat the number he had dialled.

He didn't introduce himself.

'You might wonder whether Sean Pius McAnally has gone supergrass.'

He put down the telephone.

The Secretary of State was taking his breakfast of toast and orange juice in the flat over his office in the Castle, when his civil servant brought in the morning's newspapers.

'A bit damned early, Fred.'

'I've been with the police since five. Belfast Brigade in its entirety is currently enjoying the hospitality of Castlereagh Holding Centre.'

'That's damned good.'

'It's gone like clockwork, so far.'

The Secretary of State looked keenly at his civil servant. 'You'll keep that clock wound . . . if we fail with this one we're all for the rubbish bin.'

'And if we win, sir, then it's P.I.R.A. Belfast, that's on the dust cart.'

The civil servant put down the newspapers, smiled briskly, and let himself out.

The Secretary of State reflected that his political and public career depended on a turned Provo carrying through an act of betrayal against the Organization he had sworn allegiance to.

He glanced at the front page of the *Newsletter*. More demands from the Protestant politicians for his resignation. He picked up the *Irish News*. A Catholic leader said he was tainted with bias and should be sacked as a gesture to the nationalist population. God alone knew that he did his best for the bloody place, and God alone knew where he'd find some thanks for his efforts.

Frankie turned into the Drive and braked.

Far up the road he saw the police landrovers, and beyond them, parked at the side of the road, was a removal van.

That was all he needed to see. He reversed and drove away.

Frankie Conroy had told the Chief that Gingy McAnally was playing stone statues in Castlereagh, and all the time the bugger was touting . . . Shit Almighty, Gingy McAnally had been briefed on 'Tenner' Simpson by all of the Brigade.

*

He had been strip-searched. His legs had been prised open and a cold dry hand had felt in his crutch, and the cheeks of his arse had been opened for a mirror examination. He had been weighed. He had been asked if he wished to see a doctor. He had signed for his meagre possessions. His signature was his only active co-operation in the Castlereagh reception process. The Chief sat now in a solitary cell.

He had no way of knowing how many men had been lifted with him, but he had seen the numbers of the vehicles in the yard at Springfield Road. The numbers of Saracens and landrovers added up to a big lift.

Confusion, anger, frustration, swam in his mind. What had the pigs got on him? What had the pigs got lined up and ready and waiting for him? No detective had yet bothered to talk to him. He was in bloody solitary.

They had taken the Chief's watch. He had been in the solitary cell probably for less than twenty minutes, and it seemed to be for bloody ever. Many times, dates spread over many years, he had been lifted. This was a changed time. Never before had the bastards seemed so confident.

Frankie came within sight of the maisonettes.

There were landrovers outside the block, and uniformed policemen, and as he cruised gently forward he saw two detectives coming out of the doorway and carrying a plastic bag between them that was filled with clothes.

Frankie knew the block. He knew it was where the Chief was currently sleeping.

He set off to check the homes of Ollie O'Brien and Joey McGilivarry and Tom McCreevy. He knew what he would find. His face was grim set.

When he saw the landrovers at Ollie O'Brien's in Andy'town, he muttered soundlessly to his chest: 'Gingy McAnally, you're fucking dead. So help me, you're dead, you fucking tout.'

Rennie had said to him that he shouldn't try to talk to Roisin until they were in the safe house. Rennie warned him that she would be in shock, and that he should take it slowly. Rennie played the marriage bloody guidance priest with him. Rennie had talked to him quietly by the window after the men had been brought into the yard. They would have the morning together, what remained of the morning, and after lunch Rennie would come to the safe house and he would explain to Roisin what was happening and then she'd see it easier.

Didn't see it so bloody easy now, did she? Hadn't bloody spoken to him all the time they had been in the canteen, and he'd seen the vicious look on her face when Little Patty had come to sit on his knee.

Rennie had gone when the landrovers had left for Castlereagh.

There was a uniformed Inspector at the next table to them, who cleaned his fingernails with a used match, and there were the policewomen who'd become tired of clearing up Little Patty's food and of finding new comics for Young Gerard, and there were two constables who sat at tables that were a little away from them and acted as watchdogs to stop any man using the canteen from coming too close to them.

Abruptly, the Inspector looked at his watch, like it was an afterthought and he was caught by surprise . . . Bloody liar . . . The Inspector stood, motioned for McAnally to come and waved to Roisin and the kids that they should follow . . . acting like he'd get a bloody disease if he spoke to them. Roisin had Baby Sean on her shoulder. McAnally picked up Little Patty. He put out his hand for Young Gerard to take, and the kid stuck his hands down into his pockets. He'd belt the bugger if he did that tomorrow.

The Inspector led, the family following, and after the family came the policewomen and the two constables. They came out into the yard. It was quiet outside. The family crossed the yard. It was as if they were now unremarkable and uninteresting. McAnally couldn't see anyone watching them. He could see soldiers and police going about their work, but he shifted Little Patty higher on his shoulder and tried to walk taller.

There was an escort of policemen and three landrovers waiting for them. He couldn't turn, not to face Roisin. He felt Little Patty flinching against his shoulder as he walked closer to the landrovers.

'Well done, Mr McAnally.'

He stopped. He swung and saw Ferris. Ferris was coming forward, walking fast, from behind him. He saw the officer smile hesitantly. His face was still smeared with camouflage cream.

'I really meant it when I said it before, well done. I admire what you've done.'

Roisin was at his shoulder. He felt her eyes on him. 'I told you why I did it.'

Ferris said, 'Doesn't matter why, only matters what you're doing.'

McAnally peered into Ferris's face. 'I did it so's I wouldn't go to the Kesh.'

The officer was shaking his head, laughing gently. 'Rubbish, if you'll forgive me, Mr McAnally. You turned your back on something evil, that's why I admire what you've done . . .'

Roisin was staring at him, contempt at her lips, and she seemed to mouth the word 'evil', as if it were an insult to her religion.

'You know fuck all.'

'Try me, Mr McAnally, try me some day. Come back and tell me

126

whether it was just staying out of the Kesh, or helping to destroy something that's rotten in this community . . . You should be very proud of him, Mrs McAnally.'

'Keep her out of it.'

'I read up about the kestrel, Mr McAnally. Lovely bird. Free to every limit. Free as your children should be, free as Mrs McAnally should be.'

McAnally came close to Ferris.

'Why am I important to you?' he said hoarsely.

'You want to know?'

'I want to know.'

'I can't change the course of this war, can't move it an inch. You can change it, you can cut away something that's foul. I can't but you can. Compared with what you can do, I'm wasting my time. I'm insignificant, all of us here are irrelevant, if we're compared with what you can achieve.'

'I've done it for myself, myself and my family only.'

'I don't think so.'

'Why don't you ever listen?'

'Mightn't believe what I'm told.'

McAnally went to the landrover. He waited at the back doors to help Roisin climb up inside.

10

The landrover carrying the McAnally family jerked to a halt. The rear doors opened, flooding the interior with light. The escorts jumped down. They were in the middle of a housing estate. Past the bodies of the constables he saw small front gardens with low white-painted fences, and windows slung with net curtains and decorated with pot plants. The houses were of soft brick and whitewood facing and were semi-detached. A constable reached back into the landrover to lift out the one suitcase.

'Let's get you comfortable, Mrs McAnally,' the Inspector said brusquely. 'Always get the ladies comfortable first, isn't that right, Mr McAnally?'

McAnally reckoned it would have hurt the Inspector to call her 'lady', and him 'Mister'. Roisin, beside him, snorted.

She went first, carrying Baby Sean. He went after her, with Little Patty. Young Gerard ignored his father's hand to help him down, and a constable's hand, and wriggled out on the seat of his trousers and dropped onto the roadway.

Just an ordinary estate, if McAnally kept his eyeline low. An everyday estate for everyday people. They were the end righthand house of a cul-de-sac.

The Inspector looked sharply round him, as if on an ordinary and everyday estate there could be danger. 'Straight in, please, Mrs McAnally.'

McAnally looked for further horizons. On the rising ground behind the houses he saw the corrugated iron screen fencing, and the coiled barbed wire. He saw a perimeter guard tower, blacked and draped in camouflage netting and further protected by a rocket screen. They were on a sloping hillside, the Shorts aircraft factory and the waters of Belfast Lough were below them.

Palace Barracks. Every man who had ever sworn the oath to the Organization knew about Palace Barracks, Holywood. The lore of the Palace Barracks was rooted in the activities of the Special Branch and Intelligence Corps interrogators a dozen years before, and the 'five techniques' used on the Provo suspects in the early years of the war. Hooding, the noise machine, standing against the wall on tiptoe, deprivation of sleep, absence of food, those were the Famous Five that had been imported to Northern Ireland after successful use in Aden, Cyprus, Malaya, wherever any little nationalist runt gave two fingers to the Brits. More than two thousand men had gone through Holywood before the interrogators packed up, locked up, and went to Castlereagh. Palace Barracks had reverted to its previous role, home for a long-stay married accompanied battalion of the regular army. The Palace Barracks into which Gingy McAnally and his family had been brought was base for eighteen months for the Devons and Dorsets and their families.

Across the cul-de-sac a woman was bent and was picking up by hand the last of the leaves to fall on her handkerchief lawn and was placing them one by one into a plastic supermarket bag, and when she saw the flotsam spill out from the landrover opposite she put down her bag deliberately and went back into her house and firmly closed the door.

Roisin McAnally had seen the woman. She gazed expressionless at the slammed door. At the entry to the cul-de-sac were two women, one with a push chair and baby, one with a soldier husband, and their mouths moved in unheard talk, and the woman kissed her soldier on the cheek, and they looked one last time at the family and the soldier went one way and the woman with the push chair went another. She saw the young face of a woman at a window, and when she met the stare the curtain fell and hid the face.

She followed the Inspector up the narrow front pathway, and he took a key from his pocket and opened the front door.

She turned her face away from Baby Sean and back towards McAnally.

'You know they think we're shit, don't you?'

He didn't answer.

If the Inspector had heard, he gave no sign. At a brisk pace he led Roisin McAnally around the house. It was furnished, army issue, for a junior non-commissioned officer. A through living room with a worn sofa and chairs around a gas fire, a table at the far end beside the glass doors out onto the back garden, no pictures on the walls and the last of the ducks in flight had a chipped wing.

'It's the best we could do in the time we had, Mrs McAnally . . . and it's safe here, that's the main thing. It's a bit bare, but it'll be quite comfortable.'

Of course, it was beyond the Inspector's reasoning that Roisin McAnally had never felt anything but safe in Turf Lodge, and could never feel anything but danger if she was sleeping in the heart of a Brit army barracks.

Up the stairs, feet padding on the carpet, the Inspector and Roisin McAnally and Young Gerard staying close to her, and McAnally left behind in the living room holding Little Patty's hand and carrying Baby Sean.

'Three bedrooms upstairs, Mrs McAnally. One's a double bed, one's twins, one's single. Bathroom, loo, hot water all the time, much as you want. It's not that bad, is it?'

'How long are we here?'

'That's not for me to say. Mr Rennie'll be down, he'll decide that.'

'And what do we decide?' she snapped.

'Your decision's been made, Mrs McAnally. Your husband's decided for you, that's why you're here.'

The beds were unmade. There were neatly folded piles of blankets and sheets and pillows on the mattresses.

She came down the stairs after him.

'My baby'll want milk.'

'In the fridge, Mrs McAnally.'

Everything organized, everything planned, and the Inspector seemed to tell her that after life in Turf Lodge this must be bloody paradise. She went into the kitchen to find milk from the fridge.

She heard McAnally's voice from the living room.

'Have you chucked someone out? Have you turfed someone out to make room for us?'

She heard the Inspector's voice.

'Came vacant last week. A corporal was shot in Short Strand. The bullet did his spine, paralysed him. They flew him to Stoke Mandeville in the U.K., his wife's gone with him, and their kiddies. That's why the house is free.'

129

She was frozen at the open door of the fridge, her hand was on the milk bottle. She couldn't help herself, she had to hear what her man replied. There was a long silence.

'I'm sorry,' McAnally said.

Jesus, God Al-fucking-mighty. Sean McAnally telling a Prod peeler that he was sorry a squaddie had got himself taken out of Belfast on his back.

'I'll be outside,' the Inspector said. 'Mr Rennie'll be here soon. You shouldn't go out, not till he's been, and the kids shouldn't go out.'

She heard the door close. She took the milk from the fridge, and then opened a cupboard and she saw the piles of plates and saucers, and cups, and mugs. There was a mug with rabbits on it, and she reached for it without thinking, and then she wondered if it had been left behind in the panic rush to get to a bedside in an English hospital. She wondered, and she blinked her eyes, and took down the mug. She might have smashed the mug, instead she filled it with milk.

She took the milk into the living room.

She saw pleading on her husband's face.

'It's nice, isn't it?' McAnally said. 'It's a nice house . . .'

'You're bought cheap. Running hot water, and a stair carpet, and you're happy to bloody tout.'

'It's the best for us, for all of us,' he was shouting. 'It's because I love you, you and the kids.'

Young Gerard ran from the window to clutch at his mother's waist.

'I'm sorry,' she mimicked.

He looked out of the window. He saw the landrover, and the Inspector standing by the door and smoking a cigarette. He looked the other way, down the length of the room, out of the glass doors and across the back garden and he saw the dark silhouette of a uniformed constable.

'It's a hell of a way to show you love us, Sean, bringing us here.'

Frankie crossed West Belfast many times that morning in his effort to measure the scale of the lifts. He was in Twinbrook and Suffolk, in Finaghy and Beechmount, in Ballymurphy and Whiterock, in Andersonstown and Falls. He checked the homes and safe houses of the big men of Brigade and the Battalions. He saw the smashed-down doors.

He was known in the Organization as a willing helper. He held no Brigade rank, nor any position in a particular Battalion. His friends liked to think of him as a troubleshooter, and that always raised a laugh in a snug bar or an upstairs back room. He floated from the A.S.U.s and the Volunteers up the ladder to the big shots who surrounded the Chief. He knew almost every man who had been taken to Castlereagh, and so he knew how grave the damage was.

That morning Frankie Conroy felt the fear of many men in the city. It was the fear bred by a traitor, and the fear was fuelled by the danger of the domino. If one man turned and implicated a cell block full of friends, then would one of those friends go supergrass too? Where did it end?

There was one way, one way only, in Frankie's thinking, to handle the tout. He should be handled at barrel point. The informer should be terrorized into retraction. The long arm of the Organization had to reach to the safe house of the tout. And the bastard could be in any police station in the city, or in any military barracks, or he could be up in Prot country in the north of Co. Antrim, or he could be in the Air Force compound at Aldergrove . . . where to begin to bloody look?

He had called a meeting. Without authority he had taken charge. Who could give Frankie Conroy authority to blow his bloody nose when Brigade staff was in Castlereagh, and half of the Battalion officers with them? The meeting was called for lunch hour in the bar in Clonard where there was a private room, where Frankie was comfortable.

During the morning Frankie had worked hard. He had dug into the background lives of Sean and Roisin McAnally. In Turf Lodge, the Parade and the Drive ran parallel. He parked in the Parade and cut through a garden and climbed the low common fence and came to the back door of a house in the Drive, the back door of Number 12.

He saw the old woman in the kitchen, washing her smalls.

He rapped on the window.

She came to the back door.

'It's Mrs O'Rourke?'

'Who's wanting me?'

'Not to matter who's wanting you . . . You're the Ma of Roisin McAnally? . . . You're the Gran of Gerard and Patty and Sean . . . ?'

He saw the nervousness in her face.

'Been to 63 this morning, Mrs O'Rourke?'

'I have.'

'And I'll bet you didn't get much of a welcome this morning, Mrs O'Rourke.'

'What's it to you?'

'Don't ask me questions, Mrs O'Rourke . . . What did you find, at 63, this morning?'

Between his finger and his thumb he could have broken her thin wrist, but he held her wrist lightly, like a friend, and he spoke softly, like a saviour.

'Found nothing, found them gone.' There was a dribble glistening at her eyes.

'Gone without telling her Ma?'

'She never said nothing about going.'

'You've a telephone, Mrs O'Rourke?'

'She never rung me. I've a telephone. She never rung to say she was going.'

'Where's she gone, Mrs O'Rourke?'

The wet eyes dropped. Frankie was inside the kitchen. He closed the door behind him. She didn't answer him.

'Where's your man, Mrs O'Rourke, where's Roisin's Da?'

'He's in bed, with a chest. It'd kill him to know what she's done.'

'You know what she's done?'

'Her furniture's taken, little enough of it, but it's gone.'

'Shall I make a pot of tea for us, Mrs O'Rourke . . . Sean McAnally's gone supergrass . . . Where's your kettle? . . . Your Roisin's married to a tout . . . 'Scuse me for the tap . . . Your grankids have an informer for a father . . .'

Frankie had filled the kettle. He lit the gas ring. He was looking to the shelves for the tea tin, and she pointed to it.

'It's not out yet, Mrs O'Rourke, but it's going to be out. The dad of Gerard and Patty and Sean is an informer. He's buying his freedom with the gaoling of thirty men. He's a paid perjurer. He's going to lie his way through a show trial. The men he's named, they're some of the finest Irish patriots ever born. Mrs O'Rourke . . . we'll need some milk . . . Mrs O'Rourke, Sean McAnally is going to be hated in this city wherever there is pride in the nation of Ireland. He's going to be hated, along with your daughter, along with your grankids . . . The kettle's boiled, Mrs O'Rourke.'

She made the tea in the old teapot, the pot she had been given at her wedding.

She passed Frankie Conroy his mug of tea. She put him in a spoon of sugar, and her hand was shaking, and the grains were spread on the table beside the pile of waiting washing.

'What do you want of me?'

'I want to help you, Mrs O'Rourke. I'm not asking for anything from you, I'm trying to help you, to save you from what's going to hit you when it's known that your Roisin's man's a tout.'

'What do you want from me?'

'You've got it wrong, Mrs O'Rourke, I'm helping you . . . it's good tea . . . a man's going to come to see you, a law man, he's going to ask something of you. Mrs O'Rourke, we want to get Roisin back to you, back to her home with your grankids, that's all we want. Mrs O'Rourke, if Roisin telephones for you, find out where she is. If she's not to be hated as the enemy of the Irish people then we have to know where she is . . . that's a grand cup, thanks . . . we don't want her hated like Sean McAnally, do we, Mrs O'Rourke?'

He left his tea half finished. He went out of the kitchen, and back the way he had come.

*

132

Rennie held up his warrant card at the gate barrier. The soldier on sentry scrutinized it, nodded him through, and Rennie gestured behind him to draw attention to the two following cars.

He knew the way, after a fashion. It was a dozen years since he had worked in Palace Barracks, but he remembered the layout although the married quarters had been extended since his time.

St Andrew's Close, Number 15. It was a bugger to find because all the Closes and Terraces and Gardens and Avenues were damn near the same. He asked a housewife, deciphered her Plymouth accent, and found the house with the landrover and the Inspector parked outside.

He went to the door. There were two men, younger than Rennie, behind him.

McAnally opened the door.

'Alright, Gingy?' Rennie asked, as if there could be no problem.

'She won't speak to me, fucking cutting me out.'

'Leave her to me, Gingy.'

He went through the door and the two men followed him. They were of a type, old slacks, heavy shoes, sweaters and anoraks. They were alert, interested, they were at work as if going through the door was the act of card punching.

The television was on in the living room, soap opera, trivial lives where no one thought of blasting a judge to his maker with a Soviet-built R.P.G. warhead. Rennie's nose turned. He reckoned the baby must have peed on the carpet. A fog of cigarette smoke. He saw the filled ashtray on the arm of the chair in which she sat. Half the smoke was going up the baby's nose . . . perhaps the little bugger peed on the carpet in protest.

Rennie said, 'Let's get the introductions over . . . This is John Prentice, this is Andy Goss. John and Andy are the guarantee of your safety . . .'

Roisin McAnally looked up at him, there was a sneer on her mouth. 'Are they here to see we don't run away?'

'They're here as guarantees of your personal protection, no more and no less . . . Spare me a minute, please, Mrs McAnally.'

He nodded his head back towards the door. It wasn't a request, and she stood and followed him. They went out of the room, and without comment Rennie led the way up the stairs and into the main bedroom. She had not made the bed, she had not unpacked the suitcase.

'Sit down, Mrs McAnally.'

She sat, and she stared up at him and her eyes were bright with pain and suspicion.

'A few facts, Mrs McAnally. Your Sean, in our book, is a Converted Terrorist. That means that we are prepared to give him immunity from prosecution, while he is prepared to testify in court against the men with whom he formerly engaged in criminal and illegal acts. Some men

133

who have taken a similar road have abandoned their families, left them at home to face the music. Sean insisted that you and your children should be taken into our protective care, and we are very happy to provide that care. For the next few weeks we will keep you in Belfast because there's still a hefty amount of ground for Sean to cover with us, after that you may go across the water to England or we may look further away – Cyprus, Gibraltar – but all that depends on the timing of the Magistrates' committal proceedings in which Sean will provide prosecution evidence. When that's done we'll be thinking about something permanent, a new start for you all. After the trial proper we promise to build a new identity for Sean, you, the children, a new identity in a new location. Financially you will be looked after, not luxury, but comfortable . . .'

'Sean's got immunity?'

'Correct.'

'He's guaranteed immunity?'

'Correct.'

'We're not prisoners here?'

'You're free to go whenever, wherever you wish.'

'And you'll not stop us going now . . . going home now . . .'

She stood.

'Hear me out, Mrs McAnally.'

'I'm going home.'

There was a winter smile spreading on Rennie's face. He took a folded sheet of paper from his pocket.

'Thought this might interest you, transcript of the local lunchtime radio . . . Listening, Mrs McAnally?'

Her eyes never left his face. He thought that if Sean Pius McAnally had blown Howard Rennie away, then she'd have given him an extra screw that night, to tell him he'd done well.

'This is what they said on the lunchtime . . . "Shortly after a West Belfast family were taken by police into protective care early this morning, Security Forces launched their largest arrest operation of the year. A Provisional Sinn Fein spokesman has admitted that Sean Pius McAnally of the Drive in Turf Lodge has implicated many leading Republicans after turning supergrass following his arrest a week ago in connection with the R.P.G. attack that killed Mr Justice William Simpson and two of his police bodyguards." . . . Listening, Mrs McAnally? . . . "Police sources were claiming this morning that Mr McAnally's statements had led to the arrest of the entire Brigade staff of the P.I.R.A. in Belfast and of many Battalion-ranking officers. One senior detective said, 'We now have firm evidence against some of the most vicious killers who have been preying on our community.' It is known that at least thirty men were picked up in the dawn swoops." . . . Got it, Mrs McAnally?'

Rennie replaced the sheet of paper in his pocket.

'You haven't a home to go back to, Mrs McAnally.'

'You bastard.'

'And you're a sensible woman.'

'What did you do to him?'

'Your baby's crying, Mrs McAnally.'

'You've bloody destroyed him.'

'I didn't destroy him, Mrs McAnally. I didn't kill a judge and two police officers, I wasn't staring down a twenty-five-year stretch . . . I'm bloody Father Christmas to you and your family.'

'He'll be looking over his shoulder for the rest of his life.'

'Not true . . . and even if it were true that's better than the rest of his life in the Kesh. Mrs McAnally, get used to one thing: after what he's told us there's no going back for Sean, there's no "going home". If Sean goes home he's dead in the gutter. Don't tell me you'd prefer that.'

'You *bastard*.'

'We're getting repetitive, Mrs McAnally . . . Thank you for sparing me a minute.'

Rennie went out, and closed the door on her. He heard the first sob in her throat.

He went downstairs.

He called brightly through the door. 'Did you bring those cans in, Andy?'

Inside the living room was his answer. Half a dozen Tennants cans on the low table beside the sofa. McAnally looked questioningly at Rennie.

Rennie said, 'She's had a hell of a day, Gingy. She's going to lie down for a bit, best for her.'

The Cortina car was unremarkable, eight years old, paint scraped and rusted.

There were two men in the car, and in their different ways they were as unremarkable as their transport. Perhaps they were labourers, perhaps they were a farmer's sons.

It was the third time in as many days that these two men had come south of the border and into Monaghan town. On the previous two days they had established the pattern of life inside and outside the workshop of the watch mender. These two men could blend into crowds, onto streets. It was their training. Without drawing attention to themselves they had surveyed the workshop, found the rear ground-level window to the cellar, reckoned how fire would be contained in the cellar, checked the daily movements of the watch mender. They could blend easily, if they didn't speak.

135

They had left Gough Barracks in Armagh as the afternoon light was dipping and instead of taking the direct road to Monaghan they had gone the long way, through Killylea and Caledon, before turning off the road to substitute southern car plates for northern ones.

Each man was armed with a Browning automatic pistol. It was a chance, a risk, to be armed and to be stopped at a Garda or Irish Army checkpoint, but nothing to the chance and risk of being blown by the Provos and left without means of defence.

In the boot of the car was a two-gallon can of petrol.

No record existed of their orders. Their initiative was to be given free rein. They appreciated that freedom. All the Troopers and N.C.O.s of the Special Air Service working from Northern Ireland appreciated freedom. These two men had been given the information that the watch mender in Monaghan doubled as a craftsman in explosive devices.

Mr Pronsias Reilly had driven in his lunch hour to Turf Lodge. On the way back to the city centre he had mapped out in his mind the statement that he would issue in the name of Mrs Chrissie O'Rourke. In Mr Pronsias Reilly's book it was a scandal that a woman and her kids could be 'kidnapped' by police from her home in the middle of the night at gun point.

He had told Mrs O'Rourke that he would do his certain damnedest to get her daughter back to her, and the issuing of her statement would be a positive step.

Was Mr Pronsias Reilly opposed to the Provos? Too simplistic a question for a successful young legal mind. Phrase the question again. Was Mr Pronsias Reilly opposed to violence? Definitely, he was opposed to violence, to the violence of the British army, the Royal Ulster Constabulary, the Special Air Service, the prison staff, the Ulster Defence Regiment, the Protestant paramilitary assassination squads. Was Mr Pronsias Reilly opposed to Provo violence? Ah, but with all the violence thrown against the Nationalist minority small wonder that they turned to their own army for protection.

From his own perspective he regarded himself as realistic. In the eyes of his professional colleagues, he was ambivalent.

And for their opinions he cared not a tuppenny crap.

The word had gone out, the word said that Frankie Conroy had called for a meeting at the bar in Clonard.

There were eight men in the private room, and there was a man on the staircase, and there were two more men in the long bar to watch.

'There's no pissing, no messing, McAnally's to be stiffed. McAnally's dead, from this time he's dead. McAnally will not appear in court. For what he's done, he doesn't just retract his evidence and walk back to us like nothing's different. He's dead. First I want him cringing, then I want him screaming, then I want him dead. They're crowing up there at Headquarters. They won't crow long. Wherever he is, we reach him.'

There were no interruptions.

'We reach him, and we smash him.'

The meeting settled after Frankie's address to set up the command structure that would replace the lifted Brigade organization, and to prepare the necessary intelligence network that would track McAnally to his safe house.

Eight men, drinking and smoking and plotting the death of Sean Pius McAnally, tout.

'Roisin'll take us to him, whether she knows it or she doesn't. She'll take us there, right to him. She's a good girl, she's the way to him.'

The television was on for the children, cartoons.

John Prentice had taken a chair into the hall, he'd left Andy in the living room with the kids. He thought Mrs McAnally was asleep upstairs, and Gingy had just gone up, to leak, because he'd five Tennants in him. It wasn't the first time that Prentice had played minder to a supergrass. He had been on the squad two years. The last one had been a Protestant, U.V.F. thug, who'd done his show in court and been shipped off to Australia, the last one would be good news to the bookmakers in Melbourne or Sydney or Adelaide or wherever. He was a Detective Constable in the R.U.C., he had been told that he was selected for work of the most exacting nature. Christ, he hadn't known the half of it when he started out. He had learned to play wetnurse, nanny, prison officer, confidant and bully. The first days were the hardest with a new supergrass. The first days were when he had to grope to find the personality of his man, and then learn to respond to that personality, and then to control it. The psychologist who came to Headquarters said that the relationships between a supergrass and a minder should be taken slowly the first few days. No rush, no speed, because it's ball and chain for weeks and months.

There was a P.P.K. handgun in the shoulder holster under Prentice's jacket. He was a trained marksman. There were two sides to the job of minder. There was the personal contact bit, and there was the bodyguard bit. He was three years senior to Goss, three years more service. He was responsible for getting Gingy McAnally into court as a credible witness offering evidence without corroboration. He was responsible for seeing that Gingy McAnally's nerve held up, and he was responsible for keeping the man out of the gutter and out of the sights of an Armalite.

A fair old responsibility for John Prentice, aged twenty-nine. The psychologist said that the minder had to build an atmosphere of delicate control and influence. The psychologist characterized it as 'discreet domination'. Fine for the psychologist. The psychologist wasn't going to be cooped up for weeks with a Provo murderer and a Provo murderer's wife and their kids. In a bag in the boot of his car was a spare shirt and spare socks and a plastic razor. He had nothing to go back to that he could call a home. He lived in a furnished flatlet off the Newtownards Road, had been there since his wife had kicked him out of their Glengormley bungalow. Divorce yourself from the police, or she'd divorce him, that had been her ultimatum. He had made his choice. He thought she was young enough to find some other fellow. He would sleep on the sofa in the living room of the safe house, and not think a lot about it. Andy had it coming, he had a fiancée in the Northern Bank, who didn't like the hours, and didn't like the drinking, and wasn't hot on the danger. Andy's time would come too.

He could handle Gingy, he'd decided that. He didn't know whether he could handle Roisin. He wasn't sure if Gingy could handle Roisin.

The toilet flushed. McAnally was coming down the stairs. Behind McAnally the bedroom door opened. The sleep hadn't done her much good. She came fast down the stairs, and bumped past her man and nearly spilled him, and went into the living room running as if she thought Andy might be abusing her kids.

'Alright, Gingy?'

'Not bad.'

There hadn't been any kids in his own marriage. He'd taken his chair into the hallway because he wasn't good with kids. Andy was better. Andy came from a vicarage in County Tyrone that was stuffed with kids. The older boy had problems written all over him, not responding to Gingy, shrinking from himself and from Andy, and too bloody quiet. The girl was alright, the girl was too young, but the older boy knew his father was a tout.

The cartoons were gone, on the television, and the adverts. John Prentice heard the signature tune of the news.

He heard the voices.

Mrs McAnally said, 'Leave it on.'

Andy said, 'Better you don't see it.'

The announcer spoke the name of Sean Pius McAnally.

'Leave it bloody on.'

'You'll only hurt yourself.'

The announcer described Sean Pius McAnally as the most significant supergrass the R.U.C. had yet found.

John Prentice came to the door of the living room. Andy had given way. The little girl pointed in innocence at the screen and the photograph of her father. The next picture showed a house on an estate, and

138

the boy watched it blankly and said nothing because it was his home.

Silence in the room because all eyes were on the television, then Roisin had her hand at her mouth and her fist was clenched tight.

'That's Ma . . .'

A photograph of an elderly lady on the screen. And the announcer said that the old lady was the mother-in-law of Sean Pius McAnally, and that the lady pleaded with her daughter to come back home to her . . .

'That's Gran . . .' the little girl said.

Her daughter should come back to her, because whatever her man had done, Roisin had done no wrong.

Shit, Andy bloody Goss should have bloody pulled the plug out.

Prentice strode into the room, straight to the television, switched it off.

'What's you done that for?' Roisin screamed at him.

'Because it's best off.'

'You tell me what I watch?'

'When it's for your own good, yes.'

'You think I shouldn't know what's said about me? . . . That was my Ma that you switched off.'

'For a bit it's better you don't watch.'

'You tell him,' she turned to McAnally. 'You tell him I'm watching the bloody television.'

McAnally walked away. He stepped over Young Gerard's legs, he went past Little Patty, on past the sofa where Baby Sean was sleeping. He went to the back window of the living room. He could see the line of the perimeter arc lamps circling Palace Barracks.

'Tell him to put the telly back on for me.'

He went away from the window. He was desperate, he was in agony. She stood in front of him. Her hands were on her hips, her head was tossed back. His lips quivered, but he could not speak.

She sneered, 'A man would tell him to put the telly on for me.'

Nothing for Prentice to say.

'Tell him to switch it on for me.'

McAnally howled, deep in his pain. 'I only did it for you, for you and the kids . . .'

'Lying sod.'

'It was just for you.'

'You hadn't the balls to go to the Kesh.'

'Because I love my kids.'

'The men in the Kesh are twice the man you are.'

'Because I love you.'

'You're a yellow bastard.'

McAnally hit his wife. He hit her with the flat of his hand across the face.

Goss caught Young Gerard, held him struggling as he tried to get to his father, to defend his mother.

McAnally and his wife clutched for each other. They were both weeping. Their arms were around each other, and the tears were wet on their faces. McAnally buried his kisses in Roisin's shaking, sobbing head.

Goss said to Young Gerard, 'Let's make a cup of tea for your Ma, laddie.'

The watch mender in Monaghan died that evening in the cellar below his workshop.

He was working on a booby trap when a boot kicked in the glass of the cellar's high window, when the petrol streamed down over his work bench, when the match was thrown.

The watch mender in Monaghan had never heard the name of Sean Pius McAnally.

11

Because Baby Sean's growing teeth ached in his gums the small child tossed and cried through the night, even when Roisin cuddled his body against her. Coming down the stairs Roisin was withdrawn inside herself and pale-skinned and red-eyed, and McAnally had snapped that he didn't have to shave every bloody day and his eyes were puffed and staring strangely. By morning Baby Sean was finally asleep, curled in the centre of their bed.

Goss was in the kitchen, boiling a kettle, looking for tea bags, managing a welcoming smile for Roisin. Prentice drowsed in his hallway chair. Goss greeted Roisin as if there was nothing odd in a woman coming into her kitchen and finding a detective with a shoulder holster worn over his sleeveless sweater rummaging for a teapot. He didn't bother to ask her how she had slept. One thing he had found since he'd come to Palace Barracks was that the woman was the strength of the pair. Whatever happened down the road at Castlereagh with her man, when it came to the home then it was with Roisin McAnally that the minders had to score. Goss reckoned there were never two equals in a marriage, there was one on the top and one on the bottom, and in this family it was Roisin who ruled. If he and Prentice missed with her, then they were scratching . . . and she had walls around her that would take some battering.

She moved around him in the kitchen as if he were an obstruction. With Goss awake and Prentice sleeping it was pretty obvious how they'd spent their night. Staggered duties of sleep and guard. She'd get used to it, she'd have to get used to it, and get used to the pistols worn against their chests, and to the personal radio that was clamped in Prentice's hands.

She had made a small effort to face the day. She wore a smear of lipstick, and she'd combed her hair back to the elastic band. McAnally had made no effort. Not that his cropped hair needed combing and brushing, but the fact that he hadn't washed was clear from the last evening's newsprint stains on his fingers and the sleep in his eyes. Goss sat with them at the kitchen table for toast and tea, and could smell McAnally. Goss's girl, the girl he was to marry, the girl who worked in the Northern Bank, she was a stickler for personal cleanliness. Goss's girl would have said that Andy Goss should pack it in, and get himself something half decent, something where he didn't touch dirt like this. That was another problem, Goss's girl, that was a problem that wouldn't get sorted that morning.

Roisin didn't acknowledge Goss at the table. Goss did not exist. She didn't pass him the toast, nor the butter, nor the jam. She let him pour his own tea, his own milk.

There was a key in the door. Roisin listened. Goss listened. They heard Prentice's voice, and Rennie's, a murmured confidential conversation out in the hall.

'Are we going out this morning?'

'Where?'

Roisin looked at McAnally as if he were an idiot.

'Shopping, for me, for the kids, for the kitchen.'

'Not with me, you're not.' McAnally shovelled toast into his mouth.

'Why not?'

'Because I'm out.'

'Where are you?'

McAnally didn't reply. He reached for more toast.

If it hadn't been so bloody important Goss could have had a big belly laugh. Gingy McAnally wasn't up to telling his Missus that he'd be off to Castlereagh for the morning to do a bit more touting. Gingy hadn't the bottle to chat the Missus with the happy news that he was spilling through the morning on some more of his mates, and stitching them up for Tens and Twenties.

'So, when you're out, what do I do?'

McAnally poured himself tea.

Rennie came in.

Rennie was like a big bloody bouncing ball. If he was aware of the cut in the atmosphere of the kitchen he gave no sign of it.

'Come on, Gingy . . . Start of the working day. Jump to it, lad.'

That was rich, Goss thought, because he knew from the file that Sean Pius McAnally had never held down a job in his life. Urban guerrilla on the dole, freedom fighter on Supplementary benefit.

'Morning, Mrs McAnally, settling nicely I hope . . . Come on, Gingy, shift yourself, we've got a mountain today.'

Goss had to hand it to Rennie. The old cut-throat knew what he was at. Jollying the reptile along was the name of the game, with cheerful, bruising authority. He saw the glance that Roisin gave Rennie. Prentice was well out of it, Prentice was clever to have his head down.

McAnally stood. There was a moment of indecision and then he bent quickly and kissed Roisin on the forehead, and her face seemed to say that if she had known what he was about to do then she would have ducked her face away.

Prentice went with McAnally and Rennie, out through the front door. Rennie led, and Prentice was behind McAnally and close to him.

Goss was watching Roisin. She gazed after them, and then at the slammed front door. He saw the sneer on her face. Now she stood up and walked to the back window.

Goss saw the slimness of her hips, the outline of her shoulder blades.

'It'll get better, Mrs McAnally. There are only two bad bits. This is one of the bad bits, trying to find your balance after what's happened to you. The other bit is when your husband goes into court.'

He couldn't see what sight, out of the window, held her attention.

'There's two bad bits, and a whole lot of good things. Look at it this way . . . if Sean had gone to the Kesh for life then you and the kids are wrecked for ever. You're not wrecked now, far from it. You're in good shape and you're in honest hands.'

He saw that he had reached her, that at least she listened to him. Her head jolted back. He fancied her mouth was set in derision.

'The kids have a chance now. The kids have a chance to do something decent with their lives. It's the worst thing with what goes on here that the kids are stained for the rest of their lives with what their parents have done. You don't believe you're in honest hands? We're going to show you that you're wrong.'

She turned to face him. There was a snap of a short smile on her face, and then she looked away.

'I'll be getting the kids up, making the beds.'

She went past him. He heard her tripping up the stairs.

*

142

'Tell him you want to play that draughts game.'

'I don't know how to play the game.'

'I'm not caring whether you know how. Tell him to teach you.'

Roisin was at the front bedroom window. She could see the woman from the next house but one and the woman from the house beyond that. They had their overcoats on and there was a push chair and a wheeled shopping basket.

'Gerard, you learn to play the game from him, you be sweet to him.'

'I hate the shit peeler.'

When he was very small she would have ear clipped him for swearing, when he was three or four years old. She didn't any longer. She barely noticed his obscenities.

'Gerard, if I didn't want you to play the game with him then I wouldn't be asking you. Do as I say, Gerard.'

'I have to?'

'You have to.'

Roisin went down the stairs half the flight behind Gerard. Baby Sean was still asleep, Little Patty was in her bed and turning the pages of a picture book. Roisin heard Gerard shyly ask Goss to show him the draughts game. She heard the detective's surprised and pleased reply. Oh, he'd like that, would the detective. He'd like to show the boy how to play a game like draughts. The living room door was open. Goss would be able to see the front door, would be able to watch it even though he was teaching her boy to play the game of draughts. Bloody good kid, that Gerard. Good because he did what he was told without a bloody inquest of explanations.

It was in the night that she had decided what she would do. When she was sleepless, when Gingy had been on his back and moaning his worries, when Baby Sean had been fretting on his teeth, when she had remembered the television.

The kitchen door was locked, and no key. With care she moved the saucepans off the draining board. She climbed easily onto the draining board. Away in the living room she heard the clatter of the draught pieces, and Goss's laughter. She eased the window open.

She dropped out through the window. She pushed the window shut behind her.

There was a cold, wet wind catching at her sweater. She couldn't have put on a coat, too bulky for the narrow kitchen window. She had to pass the window doors of the living room. She couldn't help herself, she peered for a moment into the lit room and saw Gerard on his knees, and Goss leaning forward from his chair and the draughts board on the carpet. She scurried past the windows. Her teeth were chattering.

The side fences separating the small back gardens were waist-high. Her foot sunk into the flowerbed as she levered herself up and over the

143

fence and into the next-door garden. The curtains at the back of the house were drawn. She climbed the second fence.

The kitchen door of the house of the woman with a push chair was unlocked.

She went inside. She tiptoed through a polished, scrubbed-down kitchen – house-proud bitch – and into the darkened hallway.

On the low table near the front door, and beside the army dress wedding photograph was the telephone.

'Remember this, Gingy, he can't touch you. The time that he could hurt you is gone. You go in there and you do your stuff, and you remember that his days for frightening folks are over.'

If Sean Pius McAnally could not confront the Chief with a direct accusation then it was a waste of time, everybody's time, to consider that the supergrass could stand up in court and survive hostile cross-examination. Rennie, pacing near the window, knew that. McAnally, sitting at the table, knew that. Prentice and McDonough and Astley, standing between the door and McAnally, knew that. Obvious to every man in the room, and unsaid, was the clear fact that McAnally had to be able to level his charge into the Chief's face.

'What's the big deal?' McAnally snarled. 'Who said there was a problem?'

'That's the boy,' Rennie said.

'He doesn't scare me, Mr Rennie.'

'Nice to hear that, Gingy.'

'Where was he when I was with the bloody R.P.G., close quarters?'

'The Chief hasn't the bottle you've got Gingy.' McDonough swallowed hard, as if speaking made him sick.

Astley said, 'He'd have been playing with himself, Gingy. What he wouldn't have been doing is putting himself up the sharp end.'

Prentice said, 'When you go in there and face him you really kick his balls. You give him interest on what he did to you.'

McAnally's cheeks were flushed. His voice was loud. 'You think I'm scared, don't you? That's what you think, isn't it?'

Rennie smiled. 'Just show us that you're not scared, Gingy.'

If he came through this then he might come through the cross-examination. If he failed this then he would fail in the witness box. Rennie was sweating. Mid-December and the central heating turned too high. He wiped his forehead.

'I'm not yellow, Mr Rennie.'

*

144

'It's not his fault, Ma. They've brained him, see . . . You have to tell people that it's not our Gingy they've got. He's like a man I don't know. Ma, I saw what you said on the telly last evening. That's why I've called you. Ma, something'll be sorted out. Ma, I don't know what's for the best. Gingy's all changed, like they've done his mind . . .'

Doggedly Mrs Chrissie O'Rourke repeated the question that had been twice asked and twice ignored. It was the question she had been told to ask until it was answered.

'Where are you, Roisin?'

A long pause, and then a small voice. 'That doesn't matter to you, Ma.'

'Where are you?'

'We have to help ourselves, Ma. You can't help us.'

'I've the right to know where my girl is, where my grankids are.'

Mrs Chrissie O'Rourke stared down at the blank sheet of paper on the pad beside the telephone. She didn't doubt what she was doing. She knew Frankie Conroy to be a decent man. Since he had called the first time to her house she had asked around about him. She had asked Father Francis when he had come to visit and commiserate. She had asked the solicitor when he had come. Both the priest and the solicitor had said that Frankie Conroy was a decent man. No doubts in her mind. She thought the solicitor was flash, but she had a small love for Father Francis. The priest was what any Ma would want of a son. And he never slagged the Provies. Slagged the Brit army, but no one in the parish had ever heard him slag the Provies. A little bit she trusted the solicitor. Father Francis she trusted all the way. She heard the words spoken in a hush on the telephone and wrote them down.

The policeman had lightly taken the Chief's arm as they came out of the cell and into the block corridor. The Chief shrugged the fist away. The policeman didn't make a big deal of it. All the policemen wore their identification numbers on their uniform tunic shoulders. They could all be identified, and they would all know that the prisoner from the last in the line cell on the ground floor of the block was rated as P.I.R.A. Brigade Commander, Belfast. The Chief knew that these were the old sods, those who worked inside at Castlereagh, old sods who had wormed their way out of postings to the front line of West Belfast or South Armagh or the Fermanagh border or Derry. The old sods looked over their shoulders, and thought of the day when a man like the Chief might have his freedom again, and might remember a policeman's face, and put the face to a name, and the name to an address. No big deal for this policeman. He allowed the Chief to walk without his fist in the Chief's sleeve.

In the hours that he had been in custody the Chief had not fathomed the evidence against him. His questioning at the hands of a Detective Sergeant and a Detective Constable had been cursory, and had seemed to involve his daytime movements of ten, eleven days back. Of course, he hadn't answered the pigs. The Chief had set himself to shut his mouth and keep it shut. What puzzled him was that the detectives seemed to think his silence a small matter. Other than the detectives and the escorting policeman he had seen no other person during his time in custody. His stomach growled, the wind bulged like a knot in his belly. They came out of the cell block and through the covered walkway and into the Interrogation Block.

The policeman knocked on the door of the third Interrogation Room on the right side of the corridor. There was an indistinct shout from inside and the policeman opened the door.

The Chief saw the two 'tecs. The same men as the time before, and the time before that. An easy smile from the older one, like they were old friends. The Chief broke wind, and went to a chair at the table. The younger one grinned too. The Chief sat. What had the bastards to smile about?

'Detective Sergeant McDonough . . .'

'Detective Constable Astley . . .'

'I know your bloody names,' the Chief said. He was sitting, they were both standing.

'Just the rule book,' McDonough said.

Silence . . . as if the 'tecs were waiting for something, as if they had no questions. The Chief saw the remote camera, aimed down at him from high on the wall.

Because the Interrogation Room was sound-proofed noises could not escape, and no outside noise could come in. The Chief did not hear the approach down the corridor outside.

The door opened. The Chief looked up sharply. He saw Rennie in the doorway. He had once ordered the killing of Rennie. He knew Rennie from his photograph, the photograph fitted the face in the doorway. The face was expressionless. Their movement had been imperceptible, unnoticed by the Chief before it was completed, but McDonough and Astley were now positioned between the Chief and the door. It was crowded in the doorway. Behind Rennie was another detective, a younger man, and behind him were two uniformed policemen. The Chief blinked. He couldn't help himself. He had seen the face that was half-hidden behind Rennie's shoulder. A nervous, peering, gawping little face, Gingy fucking McAnally's face.

Rennie said, 'Get on with it, Gingy.'

The Chief understood. The anger surged in him. His fists were clenched. He saw the hands jump from the pockets of McDonough and Astley.

'Learned your fucking lines, Gingy?' the Chief shouted.

'That man is the Chief of the Belfast Brigade. The man briefed me on the attack on Mr Justice Simpson . . .'

The Chief's voice smashed through McAnally's hesitant recitation. 'Is your bloody wallet full, Gingy? Filled your bloody wallet up, have they?'

'That man explained to me how Simpson was to be taken out . . .'

'You're going to be stiffed, McAnally.'

'He set up the whole attack. I told him that it couldn't be done, but he wouldn't have anything of that . . .'

'You won't live to spend their fucking money.'

'He said that I was the only one he could lay his hands on who had the training to use the R.P.G. without practice.' McAnally was gabbling, charging out his words.

'You've shamed your family.'

'He had the map out, he went over the plan on the map. It was his plan . . .'

'You think you'll ever be safe from us, Gingy McAnally – you, or your woman, or your brats?'

McAnally turned to Rennie. He was pulling at Rennie's coat. 'Stop him, don't let him say that . . .'

'You'll be shot. You'll be pissing down your leg when you're shot.'

'That one, the Chief, he made me do it. Without him I wouldn't have done it . . . You're going down, you're going down for bloody life, you're going to the Kesh, you bloody filth . . . I'll be fucking laughing when you're in the Kesh.'

The Chief saw the hysteria rising in Sean Pius McAnally, saw the saucer eyes, saw the opened mouth from which the shrieking spat. The Chief saw Rennie look away. The Chief saw that Rennie wouldn't help the bastard. 'Course he wouldn't help him . . . If he helped him now then he'd never stand on his feet later, not later when it mattered.

The Chief stood. Not fast, but deliberately. He came round the table. He moved very slowly. His eyes were fixed on McAnally's, he trapped the tout with his eyes. The 'tecs, McDonough and Astley, were shoulder to shoulder, and ready for him if he charged, and behind them was Rennie. He couldn't get at McAnally with his fists or his boots. He could reach the bastard only with his eyes and with his voice. He saw the fear spreading on McAnally's mouth.

'You're dead, Gingy, you're dead for what you've done,' the Chief whispered. 'You're dead in the street, Gingy, before you get near a bloody court. Look at me, Gingy . . . you're dead before you'll spend the bloody money they're paying you.'

Rennie shoved McAnally out through the door.

The Chief saw a momentary flash of the pale white face of the tout.

147

'You're gone, Gingy. You're gone to a traitor's grave.'
The door slammed shut.

Frankie Conroy smiled a wide and bright smile.

'You did well, Mrs O'Rourke. You've done the best thing that you could have done. I'll get her back to you, Mrs O'Rourke, her and the kids. You done really well.'

Frankie Conroy was hurrying on his way from the back door of Mrs Chrissie O'Rourke's house in the Drive, Turf Lodge, and out over the back fence, and across another garden to his car.

There was no rain now. The clouds had slipped away east over the city that lay scattered and sprawled below the Turf Lodge estate. The light fell on the dark slopes of the Divis mountain above him. Hidden on the wild, rock-strewn bracken-covered inclines of the mountain was the arms cache that he would draw upon when he began the process later that day of prising Roisin McAnally away from her husband. He knew the way of the supergrasses. If the woman stayed with the man then the chances of him reaching the witness box were increased. If the woman quit her man then those chances were diminished. With the weapons that were hidden on Divis mountain lay his first and best chance of reaching to the fears of Roisin McAnally.

Palace Barracks, Holywood, wasn't bad for him. Could have been worse. Could have been Thiepval at Lisburn, could have been the camps at Ballycastle or Ballyclare.

He could get close enough to Palace Barracks to scare Roisin McAnally witless. Scare her so that she reckoned she was safer at her Ma's than she was in the protective care of the squaddies and the peelers.

They had left Prentice to watch McAnally.

They were out in the corridor for the conference.

Through the high small window in the door Rennie could see McAnally in profile.

McAnally sat in his chair, and his hands were tight together around a steaming coffee mug and trembling so that he didn't trust himself to take the mug to his mouth. He lowered his chin to the rim of the mug, and when he drank there was coffee spilling from his lips.

Rennie watched Prentice offer McAnally a cigarette. McAnally took the cigarette. The coffee was smeared on the table, and Prentice wiped it away with his handkerchief, and was trying to laugh as he lit the cigarette for McAnally.

Disgust on Rennie's face.

'That's just one, and he's got to do that thirty more times . . . O.K., the Chief's the hardest one for him, but none of them are that different. There are no bloody Volunteers on McAnally's shopping list, they're all Brigade and Battalion. They're all quality, and they're all going to stick our Gingy through the hoop like the Chief did, right . . . and if the Chief can make that sort of mess of him, what state's he going to be in when he's been messed thirty times?'

He was talking aloud but to himself.

Astley didn't care. Astley socked in hard. 'Perhaps we all jumped too fast, perhaps we were running when we should have been walking.'

'What's that supposed to mean?'

'Perhaps we should have charged him, stuffed him away to remand and come back to work on him later, in six months or a year . . .'

'That's bloody hindsight. Hindsight's the biggest load of crap there is in this game.'

'You asked, Mr Rennie.' Astley was now cowed.

'I didn't ask for bloody hindsight.'

McDonough gripped Astley's arm, squeezed hard on it. It was an unspoken instruction from the Detective Sergeant for the Detective Constable to close his mouth.

'He's what we have,' McDonough said. 'He's the best we've ever had. He might be the best we're ever going to get. That's how it seems to me.'

'And the best's piss poor,' Rennie said.

'Then he's got to be stiffened, Mr Rennie.'

Astley shook off McDonough's hand. 'Ship him out then. Lose him for a few months across the water.'

'Can't,' said Rennie. 'They're talking about an early preliminary hearing at the Magistrate's, getting him into the box good and early. All bloody politics. It's the politicians' pound of flesh they're looking for in return for McAnally's immunity, our boyo in the box filling the front pages with evidence . . .' Now he laughed. 'Don't anyone talk about justice, justice has fuck all to do with it. The politicians want success, and their success is McAnally going through his routine at preliminary and then at trial. They want two bites at the bloody flesh. And I've Special Branch queuing for him, and I've got Intelligence waiting in line, and the Army wouldn't mind seeing him . . . So, he can't be lost for a few months over the water . . . a few days, that's all I can get him out for.'

Astley said, 'Then you've a problem, Mr Rennie.'

McDonough said, 'It's not worth considering, Mr Rennie, if McAnally were to fall down on us.'

'It's not worth considering because it can't happen. I'll tell you why it can't happen. The Secretary of State told the Prime Minister that McAnally would be in court. The Chief Constable told the Secretary of State that McAnally would be in court, I told the Chief Constable that McAnally would be in court if I had to bloody carry him there.

Got it? Have you got why McAnally can't fall down on us? There are no confessions, from the crowd we've pulled in? There's none of them doing McAnally's job for him?'

'You're joking,' Astley snorted.

'They're none of them opening their mouths,' McDonough said. 'Without McAnally none of them'll go down, and the bastards'll all walk out.'

Rennie stared through the window, and down onto McAnally's sunken head. He saw the shaking in McAnally's shoulders.

'I'm not going to wet nurse him. He's got to know what he's signed on for. He's to confront McGilivarry and McCreevy this morning, and O'Brien this afternoon.'

'And if he's on the floor?' Astley asked.

'Then we pick him up again.'

'And if he can't stand up?'

'Then we find a different way to prop him,' Rennie said.

Rennie and McDonough went back into the Interrogation Room, both smiling broadly. Astley went to arrange the transfer of Joey McGilivarry, Belfast Brigade Intelligence Officer, from the cell block to the Interrogation Block.

The radio message was brief.

In fifteen minutes Ferris was to rendezvous with his foot patrol at the junction of Whiterock and Glenalina Road for transport that would take him immediately to Springfield Road barracks. Just that.

The junction of Whiterock and Glenalina wasn't a good place to be standing around if the transport was late. But the transport, a Pig, was waiting for them. He'd jumped into the back and they had sped away. It was rare for transport to be punctual. Presumably something of priority required him back at the barracks. He need not have been on the foot patrol. The corporal who had now taken over command could just as well have started the job, but foot patrol enabled Ferris to be out of the barracks, beyond the wire and the fences and the high gates and the sentries.

The Intelligence Officer was waiting for the Pig in the vehicle park.

'We had to search round for you.'

'Bravo knew where I was,' Ferris said tersely.

'You're wanted again. Your friend's crying for you.'

'What's that supposed to mean?'

'Your little Provo friend . . . You don't listen, David, when you're given good advice. That's a weight of a problem you have, not listening to good advice.'

'What advice?'

'Being told not to get involved with Provo shit.'

'I've said it before: nobody asked me if I wanted to get involved.'

'Strikes most of us, David, most of us in the Mess, that you didn't try very hard to uninvolve yourself . . .'

'Who wants me?' Ferris had walked to the Weapons Pit and the I.O. had trailed him there. He cleared his rifle.

'That thug who's your second friend, the detective. Your game's getting boring for the rest of us. Hobnobbing with scum and policemen. What's with you?'

'I'll tell you what's with *me* . . . What's with me is trying to get this bloody war behind us, not trying just to serve out a four months' tour but trying to tie at least one loose end.' If he couldn't put one on the Intelligence Officer's nose, at least he could spit his words up the wretched man's nostrils. 'What we're trying to do is to put thirty bad men, evil men – am I talking the language you understand – off the streets.'

'Personal conceit's no substitute in soldiering for professionalism.'

'Thirty is more than our Battalion, six hundred of us, is ever going to put away.'

'I hope you don't fall on your face, David. I'd get a pain in the side laughing if you did.'

Ferris walked rapidly to the far side of the vehicle park. He had spotted Rennie's car.

The Intelligence Officer called after him. 'Let us know when you're murdering friend's had enough of you, so we can get you back to leading your platoon.'

Ferris stopped and turned. 'Get the fuck off my back,' he shouted.

There were two squaddies working under the bonnet of a landrover and listening.

The Intelligence Officer smiled. 'Didn't anyone tell you about my sister, about my sister's fiancé, about the week before they were to be married, about a bomb in South Armagh under a Ferret, about a Hussar who lost his legs and his balls, about a cancelled wedding. Didn't anyone tell you why I'm not fond of people who get cuddly with the Provos?'

Ferris walked on towards Rennie's car.

In the car Rennie pointed to a rug on the back seat and gestured for Ferris to put his rifle under it, to hide it. Ferris shrugged Rennie's overcoat over his military dress, and Rennie handed him his personal pistol to hold at his waist under the coat.

Rennie told him about the confrontations between Sean Pius McAnally and the arrested men of P.I.R.A.'s Belfast Brigade. It had been bad with the Chief, but better with Intelligence, grim with Operations, and worst of all with the Quartermaster. The Quartermaster had shouted at McAnally in Gaelic and it had been a shambles because Rennie and the detectives with him didn't understand a word of the language. Rennie said it was like a witch handing down a curse in a bad film.

McAnally was in poor shape. Rennie said that Ferris was the only man he knew who could breathe some bottle back into Sean Pius McAnally.

'We're all on the line, David,' Rennie said. 'Understand me, I have to use you. Whether I like it, you like it, you're my only way to him.'

The mortar had been manufactured in a light engineering factory across the border and far away, on the edges of Waterford city. The mortar was precision tooled, and as good as could be obtained when the Organization was unable to lay its hands on the regular military item. The mortar was modelled on the old two-inch variety and could throw the bombs a good 250 yards.

Frankie Conroy had yelled himself hoarse to get his hands on the mortar.

'If the men who are in Castlereagh ever get out of there and get to hear that when a mortar was called for it wasn't made available, then you'll be needing plastic in your knees.'

The mortar was a jewel.

'Christ help you, Frankie Conroy, if you don't bring it back.'

In the city, the Organization had never been short of hand guns or rifles, never wanting for fertilizer mix in the big bombs, never had to search far for industrial detonators, but the mortar was especially precious.

'Don't you go bloody leaving it where you're taking it. Four bombs you can have . . .'

And a man to sight the mortar, and a man to drop the bombs in the tube.

The afternoon light was failing. He had the mortar, and the bombs, and he had two kids out in Andy'town looking for a flat-top lorry to drive away, and he had the men to fire the mortar from the back floor of the lorry, and he had a man with bottle who was touring the small Protestant housing estate beween Palace Barracks and the Upper Sullivan School in Holywood who would find him the firing place, and he had three men out in the Falls who were hunting for cars . . . Christ, he needed a bloody army.

He went to the Falls Road offices of Provisional Sinn Fein. He was taken to a back office. The man he talked to had once done time for possession of firearms, and now reckoned there was a career ahead in community politics. Frankie snapped out his requirements, like he was speaking to dirt.

'I want a loudspeaker kit that won't come back. I want to know where

152

I can go and lift one, Public Address that'll be heard for at least two hundred yards clear.'

He was given the address of the firm that rented mobile P.A. systems to Provisional Sinn Fein.

On the way over Rennie had stopped at an off-licence.

They had arrived with three six-packs of Tennants and a bottle of Rioja, and Rennie had said that if they put the Spanish stuff down the woman's throat at least it would shut her up.

Prentice had laid in the chops and some chips and some peas, and Prentice had made a thing of how it was time for Roisin to have a night off the dishes and saucepans, and he'd cooked, and Goss had minded the kids and sat with Young Gerard and Little Patty on the floor, and Rennie had kept Roisin's glass going.

The meal was finished. The kitchen was cleared except for McAnally and David Ferris. Rennie had contrived it well. One moment the kitchen had been full, like a party time when no one was in the mood, now there were only the lieutenant and the tout at the table, and the last six-pack in front of them.

Ferris tore at the cardboard wrapping, slid a can across to McAnally.

'It's been a bastard, today?'

'Too right.' There could be a softness in McAnally's voice, as if he lost a bit of hard Belfast when he was down in the caravan beside the canal. 'Right bastard.'

'Every time they curse you, every time they threaten you, think of your kids, Gingy . . . It's all air they're talking. They can't touch you.'

'They said I was dead. Each one of them said I was dead.'

'That's all they can say. They're frightened and they're lying through their teeth.'

'Tom McCreevy said I'd be looking over my shoulder till I was dead, whether it was a month or a year or ten years.'

Ferris speaking earnestly, quietly. 'They have to make believe the world begins and ends with them . . . It's not true, the world's too big for them, for their bullying. You're going to go away to places where they can't touch you, can't reach you . . . you're going to go to places where your kids'll grow up with a better future than time in the Kesh.'

'Ollie O'Brien spoke in Irish – bloody Rennie went mad – Ollie said I'd be called the biggest whore in Ireland.'

'Gingy, you may have been a right little shit when you were in Belfast, but you went out, you learned about a different way of living when you were down south. You saw there was a different way of living than facing up the twenty-five years behind the wire.'

'You know what they are, when they come after you? You think they'll just forget about me?'

'They won't know where to go looking.'

'They'll look till they bloody find me.'

'They won't know where to start . . . You're going to be safe, Gingy, safe with Roisin, safe with the kids . . . Listen, way back the Soviets slaughtered everyone who stood in their way, everyone who turned their back on them. I give you two different men, both Soviets who went over, defected. One in Canada, one in Australia. If the Soviets had found them they were dead. They lived to be old men . . . they lived long because they had new identities.'

The doubt flickered on McAnally's face. 'And the Commies were looking for them?'

'Looking as hard as they bloody could, and not finding them.'

'You mean it, don't you? You mean it that they'd never get close to us.'

'You'll be where there are no prisons, where kids don't get knee-capped, where Roisin will know you're coming home in the evening. You'll be where proper people are.'

McAnally dropped his head down onto his hands that were splayed out over the table. 'Shit, I want to believe you.'

The van was in front, once bright red, now battered, the loudspeakers on the roof. Behind the van was the flat-top lorry, nearly blocking the street. Behind the lorry and arse about to it was the Cortina, Frankie at the wheel.

Frankie was following the second hand of his watch. When it crossed the hour he hooted his horn.

'The people you're with now, Gingy, they're not setting you up in a shooting alley. They're going to protect you, they're going to care for you. Get that straight in your mind, Gingy, it's a guarantee of safety. When you've been in the witness box, you're not just going to be chucked out on your own, you're going to be looked after. Believe me . . .'

The building shuddered, the tremors swinging the ceiling light. Then the blast of the sound of the explosion. Ferris sat rooted, the words blocked in his mouth, his mind. McAnally set his throat to scream.

The next blast and after it the sounds of crashing glass, and the curtains over the sink swept back in the draught.

'Don't just bloody sit there.' Rennie had catapulted into the kitchen. Rennie tore at McAnally's sweater, heaved him out of his chair and dragged him into the hallway. The area under the stairs was open plan. Rennie threw McAnally into the corner, covered him with his body.

Prentice was by the front door with his pistol drawn, crouched low.

A third explosion, nearer than the first, further than the second.

Ferris had watched Rennie's action, had watched the protection of McAnally. He realized he was still sitting at the kitchen table, and there was glass scattered between the Tennants cans, and there was a cold wind hammering through the window. He heard Goss shout that he had Roisin and the kids between the sofa and the interior wall.

Then there was a fourth explosion.

A guarantee of safety.

He slid off his chair and down onto the floor.

12

'Gingy McAnally is a lying tout.'

The voice spilled across the length and breadth of the Palace Barracks. The voice carried over the roofs of the old military buildings, through the doors and windows of the modern family quarters. A whole Battalion force and all their wives and all their children heard the denunciation of Sean Pius McAnally.

'Gingy McAnally is a paid perjurer.'

Buried beneath Rennie's huge body, squashed down into the corner beneath the stairs, McAnally heard his name, hugely amplified, echoed out into the night. The explosions were just a memory, a memory that was a minute old.

'Gingy McAnally is a traitor to his people.'

There was distant and sporadic gunfire, one burst from a machine gun and several isolated single shots. Then there were fire bells and ambulance sirens.

'We know where you are, Gingy. We'll always know where you are.'

Ferris ran from the kitchen down the hallway. His rifle was behind the door, still wrapped in Rennie's car rug. Ferris took his rifle, slapped a magazine into its body. He came back to the foot of the stairs. He could see McAnally's head protruding from under Rennie's armpit.

'When we're ready to come for you, Gingy, we'll know where you are, we'll know where to come.'

There was a hard knock at the front door. A clipped military report advised that soldiers were in position around the house, that it was secure against attack. Then a silence around McAnally and Rennie and

Ferris and John Prentice in the hallway. Ferris saw the way that Rennie's arm was close on McAnally's shoulders to stifle the shivering. Big, brusque bugger he might be, but he understood a tout's fear. The bellowing voice was gone. The rhythm of the shouts was broken. Instinctively Ferris knew that the attack was finished. He stood up. He stepped over Rennie's legs and went into the living room. The television was playing, and he realized that through the bombardment and the broadcast voice calls he had not heard the television. There was a comedian on the screen and the studio audience was braying with laughter. He went to the settee and looked behind, and down onto the jumble of bodies and arms and legs.

'It's alright now, it's over,' Ferris said.

Andy Goss pushed himself upright. He had a Walther pistol in his hand.

'You can put that away.'

Goss cleared his pistol, made it safe, slid it down into his shoulder holster. Roisin McAnally lay prone over her children. Her face was twisted in cold, controlled fury.

'Are they alright?'

''Course they're alright,' Goss barked back at Ferris.

Ferris went back to the kitchen. He filled the kettle, put it on the stove.

'. . . It's a guarantee of safety . . .'

He thought of the Mess at Springfield Road, and Sunray presiding at dinner. He thought of Bravo's commander who soldiered in the relaxation of knowing that a thousand Northumberland acres waited for him whenever his father thought fit to retire. He thought of the Intelligence Officer who had briefly, just once, showed the scab of his flesh, and whose friends across the water drove Porsche sports cars or Alfa Romeos. He thought of the Chaplain who drank a couple of bottles of whisky a week and preached on Sundays that God was on the side of 2 R.R.F. For Sunray and Bravo's commander and the Intelligence Officer and the Chaplain it was all a game with a playing time of sixteen weeks. Christ, but it was a bloody long game for Sean Pius McAnally, and for Roisin, and for her kids. Nothing make-believe in the game of the supergrass and his dependents. Up to that time Ferris had played the Battalion's game, up to the time of the thudding explosions of the mortar bombs inside the perimeter of a fortified army base, up to the time of a mechanical voice jeering into the night that an informer was marked down for execution.

The kettle was whistling.

Ferris heard McAnally's whimpering voice from the hallway.

'How did they know, Mr Rennie, how did the buggers know I was here?'

156

Rennie, cold and hard. 'Just a random chance, Gingy. They came up lucky, that's all.'

'They knew I was here.'

'Just a guess that proved right, they couldn't have known.'

'You told me I was safe. Mr Ferris said I was safe.'

'Listen to what I say – it was just luck.'

Ferris ignored the kettle. He stood in the kitchen doorway. Roisin had come to the living room's door. She was holding Baby Sean tight against her shoulder. She was white-faced, she was a sleepwalker. Ferris went down the hall, past Roisin, to the telephone. He dialled Brigade Ops at Lisburn Headquarters.

'Lieutenant Ferris, 2 R.R.F., on secondment to Police Headquarters. There was a mortar bombardment a few minutes ago at Palace Barracks, Holywood. Have any other military installations been targeted tonight . . . Thanks.'

One base only had been hit. The answer was clear on Ferris's face.

'Tell me how they knew.' McAnally shouted into Rennie's face.

Rennie shouted back. 'I don't bloody know . . .' Their faces were inches apart. Rennie dropped his voice. 'I didn't tell them, Gingy.'

McAnally stared at Ferris. He was crying out for reassurance. Ferris couldn't speak to him. He went back into the kitchen to make the tea.

McAnally said, 'You've got to get me out of here.'

Rennie said, 'We're not moving anywhere, not while it's dark.'

Later the owners of Loud and Clear Public Address would report that a van had been stolen from their premises out on the Twinbrook estate, and a haulage company would complain of the hijacking of a flat-top three-tonner on the Glen Road. And when Forensic had eventually finished with the van and the lorry those firms would have their vehicles returned to them.

When the soldiers ventured out from Palace Barracks and retrieved the van and the flat-top lorry there was little for them to examine. The wooden floorboards of the lorry were dented and splintered from the impact of the mortar's baseplate, and wired to the amplification system in the back of the van was an Aiwa cassette player. Neither the lorry nor the van was entered before Felix and his bomb squad had cleared them for possible booby trap devices. The bomb squad officer was always 'Felix' in Belfast. He appreciated his code name, and reckoned that a sense of humour went with the job.

'Shouldn't be too much trouble to identify the miscreants,' he said cheerfully to a Detective Inspector. 'I imagine you'll run a voice print on a hundred thousand Micks, and that'll tell you who the new Sean Connery is. Piece of cake I'd say . . . What's inside?'

157

'Four firings, all detonated.'

'We'll scratch around in daylight and see what's what,' Felix said.

The blue lights of the bomb squad convoy winked away out of the estate. Detectives moved from house to house in search of an eye witness, and the search was fruitless. Further into the night a burned-out car was found deep in the trees off the Bangor Road.

After the arrival of a Press Liaison Officer from Lisburn the Commanding Officer of Palace Barracks agreed to meet the assembled reporters at the main gate. The advice that he had been given was not to respond to questions, only make a statement and ignore interruptions.

'This was a particularly cowardly attack and I can say in all honesty that only incredible good luck prevented the death or maiming of any of my soldiers' wives and children. That no casualties were inflicted was in no way due to the terrorists' aim . . . Without regard for the safety of women and children they sprayed this base with four high explosive mortar shells . . . I'm not prepared to discuss our security arrangements . . . two shells landed harmlessly in the parade ground, thank God. One shell hit the roof of a storage shed. The fourth shell impacted against a garden fence in the married quarters area . . . A tape recording? I know nothing of a tape recording played during the attack . . . The motive of the attack is perfectly clear in my mind, the motive was to kill my soldiers and their families . . . I said, I know nothing of any tape recording, and that's all I have to say. Goodnight to you, gentlemen.'

He was flushed and angry as he walked away from the chorus of questions prompted by the reporters' sight of the Loud and Clear van. He had been given no option on whether or not he should play host to a Converted Terrorist and his brood. A bloody headquarters order . . . The Press Liaison Officer, a damned idiot, told him that he had done well.

The reporters went back to the housing estate and filled the pages of their notepads with quotes from the householders on the text of the message broadcast to Gingy McAnally, perjurer, traitor, and tout.

Frankie Conroy returned the mortar tube in person.

'You did well,' the man said shrewdly, 'to know where he was.'

Frankie chuckled, the puckered hole in his neck wobbled. 'They'll need a lorry to carry the bog paper to clear up McAnally's shit.'

'You did well, but you had the luck.'

'We're just starting,' Frankie said.

*

Roisin's bedroom was on the front of the house, and the glass there was not damaged. She could be alone there with her children. The warming ache of the Rioja had gone from her head with the first of the explosions, replaced by just a pain that needled into her mind.

She had not spoken a word since the 'tec, Goss, had heaved himself off her body, his hand on her hip. She hadn't spoken to Gingy, because she wouldn't have known what to say to him, nor to bloody Rennie, nor to Ferris. By the time that the shouting had died, and the ambulance wail had faded, she had gathered her children to her and climbed away up the stairs. None of the men had tried to stop her going, bloody good riddance on all their faces. In the way, wasn't she? All the bloody men clustered round her Gingy, bloody flies on jam, trying to put some spine in the poor bastard.

How could she have known that this would happen? She had only told her Ma where they were. That wasn't touting, that was for the good of them all, for the good of her Gingy.

In her bed, with Young Gerard against her back, with Baby Sean close against her, with Little Patty's sleeping head close to her eyes, she thought that it was a question of what was worse. Worse to be hunted out in a Brit base, or worse to be at home and amongst her own and to be reviled as a tout's woman.

Into the small hours.

Rennie had gone.

Soldiers had come with hammers and nails and chipboard, and sealed up the kitchen window from the outside.

Goss lay on the floor of the upstairs landing, his face washed by the ceiling light. He was awake and his hand rested lightly across his holster.

Prentice was perched on the chair in the hall, head lolling, but his eyes open.

Ferris and McAnally were in the lounge. Ferris sat cross-legged on the carpet, McAnally lay on the sofa. Mostly Ferris talked, softly, not disturbing the night, mostly McAnally listened.

'They never had a hope of hurting you, not a thousand to one. It was just a gimmick, Gingy, just piss and wind. They're trying to frighten you, and you can't be scared by piss and wind, Gingy.'

There was a flicker of a smile on McAnally's face, a nervous little smile. 'They scared me.'

'What did they do to scare you? They put mortars into a built-up housing estate, an estate full of young women and kids. That's what they were prepared to do to *scare* you. God, Gingy, you turned your back on those people, people who'd do that. They could have killed a

159

couple of kiddies, they could have sliced a couple of women, but that would have been all right if they'd *scared* you.'

'You ever been scared, like I was scared in there?'

'Once, maybe once.'

'You know what it is, when you don't think you can stop yourself pissing.'

'Once.'

'Probably long ago, you've likely forgotten what it was.'

'Pretty recent.'

McAnally brightened. 'Give it.'

'V.C.P. on Divis, a car broke us. We had two bursts on an Armalite. I was a bit scared then.'

'Shit.'

'That was all round me, wasn't in the bloody distance like those mortars.'

'The Armalites didn't have your name on them, the mortars had my name . . . you know the car . . . ?'

'The car in Divis?'

'I was on board.'

'Didn't you know, because you were in the car . . . ?'

'Know what?'

'That's why you were pulled, because we saw you in the car.'

'Shit . . .' McAnally leaned forward. 'I was on board, it wasn't me on the Armalite.'

'Good to know,' Ferris said dryly.

McAnally grinned, rueful. 'Wouldn't have scared you if I had been on the Armalite, couldn't hit a bloody house . . . R.P.G.'s good. You ever fired an R.P.G.?'

'Not our weapon, Gingy. Enemy weapon. We use a thing called a Milan, bigger and better, I've been on exercise when they've fired a live Milan. It's a pretty big bang.'

Gingy mused, 'R.P.G.'s right for here. Wouldn't want anything big. And you want it dead simple. When the first one reached here all the stuff about it was in Russian and Arabic . . .' Again the grin. 'That's why we made such a cock at the start. We got better.'

'That's behind you, Gingy,' Ferris said, a sharp cut in his voice.

'What's ahead of me?'

'Everything's ahead of you.'

'Easy enough to say.'

'It's true.'

McAnally swung his legs off the settee. He was crouched down, his eyes level with Ferris's eyes. His hands were groped out ahead of him and Ferris took them and held them between the palms of his own hands. McAnally stuttered for the words before finding them.

'Gingy McAnally, Provo, what's he to you? What's Gingy McAnally to David Ferris, Brit officer? You can't bloody answer.'

'I can't answer.'

'What am I to you? Find an answer for me, you bloody have to.'

'You're a loser, I want to see you win. All the time with the R.P.G. you were losing, all you were getting closer to was three lifers in the Kesh.'

'What's it to you if I *win*?'

'I told you at Springfield. It's still the same. If you win then thirty evil sods get put away. If they go away, you've won. You win, and Roisin wins, and your kids win. I'm going to help you win. I'll put it better, Gingy, I'm going to bloody make you win. I'm going to stand beside you right up till you go into the box, because when you've finshed in the box then you've won.'

'I'm a Provo, you're a Brit officer.'

'When you've won, when you've gone from this crap place, it won't matter a shit what you are, what I am.'

'You'll stand beside me . . . If they come for me, would you step in front of me?'

'Yes,' Ferris said.

Ferris saw the wetness in McAnally's eyes. McAnally pulled his hands back from Ferris's grip.

'For a Brit officer you're an idiot.'

'Probably.'

Ferris was exhausted, drained. He tipped McAnally's legs up onto the cushions, and pushed his body over so that his face was against the settee's back. He fetched two blankets and covered him and watched until the pant of his breathing subsided, until he was asleep.

A few minutes past five in the morning, and bitterly cold in the Turf Lodge estate, Mrs Chrissie O'Rourke came out of her house, and Mr Pronsias Reilly closed the door shut behind her. The low gate between the front garden and the pavement was held open by Father Francis. A black dark shivery morning, and Mr Pronsias Reilly was well pleased that Mrs O'Rourke had dressed fast and without complaint. But it was big enough bait to cause her to hurry . . . If you want to see your daughter there is no time like the time now . . . she'd responded well enough.

The solicitor's car was parked in front of the house. His fingers fumbled with the key and the lock. He was nervous, he was taking a chance being this involved. He was further over the line than he would have cared. He heard a car door open from down the Drive and under a damaged lightpost. He heard the footsteps approach quickly. Father

Francis held Mrs Chrissie O'Rourke's arm, as if she was in need of protection. Mr Pronsias Reilly saw Frankie Conroy coming close.

'You're set?'

'We're fine,' Mr Pronsias Reilly said.

'Who is it?' Father Francis asked, unable to disguise his anxiety.

'No one for you to worry yourself with,' Frankie said. He took Mrs Chrissie O'Rourke's hand. 'Do what they tell you, Missus, just as they tell you. Remember what we're trying to do – What we're trying to do is to get your Roisin and your grankids back to you. And, Missus, we're trying to save your family from the shame of touting . . .'

She had just come from the house where there was still some warmth in the pipes, and now she was in the cold, and her glasses were steaming over with mist, and her eyes were bright and blurred and wide behind the lenses, as she looked up into Frankie's face.

'Missus, all I'm doing is for your family . . . Missus, you have to slide something to Roisin, and you have to tell her that it's for Gingy. It's personal from me to Gingy. Gingy'll understand what it is and why it's sent him. It has to get to him, Missus . . . Missus, you have to do it good and quiet. No one has to see you, Missus.'

He smiled to comfort her, and to strengthen her, and then he winked to her. His hand went to his donkey jacket pocket, and he took out and palmed to Mrs Chrissie O'Rourke a small crumpled tight handkerchief.

'You'll not be forgetting, Missus?'

And Frankie was gone, striding away into the shadow deeps.

Father Francis didn't understand, and the puzzlement bit lines into the youth of his forehead. Mr Pronsias Reilly understood, and he could smile because nothing could be traced to himself. Mrs Chrissie O'Rourke plunged the handkerchief into her overcoat pocket.

Mrs Chrissie O'Rourke was harnessed into the front passenger seat, and Father Francis leaned forward from the back of the big saloon and put his hands on the shoulders of the old lady, and believed in his act of charity.

'Who else'll be there, Mr Reilly?' Father Francis asked.

'I rang the *News*, they'll be there, if the buggers can get out of bed. The *News*'ll pass the word.

Mr Pronsias Reilly drove away fast from the Turf Lodge estate and out onto the main road that would take them east from the Falls and through the centre of the city. They cut past the City Hall that was to Mr Pronsias Reilly only one more symbol of the old Protestant ascendancy, and past the Magistrate's Court where he earned his living behind the wire fences that protected the building, and he took his right turn opposite the Oxford Street bus station where more than a decade before the Provo bombs had made a Bloody Friday that matched the Brit army's Bloody Sunday in Derry. He took the Albert Bridge over the Lagan, and then left past the nationalist ghetto of Short Strand – he had clients in the dingy and near-derelict warren of Short Strand. Another left, and another right, and he was out onto the open speedway of the by-pass, and the signs at the roadside directed him towards Holywood.

When his foot touched the brake, when the car began to slow, he turned to Mrs Chrissie O'Rourke.

'Just as we told you, Mrs O'Rourke.'

Ahead of them, stretching away on the righthand side, were the perimeter lights of Palace Barracks. They passed the first corner's watch tower. Past the lit main gate, past the length of the barracks frontage onto the main road. He could not park in front of the barracks. He took the right turn into the housing estate, and he saw a crouched soldier beside a front garden hedge, and he cut his headlights. In front of him the street was sealed with white ribbon, and behind the ribbon were policemen and soldiers and behind them he could see a flat-top lorry and a van. Frankie had given it to him straight, Frankie hadn't told him an untruth. The bastard tout had been softened, and his woman and his kids had been jazzed. He parked. He was well short of the ribbon barrier.

As they left the car, a soldier approached them. The solicitor and the priest each held an arm of the elderly lady.

'Good evening, my son,' Father Francis said politely.

The soldier muttered something, inaudible, and backed away. Another quiet smile from Mr Pronsias Reilly. The Brit squaddies were always impressed by a clerical collar, like a magic bloody pass-word. They went to the main road, and both Mr Pronsias Reilly and Father Francis had tight holds on the slender arms of Mrs Chrissie O'Rourke. They walked past the high wire mesh fences, and the long coiled lines of barbed wire, and the sentry boxes, and the arc lights.

Approaching the main gate, Mr Pronsias Reilly swore quietly to himself. No bloody photographer in position yet.

They came to the gate, the big barrier confronted them. A place as bright as daylight. Soldiers watched them from the front of the Guard House.

'She's in there, Mrs O'Rourke, she's in there with your grankids,' Mr Pronsias Reilly persisted into Mrs Chrissie O'Rourke's ear, and Father Francis smiled courage into her face. 'Just as we said . . .'

She nodded her head. Mr Pronsias Reilly thought she would do them well. She was a frail and pitiful sight. Father Francis thought she would turn the heart of any sinner, even the heart of a British soldier.

They came to the barrier. A corporal came forward.

'What's your business?'

'My girl's inside there, and I've come to see her.'

'Who's your girl?' The first glimmer of confusion from the corporal.

'She's Roisin McAnally, that's her married name, to me she's Roisin

O'Rourke. She's with the tout McAnally. She's with my grankids. I've come to see her.'

'You're joking, aren't you . . . ? In the middle of the night, you've got to be joking.'

'I'm not going till I've seen her.'

The corporal shifted his weight from right foot to left foot. Officer's job, this was. 'Who are you, gentlemen?'

'Pronsias Reilly, solicitor at law.'

'Father Francis Kane. Mrs O'Rourke is my parishioner.'

'I'm here to ascertain that Mrs O'Rourke's rights are not abused.'

'I've come to offer any guidance to Mrs O'Rourke that she might seek.'

Definitely a bloody officer's job.

'I'll have to ask . . . You can't stand there, this is M.O.D. property.'

'I'm staying where I am, till I've seen my girl.'

A car pulled up on the far side of the road. A young man jumped from the passenger seat. Mr Pronsias Reilly saw the bag slung over the young man's shoulder, and a camera hung round his neck. The car drove away in search of a parking place.

Mr Pronsias Reilly was smiling.

'You'd better get your officer, Corporal.'

Rennie arrived. He was puffed with temper, barging his way into the hall of the house.

In the hall were Ferris and Prentice, and Sean Pius McAnally. Goss was on the landing, leaning over the bannister rail.

Baby Sean was howling from somewhere behind Goss, and there was the clattering of Roisin's feet in the bedroom above the hallway.

'Does she know?' Rennie snapped.

'She knows something's messing us, she doesn't know what,' Prentice said. 'Worst luck, she was already awake to get her packing done when the officer came. Andy has her boxed in the bedrooms.'

'How is she with her Ma, Gingy?' Rennie asked.

'She's as married to her as she is to me,' McAnally said. The sleep was still in his face.

'What'd she be like if she saw her Ma?'

'You couldn't depend on how she'd be. She'd bawl, that's certain. I don't know how she'd be.'

'You know the cow's sat down in the middle of the bloody road, and she's a Provo lawyer with her, and a bloody dog collar . . . and she's three photographers and a camera crew. If they don't meet, then I'll have a Habeas Corpus action in court this morning, and if the judge has Roisin in Chambers and she spills that she wanted to see her Ma

164

and was prevented, then we're in deep shit. If she sees her Ma, then that's the end of it, they can't go to the High Court.'

Rennie was thinking aloud. 'It's nothing to do with Roisin needing to see her Ma, Gingy. It's about pressure, it's about Provie pressure to break her away from you. Got it, Gingy? Is she going to stand up to that pressure, Gingy?'

'I don't know . . .' Misery in McAnally's whisper. 'I just want her with me, don't know . . .'

'She's your fucking wife, Gingy . . . How can I know if you don't know?'

'I can't lose her.'

'Give it a rest, for Christ's sake.'

'I don't want them to take her from me.'

'It's a bloody lottery, how she'll react.'

'It's not my fault, Mr Rennie, I didn't tell the Provos where I was, where my family was,' McAnally shouted. 'It wasn't me that told them where to chuck their bloody mortars. It wasn't me that told Roisin's Ma where we was.'

Ferris heard the noise at the top of the stairs. Ferris saw Roisin, and Goss was restraining her, and the kids were round her legs.

'Too late for worrying who told her. The old cow's at the gate and that's the bloody end of it . . .' Rennie's voice cut. He looked into Ferris's face, and followed his eyeline, followed it to the top of the stairs, followed it to Roisin's drawn, devastated features.

'I want to see my Ma,' Roisin said.

Rennie shook his head grimly. The world falling on his shoulders. Was it worth the effort? All the bloody effort . . . No effort at all to have slapped Sean Pius McAnally into the Kesh for three lifers . . . Made the big effort, the big bloody effort for the big bloody success.

'They're just trying to take you from me,' McAnally called to his wife.

'I want to see my Ma.'

'Don't you see, Roisin . . .'

'We're free, aren't we?' she snarled. 'We're not bloody prisoners. I want to see her.'

'You're quite right, Mrs McAnally, you're free,' Rennie had regained control. He spoke carefully. 'You are not a bloody prisoner. Of course you can meet with your mother, of course you can slide back into your bloody cess-pit if you want to, and turn your back on your husband. Of course, you can dirty your hands with Provo work if you want to. You're not a bloody prisoner. You're quite free to chuck up the chance of a new life.'

'She's my Ma.'

'And he's your husband,' Rennie said.

165

Roisin came down the stairs. She was carrying Baby Sean. The men in the hallway backed away from her, made room for her.

'I'll need my coat,' she said.

The barrier rose, and the landrover came slowly out from the barracks. There wasn't much room for the driver, but enough. He was able to bend his way between the photographers and the centre of the road where Mrs Chrissie O'Rourke sat with Mr Pronsias Reilly and Father Francis.

They had done the interviews.

'I'm just here to try to get the chance to see my daughter who was kidnapped out of her house by the Army. I want her to come home to her Ma, to come back with my grankids. I don't want her to be a part of the lies that man of hers is telling, getting good men locked up on his lies. I want the chance to tell my girl to her face that she's to come home, and have nothing of all these lies. Her Da's in bed sick with worry over this. We've always been a good family, there's never been anyone in our family that's not loyal to Ireland, that's what I've come to tell her.'

'It's my belief that Mrs McAnally is being held in these barracks against her will. As a solicitor I'm not prepared to stand idly by and watch the rights of the individual jeopardized in the interests of Show Trials.'

'The O'Rourke family are valued and loved members of my congregation, and that includes Mrs Roisin McAnally. *They* say she's in protective care, with bombs raining down on her in the night. She'd be safer where she belongs, and she belongs back in Turf Lodge.'

On they waited. From time to time flash bulbs lit the darkness, and the soldiers stood with their weapons in a hostile and frustrated line at the Palace Barracks gates.

And behind the soldiers a major stood with his head cocked down to his shoulder the better to hear the message transmitted to his personal radio.

Time slipping by.

And Mrs O'Rourke wondering whether she'd ever get the damp of the roadway out of her skirt.

And Mr Pronsias Reilly thinking of a lost breakfast.

And Father Francis concerning himself that he had made no arrangement for a colleague to take eight o'clock Mass.

A light rain in the air and the wind, and a pastel touch of morning light in the east, above the roofs of the barracks.

And breakfast television came and recorded the litany, and packaged their tape for the studios and transmission.

And the major listened to the message, acknowledged it curtly, and reckoned that soldiering in Northern Ireland was a greater shower of wet shit than he could ever have believed possible. He strode forward, through the line of soldiers, ducked under the painted barrier and came to stand in front of Mrs O'Rourke.

'You are to see your daughter. Follow me, please.'

Mr Pronsias Reilly grinned as he and Father Francis helped the old lady to her feet. Both men made a play of wiping the road dirt from her coat. They walked with her, in the steps of the major, to the barrier.

Mrs Chrissie O'Rourke doubled herself awkwardly under the lowered pole. Mr Pronsias Reilly bent to follow.

'Just Mrs O'Rourke, thank you. On her own . . . If her daughter, quite voluntarily, agrees to meet her, then she hardly requires legal advice and spiritual guidance.'

They watched her go, a tiny sparrow figure beside the major, through the doorway of the Guard House. A minute later a landrover backed up hard against the Guard House verandah's steps. The cameras clicked. There were some amongst the photographers who said they had glimpsed the dark long hair of Mrs Roisin McAnally, wife of the tout.

Roisin had taken the baby with her, never without the baby. Little Patty was between Young Gerard and Andy Goss. Goss was reading her a story, a soft-spoken voice heading for a lived-happily-ever-after climax. Little Patty was fine, would cope with whatever, but Ferris bled for the boy. He knew no way to fracture the stolid mask of contempt Young Gerard showed to his father. And Gingy seemed not to notice. He was pacing from room to room. He was passing Ferris. He grabbed at Ferris's arm.

'What you said last night . . .'

'If I said it, then I meant it.'

'You said some daft things.'

'And meant them.'

'Really meant them?'

'You're going to win, Gingy. I promised to help you to win.'

'That's your word.'

'A promise is always binding.'

'You said you'd step in front of me.'

Ferris felt McAnally's clawing through his jacket, to the skin of his arms.

'I promised.'

'When'll I see you?'

'Rennie can fix it. When you shout, then Rennie will make it work.'

The hand loosed from Ferris's sleeve. Young Gerard's head was

167

down, so that he did not have to meet his father's eye. Andy Goss read on, he too would have heard, but he stayed with the momentum of a story of ogres and a shining prince and danger.

From away across the barracks came the thunder of a landing helicopter.

She was crying. There were no sounds to her crying above the crash of the rotors. She was waist-strapped in her seat deep in the fuselage of the Wessex, and she had Baby Sean tight against her chest, and her tears ran on the thin hair of his head. With the R.A.F. loadmaster, Prentice was helping the flotsam family up through the hatch . . . Young Gerard and Little Patty and Sean Pius McAnally, and Goss was passing up the case and the bags. They were a fugitive family.

Young Gerard had taken the seat beside his mother. Without ceremony Goss yanked him out of it, dropping him down on the far side of the fuselage, and pushed McAnally in next to Roisin.

The door slid shut. The engine noise soared, and the Wessex swayed in the moment before lift-off.

'What'd she say?' McAnally shouted.

'For me to go back.'

'What'd you say?'

'That I'd married you.'

'What's that mean?'

'That I'm your wife.'

'Is that why you stayed?'

'It'll do for now.'

She twisted her head so that she could see out through the cleaned porthole windows of the helicopter. They hovered for a moment over the parade ground. She saw the tiny figures of the Brit officer and the 'tec Rennie. They were the men who had trapped Gingy. She couldn't hold the flow of the tears . . . She had met her Ma for four and a half minutes. They had been alone along with the duty roster forms on the wall and the fire buckets on the floor. Her Ma had said that her Da was ill, that if she didn't break with Gingy now she might never see her Da alive again. Her Ma had said she had nothing to fear from coming home. Her Ma had said that Gingy had made his family like lepers. Her Ma had palmed her a crumpled handkerchief, and she had felt the hardness inside the cloth. Her Ma had said to be sure to give the handkerchief to Gingy.

She had to loosen her safety strap to get her hand in her pocket, to reach for the handkerchief. She passed it to Gingy.

She looked out through the porthole at the close-set streets of the

168

city, that gave way to the greens of Ormeau Park, and the greyness of the river, and the red rust of the gasometers across the water.

Gingy screamed. She spun to see him. His eyes were closed, his chin was jibbering, and all the time the howl of his agony. She saw his feet threshing, as if to kick away something on the fuselage floor. The handkerchief was tight in his hands and he struggled for the strength to rip it, shred and destroy it. She saw a moment of light beneath his shoes.

She saw a single bullet.

Christ . . . Christ Almighty.

One bullet, on the floor of the helicopter. A small revolver bullet.

She tried to take his head in her hands.

'I didn't know . . . God knows I didn't know.'

Prentice was crawling on the floor in front of McAnally, one arm on the flailing legs, scrabbling for the bullet. And all the time the screaming of the tout's wound.

'I didn't know, Gingy . . . Believe me. My Ma just said . . .'

Prentice had found the bullet and shouted, 'You're a bitch of a woman.'

She was sobbing into Gingy's shoulder.

'My Ma just said . . . God forgive me, I didn't know, Gingy.'

Her hand was over his mouth to stifle the screaming, and when she had killed the sound then he trembled, like a naked man in snow.

13

To most of those who met him John Prentice was a rough, tough policeman, a little of a lout, who would ride his way across people's feelings, a man who didn't give a damn what he said or to whom he said it, a man without the softness of sentiment. Howard Rennie knew better. Rennie had been the older man who had nursed Prentice through his marriage break and his divorce. Rennie knew the man behind the front. On the long weekend drinking marathons, Bushmills and stout, Rennie had discovered the young detective. Rolling, staggering drinking sessions through Saturday mornings and afternoons and evenings in the little hotels on the Antrim cliff coast, had shown Rennie that Prentice had a well hidden caring streak. There if dug for. All the 'tecs drank too much, and better that it was public drinking, far better when the 'tec was falling round in full view. Better than when it was a big bottle in a lonely room, because that was the route to a police issue pistol barrel poking up into a 'tec's mouth. Rennie liked the man, liked his company when he wanted to get pissed, when he wanted to forget Godfathers and widow-makers and mercury tilt time devices. Rennie was proud to have pulled him back from the brink of resignation when his girl gave him the boot.

Prentice had sworn and spat at Roisin McAnally in the helicopter, and had pocketed the bullet, and had known perfectly well that the woman hadn't an idea what she was doing when she had passed the handkerchief to her husband.

He had seen the way she had clung to Gingy for the remainder of the flight in the helicopter. When they had landed at Thiepval in Lisburn, she had hung on his arm, like she'd fall if he didn't lift her, and Goss had been left to carry Baby Sean and Little Patty.

The house was pretty much of a disaster. Thiepval was the old barracks of Northern Ireland Headquarters. By squaddy's standards the quarter was unacceptable, which meant it was God-awful, which was why it was available. The kitchen window was broken, and the rain had come in and cracked the linoleum. The roof had a quota of tiles dislodged and the main bedroom's wallpaper peeled from the wet plaster. The furniture was chipped or torn or frayed, and most of what was portable had long since been 'possessed' by army women. They had been let into the house by an obese captain, who hadn't thought it necessary to apologize for the condition of the premises. The house was in the heart of the old barracks' married quarters, its similarity with the one in Palace Barracks began and ended with its siting at the end of a cul-de-sac. Later that morning the captain had returned with a van-load of crockery and cutlery and bedding and a television, and he had required Prentice to check the items and sign for them on three different forms.

That first morning Goss took McAnally to Castlereagh for a session with the Branch. They went in the back of an armoured police landrover, and the supergrass was fitted out in a flak jacket.

Bloody good thing to have got rid of him, Prentice thought. He'd looked bloody helpless amongst the mess in the house. As that morning drifted on Prentice felt he was right in his judgement of the debris family of Sean Pius McAnally: if there wasn't another disaster they just might come through. She hadn't spoken to her husband in the house, but she had held his arm, and when he had gone, and when the van had brought the crockery and cutlery and the bedding, then she had started to work.

Baby Sean fed and asleep, Little Patty with the morning television babbling in front of her, Young Gerard with his mother. She started on the kitchen floor. Prentice found her with a bucket of hot water – there was hot water which was a miracle – and with a brush that was worn down to a stubble. Prentice caught the mood, and he rang the number the captain had reluctantly given him, and demanded plywood to cover up the smashed kitchen window, and portable heaters to blast out the upstairs damp.

More signing of white and yellow and mauve flimsies. The soldiers who brought the three gas heaters and the plywood and the saw and hammer and nails weren't admitted to the house, were packed off with their chitty. Prentice carried the heaters upstairs and lit them, one for each bedroom, and he went outside into the rain and hammered the plywood that he had cut to size over the broken window. She had stopped her scrubbing of the kitchen floor and looked up as he had come through the kitchen door, and she would have seen him lock it after him, and pocket the key. She smiled ruefully at Prentice, and dropped back to her work, and her trousers were tight on her backside, and her jersey had ridden up to show the smooth pale skin at the base of her spine, and Prentice thought she was as good a looking woman as the one who had booted him out of the bungalow in Glengormley.

He found a vacuum cleaner in the cupboard under the stairs, and took the plug off a standard lamp in the living room, and made the vacuum cleaner operational, and he curtly set Young Gerard to work on the carpets upstairs and downstairs.

Prentice laughed to himself when he was upstairs in the small bedrooms. He moved all the beds back from the windows before laying out the sheets. The Provies had blown it. That was his belief. The bullet had been too much.

'You didn't have to do that.'

Roisin was leaning against the doorway. Her hair was streaked down over her forehead, the sleeves of her jersey were pulled up to her elbows.

'The cleaner's out of a museum, but it goes.' 'It's standard police training, getting vacuum cleaners to work,' Prentice said.

She smiled quickly, as if forgetting herself.

'There's no food in the house.'

'I'll get some down here . . . if Gingy's back we'll run you into the supermarket in Lisburn, fill a basket.'

She said simply, 'I didn't know.'

'What was in the handkerchief, I know you didn't know.'

'You called me a bitch of a woman.'

'I think I got you wrong, Mrs McAnally.'

He spread a first blanket over the single bed that filled the room, smoothed it down, and tucked in the bottom and the sides.

When he had finished the bed, admired it, he turned to the doorway for approval. She was gone.

*

171

Frankie said, 'I can't bloody say what'll happen . . . I just know that last night was bloody good . . . McAnally got himself shaken. He'd have to have had ear plugs not to have heard the tape. His woman ends up in fits of tears with her Ma, 'cos the old lady gives it her thicker than gravy. I don't bloody say it'll happen today or tomorrow, but that woman's his strength, and we've damaged her good and true . . . That's all I can bloody say.'

Sharp, nasal voices swam around the ears of Frankie Conroy.

'You had a hell of a crowd of men out last night, you won't get the likes of that again in a hurry.'

'They put them in the birdie. Who's to say where they've lifted him. Could be to Aldergrove and a flight out.'

'What're you going to do now, Frankie?'

'How're you going to squeeze him, Frankie?'

Frankie sighed. 'I bloody found him and damaged him. I don't know how I'm going to get to him again.'

Opposite Frankie in the private room of the bar in Clonard was a veteran of the movement. He had done time as an Internee in the '56–62 campaign, and again after the '71 lifts, and he had been imprisoned in Portlaoise gaol in the South for membership in '76. He was a man who was listened to.

'You've gone for a big crack, Frankie. You've come in and you've chucked your weight all over. Your crack'll have to hurt, Frankie.'

'Would you be wanting the Chief and thirty others to rot away in the Kesh?'

'Just telling you, that it's best you keep the ideas coming,' the veteran said calmly.

'Is you saying we should forget the Chief, and the Brigade staff, and the Battalions. Forget the Chief and Ollie and Joey and Tom?'

'You don't listen well, Frankie. And don't you tell me what you think I'm saying. Listen hard. *You've* got it going, *you* have to keep it going. If you don't keep it going then it's bad for all of us, Frankie, and that's bad for you.'

'Don't fucking threaten me.'

'I didn't threaten you . . .' There was a cold emphasis in the veteran's voice.

Frankie stood. His knees clipped the table skirting, shook the glasses and spilled a sea of beer. The Organization was deep with divisions on the policy of the war. There were those who called for political advancement and ultimately the black saloon cars that would take them to the negotiating table, and there were the fighters. The Chief was a fighter, and Frankie was the Chief's man. In his mind he saw the veteran in his wedding suit, or his funeral suit, smiling at the cameras as he stepped into the black car for a trip to the sell-out table. Soft old bastard . . . There were those who would have dry eyes if the Chief and thirty

172

of his fighters went down for Tenners and Fifteens and Twenties.

Frankie stared out the faces round the table, at the doorway.

'My crack'll hurt,' Frankie said.

Frankie went out and into the street, and he gulped the air, as if what he had breathed in the private room had been poison.

Ferris felt as if he had crawled through a hedge. He felt the dirt on his body and the beard gathering on his cheeks and throat and chin. He should have washed and shaved before entering the Mess, even if just for a fast coffee. Post was always on the sideboard, the sideboard was always his first stop. Bloody good . . . he saw his Sam's handwriting on a smart blue envelope. Big bold writing that could be read across a room, about all they'd taught her that had stuck from school. There was a bank statement and a letter from his mother. His mother wrote every week, about nothing, but had a notion of duty that she should write even if it were only to list the progress of the neighbours' kitchen extension.

He came from the sideboard with the letters tight in his hand, and went to the coffee urn. He heard Sunray's voice.

'You're just back, David?'

'Yes, sir.'

'From your extra-ordinary duties?'

'Yes, sir.' Ferris hovered by the urn.

'And been up all night, with the mortar business?'

'Yes, sir.'

'Your ordinary duties, here, will, I hope, permit you time to bath and shave.'

'Yes, sir.'

'Cook Corporal will keep coffee by for you, so that you can have coffee after a bath and a shave.'

'Thank you, sir.'

The Bravo Company commander and the Battalion Adjutant and the Quartermaster Captain were watching him. Sunray was by the urn, holding his own cup and saucer.

'How's your man?'

'He's fine, sir.'

'The opposition's getting the better of you.'

Pompous arsehole, Ferris thought. 'I hope not, sir.'

'David . . .'

'Sir?'

'I've a few of the locals coming for a drink tomorrow evening, Lisburn's latest on winning hearts and minds is to pour sherry down their

173

throats. You've become very close to the ground, so I'd appreciate your presence, sixish.'

'Thank you, sir.'

He searched out his Platoon Sergeant, heard that a two-vehicle mobile patrol was rostered for mid-day, and cried himself off it. The Platoon Sergeant gave Ferris a fast eyes only inspection, and his face seemed to say that in the state the officer was in they'd be better off without him.

The water was tepid. His towel was damp, which meant bloody Wilkins had used it the previous evening.

He crawled onto his bunk bed. There were three beds in the cubicle, standard for junior officers. No comfort, no privacy, for Ferris and Armstrong and Wilkins. Some idiot would say that it was good for the moulding of character. Junior officers weren't expected to sleep. Junior officers were supposed to be traipsing the streets of Andy'town and Whiterock, keeping the bloody peace, keeping the heathens from each other's throats. He meant to read his mother's letter first, then his bank statement, then finish on a high note with Sam's. Bloody good thinking, bloody poor execution.

Ferris slept for an hour. The Cook Corporal came in search of him with a tray of toast and coffee and found him stretched out, snoring lightly, grinning like a cat, with his girl's letter unopened and lying on his chest. The Cook Corporal let him be. It was a dreamless sleep without trouble. He'd thought of Sam when he'd closed his eyes, it had been his last thought before he crashed out.

There were two teenagers and an older man, past thirty, in the A.S.U. One of the teenagers, armed with a Mauser handgun, held the widow in her kitchen. The other teenager and the older man went upstairs to her bedroom. The older man carried an Armalite rifle, the other teenager carried a five-gallon petrol can, and a short stave at the end of which had been wrapped a torn string vest and the striped sleeve of a pyjama top. The other teenager unscrewed the top of the petrol can, while the older man, once and briefly, flicked back the window curtain to check his view of the front gates of the Springfield Road barracks.

The widow's bedroom soon stank of the fumes of the can's petrol and the paraffin that had been splashed on the rags around the stave.

Ferris woke.

The long-stay soldiers said it was the mark of a good young officer that he could steal an hour in an army bunk and make it count like a night at the Dorchester.

He felt good. No bloody right to, but he felt good. A bit before twelve. Must have been the combination of the shower and the shave and the shit that had knocked him out. There was a sweet scent close to him . . . Bloody Sam. She'd tipped some perfume on the envelope. He must have smelt like a hanging pheasant before he'd cleaned himself up, why he hadn't noticed Sam's scent.

He read his mother's letter . . . his mother was well, his father was well, the bank his father managed was well, the garden his mother tended was well. They had driven the previous weekend to Windermere and walked on the lakeside with his aunt and uncle, and they were well. When they had returned from Windermere, they had gone to Evensong at St Peter's and St Paul's, and the vicar was well, and had asked after him . . . 'We seem to go to church more often since you went over there. The Rev. Davies knows you're in Belfast and he said a prayer for all "our boys" who are at risk to keep us safe. Your father and I thought he did it very well. We take comfort that there has been nothing on the news since the judge was killed. Your father tells me, and he showed me a map, that you would have been in quite a different part of the city to where the poor man was murdered. Your father says there's no end to it until the army are allowed a free hand. Ernie, you remember our milkman, says Ulster should be given to the Royal Air Force as a bombing range. Ernie always makes me laugh. He hopes you are well. I've been raking the last of the leaves today from the elm, and managed to get a bonfire going, but then Mrs Frobisher put her washing on the line and I had to put a bucket on it. We're playing bridge with her next week, she's not been well.'

He was £98.72 overdrawn. He didn't bank with his father. They'd have to be patient, till after Christmas. Christmas . . . what a thought . . . Christmas in the Springfield Road barracks. Sunray serving up the brown windsor and the yellow turkey for the squaddies, paper hats in the Mess, and the Chaplain trying to pretend that for one day at least there could be hope and love on the streets of Belfast.

There was a biscuit tin in his cupboard. He stuffed his mother's letter into it, and the bank statement.

He sniffed at Sam's envelope. Cheeky girl. He ran his thumb nail under the gummed down flap. He could see Sam's tongue licking the flap down, could feel it if he half tried. Ten weeks gone, six to go. He was certain of Sam, she was the only human being in the world that he was sure of. God, what Sam would have done for the morale of a Spitfire squadron parked out on a field in Kent in 1940. Every pilot, heading for death or glory, would have thought of Sam when it was curtains time and loved her.

'Darling David, it's hells boring here – when are you coming back to me?' . . . Sam was close to being worth a desertion charge . . . 'That hideous little solicitor from Frome has been pestering me to go to

175

dinner, so I told him he should get a commission in the Parachute Reg. and then I'd look at him again, he said I couldn't go through life being flippant, I told him to naff off' . . . he believed her. The solicitor wouldn't have an overdraft of £98.72. The solicitor had a future that stretched further than six more weeks patrolling West Belfast . . . 'The papers have been full of the supergrasses, especially this smelly little turnip they've just roped in. Anyone who has to deal with him must feel like having a good bath afterwards' . . . he saw Sam in the bath, bubbles and nipples and knees, and he saw Gingy McAnally hurrying with his children to the opened hatch of a helicopter . . . 'If you've been without it for sixteen weeks will you be impotent when you come back? I met a doctor at the Mendip Hunt thrash who said that men who had been without for too long sometimes lost the urge' . . . you're a bloody tease, Sam. Fusilier Jones would have a ruder name for Sam. Fusilier Jones wouldn't like to think of a girl in Somerset getting his officer all charged up . . . 'Lots of love, David darling, from your Sam – P.S. Daddy's dived into a book about the Russian army. He says the Russians wouldn't have let N.I. go on for so long – finger out, my darling.'

It was the sixth letter he had received from her since the Battalion had travelled. He kept all her letters in a cellophane folder in the breast pocket of his denims. Sam's letters were always with him on patrol in Turf Lodge.

One last time he held the envelope to his nose, then he tore it into small pieces and put them into the black plastic bag that was the room's rubbish bin.

He stretched.

He heard the rifle fire.

He heard the crash of S.L.R.s on semi-automatic.

He heard urgent, shouted orders.

He heard the alarm bell howling through the windowless walls of his room.

Sam vanished. Ferris had slept in his boots. Standard Operating Procedure that officers slept in their boots if they cat-napped in daytime. He plunged off the bunk, grabbed his flak jacket from the nail on the door. He stuffed Sam's letter into his trouser pocket. He took his rifle from the floor under the bed, and sprinted out of the quarters and into the yard where the vehicles were parked.

Bedlam outside. Men running. Officers and N.C.O.s shouting. The Saracens with the big red crosses on them were revving their engines.

Ferris saw the smoke climbing from the street side of the screen fencing round the barracks.

'It's *your* patrol.'

He turned. He saw the Intelligence Officer running behind him.

The gates were open. Ferris ran out into the Springfield in the wake of the second Saracen.

Just down the road, to the right, on the far side, were the two land-rovers. The lead landrover was intact. The follow-up vehicle was a blackened base and above it were climbing flames. Soldiers were kicking in the door of the house beside it. Shots were fired into the upper window. Two black, scorched figures rolled, writhed, in the middle of the roadway, and the stench spread the width of the street.

The medics reached the two men.

An old lady, not an inch above five feet tall, was dragged dumb from the front door of her house.

Sunray was out in the street, and Bravo's Company commander.

Fusilier Jones was kneeling by a lamp post, his rifle at his shoulder and covering the upper windows on the far side of the street. Ferris saw his chin trembling uncontrollably. He went to him, he crouched down beside him. He felt a terrible sense of shame. His men, the men of his platoon, attacked while he was in his pit.

'Tell me, Jones.'

'It's the Sarge and Nobby. Not much to tell, really. Window breaks, a can full of gas and a fire stick came out. That's about it. We pump the window, too fucking late. Sarge's vehicle catches the gas. Harry and Rick get out O.K., Sarge and Nobby don't have the luck. Sarge's fucking bad . . .' the young Fusilier looked away from his sighting aim, looked into his officer's face. He was shouting. 'You couldn't see them . . . you couldn't hit the cunts back.'

'Easy, lad.' Ferris's hand rested on Fusilier Jones's shoulder.

Time for a bloody officer to display bloody leadership, wasn't it?

Of course, they couldn't hit back, not with rifles, not with vehicle patrols. Getting Sean Pius McAnally into the witness box was hitting back. Getting him to testify was hitting back at the bastards.

The ambulance Saracen wailed away the few hundred yards to Casualty at the Royal Victoria.

'Take the vehicle back and get a mug of tea,' Ferris said to Jones.

Rennie extricated Gingy McAnally from the Special Branch rooms at Castlereagh.

The Branch were easy on Gingy. Their concern was the structure of the Organization, the morale and thinking of the P.I.R.A. Volunteers and Officers, the tactical approach of the movement. An easy ride for Gingy. The big picture was of little use to Howard Rennie. Rennie's job was to get men into court first, to get men into the Kesh second.

Out in the corridor Rennie crowded McAnally up against a wall. He towered over the tout.

'Yesterday was pretty bloody. It won't get better till you make it better. It's in your hands, and the only way you'll make it better is by getting on with it, head down. You have to face them, and you're going to face them, all the men you've named. When you can do that, when you can spit in their bloody eyes, then it's getting better.'

Rennie punched McAnally on the upper arm, hurting him, tensing him.

'Head down, and you spit in their eyes, and you face them.'

McAnally nodded.

'And no pissing me about.'

Again McAnally nodded.

Rennie knew that he could never be certain of a supergrass. Once he had psyched a man right up to the back door of the Crumlin Road Court House, and defence had won a week's adjournment, and the supergrass had gone flat on them, walked out. He'd shouted at him, pleaded with him, threatened him, and the man had walked out on them. Rennie wouldn't risk his life on a supergrass making it to Crumlin Road, hardly depend a bloody toenail on it.

'Is the house alright, the new house?' Rennie asked conversationally. They were tramping the corridors on their way to Interrogation.

'The house is grand.'

Rennie thought McAnally would call a shit house a palace if he thought that would please. He had to find a way of planting some balls in the man if he wasn't to be crucified under cross-examination. He knew all the barristers, mostly Protestants because they'd had the places at the Law Department in Queens, and they wet themselves at the chance of turning over a supergrass in the witness box.

'Don't you bloody dare let me down.'

That afternoon Sean Pius McAnally confronted Fatsy Rawe and Eamonn Bugsy Malone and Damien Dusty O'Hara and Brennie Toibin and Phonsie McGurr and Joey Mulvaney and Billy Clinch. No hanging about, no messing as there had been with Muldoon, O'Brien, McGilivarry, McCreevy. A uniformed Inspector was present as an independent witness. Two detectives to watch the prisoner. McAnally into the doorway, reciting his accusations that were sometimes drowned in the protest shouting or the hissing threats, and out of the door. Rennie never let go of McAnally's arm, not when they were back out in the corridor, not when they were in the doorway in confrontation.

McAnally might have run a mile. He was weakening, he was sagging, and Rennie's hand held him upright, propelled him towards each of his former comrades.

'Can I go back to Roisin?' With both hands McAnally gripped a mug of tea.

'I'm laying charges tonight. You'll go on facing them till you're through your list.'

'Yes.'

Rennie softened. 'Prentice says to me that Roisin didn't know . . . he says she's as buggered by the bullet as you were.'

'She wouldn't have done it if she'd known.'

'She didn't know what she was doing . . . It's not only you that's going through the hoop, Gingy . . . Give her time, laddie.'

'What'll you do with her Ma?'

'Nothing.'

McAnally snorted. 'Possession of ammunition, there's guys doing a Fiver for possession of a bullet.'

'Don't play bloody lawyers with me . . . I'd love to book the bastard who put the bullet in her hand. To send him down I've got to heave her through the courts, as a witness or in the dock. If I do that then you lose Roisin, Gingy. They're not bloody daft, they knew we'd do damn all.'

McAnally dropped his head. 'I'm only here because of Roisin, because I wanted to do the best for her, for the kids.'

Rennie said cruelly, 'And a matter of three life sentences, that little matter too. Let's get on with it . . .'

Back to the Interrogation Block. Back to the snarling, enraged faces of the men accused by Sean Pius McAnally.

Andy Goss escorted McAnally back to Thiepval, same transport, same armoured landrover.

Goss wasn't making much of his job as 'minder' during the journey in the dimmed light of the landrover's interior. He'd been chirpy enough when Rennie had given him the afternoon to go and see his girl. She'd wanted him with her after the bank closed, for Christmas shopping in Royal Avenue. He'd said he couldn't make it. She'd wanted him at home for lunch on Sunday because her relations were coming up from Dungannon. He'd said there was no chance he could get away this Sunday.

'You're supposed to be engaged to me, not that wretched informer. You'll get known, you know. You can't help but get known. What if he runs out on you, or his wife, then those murdering Provos'll have your name. They'll come for you, to shoot you. That's a hell of a future for me, marrying a man who's a target. You didn't think of me when you walked into the job. God only knows what you were thinking about.'

She'd left him at the door of the bank.

'How did it go today, Gingy?' Goss said.

'Pretty well.' His face was in shadow. Goss couldn't see McAnally's doubt, only hear it.

A long ride to Lisburn, skirting the city centre, and time for Goss to think on what his girl had said, to think of his future if the Provos had his name as a supergrass minder.

The civil servant smiled at the aggravating persistence of the American interviewer. The audience in the United States was considered important. It was believed in Whitehall that if the British 'line' on Northern Ireland were correctly explained then funds for the Provisionals from across the Atlantic would dry up. The civil servant regarded such a belief as nonsense. He reckoned the Armalites and the dollars would still drift over however clean a figure the Secretary of State cut with the American media.

The *New York Times* had come from London.

'But surely you've considered the possibility that a supergrass, like this McAnally, will further alienate the Catholic population, make a bad situation worse?'

He'd come on the early morning flight, taken a taxi round the Falls, then beer and sandwiches with the *Telegraph*, then an ear bashing from an abstentionist Catholic politician, then another taxi to Stormont Castle. Plenty of time to become an expert, the civil servant reflected.

'You have to understand our legal system. I have nothing to do with the law. In the United Kingdom the judiciary are quite separate from the political process. It is for the judiciary to decide whether the supergrass system is acceptable.'

A good straight bat from the Secretary of State, the civil servant thought. The pity of it was that the Americans didn't play cricket.

'Wouldn't you admit that the supergrass system has been widely condemned?'

'The system has been complained about by a particular section of our society here which has shown scant respect for the rule of law, and even less respect for human life. I disregard these shrill protests from groups closely associated with the paramilitary violence that has caused so much misery in the Province.'

'An American lawyer who visited Belfast to study the supergrass system wrote that the use of supergrasses was "an extension of military policy". What do you say to that?'

Excellent . . . the civil servant had given the Secretary of State the right answer to that one. Go on, shove it down his nasty plastic microphone. Typical of the modern times. He didn't see half a dozen journalists a year who could write shorthand.

'We have a maxim here about people living in glasshouses not throwing stones. In the last fifteen years, to my certain knowledge, more than four thousand American citizens – shall I repeat the figure? – have informed on your organized crime syndicates in return for immunity.

I'm sure the Mafia have complained, but I haven't read of the complaints of the *New York Times* . . . There's something I'd like to add. If the American people want to show true concern for the community of Northern Ireland, then they should cease providing the terrorists here with guns and ammunition. Do you know that almost every soldier, every policeman, every politician, who is gunned down here, has been murdered with a weapon manufactured in the United States of America? Would you like to go to the police armoury? Would you like to see the weapons we have captured from the terrorists? American-made weapons?'

The civil servant saw the journalist hesitate.

'My flight . . . my next trip, perhaps . . . I'd be happy to. Going back to the supergrass system . . .'

'There are other priorities in Northern Ireland today, which could be of interest to you.'

'Doesn't the supergrass system only alienate middle-ground opinion?'

'You're here ten years too late if you're looking for middle-ground tolerance. Today, the middle ground's gone. How could it have survived? The civilian population of Northern Ireland has been subjected to a peace-time murder campaign of a ferocity unequalled in western Europe this century. The middle ground has been shot and bombed to exinction. There are two camps here. In one camp are those who support paramilitary violence, in the other camp are those who support a democratic rule of law and order. There can hardly be a no man's land between those two camps with 2500 already dead. I'm talking blunt reality. We are fighting a difficult and cunning enemy – regretfully that enemy has destroyed the middle ground.'

The Secretary of State eased back, drew breath.

'And the prosecution of the war justifies the use of traitors, of Judas men?'

The civil servant saw the flare of anger in the Secretary of State's eyes.

'If you view the Provisional I.R.A. as Christ then the supergrass is indeed a Judas. You won't be expecting me to take that viewpoint.'

'What I was trying to say . . .'

The civil servant stood. 'I think that ground's covered, Mr Broekweicz, and there's your flight . . .'

During the hand-shaking the telephone on the Secretary of State's desk warbled. The civil servant took it, listened, replaced the receiver.

He showed the journalist out, shut the door on him.

'Bloody good riddance. Did I do alright?'

'Perfect, sir.'

'That's no bloody answer, Fred.'

'It'll do . . . Chief Constable was on. The charges are being laid tonight, on McAnally's word. The Chief Constable's rather spare with information. He says that after yesterday's capers McAnally's as well as can be expected.'

'I'm gone, if he retracts.' The Secretary of State stared out of the window, down across the Stormont grasslands. His triumph over Conrad Broekweicz of the *New York Times* had given only short-lived pleasure.

'The Coleraine Development Board are next,' the civil servant advised.

At the door of the supermarket, a huge, basic, covered barn of a place, Prentice palmed McAnally five fivers.

He did it privately, hoping that Roisin wouldn't see. McAnally just passed the folded notes to Roisin. Prentice's effort was wasted. She put the money in her purse.

'Don't you want to get something, Gingy, something for yourself?'

'She'll get all I need.'

'What about the kids?'

'She'll get what the kids need.'

The loudspeakers in the supermarket were playing scratched carols. Prentice reckoned it must be last year's tape, recorded off the previous year's record.

> God rest you Merry Gentlemen
> Let nothing you dismay.

McAnally was like a lost man, and he held Little Patty's hand tight, and he didn't respond to her excitements and pointings and pleasures that were the shelves. He meandered without purpose, and away from Roisin who had settled Baby Sean in the food trolley's toddler seat, and away from Young Gerard who stayed with his Ma. What price all the bright tinsel and the plastic holly and the gift-wrapped presents for the family of Sean Pius McAnally? He'd made his bed, the bugger could lie on it. Prentice saw Goss fall in behind the informer, shadowing him as he went between the shelf banks. Himself he went after Roisin; not too close, not so that she would be aware of him, crowded by him.

> Jesus Christ, our Sav-i-our
> Was born on Christmas Day.

Always the shoulders and the raven dark hair of Roisin were in his sight.

*

Rennie came into the Chief's cell. With him were McDonough and
Astley and a uniformed Inspector. Astley had his notebook opened.
Rennie read from a sheet of typewritten paper.

'Kevin Majella Muldoon, no fixed abode, you are charged that
between the 1st day of November 1984 and the 1st day of December
1984 you and others conspired together to murder William Horace
Simpson, contrary to section 4 of the Offences against the Person Act
1861. Do you wish to say anything? You are not obliged to say anything
unless you wish to do so, but whatever you say will be taken down in
writing and may be used in evidence.'

'Nothing.'

'Kevin Majella Muldoon, no fixed abode, you are charged that
between the 1st day of January 1981 and the 1st day of December 1984,
you belonged to a proscribed organization, namely the Irish Republican
Army, contrary to section 21(1)(a) of the Northern Ireland (Emergency
Provisions) Act 1978 . . . Do you wish to say anything? You are not
obliged to say anything unless you wish to do so, but whatever you say
will be taken down in writing and may be used in evidence.'

The Chief belched. 'Nothing.'

The Chief turned his head to the wall, and the door shut on his back.

Out in the corridor, to Astley, Rennie said, 'If I lose that bastard
you might see me crying, sonny.'

At the next cell door McDonough passed Rennie from a thick sheaf
of papers the charge sheet of Oliver Anthony O'Brien.

'I won't just be crying, I'll be blubbering my eyes out, if I lose any
one of them.'

It would take them more than an hour to work through the charge
sheets to be served against the men named by Sean Pius McAnally.

14

Mr Pronsias Reilly had a crowded morning schedule to sandwich
between the Magistrate's hearing and his attendance at the Crown
Court.

He was pleased with his performance before the Magistrate, well
satisfied as he was led by a Court policeman down the steep steps to
the cells where he would be able to manage ten minutes with the Chief.
At the hearing he had established from a reluctant Detective Sergeant
McDonough that the evidence against his client was based on the word
of Sean Pius McAnally. And he had further established that the same

Sean Pius McAnally had been granted immunity in respect of all charges he might have faced. Serious charges? Charges of Murder? Sean Pius McAnally had been granted immunity from charges of triple murder? The solicitor had seen the flickering movement of pencils and biros at the Press Bench. He had scored the points that were there to be taken and had gone on to attack the media for what he criticized as a circus of sensationalism in their coverage of his client's arrest. A good performance.

In the cell he talked to his client within the view, but outside the hearing, of the Court policeman.

'Who's taking care?'

'Frankie Conroy. He's sworn he'll get you out. He's sworn McAnally won't testify.'

'It's one thing to swear.'

'Frankie's sworn it.' There was a quick smile at Mr Pronsias Reilly's lips. 'There's not everyone was prepared to swear the same. If Frankie fails you then you'll be waiting on the judge.'

'McAnally's for killing.'

'Frankie has to find him again.'

'Frankie has to kill him.'

Mr Pronsias Reilly slipped back on the cell chair. It was a new sight of the Chief. This was the hard man of the Organization, and the solicitor sensed the whiff of fear in the Chief's words. The charge of Conspiracy to Murder carried Eighteen or Twenty. There were some of the big men who gave the judge two fingers when they were sent down. Not this one. Bright staring eyes, and the breath coming in little pants.

'Frankie has to stiff him.'

'Frankie's sworn it, he may not get all the help he wants . . . There are some who say there's better things for the Organization to be at.'

'Which bastards?'

'I didn't hear the names.'

The Chief had hold of Mr Pronsias Reilly's hand, squeezed it, hurt him. 'If people turn their arses on me, then they're dead when I'm out; you tell every bastard that who turns his back on me.'

'Frankie knows what he has to do.'

A coasting day for McAnally.

The confrontations completed, the accused in court, a full day with the Branch.

Last night Roisin had cooked a good meal, and cooked for the minders as well, and there'd been no talk of the bullet. And she'd washed up with Prentice, and he'd heard her laugh . . . first bloody time. And she'd made something of the house. In a day she'd made the house a home.

The Branch man was an odd bugger. Grey hair onto his shoulders, and a leather jacket like he was a teenager, and jeans, and beads round his bloody throat. Proper queer one. Used a cassette tape as a notebook, so they could talk, and they could have a crack and a laugh. Not like taking the statements. Easier this, relaxed, comfortable, and McAnally talking, and the Branch man prompting, and later in the morning the snapshot book came out of a drawer in the Branch man's desk. Bloody incredible photographs. Not mug shots, photos from the long lens cameras. Funerals, street-corner meetings, men into doorways, men out of doorways, men on the pavement, men in cars. Who's that . . . ? Did you ever come across him . . . ? That a fellow you ever met . . . ? Was he ever on your side of town . . . ? The talk was kept light and cool, and McAnally warmed to the Branch man because he had mahogany stains on his fingernails, and dirt under the nails, and he hadn't shaved well, and McAnally could sniff his socks.

McAnally talked through that day. The first time that he had felt good talking. Goss was behind him, in a hard chair, managing to sleep and snoring softly, and McAnally was scratching his mind for memories of the men who had been photographed by the surveillance cameras, and when he could tell a story about a photograph the Branch man told him that he was bloody marvellous.

'He wants to go outside, can he or can't he?' Roisin challenged.

Through the living room door Prentice could see Young Gerard standing in the hall. The boy was silent, but seemed to whine like a dog that needed to get to the front gate and lift a leg. Prentice didn't know the answer. There should have been a woman on the detail, a W.P.C.

'He's a boy, he's eight and a half, he's been cooped up inside since . . .'

. . . Since the family had been lifted out of Turf Lodge to go into hiding with the breadwinner who was a tout. There couldn't be any harm in the boy going out. He could walk around. He might find some kids to play football with. Prentice hesitated.

'He's not a bloody prisoner, whatever we are.'

If Prentice said that the boy couldn't go out, then he'd be back into the living room, glowering, and park himself across the carpet in front of the television, and bicker with Little Patty.

'Not far.'

'What does that mean?'

'It means he can go out, but he shouldn't be out of sight of the house.'

Roisin stared hard at him. 'Why shouldn't he be out of sight of the house?'

'Because I say he shouldn't,' Prentice said.

'In a month's time will he be allowed out of sight of the house, in a year's time?'

He didn't know why she wanted to fight. He tried to smile, made a play at not taking offence. 'I said that the boy can go out.'

Roisin called to Young Gerard, 'You're *allowed* out, but not out of sight of the house.'

Prentice saw the boy drift down the front path. Baby Sean was sleeping on the settee. He could hear Little Patty scuffling on the floor of the upstairs bedroom, playing.

It was warm in the living room, central heating on full. A side light was lit. Prentice looked across the room at Roisin. She was in the arm chair, a large sagging chair. Her legs were splayed wide. There was shadow on her face. He couldn't read her expression. He could see her long thighs stretched out from the cushions of the chair.

'You want to screw me, *Mister* Prentice?'

He heard the tinkle of her laughter. He sat on a chair at the table at the back end of the room.

He looked out of the window, into the back garden.

'Only you wouldn't know what I'd do, if you got up out of your chair. You wouldn't know whether I'd give you a ride . . . or whether I'd scream the bloody roof off. You wouldn't know what I'd do, would you, Mister Prentice?'

He saw Young Gerard's head appear behind the fence at the end of the garden, then move off. He lost him.

'Don't bloody know, do you?'

Prentice stood up, walked through the room and out into the hall. He sat on the stairs.

She came after him, stood in the doorway. She pushed her hair back from her forehead.

'Frightened I'd scream. I might just scream . . . and then I might give you a bloody good ride . . . You're a big bloody disappointment to me. I thought you'd chance it to find whether I scream.'

He was cleaning his nails with a used match.

'Would you be frightened of screwing a Taig woman? Would you be frightened I'd be dirty? Have you ever screwed a Taig woman? Would you know if you had? 'Course you would. Taig women are different to your women, aren't they? Smell different, don't they, and their eyes are closer together. You'd know if you'd screwed a Taig, wouldn't you?'

She came close to him, stood in front of him. Her stomach was in front of his eyes. She jutted her hips towards him. 'Do we smell different to Protestant women?' She crouched so that her eyes were level with his. 'Are they closer together than your Protestant women's eyes?'

'Keep going, if you want your arse kicked,' Prentice said quietly.

'Proper gentleman,' she sneered.

'Proper bitch.'

She sat on the floor. She put her hand lightly on his knee. He took her hand in his fingers. It was a small hand, it would have been a delicate hand before it was roughened from the work of keeping a house while her man was running or in the Kesh or away in the South.

'We're all fucked, aren't we?' she said heavily. 'Me and Sean and the kids, we're bloody gone.'

'That's not true.'

'I forgot myself last night. Because we'd had some drinks, because you'd bought some decent food, I forgot myself. I thought it might bloody work. Idiot bloody thought . . . I thought it would work, and Sean came upstairs, all he bloody talked about was the Brit officer. He talked about the Brit officer like he was his bloody friend. The sun shone out of the Brit officer's bum. Sean was a right idiot last night . . . and I'd forgot myself, because I thought we might have a real life . . .'

He could talk to the tout, he couldn't talk to the tout's woman.

'There'll be a new life.'

'And you'll be doling out the pound notes.'

'Sean'll be got a job.'

'A job . . . Sean's never bloody worked in his life.' Her derision spat into Prentice's face. 'He can't hammer a nail . . . all he can do is shoot people with a fucking R.P.G. . . . . You going to get him a job doing that? I'll make a pot of tea.'

Prentice let her hand drop, and she stood.

'We're Republicans, we're Provos.'

'It'll get washed out of you,' Prentice said grimly. 'When you live amongst people who don't give a damn then it'll be scrubbed out of your system.'

'You wouldn't understand.'

'Go and make the tea.'

'You think we're better off, with you, than with our own?'

'Your decision. You should make the tea.'

She went to the kitchen. He eased himself up from the stairs and went to the front door. He looked out, and couldn't see Young Gerard in the gathering darkness of the early evening.

She called from the kitchen. 'I don't think I would have screamed.'

'Your eyes are too close together,' he shouted back. He wondered whether she heard him over the noise of the tap water bubbling into the kettle.

*

187

He had seen the patrol approaching, and he had positioned his ambush.

There were five in the patrol and they moved carelessly. They were bunched too close together, and they paid insufficient attention to the parked cars and the dustbins and they chattered amongst themselves, and there was no rear marker walking backwards to cover the way they had come.

The patrol was as sloppy as anything that the urban guerrilla fighter had ever seen. He crouched behind a low hedgerow that had holes enough for him to watch the patrol drift closer. He could hear their voices. He hadn't the experience to recognize where in Britain they came from, and it didn't concern him. They were accents from across the water of the Army of Occupation.

From his hiding place, he studied the faces of the patrol. Cheerful, happy faces, faces without fear. He loathed each of the faces equally. He blamed each of the shock blasts that had entrapped his recent life on the faces of the patrol. There were five in the patrol, and each one of them was a symbol of the disasters in his life. He thought that if he achieved total surprise he could hope not only to smash the smugness of the patrol, but also to capture a weapon. It was more than a week to Christmas, but already the members of the patrol carried shiny, bright weapons.

Young Gerard's weapons were half a brick and the broken corner of a cement building block that filled the palm of his hand. Two of the patrol carried silver chrome cowboy cap pistols. The leader of the patrol had a rifle with a crackling sound for the pulling of the trigger and a battery operated light to flash in the muzzle. The boy behind the leader carried a wooden-made Thompson sub-machine gun, put together by his father who was a Signals clerk at Headquarters. The boy in front of the leader carried an Armalite reproduction, and the butt was reinforced with sellotape because his sister's bicycle had run over it. There were five of them to the one of him, but none of their weapons could compare with the half-brick and the corner of concrete block.

They were bigger than him, every one of them was older than his eight years, but then the British army with all its numbers and tanks was bigger than the strength of the Provies. Young Gerard could understand the war that his father had once been a part of, could understand the imprisonment in the Kesh, and after that the frequent disappearances of his father on active service. After a fashion he could understand, too, his father's move away to the South. He had known that his father would come back, come back and belt the enemy, and he had seen the wreckage of the judge's car on the television. He had understood that his father could be arrested, and he had stood by his father when the bastard army had smashed into their home and taken his father. All that he could understand. The confusions began with his father's return at dawn to their home, and the packing, and his Ma

188

crying, and the drive in the armoured police landrover, and the life in the barracks, and the crash of the mortars and the amplified voice, and the helicopter flight, and a bullet bouncing on the floor of the helicopter . . . those were the confusions. Young Gerard could not believe that his father had gone supergrass. A supergrass was the lowest thing that Young Gerard knew of. He thought there must be a motive to what his father had done. He hadn't the age to work out what his father's motive might be, but he had to believe there was a motive because otherwise he was left with nothing to hold.

He was trembling. For a moment he wondered if his father trembled when he held the R.P.G. on his shoulder.

He loved his father. Before his father had come back to their home with the police and the army, he had worshipped his father. Now he could not bring himself to speak to his father. Young Gerard thought that if his attack on the patrol was successful, that then he could talk with his father. He could sit on his father's knee and talk with him, as he'd always talked with him.

Young Gerard rose up from his hiding place behind the hedge. With all his strength he hurled the half-brick at the back of the second boy in the patrol. The brick caught him sickeningly hard between the shoulder blades. As he yelped, he fell. There was a moment of stunned amazement from the boys behind him who saw him toppled over, saw his bright little pistol leap from his hand and into the roadway. Before the source of the missile had been identified, Young Gerard thrust himself through the hedge. His target was the boy with the wooden S.M.G.

He battered the corner of the concrete building block onto the boy's shoulder. He seemed not to hear the scream of pain and fear, again and again he hit the boy with the rough edge of the block. He saw blood, when he hit the boy's ear, and the boy crumpled. Young Gerard grabbed for the wooden S.M.G.

Too late he saw that the boy had learned from the television pictures of the patrols, that he had copied the technique of looping one end of the weapon's lanyard to his wrist. He was tugging the wooden barrel of the S.M.G. and the boy was being dragged across the pavement, and the blood was pumping from the boy's ear, and onto his anorak, and onto the ground.

Because Young Gerard was too late in releasing his grip on the barrel of the S.M.G., they caught him.

The leader smothered him onto the ground. The two other boys dived on top, bursting the air from Young Gerard's lungs. They kneed him, bit him, punched him.

He didn't scream. He scratched back at them, hit back at them.

The boy he had hit with the brick was shouting, and the boy with the wooden S.M.G. was shrieking, and Young Gerard tried to cover his head and his stomach from the raining blows and pains.

189

He thought of his father. He thought only that his father must be able to be proud of him.

He didn't hear his mother's voice, he didn't hear Prentice's pounding feet.

He was lifted to his feet. When the anger mist cleared from his eyes he realized that the minder detective held him by the neck of his collar and lashed the other boy's back, and his mother was trying to free him from the detective, and he kicked with his feet and punched with his hands at the body of the policeman. His fist, small and tight-clenched, hit the shoulder holster under the open jacket. His fingers found the handle of the policeman's pistol and tugged it out.

And suddenly Young Gerard was alone, and Prentice had released him, and the boys were backing and stumbling away from him, and his mother was wide-eyed and staring at him, and he held the pistol in his hand.

Prentice's hand smashed into the side of Young Gerard's head, spun him, dropped him.

He heard his mother cry out.

'You didn't have to belt him.'

'It was armed.'

His mother was kneeling over him, and his hand was empty.

'He's a child . . .'

'It was only on safety, he could have blown us away.'

His mother had her arms around him, protecting him. He felt the warmth and safety of her body.

He heard Prentice say, 'Get him home, Mrs McAnally, just get him back to the house.'

'I fought the Brit bastards.'

He saw that Prentice's shoe covered the pistol, and then the detective bent and picked up the gun, and briefly checked it, and slid it back to his holster.

His mother lifted him up. His enemies were standing back from him, five of them, hating him and frightened of him, as if they wondered if he could still strike once more at them. One of the boys held a red-soaked handkerchief against his ear. His body hurt in every place as he walked away with his mother supporting him. He was close to clinging to her.

'I'm going home . . .' There was a choke in his mother's voice. '. . . I'm bloody going home.'

Between the street lamps it was dark in the street. Young Gerard whose father was a tout, and his mother, and the minder detective, went back to the safe house.

*

190

David Ferris was late for Sunray's evening in the Mess. He had been held up in the Glen Road for an hour with a suspect car bomb, and Felix had been delayed in getting there to clear it. Ferris was in a dismal mood for a party. The guests were local West Belfast. A collection of priests, nuns, school teachers, doctors and principal tradesmen who were to be exposed to what Sunray called the Security Force Point of View.

For the Fusiliers, the Chaplain would be high profile, collar and pealing laugh leading. The Intelligence Officer would be low profile, but flitting and listening because the Commanding Officer believed that there was good intelligence to be gathered. Sunray would greet his guests at the door and then repair to the stove, and his officers would mingle and make small talk and try to cut good figures.

Ferris hadn't changed from his patrol denims. He could smell his own armpits. He was hardly kitted out for winning hearts and turning minds, and he didn't think that the whole bloody thing added up to a row of beans.

He looked around him. He wondered why the guests had bothered to show.

They all looked scared half to death of getting pissed and compromised. After a couple of gins, or a couple of sherries, they were all holding their hand over their glasses, and muttering about taking it slowly. The Mess Orderly found Ferris when he was still close to the door. Ferris took a whisky, and added the measure from another glass on the tray as reinforcement and splashed in a little water. At least the bloody drinks were on the battalion. He saw Sunray at the far end of the Mess, talking to a young priest. Sunray saw Ferris.

'David . . . To me, please.'

The bloody man ran a party as if he had the battalion out on Salisbury Plain.

'On your travels, David, have you come across . . . I'm bad with names?'

'Father Francis, Francis Kane. Have we had the pleasure?'

'David Ferris.' Ferris drained the whisky, looked behind him for more.

'David spends most of his waking hours in Turf Lodge. That's your patch isn't it, Father . . . ?'

'Father Francis . . . Yes, Turf Lodge is in my parish.'

'So, you'll have plenty to talk about.'

Sunray was off.

They eyed each other, Ferris and Father Francis. They would have been close to the same age. At once Ferris realized why he disliked the priest. He was used to men in Northern Ireland dropping away from his stare. The hostility of the young priest was overpowering.

'I don't know why you bothered to come.'

191

'By coming I can understand better you and the likes of you,' Father Francis said.

'I'd have thought that rather than avail yourself of our hospitality, you'd be busy extricating the men of violence from your flock.'

'Extricate yourself from my parish, Mr Ferris, and I'd have no men of violence to contend with. You're the source of the violence, not my parishioners.'

'Nonsense.'

'The principal causes of violence are the presence of a foreign army and a sectarian police force.'

'You believe that?'

'I know that.'

Ferris laughed aloud. 'Do you give that line from the pulpit each Sunday?'

'You're in the wrong place, at the wrong time. Go home, Mr Ferris, to where your efforts are appreciated.'

His whisky was finished. Ferris's voice was growing. He was unaware of the hush around him, of the darting glances of surprise. 'We're forced to stay here because your two communities can't live together in the same cage.'

'What you represent will never succeed here, Mr Ferris. Like all military solutions in Irish history that have been imposed by the British it will fail.' Father Francis smiled sweetly. 'Go home, Mr Ferris. May God speed your journey. And when you go, Mr Ferris, please take with you your tanks and your guns and your concentration camps and your supergrasses and your flag . . .'

Ferris laughed louder. 'That's the one that hurts . . . the supergrass, that's the one that screws your friends . . .'

He saw the flush on the priest's cheeks. 'It's an evil system.'

'Because it puts away the men of evil, is that why it's evil?'

Father Francis looked keenly into Ferris's face. He said quietly, 'What's your interest in supergrasses, Mr Ferris?'

Ferris heard the murmur of uneasy conversation around him. 'It's been a great pleasure to meet you, Father Francis,' he said. He felt that he teetered on a cliff edge. He smiled briskly, and shook the priest's hand.

When he turned away he saw Rennie standing near the door of the Mess. Rennie's overcoat was wet on his shoulders, and he was talking urgently with the Commanding Officer. When he saw Ferris he beckoned him, as if Ferris was Rennie's bloody lapdog.

Rennie was speaking urgently to Sunray.

'. . . So if I can have him tomorrow, that's when I need him. That's good, thank you, sir.'

Sunray curtly nodded his consent.

Rennie said, 'She's going . . . Roisin's walking out on him. We're

192

not arguing with her. From tomorrow morning he's to be on his own.'

'But she's all that's holding him on his feet,' Ferris mouthed.

'Then we're in the market for something else to hold the bugger up . . . I'll call for you in the morning at seven.'

Ferris drank the rest of the party away. He felt he had been separated from the family of the battalion. He was thinking of Gingy McAnally and of Roisin and of Young Gerard and Little Patty and Baby Sean when he became aware of the movement of the guests towards the door. He saw Father Francis waiting in line to pump the hands of the senior officers. He saw the smile break on the clean scrubbed features of the priest.

'That was Mr Rennie I saw you speaking with, I fancy. Interesting man is Howard Rennie. Not bad news he was bringing, I hope.'

15

At a few minutes after seven o'clock in the morning, Roisin McAnally and her children left by taxi from Thiepval barracks.

It had been the worst night of her life. The arguments were still ringing in her head when she woke, when she dressed her children. The arguments had gone on all through the previous evening, from the time that her man had come back from Castlereagh and found the army nurse and the army doctor patching the scratches and anointing the bruises on Young Gerard's face and body. She had told him she was going . . .

He could have his new life, on his own. He could make his new life how he cared. Her life was Belfast. She had lived in no other city. She was buggered if she was going to exchange what she knew for a new life in company with two detectives and their guns.

When she had first said that she was going home, said it to Prentice as they were bringing Young Gerard back to the house, then she had expected that he would fight her on the decision. He hadn't. He'd not appeared to give a damn. Not a flicker of emotion from Prentice when she had sworn that she was going . . .

Later Sean had come to the locked bedroom door, and tried the handle and found it shut on him, and he had banged with his fist on the door. He had shouted through the door. She had heard the desperation growing in his voice, like he'd told the men downstairs that she was just upset, that if he could speak to her he could change her mind, and she had lain in the bed fully dressed with her children close against her body, and she had squeezed the pillows over their ears to shut out the sounds of his pleading.

She had slept hardly at all.

When she was awake her imagination latched onto thoughts and pictures of a new life amongst soldiers and policemen and shoulder holsters and armoured landrovers, a life without friends and without family. When she was asleep fast dreams overwhelmed her, dreams of Sean bleeding in the gutter, and sometimes it was the Sean of today, and sometimes his hair was greying, and sometimes his hair was thinning and white. Always the dreams ended with Sean in the gutter. Whether Sean was shot dead this year, or in ten years, or in twenty years, he was always in the end dead in her dreams. Now she neither hated Sean, nor loved him. She was apart from her man. She was separated by a locked door and by her loyalties. She had chosen Turf Lodge and her family against her man.

In the morning she unlocked her door. From the landing she looked down the stairs to the front door of the house. Prentice was sitting on his chair. To her he seemed fresh, alert, as if he hadn't had trouble sleeping. He ducked his head to acknowledge her.

Prentice smiled up the stairs at her, a grin that gave nothing.

'Would you like some tea, Mrs McAnally?'

'I've not changed my mind.'

'I said, did you want some tea?'

'I'm going home.'

She wondered what sort of home he went back to when he was finished with Gingy McAnally. She wondered what he thought of her, the tout's woman.

'I'd like some tea.'

In the bathroom, she washed her face and hands. The water in the basin was wonderful, hot, and the soap bar was Camay and scented. She had bought the soap in the supermarket with Prentice's money. The shape of the soap was hardly disturbed. She wouldn't have bought soap like that in Turf Lodge, not on the Supplementary Benefit. When she had washed she wiped the soap bar dry with a towel, and took it back with her to the bedroom and put it in her bag.

On tiptoe, hoping that she would not wake her man, she went into the main bedroom. The double bed was empty. She took their suitcase from out of the wardrobe and began to pack her clothes.

'Your tea . . .'

Prentice was in the doorway. She had not heard him on the stairs. He passed her a mug.

'You won't forget anything,' Prentice said lightly. 'You'd hardly want to come back for anything you've forgotten.'

'Where's Sean?'

'Sleeping on the sofa.' Prentice loved to smile. 'He's out on a pill . . .

So don't have any bright ideas of talking him into walking out with you. The pill'll last him through till after you've gone.'

'You don't give a shit for him, as long as he's your fucking puppet in the witness box.'

'I care for him enough to see that you don't take him home.'

'I've the right to talk to my husband.'

'And last night you had the chance, and you turned the key on the chance . . . your tea'll get cold, Mrs McAnally.'

She heard him pad back down the stairs.

She wanted to scream, and she knew that if she screamed that no man would care, that her man would not hear her. She packed carelessly, shovelling the clothes into the case, indifferent to whether they would be creased at the end of her journey.

Back in her bedroom she told the children that they were going home. She told them that they would not be going home with their Da. Young Gerard said nothing, Young Gerard understood, and Little Patty cried and her Ma wanted to hit her. She told her children that they would have their breakfast when they were at their Gran's.

'When'll we see our Da again?' Little Patty's small voice.

'I don't know,' Roisin McAnally lied.

She looked around her. All her possessions were in the case and in two plastic bags. She led the children down the stairs. Prentice was shrugging into an anorak.

'I've rung you a taxi. We'll walk to the gates.'

Goss stood bleary-eyed at the open door of the living room. She stood on her toes and gazed into the room over his shoulder. She could see Sean's head on a cushion on the settee. She could hear the snoring regular breathing of his sleep. Goss stayed his ground, blocked her. She thought she was looking onto the face of a dead man, a dead man in the gutter.

'You bastards, for what you've bloody done to him.'

'Taxis charge waiting time, Mrs McAnally,' Prentice said.

Roisin carried Baby Sean, and she held Little Patty's hand, and Young Gerard walked beside her, and Prentice had taken the suitcase and the two plastic bags. They walked from the married quarters, and away through the administration buildings and came to the main gates. The taxi was waiting, its engine chugging quietly. Prentice opened the door for her, and she slid into the back seat and pulled Little Patty in after her and gestured for Young Gerard to follow, as if she didn't want him to be in the front seat and away from her.

'Pity all your work in the house was wasted, but we're moving on. We'll have him out of here.'

'What's that to me?'

'I'm telling you so you can tell your nasty friends that Sean isn't in Thiepval.'

'I'm not a tout.'

'Quite the heroine, Mrs McAnally. Just tell your friends that mortar bombs into Thiepval won't touch Sean.'

Prentice slammed the door behind her, and then went to the driver's window and passed him a folded note.

'It'll cover where Mrs McAnally wants to go,' she heard Prentice say.

As the taxi pulled away from the gates she turned and saw Prentice through the back window. He watched them go, didn't wave.

It was a journey of several minutes, from the Lisburn barracks to the Turf Lodge estate. She had crossed a chasm.

The houses in the Drive were still darkened when she came to her mother's home.

She knew the driver was a Protestant because when he stopped he just leaned back and opened the door from the inside, and let her crawl out from it with her children and her baggage, and when she was on the street, he slammed the door behind her and drove fast away.

She walked up the front path and rang the bell of Number 12.

'You'll not have had breakfast – I'm taking you where you'll get a decent breakfast,' Rennie said.

Ferris sat numb beside him. Bloody cold, and he had a headache from the night before.

Rennie eased off the speed once he had crossed the Peace Line, once they were clear of Provo territory and back in the land of the Protestant Ascendancy.

It was unfamiliar ground for Ferris. His knowledge of Belfast was confined to the Housing Executive estates on the west side of the city. They came off the main road into Dunmurry, and the shabby streets gave way to wide tree-lined avenues and modern bungalows and substantial detached houses, and the headlights threw up tended gardens that were stocked from the Garden Centres.

Rennie read him. 'Not all Belfast is Whiterock, Turf Lodge, Ballymurphy. There's another life. People round here don't know there's a war going on. They drive into town, they do their work, they come back here. If they come back in the evening and want a meal out, then they head for the country. People round here have never driven through Andersonstown. There's 25,000 buggers in the Security Forces protecting the people round here, and they don't want to know what we're at or why.'

They turned into a cul-de-sac. It was brightly lit, and the pavement sides were swept clean of leaves, and there were names on the gates. It might have been where his mother and father lived. There was a house at the end of the roadway, front door facing them, and Ferris

196

saw the lights burning above the garage door, and above the front door, and on the front corner of the house, and down the side of the house. Rennie had brought him home.

'Because I live here, every bugger in the road looks under his car in the morning to see if it's wired, to see if they've cocked up the address . . . but in my house you'll get a decent bloody breakfast.'

'How do you live with it, not knowing when, but knowing they'll come one day?' Ferris asked.

An old mirthless smile on Rennie's face. He had brought the car to a stop outside the house. He pointed through his window, down to the black plastic rubbish sacks that were by his gate, and Rennie saw the open cardboard box and the glint from the bottles thrown up by the lights.

'But not before breakfast . . .' Rennie said.

Rennie let himself into the house.

Ferris chuckled, embarrassed, because Rennie had to wait in the open door for him while he cleared his rifle, barrel pointing into the rose bushes, and took off the magazine.

It was a careful, tidy home. There were photographs on the walls of the hall, framed, of police presentations, there were potted plants, and he wiped his feet hard on the mat so that his boots wouldn't carry dirt onto the clean, patterned carpet.

'My wife, Gloria . . . David Ferris, dear.'

Ferris shook hands with the woman who waited for them at the entrance of the kitchen. She wore a housecoat, and no cosmetics and her face was lined and he thought that he had found her before the mascara and the foundation could hide the anxiety of a detective's wife.

There was a rich scent of bacon and sausages and coffee. Breakfast was laid.

'Can McAnally survive if his woman doesn't support him?'

'That's sharp for this time in the morning.' Rennie led Ferris to the kitchen table.

Ferris wolfed the food off his plate.

'He's hooked,' Rennie spoke through his mouthfuls. 'Because he's hooked we didn't make a big deal out of her going. We didn't reckon on going into the counselling business. She was a bloody dead loss. She's a mind of her own, that's why she was no bloody good to us. He wants to get laid, right, we'll get him laid. He doesn't need a woman now, he needs a friend . . . and he needs someone he can trust, and he thinks that's you. David, I'd not be doing my job if I didn't bloody milk you.'

Ferris stared down at his plate. 'What's to stop him walking out on you?'

'Without our help? He hasn't a chance . . . David, because you're talking to Gingy you should know why he hasn't a chance. I've never threatened him on what'll happen if he reneges on me, but you should know.'

'What'll happen?' Ferris looked up and into Rennie's eyes. They were grey, dark, pitiless.

'A couple of weeks back there was a fire across the border in Monaghan. A man died in his workshop. He was a watch mender. He did watch mending when he wasn't making P.I.R.A. bombs. It was a bad fire, spread fast, and it trapped the watch mender in his basement. Before we had Gingy we didn't know about the watch mender. The watch mender's down to Gingy McAnally. Believe me, David, if Gingy quits on me then I'd be astonished if some bloody fool 'tec didn't let slip how the watch mender got fried.'

'That's foul, that's . . .'

'Grow up, soldier.'

'That's bloody murder.'

'You're not a boy scout.'

'Why tell me?'

'So you'll be better at telling Gingy that he shouldn't quit . . . You'll have some more coffee?'

And Rennie was on his feet, and away for the pot, and two teenage girls were in the kitchen and gathering lunch boxes and scattering text books, and Rennie was a father and wanting to know about last night's homework. The faces were a blur and Ferris sagged in his chair. One of the girls had snapped on the radio, and the kitchen was filled with music, and Ferris shook his head, to try to smash down a bad dream.

'What are you doing today?'

'Double biology, English Lit, Maths. There's a hockey match this afternoon.'

'We've got netball . . . What are you doing, Daddy?'

'A day in the countryside,' Rennie said affably. 'I'm taking Mr Ferris and a friend of his for a drive in the country.'

A car horn hooted out in the roadway. The girls fled, leaving their music behind them.

'What are we going to the country for?'

'A scenic drive, where you'll be able to persuade Gingy that he shouldn't quit on me.'

Ferris retrieved his rifle from the floor. Rennie slipped on his raincoat, and shouted his goodbyes up the staircase.

There was no rain, only the low howl of the winter wind as they drove out of the cul-de-sac and away towards Lisburn.

The tout's family was back in the Drive.

Word spread through Turf Lodge. The supergrass's woman was back, with the supergrass's brats.

198

The children gathered outside Number 12, because that was where the woman of the traitor and the kids of the traitor were sheltering.

Not a policeman, not a soldier, was seen in the Drive, as the screaming insults flew to the front windows of the semi-detached house.

'Bastard touts . . . they'll stiff your Da, they'll stiff your man . . . How much is they paying your bloody man for his lies? . . . Fucking yellow, that's your man, Mrs McAnally . . .'

Amongst the crowd were relatives of Phonsie McGurr and Brennie Toibin and Fatsy Rawe, and their presence encouraged the crowd, and bricks beat on the front door, and took the glass from the front room windows.

Father Francis came, young and blushing with inexperience.

'Go home, you shouldn't be blaming a good woman. Go home, Roisin's come back to us because she's walked out on the paid perjurer. Roisin has come back to us and turned herself away from the Show Trials . . .'

He cuffed and swiped at a boy who ran forward to get a better aim with a fractured piece of paving stone.

When he came into the house, admitted by Mrs O'Rourke, he found Roisin and her children sheltering on the kitchen floor. She was trembling and red-eyed.

'You took your bloody time,' Roisin spat at the priest.

'I came when I heard.'

'I didn't know it would be like that.'

'They'll be used to you soon and they won't harm you or the children. And now that you are back, there's a man will come to see you and see that all is well.'

'Who will bloody come?'

'He'll be here tonight.'

Father Francis left her, and he went outside and sat down on the front doorstep with his back against the closed door, and the jeering tailed away, and shortly the crowd drifted down the street and dispersed. There were a few of the youngsters who threw stones at the windows of Number 63, only a few because the windows were already broken, and the door was already hanging open, and the inside of Roisin's McAnally's home was already wrecked.

'How long will this go on?'

'Till your man retracts,' her mother said.

'I'll go bloody mad.'

'It'll kill your Da.'

Roisin clung to her children. She couldn't gain the strength to crawl up from the floor. Her mother put the kettle on the rings.

'When the man comes tonight you have to tell him what he needs to know.'

'Why?'

199

'To show that they haven't spoiled you, to show you're still ours.'
She put her hand onto the table, she pulled herself up to her knees.
'I'll help you clear the mess, Ma.'

Rennie was at the wheel, with Gingy beside him and Ferris in the back
seat. Goss drove behind them, always on their tail, with Prentice. Across
Prentice's knee, and hidden by his anorak, was a Stirling sub-machine
gun.

Rennie's scenic drive took them up over the hills from Lisburn and
out past the airport, and through Antrim, and past the waters of Lough
Neagh, and through Randalstown and Castledawson, and away onto
the long open road to the Sperrins, the high rolling moorland mountains.
What had been rain in Belfast was sleet out here, with short showers
of hail. Ferris had seen that Gingy rarely smoked, but he snatched a
cigarette each time that Rennie offered it. Rennie took them off the
main road and into the wilderness beyond Lisnamuck and Moneyneany,
took them onto the side road that was wide enough for a tractor and a
hay load under the summit of Mullaghmore.

It was beautiful, lonely countryside. There were small hill farm buildings of whitewashed stone, and there were barns of rust ochre, set for
shelter in the valleys, and on the bare expanses of the hillsides there
were the scattered grazing sheep. Between the showers, where there
were gaps in the cloud, the sun beamed down with torch pools of light
on the fields and moorland.

They stopped in a picnic site lay-by. There were rough-cut tables and
benches. Christ, Ferris thought, so bloody artificial . . .

Rennie climbed out of the car. He looked pleased with himself. He
slapped his hands together against the cold. McAnally was a city man.
He followed Rennie out reluctantly. Ferris looked up at the looming
brow of Mullaghmore, and then at McAnally's feet, and he saw the
Adidas trainers. Shit, and he had his army boots . . . Shit, it was unreal
to think of McAnally climbing in winter to nineteen hundred feet in
bloody Adidas trainers.

'Get a bit of air in your lungs, Gingy, that's what you need,' Rennie
boomed. 'A good bloody hike's what you want.'

If he stayed with them then there would always be someone to tell
McAnally what he needed, what he wanted, Ferris thought.

There was a cluster of sheep watching them. 'Come on you young
buggers . . .' and Rennie waved towards the summit. 'Goss'll look after
your weapon, David.'

They set off on a springy sheep track.

All so bloody predictable. Prentice shouting from his car that he had
trouble with his indicator lights, and Rennie saying he'd have to help

because Prentice couldn't change his knickers without help and he'd catch them, and Rennie dropping back, and Ferris and McAnally alone on the hillside and trudging away from the parked cars.

In the dips in the ground there were hidden weaknesses in the peat floor, and sometimes McAnally's feet sunk down and were lost in the black mud, and his feet squelched.

Bloody ridiculous, ridiculous even to a moron supergrass.

'You like walking, Mr Ferris?'

'Not a lot.'

'I hate bloody walking.'

'I was at school in the North of England, we used to go for walks, hikes, up in the Lake District, at weekends.'

'You had school at weekends?'

'Yes.'

'And you had to go, bloody walking?'

'I suppose we had to, nobody ever said they wouldn't go.'

'I walked to school, and I walked home, that's all the walking I ever did.'

'Got you out of the house at weekends. Perhaps that's why we didn't mind.'

McAnally grinned. 'We had the aggro to get us out of our houses. Internment aggro when we put the barricades up, when the Turf Lodge was no go to the Brits. We had the Motorman aggro when they came and pulled them down. Up half the fucking night throwing rocks, half fucking asleep at school. What were you doing when we were doing aggro?'

Ferris thought. ''71, '72 . . . I was about ten, I was trying to get to the Grammar School, after I'd finished proper school I used to go to a retired teacher two evenings and Saturday mornings for extra lessons.'

'Did you want to do that?'

'I doubt it.'

'But you did it?'

'My father was pretty keen that I should get to the Grammar School.'

'Why didn't you tell him to fuck off? Why didn't you do what you wanted to do?'

'Because where we lived wasn't like Turf Lodge, Gingy,' Ferris said.

They walked on. If they paused and looked back, then the view beneath them was spreading. The clouds were thickening over to the west and Dungiven and Claudy, and there was the grey blue pencil line of the mountains of Donegal. The going wasn't hard for Ferris, but he was anxious for McAnally. McAnally didn't complain. The track wasn't wide enough for the two of them, and McAnally led, as if that were important to him.

'What's your Da do, Mr Ferris?'

'He manages a bank.'

201

'What does he make?'

'I don't know, I suppose about fifteen thousand.'

'What's that in a week?'

'That's about three hundred a week.'

'Jesus, when I was at home, on the Assistance I pulled in less than sixty.'

'He's been with the bank a long time,' Ferris said lamely.

'Do you get extra if you shoot a Provo?'

'No.'

McAnally turned momentarily to Ferris, his face was cut with disappointment. 'We heard you got extra, that's what we were told.'

'I wouldn't have thought either of us gets overloaded with the truth.'

Three sheep burst from shelter in front of them and stampeded, frightened and clumsy, away from their approach.

McAnally had stopped. He swung round to face Ferris. 'Would Rennie lie to me?'

'What about?'

'I said to him that I'd heard in the papers that a tout was paid fifty grand, he said that was just Provo propaganda. He said that with Roisin and the kids with me that I'd get more than a hundred a week. He said without Roisin and the kids I'd get forty a week. He said that was private, between us, that I wasn't to say about it . . . He said that I'd be found a place to live, that I wouldn't have to pay for anything myself, like the electricity . . .'

Ferris couldn't look at him. Jesus Christ, was that what it was about? Was it about forty pounds a week, and free electricity?

'He said that I'd have people to look after me, after I'd given evidence, and that they'd buy the food, pay for everything. That'd be my spending money, forty pounds a week . . . Would he lie to me?'

'Mr Rennie wouldn't have lied about that.'

Ferris looked at the mud-smear over his boots. Forty pounds a week, the pieces of silver. Touts came bloody cheap.

They achieved a tiny plateau, just a few yards square, and the sheep had cropped the grass short. At the side of this oasis of level ground were old scorch marks of a camp fire. They were open to the wind and to the first spitting pricks of hail on their faces, against McAnally's thin anorak and Ferris's camouflaged tunic. Ferris thought of Rennie warm in his bloody car with the radio on, and probably with a bloody hip flask, and he'd have a bloody great grin on his face as the hail tattooed on the windscreen. He heard McAnally squeal in laughter.

McAnally had bent down, examining something at the edge of the plateau, where it merged into the dead, dropped bracken. Now he stood, and held out between his fingers was a condom sheath. McAnally was cackling with laughter. He put it to his lips and blew hard and filled it like a balloon and let it go and it soared away into the wind and died and dropped in the undergrowth. Ferris swallowed. He felt sick. Kiss a used Frenchie, and you'd kiss any arse in the world, Ferris thought. McAnally was excited. He patrolled the perimeter of the grass.

He found a plastic football. It was caved in, where it had been punctured before being thrown away.

The storm hit them. The hail pellets whitened the ground. McAnally kicked the ball at Ferris. Ferris caught it, threw it back to him to kick it again. On the middle slopes of Mullaghmore, Ferris and McAnally played football, with a soft ball, and Ferris was the 'keeper and McAnally was the striker.

Ferris was the 'keeper because McAnally had to score – the poor bugger had to win something. Ferris remembered when he had been at Junior School, and they had played kick-about football, and there had always been a line in front of the 'keeper over which the strikers couldn't come, so that scoring should not be too easy . . . There was no line on the mountain slope of Mullaghmore. The laughter was gone from McAnally, his face was closed in concentration and effort. McAnally dribbled the ball towards Ferris. He came forward, across where the line should have been, and no shot. Fuck the bugger, because he was coming so close that he couldn't miss, had to win, fuck him. Ferris dived forward, over the ball, cannoning his shoulder into McAnally's legs. McAnally fell, half across Ferris, and his legs were thrashing to get his toe to the ball that was in Ferris's arms and tight against his chest. And their faces were inches apart, and the fury exploded in McAnally, and his hands surged to Ferris's throat. Eye to eye, mouth to mouth, face to face, and the hail lashing down on them . . . and McAnally sagged away, and his fingers loosened from Ferris's throat. He took the ball from Ferris and punted it away, hard and high, and set off towards the summit, blurred in the hail.

Ferris followed him, trotted to catch him.

'Forget it, Gingy.'

McAnally's head was tucked down onto his chest and he had pulled up the hood of his anorak over his short hair. Ferris spoke from the side of his mouth.

'Don't be bloody stupid, Gingy.'

They went on in silence. The winds hit them, reeled and crashed against them, as they stumbled forward towards the cairn of stones at the summit. They left the bracken and the grass and scrambled on their hands and knees over the stone scree to the top of Mullaghmore. Neither man would ask the other to turn back, head for the shelter of the cars. They were dripping from the storm, chilled to the skin.

'I'm wrecked,' McAnally said flatly. 'I'm bloody gone.'

Ferris was shielding his face from the rain. They were huddled close to each other, each trying to gain the protection of the squat cairn of rocks.

'You have to go on with it.'

'There was a reason for touting when I had Roisin, and my kids. I did it for them.'

'You asked about lies, Gingy. That's a lie. You did it to stay out of gaol.' Ferris shouted at him across the wind.

'I did it for my wife and my kids.'

'If you're wrecked, Gingy, you've no one to blame but yourself.'

'Don't fucking shout at me, don't play the big, bloody Brit with me.'

'Facts, Gingy, you did it because you hadn't the bottle to go to gaol.'

'I don't have to go through with it.'

'You're going to give evidence.'

'Smart-arse Brit, you can't touch me, I've got bloody immunity.'

'Try walking out, Gingy.'

McAnally pulled himself to his feet. His hand was on the cairn to steady himself. He yelled down to Ferris, and his arm was waving towards the distant ribbon of the main road. 'I can walk out on you, I don't have to listen to your Brit shit, I can go my way.'

'Go where?'

'Where I don't have a fucking Brit officer preaching at me.'

'Go where, Gingy?'

McAnally said, 'Go anywhere, anywhere I bloody want to . . .'

'You've nothing for a passport, you've nothing for bloody money. How far'll you go without a passport, without money – you've got to earn your precious forty pounds a week.'

'I'll go down south.'

'Like nothing's happened?'

'Like that.'

'But something has happened,' Ferris said.

There was a frost in McAnally's hair, an ice on his anorak from the hail and the sleet. 'I made a statement, others have made statements and retracted. If I walk out, they walk out too – the Chief, Ollie and Joey and Tom McCreevy, they all walk out . . .'

'You told them about a man in Monaghan, a man who mended watches.'

The fear slipped again over McAnally. 'What if I did?'

'You named him. He's dead. He burned to death . . . Gingy, you think that wouldn't get known, you think Rennie would just wave you goodbye? You think Rennie wouldn't let it be known how they fingered the man in Monaghan? Gingy, don't give me that crap about walking out.'

McAnally slid down to sit beside Ferris. He was shivering and squeezing his arms against his body for warmth.

'Would Rennie tell?'

'You're a big clever boy, Gingy. Do you think he'd tell? You named a man, Rennie passed on what you said, the man was burned to death.

That's Rennie's way, that's how far his claws are in you. That's why you won't walk out on him. Don't ask me if I think he'd tell.'

Ferris pulled McAnally to his feet. Into the teeth of the wind they started down the mountain.

'You made me a promise.'

'I did.'

'You promised you'd stand in front of me.'

'Let's hope it doesn't happen.'

'Was that just bloody words?'

'It was a promise, Gingy.'

Ferris held McAnally's arm, to steady him, all the time of the long descent to the picnic lay-by.

Half way down the hill Ferris saw the bird that hovered in the driving wind away to his right. The bird was trying to hold a position through the buffeting. He yelled in McAnally's ear, and pointed to the bird. McAnally looked at the fluttering wing beat of the hunting kestrel. He gazed with a longing at the bird, then ducked his head down and pulled Ferris forward.

When they reached the lay-by, Rennie wound down his window.

'I managed to fix the indicator light. You had a good walk?'

They had done a round dozen of bars between the Sperrins and Thiepval Barracks.

Drunk in charge of two cars were a detective chief inspector of the Royal Ulster Constabulary and a platoon commander of 2 Battalion Royal Regiment of Fusiliers and two detective constables and a super-grass. There was a line of parked cars in Antrim that were paint-scraped from Rennie's tail bumper, and a lorry coming away from the airport had done an emergency stop as Prentice cut him up. Otherwise it hadn't been a bad journey, and McAnally had shown that he could sing.

Prentice and Goss manoeuvred McAnally into the house.

Rennie said, 'You chirped him right up. Bloody well done.'

Since breakfast Ferris hadn't eaten and he had drunk twelve Black-bush and he felt sick.

'Thanks.'

'What did you tell him?'

Ferris swayed in his seat. 'I said that if he didn't quit every Presbyterian Minister in the Province and all the Church of Ireland bishops would sing psalms of gratitude for the arrival of Gingy McAnally.'

'Don't pull my pisser, sonny.'

'I said he was better off alive with forty quid a week of yours in his pocket, than with his pockets empty and a Provo bullet packing his head.'

'Is he going to hold up?'

'I don't know – perhaps, perhaps not.'

'I'll drop you back,' Rennie said.

The man filled the doorway.

The ceiling light in the hallway shone over Roisin's shoulder and onto his face. It was a grim face, pocked and without kindness. She saw the hole in his throat where the stitches had knitted the skin back, a blotch on a white throat.

'It's Roisin . . . ?'

'Yes.'

'We'll try a few drinks first, then a few words.'

'My baby's in the bath.'

'Your Ma'll do your baby.'

'What's your name?'

'Frankie . . . You'll want your coat . . . Frankie Conroy.'

16

There had been singing in the Bar, two young men and a pair of guitars and the amplifiers turned high enough to give them a chance over the talk and the crack.

She wouldn't have chanced her luck on her own, but she'd seen the sour faces soften when Frankie was seen to be her escort. He drank pints of stout, she had three vodka and orange, without ice, because there never was any bloody ice, and he had talked about everything that was nothing to do with Gingy McAnally, her man, going supergrass. Where Frankie sat he held court. Men came to him and nodded to her and then whispered in his ear, and bent their heads down so that Frankie could whisper his answer back. She had known Frankie for many years, since she was young, since before Gingy and the children, everyone knew everyone in the 'Murph and the Whiterock and the Turf Lodge. She had known Frankie when he was a gangling courier of messages for the Organization, when he was a growing man in the Provos, when he came out of the Kesh after the sentence for attempted murder. She had known him as a part of the movement, but she had never before seen the respect that was accorded him that night. The protection of Frankie Conroy was gold dust to her. She recognized that. And she was irritated that she hadn't taken the time to go upstairs at her Ma's and make her face, that she had just slid on her coat and gone with him.

When Frankie took her out of the Bar, he held her arm and steered her between the drinkers. He made a display of her, as if to say that Roisin McAnally had come home to the protection of Frankie Conroy.

He took her out to his car, and drove her away from the estates and up to the slopes of Divis, and he parked in the darkness at the entrance to the rubbish tips. He cut the headlights.

She could hear his breathing, sense the warmth of his body. She stared ahead of her, into nothing.

'How's Gingy?'

'How you'd expect.'

'You did well, telling us where to look.'

'I told my Ma, I didn't know who she'd tell.'

His arm looped behind her and his hand was on her shoulder. He gripped the bones of her shoulder, and if she'd wanted to she couldn't have shrugged him away.

'How'd he take it?'

'The bombs, I didn't see him . . . he was in the hall, I was in the living room . . .'

'How'd he take it, Roisin?'

'I'm not touting on my man. I'm not touting on him just because he's touted on others.'

The fingers bit harder into her flesh, onto her bones. 'How'd he take it?'

The pain was cruel in her shoulder. 'Shaking, frightened.'

'Did he see the bullet?'

'That was bloody evil, how did you . . . ?'

'Did he see the bullet?'

'He was pig screaming at the bullet. It was in the helicopter.'

His hands spread over her. A hand tugging up her sweater and her vest from the waist of her jeans, and a hand grappling with the bra fastener at her back. Calloused hands on her skin. And the taste of his beer and his cigarettes on her mouth.

'Is he going to follow you?'

'He's frightened as a dog. He'll come back.'

'How soon?'

'Without the soldier he'd be back now . . .'

He had loosened the fastener. His hands were on her breasts.

'Get your hands off me.'

She was wriggling to be away from him, clawing at the hand that cupped her breast. And he was laughing at her.

'You going to fight me, you going to fight Frankie Conroy?'

'Get your filthy fucking hands off me.'

'Heh, Missus, you start shouting . . . Who's coming to help a tout's woman? Without me you're in bad shit. You be bloody thankful you're with me . . .'

He was huge, heavy, overwhelming her. His hands were away from her breasts and scraping at the zip of her jeans. She brought her knee up sharply into his groin, and he gasped, and sagged away from her. He was staring at her, panting.

'You come near me again and you'd better have a saucepan over it. I'll kick it till it's fucking blue.'

'Without me . . .'

'You don't buy me, Frankie Conroy . . . If I want to get laid, I get laid. But I don't get laid on anyone's say so. I want to take my trousers off, I take them off, I don't need any lout telling me.'

'You hurt me.'

'Keep your hands under your bum.'

There was a slow smile on Frankie's face that was dimly lit from the dashboard. He shrugged. She leaned forward, and without thinking Frankie refastened the bra catch. Frankie's arm was round her shoulder, but gently. She stared up at the car roof.

'What'll happen to him?'

'We'll try to kill him.'

'If he comes home?'

'He's gone, Missus. To us he's dead. To Turf Lodge he's dead. You walked out on him. He's dead to you.'

Frankie lit two cigarettes, passed one to her.

'Who's with him?'

'Rennie's there . . . There's one called Prentice, one called Goss.'

'Is one of them the soldier?'

'What's it to you?'

'Don't mess with me, Missus. You came back, remember. You came back to your people . . .'

'You want me to tout on my man, so's it's easier for you to kill my man.'

'You help Frankie Conroy and you might just be able to live in Turf Lodge. You mess me and fuck knows where you're going to have to run to. Didn't you think it out, Missus?'

Jesus, that was rich. When was the time to think it out? With the mortars landing, with the loudspeaker, flying from Palace to Lisburn with a bullet bouncing on the floor, bloody good time to think it out. With Young Gerard pointing a loaded pistol at Prentice, with the door locked on Gingy's shouting, bloody good time . . .

'I didn't think it out.'

'You'll think it out now.'

'Yes.'

She had Young Gerard and Little Patty and Baby Sean, and she had her Ma, and she had a house in Turf Lodge.

'Who counts with Gingy?'

A small voice. 'The soldier.'

'Who's the soldier?'

'The one that took him the first time.'

'What's the soldier's name?'

'He's from the barracks at Springfield.'

'What's his name?'

'Ferris . . .'

'Why's he special?'

'He's the one Gingy listens to.'

'His name's Ferris, and he's Springfield? Thank you, Missus. You're back with your own.'

'You don't have to kill him.'

'Gingy? What's he to you now?'

'He's my husband, he's the . . .' Her voice died. She took the handkerchief from the sleeve of her jersey and noisily blew her nose. 'He's my man, you bastard.'

He drove her back to her mother's house.

He leaned across her, opened her door for her.

'You don't have to kill him.'

'Might not have to do anything to him.'

Rennie put down the telephone and went back into the living room.

McAnally was on the settee. He was lying on his back snoring and there was a blanket over him. He looked at peace, as if his mind had shut down. Best thing for him, to be pissed and not be dreaming. Goss was feeding himself instant coffee.

Prentice turned from the window.

'Marching orders?'

'You've drawn the jackpot, John. Christmas in a U.K. army camp. You two, and him. You fly tomorrow morning.'

'About time.'

'Time to make the bugger start earning his keep.'

Prentice looked at Rennie. 'He's got to learn to stand on his own feet, without Ferris holding him up. That's the difficulty.'

'Right now I'm just thankful he's standing. I'm not fussed who's propping him.'

'You can't walk away from the difficulty, Mr Rennie . . .'

He was tired, he wanted to be home. Suddenly Rennie was bored sick with the supergrass, with the 'difficulty' of the supergrass. He

209

exploded, 'So McAnally needs his soldier friend to keep him standing, so he has him, so he will continue to have him . . .'

'He won't stand up without him, Mr Rennie.'

'He will continue to have him.' He savaged the two young detectives with his gaze. Rennie remembered the days when convictions were obtained by evidence. The days of fingerprints, and of identification parades, and the matching of fibres of hairs under microscopes, the days of interrogation. These two detectives were spoiled brats. Their police work was done for them by an informer. Lazy spoiled brats, because all that was asked of them was to keep the informer on his feet until his time came for the witness box . . . The anger evaporated. He thought that he could be a boring old bugger when he tried, and he wanted his bed and his woman's backside against his, and he wanted Sean Pius McAnally out of his mind.

'You don't have to shout, Mr Rennie.'

'I'll see you in the morning, lads, and thanks . . .'

He had the back room of a widower's terraced house off Beechmount. He was a good tenant, paid regular. Bank money and Post Office money, rolled in the South, and changed in the border villages from Punts to Sterling, enabled Frankie to pay his rent on the nail.

It was a small room. Bed, table, chair, and a wardrobe. The widower swept up after him because he paid regularly and he paid above. He drew a hundred a week from the Organization and forty a week from the Unemployment. He was supported by the South's taxpayers and the United Kingdom's taxpayers, and between the two of them they gave him enough for his needs. He would have needed more, of course, if he had had a wife or a steady woman living in. There never had been a wife. There had been a girl who might have been a wife until she went away. The girl was in her eighth year in Armagh prison, pub bombing and Frankie had never been much at writing letters, and worse at visiting.

Lying on his bed Frankie Conroy squirmed with pleasure at the thought of Roisin McAnally, and the thought of what she had given him.

The name of Ferris.

David Ferris of the Royal Regiment of Fusiliers, who were garrisoned at Springfield Road.

In his mind he saw a cripple who moved with the help of a crutch. The crutch kicked away, and the cripple fell helpless, and the crutch was the soldier called Ferris.

He'd not have believed it, that Gingy McAnally would depend himself on a Brit officer.

*

The Chaplain had come to talk.

The cross on his shoulder flash gave him an access to the officers and men alike that was denied to any other man in the battalion.

From the gap under the door he saw that the ceiling light was on. He eased the door open. He smelt the reek of whisky.

After the night in the Mess he had chided himself for not taking a keener interest in young Ferris. There was no doubt that he *was* bending – not cracking, not yet, just bending – anyone in the Mess and hearing Ferris and the little wart of the local clergy could have recognized that Ferris was bending. He might have left it a few more days, but he had come from the Intelligence Officer's room, and there he had heard the gossip that Ferris had come back drunk from his day out with the police. Word of it had not yet reached the Commanding Officer. Sooner or later it would, and if the Chaplain wasn't quick about it, he would be too late to salvage the record of David Ferris.

He saw on the floor an ugly heap of wet uniform and a pair of muddy boots. Ferris was asleep on the top blanket, in his vest and underpants and his socks. He held against his face a sheet of notepaper, a handwritten letter. Moving carefully, the Chaplain gathered up the clothes, carried them like a housewife to the hot radiator pipes and hung them out.

The Chaplain closed the door and went as discreetly as he had come. No point in waking the poor devil. He knew Ferris's file, knew all the officers' files, he knew of the failed University entrance and the failed Special Air Service application, but for all those failures he was a good young man, conscientious and sincere, a bit of a prig but nothing of a snob. He wanted to do right by Ferris.

He went to Sunray's room, found him pyjama-clad and writing a letter.

'What's your prob, Billy, temporal or spiritual?'

'Young Ferris, Bravo Company . . .'

'Quite wretched behaviour in the Mess. I haven't caught up with him yet.'

'He's under stress,' the Chaplain said flatly.

'Every man here's in stress.'

'His normal soldiering, that's one thing, but his dealings with the police are too much on top. The I.O. tells me they're using him to hang onto their prize supergrass. That's why he's in a bad way.'

'Have you got him outside?'

'He's out on his feet. He's drunk, I am afraid.'

'God Almighty.'

'Ship him out, sir, if you can, three days, four days, give him some leave.'

'We're a week from Christmas, Billy, we'd all like some leave.'

'He's doing two jobs here, when the rest of us have one.'

'We're all flat out.'

'I'll put it another way, sir . . . You have allowed one of your officers to be manipulated by the police . . . I wouldn't have thought the police will be greatly concerned with young Ferris once they've bled him for what he's worth to them. They'll drop him like he never existed.'

'That's rather bold, Billy.'

'Do you like what he's doing, sir?'

'I wasn't asked.'

'And neither was he . . . What he needs now is help, not a reprimand. He's one of your best young officers. He's worth helping. He's got a lovely girl at home, and when he's done the right thing by her, as I'm sure he will, he'll lose a few of these sharp edges, and he'll be a better soldier for it. I'm going to be bolder, sir . . .'

'I'm sure you are.'

'By allowing Ferris to get mixed up in this squalid affair, I don't think you've done him well.'

Sunray grinned. 'You're bloody preaching, Billy. You're hiding behind your cloth . . . you'll take a wet?'

'I'll have a drink, if you'll give him three or four days.'

'You'll have to concoct some fool excuse for it.'

'Whisky, please.'

A Wessex helicopter lifted Sean Pius McAnally and his minders from Thiepval to the Royal Air Force section of Aldergrove Airport. Rennie didn't take the ride, he contented himself with an early morning lecture to the informer in the front room of the house. He told him he was saving lives, he told him that whatever he had done in the past could be wiped out by his evidence. He used thick paint to make the images of widows and fatherless children. Nothing too sophisticated for a creature like McAnally.

Through the helicopter's porthole windows as it rose above Lisburn McAnally could see the city in which he had lived all his life before the escape to the caravan in the South. It was a rare sunny morning, and the light caught the rows of grey houses that were the estates of West Belfast, and he could see the needles of smoke rising from the chimneys before the sweep to the west and the run to the airport. He sat on his own opposite Prentice and Goss.

There had been no calls for Prentice to make. There was no one in his life who would care whether he was out of the city for the holiday. Goss had spoken to his fiancée. He would be away over Christmas, and it wasn't a bloody holiday, and no, he couldn't say where he was going.

At Aldergrove they were told they were late, that the Hercules transporter had been held for them. They were hurried across the tarmac

212

from the helicopters' park to the aircraft. There were ground crew round the Hercules, muffled against the cold, and they looked with shameless curiosity at the three passengers. They could recognize policemen, something in the manner, something in the walk, but the man between them was the odd man out. Way out. The Adidas trainers on McAnally's feet were still mud-caked, and his jeans were torn, and his anorak was too thin for this cold, and his head was ducked down as if he were fearful of being recognized.

The Hercules was carrying freight. They were found three canvas-bottomed seats forward in the fuselage, close to the bulkhead ladder up to the cockpit, they were shown the piss bucket. They were led to believe they were a bloody nuisance for delaying take off.

Over the roar of the engines revving for power, Prentice said, 'Good case for a Redeye. If any of your friends have a spare heat-seeker lying around then these buggers should be first on the list.'

Goss thought it a hell of a crack. Gingy McAnally didn't laugh, the men in the city who had the rockets and the Armalites and the Kalashnikovs and the Remingtons and the Thompsons were no longer his friends. The men in the city who might one day lay their hands on a heat-seeking Redeye missile would be glad to fire it up his arse.

The Hercules lumbered into the air.

Temporarily Belfast was behind Sean Pius McAnally.

He was tall, he had no belly on him, he always carried a rifle, he was the only officer who came out on foot patrol in Turf Lodge.

That was where Frankie Conroy started. And he built on that small foundation, gathering bricks of information.

He learned that in the mornings the patrols were mostly in open landrovers and that in the afternoons they came on foot. You wouldn't be setting a clock on it, but mostly the foot patrols came as the light was going. There was one platoon from Springfield that did the Turf Lodge, it was pretty much always the same platoon. They used the eight-man patrol, four on each pavement. Those that he asked didn't question why the information was required, merely gave him help and closed the door on him.

When he had established the pattern of patrolling in Turf Lodge, cursorily and not at firsthand, he sought out the driver of a delivery van. The van was regular round the Upper Falls and the Whiterock. By the familiarity of its rounds the van had a certain immunity from search, and the driver always had a smile for the troops and the police at road block checks.

'You want a bloody Armalite? What for?'

'For a snipe.'

213

'On whose say?'

'My say.'

'Brigade has to say it.'

'Brigade's in the Crumlin Road gaol.'

'How long would you want it for, just an afternoon?'

'Four or five days, till I've done my snipe.'

'That's daft, you'll not get an Armalite for that time, not without someone's say-so.'

'It's my say-so . . . when the Chief's out, it would go bad for the man who didn't help with an Armalite to speed him out.'

'To get the Chief out . . . ?'

'And all those with him.'

The driver shrugged. 'It's on your head.'

'Your neck if I don't get an Armalite.'

Frankie fixed his rendezvous for the collection of a weapon and a full magazine.

The days and the nights drifted closer to Christmas, and Frankie found for himself the detail of Turf Lodge. Of course he had a map, but a street map told him nothing. For two days he padded the pavements by day, and was a fleeting shadow figure in the darkness of the night as he examined the back entries to the houses and their back fences and their back gardens. Carol singers moved through the estate, and the mothers and children came from the city in the black taxis with arms bulging from shop-wrapped parcels, and the men who were in work laid in drink for the holiday, and a sort of truce invaded the area.

If the sniping of the soldier had been given to an A.S.U. then it would have been simple work. One on the gun, one on the lookout, one with the covering fire, one to drive the getaway . . . But Frankie was alone. He searched in Turf Lodge for a sniping site . . . If an A.S.U. was making the hit then a house could be taken over. That was standard. The family held and the marksman in the front bedroom to while away the hours till target time . . . But Frankie on his own could not hold a family and snipe.

There was a house on the corner of the Drive and the Crescent. The house was derelict. The last woman who had lived there had been prominent in the Peace Movement, and when her windows had been broken and she had gone overseas with her husband and her children the mob had finished inside what they had started outside. The final act had been to pour petrol over the hallway and ignite it. Turf Lodge had hated the Peace Movement women, seen them as Brit stooges, and Prot stooges, and as traitors to the community. When the petrol was poured, when the match was thrown, one of the raiding youths had been still inside, and upstairs. It was said later that he had been trying to wrench the taps off the bath. The youth burned to death and in the perverse way of Turf Lodge the death that had been agonized and noisy was

214

blamed on the Peace Movement women. In the lore of the community the house was tainted. It had never been made habitable. It had been boarded up with chipboard by the Housing Executive workmen and abandoned. Frankie reckoned the combination of the first floor small bedroom and the next door bathroom could give him a shot down either the Drive or the Crescent. It had to be a daylight shot . . . None of the street lights functioned within two hundred yards of the junction . . . no bloody way an officer could be identified in darkness, and no bloody way that Frankie would ever get his hands on an Image Intensifier Night Sight.

Frankie Conroy had played the big man in the private room of the bar in Clonard, and he had put his weight around the man who would provide the Armalite. Frankie Conroy had let it be known that he had dedicated himself to breaking Gingy McAnally, and winning the freedom of the Chief and Brigade Staff and Battalion Staff. Frankie Conroy had opened his fat fucking mouth. Easy enough to open his mouth before it was a daytime shot and a charge across the back fences to a getaway car that didn't have the bloody engine switched. Because he had opened his fucking mouth, he was afraid.

He had no woman, he had no children, he was alone.

He drove to the Andersonstown supermarket. He bought a box of coloured lights, and three packets of tinsel glitter, and outside he paid four pounds for a Christmas tree. He went to the Drive, to Number 12.

He carried the lights and the tinsel and the tree to the door, and rapped the knocker.

She opened the door. He had hoped it would be her that came to the door.

'What's that for?' Roisin asked coldly.

He thought she looked bloody awful. She hadn't bothered with her hair, and her face was pasty pale, and there were grey sacks beneath her eyes.

'For you and the kids,' Frankie muttered.

She sighed, her hands were on her hips, sud-covered. 'It's going to be a *great* Christmas . . .'

Inside he could hear Mrs O'Rourke scolding, and Little Patty crying.

'Better here than where you were,' Frankie said.

Without warning, the voice, the foreign accent, belted his ears.

'Good evening, Mrs McAnally . . .'

Frankie spun. He hadn't heard the footsteps of the soldiers.

'. . . Getting ready for the festive season?'

Frankie stared into the young face of the officer. Tall and with no belly and carrying a rifle, and standing by the gate. There was a grin curling the officer's mouth, as if he were teasing a puppy.

'. . . Have a very Merry Christmas, Mrs McAnally.'

The soldiers on the far pavement ran forward, moving away. The officer looked behind him, then trotted off.

'That's him,' Roisin whispered. 'That's your Ferris.'

She took the tree and the lights and the tinsel from him and closed the door on him.

Before, there had been a name locked in Frankie's mind. In place of the name there was now a face.

'It was all pretty routine . . . I've nothing for you really,' Ferris said.

'You were pavement bashing more than three hours, there must have been something.' The Intelligence Officer sipped at his coffee. He hadn't offered Ferris a mug.

Ferris said, 'It's not my fault if they take a day off from running round with Armalites. Turf Lodge, Whiterock, were just anywhere that's getting ready for Christmas. Bags and parcels and shopping, that's about it.'

'Did you consider that any of those bags and parcels and shopping might be the cover for the movement of weapons, of explosives? Did you open any of those bags and parcels and shopping?'

'I didn't.'

'That's damned lame, David.'

'Well, I didn't.'

The sarcasm spat from the Intelligence Officer. 'Your *especial* knowledge of the P.I.R.A. would surely have told you that they don't hang up their boots because it's Christmas.'

Ferris grinned. What a boring arsehole, he thought. On this tour the I.O. would have put in as much foot slogging as he, Ferris, endured in a couple of days.

He said brightly, 'I saw Mrs McAnally.'

'Did you call in for tea?'

'A chappie was dropping a Christmas tree off at her door, that's all.'

'What did she say to you?'

'I wished her a Merry Christmas . . . she didn't reciprocate.'

'Who was the chappie?'

'I don't know.'

'It's S.O.P. to do a P.-check on any man at a Provo house.'

'Well, I didn't,' Ferris said. He wanted to get the hell out. Yes, it was Standing Operating Procedure to do a Person check on anyone calling at a suspect address, and he hadn't.

The Intelligence Officer looked curiously at him. 'You alright, David?'

' 'Course I'm alright,' Ferris flared. 'Why shouldn't I be alright?'

'Sky pilot's been asking for you.'

Ferris went in search of the Chaplain. He was angry with himself. Of course he should have done the check on the man with the Christmas tree. He found the Chaplain writing a letter for a Fusilier from Headquarters Company. He waited at the door. The little bugger couldn't write his own letter home to tell his Ma that his girlfriend was in the family way, and there'd be a wedding at the end of the tour. Ferris shuddered. If the army was somewhere in between eighteen-year-old Fusiliers who couldn't write and arseholes like the I.O. then it had to be scratching when it came to solving the bloody Province's problems. Now he snorted . . . Bloody Provo house, bloody load of rubbish. He thought there was more charity waiting for Roisin McAnally in Turf Lodge than there would be in a police safe house. He thought the chappie had looked quite decent, the one who'd brought her the Christmas tree. He thought she might just have been right, doing what was best for her kids, walking out on Gingy. Poor Gingy, he might just have been wrong . . . The trouble with arseholes like the I.O., stuck in an office, or in Operations, or in the Mess, was that they saw every male between fourteen years old and seventy as a Provo, and every woman too . . . He had been far away, and the Fusilier was thanking the Chaplain and squeezing past him, and the Chaplain was making nice noises, and carting him off to Sunray.

Hard to believe what the Commanding Officer told him.

'This is a caring battalion, David. We care for our men, and we care for their families. I know you've been to see him a couple of times, but you may not have heard. Sergeant Tunney has been transferred to England for burns treatment. I'd like Mrs Tunney to know that we care for his welfare, and for hers. I think she'd appreciate it if you were to visit him, in England. He'll have Mrs Tunney and his children at the hospital over Christmas. I thought the New Year would be a good time for you to go over . . . I reckoned you'd be away three days. Adjutant'll fix your movements . . . Your policeman rang me. The informer's been shipped out of the country, until his case comes up, I expect. I'm glad that preoccupation's over . . . That's all, David, and never forget that this is a caring battalion.'

Out in the corridor, Sunray's door closed on them, the Chaplain said, 'First-class idea of his. Your presence will be of great comfort to Mrs Tunney . . . I like that, a caring battalion . . . You'll be in good voice tomorrow night, Christmas Eve carols in the vehicle park, another of the old man's good ideas.'

'He's not about to join the human race, is he?' Ferris smiled.

*

217

Under the cover of darkness, Frankie Conroy entered the house on the junction of the Drive and the Crescent. By torchlight he climbed the damaged staircase, testing his weight on each step. He had prised away the chip boarding on the window.

He preferred to come at night, and he had prepared himself for a bivouac. He carried an Armalite rifle, a sleeping bag and a rucksack in which were two cartons of milk, a dozen slices of ham, a loaf, and a supermarket fruit cake. At the bottom of the rucksack was a can of Harp, for Christmas Day.

The bastard officer better come on Christmas Eve. A fucking good Christmas it would be, stuck in the house, if the officer didn't patrol on Christmas Eve.

On the landing he switched off the torch and groped his way into what had been the front small bedroom.

He laid out his sleeping bag, and made the rucksack for a pillow, and propped the Armalite against the dark, charred, stinking wall, and settled himself to wait. His hands were damp wet under the rubber kitchen gloves that he wore.

17

The patrol moved out.

For a few seconds the gates of the Springfield barracks were opened sufficiently to permit the soldiers to squeeze through. As the gates swung shut on them they sprinted away up the Springfield Road. Ferris had taught his platoon always to run for the first fifty yards from the barracks' gates. He had learned that at Crossmaglen on the South Armagh border. At XMG the squaddies came out of the barracks like it was the Greyhound Derby, like they thought there was a chance of catching the hare. The departure from the barracks, and the return, were the two most vulnerable moments for the patrol, and Ferris had drilled the message into the heads of his platoon.

They dashed for their first cover, for a lamp post, for a doorway, for a parked car. They seemed to scatter without cohesion, but when those first crouched hiding places were found the patrol had established its pattern. Eight men, four on each side of the road, and the officer on the righthand side and third in the 'brick', and Fusilier Jones behind him and walking backwards because the protection of the officer's back was his first priority.

It was a few minutes after three o'clock in the afternoon. There were

218

no clear-cut shadows for them because the sun hadn't been seen that day, and there was a light mist rain. The cars and vans had their side-lights switched on already.

Sometimes trotting, sometimes walking, sometimes stationary and watching, the patrol covered the Springfield Road. They passed the Kashmir Road and Cupar Street entrances to the Nationalist enclave of Clonard; a bad place, a place to be wary of if you hadn't celebrated your nineteenth birthday and you were wearing the beret and the red and white Fusilier hackle of 2 R.R.F. Past the Mackie's factory gate, the pride of the Protestant engineering industry, where the squaddies relaxed. On towards Nationalist Ballymurphy, and past the barricades across the Springmartin Road that were in place to frustrate the attack routes and the escape routes of random sectarian assassins, whether they were coming from Protestant Springmartin to prey on Catholic Ballymurphy, or vice versa.

On and into Ballymurphy. Off the wide Springfield Road, and into the estate, into Divismore Way and Glenalina Road, and heading for the Ballymurphy Bullring. They'd have liked to have had a bloody British squaddy alone in their bullring, liked to have tossed knives and swords in his guts, and stoned him till he was bleeding . . . Christ, and it was Christmas Eve, and he didn't usually think like that, didn't usually loathe the natives, one and all, and lump them together as if each and every bloody one was a Provo-lover.

'Been a sight better off in the rovers, sir.' Behind Ferris came the bleat from Fusilier Jones.

'You'll be back in time for the carols, Jones.'

'That wasn't what's bothering me, sir.'

'Chilblains playing up?'

'Bloody footrot's playing up.'

'Footrot won't be your problem if you don't open your eyes and shut your mouth, a bloody bullet up the arse'll be your problem.'

'Just so, sir.'

Hard enough to drill into the soldiers the need for patrolling, and harder still to persuade them that foot patrolling was more effective than riding in the landrovers. Ferris reckoned that he and his squaddies could see and note twice as much when they were on foot as they could from a vehicle. The bloody police were never out of their landrovers. The squaddies each had a sheet page of photographs for the week, to memorize. Mug shots of the top men on the wanted list who might frequent these West Belfast estates. The photographs were pretty awful, and they'd all have grown beards or cut them off, but at least it was bloody trying . . . Men wanted for the Maze escape, and for the kidnapping across the border, and for all the little jollies that kept them busy.

They were in the Bullring. They were surrounded by the grey walls of the estate's houses, and the grey roofs, and the aerosol graffiti of

Provo power . . . The thought was a recurring tick in Ferris's mind. If he had lived in Ballymurphy, or Whiterock, or Turf Lodge, and the British army had come through twice a day with their cocked rifles and their swagger, then would David Ferris have been a Provo . . . ?

There was a pretty girl coming past the patrol on the far pavement. She'd be fifteen, she still had her looks, she'd have faded in a few short years, she'd be bloody ancient at twenty if she stayed in the Bullring, Ballymurphy. He heard the banter of the squaddies as the girl came past them. Crude little sods, David Ferris's squaddies.

'Will you bloody shut up,' Ferris shouted. He saw the faces of the soldiers spin to him in surprise that gave way to resentment. 'Just bloody concentrate on what you're doing.'

Because he had shouted at them in the hearing of the girl and the woman who was banging her front mat on the garden gate post and of the women who were talking beside the leaning lamp post, they were coldly angry. But their eyes were back on the rooftops and the upper windows, back on the street corners, and on the car reversing on the far side of the Bullring.

'Do as your teacher tells you,' the girl cackled. 'Do as he tells you, or the Provies'll get you.'

It had started to rain more heavily. The girl had gone her way, but her shrill laugh hung around the patrol. It would be the talk of the Bullring, that an officer had shouted at his men.

The patrol came out of Ballymurphy and into the Whiterock Road. Two police landrovers passed them, the rifles jutting uneasily from between the rear doors. The squaddies ignored the landrovers, but each man was pleased to see them after the loneliness of the estate. The landrovers seemed to say to them that they were part of a larger brotherhood.

The rain ran from Ferris's beret down onto his nose, down across his mouth. It would rain, but it wouldn't snow. Not cold enough for snow.

He wondered where Gingy was and why Rennie hadn't telephoned him or called by for him. Bloody silly, to feel as if he had been stood up by a girl, because Rennie hadn't called by, and he didn't know where Gingy was . . . he reckoned that Gingy McAnally's would be a black bloody Christmas, snow or no snow.

At the top of the Whiterock, the patrol P.-checked a group of youths. They gave their names. The names were radioed back to Springfield Road Ops Room, and fed to the computer. Every name was clean.

The pace of the patrol quickened as they came to the northern end of Turf Lodge. Downhill, half way through the bloody patrol.

He was almost certain of it. If he had been brought up in Ballymurphy or Whiterock or Turf Lodge, he would have been a Volunteer.

220

They hurried past the big Christian Brothers Primary School before swinging back into the narrow streets of the Turf Lodge estate.

He had been in the house for twenty hours.

In the night a tramp had come and rattled at the back door to see whether it was fastened, and not found the place where Frankie Conroy had made his entry and replaced the chip-board window cover. Other tramps had been in the house, the smell told him, and the slime he had slid on at the top of the stairs. In the morning he had eaten a little of his food. He had been hungry and cold in his sleeping bag, but only a little of the food because he had determined to wait for the officer, for as long as it took. Difficult to eat in the gloves that hid the points of his fingertips from anything he touched. At lunch time he had heard two young voices outside the kitchen door, and giggling, and after a few minutes he had seen a girl slip away into the Crescent tucking her blouse into the waist of her skirt, and a boy followed her a minute later.

When he crossed between the small front bedroom and the bathroom he walked on his toes, and with whatever care he took the boards creaked, and the sounds seemed to him to scream in the empty house. From daybreak he had been continuously on the move, between the two rooms, searching down the Drive and then down the Crescent, hunting for the patrol.

It was the half light now, the light that he wanted, the grey light. It would be right for him if they came at this time. He checked his watch. If they came within ten minutes, fifteen minutes, it would be good for him. Not after fifteen minutes. He wouldn't have the half light after fifteen minutes.

Backwards and forwards, between the two rooms, Frankie Conroy watched and waited for his target. He could come close to the broken glass of the windows, where the chip-board had rotted in the weather, because he had smeared his face with blackening from the damp charred beams at the top of the stairs. His features merged with the darkness of the interior of the derelict house.

Each day since she had been back, her Ma had told Roisin that she should get herself down to Gingy's people. On the afternoon of Christmas Eve she had exhausted her excuses, which had nothing to do with her dislike of them at any time and her unwillingness to speak to them at this time.

Mrs Chrissie O'Rourke had persisted. The McAnallys had the right to see their daughter-in-law, wasn't their fault that Gingy had done what he had.

Her kids didn't need her for an hour, her Ma didn't need her in the kitchen, she had no reason not to go.

The tree stood well in the living room, the lights twinkling into the gloom behind the drawn curtains, and the tinsel was bright and glittering, and the fire was lit and the kids had the telly and were watching B.B.C. with the bloody Brit accents and were sticking the links of a paper chain, and weren't arguing. Her kids didn't need her. Her Ma was baking, and the kitchen wasn't big enough for two to be working there.

Her Da was coughing upstairs. Her Ma said that her Da might get up for Christmas lunch and try some breast of chicken.

She couldn't take her Ma lecturing. It was easier to go and see the McAnallys than scratch another excuse together, and fight.

She had to walk the length of the Drive, almost to the junction with the Crescent. She had to walk past her home. There had been workmen there the previous day, making a start at sealing the broken windows. They'd come to her Ma's and then they had gone down the Drive to Number 63. After the holiday she'd have to find out when they could get her furniture back. She couldn't live with her Ma, not permanent. She'd have to get back to her own home after Christmas. It didn't look like her own home, not with the wood sheets guarding the windows and broken glass up the front path. But if she didn't go back into her own home after the holiday then the house would be lost to her, would become like the house on the junction with the Crescent that had been burnt and abandoned.

There were never any bloody men to be seen in the Drive, always only the women. There were two women struggling along the pavement, loaded with their shopping, dropped by a black taxi on the Glen Road. They neither of them noticed her, though she had to get off the pavement to let them by. They, neither of them, looked at her, smiled at her. Bitches . . .

Frankie Conroy took me out the first night I was back, isn't that fucking good enough for you? Bitches . . .

And it would bloody go on. If she had a legal separation from Sean, if she had a civil divorce, she would still be known in the Drive as the tout's woman, and he'd be across the papers for the Magistrate's court, and he'd be on the telly with his Crown Court evidence. She'd be bloody known for ever as the tout McAnally's woman. The women with their shopping wouldn't look at her until they were past her, then they'd bloody look at her. They'd look at her back.

They lived at Number 97.

The aerosol heroes had been active. The walls beneath the front windows were all sprayed.

'Touts will be stiffed.'

'Provos Rule, Not Traitors.'

'No Show Trials. No Paid Perjurers.'

It was like a house where there had been a bad death. There were good deaths and bad deaths. There were deaths that were natural. It was like a house where there had been a bloody awful death.

She knew Sean's father as a big man, bigger than his son. He had shrivelled. She had never seen his shoulders gone before, not when his son was off to the Kesh, not when he was running, not even when he quit and went down South. Sean's father seemed to thank her with his eyes at the doorway, for coming.

'You'll have a cup, we'll put the kettle on.'

Sean's mother smiled at Roisin vaguely, from the kitchen door at the back of the hall. She understood the look, she knew what the Valium did, or the Librium, or whatever new pill it was that the doctors were peddling. She was shown into the front room. She looked straight for the mantelpiece. She saw the photograph frame. She had given them the photograph frame for Christmas three years earlier to hold the photograph of Sean in his confirmation suit. She saw the frame was lying face down. She saw that his father and mother couldn't look at the face of their son.

Sean's father blurted, 'I'd kill him myself, God forgive me, but I'd kill him . . . Does he know what he's done to us? . . . When we went to Mass, the Sunday after he'd gone supergrass, do you know that no one would sit near us, not in our row, not in front of us, not behind us . . . You seen his mother, you wonder she's like that . . .'

'I tried to tell him.'

'Why . . . his mother keeps asking me why he did it . . . So he got himself caught, but there's plenty of fellows get caught, the Kesh is full of them, but he didn't have to do this to us.' Sean's father pleaded for the answer. 'Will he change his mind?'

'He doesn't have a mind any more, not of his own,' Roisin said.

Sean's mother came into the front room. She was carrying two mugs of tea and her hands were shaking, and the tea was spilling from the mugs.

'You didn't bring the little ones,' Sean's mother said. 'You haven't brought our grankids for us to see.'

'They'll be round tomorrow . . . You'll find Young Gerard a bit funny, you're not to take notice of him. You mustn't mind him . . .' Roisin gulped down her tea, scalded her throat.

The patrol came down the Crescent.

They were soaked, they were on the home run, and Ferris wasn't bothering with any more P.-checks. Showing the bloody flag would have to be enough for Christmas Eve.

*

223

He saw the one he wanted. He couldn't fail to see him.

Taller than the men in front of him and behind him. Not ducking and weaving like they were. Like they were scared and this one wasn't. Frankie Conroy eased the Armalite up to his shoulder. The hard steel of the extended stock pressed back into his shoulder. Hold it tight, the bread delivery man had said, lock it against the bone of your shoulder. Have your fingers fast on it, the bread delivery man had added, and don't bloody tremble, and don't bloody think what it's for and what's going to happen.

Hard not to tremble. Frankie Conroy was on one knee. The anti-flash cover and the needle sight on the forward end of the barrel protruded three, four inches through the gap in the rotten chipboard at the window. The officer was a hundred yards from him, coming down the Crescent steadily. The officer would be forty yards from him when he fired, but already Frankie Conroy was lining his aim.

He had listened well to the bread delivery man. There was nothing in his mind about what it was for, what would happen, no crap like that. No troubles in his mind, that sort of shit, about taking the life of a British soldier on the day before Christmas. What concerned Frankie Conroy, waiting and watching, aiming through the half light, was whether he could hold the barrel steady, whether he could put the bastard down first shot.

There would only be one shot, the first shot.

He was sweating. The wetness was clinging on his skin. And he couldn't take his hands from the Armalite to wipe his forehead or smear the dampness out of his eyelids.

It was to save the Chief from the Kesh that the officer would be blown away with a high velocity bullet. That's what it was for, that's what would happen.

The barrel was steady. The leaf sight and the needle sight met on the chest of the officer.

The officer seemed to be talking to himself. Frankie Conroy could see his lips move. He heard only the soft slither of the patrol's boots on the pavements, and the moan of distant traffic. He couldn't help himself, he wondered what the bastard was saying to himself.

His finger was on the trigger, round it, starting to squeeze on it, like the bread delivery man had said he should.

The barrel traversed, followed the officer to the corner of the Crescent and the Drive. He'd fire at forty yards.

He was trying not to think about Sam. Thinking about Sam was too damned dangerous when strolling in Turf Lodge. He was going to ring Sam in the morning, Christmas morning, to tell her that he was coming across the water, to try to fix something with her. He'd have to spend a day with his parents in Lancashire, and then there was the day with Sergeant Tunney at the hospital, but he should be able to manage the last evening with Sam before the long bloody trek back, and if he was really bloody trying he might just make a night with Sam . . . He reckoned it would be New Year's Eve. Sam was hardly going to be sitting round on New Year's Eve waiting for poor old Ferris to give her a bell from Belfast. He should have rung her straight off, as soon as Sunray had told him he was going cross-Channel . . . Arseholes . . .

'Arseholes . . .' Ferris said out loud.

'Beg your pardon, sir,' Jones said cheerfully, from behind.

That was the moment Ferris turned to smile at Fusilier Jones.

It was the moment of the shot.

The whip crack of the shot belted Sam, New Year's Eve, every bloody thing out of Ferris's head.

He was spinning, couldn't stand, the blow turned him like a top. Lost the control of his legs, and the pavement was rising to take him, and he couldn't hear anything after the shot.

The pavement smashed into his face.

Frankie charged down the staircase. One step broke under him, and he was close to losing his balance, and he careered through the kitchen and put his shoulder into the chipboard masking the window, and he climbed out into the late afternoon murk and the back garden of the house.

He'd seen the officer twist away at the moment he'd fired.

There were shouts in the street, the wrong side of the house from him, panic shouts, squealed shouts in the bloody Brit accent.

He went over the garden fence, and into the back path that went to the garages, and he ran till the wind sobbed in his throat.

He reckoned he'd done pretty bloody well because he had seen the officer twist and go down.

And the shouts were far away, and behind him.

Roisin stood in the opened door of the McAnallys' house.

Over the top of the hedge she could see the backs of the soldiers as they bent low. She could hear the frantic, frightened cursing. Past the hedge where the gate was open, she could see the boots and legs of a squaddie on the ground, but not his face. She could hear the atmospheric and staccato replies of their radios.

'What's happened?' The call was from behind her, far back in the hall.

225

'A soldier's been shot,' Roisin said over her shoulder.

'Are you coming back to your tea?'

She closed her eyes, she shook her head. She closed the door on the street.

She turned to Mr McAnally. She smiled brightly. 'I have to help my Ma, but I've time for another cup.'

His hearing was back.

The carols out in the vehicle park were a pain in his ears, and the M.O.'s voice was an agony.

The M.O. swabbed at the blood round his nose.

'No Purple Heart for you, Mr Ferris, but by Christ there's someone up there with a sense of the festive spirit and smiling on you . . . do you know that the incoming round *actually* hit the mag on your S.L.R., not full-face of course, but glanced it, and the mag was enough to ricochet it. Head-butting the pavement wasn't sensible, giving yourself a nose-bleed doesn't exactly fit the hero slot . . .'

'They didn't get the shit,' Ferris said bleakly.

'Didn't even get a shot back, too much powder in their bloody tea . . . you've got leave, haven't you? Well, don't expect a good time with the crumpet, not with the way your hooter's looking . . . bloody great excitement here when the Contact came over the air, your lads must be fond of you, they were half hysterical, bellowing for an ambulance, the way it sounded at this end the Sky Pilot was reaching for his beads and prayer book . . . You'll dine out on that one, your mag getting in the way. You'll bore the pants off your grandchildren . . . There you are, laddie, perfect though not pretty.'

Ferris straightened on the surgery couch. 'I'm clear?'

'Free to get pissed. You'll have an expensive night in the Mess.'

Gingerly Ferris touched his face. 'It feels a bit wretched.'

'Not half as wretched as the bugger who sniped you . . . Your bill of health'll put him right in the mood for Christmas. He'll be boasting to all his mates, till *News At Ten*. Merry Christmas . . .'

Ferris went out to the vehicle park. He was in time to join the singing of the final two carols.

He had cut his knee when he had stumbled in his flight over a rusted, scrapped bicycle frame.

Frankie Conroy sat on his bed in the room that he rented from the widower, and he had pulled his trouser leg up to his knee, and he held a handkerchief against the wound to staunch the bleeding. His door was open. He could hear the television downstairs, in the widower's front room.

'. . . the Cardinal concluded his statement by saying that he hoped that all members of the community would examine their consciences during the Christmas holiday, and remember the true spirit and meaning of Christmas, and renounce the ways of violence.

'In West Belfast, an officer in the 2nd Battalion the Royal Regiment of Fusiliers had an extraordinary escape when a sniper's bullet glanced off the magazine of his rifle. The officer, leading a foot patrol, was unhurt. An army spokesman described the escape as a "miracle".

'In Part Two, we will be seeing how they are getting ready for Christmas on an oil platform in the North Sea, and we'll be reporting on Pope John Paul's visit to a young people's reformatory in Rome. Join us again . . .'

He could have bloody wept, because he had seen the officer go down.

He could have bloody screamed, because he had seen the face of David Ferris over the leaf sight of the Armalite.

The train rocked and rolled through the outer London suburbs.

The lights were on in the back rooms of the houses. When the curtains hadn't been drawn across Ferris could see into the warm homes. The food was being laid out for parties in the dining rooms, and there were aproned women over their stoves in the kitchens, and upstairs there were youngsters in their bedrooms preening themselves in front of mirrors, preparing for the celebrations at the year's end . . . All so bloody safe, and so bloody relaxed. Hundreds and hundreds and hundreds of safe, relaxed, warm homes, that were the homes of families who were far from the front line of David Ferris's war.

He wasn't in uniform. He wore a grey suit under his anorak, and his other civilian clothes were in the canvas grip between his feet. There was nothing about him to show that he was a soldier. He was any young man who was going to visit a friend in hospital, any young man who was then going to meet his girl and celebrate the passing of an old year.

His newspaper was discarded on the luggage rack above his head. He had gutted it for news of the war, and found nothing. He knew that he had made the newspapers, one paragraph after Christmas, and no name, but a few words about a miracle, and he knew that it had been reported on the box. An 'escape' had to be pretty miraculous to make the papers and the box when a death couldn't guarantee getting a column inch or a few seconds of airtime.

The previous day he had travelled from Belfast on the ferry to Liverpool, and he had taken the train to Preston and his parents' home. He hadn't told them about the stunning impact of a high velocity round

227

against the magazine of an SLR. No bloody point. He had told them, and made a laugh of it, that he had slipped on an icy pavement and clipped his nose on the kerbstone. They'd accepted the explanation, because they knew nothing of the grey world that was Turf Lodge. There had been some of their friends invited round for supper, and the talk at the table had been about everything but Northern Ireland. They wouldn't have discussed cancer or incurable leukaemia at the supper table, and there was no reason why they should discuss Northern Ireland. His mother had watched over him and seemed to wonder why her boy drank so often and so deeply. After the guests had gone when his mother was in the kitchen, his father had sidled close to him and asked if 'things were alright' over there, and David had said they were 'alright'. There was a sharp nervous smile on his father's face as he had supposed that his son didn't see much of the 'difficulties', and David had said that he never seemed to see anything of the 'difficulties'. Not their war, they hadn't volunteered for warfare across the Irish Sea. His father had made a play of seeming satisfied.

He had travelled down to London that morning, and crossed London by underground, and taken a stopping train to a station near Roehampton. It wasn't a bad day for the last of December, quite a bright sun. Until he had gone through the front doors the hospital had seemed a fairly decent sort of place. Not that there was anything wrong with the inside of the buildings, it was the people inside that bruised him. They were all of his age, the men who were learning to walk with artificial limbs, and on crutches, and on sticks, and the men who were learning to get themselves down a corridor when their eyes were shaded with dark glasses.

'Why didn't you tell me earlier?' Rennie snapped into the telephone.

'I thought we could get over it, and I was wrong . . .' Prentice's voice was faint on the line.

'Have you taken him boozing?'

'He's pissed every night.'

'Get him a woman.'

'He'd run a bloody mile – that's not his problem. His problem is that he's talking about scratching out.'

'He knows what'll happen to him?'

'I've told him, Goss's told him. He's not in the mood to be told.'

'Have you talked money with him?'

'Like we're a couple of investment brokers. It's not about money.'

'What in Christ's name is it about?'

'He's lost his balls.'

'If he ever had any,' Rennie muttered.

228

'Come again, Mr Rennie . . .'

'I said that it's your job to lift him.'

'We can hold him up, Mr Rennie, Goss and me'll hold him up till he's in the box. When he's in the box and we can't hold him then he'll fall flat on his bloody face.'

'Will he get better?'

'My opinion only, but he'll get worse. My opinion, you have to get him through the Magistrate soonest, it might show there's nowhere else to go but the Crown Court. Doing his act at the preliminary hearing might just toughen him, steel him – but I wouldn't put money on it – it might just fold him. We're in a bad way.'

'If you let McAnally through your fingers . . .'

'You've no call to be threatening me, Mr Rennie.'

Rennie sat in his office. The telephone in his hand was sheened with the sweat from his palm. New Year's Eve, and the end of the week when he had come near to forgetting Sean Pius McAnally. New Year's Eve, and he had been hoping to take Gloria to the rugby club for the dinner dance. Just about cleared his desk, when Prentice had rung. He shouldn't have been doubting Prentice. Prentice was as good as any he had. Prentice had been nursing the problem, hoping it would go away.

'John, give it me again.'

'I told you all of it, Mr Rennie.'

'Just give it me again.'

'We let him ring home on Christmas morning, mid-morning. It couldn't have been worse. His little girl had gone down to McAnally's parents, just down the Drive – this is what Roisin told him – she was chased by some kids. Bloody Christmas morning, and they chased her, they were shouting "Tout's brat" at her, something like that . . . she ran into the road. There was this car, it swerved in time. It didn't hit the girl, it frightened the wits out of her. The car hit a hedge. His Missus came out, she was screaming up and down the road, that's what she told Gingy. The girl wasn't hurt, but she could just as well have been killed . . . Gingy caught the lot of it. She'd just got the girl indoors when he rang, she was still hysterical. She told Gingy that if Little Patty had been killed then her blood would have been on his head . . . I don't think she meant it, it was just bad luck he phoned when he did.'

'Fucking animals . . . right, that's Christmas Day.'

'Next day we let him ring again – we reckoned she'd have calmed down. The boy, Gerard, picked up the phone. Gingy said who he was and the boy cut him, just cut the call. They must have left the phone off after that, because Gingy tried twice more and it was engaged both times.'

'I see your problem,' Rennie said heavily.

'We gave Gingy the chance to call again last night, late, after the kid would have been in bed. Gingy dialled it, he went pretty white, he just put the phone down. A fellow answered it . . . Gingy won't say who it was . . . he just went to pieces then. Look, this morning we were trying him with his evidence. He was awful. If he were like that in court, up against Counsel, he'd be massacred.'

'You took your bloody time telling me.'

Rennie pondered. He was bleak-faced. He was searching his memory, recalling his last conversation with the Commanding Officer of 2 R.R.F. He remembered what had been said about David Ferris.

'John, where are you tonight?'

'Some awful dive that Andy's found.'

'In the town?'

'Yes.'

'For midnight?'

'Yes, we've a hell of a lot to celebrate.'

'What's it called?'

'The Midnite Club – you coming over, Mr Rennie?'

'Don't fuck me about, boy . . . You be in the Midnite, you better be there.'

'That the lot, Mr Rennie?'

'It'll be the lot for now.'

Rennie put down the telephone. He began to search in his book for the direct line to the Commanding Officer of 2 R.R.F.

Alone in his cell, the Chief brooded on what he had learned on that day, the last day of the year. His lunch tray was on the floor in front of him, untouched.

Mr Pronsias Reilly had made, in the late afternoon, a solicitor's call to his client.

'You'll not credit it of Gingy McAnally, but the word is that he's under the thumb of a Brit officer, that the officer's got him wrapped round the finger. The officer's what's holding Gingy up . . . So the name of the officer was learned . . . Frankie Conroy had the name. Frankie went for him, set up a snipe on him, and hit his bloody rifle. Without that officer, McAnally's gone, and Frankie hit the officer's rifle. That was Christmas Eve, and the officer hasn't been seen since. We've lost track of Gingy, most likely he's across the water, but the officer was the way to him, and he's not been seen since the snipe . . . If you're to break the charges then Gingy's got to lose that officer. That's about all there is, but I reckoned you'd want to know.'

The Chief had access to newspapers and to a pocket transistor radio. He knew the war was scaled down in his absence, and the absence of the Brigade Staff, and the absence of the Battalion Officers, all in the cells alongside him, there on the word of Gingy McAnally. The

Organization always hit hard before Christmas, and then allowed a lull, and came back kicking the New Year in.

'Why Frankie? Why that donkey on the rifle?' the Chief hissed out of earshot of the watching prison officer.

'The only one who was interested,' Mr Pronsias Reilly muttered.

'There's plenty of men who wouldn't have hit the rifle.'

'None of them interested enough to try.'

'Only Frankie?'

'Who you'd depend your freedom on? Only Frankie.'

'He's useless.'

'He's what you've got.'

The Organization was stagnated. It was castrated without the influence of the Chief and his Brigade Staff and his Battalion Officers. He hated to lie on his cell bunk because then his head was close to the whitewashed wall and the cell seemed to close around him, and his ears seemed to ring with the crash of closing doors, and the scrape of bolts, and the tinkle of the key chains. He hated to lie on his bed blanket with his head close to the wall because then the knowledge of the months and years in the Kesh seemed to overwhelm him.

He sat on his bed, and he stared at the door, and he cursed, because the only man who would champion him was the donkey, Frankie Conroy.

He spent an hour and a half with Sergeant Tunney . . . for David Ferris it was a hard hour and a half, and he tried not to look too often at the scorched raw flesh of the sergeant's face and hands. He told the sergeant what had happened to him, out in Turf Lodge, and he lied a bit and said they might have hit the bugger with return fire, because that would please the sergeant. He told him about Christmas Day, and Sunray serving soup for the Fusiliers, and the 2 i/c carving the turkeys, and the Adjutant dropping a two-dozen tray of cans and the beer foaming when the rings were pulled and making a hell of a mess, and Fusilier Jones losing a tooth filling on a 5p piece in the Christmas pudding. When he left, when he touched gently onto Sergeant Tunney's shoulder, he thought there was the dribble of a tear at his platoon sergeant's eye. He couldn't shake the sergeant's hand, so he had to touch him on the shoulder, and he couldn't be sure whether it was tears or not because there was so much mucus and ointment on the sergeant's face.

'You give the fuckers hell, Mr Ferris, when you get back.'

'We'll leave a few for you, Sergeant Tunney, for when you're with us again.'

He smiled with as much confidence as he could muster, and he walked out of the ward.

The sergeant's wife was sitting on a hard bench in the corridor. She looked away from him, and he pretended that he hadn't seen her. He thought that each of the days of the year the Ministry should bring the cameras into the wards and the corridors of this hospital to record what his father called the 'difficulties' of Northern Ireland. Let the people, the voters, see the real price of keeping the peace in the Province. Let them see the men without legs, without stomachs, without sight, without skin on their faces and hands. The sergeant's wife had the right to look away from him.

'David . . .'

She was coming down the corridor towards him. His Sam, his girl. A full swinging skirt. Shined Italian boots. A suede coat open over a cashmere sweater. Long hair darting golden over her face. His Sam, coming towards him with excitement loud on her cheeks. She was light in darkness. She was love in a place of misery.

He saw the wide open newspaper that hid from him the face of the sergeant's wife. He was meeting his girl, he was whole. She was waiting on her man, he was damaged. Fucking Northern Ireland, fucking Belfast . . .

'Sorry I'm late, David darling, bloody traffic, God knows where it all comes from. Heavens you look well. Got your business done?'

She came into his arms. He was embarrassed, Sam wasn't. Sam hugged him, kissed him. Sam didn't see the newspaper of the sergeant's wife.

He felt the tackiness of her lipstick on his mouth, on his face. He felt the warmth of her coat on his neck. He felt the shape of her pressed against his chest.

'It's wonderful to see you,' Ferris said, into her ear.

'Too damned right it's wonderful. You finished?'

'Yes.'

She was still kissing him.

'Let's get the hell out. It's got the smell of death, this place.'

His voice would have carried across a parade ground. They walked away together down the corridor, and from Mrs Tunney.

'We're well fixed up – Christ, you didn't give me much time . . . We're going to someone called Penny's for supper – we were at school – lives in Farnham – then we're going dancing. We're staying at Penny's. Alright?'

'Brilliant.'

'Penny says she's dying to meet you. She says any man that keeps me celibate must be worth meeting. She's married to an accountant, so no army talk . . .'

He pushed open the rubber doors at the end of the corridor and they came out into the Reception hallway of the hospital. He kissed her forehead, she kissed him back on the mouth.

'Who were you seeing in there?'

'My platoon sergeant.'

'What's his problem?'

'He's just a bit ill.'

'You've got to go back tomorrow, to Belfast?'

'Got to.'

'Wouldn't you desert for me?'

In the centre of the Reception hallway, David Ferris held Samantha Forster. Held her, squeezed her, buried his head in her soft, scented hair. He didn't see the nurses, nor the visitors, nor the doctors.

The voice in his ear was respectful, even quiet.

'Excuse me, it's Mr Ferris, isn't it?'

He turned. A receptionist was beside him. He nodded.

'There's a telephone call for you, long distance.'

There was a frown on his forehead.

'Not the bloody army . . .' Sam said.

'They're holding on for you.'

He let go of Sam. He thought she sounded quite amused, himself he felt bloody furious. He walked after the receptionist to the front desk. The telephone was lying beside its cradle. For one moment he considered ignoring the call. It was a short moment. He looked round at Sam. She was lovely, she was pulling a face at him.

'Hurry it up, David, Penny'll be pouring the gin by now.'

He picked up the telephone.

'Ferris . . .' he said curtly.

'Thank Christ for that. It's Rennie . . .'

It was a good line. Ferris could hear Rennie clearly enough to sense the relief.

'Happy New Year's Eve, Mr Rennie.'

'This isn't a secure call, so watch what you say. I know it's New Year's Eve, I know you're on leave, I know you're with your lady – and I'm making no apologies. We're in deep shit, David. The word I have is that our friend is likely to walk out on us . . . Don't argue, just listen. If it wasn't important I wouldn't have tracked you . . . David, the boys say that our friend's going through the floor – doesn't matter why, but he's in maggots. Don't tell me you've got plans for tonight . . . David, you're in Roehampton now. Before midnight I want you in Aldershot . . . Before midnight I want you in Aldershot . . . Before midnight I want you at a club in Aldershot. Our friend's going to be there. He's got to be lifted, he's got to be helped. David, if you don't lift him, then the whole thing's over. Got your pencil, I'll give you the address.'

Ferris gripped the telephone between his ear and his shoulder, and reached in his pocket for a pen.

He met Sam's eyes.

'I'm dying for that drink. Hurry up, darling.' Sam blew him a kiss.
He wrote the address.

Rennie said, down the long line, that if David Ferris ever did the
decent thing by the girl that he'd buy them a wedding present, and in
the meantime a Happy New Year to both of them.

It was an hour before midnight.

Sam was bloody extraordinary. He'd thought she might have ditched
him, might at least have gone acid on him. She had shrugged, said that
it might be fun, said that Penny's accountant was a boring pouf, said
that they might have a good laugh out of it. He'd just told her that it
was something to do with his work, that there was a man he had to
meet.

They'd eaten Penny's dinner. He'd drunk three gins and the best part
of a bottle of wine and he hadn't a lot to say for himself, and Sam didn't
seem to notice and had rabbited about school days, and the accountant
had watched him morosely each time he'd filled his glass. Sam didn't
seem to mind, and there was a double bed waiting upstairs, and turned
down, and Sam's nightdress on the pillows.

He was holding her hand and they were walking past shop windows.
He heard the disco music.

'Sam, don't ask me who this man is. Please just help me cheer him
up, just make a fuss of him. All we've got to do is give him a bloody
good evening.'

'And have one ourselves.'

Some bloody chance.

There was a muscled bouncer on the door. The place called itself the
Midnite Club, and there was a pound surcharge because it was New
Year's Eve, and fancy dress was optional, and denims weren't.

'It'll be full of Other Ranks, Sam, sorry . . .'

'Don't be so pompous. You're worse than bloody Daddy.'

She tugged him to the door, smiled sweetly at the bouncer, and won
a bow. Ferris paid them in.

They went down the stairs inside and thoughts of Sean Pius McAnally,
supergrass and cracking, were blown clean out of his head by the
explosion that was the music.

18

The lights flashed from the ceiling through revolving prisms over the dancers. They were early. Jackson and Boy George pounded their ears. He'd looked around him as soon as they were inside. There were tables and chairs around the edge of the dance floor, but the action was middle-stage. The minders and the supergrass hadn't shown. There was a bar, but Sam said that she had to drive, and she didn't want him falling over and he didn't need any more to drink, and she'd come to dance. She took his hand and led him to the centre of the floor. Now, for the first time, she joked about his damaged nose and he gave the same lie that had stopped his mother's fussing, and the lie was good enough for Sam as well.

She wore a full black skirt, and she showed her glorious legs when the tempo was going hard and she twirled from the ends of his fingers. She wore a tight-fitting polka dot blouse, and he felt the warmth of her against his shirt when the music was slow, loving. And she told him he was a damned heifer when he scraped her toes and that he wasn't that bad close to, and she nibbled his ear and chewed his lobe.

He was a prisoner who had escaped. For twelve weeks he had been incarcerated in the Springfield Road, and he had bust out. Belfast was ancient bloody history . . . There was nothing in his mind of the Turf Lodge, or of a hidden marksman, or of Sunray or the I.O. The present was Sam, and the sweat streaking the fair strands on her forehead, and the damp lovely warmth of her, and her hips that were swinging and drifting against him. She was a bad bloody woman, and she knew it, and he thought he might just love her for it.

Sam kept Ferris to the centre of the dance floor, and she grinned because her elbows made room for them to dance without being buffeted by other couples. And the Midnite Club was O.R.'s territory, and O.R.s and their girls gave space to an officer and an officer's woman. Obvious she was an officer's woman when she didn't care that his cheek had lipstick smears, when she wore a string of pearls at her throat, when she didn't give a damn who saw her thighs. Ferris thought that Sam was the best-looking woman in the Midnite Club.

They didn't talk. The bedlam of the noise was too much to talk across. He no longer looked every minute or so to the entrance steps. He was close to forgetting what he was there for. Her hands were locked on the nape of his neck and her lips nuzzled under his chin.

Midnight was closing on the Club. The floor was emptier as the dancers struggled to reach the bar and gain the refills for the twelve o'clock toasts. Ferris and Sam danced on. Ferris heard nothing around him but the gentle breathing of Sam. He danced as if he were unaware of the music, he moved in the world that was Sam and himself. And Sam was lovely, the loveliest.

The voice rabbit punched him.

The accent carved through the music, through Ferris's preoccupation with holding Sam tight to him.

The accent rasped in his mind for recognition.

'If we's wants a bloody drink, we'll have a bloody drink.'

He could pinpoint the accent. The accent was Gingy McAnally's.

'So get your fat arse out the way, so's we can get a bloody drink.'

The accent was drunk.

Ferris had stiffened, he no longer moved with the music. He felt Sam pulling him, trying to drag him back to the dancing steps. There was a puzzlement in her face, merging with annoyance.

'Where's the bloody bar? . . . and it's your bloody shout, Goss.'

He turned slowly, towards the door. He saw McAnally shove himself past the bouncer, and as the bouncer reached to grab him, then Prentice's arm was out and restraining, and Goss was grimly flashing his warrant card. The bouncer backed off. On the edge of the dance floor McAnally seemed to lose his footing and he careened into a girl who was dancing, and half tripped her, and the girl's fellow was squaring up when again Prentice's hand dropped on the arm. At the bar McAnally tunnelled for space and service and Prentice and Goss were hard in behind him.

'Scotch for me, Goss . . . whatever you's having, Scotch for me.'

It was ten days since he had seen McAnally, since they had walked on the mountain of Mullaghmore.

'Shift your arse . . . three Scotches, he's paying.'

The man was devastated. There was a new suit on him, three-piece Burton's in the High Street, but that couldn't conceal the devastation, nor could the centre-parting hair salon job hide the damage.

'Come on, Goss, for fuck's sake, show her your fucking money so's we get served.'

McAnally had put on half a stone that bulged his waist under his unbuttoned waistcoat, and his shirt tail was out of his trousers, and his tie of brilliant green was loose at his throat. His face was a blotched red mess, and his eyes blinked as if to focus on his nose, and a cheroot cigar hung from the side of his mouth and jerked when he shouted. Prentice was bent over his shoulder, whispering in his ear.

'Don't tell me to shut up, Prentice.'

The drink from Goss was in his hand, and swigged.

'Piss poor measures they give here.'

Prentice had him by the throat.

'Don't tell me to behave . . .' McAnally drained his glass. 'Goss, keep shouting, same as before.'

Ferris shuddered. The sight of McAnally appalled him. He understood why Rennie had tracked him down.

'Sam . . .' Ferris spoke softly in her ear. 'I'm sorry, you should go back to Penny's. I'll catch you there.'

She stared at him, astonished. 'I'm not going anywhere.'

'Please, Sam.'

'We're in this ghastly place to meet your friend who hasn't come. So we enjoy ourselves. I'm not going anywhere.'

'Come on, darling.' He tried to gently pull her off the floor.

She held her ground. 'It's five to midnight, David.'

'I don't want you to stay here.'

'Because a drunk's making a bit of noise, don't be so wet . . . I'm not going at five minutes to midnight and neither are you.'

She kicked him sharply on the ankle. As he hopped she swung him back into the rhythm of the music. As he danced he twisted his head, always watching McAnally. She tweaked his nose, hurt him.

'What's special about the drunk?'

'Don't ask,' Ferris said.

'Why not . . . ?' She was laughing happily into his face. 'Is *that* your friend?'

'I said, don't ask.'

'You can't *actually* know him.'

'Sam, be quiet.'

'Aren't you going to introduce me?'

'When I bloody have to, not before.'

The disc jockey, an excited sallow youth with a purple streak in his hair, was calling for the floor to be filled, the last spin of the old year. Sam danced mechanically, distant from Ferris.

He heard McAnally's voice.

'There's no bloody offence meant, so's you needn't be taking offence.'

He heard Prentice's voice.

'Just close your hole up, Gingy, do us a bloody favour.'

'I was just telling the man that there's no offence meant . . .'

'He got your message.'

Goss was trying to pour water from a jug into McAnally's new whisky, and McAnally's hand was wobbling, and the water had flowed into the lap of a lady, and her husband was on his feet and remonstrating. Ferris reckoned the husband to be at least a colour sergeant and an evil little toad whatever he was, the sort of little toad who'd break the bottom off a bottle.

'Apologize, you silly shit,' Prentice shouted.

'No offence meant, that's a bloody apology.'

The man was apparently satisfied.

His lady was standing and squeezing the water out of her frock.

Ferris closed his eyes. A bloody nightmare.

The disc jockey was on the countdown. The dancers were shouting the numbers with him. Ferris looked at Sam, she wasn't shouting, she was staring straight ahead, at Sean Pius McAnally, fascinated.

'I'm sorry . . . Sam, I'm sorry.'

He tried to kiss her lips and she turned her head away and his mouth brushed her cheek.

'It's a bit different to what Penny had in mind for us, and that would have been bloody boring. You're a right laugh, darling.'

'Happy New Year . . . Happy New Year . . .' the disc jockey shrieked.

'Happy New Year, Sam,' Ferris said softly.

'Happy New Year yourself,' she said, from the side of her mouth. 'Level with me. Are we here to meet that drunk?'

The dancers linked arms, made a long bent line that circled the dance floor.

Auld Lang Syne on the turntable, and everyone singing, and Ferris singing and trying to wake up from a bad dream.

The line stamped across the dance floor, squashing itself together. Bodies barged together, elbowed each other, kneed each other. He held tight onto Sam's hand. The faces in front of him were blurred, blurred as the noise of the singing.

'It's the fucking officer . . .'

He saw McAnally. McAnally was in the line opposite him, pinioned by Prentice and Goss.

'Look, you daft bugger . . . look, Goss, it's our bloody officer.'

The line swept back. Across the floor McAnally's feet scrabbled for a grip on the boards as Prentice and Goss hoisted him away with the motion of the line. McAnally's eyes were locked on Ferris.

'Don't you see? It's bloody Ferris . . .'

Sam jabbed her elbow into Ferris's side.

'Who is he?'

'He's nothing you need to know about.'

McAnally leered across the floor.

'That's a great bit of fanny, Ferris,' McAnally shouted. 'You're on a better bloody promise than I am . . . You've got a right looking raver, I've got these jerks . . . I hope it's a promise, hope it wasn't her that did your nose.'

Prentice was laughing, and Goss was trying not to look pained, and McAnally was laughing with Prentice and giggling with Goss, and leaning on their arms, and the singing died and the arm chains broke.

'Is this some crack of Rennie's?' To Prentice it was a hell of a joke.

'Did Rennie put you up to being here?' Goss, embarrassed, trying

for his answers. 'I mean you're hardly in this dump out of choice.'
Ferris turned his back, he turned away so that he faced Sam.

'He's Belfast,' Ferris said simply. 'He's nothing to do with here.'

'What is he in Belfast?'

'He's . . . Sam, I can't plead the bloody Official Secrets Act with you.'

'What is he?'

'He's . . .'

He felt the fingers grappling with the shoulder of his jacket. He spun, McAnally was hanging to his clothes, and he stank of Scotch and the cheroot was still in his mouth. Prentice and Goss were holding McAnally upright.

'Mister bloody Ferris . . . Happy New Year, a fucking happier New Year than the last one was . . . You've forgotten your Gingy, haven't you? You wouldn't be thinking about Gingy when you've that fanny with you . . . aren't you going to introduce us? You're friendly enough with Taig filth, with Gingy McAnally, when you're 'cross the water. Aren't you going to be friendly now?'

'I'd *love* to meet your friends, David,' Sam said, and she rolled her south-of-England accent, and Ferris thought she might have winked at the minders.

Ferris said unhappily, 'Sam, this is Sean McAnally, and this is John Prentice, and this is Andy Goss . . . gentlemen, this is Samantha Forster . . .'

'Pleased to meet you, Mr McAnally.'

'Fucking pleased to meet you, Samantha.'

'Watch your foul mouth, Gingy . . .' Prentice snapped.

'You're talking to a lady, Gingy . . .' Goss snapped.

'Good-looking fanny, and all . . .' McAnally belched.

'I hear you're a friend of David's, Mr McAnally.'

'Prefer to be your fucking friend, lady . . . Get some drinks, Goss, for my friend and his fucking lady . . . Piss off and get the drinks.'

'Gingy . . .' Ferris's voice was cold, quiet. 'You are behaving like a silly shit, Gingy.'

'"A silly shit, Gingy",' McAnally tried to mimic Ferris. 'Not good enough for the officer, are we? Not good enough when he's going to get laid by this lady . . . Where're those drinks, Goss?'

She was laughing. Her head was back, her hair was back. She was laughing through her open mouth, her open lips.

'If I was you, Mister officer, I wouldn't be hanging round the likes of us when you could be laying that lady.'

The laughter was pealing in Ferris's head.

Ferris smashed his fist into the right-side cheek of Gingy McAnally's face.

The fist slapped into the soft flesh of the cheek, crunched against the jaw bone. Ferris had never before hit a man with the bare knuckles of his fist.

There was a moment of bewilderment spilling over McAnally's face, then his mouth screwed tight with the pain.

'He's only drunk, there's no call . . .' Sam shouted.

'You daft bugger,' Prentice growled.

McAnally's knees buckled. He crumpled down onto the floor, down amongst their feet.

The bouncer piled into the knot of Prentice and Goss and Ferris and Sam. When he pulled Goss's jacket the button cotton snapped and the jacket came open and the bouncer saw the shoulder holster and the wood handle of the P.P.K. Walther, and he backed away. The music soared around them, and the dancers cocooned them.

McAnally held his hand over the right side of his cheek.

The bewilderment was past, and the pain was overcome, he was suffused with fury.

'I tell you what, Ferris, I'll tell you this . . . if I ever had any doubts, I've no doubts now . . . I'm out, I'm gone. You get on the phone to Mister bloody Rennie, and you tell him from me, tell him that Gingy McAnally's on his bike. He can stuff his fucking immunity, he can shove his evidence up his arse . . . You tell him that, you tell Mister bloody Rennie that Gingy McAnally's not part of his bloody plans, not any more . . .'

Goss bent to placate McAnally, and was shoved away.

'Don't play the bloody soft soaper with me. I'm gone . . .'

There were tears welling in McAnally's eyes. He gazed up at Ferris.

'All the bullshit about friendship . . .' He tried to imitate Ferris's accent. 'I'll stand beside you, I'll step in front of you – horseshit. I'm scum to you, to you I'm just a Taig tout. I'm not a person, I'm just a Taig informer to be pissed on . . .'

A crack in Sam's voice. She rounded on Ferris. 'Is he a supergrass?'

'He's a fucking supergrass, lady, he's a fucking stoogie.' McAnally choked out the words, smeared his sleeve across his eyes.

'You're mixed up with people like this?'

'Didn't he tell you what shit he's mixed with, doesn't he tell his fanny?'

Ferris saw that Prentice's fists were clenched, that Goss was poised to come forward.

McAnally crawled onto his knees, pushed himself up, and stood in front of Ferris.

'I'm out, I've quit.'

For a few steps McAnally staggered, then he seemed to regain his balance, and he spun to the exit light. His head was down on his shoulders, he seemed not to look ahead of him as he ploughed through the dancers.

240

'That was hell's clever,' Prentice said.

'You could have walked away,' Goss said. 'Or did Rennie send you to cheer us all up. If he did, haven't you made a bloody good job of it?'

Prentice sighed. He set off to follow McAnally. Ferris looked from Sam away to the back of McAnally's head that was bobbing on the steps to the exit. He muttered something, he didn't hear his own words and Sam wouldn't have heard them, it was something of an apology.

Ferris ran across the floor, and he pushed Prentice back from the door, back down the steps. The bouncer was shouting in his ear that it was a respectable club, that his behaviour was a bloody disgrace.

The night air hit him. He tripped on a dustbin, clattered the lid off. He was in an alleyway at the side of the club. He ran up the alley to the main street. He looked right, then left, when he looked left he saw McAnally.

There was an oath from the alleyway behind him. He knew that Prentice had found the dustbin.

McAnally was holding onto a lamp post, and was vomiting. And he was crying, and Ferris could hear his sobs. A couple, arm in arm and in fancy dress, crossed the road to avoid contact with McAnally.

He walked towards McAnally. McAnally would have heard his footsteps, and he looked up and saw Ferris closing on him.

'I said I'd bloody gone, I said I'd quit,' McAnally shouted. The vomit gleamed on his shoes. He turned and shambled away up the street, and Ferris followed.

Ferris reached him at the traffic lights. McAnally stood, listless and with his head shrunk down into his shoulders, and waited for the lights to change. They crossed the road together. He smelt the vomit on Gingy's waistcoat. Just as the comedians said, it was always diced carrot. They walked past the shop windows, past a patrolling policeman. In silence they walked until they came to a park. There was a bench that was too near to the street and the lights for the couples who shivered and sought warmth from each other's hands. Gingy had fought back the tears, Ferris no longer heard the sounds of his crying.

Gingy sat on the bench. Ferris sat beside him.

'I said I was quitting.'

'It was pretty daft what happened in there.'

'I was going to quit, what happened inside's not to do with it.'

'I'm sorry I hit you,' Ferris said simply.

'I was pissed . . . shit . . .' McAnally found the vomit on his hands. 'It was the drink I'd taken.'

'I didn't have to belt you.'

'I'd have fucking belted me, if I'd been with the bird . . .'

'So it happened, so it's history.'

'Did you walk out on your bird?'

241

Ferris took his handkerchief from his pocket and wiped the mess from Gingy's mouth, and took his hands and cleaned them, and he threw the handkerchief behind him into the Corporation's flowerbed.

'I meant it, what I said, that I'm quitting.'

'They'll wreck you, they won't let you walk out. They'll put the mark on you.'

'You get so's you don't bloody care.'

'Rennie'll let it be known that you named the Monaghan man. He burned to death, there'll be no love for you after that's known.'

'Don't you listen, you get so's you don't bloody care.'

'What happened, Gingy?'

Sean Pius McAnally told David Ferris about the telephone calls.

'There's nothing any of us can do about it,' Ferris said.

'That's a bloody good help.'

'I mean it, Gingy. You stayed in, she didn't.'

'She's my wife, they're my kids.'

'It was her decision not to stay with you. She might change her mind.'

'She's never changed her mind yet,' McAnally laughed shrilly. And the laugh was killed. Bright eyes staring at Ferris. 'You want to know what it's like here?'

'Tell me.'

'I'm never out of their sight. It's all pals, isn't it? It's all Gingy and Johnny and Andy, it's all like we're bloody muckers in it together . . . That's a lie. They say they're close on me because I need protection . . . bollocks, they're with me so's I don't quit . . . but they can't stop me quitting . . . I'm a bloody puppet to them. They tell me I need some clothes, so's we're out to the shops. I don't choose this suit, Prentice chooses it. Prentice goes down the line and he decides what I'm going to wear . . . I hate this bloody suit. Nobody asks me if I like the bloody suit. I'm not to open my bloody mouth, I'm just a parcel of shit that has to be tarted up. They don't want Gingy the way he is, used to be. They want him so's he's theirs. They want the old Gingy buried, they want him like a bloody puppet, that they can sit on their knee, that they can talk through. What do you call that?'

'They call it a ventriloquist's dummy, Gingy.'

'That's what they want, Gingy for a dummy. I'm not having it . . . They want to put the mark on me, let them . . . We're in a para barracks. The cover is that we're 'tecs over for a course. No sod's buying that. We're in a flat, top floor, end of corridor. The door's always locked. They put me to bed, like I was a kid. I can hear them when I'm in bed, I can hear them bloody laughing. The bloody walls are like cardboard, every time they bloody laugh I hear them. We go out each night, go on the booze, and if I come out of the room after I've gone to bed, for a leak, then the laughing stops. There's never any bloody laughing when I can get myself close to them.'

242

Ferris shuddered in the cold, and Gingy's teeth were chattering, and he was gushing out his talk, as if speaking kept him warm. When he looked behind him he saw the outline of Prentice sitting on a low wall of the park, fifty yards from them, sitting and watching a man who was blown out.

'I'm not a bloody fool, I know what they're at. They're at taking myself away from me, they're at changing me. The clothes is changing me, and the bloody haircut's changing me . . . We went to church on Christmas morning, the local R.C. They looked a bit nervous, and they was watching everyone else so they'd get the movements right. I said I wanted to go to Confession, that was a morning after Christmas. I didn't really want to go, I was chancing, but they said no, that I couldn't . . .'

'What would you have confessed, Gingy?'

'That's not your business.'

'Would you have confessed that you were an informer?'

'Confession's not for blabbing about, not to the likes of you.'

'Or would you have confessed that you'd killed a judge and two detectives?'

'Not your business.'

'Or that you were running scared?'

'What do you know of running . . . you've a bloody great army behind you. You're not on your bloody own. If you were ever on your own, against them, then you wouldn't give me talk about running scared.'

Again Ferris looked behind him. Prentice would have seen his face, white from the high street light. He saw Prentice raise his hand in acknowledgement. He knew that Prentice wouldn't approach. He knew Prentice would leave him to do the graft alone, to bend McAnally once again back on course . . . bastard.

'What else have you been playing at, Gingy?' Ferris asked briskly.

'Rehearsing, isn't that your word?'

'Could be the word.'

'They've brought my statements over. We've been taking a morning on each statement. Today it was what I said about Phonsie McGurr, yesterday it was Dusty O'Hara, day before was Fatsy Rawe. It's Brennie Toibin tomorrow . . . wrong, not Brennie Toibin, because I've quit . . .'

'How do you rehearse the statement?'

'I have to be able to speak the statement without looking at it. They start shouting at you, trying to interfere with what you're saying, and they tell you you're a liar, that you're making it all up.'

'Like it would be in court?'

'That's what they say it would be like in court – only I'm not finding out what it's like in court, I'm quitting.'

'That's what you said, Gingy.'

'And meant it.'

'What'll you do?'

'When I've quit . . . ? I'll lie up for a bit, then I'll put the word out, that I'm looking to go back . . .'

'Go back?'

'Go back home.'

'You'll be dead before you get a mile off the boat.'

Gingy seemed not to hear him. 'If the word's right I'll go back home.'

'What's home?'

'Home is Roisin, home is the kids.'

Ferris breathed the cold air deep into his lungs. 'She'd not have you back.'

'Don't mess me,' Gingy snarled.

'You know a big man . . .'

'I know a hundred big men.'

'Do you know a big man with a bullet scar in his throat?'

Gingy hesitated, he was trying to read Ferris and could not. 'What if I do?'

'Do you know him?'

'I know Frankie Conroy, so what if I do?'

'Does he know Roisin?'

'She might know him.'

'Does she know him very well?'

'She's no reason to.'

'Does she know him well enough for him to be calling with the presents and the tree for Christmas and the lights, does she know him that very bloody well?'

Gingy's head dropped into his hands. His shoulders were shaking, his face was hidden from Ferris. His voice was muffled through his fingers. 'Do you know what the fear is? Does a Brit soldier know that?'

'Yes.'

'You'd not have the chance of knowing.'

'We had a sniper, when I was out on patrol last week, we were hit by a sniper, that was pretty scary.'

'One of your squaddies got hit, you wondered how you didn't?'

'I was the target,' Ferris said. 'I just stopped, I can't remember why, I must have broken his aim as he was on the trigger. His bullet glanced off the mag on my rifle, the impact put me down on the deck, which is why my nose isn't healthy, wasn't Sam. Knowing the rifle had been on you, the aim on you, that was pretty scary. Knowing that you'd been chosen, out of eight and he'd chosen you. I suppose it was because I was the officer . . .'

Gingy shook his head, he looked up from his hand. There was pity for Ferris in his eyes. 'You know fuck all of nothing.'

'He'd taken a derelict house, on the corner of the Drive and the Crescent in Turf Lodge, he had food there and a sleeping bag.'

'Don't go back,' Gingy said hoarsely.

Ferris smiled, sadly. 'Have to go back, and lightning never strikes twice.'

'How many snipes in your platoon area, the last month?'

'No snipes, not in the last month.'

'Not in your Battalion?'

'Not one, we had a petrol attack . . .'

'And it's the first snipe, and it's you that's the target . . . and Roisin's gone home, and Frankie Conroy's sniffing at her fucking door . . . You think you were bloody random?'

Ferris gazed at Gingy, opened-mouthed. 'Roisin would have . . . ?'

'They've got you down as the way to me. Don't go back . . . 'Course Roisin would have, you're her fucking enemy, you're the enemy of every bastard in Turf Lodge. You're the friend of the supergrass . . . If you go back you know fuck all of nothing. You tell me if I go home I'm dead. I'm telling you that if you go back you're sniped.'

'I have to go back. Because I said I'd stand beside you, and I will.'

'You're bloody mad.'

'I'm going to go back, and you're going to give evidence, Gingy.'

'What's you going back going to get you?'

'Gingy, believe me, me going back is going to get you into the witness box.'

'You're all crap, Ferris.'

'We're going back, you and me, Gingy . . .'

'You'll be in the bloody gutter.'

'So you can put the bastards away.'

'You'll be in the gutter and the kids'll be jumping round you, fucking clapping.'

'Not you, not me, neither of us are running scared from the bastards.'

Ferris stood up, and Gingy McAnally followed. The light from the street lamp beamed onto their faces. Ferris managed a sharp smile, and Gingy grinned and then shook his head. Their hands were clasped for a moment.

'What'll have happened to your girl?'

Ferris walked away.

He passed Prentice, who nodded curtly, and further down the street he saw Goss who was lolling head back and asleep in a parked car.

He thought of a man waiting in the upper room of a derelict house with his food and his sleeping bag and his Armalite rifle, and the face of David Ferris in his mind. He thought of a gutter in Turf Lodge, and he thought of the children's feet jumping before his fading sight, and he thought of their shouts in his dying ears. He thought of his father who was embarrassed to speak of the 'difficulties'. He thought of Sergeant Tunney who wanted a few left for him and who would never again wear a uniform over his re-grafted skin. He thought of the Chief of the Belfast Brigade, pulled from a hiding place under a bed. He thought

245

of the faces of Turf Lodge, all anonymous, all without names, all joined in their loathing of David Ferris, friend of Gingy McAnally.

The door of the Midnite Club was padlocked. The windows were darkened. He looked both ways on the street, and didn't find her.

He went to the car park, where she had left her car. The car park was empty.

He walked the eight miles from Aldershot to Farnham, and revellers who were returning to their homes hooted at him and swept past.

He walked into the estate of new Wates houses. He walked up the cul-de-sac to the accountant's home. He saw Sam's car, parked with the near front wheel among the pruned roses.

He walked round the side of the house, and looked up at the back room where the double bed was, and shouted Sam's name.

When the kitchen door opened, when she stood in her nightdress in the doorway, he saw that Sam who had laughed in the Midnite Club had wept in her friend's bedroom. She clung to him, he clung to her. Big, bold Sam, crying like a baby.

'I so wanted you to come back here . . .'

'You're going to be mine, Sam, I'm going to be yours. Soon as I'm out of that dreadful place.'

'Promise.'

She was smiling and she was crying. A rainbow in the night, crying and loving.

'I promise.'

'Thank God you came back . . . That creature, is he really your friend?'

'I have to be his friend. If I'm not his friend then he's had it.'

'You promise you'll come back to me.'

'Promise, Sam.'

She kissed him all the way up the stairs, all the way to the back bedroom.

19

The landrover was waiting for David Ferris in the car park outside the Customs hall. It had been a rough night on the boat, force eight, he had hardly slept in the hard seat in the passenger lounge. Since they had sighted land, a blur in the dawn light, he had been on deck, leaning on the rail, watching the coast line. He was chilled from the sea's climbing spray.

The faithful Jones, with two squaddies to ride shotgun, had brought the landrover to meet him.

Ferris was unshaven. He wore the same shirt and socks as in the Midnite Club. His suit trousers were holed from the collision with the dustbin, the skin on his right knuckle was bruised.

Fusilier Jones arched his eyebrows. 'A good leave, sir?'

'Excellent,' Ferris said.

'How is Sergeant Tunney?'

'In good shape, Jones, looking forward to getting back so he can bawl your arse off you.'

'You gave him our love, sir?'

'I told him you were all wetting your beds because he wasn't there to tuck you up each night . . .'

They drove through the city that was awakening from the Christmas and New Year holiday. They queued in the traffic lines, and saw the files that were waiting for the Sales doors to open on Royal Avenue and in Donegal Square. All the greasepaint normality of Belfast was on show for his homecoming, all the fraud that pretended this was just another community in the United Kingdom lurching back to life. In the cars around their landrover were the civil servants and the representatives and the bank clerks and the insurance men, and on the pavements beside the landrover were the housewives and the secretaries and the shop girls who were late and running, and none of them would care a shit for Ferris's war and the supergrass's war.

And then they were on the Falls. He had Jones's rifle across his knee, and he had cocked it. He saw the bomb sites and the graffiti, and the end of terrace wall that had long ago been painted white so that a passing patrol would show up for a marksman's aim, and he saw the bar that was caged in wire against petrol bombs, and the Housing Executive office that was protected by concrete dragon's teeth against a close-quarters car bomb, and he saw a cruising R.U.C. mobile, and a foot patrol of Charley company. His eyes were on the roof-tops, and were searching for the missing slates, and for the darkened holes in bricked-up doorways. He was watching the gable walls that would give a sniper cover until the moment he was prepared to fire. He watched the dustbins that could be the hiding place for a pack of explosives linked to a command wire. He watched the Falls as he had never watched it before.

He remembered Gingy McAnally's warning and the clasp of McAnally's fingers on his, and in that moment he thought he might throw up because he was so bloody scared to be back in the Falls.

The landrover swung through the gates at Springfield.

Jones cut the engine. 'I'd get yourself changed, sir,' he said confidentially, 'and get your face scraped . . . I'd do it soonest, sir.'

Back in uniform, with his face burning from a new razor blade, he went to the Armoury and drew out his rifle and signed his name for two magazines of 7.62 mm ammunition.

On his way to Bravo's Ops he met the Intelligence Officer.

'Have a good leave?'

'Fine,' Ferris said.

The Company Commander greeted him like a malingerer.

'How was your leave?'

'Fine.'

He passed the Chaplain in a corridor.

'Nice to see you back, David. A good leave I hope.'

'Very good, thank you.'

He went to the Commanding Officer's room.

'What shape's Tunney in?' Sunray asked.

'First-class, sir, raring to be back.'

'Damn good. You had a good leave?'

'Very good, sir.'

There was what they wanted to hear, and there was what they didn't want to hear.

The Battalion area, Ferris learned, had been as quiet as a cemetery during his absence. The locals were still sleeping off their New Year's liquor intake. He had missed nothing, so he was told.

They met in the city centre and went together into Boots on Royal Avenue.

Mr Pronsias Reilly had set up the meeting with Frankie Conroy, scrambled it into his lunch break from the Crown Court. He preferred to meet among the crowds of the Belfast shopping area, rather than risk himself against the hidden electronic surveillance systems that operated on the Falls and throughout Nationalist West Belfast. He would have preferred Frankie to have used his bloody loaf, to have dressed with a little more care, not to have appeared as if straight off an Assistance queue. They made a rare pair – Mr Pronsias Reilly, suit and black overcoat and blue shirt and white collar, and Frankie Conroy, mud-scarred Docs and jeans and donkey jacket and a wool cap – working their way past the cosmetics counters and the garden tools and the hardware electricals.

'They're galloping, they're rushing into court,' Reilly said quietly.

'What does that mean?'

'They're going for an early Preliminary hearing in front of the Magistrate. They've delivered the prosecution statements, they're going ahead in a week or so . . .'

'Normally it's bloody months.'

'They're going to get McAnally into court, get the boys committed

248

for trial, then they'll put him out to clover for a year, then we'll have the main show.'

'Why're they rushing?'

'Perhaps because he's going to be better sooner rather than later . . . there's fuck all the defence can do about it, whatever the reason.'

'I've lost him,' Frankie said simply.

'Lost who?'

'Lost his *friend*, lost the Brit officer who holds his hand.'

Since St Stephen's Day, the day after Christmas, Frankie Conroy had trudged the streets of Turf Lodge, looking for the officer whose face was drawn in his mind. He had seen the mobiles and the foot patrols, and the V.C.P.s and the P.-checks. He had been out early in the morning, and in the late afternoon, when the patrols came. He had wondered whether the television and the papers had lied. They had said the officer wasn't hurt, that the magazine of his rifle had deflected an aimed shot. He had wondered whether that was a bloody lie. He had recognized some of the Brit soldiers from Ferris's platoon, but their officer had never been with them.

'You promised . . .'

'There's fuck all I can do if he's not out on the streets.'

'I told the Chief you were taking care of him.' The ferret eyes of Mr Pronsias Reilly gleamed in anger. He should never have gone in so bloody deep. Direct association with the Organization was walking him out of his depth, too bloody deep.

'He's not where I can get at him.'

'You bloody said you'd get at him.'

'I can't bloody ring up the barracks and ask . . .'

'You said you'd stiff him.'

'If he's not on the streets, I can't get him.'

'Then you keep looking for him, laddie, because the Chief's waiting on your word.'

They went their separate ways. Mr Pronsias Reilly walked back to the Crown Court and the canteen and a sandwich, and Frankie Conroy took himself off in search of a black taxi and a ride to Turf Lodge.

Rennie rang Aldershot.

In staccato sentences he spelled out to Prentice what he had achieved with the office of the Director of Public Prosecutions.

The Preliminary in court opening in a week, two days for the Prosecution counsel before the weekend. McAnally to come in on the Friday, and be ready to perform on the Monday.

'We reckon he'll be in the box for the rest of the week. He has to see that through . . . you've got a holiday after that. It's fixed that you're for Cyprus once he's past the Magistrate. You're bloody lucky, Prentice, sunshine and cheap plonk to calm down with. You'll have forgotten what bloody Belfast is by the time you get back. You'll have him ready?'

Prentice said he would have him ready.

'How's his chin?'

Prentice said that Sean Pius McAnally's chin was mended.

'He'll be alright?' No more certainty from Rennie.

There was an age-long pause on the line, like Prentice had gone away to have a leak.

'I'll have him ready, and his chin won't look like he's been scrapping. He'll know his lines, he'll know what to expect, but that's all I know for sure. He doesn't talk to us any more. He's inside himself. The Brit talked to him, you know that. I don't know what he said because McAnally won't tell me, and because Ferris isn't around to be asked. McAnally's gone inside himself so's I can't reach him. As I said, Mr Rennie, he knows what he has to say, but whether he's going to say it I just don't know. You won't know whether he's going to deliver right up to the time he goes in the box.'

'You mean he might fall down on his arse.'

'I just don't know.'

'You're a bloody comfort. I'll have his friend on ice for him.'

'You do that, Mr Rennie.'

'Not good news, David, I'm afraid,' the Adjutant said. 'Cast your memory back. The day you were shot up in the Falls, the McAnally fellow, that business. You were running down to Hastings Street R.U.C. because there'd been a complaint from a newsagent chappie or something, about your apes wrecking his place. We thought the peelers had forgotten about it, seems they haven't, seems you're required in the afternoon for your statement.'

'I'm supposed to be patrol leading.'

'If your chaps can't manage without you then you're a pretty poor platoon commander. Most mortals would be grovelling thanks at the thought of spending time in the cop shop rather than pavement bashing . . . You alright, David?'

Frankie Conroy had a bicycle and a ladder and a bucket, and he smear-wiped front windows in Turf Lodge, and didn't ask for money, and those that didn't know thought he was a fucking eejit, and those that knew him saw the way that his head was most of the time twisted away from his work and watching the Drive and the Crescent and the Avenue.

250

And still no officer with them when the patrol came through. And there was a biddy at his shoulder, shouting that the glass was dirtier than when he'd started.

In a corner of the Mess the Bravo Company commander collared him.

'You're in luck, David. Sunray's got it into his head that the Battalion's short of range firing. You're going down to Ballyclare tomorrow, you and 2 platoon from Alpha. I don't want Henry crowing over me that my lads can't shoot. If Alpha put one over us, I'll kick you where it hurts . . . Well, don't look so damned miserable.'

Ferris went back to his chair and the dog-eared *Illustrated London News*. The pages were bouncing in front of his eyes. For another day he was spared patrolling. He had stiffened himself to accept that in the morning he would be on the streets of Turf Lodge, a target. There was no one he could tell . . . he couldn't ask for a desk job, or a transfer, or to be shipped out. His pact was made with Gingy McAnally. It was the third time that he had tried the page and the report of last season's Calcutta Cup match. He couldn't read the words, and couldn't absorb the photographs. He was obsessed by the narrow streets of the Falls, and by the estates of Whiterock and Ballymurphy and Turf Lodge.

'If you saw Frankie then you'd know he was trying.'

Mr Pronsias Reilly was hunched over the interview table. The Chief's face was a few inches from his. The lawyer saw the licking nervous strokes of the Chief's tongue against his lips.

'Frankie's doing his best, but his man's off the face of the earth.'

'What else is there?'

'There's nothing else, there's only the officer.'

'Without the officer . . .'

'Gingy might retract.'

'With the officer?'

'They're going ahead, rushing it, because they reckon he won't retract if they can get in fast. If he's got the officer . . .'

'What if he's got the officer?'

'Then it's bad for us, that's all I can say.'

'Why isn't there anything else?'

'Because there isn't.'

'What about his wife?'

'Wouldn't matter a shit to him.'

'What about his kids?'

Mr Pronsias Reilly gazed into the face of the Chief. He felt the fear tremor in his belly. He knew of Mattie Blaney's boy . . .

251

'I didn't hear that,' he said. 'If one of those kids is harmed – so help me, I'll stand in court and cheer when you go down. I'll cheer if you go down, for twenty –'

The Chief grinned. 'I didn't make a threat.'

'Then be careful with your words.'

'The Brit officer's different?'

Mr Pronsias Reilly shuffled together his papers. Finally he said, 'I'll do my damnedest to see you walk out a free man, but not if the McAnally kids are harmed.'

'You get that officer, you and Frankie.'

'I put it to you, McAnally, that you have told a tissue of lies.'

He said stubbornly. 'I've told the truth.'

'I put it to you, McAnally, that you have lied for one simple reason, to save your skin.'

'No.'

'You are a man with a violent criminal record, a record of murderous terrorism, for which you deservedly faced a life sentence of imprisonment, and now you're lying to wriggle clear of that sentence.'

Prentice walked the room. McAnally sat on a hard wooden chair, and just behind him and cross-legged on the carpet was Goss.

'I'm telling the truth.' McAnally swung to face Prentice, his control was sliding. 'It's not lies.'

Goss's hand came up to McAnally's shoulder. 'Never turn and face them, it's to goad you into facing the dock, facing the relatives. You just look in front of you, just at the Magistrate.'

'Would it not be correct to say, McAnally, that by naming names you have won immunity from prosecution for a number of serious crimes?'

Gingy's hand, clasped tight, slapped down onto his thigh. 'It's all bloody rubbish this . . .'

'Just answer my question. I am suggesting that you concocted events to go with the names of quite innocent men.'

Gingy had turned again to Prentice. 'I know what happened, I know what I've got to say.'

Goss gestured for Prentice to hold off. He spoke quietly, urgently, in McAnally's ear. 'Gingy, I've told you every bloody day, and I'll tell you again. It's your word against their word. What it comes down to is this. They are going to try to destroy you, to cut you up in little pieces.'

Gingy sighed dramatically. Prentice caught Goss's glare of annoyance. Prentice didn't hold back. There was no requirement for him to mollycoddle the supergrass. His requirement was to toughen him, strengthen him, so that when the barristers got their hands on him, he'd have some defence, some armour.

252

'You say that you were brought back from the South against your will.'

'Yes.'

'And you were then dropped at your home?'

'Yes.'

'I put it to you, McAnally, that if you had been brought back from the South against your will, that when you were dropped at home, you were then perfectly free to return to the South.'

'You don't understand . . .'

'I suggest to you that you were a willing member of a murder gang, who when arrested plucked names out of the air and signed a statement which was traded in for immunity for a life sentence of penal servitude.'

'That's a bloody joke . . .'

'Try, Gingy,' Goss hissed. 'Try and help yourself.'

'Is that what they're going to say to me?'

'That's what they're going to say to you,' Prentice said. His voice had roughened, lost the court-room gloss.

'Jesus . . .' McAnally had slumped forward in his chair, his hands covered his face.

'Do you know what's happening now, if this was the court?' Prentice crowded close to McAnally's chair.

'What's happening?' The reply muffled from behind McAnally's fingers.

'Defence are on their feet. They're pleading there's no case to answer, that it doesn't even go to the Crown Court, because the witness is a half-wit, and they might just get away with it . . . and the Chief's cracking a bloody smile, because he might be walking down the steps of the Crumlin in half an hour's time. And if he's walking out then he's thinking bloody well of Gingy McAnally. And if the Chief's out, then out with him are Shay and Dommy and Fatsy and Bugsy and Phonsie and Dusty, and they're all talking bloody well of Gingy McAnally, tout . . . Don't be a pathetic bastard, McAnally.'

Goss waved Prentice back. McAnally's shoulders were shaking, convulsing, and his hand couldn't steady them. His mouth was against McAnally's ear. 'We have to do this, Gingy, it's for your own good. By hurting you now, we're trying to make sure they don't hurt you in court. You sit in the box, you don't turn round, you take your time.'

'I didn't know . . .'

'. . . it would be like this? We're teaching you because it's better you find out now, than find out when you're in the box.'

'I can't . . .'

'I don't know that bloody word,' Prentice shouted.

'I gave you your statement. I'm not going through with being ripped.'

'Your statement didn't buy you immunity.'

'Where's Ferris?' McAnally's head jerked up. He stared at Prentice.

253

'Back in Belfast,' Prentice said warily.

'He's really back there, no bloody lie?'

'He went back to Belfast, back to his unit.'

'He's not transferred out?'

'He's back on the Springfield Road.'

'You know that? You're not lying to me?'

A puzzled frown cut Goss's forehead. 'Why, Gingy?'

'You wouldn't lie to me?'

'He's with his unit, soldiering. That's certain. Rennie rang him. We're going back on Friday, right. We're staying up the coast of the Lough for the weekend. Rennie's called him out for a piss-up on Friday night, that's how I know that Ferris is in Belfast.'

'Could he sit in court?'

'Christ, Gingy, what for?' Prentice stalked away from McAnally's chair.

'Where I could see him,' McAnally said quietly.

Goss summoned a little gentleness, didn't bloody know where he found it. 'I'll get it fixed.'

'And he went back to Belfast?'

Prentice leaned against the wall behind McAnally. He said keenly, 'Why shouldn't he have gone back to Belfast?'

McAnally stared at the carpet pattern between his feet. He pursed his lips in concentration and he drove his fingers through his hair, and he lit a cigarette, and drew deeply onto the butt.

A calm settled on his face, and his shoulders no longer shuddered.

Without warning, he smiled, and shrugged.

'Can we go over that again?' McAnally asked.

Goss shook his head at Prentice, nothing for either of them to say. He went and sat at the table. He was to the left of McAnally's eyeline, but McAnally could see him if he was staring straight ahead. He sat where they would fix for the officer to sit.

Prentice stated, 'I suggest to you, McAnally, that you were a willing member of the murder gang, who, when you were arrested, plucked names out of the air and signed a statement which was traded in for immunity from a life sentence of penal servitude.'

McAnally gazed at Goss who sat in front of him. He seemed to see the officer, and he saw a mountainside and the rain was lashing from the officer's face, and he heard the words of the officer, quiet and caring, in his ears.

'What I said is the bloody truth,' McAnally said.

*

254

In the early morning dark the patrol slipped out of the Springfield barracks. Eight men, shadowed and silent figures, jogging between the doorways, crouching in cover. And raining over West Belfast.

The Bravo company officer had suggested that the patrol should be a Mobile. Ferris had requested that they should be on foot. The company commander had cocked his head in surprise, but made no objection. Each day that he had not been out on patrol had been worse for Ferris. There had been the Hastings Street visit, and then the day on the range where he'd shot like a blind pig, and there had been the day when the local scribbler from the North East had come to Springfield to write 'home town stories' of the squaddies and she'd been fifty and fat and thought it a bloody adventure to get as far as the barracks. The police station and the range and the minding of the reporter had kept Ferris off the streets. Each day had been worse than the one before.

On his upper body were his vest and his shirt and his heavy knit sweater and his camouflage tunic and his flak jacket, and he was shivering. In the first sprint across the Springfield Road from the gates he had nearly dropped his rifle, and he had stumbled down into his first cover and torn the skin from his knees. If a squaddie had come to him and said he was shit scared of stepping outside the barracks' perimeter, Ferris would have played the good officer, and slapped him cheerfully on the shoulder, and told him there was nothing to fear, and that he was a member of a highly trained group of young men, that his back was always covered, and not to talk such crap. If an officer was afraid then he was a case of L.M.F. You couldn't hide Lack of Moral Fibre. All the Battalion would know that David Ferris had been categorized as L.M.F. Right down to Fusilier Jones they'd know. His mother and his father would know. And Sam would know.

David Ferris didn't think he had the balls to go to the Commanding Officer and request a transfer, on the grounds that he was a possible specific target. So he led his foot patrol out into the warren of West Belfast, and each time he was stationary the foresight of his rifle flickered on the rooftops and the chimneys and down the dark unlit alleyways.

He didn't think of Sam. He didn't think of Gingy, nor of Rennie who had telephoned to request his presence at a hotel bar on Friday evening. He didn't think of twenty-one more days in Belfast before the Battalion up-sticked for home.

Dangerous to think of anything but the shadows of the doorways and the marksman's possible hiding places, and the plastic bags and the dustbins and the lengths of discarded piping.

The patrol found two youths acting as though they were about to teach themselves a lesson in larceny, and over the radio they whistled up a police wagon, and handed the brats over along with their bag of tools.

They were almost into Ballymurphy when, high on the Springfield, there was the crash of a single shot. Ferris was aware of his men flinging themselves to the pavements, crawling towards shadow. Outgoing, from one of his own. And then the swearing from across the road, and the section corporal giving out, and then running across the road to where Ferris lay.

'That silly cunt Conville, Mr Ferris. Tripped over an old push chair, and his thumb flicked off the safety. Accidental Discharge . . .'

Ferris hauled himself up. He tried to keep his voice flat and calm. 'Thank you, corporal. Make a note of the details. It'll have to be reported.'

'Wouldn't have thought so, sir,' the section corporal said easily. 'There's a few rounds spare from the range . . .'

'Don't know what's the matter with the bugger, mind you keep your eye on him. And mind you make up his ammo.'

'Best way, sir. Wouldn't want 3 Platoon knowing, never hear the bloody end of it.'

When the shot had been fired he had been terrified. He banged the sharp corner of his magazine into his knee-cap. Pain was preferable to fear.

The morning was coming, the light was hazing through the streets as the patrol entered Turf Lodge.

She slid her legs off the bed and reached for her dressing gown and slipped it over her shoulders.

Frankie was on his back, snoring, the blankets lying low on his bare stomach.

It had been Roisin's first night back in her old house. The workmen had been the previous morning and finished the repairs to the windows and the door, days bloody late and a piss awful job they'd made of it, and the van had come in the afternoon with her furniture. Not one of the neighbours had stirred a fist to help her move her furniture, and she'd been struggling on her own, and with Young Gerard, when Frankie had appeared on his bicycle. He'd parked the bicycle round the back, with his bucket and his ladder, and he'd shifted the furniture with her.

And his bicycle and his ladder and his bucket were still round the back, against the kitchen wall.

She'd surprised herself because it hadn't seemed that important to her, going up the stairs with Frankie Conroy, him going to bed with her and settling onto Sean's side like he had the right to be there. She'd reminded him of what she had said in his car. Nobody took her trousers off her, she took them off when she wanted them off. She'd thought she wanted Frankie Conroy in her bed that night. Not that important, not a big deal, when she'd carried Baby Sean out of her bed and put him down with Little Patty. He was a clumsy sod, and he wasn't clean, but he'd been good to them. God knows where she and her Ma would have found the money for the Christmas tree and the lights. They'd have been without if Frankie hadn't showed. And he'd bought the supper that night, before she'd taken him up the stairs. He'd given Young Gerard the money to run down to the chipper van, four cod and six chips. They'd had a good crack round the table, and even Young Gerard had smiled. Young Gerard liked the big fellow. And there wasn't a man who she should be keeping herself for, not since she'd taken the taxi and her kids away from Thiepval Barracks.

It was good to be back in her house even if the workmen had made a bloody awful job of it. It was good to have a man in her bed even if he bloody snored.

She pulled back the curtain.

The soldier crouched by her front gate, and he must have seen the curtain move because his rifle swung to aim at the window. She saw the grin explode on the soldier's face and pulled the dressing gown tight around her. Then saw Ferris.

'Sean's friend,' she said, to herself out loud.

'What's you say?' Frankie propped himself up on his elbow.

'I said, it's Gingy's friend.'

She spoke her husband's name flatly, as if he were gone from her, as if he had never been part of her.

She saw Ferris's face, and his hollow deep-set eyes, and the way his rifle barrel traversed over the rooftop above her before he went away up the road, a loping loose stride.

Frankie was beside her, white-skinned, naked, bulging his stomach against the window sill. Together they watched the officer's back until it was gone from their sight.

Frankie left her at the window. He dressed fast.

'What's your bloody hurry?' She didn't turn to look at him.

'I've got to be away.'

'Where to?'

'Limerick . . .'

'Down south?'

'I'll call by when I'm back.'

She heard him go down the stairs and into the kitchen. She heard him open the back door. She heard the squeaking of his bicycle and the ring of his bucket in the hall.

Frankie Conroy rode away down the Drive, away from the patrol, wobbling on his bicycle because he balanced his ladder on the handlebars, a shadow figure in the early morning light.

*

257

Thursday, early. January's wet low cloud hovering on the Crumlin Court House. They had to be in the Crumlin for the Preliminary because the city centre Magistrate's court on Chichester Street didn't have the capacity to hold so many defendants.

A few minutes before 10 a.m., the prisoners filed into the dock. They'd had to squeeze their way up the stairs from the basement cells, because there was a prison officer flanking each of them, and more prison officers waiting for them in the dock, and the dock itself was ringed by uniformed policemen. There were policemen at each corner of the courtroom, and two cradled their carbines, and some rested their hands on the handles of their holstered hand guns.

As each of the prisoners came up the steps, appeared at the back of the dock, there was clapping from the public gallery where the friends and relatives were herded close together. More policemen in the public gallery. The prisoners were at this moment stars greeted by their faithful admirers.

The barristers and solicitors and clerks gathered together in the sectarian knots of Defence and Prosecution, and talked earnestly and quietly and seemed to make the pretence that this was an everyday occasion, not special. Every seat taken on the hard wood benches of the journalists, their sharpened pencils laid out with new shorthand notebooks.

The prisoners talked loudly amongst themselves and waved back to the public gallery. All except one made a show of cheerfulness and bravado and camaraderie. The Chief was alone. The Chief didn't look up to the gallery, didn't acknowledge the particular ripple of applause that greeted his entry into the dock. The Chief allowed his chin to be on his chest and his shoulders to droop.

It would be different on Monday. There wouldn't be the clapping and the applause and the waving on Monday. On Monday all eyes would be on the small low door at the back of the courtroom through which the witness would come. There would be a tension and expectancy on Monday, because Sean Pius McAnally must come through that door on his way to the witness box to supergrass on the Brigade and Battalion officers of Belfast's Provisionals.

There was a straightbacked wooden chair, not taken, against the wall of the courtroom, to the left of where the Magistrate would sit and below his raised dais.

20

Ferris had the billet to himself. Armstrong was on early stag in Ops, Wilkins was taking his turn on the range.

Soft disc jockey patter and the easy music through the ply-board partitions that separated this billet from half a dozen like it.

He lay in bed, the notepad on his pillow, writing to Sam.

My dearest Sam,

It's been a pretty soft week. I've had masses of time to think about you, to think about us. I want us to make the announcement as soon as I can get you to a shop and get you the RING.

I've got a really soft week coming up. From Monday I'm going to sit in court and hear the supergrass give his evidence. They've got some daft idea that if he can see me while he's in the witness box he'll have the guts to go through with it. He's flying in tonight from England and I'm being taken off for a few drinks with him, which means I'll be dumped back here legless. If you didn't know what he'd done, you'd say that he's quite a fair chap really. He's wrecked himself. I shouldn't really have got involved, but you get no choice.

I was talking to our Sky Pilot, and he put in a bid to do us in the Depot chapel – we'll talk about it. I showed him your picture – he said you had child-bearing hips! See you soon, Sam, see you at home, see you away from this awful place. Look after those hips.

Lots of love,
David

He put the single sheet of paper in a coarse brown envelope, licked down the flap and addressed it.

He shaved carefully that morning, as if there was to be a special purpose for the day. He thought his face was that of an old man. He saw the worry lines when the razor was close to his mouth, and he saw that his eyes were sunken. He shouldn't have recognized the bloody face in the mirror. He had to shave with great care because the blade was new and his fingers shook.

He went to the Mess, and at the mahogany table he hid himself behind a newspaper and drank three cups of coffee.

'David, jolly good, glad I've caught you.' The Adjutant breezed towards him. 'What are you on today?'

'Rennie, the detective, is picking me up this evening – he cleared it with you.'

'This evening . . . what about today?'

He said heavily, 'I've a mobile going out in the morning, in the afternoon I've two sections for foot patrol.'

'Excellent . . . you're out yourself this afternoon.'

He hesitated. 'I'm not sure yet . . . I've got Rennie coming.'

'Rennie's this evening. Whatever you do this evening, kindly remember that for today you are a member of 2 R.R.F. You won't need a whole day off to ready yourself for junketing with the police.'

'I'll probably be out with one of the foot patrols, probably not out with the mobiles.'

'That's more like it. I've a couple of Scots Guards in. They take over from us. It would thrill the pants off them if you take the lieutenant on walk-about, show him the ropes, give him a feel of things.'

Ferris swore to himself. No bloody chance of quitting foot patrol now.

'Be a pleasure.'

'That's grand . . . nothing wrong is there, David?'

'Never been better.'

'Excellent. What time do you want him?'

'Ops Room at fifteen hundred.'

The Adjutant tramped noisily away, whistling.

Ferris finished his breakfast and went off to beg a stamp from the kitchen corporal.

'They said you was a tout.'

'And I never was.'

'I know you was never a tout.'

Frankie smiled down at the pinched defiant face of Mattie Blaney's boy. The boy was the last of the cogs for the wheel trap that he had fashioned in the fifty hours since he had seen the officer from the window of Roisin's bedroom.

The boy supported himself with a metal stick. He was mobile, after a fashion. He was as agile as any of the others who had had the plastic knee-cap fitted at the Royal Victoria Hospital.

'Does it hurt you much?'

'Not so's I'd notice,' Mattie Blaney's boy lied.

'You can stand on it?'

''Course I can stand on it. Standing now on it, aren't I?'

'Could you stand on it a long time?'

'I could.'

'Like two hours?'

'If I wanted to I could. Why should I want to?'

'They made a mistake with you.'

'I was never a tout,' the boy blurted.

'You was blamed for something you never did.'

'Right I was.'

'We think you're too good a kid to walk away from us. We think you're still one of us, even after what we did to you.' Frankie gave the boy a cigarette, and struck the match for him, and watched the boy choke on his first inhalation, and cough the smoke out of his mouth. 'There's been a hell of a row about what happened to you . . . I still trust you, boy.'

'Wha's you want from me?'

'Not what I want from you, it's what the Organization wants from you. We want you to mind something.'

'What do you want minded?'

'You don't ask questions, not when you work for us. We're trusting you. We's saying you wasn't a tout. No bugger'll ever again say that Mattie Blaney's boy touted.'

'You know what they did to me?'

'They was wrong to do it, they'd no cause to do it.'

'They burned me with a fag . . .' The boy held the cigarette close to Frankie's nose, close enough for him to feel the ash heat. 'They put the boot in on me, then they hooded me, then they shot me fucking knee off . . . I told them I was never a tout.'

'If any man says you're a tout, he'll have to say it to my face, if you's help me.'

Mattie Blaney's boy wasn't much more than a child. He was a thin little scarecrow. He wore running shoes split at the toes, and jeans that were knee-patched, and a sweater that had come down from three brothers. Mattie Blaney's boy nodded his trust to Frankie Conroy. When they walked away Frankie had to curb his impatience because the boy hobbled awkwardly after him.

Frankie took him from the Drive into the narrow footpath that divided the gardens of 50 and 52. They could just walk side by side. The alley was wide enough for a running man, or for a man on a motorcycle. He felt bloody tired. It had been a hell of a drive to Limerick, and he'd had to find the cottage out on the Clare side of the city. And when he'd found the man the bastard had said that for that sort of work he needed clearance from Army Council, and he needed permission from the Quartermaster General for the gelignite and for the detonator. They were funny bastards down south when it was joining-up time with Northern Command or Belfast Brigade. Frankie had pleaded that he didn't have the time to wait on the authorization, and the bastard hadn't been easy to twist because he'd wondered who'd dropped his name. Frankie had said that the name came from the Chief, and that was true. The bastard had been suspicious as a virgin nun, and hard bloody going because Frankie couldn't understand all the Clare accent chatter, and the bastard blinked at the Belfast talk . . . What did Frankie want? Frankie wanted the same as the bastard had done before . . . Four hours of talking, and a half-bottle of Paddy, and finally the bastard had said he'd do it.

Frankie had gone to sleep in the chair by the fire. The bastard had woken Frankie in the chair and handed him the cardboard box, and the bastard had told Frankie how it should be done. He had come back over the border on an Unapproved Crossing. He hadn't met a block. He'd been wetting himself all the way towards the border in case he hit a block and the cardboard box was opened.

The rough back road at the end of the alley that served the pre-cast concrete garages for the residents of the Drive and the Avenue was rutted and pot-holed. He was certain it would work. Frankie Conroy had to be certain. It was down to him. Fucked if he was going to sit in another bloody house with an Armalite and wait for a patrol and for the officer. He thought that with his plan he could guarantee that the officer would come. Guarantee? . . . that was bloody rich. Christ, he was doing his bloody best.

He led Mattie Blaney's boy to the third garage in the back road. The doors were old and sagging, but there was a new padlock on the clasps. He had the key and he opened the door. He checked both ways and saw nothing and nobody to disturb him. He pushed Mattie Blaney's boy in ahead of him, into the dark interior of the garage. The boy hadn't gone easily. Frankie wondered if they'd done his knee in a place like this. The garage was empty . . . there were few enough cars owned in the Drive or the Avenue, if a bugger had a car then he kept it in front of his windows, where he could see it. He went to the back wall, to a heap of plastic sheeting. He pulled back the sheeting and displayed to Mattie Blaney's boy two Suzuki 125cc motorcycles, blue painted, identical. He bent down and pointed behind the far wheels of the motorcycles, showed the boy two black mouth-guard crash helmets. He unwrapped a strip of sacking and stood back to let the boy see two Luger pistols.

Jesus, and hadn't he worked since he had flogged back from Limerick . . . worked to 'loan' the motorcycles, worked to 'borrow' the helmets, worked for the Lugers, worked to 'acquire' the garage, worked to find the trap for the officer.

He covered the pistols and laid the sheeting back over the motorcycles.

The boy watched him. There was no awe on his face, no admiration.

'He'll have to be a right fool,' the boy said coldly.

'Who?'

'Who you're going for.'

'Why's he have to be a fool?'

There was almost a sneer at the boy's mouth. 'They did this two years ago, the I.N.L.A. did it. The peelers'll know this one.'

'It's not for the police,' Frankie said angrily.

'If it's for the Brits it might work. The Brits isn't permanent here like the peelers, they mightn't know about it.'

Frankie smiled and tried to be the boy's friend and patiently explained to him what he wanted.

The tunnel corridor echoed to the crack of the warder's shoes.

The Chief thought that the shits always shod their shoes with metal, toe and heel, as if it gave the shits some authority. Each man in the long file was escorted by a warder down the steps from the gaol, through the tunnel corridor under the Crumlin Road, up the steps and into the basement of the Crown Court.

He felt the winter dampness on the prison walls. The younger men in the file looked to him for leadership, for defiance, and he had nothing to give them . . . Shay and Eug and Dommy looked to him, and Fatsy and Bugsie and Dusty and Phonsie. They looked to him as if he had some bloody magic . . . and when he turned to them suddenly, when they hadn't expected it, he could see their resentment, their belief that he was to blame for having called back Sean Pius McAnally from the South.

Beneath the court he was locked into a cell by himself.

The Chief sat on a wooden bench. There were names scratched and biroed and pencilled on the walls. He saw names that he knew, the names of the men who were his contemporaries as he had come up in the Organization, men who were rotting in the Kesh on Tenners and Fifteens and Lifes.

There was a rattle of keys. The cell door opened, and Mr Pronsias Reilly bobbed inside. The Chief smelt the aftershave and the talc powder.

Mr Pronsias Reilly came close to the Chief.

'Frankie's going this afternoon, going for bloody broke. If you're a praying man, you should be bloody praying the sun's shining on Frankie's arse this afternoon . . .'

The saloon bar of the big road house on the A31 beyond Guildford was empty but for them.

Goss leaking in the jacks, and McAnally at a corner table with his back to the wall and trying to pretend he could read a newspaper, and Prentice drumming his fingers on the counter and waiting for the skimpy girl to take time off from glass polishing. Rennie had said that McAnally should arrive pickled, and stay pickled through Friday evening, and through Saturday, and they'd dry him out on Sunday and give him a bomb to get him to sleep, and bounce him into court on Monday morning.

He reckoned they'd managed to get McAnally quite respectable. The suit had been dry-cleaned, and unless you looked hard you couldn't see the vomit stains. Not that the runt was saying much, so the sooner the pickle was inside him the better. For himself, he wasn't fussed about getting back to Belfast, but Andy was. Andy was bloody fretting over his lady. He'd learn. When the door was slammed in his face, he'd learn.

'Two halves of draught lager, love, and a large Scotch.'

Fine for McAnally to be pissed on the flight, not so fine for Goss and himself. Goss came to him at the bar as he was paying. Goss was staring along the bar at McAnally.

'He's a horrible little turd, isn't he?'

Prentice laughed out loud. 'Did you expect a bloody saint?'

'I was standing in there, having my pee, and I thought – up your zipper, Andy, on with your smile, and go back out there to that horrible little turd.'

'Like I said, he's no more than you'd expect,' Prentice said quietly.

'You know what I hate about him? He's never been one bloody bit sorry for what he did. You ever heard him say that he regrets blowing away an old man and two young coppers? Have you hell.'

'It's your bloody job, Andy,' Prentice said.

'Then it's a rotten bloody job.'

Prentice took his glass of lager and McAnally's Scotch and walked to the corner table. He saw Goss drain his glass and head for the door. He'd have gone to sit in the car. No one said it was easy, cuddling up to a supergrass. He thought that he didn't care who he was cuddling with. He thought he was a good bloody 'tec for a rotten bloody job. And in the evening it wouldn't be John Prentice who'd be cuddling up to the supergrass, it would be the Brit officer, and John Prentice would be at the bar, and getting well pissed.

A warm smile gathered at Prentice's mouth.

'Double Scotch, Gingy, what the doctor ordered. Crack it down you, lad.'

'What's with him?' McAnally gestured towards the door.

'Something about the car. Get it down, Gingy, then we've time for one more. We'll not get any more once we're with the Air Force . . .'

'What was he saying to you?'

'He was saying the car had a rotten bloody engine. Myself, I don't care. If the engine gets us where we want to go then I'm happy. I'm not fussed as long as we get where we want to go. You understand me, Gingy? Another of the same won't see you wrong, right?'

He was still smiling when McAnally drained the Scotch and belched, and he went back to the bar to get the glass refilled.

He had been in the pub, and he'd tried to pee away the pints that he had drunk while Mattie Blaney's boy waited outside with a packet of crisps and a chocolate bar. It was a cold afternoon, but Frankie Conroy was sweating. He thought now that he might have been better on an Armalite, that what he'd managed was too bloody elaborate, but he had got it, and he was stuck with it.

He pushed the motorcycle down the alley and into the Drive, and the boy came after him with the crash helmet under his arm. He took the motorcycle fifteen, twenty yards down the Drive from the entrance to the alley so that it couldn't be seen by a man standing at the top of the alley at the garages.

The two pounds of industrial gelignite were strapped to the inner top of the helmet, with the detonator and the bicycle lamp battery that provided the power to explode the gelignite when the circuit was tripped. Frankie had the coat collar of his jacket turned up and he wore his wool cap low down on his forehead as if for disguise. He laid the Luger pistol on the pillion seat of the motorcycle and placed the crash helmet carefully over it, and lifted the tinted visor so that when he looked through the space he could see the weapon. There was a single, short length of fishing line hanging from the helmet. Irritably, because he was frightened, he waved the boy back from him, not for the boy's safety, but because he needed the light to complete the arming of the booby trap. He fingered the line down to the iron bar underneath the padded pillion seat, and gently inserted it round the bar, and tightened it so that it was taut. He was breathing heavily. He had seen the six-inch steel nails that were held round the gelignite with binding tape, as he knotted the line.

If the helmet was moved, lifted, picked up, then the line would be tugged, then the power circuit would be opened.

He wiped the sleeve of his jacket across his forehead. The boy watched him, detached and unexcited. The boy watched him as if Frankie were a craftsman mechanic. He was angry that the boy had to see him when he was sweating.

He told the boy that Mattie Blaney, in the Kesh, would be proud of his son. He repeated his instructions to the boy, stabbing with his finger for emphasis.

When Frankie had gone, the boy lowered himself down onto the pavement and sat beside the rear wheel of the motorcycle. There were no scratches on the vivid blue paintwork and on the chrome finish to the engine parts, and he could see his own face reflected and distorted on the curve of the crash helmet. And when he looked through the opening of the helmet he could see the Luger. The idea wasn't new, but it might work on the Brits.

The motorcycle stood outside Number 46. After Frankie had gone, the woman came out from 46 and asked the boy what he was at, and the boy told her shrilly not to ask, and that she'd be better in the back, in her kitchen. She went into her house to fetch her man. The man came close to the motorcycle and the boy waved him away with his steel stick, and the man went back into his house and drew the curtains of the living room and of the upstairs front bedrooms so that he would see nothing.

Two women, with their push chairs and their older kids around their skirts, came towards the boy, and the kids ran ahead and wanted to touch the motorcycle because it was new, expensive, shining. The boy flailed at them with his crutch, and the mothers saw the cold determination on his face, and gripped the hands of their kids and dragged them on down the pavement.

All those who looked from their windows, or who paused to stare out from their front doors, or who walked past the motorcycle, saw Mattie Blaney's boy guarding it and taking care of the crash helmet on the pillion seat, and they knew what was planned. There were telephones in some of the houses, but none of those who knew even considered ringing the confidential number at Police Headquarters. Hadn't a wee boy been shot dead by the peelers in Short Strand the week after Christmas, and him taking sugar to his Gran, and him claimed by the peelers as a gunman, and him not fifteen? The man in Number 46 systematically removed the family china from the mantelpiece above the fire in his living room and stacked it on the kitchen table.

Half an hour after Frankie had left Mattie Blaney's boy there were no children playing on the pavements of the Drive. A silence had crawled over the street, a silence of waiting.

Within minutes of their meeting Ferris had been told that the Scots Guard lieutenant liked to be known as 'Roddy', being an abbreviation for Roderick. He was a veteran of the hike to Port Stanley. He was hating the prospect of four months in Belfast because he gathered that he wouldn't get to a decent party all the time he was there. He was disappointed to hear that they would be going on foot.

Ferris didn't say much.

Ferris said less when they were out on the Springfield, when they were clear of the covering fire of the barracks' perimeter.

266

Roddy ambled beside Ferris. He seemed unimpressed with the sudden charging runs of the squaddies, and didn't take part in the frequent dives for cover behind the base of lamp posts and the privet hedges and in the doorways. They were at the top of the Springfield, hemmed in by the estates. In front of Ferris a squaddie sprinted, bent low, across the road, causing a black taxi to swerve to miss him. Ferris was crouched down on his haunches, his rifle at his shoulder rotating over the roofs and upper windows. Roddy stood beside him. He had been issued with a Browning automatic pistol, and the strap of the holster was still fastened down. Ferris's face and the faces of all of his section were blacked with camouflage cream, Roddy's cheeks were pinkly fresh.

'Do you always behave like this?'

'What do you mean?'

'All this scampering about . . . I'm not a bloody general, you don't have to impress me. If it's for my benefit . . .'

'It's not for your benefit,' Ferris muttered. From the corner of his eye he saw the flash of a movement at a chimney stack . . . and a seagull flapped itself airborne.

'Well, you're hardly impressing the natives. If I lived here – what do say this place is? Bally what? Whatever the place is called – if I lived here then I'd say the British army is half scared to death. You're like rabbits bolting out of a cornfield. When we were in the Falklands . . .'

'Shut up,' Ferris said quietly, too faintly.

'. . . In the Falklands we *dominated* the Argies. Didn't have manpower superiority or logistics superiority, but we dominated them, enough for them to crumble.'

'Belt up,' Ferris snarled.

'Did I hear you right . . . ? Please yourself. If one can't make an observation . . .'

'When you're in charge you can walk up here in fucking red coats. For as long as you're with me, for Christ sake, shut up.'

Ferris ran across the street, and Roddy loped after him. Ferris saw the surprise beetling the Guards officer's brow. Jones came after them, grinning hugely.

'Wipe that off your face, Jones, and concentrate,' Ferris said.

Roddy said, 'Where are we?'

'Coming out of Ballymurphy, going into Turf Lodge.'

'What's Turf Lodge?'

'Turf Lodge is the enemy – just like Longdon and Tumbledown were the enemy, only you won't see any bloody white flags because we don't have any Argie conscripts here.'

Ferris could have kicked himself. The Guards officer would go back to his depot and report that the Fusiliers had the wind up.

'Listen, I'm sorry for shouting . . . every doorway, alleyway, derelict house, is danger. You get used to that and that way you stay alive.'

267

His apology was acknowledged. Roddy ignored him as he would have ignored a bore at Sunday morning drinks.

Over his radio Ferris reported his position to Ops, and then he waved the section forward, into Turf Lodge.

McAnally stumbled down the steps of the Hercules. Prentice hung to the collar of his jacket.

Rennie was by the cars. He nodded with approval to Prentice as the minders brought McAnally to the transport.

Prentice said softly to Rennie, 'I wouldn't bet on him, sorry.'

Rennie seemed not to hear. A big jovial smile for McAnally.

'Welcome back, Gingy . . . They've not been force-feeding alcohol down your throat, I hope. You'll need to have left a corner, we've a bit of a thrash tonight. I'm dropping you off, then I'm going for David.'

The doors snapped shut on them. Rennie and his driver in the front, McAnally sandwiched between Prentice and Goss in the back. Behind them was a back-up. They swept away for the forty-minute drive to the seaside hotel on Belfast Lough.

Roisin was on her knees in the kitchen. It was the third time she had scrubbed the kitchen floor since they had moved back. When she was close to the linoleum, when her nose was near to it, she could smell what the mob had done on the floor of her kitchen.

'Ma, have you been out the front?' Young Gerard was in the kitchen doorway, excited and bubbling.

'How've I been in the front when I'm on my knees out here?'

'They're going to do a fucking Brit, out in our road.' It was her son that spoke, her child. Roisin shuddered.

'Honest, Ma, they're going to do a Brit, the Provies are.'

Young Gerard didn't speak of his father any more, not after he'd put the phone down on him. She had tried, twice, three times, haltingly, to make an excuse to the child for what his father had done, and Young Gerard had walked away from her.

She wiped her hands on her apron.

Young Gerard ran in front of her to the front door. As his hand was on the latch she caught him, swung him behind her. She opened the door, she looked out. She looked right and the Drive was deserted. She looked left and she saw the bright blue of the motorcycle and Mattie Blaney's boy standing beside it.

'Look, Ma . . . the bike, Ma . . . that's for the Brits.'

She remembered the hunting keen glare on Frankie's face when she had called him to the window, pointed down to the street for him to see the officer who was Gingy's friend.

She swore at Young Gerard that she'd half bloody murder him if he followed her out.

She slammed the door shut after her. She was wearing her slippers and her apron and she had her hair tied up in a scarf.

She walked to the motorcycle and Mattie Blaney's boy. The boy watched her coming and his eyes were alive with suspicion, dislike.

'What's happening here?'

'It's nothing to you, what's happening.'

'Don't give me lip.'

'You'd be best in your house, Missus.'

'What's special about the bike?'

'Wouldn't be telling you, wouldn't be telling a supergrass woman.'

'What's the bike there for?' She was shouting at the boy.

Mattie Blaney's boy was coldly calm. 'You wouldn't need to know.'

She took a step nearer to the motorcycle, and the boy raised his stick, and its tip pointed at her stomach. She walked round the motorcycle, out of the range of the stick if the boy lunged for her stomach. Through the visor space of the crash helmet she saw the barrel of the pistol.

The light was beginning to slide. The afternoon was falling fast away. The patrols always came in the grey half-light. Usually she saw the officer in the dusk patrols.

'They'll stiff you if you tout, Missus,' Mattie Blaney's boy said. 'And they'll burn the roof off over the head of your brats.'

She turned, very slowly, and walked back to her house.

She took Young Gerard and Little Patty and Baby Sean into the kitchen, and she locked the door on the inside and put the key in the pocket of her apron, and worked with the brush and the bucket at the linoleum flooring.

Frankie sighed the air deep into his lungs.

He kicked down the support leg of the motorcycle, left it gleaming blue and chrome with the engine ticking. The crash helmet was a tight fit on his head, awkward, hard for his face to twist behind the tinted mask. He took the Luger from his pocket, cocked it, and ran towards the doorway of the Post Office.

He cannoned through the door. His voice reverberated inside the helmet as he screamed for money. It was dark in the Post Office, and he saw women cringe away from him, indistinct shadowed figures. He fired twice into the ceiling, and the pistol shots were muffled. The Post Office on the Glen Road was hit regularly, five times the last year. The Post Master was protected by a bullet-proof glass from counter to ceiling. Frankie waved his Luger at a woman and fired into the wall, over her head as she knelt on the floor. The woman was weeping. The woman was Mrs Deasy, and he'd been to school with her twins. The Post Master thrust a bundle of notes into the sliding tray under the counter glass. Frankie grabbed for the money, dropped some, pocketed some, and ran for the door.

The Suzuki roared to life. Every man and woman and child walking in the Glen Road on the southern edge of Turf Lodge saw the motorcycle and its black-helmeted rider career away towards the roundabout and the junction with Kennedy Way and the Monagh by-pass.

He cornered on the roundabout, and the grin split his face pressing his cheeks against the glass. He saw the grey toad shape of a police landrover coming circumspectly down the Monagh by-pass. Fucking good . . . It was more than a hundred yards from him. Still turning on the roundabout, he fired twice at the landrover's windscreen. Fucking liven up the pigs. He accelerated back down the Glen Road, the siren in his ears, piercing the helmet. Now the air waves would be jumping.

Twice he turned to check that the landrover was in sight, in touch with him, then he turned off, skidding and fast, into the Crescent of Turf Lodge.

'BRAVO 41 . . . BRAVO 41 . . . COME IN . . . URGENT YOU COME IN BRAVO 41.'

'Bravo 41 . . .' Ferris said into the radio mouthpiece clipped to his tunic collar. Around him the patrol had sunk to cover and defensive fire positions. Roddy's face was misting with a flicker of interest.

'BRAVO 41 . . . GLEN ROAD POST OFFICE ROBBED BY ONE ARMED MALE. DESCRIPTION IS BLACK JACKET, BLACK CRASH HELMET. ESCAPED ON BLUE MOTORCYCLE INTO TURF LODGE. POLICE MOBILE IN CHASE. YOUR POSITION? OVER.'

'The Avenue, Turf Lodge.'

'WAIT OUT . . .'

Ferris shouted, 'Post Office on the Glen Road. One armed male. Black crash helmet. Blue motorcycle.'

He saw his squaddies checking that their rifles were armed. He saw Roddy groping numbly for the fastening strap of his waist holster.

Frankie sped down the Crescent. As he swung into the alleyway linking the Crescent to the garages, the police landrover was reaching the entrance to the Crescent. He bounced down the alleyway, and swerved among the ruts to get to the garage entrance. He heaved the door open, drove inside, cut the engine. He shed the crash helmet and tossed the

Luger into a corner. He went out and closed the garage door behind him and fastened the padlock. He crossed to a back garden and climbed over the fence and was gone.

'BRAVO 41 . . .'
  'Bravo 41.'
  'POLICE MOBILE'S LOST HIM. WENT DOWN AN ALLEYWAY BETWEEN TURF LODGE CRESCENT AND TURF LODGE DRIVE. POLICE MOBILE NOT KEEN TO FOLLOW ON FOOT. GET YOURSELF THERE AND SWEEP. OUT.'
  'Out.'

The section came fast into the Drive.
  Oldest bloody trick in the book, Ferris thought, as he pounded up the pavement hill, using a motorbike to get down an alley that was too narrow for a landrover to follow.
  There was something hostile about the street, something that he couldn't finger, something about there being no one on the street.
  'What are you going to do, David, what's your procedure?' Roddy was at his shoulder, heaving. His questions snuffed out Ferris's thoughts.
  Roddy was panting as if he hadn't run two hundred yards since he crossed East Falkland island. For Christ's sake . . . it wasn't a bloody chat-up in the Mess. This was hunting an armed man. There was something . . . Shit, something, and he couldn't find it.
  He saw the boy limping down the hill of the Drive towards him. He saw the boy with his stick. The face of the boy was familiar. He had seen the face in torchlight when it was screwed in pain, and he had seen the face in the headlights of the vehicle park as the boy was lifted into the ambulance. He felt the weight of the boy in his arms.
  'Hello, you won't remember me . . .'
  The boy stared up at Ferris, no sign of remembering him.
  'I took you down to hospital when you were . . . when you were hurt.'
  The boy looked away from Ferris. He seemed to wait for permission to walk on.
  'Have you seen a man on a blue motorcycle, with a black crash helmet?'
  The boy gestured with his stick behind him.
  'Is that where you saw the man and the bike, lad?'
  Again the boy pointed.
  'How long ago?'
  'No time ago, mister.'
  The section ran forward, and the boy lurched away.

271

There was a shout from a squaddie on the far pavement to Ferris. A shout of triumph and success.

Ferris saw the motorcycle. Ahead of him, in the failing afternoon, the motorcycle was stood at the side of the road, against the gutter of the pavement, and there was the shine of a crash helmet that was placed on the pillion seat. Ferris didn't have to tell them, the squaddies had fanned out on either side of the motorcycle, and his corporal had taken one squaddie and gone up the alleyway to secure the rear of the homes on the side of the Drive where the motorcycle was parked. Ferris looked ahead of him, and behind him. No sign of the boy, and the Drive was empty. He looked at the windows of the houses and there were no lights lit, and there were no pale faces staring out at the patrol.

There should have been . . .

'That's a good show, latching onto it so soon,' Roddy drawled.

'Please don't talk to me,' Ferris snapped.

'You don't have to be scratchy. It's not the Maze break-out, it's only a Post Office . . .'

'Don't you see something's wrong . . . ?'

Ferris's voice tailed into the quiet of the Drive. His squaddies were watching him. Jones was at his shoulder, and his lips were narrow and his finger white against the trigger guard. A cat scurried from under a car, and from instinct four rifle barrels followed it over the first yards of the dash.

He walked to the motorcycle, and Jones walked behind him, backwards and covering his officer, and Roddy went with them and thanked the Lord they didn't have the likes of this one in the Guards.

Ferris stood at the side of the motorcycle. His thighs were within a foot of the rider's seat. He crouched down and the dome of the crash helmet was level with his eyes.

Something was wrong.

Ferris laid his rifle on the tarmac. He slipped to his knees. He edged the fingers of his right hand forward towards the engine parts. The tips of his fingers hovered over the metalwork, feeling for heat. A slow smile spread on his face. He dropped his fingers onto the metal, and felt nothing, no warmth. He had found the something that was wrong. Jones was looking down at him.

Ferris winked at Jones.

He depressed the 'Speak' button on his radio.

He spoke quietly, privately into his microphone. 'Bravo 41, Bravo 41 . . .'

'COME IN BRAVO 41 . . .'

Roddy strolled to the far side of the motorcycle.

'Bravo 41. Clever games in the Drive. We are outside Number 46. We have a blue Suzuki motorcycle like the one in the Glen Road, we

272

have a black crash helmet, and the engine's cold. This machine hasn't moved anywhere . . .'

'Take a peep at this,' Roddy called.

'. . . There's not a soul on the Drive. It's never like that, not at this time . . .'

'Here's his shooter, David.'

'I'm requesting the help of Bomb Disposal. In the meantime I'm going to have my hands full evacuating the nearest houses. I'm not in much of a position to mount a search. Over.'

'BRAVO 41 . . . WAIT OUT.'

Ferris turned to the Scots Guard officer. 'Sorry, what was it?'

'He left his shooter here.'

To prove his point, to display the Luger, Roddy lifted the crash helmet from the pillion.

Rennie came into the bar.

They were playing cards. Prentice and Goss, Gingy, McDonough and Astley. They were playing poker for pennies.

Gingy saw him first. Gingy saw that Detective Chief Inspector Howard Rennie had been weeping, crying his bloody eyes out.

21

In the rain, the crowd stood on the pavement outside the cream and honeysuckle majesty of the Crown Court. They were mostly women in the crowd, and some had brought their toddler children, and some held placards that had been made and given them by the Sinn Fein workers. Mostly they were from the families of the accused men. There were the wives and the mothers and the cousins of Fatsy Rawe and Bugsy Malone and Noel Connelly and Brennie Toibin and Joey Mulvaney and Dusty O'Hara and Billy Clinch and Ollie O'Brien and Joey McGilivarry and Tom McCreevy. There was the brother of Mrs Oona Flaherty. There was the aunt of the Chief . . . Waiting on the pavement outside the Crown Court building was someone who was family to each of the men named by Sean Pius McAnally, the supergrass. They had been on the pavement since dawn, just as they had waited all through the previous morning, the Monday morning, before the word had spread that the Prosecution had sought and obtained an adjournment of a day. On the

Monday morning the crowd had been raucous in its denunciation of the Show Trials and the Paid Perjurers to the microphones of the television crews and of the B.B.C. radio and downtown. Then, running from the Court House, Mr Pronsias Reilly brought word that the Prosecution had won an adjournment. The word was that the Prosecution didn't have their tout to crawl into the witness box. And the word, spoken quietly, was that the death of a Brit officer before the weekend had shattered the resolve of the informer.

Amongst the Sinn Fein workers and the local journalists who knew the habits of the police, it was said that the supergrass was always brought early in the morning to the Court House in an armour-protected saloon car with a back-up behind and hurried into the building through a side door at least two hours before the court was due to sit. Some of the workers and some of the journalists had been at the main gates of the Crumlin court since six in the morning. They said that McAnally was not inside. They said that they would swear that McAnally had not shown. The Magistrate had come with his bodyguards, and the Prosecution had come with the detective who had been assigned to him for the duration of the Preliminary hearing, but of the star and the centrepiece of the Prosecution case there was no sign.

The camera crews and the journalists were no longer interested in the relatives and their slogans – yesterday's news, yesterday's chip wrappers. There was a growing excitement amongst them, a feeling of anticipation. If the supergrass didn't show, if the Prosecution collapsed, if the accused walked free, then that was one hell of a story, that was front-page, that was the lead on the lunchtime bulletins.

Suddenly there was movement. The cameramen jerked their heavy equipment onto their shoulders. The crowd of relatives surged towards the gates and the stone-faced policeman.

Mr Pronsias Reilly skipped down the steps of the Court House and jogged to the gate. The crowd pushed round him, and the cameramen jostled for vantage views of his beaming face, and the microphones were clustered under his chin.

'I have just come from the meeting in the Magistrate's room, a meeting which was called for by counsel for the Crown. The Prosecution asked for a further adjournment. I can tell you that I and my colleagues objected strongly to further delay and pointed out to the Magistrate that this case was being heard with considerable and unusual speed at the demand of the Crown. His Worship has compromised. The court will sit at two this afternoon, and if the Prosecution are then unable to produce their witness, then their case is over, finished. I hope for a satisfactory outcome at two o'clock this afternoon . . .'

The wife of Ollie O'Brien kissed Mr Pronsias Reilly wetly on the cheek, and repeated it for the photographers who had missed the first time.

The Secretary of State said, 'You know what I should be doing now, Fred? I should be emptying my drawers, piling my papers in the middle of the carpet, and setting fire to them. Isn't that what a general does when he's in full retreat?'

The civil servant said, 'Not your fault, Minister. It shouldn't be your head.'

'The Prime Minister rang this morning, before I'd even had breakfast. The Prime Minister said that as a result of my advice, the Cabinet had been led into a cul-de-sac from which it could not escape without humiliation. McAnally not showing in court, that's humiliation in the P.M.'s book . . . God, this bloody place . . . I'm not prepared to wriggle over a resignation. I'm going to get it over with.'

'I'd leave it until after lunch if I were you, sir,' the civil servant said.

'To what purpose?'

'Only that the ending of a political career is not something to be rushed . . . Now, Confederation of Industry's outside, you've an hour with them. Security meeting's at eleven. Lunch is with the G.O.C. and the Chief Constable . . . Oh, and the flowers you wanted were sent.'

The wind blustered round the flowers, and the rain burgeoned on the petals. The colour bloom would be short-lived in the cemetery in winter. He could not see the grave because his view was obscured by the ranks of the umbrellas and the backs of the Honour party. There was the volleyed crash of blank cartridges. His own flowers, a bunch of early daffodils, were buried beneath the carpet of wreaths. He thought it was a good turn-out, considering the weather. He thought it was the same sort of turn-out that he would have had if he'd been blasted when he was with the R.P.G., when he was hitting 'Tenner' Simpson. The Last Post was played, and the face of the young bugler quivered. One by one the mourners left. He saw David's father and mother, and he saw his Commanding Officer who walked crisply with his hands clasped behind his back inside a knot of the Battalion's officers, and he recognized the girl who had been at the Midnite Club who wore a black silk coat and who held a crumpled envelope in her black-gloved hand. When the people had gone, when the troops had marched away, when the gravediggers had had their fags and set about their work, Rennie came to his side. For the service at the graveside, Rennie had stood away from him, behind him, with Prentice and Goss. He was looking at the flowers, at the love that had brought the flowers to the cemetery.

'Your decision, Gingy . . . Your choice,' Rennie said.

The wind was on his face. The rain was on his suit jacket.

The wind of the slopes of Mullaghmore. The rain of the summit of Mullaghmore.

When Rennie had come into the bar, and ignored his soft swollen eyes, and told in a stern hard voice of the explosion in Turf Lodge and the casualties in Turf Lodge, then Gingy had fled to his bedroom in the small hotel. He had cried the night away into his pillow. It was Gingy who had asked to be brought to the funeral, and Rennie had made the arrangements. Over the weekend, during the flight to Manchester, through the evening in the hotel outside Preston, Rennie had never asked Gingy for his intentions.

'I can't force you, Gingy . . . I can't be twisting your arm,' Rennie said.

He watched the men who shovelled earth onto the coffin. He gazed over the flowers. He didn't feel the wind, nor the rain.

He turned to Rennie, he nodded. It was Gingy's decision, it was his choice.

They drove fast to the airport with a siren escort of the Lancashire police.

They by-passed formalities and were last on board the British Airways flight.

They were met at Aldergrove by a convoy of unmarked police cars.

They came through Ballysillan and Ligoniel and past Ardoyne, they came down the Crumlin, and there was a Smith and Wesson revolver in Prentice's hand, and a Sterling sub-machine gun on Goss's lap, and Rennie was glancing at his watch and talking into the car radio to announce their approach. Gingy was hunched down between his minders, but he could see the gate towers of the gaol and the high painted walls of the Court House.

They were seen by the crowd, and the women threw themselves at the linked arms of the policemen, and a placard hit the roof of the lead car, and the line of policemen bulged, and held. And Gingy, low in his seat, masked by the minders, heard the cat-calls of abuse that were hurled at the bullet-proof windows. And he covered his face from the photographers and their flash bulbs.

He was hustled into the side of the Court House, and they pounded him up the back staircase to a second-floor room. He was breathing hard.

'Your decision, Gingy,' Rennie said.

Goss detached the magazine from his Sterling, clattered it down onto the table.

There was a light knock at the door.

'It's straight in, Gingy. Good luck, lad.'

He stood alone. They were all watching him. The knock came again at the door, sharper. Rennie and Prentice and Goss were watching him. He straightened his tie. It was the tie of brilliant green that he had worn to the funeral.

276

'It's not for you,' Gingy said. 'I'm not doing it for you . . . just so's you know that.'

After the darkness of the staircase and the corridors he blinked when he came into the court room.

He heard the growl of interest as he was seen. He hesitated, he seemed to those who craned to see him to freeze, then the weight of Rennie shoved him forward. He looked straight ahead of him. He saw the Magistrate whose body was huge under the black gown and he knew that the Magistrate wore a bullet-proof vest. He saw an R.U.C. constable in the corner ahead of him, expressionless, and holding his carbine. He saw the barristers and the solicitors and the clerks peering at him shamelessly. He saw beyond the witness box an empty straight-backed wooden chair. As he came forward he locked his eyes into the empty straight-backed wooden chair as if it were his talisman.

No longer the growl of interest. The shouts from the dock bleated into his ears.

'Filthy traitor, McAnally.'

'Sold out your country.'

'A disgrace to your people, McAnally, that's what you is.'

'McAnally, you're in your fucking grave.'

The hate spat down at him from the dock. The prison officers fingered their truncheons. The policemen ringing the dock tensed themselves to prevent an attack on the supergrass. He didn't turn to see the faces of the prisoners. He never saw the loathing and the anger and the bitter twists on the mouths of the men who had been his comrades in arms. He didn't see that the only man who was silent in the dock and who hadn't stood to shout and finger-jab was the Chief. Rennie and Prentice and Goss were close on him, breathing to him.

'How much did they pay you, McAnally, thirty pieces of silver?'

He seemed to stumble and Prentice and Goss were reaching to hold him, and when he felt their hands on his arms he shook them away.

He walked through the floor of the court. He didn't look behind him, nor to his side. The shouting from the dock had died. A great silence slipping on the court room. He looked ahead to the empty straight-backed wooden chair against the wall.

He stood in the low-sided witness box. He felt the blood pumping in him, he felt the stampede of his heart.

'You are Sean Pius McAnally?'

The clerk was in front of him.

'Yes.'

The clerk passed him a worn bound bible. 'Repeat after me . . .'

After he had spoken the words of the oath of truth he was told to sit by the Magistrate.

He stared at the empty straight-backed wooden chair. He tried to find the face of the man who had been his friend. He prepared himself to give his evidence.

Harry's Game

To William Kean Seymour

1

The man was panting slightly, not from the exertion of pushing his way through the shapeless, ungiving mass of the crowd but from the frustration of the delay.

He drove himself at the knot of people that had formed a defensive wall round the Underground ticket machine, reaching out through their bodies with his money for the slot, only to be swept back as the crowd formed its own queue out of the rabble. It took him fifteen seconds more than two minutes to insert his ten-pence piece and draw out a ticket, but that was still quick set against the endless, shuffling line approaching the ticket kiosk.

He moved on to the next piece of gadgetry, the automatic barrier. He inserted his ticket into the machine, which reacted and bent upwards to admit him. There was space around him now. His stride lengthened. Bottled up amongst the mass on the far side of the barrier, with the clock moving, he'd felt the constriction, his inability to get away.

Now, in the open at last, he cannoned off an elderly man, deep in his paper, making him stumble. As he tried to sidestep his way out of the collision he knocked into a girl loaded for the laundrette, hitting her hard with his left elbow. She looked startled, half focusing on him, half concentrating on holding her balance, her arms out of action clinging to the plastic bag pressed into her breasts. He saw the look of surprise fill her face, watched her as she waited for the explanation, the mumbled apology and helping hand – the usual etiquette of Oxford Circus Station, top hall, at 8.45 in the morning.

He froze the words in his mouth, the discipline of his briefing winning through. They'd told him not to speak on route to the target. Act dumb, rude, anything, but don't open your big mouth, they'd said. It had been drilled into him – not to let anyone hear the hard, nasal accent of West Belfast.

As the man sped from the fracas, leaving the elderly man to grope amongst a mass of shoes for his paper, the girl to regain her feet with the help of a clutch of hands, he could sense the eyes of the witnesses boring into him; it was enough of an incident to be remembered. The briefing had said 'Don't speak' . . . but while the crowd acknowledged people's need to hurry it demanded at the least some slight apology for breaking the etiquette of the rush hour. The failure to conform was noted by the half-dozen or so close enough to examine the man, who now ran away towards the tunnel and the escalator leading to the Victoria Line. They'd had at least three seconds to see his face, to take in his clothes and, above all, to note the fear and tension in his face as their stares built up round him.

When he reached the escalator he swerved left to the walking side of the moving stairs and ducked down behind the moving line, past the stationary paper-readers and the bikini-advertisement watchers. Here the eyes were away from him, on the financial pages, the sports pics, or the hoardings floating tantalizingly by.

He was aware of his stupidity in the hall area, conscious that he'd antagonized people who would recognize him, and he felt the slight trembling again in his hands and feet that he'd noticed several times since he'd come across the water. With his right hand, awkwardly and across his body, he gripped the rubber escalator rail to steady himself. His fingers tightened on the hard rubber, holding on till he reached the bottom and skipped clear of the sieve where the stair drove its way under the floor. The movement and the push of a young man behind him made the man stumble a little, and with his right hand he reached out for the shoulder of a woman in front of him. She smiled warmly and openly at him as he found his feet again, and a little hesitantly he smiled back, and was away. Better that time, he thought, no tension, no incident, no recognition. Cool it, sunshine. Take it easy. He walked through, carried forward by the crowd on to the platform. They'd timed the frequency of the trains; at worst he'd wait less than a minute.

His left arm, pressed against his chest, disappeared into the gap between the buttons of his raincoat. His left hand held tightly on to the barrel of the Kalashnikov automatic rifle he'd strapped to his body before leaving the North London boarding house two hours and twenty minutes earlier. In that time the hand had never left the cold metal and the skin under his thumb was numb with the indentation of the master sight. The barrel and weapon mechanism were little more than twenty inches long, with the shoulder stock of tubular steel folded back alongside it. The magazine was in his hip pocket. The train blurted its way out of the darkened tunnel, braked, and the doors slid back. As he wormed his way into a seat and the doors closed, he edged his weight off the magazine, and the thirty live rounds inside it.

It was 8.51 by the cheap watch on his wrist, just visible if he moved the gun towards the coat buttonholes. Five minutes maximum to Victoria, three minutes from the Underground platform to the street, and, taking it gently, seven minutes from there to his target. 9.06 on location. The train pulled abruptly into Green Park Station, waited little more than forty-five seconds as a trickle of passengers got off, a few moments more to let others on, and the doors, to the shout of the big West Indian guard, were closing.

9.06 on location meant that he had two minutes in hand, perhaps three at the most, primarily to assemble the gun and pick his firing position. It was a close schedule now, and he began again to feel the trembling that had dogged him since Rosslare and the ferry, and that he had first felt acutely at Fishguard as he walked with the Kalashnikov past the cold eyes of the Special Branch section watching the ferry passengers coming over from Ireland. He'd gone right by them then, waving furiously to a non-existent relative in the middle distance beyond the check-point and suddenly realizing that he was through and on his way. At his briefing they'd told him the worst part before the shooting would be at Fishguard. He'd seen when he was at the back of the queue how they watched the men coming through, watched hard and expressionless, taking them apart. But no one from his ferry, that he'd seen at any rate, had been stopped. At the briefing they explained that in his favour was his lack of form, never fingerprinted, never photographed, that he was an unknown face, that if he kept his nerve he'd get away with it and make it out as well. No sympathizers' homes in London were being used, no contact with anyone, keep it tight as an Orangeman's drum, one said. They'd all laughed. The train jolted to a halt, the carriage emptied. Victoria. He pulled himself up with his right hand on the pole support by the door, and stepped out on to the platform. Instinctively he began to hurry, then checked himself, slowed and headed for the neon 'Way Out' sign.

By the start of the nine o'clock news something approaching order was returning to the Minister's home. Three children already on their way to school, two more still wrestling with overcoats, scarfs, hockey sticks and satchels. The au pair in the hall with them. The Minister's Afghan tangled round their legs.

The Minister was alone at the long refectory table in the breakfast-room, newspapers spread out where the children's cereal bowls had been. First he gutted the editorial columns, then on through the parliamentary reports, and finally to the front-page news. He read quickly, with little outward sign of annoyance or pleasure. It was said that only his closest parliamentary colleagues, and that meant about four in the Cabinet, could spot his moods at a time like this. But the selection of papers offered him little more than the trivial interest in the fortunes of his colleagues. Since his eighteen months as second man in Belfast, and the attendant publicity, his promotion to Social Services Overlord and a place in the Cabinet had taken him back out of the public eye and reduced his exposure. His major speeches in the House were fully reported, but his monolithic department ticked along, barely feeling his touch at the helm. This morning he wasn't mentioned, and his department figured only in the continuing story of a grandmother in the

North-East who had been taken to hospital penniless and suffering from malnutrition and then told local officials that she'd never drawn her pension, and believed people should look after themselves anyway. Lunatic, stupid woman, he muttered.

The news was mostly foreign, South Africa and the mine strike, Middle East cease-fire violations, Kremlin reshuffle. 'In Belfast' – suddenly he was concentrating – 'a city centre pub was destroyed by a car bomb. Two masked men had warned the customers to leave, but the bomb went off before the area could be fully evacuated. Three men were taken to hospital suffering from shock, but a spokesman said no one was seriously hurt.' Belfast was pretty far down these days, he reflected. Just time left to see what football manager was leaving where, and then the weather, and it would be five-past. He shuffled his papers together and reached for his briefcase under the table; the car would be at the door in three minutes. 'Moving off, sweetheart,' he called, and made for the hall.

The Afghan was now sitting quietly on the doormat, the children ready, as the Minister put on his heavy, dark-blue overcoat, paused and contemplated the scarf on the hook, decided against it, gave his wife's offered cheek a kiss and opened the door into Belgrave Square. The Afghan and au pair led the way down the steps to the pavement, then the children and after a moment the Minister and his wife. To his right he saw the black Austin Princess turning out of Halkin Street, seventy-five yards away, to pick him up. The children, dog and au pair walked left towards Chapel Street, and across the road a short, dark-haired man who had been leaning against the square's fence stiffened and moved forward.

The Minister's huge voice bellowed after his children: 'Have a nice day, darlings, and don't do any damage with those sticks.' He was still smiling at the over-the-shoulder grimace from the elder girl down the street, when he saw the rifle come from under the coat of the man across the street and move to his shoulder. He was out on the pavement now and some yards away from the house as he turned and looked for the sanctuary of the door in front of which his wife was standing, intent on her children.

He had started to shout a warning to her when the man fired his first shot. For the Minister the street exploded in noise, as he felt the sledge-hammer blow of the 7.62 mm shell crashing into his chest, searing into the soft flesh on its way through a splintered rib cage, puncturing the tissue of his lungs, gouging muscle and bone from his backbone, and bursting out through his clothes, before, a shapeless mass of lead, it buried itself in the white façade of the house. The force of that first shot spun and felled the Minister, causing the second shot to miss and fly into the hallway, fracturing a mirror beside the lounge door. As the man aimed for his third shot – 'Keep steady, aim,' they'd told him, 'don't blaze, and for Christ's sake be quick' – he heard the screaming. The Minister's wife was crawling down the steps to where her husband writhed in his attempt to get away from the pain. The man fired two more shots. This time there were no misses, and he watched with detached fascination as the back of the sleek, groomed head disintegrated. It was the last chance he had to see the target before the woman who had been screaming flung herself over it, swamping it from his view. He looked to his left and saw the big car stranded, its engine racing, in the middle of the road. To the right on the pavement he saw the children, immobile like statues, with the dog straining at its leash to escape the noise.

Automatically the man flicked the safety catch to 'on', deflated the catch at the top of the stock, bent the shoulder rest back alongside the barrel and dropped the weapon into the sheath they'd built to be strapped under his coat. Then he ran, jumping out of the way of a woman as he went. He turned into Chapel Street, sprinting now. Right next into Grosvenor Place. Must get across the road, get a line of traffic between you and them, he told himself. Alongside him was the high, spiked wall of Buckingham Palace. People saw him coming and moved out of his path. He clutched his unbuttoned coat tight to his body. The rifle was awkward now, with the curved magazine digging into his ribs. As he was running he was vulnerable, he knew that. His mind didn't tell him that no one had cause to stop him, but focused almost exclusively on the road, the traffic, and at what moment he would see a hole in the river of buses and cabs and lorries. Get across Buckingham Palace Road and then into the safety and anonymity of the tube station at Victoria. Hard out of breath he stumbled into the station. He took a ten-pence piece from his pocket. Relaxed now, he could take his place in the queue. He pushed the coin into the automatic machine. Remember, they'd said, the law will expect a car; you're better on the tube. They'd given him a route, Victoria to Oxford Circus on the Victoria Line, the Circus to Notting Hill Gate on the Central Line, then the District Line to Edgware Road, then Bakerloo to Watford. He was on a train and moving and his watch showed 9.12.

The sirens of the patrol cars blotted out the screaming of the Minister's wife as she lay over the body. They'd been diverted there just ninety seconds before with the brief message, 'Man shot in Belgrave Square.' The two constables were still mentally tuned to the traffic blockages at the Knightsbridge underpass as they spilled out into the street. George Davies, twenty-two years old and only three years in the Metropolitan police, was first out. He saw the woman, the body of the man under her, and the brain tissue on the steps. The sight stopped him in mid-stride as he felt nausea rising into his mouth. Frank Smith, twice his age, screamed, 'Don't stop, *move*,' ran past him to the huddle on the steps, and pulled the Minister's wife from her husband's body. 'Give him air,' he yelled, before he took in the wrecked skull, the human debris on the flagstones and the woman's housecoat. Smith sucked in the air, mumbled inaudibly, and turned on his knees to the pale-faced Davies ten paces behind him. 'Ambulance, reinforcements, tell 'em it's big, and move it fast.' When Smith looked again at the Minister's wife he recognized her. 'It's Mrs Danby?' he whispered. It was a statement, but he put the question into it. She nodded. 'Your husband?' She nodded again. She was silent now and the children had edged close to her.

Smith took the scene in. 'Get them inside, Ma'am.' It was an instruction, and they obeyed, slowly and numbly going through the door and off the street.

Smith got up off his knees and lumbered back to the squad car.

'Davies, don't let anyone near him. Get a description.'

On the radio he put out a staccato message: 'Tango George, in Belgrave Square. Henry Danby has been shot. He's dead, from all I can see. Ambulance and reinforcements already requested.'

The street was beginning to fill. The Ministry driver of the Austin Princess had recovered from the initial shock and was able to move the car into a parking-meter bay. Two more police cars pulled up, lights flashing, uniformed and CID men jumping clear before they'd stopped. The ambulance was sounding the warning of its approach on the half-mile journey from the St George's Hospital at Hyde Park Corner. The Special Patrol Group Land-Rover, on stand-by at Scotland Yard, blocked the south side of the square. One of its constables stood beside it, his black, short-barrelled Smith and Wesson .38 calibre in his hand.

'You can put that away,' said his colleague, 'we're light years too bloody late.'

At Oxford Circus the man debated quickly whether to break his journey, head for the Gents and take the magazine off his Kalashnikov. He decided against it, and ran for the escalator to bring him up from the Victoria Line to the level of the Central Line. He thought there would be time to worry about the gun later. Now distance concerned him. His mind was still racing, unable to take in the violence of the scene behind him. His only reaction was that there had been something terribly simple about it all, that for all the work and preparation that had gone into it the killing should have been harder. He remembered the woman over the body, the children and the dog on the pavement, the old woman he had avoided on the pavement outside the house. But none of them registered: his only compulsion now was to get clear of the city.

*

288

The first reports of the shooting reached the Commissioner's desk a mile away at Scotland Yard at 9.25. He was slipping out of his coat after the chauffeur drive from Epsom when his aide came in with the first flashes. The Commissioner looked up sharply, noting there had been no knock on his door, before the young officer was in front of him, thrusting a piece of paper at him. As he read the message he saw it was torn at the bottom, ripped off a teleprinter. He said, 'Get me C1, Special Branch and SPG, here in five minutes.' He went over to his desk, pressed the intercom button, announced sharply, 'Prime Minister, please,' and flicked the switch back.

When the orange light flashed in the centre of the console the Commissioner straightened a little in his seat, subconsciously adjusted his tie, and picked up his phone. A voice remote, Etonian and clipped said on the line, 'Hello, Commissioner, we're just raking him up, won't be a second.' Then another click. 'Yes, right, you've found me, good morning, Commissioner, what can I do for you?'

The Commissioner took it slowly. First reports, much regret, your colleague Henry Danby, dead on arrival in hospital. Seems on first impression the work of an assassin, very major police activity, but few other details available. He spoke quietly into the phone and was heard out in silence. When he finished the voice at the end of the line, in the first-floor office overlooking Downing Street and the Foreign Office arch, said, 'Nothing else?' 'No, sir. It's early, though.' 'You'll shout if you want help – army, air force, intelligence, anything you need?'

There was no reply from the Commissioner. The Prime Minister went on: 'I'll get out of your hair – call me in half an hour. I'll get one of our people to put it out to the Press Association.'

The Commissioner smiled to himself bleakly. A press release straight away – the political mind taking stock. He grimaced, putting his phone down as the door opened and the three men he'd summoned came in. They headed critical departments: C1 – the élite crime investigation unit; the Special Branch – Scotland Yard's counter-terrorist and surveillance force; and the Special Patrol Group – the specialist unit trained to deal with major incidents. All were Commanders, but only the head of the SPG was in uniform.

The Commissioner kept his office Spartan and without frills, and the Commanders collected the armless chairs from the sides of the room and brought them towards the desk.

He spoke first to the Special Patrol Group Commander and asked him abruptly what was known.

'Not much, sir. Happened at 9.07. Danby comes down his front steps regular time, regular everything – he's waiting for the Ministry car. A man steps out into the street on the other side, and lets fly, fires several shots, multiple wounds, and runs for it in the direction of Victoria. Not much good for eye-witnesses at this stage, not much about. There's a woman on the pavement had a good look at him, but she's a bit shocked at the moment. We've got he's about five-eight, younger than middle-aged, say thirtyish, and what she calls so far a pinched sort of face, dark hair. Clothes aren't much good – dark trousers under a biscuit-coloured mac. That's it.'

'And the gun?'

'Can't be definite.' It was the Special Branch man. 'Seems from what the woman said it's an AK 47, usually called a Kalashnikov. Russians use it, VC in Vietnam, the Aden people, the Black September crowd. It's Czech-designed, quite old now, but it's never showed up here before. The IRA have tried to get them into Ulster, but always failed. The *Claudia* – that fishing boat up to the gills in arms – was running them when intercepted. It's a classic weapon, semi-automatic or virtually automatic – 400 rounds a minute, if you could get that many up the spout. Muzzle velocity around 2000 feet a second. Effective killing range comfortable at half a mile. The latest version has a folding stock – you could get it into a big briefcase. It's accurate and doesn't jam. It's a hell of a weapon for this sort of thing. Its calibre is fractionally bigger than ours so it fires Iron Curtain ammo, or ours at a pinch. We've found four shell cases, but no detail on them yet. It's got a noise all of its own, a crack that people who've heard it say is distinctive. From what the woman said to the people down there it fits with the Kalashnikov.'

'And the conclusion?'

'It's not an amateur's weapon. We haven't traced them coming in here yet. If it is a Kalashnikov we're not up against second division. If they can get one of these things then they're big and know what they're about.'

That struck the chord. All four stayed quiet for a moment; it was a depressing thought. The professional political assassin on their hands. It went through the Commissioner's mind before he spoke that a man who troubled to get the ideal gun for the killing, the favourite terrorist weapon in the world, would spend time on the other details of the operation.

He lit his first cigarette of the day, two hours ahead of the schedule he'd disciplined himself to after his last medical check, and broke the silence.

'He'll have thought out his escape route. It'll be good. Where are we, how do we block him?'

The murder squad chief took it up. 'Usual, sir, at this stage. Ports, ferries, airports, private strips as soon as we can get men to them. Phone calls ahead to the control towers. I've got as many men as possible concentrated on tube stations, and particularly exit points on the out-skirts. He went towards Victoria, could be the tube, could be the train. We're trying to seal it, but that takes a bit . . .'

He tailed away. He'd said enough. The Commissioner drummed his desk top with the filter of his cigarette. The others waited, anxious now to get the meeting over and get back to their desks, their teams and the reports that were beginning to build.

The Commissioner reacted, sensing the mood.

'Right, I take it we all accept Danby was the target because of his work in Northern Ireland, though God knows a less controversial Minister I never met. Like a bloody willow tree. It's not a nut, because nutters don't get modern Commie assault rifles to run round Belgrave Square. So look for a top man, in the IRA. Right? I'm putting Charlie in over-all control. He'll co-ordinate. By this afternoon I want the whole thing flooded, get the manpower out. Bank on Belfast, we'll get something out of there. Good luck.'

The last was a touch subdued. You couldn't give a pep talk to the three men he had in the room, yet for the first time since he'd eased himself into the Commissioner's chair he'd felt something was required of him. Stupid, he thought, as the door closed on the Special Patrol Group Commander.

His yellow light was flashing again on the telephone console. When he picked up his phone his secretary told him the Prime Minister had called an emergency Cabinet meeting for 2.30, and would require him to deliver a situation report to Ministers at the start of their meeting.

'Get me Assistant Commissioner Crime, Charlie Henderson,' he said, after he'd scribbled down the message from Downing Street on his memory pad.

At a quarter to eleven the BBC broke into its television transmissions to schools, and after two seconds of blank screen went to a 'Newsflash' caption. It then dissolved to a continuity announcer, who paused, hesitated for a moment, and then, head down on his script, read:

Here is a newsflash. Just after nine this morning a gunman shot and killed the Secretary of State for the Social Services, Mr Henry Danby. Mr Danby was about to leave his Belgrave Square home when he was fired on by a man apparently on the other side of the street. He was dead on arrival in hospital. Our outside broadcast unit is now outside Mr Danby's home and we go over there now to our reporter, James Lyons.

It's difficult from Belgrave Square to piece together exactly what happened this morning, as Mr Henry Danby, the Social Services Minister, left his home and was ambushed on his front door step. The police are at the moment keeping us a hundred yards back from the doorway as they comb the street for clues, particularly the cartridge cases of the murder weapon. But with me here is a lady who was walking her dog just round the corner of the Square when the first shot was fired.

291

Q. What did you see?

A. Well, I was walking the dog, and I heard the bang, the first bang, and I thought that doesn't sound like a car. And I came round the corner and I saw this man holding this little rifle or gun up to his –

Q. Could you see the Minister – Mr Danby?

A. I saw him, he was sort of crouched, this man in his doorway, he was trying to crawl, then came the second shot. I just stood there, and he fired again and again, and the woman –

Q. Mrs Danby?

A. The woman in the doorway was screaming. I've never heard such a noise, it was dreadful, dreadful . . . I can't say any more . . . he just ran. The poor man was lying there, bleeding. And the woman just went on screaming . . . it was awful.

Q. Did you see the man, the gunman?

A. Well, yes and no, he came past me, but he came fast, he was running.

Q. What did he look like?

A. Nothing special, he wasn't very tall, he was dark.

Q. How old, would you guess?

A. Not old, late twenties, but it was very fast.

Q. And what was he wearing? Could you see?

A. He had a brown mac on, a sort of fawn colour. I saw it had a tartan lining. I could see that he put the gun inside, in a sort of pouch. He just ran straight past me. I couldn't move. There's nothing more.

They'd told the man that simplicity would see him through. That if they kept it easy, with no frills, they'd get him back. He got off the train at Watford Junction, and began to walk towards the barrier, eyes going 180° in front of him. The detectives he spotted were close to the ticket barrier, not looking down the platform, but intent on the passengers. He walked away from the barrier towards the Gents, went into the graffiti-scrawled cubicle, and took off the coat. He hung it carefully behind a door. He unfastened the shoulder strap, unclipped the magazine from the gun, took off his jacket and put the improvised holster back on. With the jacket over the top, the rifle fitted unseen close to his armpit. It gave him a stockiness that wasn't his, and showed his jacket as a poor fit; but that was all. Trembling again in his fingers he walked towards the barrier. The CID men, both local, had been told the Minister had been shot at home in Belgrave Square, they'd been told the man might have got away by underground, they'd been told he was in a fawn-brown macintosh and was carrying an automatic rifle. They hadn't been told that, if the killer was on the tube, his ticket might not have been issued at Victoria – could have been bought at another station during the journey. Nor had they been told the Kalashnikov could be folded. They ruled him out in the five yards before he handed over his ticket.

He walked away from them, panting quietly to himself, his forehead cold with sweat, waiting for the shout behind him, or the heavy hand falling on his shoulder, and felt nothing. He walked out of the station to the car park, where the Avis Cortina waited. He stowed the gun under his driving seat and set off for Heathrow. There's no way they'll get you if you stay cool. That was the advice.

In the late morning traffic the journey took him an hour. He'd anticipated it would, and he found he'd left himself ninety minutes for his flight when he'd left the car in the No. 1 terminal car park. He locked the car, leaving the rifle under his seat with its magazine along with it.

The police were staked out at all corners of the terminal. The man saw the different groups, reflected in their shoulder markings: Airport Police – AP, T. Division of the Metropolitan – T, and the Special Patrol Group men – CO. He knew the last were armed, which gave him a chilled feeling in his belly. If they shouted and he ran, would they shoot him? . . . He clenched his fist and walked up to the BEA ticket desk.

'The name is Jones . . . you've a ticket waiting for me. The one o'clock to Amsterdam, BE 467.'

The girl behind the counter smiled, nodded, and began to beat out the instructions of the flight into her personal reservations computer. The flight was confirmed, and as she made the ticket out the terminal loudspeakers warned passengers of delays in all flights to Dublin, Cork and Shannon and Belfast. No reason was given. But that's where all the effort will be, they'd told him. They haven't the manpower for the lot.

The man brought out the new British passport supplied for him by his unit quartermaster and walked through immigration control.

2

Normally the Commissioner travelled alone, with only the elderly driver for company. That afternoon sitting in the front with the driver was an armed detective. The car turned into Downing Street through the crash barriers that had been put into position half an hour after the shooting was reported. The dark, shaded street was empty of Ministerial cars, and sightseers were banned for the day. By the door two constables had established their will on the group of photographers gathered to record all comings and goings, and shepherded them into a line stretching from the railings, over the pavement and out into the parking area. The Commissioner was met in the hall, warm with its red carpets and chandeliers, and escorted to the lift. As he passed the small room to the right of the door, he noted the four plain-clothes men sitting there. His order that the Prime Minister's guard should be doubled had been carried out. Two floors later he was led into the Prime Minister's study.

'I just wanted to see if there was anything you wanted to say before we get involved in the main scene downstairs.'

'All I can do now, sir, is say what we know, what we're doing. Not much of the first, a lot of the second.'

'There'll be a fair amount of questioning about the security round the Minister . . .'

The Commissioner said nothing. It was an atmosphere he was not happy in; he reflected that in his three years as Commissioner and the country's top policeman he'd never got into this marble tower before, never got beyond the first-floor reception salons. On the way to Whitehall he had primed himself not to allow the police to become the scapegoat, and after thirty-six years in the Force his inclination was to be back at Scotland Yard hovering on the fifth floor by the control room, irregular as it was, but at least doing something.

There was little contact, and both acknowledged it. The Prime Minister rose and motioned with his hand to the door. 'Come on,' he murmured, 'let's go and meet them. Frank Scott of the RUC and General Fairbairn are coming in from Belfast in an hour or so. We'll hear them after you.'

The man was striding his way along the vast pier of Schipol Airport, Amsterdam, towards the central transit area. If his connections were working he had fifty-eight minutes till the Aer Lingus 727 took off for Dublin Airport. He saw the special airport police with their short-barrelled, lightweight carbines patrolling the entrance to the pier where the El Al jumbo was loading, and had noticed the armoured personnel carriers on the aprons. All the precautions of the anti-hijack programme . . . but nothing to concern him. He went to the Aer Lingus desk, collected the ticket waiting for him, and drifted away to the duty-free lounge. They'd told him not to miss the duty-free lounge; the best in Europe, they'd said. Belgrave Square and the noise and the screaming were far away; for the first time in the day he felt a degree of calm.

In the first-floor Cabinet Room the Commissioner stood to deliver his briefing. He spoke slowly, picking his words with care, and aware that the Ministers were shocked, suspicious and even hostile to what he had to say. There was little comfort for them. On top of what they had seen on the television lunchtime news they were told that a new and better description was being circulated . . . for the first time the policeman had the full attention of his audience.

'There was a slight jostling incident at Oxford Circus this morning. A man barged his way through, nearly knocking people over, and noticeably didn't stop to apologize. Not the sort of thing that you'd expect people to remember, but two women independently saw the television interview from Belgrave Square this morning, and phoned the Yard – put the two together. It's the same sort of man they're talking about as we'd already heard of, but a better description. We'll have a photokit by four o'clock –'

He was interrupted by the slight knock on the door, and the arrival of the Royal Ulster Constabulary Chief Constable, Frank Scott, and General Sir Jocelyn Fairbairn, GOC Northern Ireland. When they'd sat down, crowded in at the far end of the table, the Prime Minister began.

'We all take it this is an IRA assassination. We don't know for what motive, whether it is the first of several attempts or a one-off. I want the maximum effort to get the killer – and fast. I don't want an investigation that runs a month, two months, six months. Every day that these thugs get away with it is a massive plus to them. How it was that Danby's detective was withdrawn from him so soon after he'd left the Ulster job is a mystery to me. The Home Secretary will report to us tomorrow on that, and also on what else is being done to prevent a recurrence of such attacks.'

He stopped. The room was silent, disliking the schoolroom lecture. The Commissioner wondered for a moment whether to explain that Danby himself had decided to do without the armed guard, ridiculing the detective-sergeant's efforts to watch him. He thought better of it and decided to let the Prime Minister hear it from his Home Secretary.

The Prime Minister gestured to the RUC man.

'Well, sir . . . gentlemen,' he started in the soft Scots burr of so many of the Ulstermen. He tugged at the jacket of his bottle-green uniform and moved his blackthorn cane fractionally across the table. 'If he's in Belfast we'll get him. It may not be fast, but it's a village there. We'll hear, and we'll get him. It would be very difficult for them to organize an operation of this scale and not involve so many people that we'll grab one and he'll bend. It's a lot easier to get them to talk these days. The hard men are locked up, the new generation talks. If he's in Belfast we'll get him.'

It was past five and dark outside when the Ministers, and the General and the Prime Minister again, had had their say. The Prime Minister had called a full meeting of all present for the day after tomorrow, and reiterated his demand for action and speed, when a private secretary slipped into the room, whispered in the Commissioner's ear, and ushered him out. Those next to him had heard the word 'urgent' used.

When the Commissioner came back into the room two minutes later the Prime Minister saw his face and stopped in mid-sentence. The eyes of the eighteen politicians and the Ulster policeman and the General were on the Commissioner as he said:

'We have some rather bad news. Police officers at Heathrow have discovered a hired car in the terminal car park near No. 1 building. Under the driver's seat was a Kalashnikov rifle. The car-park ticket would have given a passenger time to take flights to Vienna, Stockholm, Madrid, Rome and Amsterdam. The crew of the BEA flight to Amsterdam are already back at Heathrow, and we are sending a photokit down to the airport, it's on its way, but one of the stewardesses thinks a man who fits our primary description, the rough one we had at first, was in the fifteenth row in a window seat. We are also in touch with Schipol police, and are wiring the picture, but from the BEA flight there was ample time to make a Dublin connection. The Aer Lingus, Amsterdam/ Dublin flight landed in Dublin twenty-five minutes ago, and they are holding all passengers in the baggage reclaim hall.'

There was a common gasp of relief round the Cabinet Room, as the Commissioner went on.

'But the Dublin Airport police report that those passengers without baggage went through immigration control before we notified them.'

'Would he have had baggage?' It was the Prime Minister, speaking very quietly.

'I doubt it, sir, but we're trying to establish that with the ticket desk and check-in counter.'

'What a cock-up.' The Prime Minister was virtually inaudible. 'We'll need some results, and soon.'

From Heathrow, the Kalashnikov, swaddled in a cellophane wrapping, was rushed by squad car to Woolwich on the far side of the city, to the police test firing range. It was still white from the chalk-like fingerprint powder brushed on at the airport police station, but the airport's resident fingerprint man declared it clean. 'Doesn't look like a gloves job,' he said, 'he must have wiped it – a cloth, or something. But it's thorough; he's missed nothing.'

In the suburbs of Dublin, in the big open-plan newsroom of RTE, the Republic of Ireland's television service, the central phone in the bank used by the news editor rang at exactly six o'clock.

'Listen carefully, I'm only going to say this once. This is a spokesman for the military wing of the Provisional IRA. An active service unit of the Provisional IRA today carried out a court-martial execution order on Henry DeLacey Danby, an enemy of the people of Ireland, and servant of the British occupation forces in Ireland. During the eighteen months Danby spent in Ireland one of his duties was responsibility for the concentration camp at Long Kesh. He was repeatedly warned that if the regime of the camp did not change, action would be taken against him. That's it.'

The phone clicked off, and the news editor began to read back his shorthand.

Ten hours later the Saracens and Pigs, on dimmed headlights, were moving off from the Belfast police stations, heading out of the sand-bagged tin- and chicken-wire fortresses of Andersonstown, Hasting Street, Flax Street, Glenravel Street and Mountpottinger. Sentries in steel helmets and shrapnel-proof jerkins, their automatic rifles strapped to their wrists, pulled aside the heavy wood and barbed-wire barricades at the entrances of the battalion and company headquarters and the convoys inched their way into the darkness. Inside the armoured cars the troops huddled together, their faces blackened with boot polish, their bodies laden with gas masks, emergency wound dressings, rubber-bullet guns, truncheons and the medieval Macron see-through shields. In addition they carried with them their high-velocity NATO rifles. Few of the men had slept more than a few hours, and that cat-napping in their uniforms, their only luxury that of being able to take off their boots. Their officers and senior NCOs, who had attended the operational briefings for the raids, had slept even less. There was no talk, no conversation, only the knowledge that the day would be long, tiring, cold and probably wet. There was nothing for the men to look at.

Each car was battened down against possible sniper attacks; only the driver, the rifleman beside him and the rifleman at the back, with his barrel poked through the fine visibility slit, had any sight of the darkened, rain-swept streets. No house lights were on, no shop windows were illuminated, and only occasionally was there a high street lamp, one that had survived the attempts of both sides over the last four years to destroy its brightness.

Within a few minutes the convoys had swung off the main roads and were splitting up in the housing estates, all but one on the west side of the city. Two thousand troops, drawn from six battalions, were sealing off the streets that have the Falls Road as their spinal cord – the Catholic artery out of the west side of the city, and the route to Dublin. As the armoured cars pulled across the streets, paratroopers, marines and men from the old county infantry units flung open the reinforced doors and ran for the security of their fire positions. In the extreme west, on the Andersonstown and Suffolk border, where the houses are newer and the sight therefore more incongruous, the troops were from a heavy artillery unit – men more used to manœuvring with the long-range Abbot gun than looking for cover in front gardens and behind dustbins. Away across the city from the Falls more troops were spreading into the Ardoyne, and across on the east side of the Lagan the Short Strand area was sealed.

When their men were in position the officers waited for first light. Cars that tried to enter or leave the cordoned streets were sent back. In a gradual drizzle the troops lay and crouched in the cover that they had found, thumb on the safety catch. The selected marksmen cradled their rifles, made heavier by the attachment of the Starscope, the night vision aid.

The noise started as the soldiers began the house-to-house searches. Women, mighty in dressing-gowns with hair piled high by their bright plastic-coated curlers, surged from the houses to blow whistles, howl abuse and crash the dustbin lids. Amid the cacophony came the beating of rifle butts on doors, and the thud of the axes and sledge-hammers when there was no ready answer. Within minutes there were as many civilians on the street as soldiers, bouncing their epithets and insults off the unmoving faces of the military. Protected by small knots of soldiers were the unhappy-looking civilian police, usually with their panting, gelignite-sniffer Labradors close by. Occasionally there would come a shout of excitement from one of the small terraced houses, the accent North Country or Welsh or Cockney, and a small shining rifle or pistol would be carried into the street, wrapped to prevent the loss of the clues that would convict the still half-asleep man bundled down the pavement and into the back of an armoured truck. But this was not often. Four years of searches and swoops and cordons and arrests had left little to find.

By dawn – and it comes late as far north as Belfast, and then takes a long time coming – there was little to show for the night's work. Some Japanese-made Armalite rifles, some pistols, a sackful of ammunition and crocodile lines of men for questioning by the Special Branch, along with the paraphernalia of terrorism – batteries, lengths of flex, alarm clocks, and sacks of potent weed killer. All were itemized and shipped back to the police stations.

With the light came the stones, and the semi-orderliness of the searches gave way to the crack of rubber bullets being fired; the streets swirled with CS gas, and always at the end of the narrow line of houses were the kids heaving their fractured paving stones at the military.

Unaware of the searches, bus drivers down the Falls Road, stopping at the lights, found youths climbing into their cabs, a variety of pistols threatening them, and handed over their double-deckers. By nine o'clock the Falls was blocked in four places, and local radio bulletins were warning motorists once again to stick to alternative routes.

As the soldiers withdrew from the streets there were infrequent bursts of automatic fire, not pressed home, and causing no casualties. Only on one occasion did troops have enough of a target to fire back, and then they claimed no hit.

For both sides the raid had its achievements. The army and police had to stir up the pool, and muddy the water, get the top men on the other side on the move, perhaps panic one of them into a false step or a vital admission. The street leaders could also claim some benefit from the morning. After the lull of several weeks the army had arrived to kick in the doors, take away the men, break up the rooms, prise out the floorboards. At street level that was valuable currency.

The man had seen the police convoy racing into the airport as he'd left, carrying as his sole possessions the Schipol duty-free bag with two hundred cigarettes and a bottle of Scotch. As he'd come through a young man had stepped forward and asked him if he were Mr Jones. He'd nodded, nothing more was required of him, and followed the young man out of the new terminal and into the car park.

It was as they had driven past the airport hotel they'd seen the Garda cars and a van go by. Neither driver nor passenger spoke. The man had been told he would be met, and reminded that he must not speak at all on the journey, not even on the home run. Speech is as identifiable as a face, they explained. The car took the Dundalk road, and then on the stretch between Drogheda and Dundalk turned left and inland towards the hills.

'We'll be away over near Forkhill,' muttered the driver. The man said nothing as the car bumped its way down the side road. After fifteen minutes at a crossroads, where the only building was a corrugated-iron-roofed store, the driver stopped, got out and went inside saying he'd be a minute and had to telephone. The man sat in the car, the light-headedness he'd felt at Schipol that afternoon suddenly gone; it was not that he was alone that worried him but that his movements and immediate future were not in his own hands. He had started to conjure up images of betrayal and capture, of himself left abandoned near the border and unarmed, when the driver walked back to the car and got in.

'Forkhill's tight, we're going farther down towards the Cullyhanna road. Don't worry, you're home and dry.'

The man felt ashamed that the stranger could sense his suspicion and nervousness. As a gesture he tried to sleep, leaning his head against his safety belt. He stayed in this position till the car suddenly jerked and flung his head hard against the window of the door. He shot forward.

'Don't worry' – again the self-assured, almost patronizing approach of the driver. 'That was the crater we filled in two years ago. You're in the North now. Home in two hours.'

The driver cut back to the east, through Bessbrook and on to the north of Newry and the main road to Belfast. The man allowed himself a smile. There was dual carriageway now, and a good fast road, till the driver pulled up outside Hillsborough and motioned to the duty-free bag on the back seat under the man's coat.

'Sorry, boy, I don't want that as we come into town. Ditch it.'

The man wound down his window and flung the plastic bag across the lay-by and into a hedge. The car was moving again. The next sign showed Belfast to be five miles away.

On his return from London the previous evening, the Chief Constable had put a picked team of detectives on stand-by to wait for information over the confidential phone, the heavily publicized Belfast phone numbers over which information is passed anonymously to the police. They waited through the day in their ready room, but the call they hoped for never came. There was the usual collection of breathy messages naming people in connection with bombs, shootings, locating the dumping of firearms . . . but not a word even of rumour about the Danby killing. In three pubs in the centre of Belfast, British army intelligence officers met their contacts and talked, huddled forward in the little cubicles they favoured. All were to report later that night to their controller that nothing was known. While they talked, threatening, cajoling, bribing their sources, military police Land-Rovers cruised close by. The Red Caps had not been told who they were guarding, just detailed to watch and prevent the sudden entry of a number of men into those pubs.

The blowing of the laundry van intelligence surveillance unit, when soldiers kept watch on an Ira base area from the false ceiling of a laundry van while their colleagues plied for trade below, had woken the operation directors to the needs for safeguards when their men were in the field. That was thirty months back. The tortured and mutilated body of a Royal Tank Regiment captain found just three months before had demonstrated the probability of a security leak close to the heart of the unit, and the public outcry at home at the exposing of soldiers to these out-of-uniform dangers had led to a Ministry directive that military personnel were no longer to infiltrate the Catholic community, but instead stay out and cultivate their informers. Funds and the availability of one-way air tickets to Canada were stepped up.

Quite separate from the military intelligence team, the RUC's Special

300

Branch was also out that night – men who for three years had slept with their snub-nosed PPK Walthers on the bedside table, and kept a stock of spare number plates at the back of the garage, who stood to the side at the well-photographed police funerals. They too were to report that there was no talk about the Danby killing.

In the small hours Howard Rennie settled on to a hard wooden chair on the first floor of headquarters down the Stormont Road, and began with painful awkwardness to type out his first report. Some of his colleagues had already been in with the news that they had discovered nothing, that their informants were pleading total ignorance of this one; others would come after him to tell the same story. Even the recording tapes – the 'Confidential Line' – had failed them.

As a chief inspector, Rennie had been hammering the typewriter keys for statements, criminal assessments and incident report sheets for eighteen years, but he still maintained the right-index-finger, left-index-finger patter.

From his time in Special Branch Rennie knew the way the city would buzz after a Provisional spectacular, how rumour and gossip passed from ghetto to ghetto, carrying the message of success and with it a degree of indiscretion. That was where the Branch came in, men trained to be sensitive enough to pick up the murmurs of information. But the days of Special Branch glory in Belfast were long past.

Rennie could remember the courses he'd been on in the early days before it all went haywire, and the troops arrived, when he'd been told across in England by dour-faced men with biscuit tans from long service in the Far East and Africa that the inside work by the police was the only hope of breaking a terrorist movement in its infancy. 'When you get the army in, lording it over your heads, telling you what to do, knowing it all, then it's too late. It's out of your hands by that time. The military on the streets means the enemy are winning, and that you are no longer a force for the opposition to reckon with. The army are bad news for policemen, and the only way for a counter-terrorist operation to be successful is for the Special Branch to be in there, infiltrating, extracting knowledge at ground level.'

And they'd been right. Rennie could see that now. He and his colleagues didn't poke their noses into the corners and crannies of the Provisional heartland. They let the army do that with their fire-power and their armour plating, while the detectives sat back and contented themselves with the interrogation of the flow of arrested men. It was next best thing, but not good enough.

He'd never been much for the cloak and dagger stuff himself. Too big, too heavy, too conspicuous, not a man to flake his way into a

301

crowd, not ordinary enough. But there were others who had been good at it, till the funerals became too frequent, and the Chief Constable had called a halt.

One man, for instance, had been the king of the Branch men till he died up the Crumlin in a hail of automatic fire. Just watching the nightly riot when the sniper spotted him, and gone was a card-index memory, a walking filing system.

Rennie's report turned out to be a drab document. A succession of negatives after a score of calls and a search through the big tin drawers that carried the buff folders and the photographs and case histories. The Chief Constable came into the room as Rennie was pushing the typewriter back across the table.

'Nothing?'

'Nothing at all, sir. It's a blind alley so far. No one saying anything. Not a word.'

'I told them in London that it'll come at this end, the man they're looking for. His equipment was too good for anyone based in London. He'll be here. How many do we know who're capable of it, capable of the discipline, of that sort of training?'

'There are quite a few,' said Rennie, 'but none of them out. I could name half a dozen in Long Kesh who we would be looking for if they were free. But, taking them out of the game, I can't see anyone. A bit ago, yes, but not now.'

'I'm calling for a very big effort, maximum effort,' the Chief Constable had walked away from the table and was talking half to himself, half out into the darkness beyond the shatterproof taped windows. 'London have said in the past that they don't get the co-operation they're looking for when there's a big one in England, and they come here for our help. I don't want them saying that this time. God, it's a damned nuisance. All the manpower, all the effort, everything that has to be dropped for a thing like this. But we have to have him.'

He looked a long time into the black distance beyond the floodlit perimeter fence. Then swung on his heel. 'Good night,' he said, and closed the door carefully behind him.

It'll go on a bit now, thought Rennie, every night here for the next few weeks, typing away, and with little to show for it, unless we're just lucky. Just lucky, and that doesn't happen often.

But just before midnight came the first positive identification of the killer back in the city. The duty major in intelligence section at Lisburn military headquarters, leafing through the situation reports of the evening, read that a patrol of the Lifeguards had for fifteen minutes closed the Hillsborough to Banbridge road while they investigated a package at the side of the road. It was cleared after the bomb disposal expert arrived and found the bag contained a carton of cigarettes and a bottle of Scotch, duty free and bought at Schipol airport. He hurriedly

302

phoned his chief at home, and the RUC control centre. But, nagging at him, was the question of how such an operation as the Danby killing could have been mounted, with no word coming out.

The man was asleep now, in the spare back bedroom of a small terraced house off the Ballymurphy Bull Ring. He'd come at 11.25 up from Whiterock where he had stayed since arriving in Belfast. Round him a safety system was building, with the arrangement that he'd sleep till 5.30, then move again up into New Barnsley. The Brigade staff in Belfast were anxious not to keep him long in one place, to hustle him round. Only the Brigade commander knew the value of the man the precautions were made for . . . no one else was told, and in the house he was greeted with silence. He came in fast over the back fence, avoiding the kids' bikes, ducked under the washing lines and made his way through the damp, filthy scullery into the back room. The family was gathered in semi-darkness with the television on loud – Channel 9. His escort whispered into the ear of the man of the house, and was gone, leaving him. The man was not from this part of the city, and was not known anyway.

His arrival and needs, after four years of warfare, were unremarkable. In the 'Murph' his name could be kept secret, not his reason for running – not after the Scotland Yard photokit had been flashed up on to the screen during the late-night news. On orders from London the photo had been withheld until after the intelligence and Special Branch officers had attempted to identify the killer. With their failure the picture had been released.

The family gathered round the set to hear the announcer.

Scotland Yard have just issued a photokit picture of the man they wish to interview in connection with the murder of Mr Henry Danby, the Minister of Social Security, at his home in central London yesterday morning. The picture has been compiled from the descriptions of several eyewitnesses. Scotland Yard say the man is aged about thirty, has short hair, with a parting on the left side, a narrow face, with what a witness calls 'pinched cheeks'. The man is of light build, and about five feet nine inches tall. When last seen he was wearing grey trousers and a dark brown jacket. He may also have a fawn-coloured macintosh with him. Anyone who can identify this man is asked to get in touch immediately with the police on the Confidential Line of Belfast 227756 or 226837.

High on the fireplace over the small fire grate was a carved and painted model of a Thompson machine-gun, the present to the family from their eldest son, Eamon, held for two years in Long Kesh. It was dated Christmas 1973. Below the gun the family registered no reaction to the picture shown on their screens.

In the small hours Theresa, Eamon's sister, tiptoed her way round the scarred door of the back room. She eased her path over the floorboards, still loosened and noisy since the army came to look for her brother. In the darkness she saw the face of the man, out from under his blankets with his arms wrapped around his pillow, as a child holds a favourite doll. She was shivering in the thin nightdress, transparent and reaching barely below her hips. She had selected it two hours before to put on before waiting to be sure her people were asleep. Very gently at first, she shook the shoulder of the man, till he started half out of bed, gripped her wrist, and then in one movement pulled her down, but as a prisoner.

'Who's that?' he said it hard, tautly, with fear in his voice.

'It's Theresa.' There was silence, just the man's breathing, and still he held her wrist, vice-like. With her free hand she moved back the bedclothes and moved her body alongside his. He was naked and cold; across the room she saw his clothes strewn over the chair by the window.

'You can let go,' she said and tried to move closer to him, but only to find him backing away till the edge of the single bed stopped his movement.

'Why did you come?'

'To see you.'

'Why did you come?' Again harsher, louder.

'They showed your picture . . . on the telly . . . just now . . . on the late news.'

The hand released her wrist. The man flopped back on the pillow, tension draining out of him. Theresa pressed against his body, but found no response, no acknowledgement of her presence.

'You had to know, for when they move you on. I had to tell you . . . we aren't your enemies. You're safe with us . . . there's no danger.'

'There are six men in the city who know I'm here – and you . . .'

A little more nervously she whispered back, 'Don't worry yourself, there's no narks here, not in this street . . . not since the McCoy girl . . . they shot her.' It was an afterthought – Roisin McCoy, soldier's girl-friend, part-time informer, found shot dead under Divis mountain. Big outcry, no arrests.

'I'm not saying anything.'

'I didn't come to talk, and it's freezing, half out of the bloody clothes.'

He pulled her down, close now against him, the nylon of her nightdress riding up over her hips and her breasts. She pushed against him, screwing her nipples against the black hair of his chest.

304

'Not much, are they?' she murmured. 'Couple of bloody bee stings.'

The man smiled, and the hand that had grasped her wrist to the point of half stopping the blood flow now stroked and rubbed urgently at the soft white inside of her thighs. She reached down and felt his stomach back away as she took hold of him, limp and lifeless, pliable in her hand. Slowly, then frantically, to match her own sensations she stroked and kneaded him, but without success.

Abruptly the man stopped his movements, pulled his hand away from the moist warmth.

'Get out. Bugger off. Get out.'

Theresa, nineteen years old, four of them spent on the mill weaving line, had heard and seen enough in her life to say, 'Was it that bad . . . London . . . was it . . . ?'

The interruption was a stinging blow across the right side of her face. His cheap onyx wedding ring gouged the skin below the eye. She was gone, out through the door across the passage to her bed; there she lay, legs clenched together, fascinated and horrified at the knowledge she had.

In her half-sleep she heard the whisper of voices and the footsteps on the stairs as the man was taken to his next place of hiding.

In the Cabinet Room the Prime Minister was showing little patience for the lack of a quick arrest. He had heard the Commissioner say that the case was static in London now, and that the main police effort was to establish how and where the man had entered the country. The boarding house in Euston where he had slept the night before the shooting had been searched, but nothing found. As expected the gun had yielded no fingerprints, and the same process of elimination was being used on the car. Here it was pointed out that the police had to identify the finger-prints of everyone who had handled the car over the previous six weeks or so before they could begin to come up with a worthwhile print and say this was the killer's. It would take a long time, said the Com-missioner, and involved drivers, Avis staff, garage personnel. Nothing had been found on the basics – steering wheel, door handle, gear lever. He reported on the new security measures surrounding Ministers, pointed out that they were nearly if not totally a waste of time if poli-ticians did not co-operate, and urged no repetitions of the situation by which the murdered Minister had been able to decide for himself that he no longer wanted protection. He finished by putting the proposition that the killer had no contact in Britain, and had operated completely on his own. Reservations for tickets in Dublin, Heathrow and Amster-dam had all been made over the phone and were untraceable. He fell back on the theme that the solving of the crime would happen in Belfast, and that yesterday a Chief Superintendent from the Murder Squad had gone to Belfast to liaise with the RUC.

Frank Scott, the Chief Constable, reported nothing had come in on the confidential phones, and as yet there had been no whisper on the Special Branch net. 'Now we know he's in the city we'll get him, but it may not be fast – that's the situation.' It had been left to him to report the finding of the Amsterdam duty-free bag.

'That's what you said two days ago,' snapped the Prime Minister.

'And it's still the situation.' The Chief Constable was not prepared to give ground. The Northern Ireland Secretary chipped in, 'I think we all accept, Frank, that it's near impossible to stampede this sort of operation.'

'But I have to have results.' The Prime Minister drummed his knuckles on the table. 'We cannot let this one hang about.'

'I'm not hanging about, sir, and you well know that no one in my force is.' The Ulster policeman's retort caused a certain fidgeting down the sides of the table from Ministers who had begun to feel their presence was irrelevant to the matter in hand – other than that by their arrivals and departures the cameras could witness the activity and firm hand of government. The Commissioner wished he'd come in faster. One up to the RUC.

The Prime Minister, too, sensed the chilliness of the situation, and invited the opinion of General Fairbairn. As the GOC Northern Ireland, commanding more than fifteen thousand men there, he expected to be listened to. He weighed his words.

'The problem, sir, is getting inside the areas the IRA dominate. Getting good information that we can trust and can then act on fast enough while the tips are still hot. Now, we can thrash around as we did yesterday morning, and as we have done to a more limited degree this morning, and though we pick up a bit – a few bodies, a few guns, some bomb-making equipment – we're unlikely to get at the real thing. I would hazard the motive behind the killing was to get us to launch massive reprisal raids, cordon streets off, taking house after house to pieces, lock hundreds up. They want us to hammer them and build a new generation of mini-martyrs. It's been quiet there these last few weeks. They needed a major publicity-attracting operation, and then a big kick-back from us to involve people at street level who are beginning to want to disengage. The raids we have been mounting these last thirty-six hours are fair enough as an initial reaction, but if we keep them up we'll be in danger of reactivating the people who had begun to lose interest in the IRA.'

'What about your intelligence men, your men on the inside?'

'We don't go in for that sort of thing so much now, we tend to meet on the outside – after the young Captain was murdered three months ago, horrible business . . . the Ministry wasn't happy, we suspended that sort of work.'

306

'Suspended it?' The Prime Minister deliberately accentuated the touch of horror in his voice.

'We haven't had an operation of anything like this size to handle for around a year; things have been running down. There hasn't been the need for intelligence operatives. Now we would have to set up a new unit completely – the men we have there at the moment are too compromised. I don't think in your time-scale, Prime Minister, we have the time to do it.'

He said the last drily, and with only the faintest hint of sarcasm, sufficiently guarded to be just about permissible for a Lt-General in the Cabinet Room at No 10 Downing Street.

'I want a man in there . . . nothing else to think about,' the Prime Minister was speaking deliberately, the Agriculture man thought – nice and slowly, just right for the transcript being scribbled in the corner.

'I want an experienced agent in there as fast as you can make it. A good man. If we've picked the killer up by then, nothing lost, if not . . . I know what you're going to say, General: if the man is discovered I will take the rap. That's understood. Well?'

The General had heard enough to realize that the interchange of ideas had been over several minutes earlier. This was an instruction by the Head of Government.

'For a start, sir, you can get the gentleman taking the notes over there by the door to take his last page out of the book, take it over to the fire and burn it. You can also remind everyone in the room of the small print of the Official Secrets Act. Thank you.'

The General got up, flushed high in his cheeks, and, followed hurriedly by the Chief Constable, who was sharing his RAF plane back to Belfast, left the room.

The Prime Minister waited for the door to close, and the angry footsteps to hasten down the corridor.

'They're free enough with advice when they want us to play round with political initiatives, but the moment we come up with a suggestion . . . That's the way it's always been. I've had four generals in my time at Downing Street telling me it's all about over, that the Provisionals are beaten, that they're finished. They reel off the statistics. How many sticks of gelignite they've found, how many rifles, how many houses have been searched, how the back of the opposition is broken. I've heard it too often – too often to be satisfied with it.'

His eyes ranged up the shining mahogany table, along the line of embarrassed faces till they locked on to the Minister of Defence.

'Your people have the wherewithal for this sort of thing. Get it set up, please, and controlled from this end. If our friend the General doesn't like it, then he won't have to worry himself.'

*

That afternoon in an upper room above a newsagent's shop near the main square in Clones, just over the border in County Monaghan, half of the twelve-man Army Council of the Provisional IRA met to consider the operation mounted two days earlier in London. Initially there was some anger that the killing had not been discussed by all members in committee, as was normal. But the Chief of Staff, a distant, intense man with deep eyes and a reputation for success in pulling the movement together, glossed over the troubles. He emphasized that, now the shooting had taken place, the priority in the movement was to keep the man safe. Unknowingly he echoed the British Prime Minister five hundred miles away in Whitehall when he said, 'Every day we keep the man free is a victory. Right? They wanted to pull two battalions out next month; how can they when they can't find one man? We have to keep him moving and keep him close. He's a good man, he won't give himself away. But at all costs we have to keep their hands off him. He's better dead than in Long Kesh.'

It was getting dark when the RAF Comet took off from Tempelhof Airport, Berlin, with its three passengers. Half-way back and sitting in an aisle seat Harry still felt bewildered. Two hours earlier he had been called to the Brigade commander's office at HQ under the shadow of the old Nazi Olympic stadium, and instructed he was going to London on urgent military business. He was told he wouldn't need to go home to get his bag, that was being done, and no, it would not be suitable for him to phone home at this moment, but it would be explained to his wife that he had been called away in a hurry.

Three and a half hours later the plane landed at Northolt and then taxied two hundred yards beyond the main reception area to an unmarked square of tarmac where a solitary set of steps and a civilian Morris 1800 were waiting.

For a captain in transport it was a very remarkable set of circumstances.

3

Harry was awake at first light.

He was in a large room, painted soft pastel yellow with fine hard moulding round the ceiling. A study of a Victorian matron with a basket of apples and pears faced him from across the room. An empty bookcase against the same wall, a basin, small Ministry-issue thin towel hanging underneath it. There was a chair and table, both with his uniform draped over them. At the foot of the bed he could see the suitcase they said they'd packed for him, with no baggage labels attached to it.

They'd avoided all checks at Northolt, and Harry hadn't been asked to produce his passport or any travel documents. As soon as he was inside the car the two military policemen who had travelled with him had peeled away from his side and moved back into the shadows. He'd heard the boot bang shut to notify that his suitcase was aboard. Then the car had moved off.

'My name's Davidson.' The man in the front passenger seat was talking. 'Hope you had a good flight. We've got a bit of a drive now. Perhaps you'd like to sleep a bit.'

Harry had nodded, accepted the situation with what grace his position allowed, and dozed off.

The car had gone fast out of London, the driver taking them on to the A3, then turning off down to Leatherhead, south to Dorking and then into the narrow winding side-roads under Leith Hill. Davidson was beside the driver and Harry had the back seat to himself, and it was only when the night sky was blotted out by the arch of trees over the sunken road that he woke. The car had driven on some miles, with evident care, before it swept through the wrought-iron gates of one of those great houses buried deep amongst their own woods that lie hidden in the slopes. The drive was rough and in need of repair. Abruptly the rhododendrons gave way to lawns and the car pulled up at a huge porticoed front door.

'Bit formidable, isn't it? The Ministry maintains it's all they could get. Delusions of grandeur. A convent school went broke. Kids all died of exposure, more likely. Come on in.'

Davidson, who had opened the door for him, was speaking. Harry was aware of several other men hovering in the background. The bag was collected, and Davidson went in, followed by Harry.

'We've a long day tomorrow. Lot of talking to do. Let's call it quits, have a good night, and breakfast at seven. Okay?'

Sandwiches and a vacuum flask of coffee were waiting in Harry's room.

The plate and dirtied cup were on the rug by his bed. He put his feet down gingerly and moved to his case. His shaving bag was on top of his neatly folded clothes. He wondered what on earth Mary was making of all this. If they'd sent that dreadful adjutant down to tell her he was called away on urgent business it would be enough to get him a divorce

– better be someone with a little experience in the world of untruths.

No one he'd seen last night had been in uniform. After shaving he put on a checked shirt, Transport Corps tie and his grey suit. He folded away his uniform in the wardrobe and dispersed his other clothes to the various drawers and cupboards. He sat by the window waiting for someone to come to tell him breakfast was served. From his room on the second floor he could see he was at the back of the house. Overgrown tennis courts. A vegetable garden. A great line of trees before the ridge of Surrey hills.

Harry was not naïve and had realized he was to be briefed for an intelligence mission. That didn't bother him, he'd decided. It was a little flattering, and was welcome after brigade transport. Perhaps the remarks about nervous collapse had been rather over-stressed on his post-Aden reports. Anyway, little had come his way that had stretched him to the degree he thought he was capable of. If they'd brought him from Germany then the hard assumption would be that they were going to use him for something in Berlin. This pleased him, as he prided himself that he had taken the trouble to learn passable German, have a near taxi-driver knowledge of the city and keep himself discreetly abreast of the trade techniques. His thoughts were full of the Reichstag, watch-towers, walls and clumps of flowers by the little crosses when the sharp knock came and the door opened.

It began in earnest in what must once have been the drawing-room, now furnished in the fashion of the Defence Ministry. Heavy tables, sofas with big pink flowers all over them and deep army chairs with cloth squares at the back to prevent greased hair marking the covers.

Davidson was there, and three others.

Harry was given the armchair to the right of the fireplace, dominated by the oil painting of the Retreat from Kabul in the snows of the Afghanistan passes. One man sat behind him by the window; another, not ostentatiously, close to the door. The third sat at a central table, his files spread out on the drapes that covered the polished oak surface. One was of stiff blue cardboard, its top crossed with red tape. 'SECRET' had been written across the front in large letters, and underneath were the words: 'BROWN, HARRY JAMES, CAPT.' Four sheets of closely-typed paper were inside – Harry's life history and the assessments of his performance by each of his commanding officers. The first page carried the information they had sought when they had begun the search for the officer they wanted.

Name: Brown, Harry James
Current rank: Captain
Age: 34 years

Born: Portadown, NI, November 1940
Distinguishing marks and description: 5' 11" height, medium build, brown hair, blue eyes, no distinguishing marks, no operation scars
Service UK: Catterick, Plymouth, Tidworth, Ministry of Defence
Service Overseas: Cyprus (2nd Lt), Borneo (2nd Lt), Aden (1st Lt), Berlin (Capt.)
Decorations: Cyprus – Mentioned in Despatches. Aden – Military Cross

In the last quarter of the page was the passage that ensured that Harry came into the operation.

Aden citation: For three months this officer lived as a native in the Arab quarter of Sheik Othman, moving inside the community there and supplying most valuable intelligence concerning terrorist operations. As a result of his work many important arrests were made. It should be stressed that this work was extremely dangerous to the officer, and there was a constant risk that if discovered he would face certain torture and death.

Too right, Harry would have thought if anyone had let him see the file. Day after day, living with those filthy bastards, eating with them, talking with them, crapping with them. Watching for new cars, watching for movement after curfew, observing the huddles in the coffee shops. And always the fear, and the horror if they came too close to him, seemed too interested, talked too much. The terrible fear of discovery, and the pain that would follow. And the know-alls in intelligence back at headquarters who only met an NLF man when he was neatly parcelled up in their basement cells, and who pass discreet little messages – about hanging on a few more days, just a little bit longer. They'd seemed surprised when he just walked up to an army patrol one hot, stinking morning, and introduced himself, and walked out of thirteen weeks of naked terror. And no mention in the files on him of the nervous breakdown, and the days of sick leave. Just a metal cross and an inch square of purple and white cloth to dangle it from, all there was to show for it.

Davidson was moving about the room in sharp darts around the obstacles of furniture.

'I don't have to tell you from your past experience that everything that is said in this room this morning goes under the Official Secrets Act. But I'll remind you of that anyway. What we say in here, the people you've seen here, and the building and its location are all secret.

'Your name was put forward when we came into the market for a new man for an infiltration job. We've seen the files on the Aden experience, and the need has now come up for a man unconnected with any

311

of the normal channels to go in and work in a most sensitive area. The work has been demanded by the Prime Minister. Yesterday afternoon he authorized the mission, and I must say frankly it was against, as I understand it, the advice of his closest military advisers. Perhaps that's putting it a bit strong, but there's some scepticism . . . the PM had a brother in SOE thirty years ago, he has heard over Sunday lunch how the infiltration of agents into enemy country won the war, and they say he's had a bee about it ever since.

'He wants to put a man into the heart of Provo-land, into the Falls in Belfast – a man who is quite clean and has no form in that world at all. The man should not be handled by any of the existing intelligence and undercover groups. He'd be quite new, and to all intents he'd be on his own as far as looking after himself is concerned. I think anyone who has thought even a little about what the PM is asking for knows that the job he has asked us to do is bloody dangerous. I haven't gilded it, Harry. It's a job we've been asked to do, and we all think from what we've read of you that you are the ideal man for it. Putting it formally, this is the bit where you either stand up and say "Not effing likely", and walk out through the door and we'll have you on a flight to Berlin in three hours. Or it's the time when you come in and then stay in.'

The man at the table with the files shuffled his papers. Harry was a long way from a rational evaluation of the job, whatever it was they were offering. He was just thinking how large a file they'd got on him when he became aware of the silence in the room.

Harry said, 'I'll try it.'

'You appreciate, Harry, once you say "yes", that's it. That has to be the definitive decision.'

'Yes, I said yes. I'll try it.' Harry was almost impatient with Davidson's caution.

The atmosphere in the room seemed to change. The man behind Harry coughed. Davidson was on the move again, the file now open in his hand.

'We're going to put you into the Falls with the express and only job of listening for any word of the man who shot the Minister, Danby, three days ago. Why aren't they doing it from Belfast? Basic reason is they've no longer got an infiltration set-up that we're happy with. They used to do it, lost out, and have pretty much withdrawn their men to let them stooge on the outside and collect the stuff they want from informers. The activity has been down over the last few months, and with the risk that exists – I'm being straight with you, Harry – of an undercover man being picked off, and the hullabaloo when it hits the fan, those sort of operations have been scaled down. There is a thought that the intelligence division over there is not as tight as it ought to be. We've been asked to set up a new operation. Intelligence in Belfast won't handle you, we will. The Special Branch over there won't have heard of you. Whatever else your problems may be they won't be that someone is going to drop you in it over there, because no one will know of your existence. If you have a message you pass it to us. A phone call to us, on the numbers we give you, will be as fast – if you want to alert the military – as anything you could do if you were plugged into the regular Lisburn net, working under their control.

'I stress again, this is the PM's idea. He raised it at the security meeting yesterday and insisted we push it forward. The RUC don't want you, and the military regard it as something of a joke. We reckon we'll need you here for two weeks before we fly you in, and in that time they may have the man, or at least have a name on him. If that happens then we call the whole thing off, and you can relax and go back to Germany. It's not a bad thing that they don't want to know – we won't have to tell them anything till it's ripe, and that way we keep it tight.'

He'd wondered whether to mention the Prime Minister's involvement, and thought about it at length the previous evening. If this man were to be captured and talk under torture the balloon would be sky high, the reverberations catastrophic. But there was another side to it. Any man asked to do as dangerous a job as the one envisaged had the right to know where the orders originated; to be certain he wasn't the puppet on the end of wire manipulated for the benefit of a second-rate operation. It was Davidson's own inclination to be open, and he reckoned that apart from everything else a man in these circumstances needed all the morale-building he could get.

'So far the police and military have put out pictures, appeals, rewards, launched raids, checked all the usual angles, and they haven't come up with anything. I don't know whether you would. The PM's decided we try and that's what's going to happen.

'I'm sorry, but on this there cannot be a phone call to your wife. We've told her you've been called away on urgent posting. This morning she's been told you're on your way to Muscat, because of your special Aden knowledge. We have some postcards you can write to her later and we'll get them posted by the RAF for you.

'I said at the beginning this would be dangerous. I don't want to minimize that. The IRA shoot intelligence men they get their hands on. They don't rough them up and leave them for a patrol to find, they kill them. The last man of ours that they took was tortured. Catholics who work for us have been beaten up, burned, lacerated, hooded and then killed. They're hard bastards . . . but we want this man badly.'

Davidson paused in his stride, jolting Harry's attention. Harry fidgeted and shifted in the chair. He hated the pep talks. This one was damn near a carbon copy of the one he'd had in Aden, though then

313

the PM's name had been left out, and they were quoting top secret instructions from GOC Land Forces Mid East.

Davidson suggested coffee. The work would start after the break.

The Prime Minister had been hearing a report on the latest speech to a Bulawayo farming conference of the rebel Prime Minister – his 'illegal counterpart', as he liked to call him. He scanned the pages quickly and deftly, assimilating the nuances the Rhodesian's speech writers had written in for the reader on the other side of the world. It was a static situation, he decided, not one for a further initiative at this stage. When his secretary had left him he turned back to his desk from the window and dialled an unlisted number at the Ministry of Defence.

The conversation was short and obviously to the point. It lasted about twenty-five seconds. The Prime Minister put his opening question, listened, and rang off after saying, 'No . . . no . . . I don't want to know any more . . . only that it's happening. Thank you, you'll keep me informed, thank you.'

Off the Broadway, half-way up the Falls, the man and his minder locked the doors of the stolen and resprayed Cortina and moved through the protective cordon of white-painted petrol drums to the door of the pub. The minder had been there from the morning, not knowing and not asking who was the man he had been set to protect. With the job went the PPK Walther that pulled down his coat pocket. The gun was a prize symbol of the old success days of the local IRA company – taken from the body of a Special Branch constable ambushed as he cruised late at night in the Springfield Road. It was now prized, partly for its fire power, partly for its value as a trophy.

The man led the way into the pub. It was the first time he had walked the streets of the city since his return, and after two days on the move from house to house and not a straight night's sleep at any of them he showed the signs of a life on the run. The Army Council had anticipated this and had decided that for his own safety the man should as soon as possible be reintroduced to his old haunts, as the longer he were away the more likely it was that his name could become associated with the shooting in London.

The pub boasted a single bar, dark, shabby and with a pall of smoke hanging between shoulder height and the low ceiling. A sparse covering of worn lino was on the floor, pocked with cigarette burns. As always most eyes were facing the door, and conversation died as the man walked in and went towards the snug, away to the left of the serving area. The minder gripped him by the arm, and mouthed quickly in his ear.

'They said in the middle of the bar. Show yourself. That's what they told me.'

The man nodded his head, turned to the bar and ordered his drinks. He was known only slightly here, but the man with him was local, and that was the passport to acceptance. The man felt the tension easing out of him, as the conversation again spread through the bar.

Later he was asked by one old man how come he'd not been in. He replied loudly, and with the warm beer moving through him, that his Mam in Cork had been unwell. He'd been to see her, she was better now and he was back. His Mam was better known in these streets than he was, and it was remembered by a few that she'd married a railwayman in Cork three years after her first husband died, and moved away to the South from Belfast. Lucky I was too, she'd say. The railwayman himself had died now, but she had stayed south. The man's explanation was more than adequate. There were mutterings of sympathy, and the subject closed.

His main worry had been the photokit picture. He had seen it reproduced on the front page of the Belfast *Newsletter* on his second day back and read of the efforts to track him down. He'd seen pictures of the troops sealing streets off, looking for him, and looked at quarter-page advertisements taken by the Northern Ireland office urging people to tell all they knew about the killing to the police via the Confidential phone. There were reports that a huge reward was to be offered for his capture, but if any of the men in the bar linked him with the picture there was no sign of it. The man had decided himself that the picture was not that similar to his features, too pinched in the face, the word the woman had used, with the hair parting too accentuated.

He was on his third pint when the patrol came into the pub.

Eight soldiers, crowding the small area, ordered everyone to stay still and keep their hands out of their pockets. With the shouting from the troops and the general noise of their entry, no one noticed the minder leaning against the bar slide his gun down towards the washing-up bowl. Nor did they see the publican, ostensibly drying his hands before displaying them to the troops, put his cloth over the dark gun-metal. With his final action he flicked cloth and gun on to the floor and kicked them hard towards the kitchen door. The design of the building prevented any of the soldiers seeing the young girl's hand that reached round the door in answer to her father's short whistle, gather up the gun, and run with it to the coal shed. The men in the bar were lined against the side wall by the empty fireplace and searched. The man's search was no more, no less thorough than that of the other men. They searched the minder very thoroughly, perhaps because he was sweating, a veil of moisture across his forehead, as he waited for their decision on him, not knowing what had happened to the gun that bore his palm prints and could earn him five years plus in the Crumlin Road.

315

Then, as suddenly as the soldiers had come they were out, barging their way past the tables, running into the street, and back to their regular routine of patrolling. There was noise again in the bar. The publican pushed the washing-up cloth, now filthy with coal smuts, across the wooden bar to the minder. The man felt noisy. He'd come through the first big test.

At the big house in Surrey the team round Harry had worked him hard the first day. They'd started by discussing what cover he would want, and rejected the alternatives in favour of a merchant seaman home after five years, but with his parents dead some years back.

'It's too small a place for us to give you a completely safe identity you could rely on. It would mean we'd have to bring other people in who would swear by you. It gets too big that way. We start taking a risk, unnecessarily.'

Davidson was adamant that the only identity Harry would have would be the one he carried round on his back. If anyone started looking into his story really deeply then there was no way in which he could survive, strong background story or not.

Harry himself supplied most of what they needed. He'd been born a Catholic in one of the little terraces off Obin Street in Portadown. The houses had been pulled down some years ago, and replaced by anonymous blocks of flats and small houses, now daubed with the slogans of revolution. With the destruction of the old buildings inevitably the people had become dispersed.

Portadown, the Orangeman's town with the ghetto round the long sloping passage of Obin Street, still had its vivid teenage memories for Harry. He'd spent his childhood there from the age of five, after his parents had been killed in a car crash. They'd been driving back to Portadown when a local businessman late home on his way back from Armagh had cut across them and sent his father into a ditch and telegraph pole. Harry had stayed with an aunt for twelve years in the Catholic street before joining the army. But his childhood in the town gave him adequate knowledge – enough, Davidson decided, for his cover.

For four hours after lunch they quizzed him on his knowledge of the intricacies of Irish affairs, sharpened him on the names of the new political figures. The major terrorist acts since the summer of 1969 were neatly catalogued on three closely-typed sheets. They briefed him particularly on the grievances of the minority.

'You'll want to know what they're beefing about. You know this, they're walking encyclopaedias on every shot we fired at them. There's going to be a lot more, but this is the refresher.'

Davidson was warming to it now, enjoying these initial stages of the preparation, the thoroughness of which would be the deciding factor whether their agent survived. Davidson had been through this before. Never with Ulster as the target, but in Aden before Harry's duty there, and Cyprus, and once when a Czech refugee was sent into his former homeland. That last time they heard nothing, till the man's execution was reported by the Czech news agency half an hour after a stony protest note was delivered to the British Ambassador in Prague. Post-war Albania had involved him too. Now it was a new operation, breeding the same compulsion as the first cigarette of the day to an inveterate smoker.

Harry had come up to the table. The papers were spread out in front of him, fingers reaching and pointing at the different essentials for him to take in.

Later he was to take many of them to his room, ask for some sandwiches and coffee and, sprawled in front of the gas fire, read them into the small hours till they were second nature. On his own for the first time in the day he too was able to assess the importance of the preparation he was undergoing, and alone in the room he allowed himself to think of the hazards of the operation in which he was now involved.

It was past two in the morning when he undressed and climbed into bed, the papers still strewn on the rug in front of the fire.

4

Over the next fortnight the street scene in Belfast returned to its pre-Danby level of violence. It was widely recognized that in the wake of the killing the level of army activity had risen sharply, initially in the use of major cordon and search operations, merging into an increase in the number of spot raids on the homes of known republicans on the run. The army activity meant more men were charged with offences, but alongside their appearances in court was an upsurge in street rioting, something that had previously been almost eradicated. The army's posture was sharply criticized by the minority politicians, who accused the troops of venting on innocent Catholic householders their frustrations at not being able to find Danby's murderer.

The Secretary of State for Northern Ireland agreed to appear on the local Independent TV station and the regional BBC news programme to answer the allegations of Protestant papers that not enough was being done – that a British Cabinet Minister had been shot down in cold blood

317

in front of his wife and children yet his killers were allowed to go free for fear of offending Catholic opinion.

Before appearing on television the Secretary of State called a meeting of his security chiefs, and heard both Frank Scott and General Fairbairn urge caution and patience. The General in particular was concerned lest a show of strength spread over several weeks undo the gradual return to something like normality. The three men were soon to leave for their various destinations – the politician for the studio, the General for Lisburn and the Chief Constable for his modern police headquarters – but first they walked on the lawn outside the Stormont residence of the Secretary of State. Away from the listening ears of secretaries, aides and bodyguards the General reported that his intelligence section had heard nothing of the killer in Belfast and there was some concern about whether the man they sought was even in the city. The Chief Constable added to the politician's cross in reporting that his men too had been unable to uncover any hard information on the man. But the head of his Special Branch favoured the belief that the killer was in the city, and probably back in circulation. The Chief Superintendent in charge of picked detectives had a fair insight into the workings of his enemies' minds, and had correctly read the desire of the Provisional IRA Army Council to get their man back into the main stream.

For three minutes they talked in the centre of the lawn. The conversation ended when the Secretary of State quietly, and more than a little hesitantly, asked the General:

'Jocelyn, no news I suppose on what the PM was talking about?'

'None, nor will there be.'

The General made his way back to his car, turned and shouted a brusque farewell.

As the military convoy pulled away, the politician turned to the policeman. 'We have to have this bastard soon. The political scene won't hold up long otherwise. And there's a lot of restiveness among the Loyalists. We need him quick, Frank, if the sectarianism isn't to start up again. There's not much time . . .'

He walked quickly now to his big maroon Rover with its reinforced sides and extra thick windows, with machine-guns, field dressings and gas masks alongside his official cases in the boot. He nodded to his driver, and then winced as the detective sitting in front of him loaded the clip of bullets into the butt of the 9 mm Browning.

The car swung out into the open road for the drive into the city, with his escort close behind to prevent any other car clipping between them. 'What a bloody carry-on,' the politician observed as they swept through the traffic towards the television studios.

*

The interview of the Secretary of State was embargoed until 18.01 hours; its full text was issued by the Northern Ireland press office to Belfast newspapers. In essence the BBC and ITV transmissions were the same, and the public relations men put out only the BBC interview.

Q. Secretary of State, can you report any progress in the hunt for Mr Danby's killer?
A. Well, I want to emphasize that the security forces are working flat out on this one. I myself have had a meeting just before this broadcast with the army commander and chief constable, and I am perfectly satisfied with the investigation and follow-up operations they are mounting. I'm confident we'll round up this gang of thugs quickly.
Q. But have you any leads yet to who the killers are?
A. I think we know who the killers are, they're the Provisional IRA, but I'm sure you wouldn't expect me to talk on television about the details of a police investigation.
Q. It's been pretty quiet for some time in Belfast, and we were led to believe that most of the IRA commanders were imprisoned . . . Isn't it justifiable to expect rather quicker action, even results at this stage?
A. If you mean to imply we have claimed the IRA weren't capable of mounting this sort of operation I don't think we have ever made that sort of assumption. We think this is the work of a small group, a very small group. We'll get them soon . . . there's nothing to panic about – (It was a bad word, panic, he saw it as soon as he said it. The interviewer nudged him forward.)
Q. I haven't heard the word 'panic' used before. Are you implying the public have over-reacted towards the killing of a Cabinet Minister in broad daylight in front of his children?
A. Of course, this was a dreadful crime. This was a colleague of mine. Of course, people should feel strongly; what I'm saying is that this is a last fling of the IRA . . .
Q. A pretty successful last fling.
A. Mr Danby was unarmed –
Q. In Loyalist areas of the city the government are accused of not going in hard to find the killer because the results could antagonize Catholic opinion.
A. That's untrue, quite untrue. When we have identified the man we intend to get him. There'll be no holding off.
Q. Secretary of State, thank you very much.
A. Thank you.

Most of the young Protestants who gathered in the side streets off the Albert Bridge Road, pelting the armoured vehicles as they went by, hadn't seen the interview. But word had quickly spread through the loyalist heartlands in the east and west of the city that the British had in some way glossed over the killing, not shown the determination to rout out those Provie rats who could murder a man in front of his bairns. The battalion on duty in Mountpottinger police station was put on fifteen minute readiness, and those making their way to the prosperous suburbs far out to the East of Belfast took long diversions, lest their cars became part of the sprouting barricades that the army crash-charged with their Saracens. Three soldiers were hurt by flying debris and the Minister's broadcast was put down as the kindling point to the brushfire that was to smoulder for more than a week in the Protestant community.

Meanwhile Harry was being prepared for the awesome moment when he would leave the woods of Surrey and fly to Belfast, on his own, leaving the back-up team that now worked with him as assiduously as any heavyweight champion's.

Early on Davidson had brought him a cassette recorder, complete with four ninety-minute tapes of Belfast accents. They'd been gathered by students from Queen's University who believed they were taking part in a national phonetics study, and had taken their microphones into pubs, launderettes, working men's clubs and supermarkets. Wherever there were groups gathered and talking in the harsh, cutting accent of Belfast, so different to the slower more gentle Southern speech, tapes had attempted to pick up the voices and record them. The tapes had been passed to the army press officer via a lecturer at the University, whose brother was on duty on the Brigade commander's staff, and then, addressed to a fictitious major, flown to the Ministry of Defence. The sergeant on Davidson's staff travelled to London to collect them from the dead letter box in the postal section of the Ministry.

Night after night Harry listened to the tapes, mouthing over the phrases and trying to lock his speech into the accents he heard. After sixteen years in the army little of it seemed real. He learned again of the abbreviations, the slang, the swearing. He heard the way that years of conflict and alertness had stunted normal conversation; talk was kept to a minimum as people hurried away from shops once their business was done, and barely waited around for a quiet gossip. In the pubs he noticed that men lectured each other, seldom listening to replies, or interested in opinions different to their own. His accent would be critical to him, the sort of thing that could awake the first inkling of suspicion that might lead to the further check he knew his cover could not sustain.

His walls, almost bare when he arrived at the big house, were soon covered by aerial photographs of Belfast. For perhaps an hour a day he was left to memorize the photographs, learn the street patterns of the geometric divisions of the artisan cottages that had been allowed to

320

sprawl out from the centre of the city. The developers of the nineteenth century had flung together the narrow streets and their back-to-back terraces along the main roads out of the city. Most relevant to Harry were those on either side of the city's two great ribbons of the Falls and Shankill. Pictures of astonishing clarity taken from RAF cameras showed the continuous peace line, or the 'interface', as the army called it, the sheets of silvery corrugated iron that separated Protestant from Catholic in the no man's land between the roads.

The photographs gave an idea of total calm, and left no impression of the hatred, terror and bestiality that existed on the ground. The open spaces of bombed devastation in any other British city would have been marked down as clearance areas for urban improvement.

From the distance of Germany – where theorists worked out war games in terms of divisions, tank skirmishes, limited nuclear warheads, and the possibility of chemical agents being thrown into a critical battle – it had become difficult for Harry to realize why the twenty or so thousand British soldiers deployed in the province were not able to wind up the Provisional campaign in a matter of months. When he took in the rabbit warren revealed by the reconnaissance photographs he began to comprehend the complexity of the problem. Displayed on his walls was the perfect guerilla fighting base. A maze of escape routes, ambush positions, back entries, cul-de-sacs and, at strategic crossroads, great towering blocks of flats commanding the approaches to terrorist strongholds.

It was the adventure playground par excellence for the urban terrorist, Davidson would say, as he fired questions at Harry till he could wheel out at will all the street names they wanted from him, so many commemorating the former greatness of British arms – Balkan, Raglan, Alma, Balaclava – their locations, and the quickest way to get there. By the second week the knowledge was there and the consolidation towards perfection was under way. Davidson and his colleagues felt now that the filing system had worked well, that this man, given the impossible brief he was working under, would do as well as any.

Also in the bedroom, and facing him as he lay in bed, was the 'tribal map' of the city. That was the army phrase, and another beloved by Davidson. It took up sixteen square feet of space, with Catholic streets marked in a gentle grass-green, the fierce loyalist strongholds in the hard orange that symbolized their heritage, and the rest in a mustard compromise. Forget that lot, Davidson had said. That had meant something in the early days when the maps were drawn up.

'Nowadays you're in one camp or the other. There are no uncommitted. Mixed areas are three years out of date. In some it's the Prods who've run, in others the other crowd.'

It had been so simple in Sheik Othman, when Harry had lived amongst the Adeni Arabs. The business of survival had occupied him so fully that the sophistications they were teaching him now were unnecessary. And there he had been so far from the help of British troops that he had become totally self-reliant. In Belfast he knew he must guard against the feeling that salvation was always a street corner away. He must reject that and burrow his way into the community if he was to achieve anything.

Outside the privacy of his room Harry seldom escaped the enthusiasm of Davidson, who personally supervised every aspect of his preparation. He followed Harry in the second week down beyond the vegetable garden to the old and battered greenhouse, yards long and with its glass roofing missing, and what was left coated in the deep moss-green compost that fell from the trees. There were no nurtured tomatoes growing here, no cosseted strawberry cuttings, only a pile of sandbags at the opposite end to the door with a circular coloured target, virgin new, propped against them. Here they retaught Harry the art of pistol shooting.

'You'll have to have a gun over there – and not to wave about, Harry,' Davidson laughed. 'Just to have. You'd be the only physically fit male specimen in the province without one if you didn't have a firearm of some sort. It's a must, I'm afraid.'

'I didn't have one in Aden. Ridiculous, I suppose, but no one suggested it.'

He took the gun from the instructor, grey-haired, hard-faced, lined from weather, wearing a blue, all-enveloping boiler suit and unmarked beret. He went through the precautionary drills, breaking the gun, flicking the revolving chamber that was empty, greased and black. The instructor counted out the first six shells.

Five times he reloaded the gun till the target was peppered and holed and askew.

'It's not the accuracy that counts so much with the first ones, sir,' said the older man, pulling off his ear muffs, 'it's the speed you get the first one or two away. If you're shooting straight enough for your opponent to hear them going by his ear that tends to be enough to get his head back a bit. But it's getting the first one away that matters. Gets the initiative for you. There aren't many men as will stand still and aim as you're pulling the trigger for the first one. Get 'em going back and then worry about the aim for the third and fourth shot. And try not to fire more than the first four straight off. It's nice to keep a couple just so that you have a chance to do something about it if things don't turn out that well. Remember with this one it's a great little gun, but it's slow to load. That's its problem. Everything else is okay.'

They went over the firing positions. Sometimes the classic right-arm-extended, sideways-on stance. 'That's if you've got all night, sir, and you don't think he's armed. Take your time and make sure. Doesn't happen that often.' Then they worked on the standard revolver-shooting

322

posture. Legs apart, body hunched, arms extended, meeting in front of the eye line, butt held in both hands, the whole torso lunging at the target. 'You're small yourself then, sir, and you've got your whole body thrown in with the gun to get it away straight. You won't miss often from that, and if you do you'll give 'im such a hell of a fright that he won't do much about it.'

'What's he like, Chief?' Davidson said to the instructor.

'We've had better through here, sir, and we've had worse. He's quite straight but a bit slow as of now. I wouldn't worry about that. If he has to use it he'll be faster. Everyone is when it's real.'

Harry followed Davidson out of the greenhouse and they walked together up the brick and weed path amongst the vegetables. It was mild for November; the trees, huge above them, were already without their load of leaves and above the trees the soft meandering grey clouds.

'I think it's going quite well, Harry – no, I mean very well at the moment. But I don't want to minimize anything that you're going to have to go through. It's all very well here, swotting for an exam if you like . . . but the questions themselves are very tough when you get to the actual paper. Forgive the metaphor, Harry, but it's not an easy road over there, however much we do for you here. There are some things we can iron out at this end. Accent. It's critical for immediate and long-term survival. You can spare your blushes but I think that's coming along very well. Your background knowledge is fine, detail of events, names, folklore – that is all good. But there are other more complex factors, about which we cannot really do very much, and which are just as vital.'

They stopped now some twenty-five yards from the house on the edge of the old tennis court. Davidson was looking for the words. Harry wasn't going to help him: that wasn't his style.

'Look, Harry. Just as important as the accent, and getting the background right, and knowing what the hullabaloo is about, is how you are going to stand up to this yourself. It's my job to send you in there as perfectly equipped as possible. Right? Well, the thing I cannot accurately gauge is how you'll soak up the punishment of just existing there. You could have an isolation problem . . . loneliness, basically. No one to confide in, not part of a local team, completely on your own. This could be a problem. I don't know the answer to it, I don't think you're liable to suffer too greatly from it – that's my reading of your file. Sorry, but we go through it most nights with a fine blade. Unless you're aware of it, and bolt it down, there'll come a time when you'll want to tell someone about yourself, however obliquely, however much at a tangent. You'll say now, never, never in a month of whatevers, but believe me it'll happen, and you have to watch it.'

Harry searched his face, noting for the first time since he'd come to the big house the concern of the other man. Davidson went on, 'After

Aden we're pretty confident in your ability to look after yourself. There's a lot in the file on that. I've no reason to disbelieve it, you've shown me none. The simple day-to-day business won't be pleasant but will be bearable. The other thing you have to consider is if you're discovered – what happens then? There is a fair chance that if they spot you we may be getting some sort of feedback as they build up information and we'll have time to shift you out in a hurry. You may notice something, a tail, a man watching you, questions being asked. Don't hang about then, just come back. What I'm getting at is difficult enough to say, but you have to face it, and you'll be better for facing it. You have to work out how you'll react if they take you alive.'

Harry grimaced weakly. The older man was fumbling about trying to say the most obvious thing of the whole operation, stumbling in his care not to scratch the varnish of morale that was coated sometimes thickly, sometimes sparsely on all these jobs.

'I think I can help you,' Harry smiled at him. 'You want to know whether I've considered the question of being taken, tortured and shot. Yes. You want to know whether I'm going to tell them all about here, you and everything else. Answer, I don't know. I think not, I hope not. But I don't know. You don't know these things, and there's no absolute statement I can make that would be of any use. But I've thought of it, and I knew what you'd hope from me. Whether you'll get it I just don't know.'

They began to walk again. Davidson swung his right arm round behind Harry's back and slapped his far shoulder. Like a father, thought Harry, and he's scared stiff. It's always been nice and comfortable for him, sitting at a desk packing the nameless numbered men off to heaven knows where, but this time the jungle's been creeping a bit close.

'Thank you, Harry. That was very fairly put. Very fair. There's things that have to be discussed if one's to keep these things professional. I'm grateful to you. I think your attitude is about right.' Thank God for that, Harry thought, now he's done his duty. We've had our facts of life talk, ready to go out into the big nasty world, and don't put your hands up little girls' skirts. God, he's relieved he's got that little lot over.

As they came to the paint-chipped back door, Davidson started again. 'You know, Harry, you haven't told us much about home, about your wife. The family. It's an aspect we haven't really had time to go into.'

'There's nothing to worry about there. Not that I know of. I suppose you never do till it's too late to be worrying about that sort of thing. She's very level. Not complicated. That sounds pretty patronizing, but I don't mean that. She's used to me going away in a hurry, at least was used to it when we were younger. It's not been so frequent over the last few years, but I think she's okay.'

'Did she know what you were doing in Aden?'

324

Harry said it slowly, thoughtfully, 'No. Not really. I didn't have time or the opportunity to write. There had been those little sods rolling grenades into the married quarters and smuggling bombs in with the food and things like that. The families went home before I became involved in the special stuff. I didn't tell her much about it when it was all over. There wasn't much to tell, not in my terms.'

'I'm sorry you had to come over here without being able to see her.'

'Inevitable. It's the way it is. She's not very service-minded. Doesn't live off married mess nights. Doesn't really get involved with the army scene. I think I prefer it that way. She'd like me out, but I tell her earning anyone else's shilling than the Queen's isn't that easy these days. I think she understands that.'

'The postcards will start arriving soon. The first lot that you did. And you'd better do some more before you move on.' Davidson sounded anxious, wanting to do it right, thought Harry. As if there was anything he could say about – what was the word he used? – this 'aspect' of the job. Of course she'd want to know where he was, of course if she knew she would be stunned with worry. What else could she be, and what could be done about it? Nothing.

They hesitated outside the door of the big room where the work was done.

Davidson said, 'I wanted to be sure that you wouldn't be too concerned about your family while you're over there. It could be important. I once had a man . . .'

Harry cut in, 'It's not a problem. Not compared with the other ones. She'll cope.'

They went into the room where the others were waiting. Davidson thought to himself, he's a cold enough fish to succeed. It went through Harry's mind that his controller was either very thorough or on the reverse slope and going a touch soft. It was the only time the two men had anything approaching a personal conversation.

Later that afternoon it was suggested that Harry should personally meet the eye-witnesses who had been in Belgrave Square, or who had reported the jostling incident with the hurrying man in the Underground ticket area at Oxford Circus. Harry could have gone in the guise of a detective, but Davidson, after mulling it over for thirty-six hours, decided it was an unnecessary risk and sent a video camera from the Ministry round to their homes with one of the young officers in order that they could relive the moments they had been face to face with the gunman. For about fifteen minutes the elderly man who had seen a flash of the face while reading his paper, the girl with the bag of laundry, the woman exercising her dog, the driver of the ministry car and the woman who had stood immobile as the man weaved a way past her had spelled out their recollections. They were taken again and again through the short experience, milked till their impatience with their questioner grew pointed, and then left wondering why so much equipment and time was spent in merely reiterating the statement they had made to the police the previous week.

Endlessly the tapes were rerun, so that the strength of each witness's description could be tested. Hesitations about hair styles, eye colours, cheekbone make-up, nose size, all the details that make each face unique as a fingerprint were analysed. Davidson made up a chart where all the strong points were listed in green ink, the next category in red, the doubtful points in blue. These were placed against the photokit picture already issued by the Royal Ulster Constabulary and Scotland Yard.

There were differences, they found. Differences that would have been sufficient to prevent the young soldiers in the pub off the Broadway eight days earlier from connecting the picture they had memorized with the man they had studied, arms up and legs apart, against the wall.

'You have to know him,' said Davidson – so often it became like a holed record – 'You have to know about him, have a sense that when he's on the pavement and you're at the other side you'll have him straight away. It's chemistry, my boy.'

Harry thought of it a different way. He thought in a job as daft as this you need everything on your side. He reckoned his chances of seeing the man about minus nil, though he maintained a more public optimism with Davidson.

The Ministry had designed their own photokit of the man, using the Scotland Yard one as a basis, but from the eye-witness tapes they slightly altered various features, particularly the profile of the face. Their own picture was displayed around treble life-size in the rooms where the team worked, the big living-room, and the dining area at the back – and more space on Harry's wall was taken up with it, alongside the maps and aerial photographs.

By the fifteenth day they were ready to push Harry out into the field, and cut the cord that held him to the security of the big house amongst the trees. Other than his sleeping time, and those hours he'd worked in his room on the voice tapes and the maps, he'd been allowed to spend little time on his own. That was Davidson's idea – 'For Christ's sake, don't let him brood on it,' he told the others.

Davidson had wondered whether there ought to be some celebration on Harry's last night, and then decided against it in favour of a few glasses of beer after their final session, and another early night.

'Don't believe all that *Daily Telegraph* stuff about them being beaten, smashed, in their final death throes. It's nonsense. They need time to regroup, and they needed a big morale booster. They've got that, not in the killing itself, but in our failure to nab their man and lock him up. The Prods are restless now, not critical yet, but stirring the pot – just as the Provos want it.

'To be frank, Harry, we all thought they'd have had the killer by now, and for the first week at least we may have handled your preparation on that basis. The word I had last night is they haven't identified any positive clue yet. No one's losing anything by you going in. But in a strange idiotic way you have a better chance than the military clumping round and the police. It's not a great chance, but about worth taking.'

They wished him luck. A little formal. Harry said nothing, nodded and walked into the hall and up the stairs to his room. They let him go alone.

The fire position was in the roof of a derelict house just to the north of the Falls road, beyond its junction with Springfield. Four of the houses had been demolished when a nineteen-year-old volunteer in the First Battalion had stumbled, knocking the arm of the battalion's explosive officer as he was putting the final touches to a seventy-five-pound gelignite bomb. The officer's fingers had moved some three-eighths of an inch, enough to connect momentarily with the terminals that in another few minutes would have been attached to the face of a cheap alarm clock.

The explosion had left a gouged hole in the line of the street. The first house to the right after the gap was left naked and exposed to the open air. The next house down was in better shape. There was a door still in place, and the roof was largely intact. The house was empty because local housing officials had condemned it as unsafe, and gas and electricity had been switched off. The five houses beyond were occupied.

The man had wedged himself in the angle between the beams and the horizontal struts of the roof. Part of the time his legs were astride the struts, which cut deep into his thighs in spite of the cushions he had brought with him. Otherwise he knelt, spreading his weight over two of the struts. In that position his balance was more stable, but it hurt more.

Looking down he could see through a gap in the roof where a tile had slid down into the street, shaken loose by the blast from the explosion. The tile had been only slightly above the level of the guttering and from his position his eyes were little more than four feet from it. From the hole his line of visibility took him left to the corner of the street, and across to the right the length of the frontage of three houses. On the same side of the street as the man's hiding place was the home of a Mrs Mulvenna, whose husband was currently held in Long Kesh. She always kept her front-room light on, with the curtains drawn back, so that the light illuminated the pavement just beyond the extremity of the man's field of fire, and threw shadows into the area covered by his line of vision. It was his hope that a night patrol, their faces blackened, rubber soles on their boots, would edge away from the brightness in favour of the side of the road where they could find some false refuge in the greyness, but where they would be covered by the man's sights. He knew enough of the habits of the soldiers to be able to bank on one of the troops in the middle of the patrol lingering uncertainly on the corner. The soldier would need to pause for only two or three seconds to make the man's vigil worthwhile.

The army were never consistent with their patrol patterns, and in the three days that he had been in the roof the man had seen only one group of soldiers. That had been in mid-morning and then, without Mrs Mulvenna's light to drive them across the street, they had come by, right underneath the hideout, and virtually out of sight. He had seen one of them momentarily then, heard their fresh, young English county voices as they passed by unaware of his presence above.

Across the man's knee was an Armalite rifle. Small, lightweight, with shocking high velocity hitting power. The bodywork of the rifle was of black plastic, made in Japan, built under licence as a copy of the American infantry's M16 weapon. The Kalashnikov in London had been a luxury, an eccentricity . . . for the more routine job in which he was now engaged the Armalite was totally suitable.

And so he waited in the dark and freezing draughts of the roof for the twenty seconds or so it would take an eight-man patrol to move past the shadows of the three houses opposite. His eyes strained at the darkness, his ears keen to the noise of feet and the different types of shoes the civilians wore. He had cat-napped through the day to reserve his concentration for the time, fast and silent, that the soldiers would come.

5

The lady who had been walking her dog in Belgrave Square now left it at home each morning when she went to the doctor's surgery. The elderly GP allowed her to talk for at least ten minutes each morning before gently shooing her back to her flat and the hysteria and depression that had engulfed her since the shooting. The doctor appreciated the need of the widow, who had been his casual and infrequent patient for twenty-three years, to talk to some friend who could comprehend her meticulous description of the screaming woman, the man with that awful banging gun at his shoulder, the petrified children, the sirens, and the shouting, helpless policemen.

He gave her mild sedatives, but had been unwilling to prescribe habit-forming doses in the hope that time would eventually erode the images of the killing. He had been surprised and annoyed when she had told him that the detectives had been to see her again, a clear week after they had received her signature on what was described as the final and definitive statement she would need to make. She had told the doctor of the queer equipment they had brought, and how over and over she had been made to describe the man with the gun.

It had been sufficient of an ordeal for her, this last visit, to set back her recovery, and accordingly the doctor had phoned the Scotland Yard officer who was named in the papers as heading the enquiry. But such was the pressure on his time, and the size of his register, that he had taken the matter no further when told that no policeman had been to visit his patient in the last nine days. He had blustered a bit when he was told that, protested about the obvious inconsistency between the police story and his patient's, and then rung off. It still puzzled him.

The Secretary of State for Defence was in his office early, clearing his desk for the start of a short holiday, and arming himself with persuasive and informed argument that he would need for his nine holes with the Prime Minister. The civil servant who was briefing him on the missile gap and the sagging morale of denuded unit in Germany continued his lecture in his usual professorial manner. He had a turn of phrase that had infuriated a series of Ministers as the civil servant had progressed upwards to his position of a Man Who Ran Things. His role in the vast department was all-commanding, his power and influence huge. One of the smaller cogs in his well-oiled machine was Davidson, and one of the less frequently mentioned properties on his books was the house near Dorking.

Tentatively the Minister spoke to him.

'That suggestion of the PM about the Danby killing – you remember, putting a chap in there. He'll want to know . . . what's happening?'

'Yes. He phoned last week. I wouldn't worry about it, Minister. We're still going over feasibility et cetera at the moment. It's not a fast business, you know; not a thing we can successfully knock off overnight.'

'Nothing definite yet, then? You've already spoken to him? That's a bit odd, isn't it? On to you direct, and by-passing me? He may be in charge of security and all that, but it's a bit off. What did you tell him?'

'That things were in hand. That he'd get a briefing the moment there was something to report, when there were developments.'

329

'I think you see me as some sort of security risk or something.' The Minister grimaced. The civil servant smiled generously. The subject was terminated. It was back to rocketry and more conventional theatres of war.

Twenty-five thousand feet up, between Liverpool and the Isle of Man, Harry was working things out. The reality of it all had been brutally clear as he had stood in the queue waiting to be searched by the Securicor team at the departure gate. Whoever heard of an agent getting his own bags taken apart by his own bloody side? It was painfully clear why his promised Smith and Wesson would have to be picked up at the Belfast main post office, where Davidson was to send it to await collection. He tried to concentrate on his cover story. Merchant seaman going home after years away, land in turmoil, oppression over the minority. Time for all true Irishmen to get back to back, together to withstand the English bastards. Three hundred years post Cromwell, and nothing changed. Blood of martyrs on the streets again. Would anyone be daft enough to come back to that stinking hole, just because things were getting worse? Be out of their minds. Irish might be daft enough, have to be daft. One thing – bloody English wouldn't come home, they'd all go off to Australia or South Africa. Wouldn't catch them risking their precious lilywhite backsides.

The story was as firm in his mind as it ever would be.

He lay, half awake, half asleep, in no man's land. What of the commitment he had taken on? Motivation was vague and unthought-out. It wouldn't be as strong as the other side's. No chance. Motivation was against the code with which he had been instilled. Officers didn't need motivation. It wasn't all clear.

Rights and wrongs, pluses and minuses, blacks and whites were all vague. In Northern Ireland things don't divide and coalesce neatly. That's too easy. What was it the politician had said? 'Anyone who thinks he knows the answer to Northern Ireland is ill-informed.' Good, that. Lots of ill-informed types in the mess in Germany then. Came back with the solution worked out. One big swoop, one big push, the tough hand, the gentle hand, the 'saturate them', the 'pull the plug and leave them'. All the answers, none the same, but all spoken with such authority, Amazing how you can learn three hundred years' bigotry in four months looking after five blocks in a scruffy council estate.

Harry, heavy with sarcasm, had once congratulated a brother in uniform on the good fortune the other had in being able to see things so clearly. To be able with such confidence to apportion his blame and praise, culpability and credit – that made him a lucky man. In Mansoura, just out of Sheik Othman, where the gunmen were running round while

330

the boyos in Ulster were still on their iced lollies and sing-songs, it had been so much easier. The Red Cross man from Switzerland, in his little white suit, even with a big bright cross on his hat so they wouldn't throw a grenade at him from a rooftop, had come to visit the unit once. He'd said to the colonel something like, 'One man's terrorist is another man's freedom fighter.' The colonel hadn't liked that. Pretty heady stuff, they all thought in the mess. Such rubbish. Terrorists they were then, wog terrorists at that.

But in Aden Harry had thought it was obvious to even the most stupid that British society was in no way being protected by their efforts . . . business perhaps, but nothing else.

Whatever else men died for in the sharp staccato engagements of small-arms fire, the green fields of home were a touch removed from the Mansoura roundabout picket, Checkpoint Golf or the Chartered Bank in Crater. As an Ulsterman, and so never allowed a posting home to fight, Harry had often wondered whether soldiering there was any different to Aden. Did all the stuff about duty, purpose and reason mean that much more just because the fighting was down by the local supermarket and not six hours away on a VC10? He reckoned he was as disinterested now in the welfare of the great body of society as he had been then. He had been given a job to do, and he was doing it because someone had to, and by a series of accidents he was better equipped than most.

But by the time the Trident was arching over the landfall to the south of Strangford Lough, Harry had decided he was not a little flattered he'd been asked. He had been chosen for a mission, after all, called for by the Prime Minister. In the close heat of the plane he thought of his wife, warmth and closeness flooding through him. It was a pity she couldn't share in his pride. The passenger across the aisle noticed the slow smile spreading across the cheeks of the man slumped by the window.

For a few more seconds Harry indulged himself, conscious of the softness of the moment. He knew from the other times of great danger that he had faced that he could cocoon himself in sentimentality for his family, for Mary and the boys. It was part of the mechanism of protection which Harry understood and cherished.

As the airliner began its approach across the small fields towards Aldergrove Harry fastened his belt strap, and let his thoughts turn to the man whose image was imprinted in his mind. He could see the man, could put flesh and colour and dimensions on to the dark lines of the photokit. The target. Was he an enemy? Not really. What, then, if not an enemy? Just a target. Still to be killed, no question of that. *Eliminate* – it rolled off Harry's silent tongue. It was the word he liked.

He was jolted awake as the wheels suspended below the wings banged down on to the scarred tarmac. The plane surged forward in the air at

331

a little more than ninety miles an hour, bounced again, and began to slow with the application of the engine's reverse thrust.

Terminal 1, Heathrow, the first-floor cafeteria. Davidson was breakfasting with the team who had come up to see Harry off. It was a subdued meal without the frills of conversation. Not much had been said after Harry had disappeared towards the security checks. Davidson had muttered, almost audibly, 'Gutsy little sod.'

'I'll take the bill,' he had added, as they rose from the table, and then, as an afterthought, 'I think we've told him all we could in three weeks, but it's bloody little time. To do that job properly you'd need six months. And then you couldn't be sure. Always the same when the politicians dip their toes in – short cuts. That's the order of the day. To come through with three weeks behind him he'll need to be lucky, bloody lucky.'

The anomaly of going to war in your own country was not lost on Harry. He came down the steep steps from the plane and hurried past the RAF Regiment corporal, who held his rifle diagonally across his thighs, right-hand forefinger extended along the trigger guard. There were coils of barbed wire at the flanks of the terminal building, sprawled across the flower beds that had once been sufficient in themselves to mark the perimeters of the taxiing area. The viewing gallery where people used to wave to their friends and relatives was now fenced with high chicken wire to prevent a missile being thrown on to the apron; it was out of bounds to civilians, anyway. After getting his bag in the concourse Harry walked out towards the coach pick-up point. Around him was an avenue of white oil drums with heavy planks slung between them – a defence against car bombers moving their lethal loads against the walls of the buildings. He moved by a line of passengers waiting to take the Trident back to London. They stood outside, occasionally shuffling forward with their baggage. Up at the front the searches went on in two green prefab huts. Only rarely did the faces of the travellers match the brightness of their going-away clothes: children silent, women with their eyes darting round, the men concerned with getting the cases to the search and then eventually to the plane. Greyness, anxiety, exhaustion.

Harry climbed on to the bus, and was quick enough to ensure himself a window seat near the back.

By the time the coach had left the fields behind and was into the top of the Crumlin Road the man directly behind Harry was in full voice. Taking upon himself the role of guide and raconteur, outmatching those who lead crocodiles of tourists round the Tower of London and Hampton Court, he capitalized on the quiet of the bus to demonstrate his intimate knowledge of the campaign as fought so far.

'Down there on the right – you see the small lane – just round the corner where you can't see – that's where the three Scottish soldiers were murdered . . . the pub . . . the one that's blown up – the one we're passing – they took 'em from there and killed them down the road when they were having a slash. There's nothing to see there now . . . people used to put flowers, but not now, nothing to see except there's no grass in the ditch where they got it . . . Army dug it all up looking for bullets, and it never grew since. Now on the left, where the road climbs up, towards the quarry, that's where the senator was killed . . . the Catholic senator with the girl, they were killed up there, stabbed. Last year it was, just before the elections. Look now in front, there she is, the greatest city on earth. Down below, left, not hard left, that's Ardoyne . . . over to the right that's Ballymurphy . . . we're coming into Ligoniel now.'

It'll be bus trips for the Japanese next, thought Harry. Once they've stopped looking round Vietnam you'll be able to flog them Belfast. By special demand after the world's greatest jungle conflict, we offer you reduced rate to the longest-ever urban guerilla war. Roll up! Roll up! Get your tickets now!

'Now wait for the bumps.' The man behind was away again, as the bus had slowed to a crawl. 'Here we go now. See we're outside a barracks . . . there on the left . . . they all have bumps outside now . . . stops the Provos belting past and giving the sentry a burst with a Thompson. They used to have luminous paint on them, the bumps, that's gone now . . . if you don't know where they are you give the car a hell of a bang . . . hit one of those at fifty and you know about it . . . that's Ardoyne, now, over on the left, where the policeman is. That's a sight for the English, policemen with bullet-proof coats and machine-guns . . . won't use the army flak jackets, have their own. We cut across now, they don't rate going down the Crumlin in Ulster buses. We'll use the Shankill. Looks all right, doesn't it, quiet enough? See that hole on the right? That's the Four Steps bar . . . killed a fair few when that went up. Not a breath of a warning. Look there on the same side, see it? That hole . . . that was a furniture shop . . . two kiddies died there – not old enough to walk.'

'Shut up, Joe, nobody wants to know. Just wrap it.'

Perhaps Joe felt he had given his virtuoso. He fell silent. Harry watched out of the window, fascinated by the sights. At the traffic lights the driver nudged up to the white line alongside a Saracen armoured car. Soldiers were crouched inside the half-open steel back doors, rifles in hand. On the other side of the crossroads he watched a patrol inching its way through the shopping crowds. On all sides were the yards of pale-brown hardboard that had taken over from glass in the display windows of the stores. The policemen here had discarded their sub-machine-guns, but let their right hands rest securely inside their heavy dark coats. It surprised Harry how much there was to see that could have been a part of any other British industrial city – buses, cars, people, clothes, paper stands – all merging in with the great military umbrella that had settled itself on Belfast.

At the bus station Harry switched to another single-decker that went high up on the Antrim Road to the north, speeding past the troubled New Lodge Junction before cutting into residential suburbs. The houses were big, old, tall, red-brick and fading. Davidson had given him the name of a boarding house where he'd said Harry could get a room, three stops up past the New Lodge.

Harry got off the bus at the stop, and looked round to find his bearings. He spotted the house they had chosen for him and moved away from it farther down the long hill till he was one hundred and fifty yards from the seedy board with its 'vacancies' sign. Then he waited. He watched the front door for twenty-five minutes before he saw what he'd half expected. A young man came out down the steps that led to the short front path. Clothes not quite right, walk too long, hair a fair bit too short.

Harry boiled. 'Stupid bastards. Davidson, you prime bastard. Send me to one of your own bloody places. Nice safe little billet for soldiers in a nice Proddy area. Somewhere you won't find anything out, but you won't get shot. No, not Davidson, some bugger in intelligence in Belfast, having his own back because it isn't his caper. Sod 'em. I'm not going through all this to sit on my arse in Proddyland and come out in a month with nothing to show. No way.'

He took the next bus into central Belfast from the other side of the road, walked across to the taxi rank in Castle Street, and asked for a lift up to mid-Falls. Not Davidson's game, that. He wouldn't know addresses in Belfast, it would have to be one of the minions, flicking through his card index, this looks right to keep him out of mischief. Couldn't infiltrate Mansoura from bloody Steamer Point, nor the Falls from Prod country.

To the cab driver he said, 'I'm working about half-way up, and looking for someone who takes in lodgers. Not too pricey. Yer know anyone? About half-way, near the Broadway. Is there anyone?'

He waited in the cab for several minutes for the other seats to be taken up in the shuttle service that had now largely replaced the incon-sistences of the bus timetable. The journey he'd made in from the airport, out on to the Antrim Road, his wait there, the trip back, the walk to the taxi rank, that delay sitting in the back waiting to go, all had taken their toll in time.

Deep greyness was settling over the city, rubbing out its sharp lines, when the taxi, at last full, pulled away.

The first soldier in the patrol was up to the corner and round it before the man had reacted to the movement. The second gave him a chance to identify it as an army patrol. On the third and fourth he had begun to get an aim, and for the next man he was ready. Rifle at the shoulder. The upper part of the shadow cut out by the V of the leaf mechanism of his rear sight, and sliced by the upward thrust of the front sight at the far tip of the barrel. The fifth soldier had come fast round the corner, too close to his colleague in front, and paused for the other to move farther away before starting off again himself. He was stationary for one and a half seconds before the man fired. The shadow fell out from the darkness of the wall towards the corridor of light from Mrs Mulvenna's front room.

The man had time to see the stillness of the form, half on the pavement and half on the street, before he wormed and scrambled his way to the centre of the roof space – and ran. His escape route took him along a catwalk of planks set across the gaps between the roof beams, in all traversing the roof space of four homes. In the last house the light shone up among the eaves where the ceiling door had been left open for him. He swung down on to the landing, and then moved to the stairs leading to the back of the house and the kitchen. The Armalite was grabbed from him by a teenager who had been listening for the clatter of the escape across the ceiling. Within three minutes it would be in a plastic bag, sealed, and dropped under the grating in the back yard, with a thin line of dark cord tied to the bars to retrieve it later.

The man went out into the back yard, scrambled over the five-foot-high fence, ducked across the back entry, and felt for the rear doors on the far side till he came to the one off the hook. It remained for him to cut through that house, and he was out in the next street. Here he didn't run, but ambled the three hundred yards farther away from the killing where he rang a front-door bell. A youth came out immediately, motioned him to a waiting car, and drove him away.

There had been no pursuit. No soldier had seen the fractional flash of the barrel as the man fired. Five of them, shouting and waving, fear in their eyes, had sunk to firing positions in the doorways of the street. Two more gathered beside their dead colleague. Before the ambulance came it was plain that their efforts were pointless, but they fumbled the medical dressing clear from his webbing belt and placed it over the bloody chest wound.

Harry heard the single shot from far up the road when the taxi was caught in stationary traffic at the lights just beyond the huge bulk of the hospital building. As the taxi stayed unmoving, log-jammed in the sea of vehicles, a convoy of armoured cars swept by up the wrong side of the road, horns blaring and headlights on. Soldiers jumped from the moving column to take up their shooting positions on the main road, while others poured into the side streets. Harry saw the blue flashing light of an ambulance swing sharply out of a side street, one hundred and fifty yards up on the right, and turn down towards them. The ambulance was a Saracen with huge red crosses on white background painted on the sides. Turning his head Harry saw through the flapping open doors at the back two dark shapes bent over the top end of the stretcher. The handles of the stretcher, between them a pair of boots stuck out beyond the tailboard of the armoured car.

It was some minutes before the traffic moved again. None of the other passengers in the cab – the old lady with her month's best shopping, or the two office girls from Andersonstown – spoke a word. When the cab reached the street corner where the ambulance had emerged the soldier in the middle of the road waved them out and to the wall. He ran his hands fast and effectively over the shoulders, torsos and legs of Harry and the driver, contenting himself with examining the woman's shopping holder and the girls' bags. He looked very young to Harry.

'What happened?' Harry asked.

'Shut your face, you pig-arsed Mick.'

The taxi dropped him off seventy-five yards farther on. He was to try Mrs Duncan's. First left, twelfth door on the right: 'Delrosa'.

It didn't take Harry long to settle into the small room that Mrs Duncan showed him at the back of her two-storey house – about as long as it takes to unpack the contents of a small suitcase and put them into a medium-size chest of drawers and a wardrobe. She suggested he wash his hands and then come down to the big room where the other guests would gather, first for tea, then to watch television. She asked no questions about him, obviously prepared to give the stranger time to fill in his background at his own pace.

Looking across from his window, Harry could see the Falls Road where the army Land-Rovers and Saracens still criss-crossed back and forth.

There were six at tea, all eating urgently and with concentration. The way to avoid talking, thought Harry. Stuff your face, with just a mutter for the milk or the sugar, or the fresh-cut bread, and you don't have to say anything. No one mentioned the shooting, but it came into the room with the BBC local television news. Mrs Duncan came from the kitchen to the doorway, leaning there, arms folded, in her apron. A single shot had killed the first soldier to die in Northern Ireland for three weeks.

The pictures showed troops illuminated in doorways and manning road blocks. Over the sound track but half drowned by the report came the words 'Put that bloody light off.' Then there was only the meaningless picture of the tarmacadam with the dark stain on it, something for the colour TV people but just a shapeless island on Mrs Duncan's set. Then out of the blackness the overlit whitened face of the young reporter as the hand light picked him up at close range.

He had little to say. A routine foot patrol in the Broadway district of the Falls had been ambushed. A single shot had been fired, fatally wounding a soldier just as darkness was falling. He said that an extensive follow-up operation was still in progress, that the area had been cordoned off, and that all cars leaving it were being searched. The camera cut to a harassed-looking officer.

Q. What happened here, Colonel?
A. This is really a most shocking attack, a most cowardly murder. One of my soldiers was shot down in cold blood, quite without warning. A horrible, despicable crime.
Q. Did your men get a sight of the gunman?
A. No, it wasn't till we were engaged in an extensive follow-up operation – which you will have seen for yourself – that we found the place where the gunman was hiding. He was up in the roof of a derelict house, and he aimed at my patrol through the gap left by a missing tile.
Q. Would this have been the work of an expert?
A. An expert – in terrorism, yes, in killing, yes. We found sixty-eight cigarette butts in the roof. He'd been there some time. He'd put four chairs on the staircase of the house – it's very narrow anyway. If we'd been chasing him and had run into the building those chairs would have lost us several seconds. That's the work of an expert killer. He'd chosen a house which had a communicating passage down the length of the terrace roof. That's the way he got out.
Q. Did anyone see anything on the street?
A. I'm sure half the street knew what was going on. Lots of people, masses of them, must have known a young man was going to be shot down in the gutter outside their homes. But I think your question is, did they identify the gunman to us? The answer there is decisively, No, they didn't. But many of them must know who the killer is – I appeal to them to use the police Confidential phone and stamp out this type of cruel, cowardly attack.
Q. Thank you, Colonel.

The programme changed to an interview in the studio. A Protestant politician and a Catholic politician were arguing over the same ground, with some minute variations, that they'd been debating on the same

337

channel for the last four years. Between them was a link man who had been hosting them, feeding them their questions and winding them up over the same period. Before the talk was a minute old Mrs Duncan came forward like a battleship under power, and reached for the off switch.

'There's enough politics on the street without bringing them into my house. Just words. Won't do that young man any good. Mother of Jesus rest with him.'

A youngish man, opposite across the table from Harry, said, 'If they stayed in their barracks they wouldn't get shot. If they weren't here there wouldn't be any shooting. You saw what they did when they came round here a few days ago. Taking the houses apart, lifting men, and blocking the streets. Claimed then it was because of that man that got shot in London. But the searches they did were nothing to do with it. Aggro, what they were looking for, nothing more. Harassment.'

Nobody in the room responded. The young man looked round for someone to join in argument with. Harry sided with him. 'If they were as busy chasing the Prods as us, they'd find things easier for themselves.'

The other looked at him, surprised to find support, if not a little disappointed that it was an ally who had put his cap in the ring. Harry went on, 'I've been away a long time, but I can see in the few hours that I've been back where all the troops are. I've been abroad, but you still read the papers, you still see the news on the telly bought from the BBC. You get to feel the way things are going. Nothing's done about those Prods, only us.'

It was not easy for Harry, that first time. With practice he would gain the facility to sing the praises of the IRA. But the first time round it was hard going. Never like this in Mansoura. Never went down the souk and shouted the odds, about what a fine bloke Quahtan As-Shaabi was, victory to the NLF, out with the imperialists. Just kept quiet there, and scuffed around in the dirt, and watched. But a different scene here. Got to be in the crowd. He excused himself, saying he was tired and had been travelling all day, and went to his room.

6

It was just after seven when Harry woke. He knew soon enough that this was the day he started working and moved on to active service. The euphoria of the farewells, the back-slaps and good-luck calls, were over. He had arrived. Now would begin the hard work of moving on to the inside. He checked his watch. Well, twenty minutes more and then it could all begin, then he would get up.

He'd known since his training started that the initial period of infiltration was going to be the difficult part. This was where the expertise and skill entered in his file after Mansoura would count. They had chosen him after going over those files, and those of a dozen other men, because they had thought that he above all of them stood the best chance of being able to adapt in those early critical hours in the new environment.

They'd told him he must take it slowly, not lambast his way in. Not make so much of his presence that he attracted attention and with that, inevitably, investigation. But they also stressed that time was against him. They pointed to the enormous benefits the opposition were gaining from the failure of the vast military force to catch the assassin.

The dilemma was spelled out to him. How much speed could he generate? How fast could he move into that fringe world which had contact with the gunmen? How far into that world must he go to get near the nucleus of the organization where the man he hunted was operating? These were his decisions. The advice had been given, but now he had to control his own planning.

They had emphasized again and again at Dorking that his own death would be bad news all round. Enormous embarrassment to HMG. No risks should be taken unless absolutely essential. It had amused him, drily. You send a man to infiltrate the most successful urban terrorist movement in the world over the last twenty-five years, and tell him if he gets shot it would be awkward. Not much time to mess about with the frills. They'd said if it was going to work out for him it would be in the first three weeks. By then they expected something to bite on . . . not necessarily the man's full name but a regular haunt, the address of a friend. A hint. Anything on to which they could turn the huge and formal military and police machine. The great force was poised and waiting for him to tell it where to hit, and that pleased him.

He was starting with little enough to go on. The same available to everyone else in the city – or virtually the same. He had in his mind the photokit picture, with the knowledge that it was superior to the one issued in police stations and army posts. But that was all that tipped the scales in his favour. Nothing else, and not much to set against the disadvantages of arriving as a stranger in a community beset by informers and on its guard against them. His first problem would be the infiltration of the Catholic population, let alone the IRA, and becoming known to people already haunted by the fear of army plain-clothes units cruising in unmarked cars, laundry vans and ice-cream trucks with hidden spy holes, of the Protestant UVF and UFF killer squads. He had to win a degree of confidence among some small segment of these people before he could hope to operate with success.

Davidson had struck a chord when he said, 'They seem to have the ability to smell an outsider. They close ranks well. It's like the instinct of a fox that's learned to react when there's a hostile being close by. God knows how they do it, but they have a feeling for danger. Much of it is how you look, the way you walk, the way you go along the pavement. Whether you can look as though you belong. You need confidence. You have to believe that you're not the centre of attention the whole time. The first trick is to get yourself a base. Establish yourself there, and then work outwards. Like an upside-down pyramid.'

The base was clearly to be the good Mrs Duncan. She was in the kitchen and washing up the first sitting of breakfast when Harry came down the stairs.

'Well, it's good to be back, Mrs Duncan. I've been away a while too long, I feel. You miss Ireland when you're away, whatever sort of place it is now. You get tired of the travelling and the journeys. You want to be back here. If these bastard British would leave us to lead our own lives then this would be a great wee country. But it can't be easy for you, Mrs Duncan, running a business in these times?'

The previous evening he had formally given his name as Harry McEvoy. That was what she called him when she replied.

'Well, Mr McEvoy, they're not the easiest of times, to be sure. One minute it's all quiet and the place is full. Then you'll have a thing like last night, and who is going to come and sleep a hundred yards or so from where a soldier was shot dead? The travellers from the south find all this a bit near. They like it a bit farther away from where it all happens. Having it full like it is now is a luxury. What did you say your business was? I was flustered up a bit when you came, getting the teas and all, yesterday.'

'I've been away, ten years or so, just under in fact, at sea. In the Merchant Navy. Down in the South Atlantic and Indian Ocean, mainly.'

'There's a lot you'll see has changed. The fighting's been hard these last years.'

'Our people have taken a bad time, and all.'

'The Catholic people have taken a bad time, and now the Protestants hate us as never before. It'll take a long time to sort it out.'

'The English don't understand us, never have, never will.'

'Of course they don't, Mr McEvoy.' She flipped his egg over expertly, set it on the plate beside the halved tomatoes, the skinned sausage, the mushrooms and the crisp fried bread. 'Look at all the ballyhoo and palaver when that man of theirs was shot – Danby. You'd think it was the first man who had died since the troubles. Here they are, close to a thousand dead and all, and one English politician gets killed . . . you should have seen the searches they did, troops all over. Never found damn all.'

'He wasn't mourned much over here.' Harry said it as a statement.

'How could he be? He was the man that ran the Maze, Long Kesh. He brought all his English warders over here to run the place for him. There was no faith in him here, and not a tear shed.'

'They've not caught a man yet for it?'

'Nor will they. The boys will keep it close. Not many will know who did it. There's been too much informing. They keep things like that tight these days. But that's enough talk of all that. If you want to talk politics you can do it outside the door and on the streets all the hours that God gave. There's no shortage of fools here to do the talking. I try and keep it out of the house. If you're back from the sea, what are you going to do now? Have you a job to be away to?'

Before answering, Harry complimented her on the breakfast. He handed her the empty plate. Then he said, 'Well, I can drive. I hoped I could pick up a job like that round here. Earn enough so that with a bit of luck I can pay you something regular, and we can agree on a rate. I want to work up this end of town if I can, not in the centre of town. Seems safer in our own part. I thought I might try something temporary for a bit while I look round for something permanent.'

'There's enough men round here would like a job, permanent or not.'

'I think I'll walk around a bit this morning. I'll do the bed first . . . an old habit at sea. Tomorrow I'll try round for a job. Wonderful breakfast, thanks.'

Mrs Duncan had noticed he'd been away. And a long time at that, she was certain. Something grated on her ear, tuned to three decades of welcoming visitors and apportioning to them their birthplace to within a few miles. She was curious, now, because she couldn't place what had happened to his accent. Like the sea he talked of, she was aware it came in waves – ebbed in its pitch. Pure Belfast for a few words, or a phrase, then falling off into something that was close to Ulster but softer, without the harshness. It was this that nagged as she dusted round the house and cleaned the downstairs hall, while above her Harry moved about in his room. She thought about it a lot during the morning, and decided that what she couldn't quite understand was the way he seemed to change his accent so slightly mid-sentence. If he was away on a boat so long then of course he would have lost the Belfast in his voice – that must have happened. But then in contradiction there were the times when he was pure Belfast. She soundlessly muttered the different words that emphasized her puzzlement to herself, uncomprehending.

*

341

They don't waste time in Belfast lingering over the previous day. By the time Harry was out on the pavements of the Falls Road and walking towards town there was nothing to show that a large-scale military operation had followed the killing of a young soldier the previous evening. The traffic was on the move, women with their children in tow were moving down towards the shops at the bottom end of the Springfield Road, and on the corners groups of youths with time on their hands and no work to go to were gathering to watch the day's events. Harry was wearing a pair of old jeans he had brought from Germany, and that he'd used for jobs round his quarters in the base, and a holed pullover that he'd last worn when painting the white surrounds to the staircase at home. They were some of the clothes the officer had collected when he'd called and told his wife that her husband was on his way to the Middle East.

The clothes were right, and he walked down the road – watched, but not greatly attracting attention. The time had been noted when he came out of the side road where Mrs Duncan had her guest house, and into the Falls. Nothing went on paper, but the youth that saw him from behind the neat muslin curtain at the junction would remember him when he came back, and mentally clock him in. There was every reason why he should be noticed, as the only new face to come out of the road that morning. Last night when he had arrived it had been too late to get a decent look at him. All Mrs Duncan's other guests were regulars, discreetly vetted and cleared by the time they'd slept in her house enough for a pattern to emerge.

Harry had decided to walk this first morning, partly because he thought it would do him good but more importantly to familiarize himself with his immediate surroundings. Reconnaissance. Time well spent. It might save your life, they'd said. Know your way round. He came down past the old Broadway cinema where no films had been shown for two years since the fire bomb exploded beside the ticket kiosk, and the open space of the one-time petrol station forecourt where pumps, reception area and garages had all long since been flattened. Across the road was the convent school. Children were laughing and shouting in the playground. Harry remembered seeing that same playground, then empty and desolated, on West German television when the newsreader had described the attack by two IRA motor-cyclists on William Staunton. The Catholic magistrate had just dropped his two girls at school and was watching them from his car as they moved along the pavement to the gate when he was shot. He had lingered for three months before he died, and then one of the papers had published a poem written by the dead man's twelve-year-old daughter. Harry had read it in the mess, and thought it of rare simplicity and beauty, and not forgotten it.

> 'Don't cry,' Mummy said
> 'They're not real.'

But Daddy was
And he's not here.

'Don't be bitter,' Mummy said
'They've hurt themselves much more.'
But they can walk and run –
Daddy can't.

'Forgive them and forget,' Mummy said
But can Daddy know I do?
'Smile for Daddy, kiss him well,' Mummy said,
But can I ever?

He was still mouthing the words as the Royal Victoria Hospital loomed up, part modern, part the dark close redbrick of old Belfast. Staunton and scores of others had been rushed here down the curved hill that swung into the rubber doors of Casualty.

Harry turned left into Grosvenor Road, hurrying his step. Most of the windows on either side of the street showed the scars of the conflict, boarded up, bricked up, sealed to squatters, too dangerous for habitation, but remaining available and ideal for the snipers. The pubs on the right, a hundred yards or so down from the main gate of the RVH, had figured in Davidson's briefings. After a Proddy bomb had gone off the local Provos had found a young bank clerk on the scene. He came from out of town and said he'd brought a cameraman to witness the devastation. The explanation hadn't satisfied. After four hours of torture, and questioning, and mutilation, they shot him, and dumped him in Cullingtree Street, a little farther down towards the city centre.

Davidson had emphasized that story, used it as an example of the wrong person just turning up and being unable to explain himself. In the hysteria and suspicion of the Falls that night it was sufficient to get him killed.

The half-mile of the street Harry was walking down was fixed in his mind. In the log of the history of the troubles since August 1969 that they'd given him to read, that half-mile had taken up fifteen separate entries.

Harry produced a driving licence made out in the name of McEvoy and the post office counter clerk gave him the brown paper parcel. Harry recognized Davidson's neat copper-plate hand on the outside – 'Hold for collection'. Inside was a 0.38 calibre Smith and Wesson revolver. Accurate and a man-stopper. One of nine hundred thousand run off in the first two years of World War Two. Untraceable. If Harry had shaken the package violently he would have heard the rattling of the forty-two rounds of ammunition. He didn't open the parcel. His instructions were very plain on that. He was to keep the gun wrapped till he got back to his base, and only when he had found a good hiding place was he to remove it from the wrapping. That made sense, nothing special, just ordinary common sense, but the way they'd gone on about it you'd have thought the paper would be stripped off and the gun waved all over Royal Avenue. At times Davidson treated everyone around him like children. 'Once it's hidden,' Davidson had warned, 'leave it there unless you think there's a real crisis. For God's sake don't go carrying it round. And be certain if you use it. Remember, if you want to fire the damn thing, the yellow card and all that's writ thereon applies as much to you, my boy, as every pimpled squaddie in the Pioneers.'

With the parcel under his arm, for all the world like a father bringing home a child's birthday present, Harry walked back from the centre of the city to the Broadway. He wanted a drink. Could justify it too, on professional grounds, need to be there, get the tempo of things, and to let a pint wash down the dryness of his throat after what he'd been through the last thirty-six hours. The 'local' was down the street from Mrs Duncan's corner. Over the last few paces to the paint-scraped door his resolve went haywire, weakened so that he would have dearly loved to walk past the door and regain the security of the little back room he had rented. He checked himself. Breathing hard, and feeling the tightness in his stomach and the lack of breath that comes from acute fear, he pushed the door open and went into the pub. God, what a miserable place! From the brightness outside his eyes took a few moments to acclimatize to the darkness within. The talk stopped and he saw the faces follow him from the door to the counter. He asked for a bottle of Guinness, anxiously projecting his voice, conscious that fear is most easily noticed from speech. Nobody spoke to him as he sipped his drink. Bloody good to drink, but you'd need to be an alcoholic to come in here to take it. The glass was two-thirds empty by the time desultory conversation started up again. The voices were muted, as if everything said was confidential. The people, Harry recognized, had come to talk, as of an art, from the sides of their mouths. Not much eavesdropping in here. Need to Watergate the place.

Across the room two young men watched Harry drink. Both were volunteers in E Company of the First Battalion of the Provisional IRA, Belfast Brigade. They had heard of the cover story Harry was using earlier in the morning just after he'd gone out for his walk. The source, though unwittingly, was Mrs Duncan. She had talked over the washing line, as she did most mornings, with her neighbour. The neighbour's son, who now stood in the bar watching Harry, had asked his mother to find out from Mrs Duncan who the new lodger was, where he came from, and whether he was staying long. Mrs Duncan enjoyed these morning chatters, and seldom hurried with her sheets and pegs unless rain was threatening. It was cold and bright. She told how the new guest had turned up out of the blue, how he hoped to find a job and stay indefinitely, had already paid three weeks in advance. He was a seaman, the English Merchant Navy, and had been abroad for many years. But he was from the North, and had come home now. From Portadown he was.

'He's been away all right,' she shouted over the fence to her friend, who was masked by the big, green-striped sheet suspended in the centre of the line, 'you can see that, hear it rather, every time he opens his mouth. You can tell he's been away, a long time and all, lucky beggar. What we should have done, missus. Now he says he's come back because Ireland, so he says, is the place in times of trouble.' She laughed again. She and her friend were always pretending they'd like to leave the North for good, but both were so wedded to Belfast that a week together at a boarding house north of Dublin in the third week of August was all they ever managed . . . then they were full of regrets all the way back to Victoria Street station.

The son had had this conversation relayed to him painfully slowly and in verbatim detail by his mother. Now he watched and listened, expressionless, as Harry finished his drink and asked for another bottle. In two days' time he would go to a routine meeting with his company's intelligence officer, by then sure in his mind if there was anything to report about the new lodger next door.

Harry walked quickly back to Delrosa after the second glass of Guinness. He'd never been fond of the stuff. Treacly muck, he told himself. He rang the door bell, and a tall, willowy girl opened the door.

'Hullo, McEvoy's the name. I'm staying here. The room at the back.'

She smiled and made way for him, stepping back into the hall. Black hair down to the shoulders, high cheekbones, and dark eyes set deep above them. She stood very straight, back arched, and breasts angled into the tight sweater before it moulded with her waist, and was lost in the wide leather belt threaded through the straps of her jeans.

'I'm Josephine. I help Mrs Duncan. Give her a hand round the house. She said there was someone new in. I do the general cleaning, most days in the week, and help with the teas.'

He looked at her blatantly and unashamed. 'Could you make me one now? A cup of tea?' Not very adequate, he thought, not for an opening chat-up to a rather beautiful girl.

She walked through into the kitchen, and he followed a pace or so behind, catching the smell of the cheap scent.

'What else do you do?' Perfunctory, imbecile, but keeps it going.

'Work at the mill, down the Falls, the big one. I do early shift, then come round and do a bit with Mrs Duncan. She's an old friend of my Mam's. I've been coming a long time now.'

'There's not much about for people here now, 'cept work, and not enough of that,' Harry waded in, 'what with the troubles and that. Do you go out much, do you find much to do?'

'Oh, there's bits and pieces. The world didn't end, and we adapted, I suppose. We don't go into town much – that's just about over. There's not much point, really. Go to a film and there'll be a bomb threat and you're cleared out. The Tartans run the centre anyway, so you have to run for dear life to get back into the Falls. The army don't protect us, they look the other way when the Tartans come, Proddy scum. There's nothing to go to town for anyway 'cept the clothes, and they're not cheap.'

'I've been away a long time,' said Harry, 'people have been through an awful time. I thought it time to get back home. You can't be an Irishman and spend your time away right now.'

She looked hard at him. The prettiness and youth of her face hardened into something more frightening to Harry. Imperceptibly he saw the age and weariness on the smooth skin of the girl, spreading like the refocusing of a lens, and then gone as the face lightened. She reached into the hip pocket of her jeans, straining them taut as her fingers found a crumpled handkerchief. She shook it loose and dabbed it against her nose. Harry saw the green embroidered shamrocks in the corners, and fractionally caught the motif in the middle of the square. Crossed black and brown Thompson machine-guns. She was aware he was staring at her.

'There's nothing special about these. Doesn't mean I'm a rebel and that. They sell them to raise funds for the men and their families, the men that are held in the Kesh. "The Men Behind the Wire." Look. It's very good, isn't it – a bit delicate? You wouldn't think a cowardly, murdering thug would have the patience to work at a thing so difficult, be so careful. They think we're all pigs, just pigs. "Fenian pigs", they call us.'

She spat the words out, the lines round her face hard and clear cut now, then the tension of the exchange was gone. She relaxed.

'We make our own entertainment. There's the clubs, social nights. There's not much mid-week, but Saturday night is okay. Only the bloody army comes belting in most times. They always say they're looking for the great commander of the IRA. They take ten boys out, and they're all back free in twenty-four hours. They stir us up, try to provoke us. We manage. I suppose all you've heard since coming back is people talking about their problems, how grim it is. But we manage.'

'That handkerchief,' said Harry, 'does that mean you follow the boyos, have you a man in the prisons?'

'Not bloody likely. It doesn't mean a damn. Just try and not buy one. You'll find out. If you don't buy one there's arguing and haggling. It's easier to pay up. You've got to have a snot-rag, right? Might as well be one of these and no argument, right? I'm not one of those heated-up little bitches that runs round after the cowboys. When I settle it'll be with a feller with more future than a detention order, I can tell you. And I'm not one of those that runs around with a magazine in my knickers and an Armalite up my trousers, either. There are enough who want to do that.'

'What sort of evenings do you have now? What sort of fun do you make for yourselves?'

'We have the caelis,' she said, 'not the sort they have in the country or in the Free State, not the proper thing. But there's dancing, and a bit of a band, and a singer and a bar. The army come lumping in, the bastards, but they don't stay long. You've been away, at sea, right? Well, we've got rid of the old songs now . . . 1916 and 1922 are in the back seat, out of the hit parade. We've the "Men Behind the Wire" – that's internment. "Bloody Sunday." "Provie Birdie", when the three boys were lifted out of Mountjoy by helicopter. Did you hear about it? Three big men and a helicopter comes right down into the exercise yard and lifts them out . . . and the screws was shouting "Shut the gates!" Must have been a laugh, and all. Understand me, I'm not for joining them, the Provos. But I'm not against them. I don't want the bastard British here.'

'On the helicopter, I was going through the Middle East. I saw it in the English paper in Beirut.'

She was impressed, seemed so anyway. Not that he'd been to an exotic sounding place like Beirut, but that the fame of Seamus Twomey, Joe O'Hagen and Kevin Mallon had spread that far.

'Do the army always come and bust in, at the evenings?'

'Just about always. They think they'll find the big boys. They don't know who they're looking for. Put on specs, tint your hair, do the parting the wrong way, don't shave, do shave . . . that's enough, that sorts them out.'

Harry had weighed her up as gently committed – not out of conviction but out of habit. A little in love with the glamour of the men with Armalites, and the rawness of the times they lived in, but unwilling to go too close in case the tinsel dulled.

'I think I'd like to come,' said Harry. 'I think it would do me good. I'm a bit out of date in my politics right now, and my voice is a bit off tune. James Connolly was being propped up in his chair in Kilmainham in my time, and they were wearing all their Green. It's time I updated and put myself back in touch. A lot of brave boys have died since I was last here. It's time to stand up and be counted in this place. That's why I came back.'

'I'll take you. I'll pick you up here, Saturday, round half seven. Cheers.'

She was away into the kitchen, and Harry to his room.

7

The man was moving the last few yards to his home. It was just after two in the morning. Two men had checked the streets near his house and given an all-clear on the presence of army foot patrols.

It was his first visit back into his native Ardoyne since he had left to go to London nearly a month ago. His absence had been noted by the local British army battalion that operated out of the towering, near-derelict, Flax Street mill complex on the edge of the Ardoyne. It was entered in the comprehensive files the intelligence section maintained on the several thousand people that lived in the area, and a week before two Land-Rovers had pulled up outside the man's house, made their way to the half-opened front door and confronted his wife. She could have told them little even if she had felt inclined to. She didn't, anyway.

She told them to 'Go fuck yourselves, you British pigs'. She then added, nervous perhaps of the impact of her initial outburst, that her husband was away in the South working for a living. The army had searched the house without enthusiasm, but this was routine, and nothing was found, nor really expected to be. The intelligence officer noted the report of the sergeant who had led the raid, noted too that it would be nice to talk to the occupant of No. 41 Ypres Avenue at some later date. That was as far as it had been taken.

If Harry had been chosen for his role because he was clean, the same criterion had operated with the other man's superiors when they had put the cross against his name midway up the list of twenty or so who were capable of going to London and killing Danby.

Ypres Avenue was a little different from the mass of streets that made up the Ardoyne. The battle it was named after gave a clue to its age, and so its state of repair was superior to those streets up in the Falls where Downs had been hiding the last three weeks and where the streets took their names from the Crimean and Indian Mutiny battles, along with the British generals who had led a liberal stock of Ulstermen into their late-nineteenth-century fighting. But fifty-nine years is still a long time for an artisan cottage to survive without major repairs, and none had been carried out on any considerable scale in the Avenue since the day they had been put up to provide dwellings for those working in the mill, where the army now slept. The houses were joined in groups of four, with, in between, a narrow passage running through to the high-walled back entrance that came along behind the tiny yards at the rear.

The blast bombs, nail bombs and petrol bombs of four years of fighting had taken their toll, and several of the houses had been walled up. The bottom eight feet of a wall at the end of the Avenue had been whitewashed, the work of housewives late at night at internment time, so that at night, in the near darkness of the Ardoyne, a soldier's silhouette would stand out all the more clearly and give the boyos a better chance with a rifle. Most corners in the area had been given the same treatment, and the army had come out in force a week later and painted the whitened walls black. The women had then been out again, then again the army, before both sides called a mutual but unspoken truce. The wall was left filthy and disfigured from the daubings.

The army sat heavily on Ardoyne, and the Provos, as they themselves admitted, had had a hard time of it. This was good for the man. A main activist would not be expected to live in an area dominated by the military and where IRA operations had virtually ceased. He had been careful to link all his work with the Falls, away in a quite separate Catholic area from the Ardoyne.

Each house was small, unshaped, and built to last. Comfort played only a small part in its design. A front hall, with a front room off it, led towards a living area with kitchen and scullery two later additions and under asbestos roofing. The toilet was the most recent arrival and was in the yard against the far wall in a breeze-block cubicle. Upstairs each house boasted two rooms and a tiny landing. Bathing was in the kitchen. This was Belfast housing, perfect for the ideological launching of the gunman, perfect too as the model ground for him to pursue his work.

In the years the man had lived there he could find his way by the counting of his footsteps and by touch, when he came to the door of his own yard. The door had been recently greased, and made no sound when it swung on its hinges. He slipped towards the kitchen and unlocked the back door and went upstairs. That back door was never bolted, just locked, so that he could come in through it at any time.

It was the longest he had ever been away. The relief was total. He was back.

He moved cat-like up from the base of the stairs, three steps, then waited and listened. The house was completely dark and he had found the banister rail by touch. There were the familiar smells of the house, strong in his nose – the smell of cold tea and cold chips, older fat, of the damp that came into the walls, of the lino and scraps of carpet where that damp had eaten and corroded. On the stairs while he waited he could hear the sound of his family clustered together in the two rooms, the rhythm of their sleep broken by the hacking cough of one of the girls.

There was no question of using the lights. Any illumination through the sparse curtains would alert the army to the fact that someone in the house was on the move unusually late, coming home or going out. A little enough thing, but sufficient to go down into the files and card system that the intelligence men pored over, and which gave them their results. In the blackness the man inched his way up the stairs, conscious that no one would have told his wife he was coming home this particular night, and anxious not to frighten her.

He moved slowly on the landing, pushed open the door of the back room where he and his wife slept, and came inside. His eyes were now accustomed to the dark. He made out her hair on the pillow, and beside it the two small shapes, huddled close together for warmth and comfort. He watched them a long time. One of the children wriggled and then subsided with the cough. It had just been coming on when he had left home. He felt no emotion, only inhibition over how to break in and intrude on their sleep. Gradually his wife became aware of his presence. At first she was frightened, moving quickly and jerking the head of one of the sleeping children. She was defensive in her movement, the mother hen protecting her nest. The aggression went when she saw it was him. With a half-strangled sob she reached out for her man and pulled him down on to the bed.

Beneath him he felt the children slide away to continue their sleep uninterrupted.

'Hullo, my love. I'm back. I'm okay. Safe now. I've come back to you.'

He mouthed the words pressed hard into the pit of her neck, his voice sandwiched between her shoulder and ear. She held him very tightly, pulling at him as if some force were working to get him away from her again.

'It's all right, love. I'm home. It's over.'

He rose to his knees and kicked off his shoes, wrenched at his socks and pulled away the trousers, jacket and shirt. She passed one of the sleeping children over her body and pulled back the clothes of the bed for him to come into the empty space.

Desperately she clung to him there, squeezing the hardness and bitterness and strength out of him, demolishing the barriers of coldness and callousness with which he had surrounded himself, working at the emotions that had been so suppressed in the last month.

'Where've you been?'

'Don't . . . don't . . . I've missed you, I've wanted you.'

'No, where've you been?' she persisted. 'We thought you were gone

350

– were dead. There was no word, not anything. Where? There's always been a word before when you've gone.'

He clung to her, holding on to the one person that he loved and whom he needed as his lifeline, particularly over the last weeks of tension and fear. He felt the tautness draining out of him as he pressed down on to her body. It was some moments before he realized that she was lying quite still, rigid and yielding nothing. His grip on her slackened and he rose a little from the bedclothes to see her face, but when he was high enough to look down at her eyes, she turned them away from him towards her sleeping children.

'What's the matter? What's this for?'

'It's where you've been. Why you've been away. That's the matter. I know now, don't I?'

'Know what . . . ?' He hesitated. Stupid bitch, what was she blathering for? He was here. Flesh and blood. But what did she know? He was uncertain. How much had she realized through the frenzy in which he had held her? What had that crude and desperate weight of worry communicated to her?'

'Are you going to tell me about it?' she said.

'About what?' His anger was rising.

'Where you've been . . .'

'I've told you. Once more. Then the end of it. I was in the South. Finish, that's it.'

'You won't tell me, then?'

'I've said it's finished. There's no more. Leave it. I'm home – that should be enough. Don't you want me here?'

'It said in the papers that his children were there. And his wife. They saw it all. That the man went on shooting long after he'd gone down. That the children were screaming, so was his wife. It said she covered him from the bullets. Put herself right over him.'

She was sitting right up now with her hands splayed behind her, back straight, and her breasts, deep from the children she had suckled, bulging forward under the intricate pattern-work of her nightdress. Downs's longing for her had gone, sapped from him by her accusation. The moment he had waited for, which had become his goal over the last few days on the run, was destroyed.

She went on, looking not at him but straight in front of her into the darkness. 'They said that if it took them five years they'd get the man who did it. They said he must have been an animal to shoot like that across the street. They said they'd hunt for him till they found him, then lock him up for the rest of his natural. You stupid, daft bastard.'

Her point of focus was in the middle distance way beyond the walls and confines of their back bedroom. In his churning mind the replies and counter-attacks flooded through him. But there was no voice. When he spoke it was without fight.

351

'Someone had to do it. It happened it was me. Danby had it coming. Little bastard he was. There's not a tear shed for him; they haven't a clue to bring them to me. There's no line on me. The picture's no good. The kids wouldn't recognize me on that. They didn't, did they?'

'Don't be so stupid. Do you think I'd hold up two four-year-olds and show them a picture and say "Do you recognize your Dad? He's a killer, shot a man in front of his kids." That what you want me to do?'

'Shut your face. Finish it. I told you there'll be no more. You shouldn't have known. You didn't need to know.'

'It'll be bloody marvellous. The return of the great and famous hero, with half the sodding army after him. What a future! "We weren't supposed to know." What sort of statement is that? If they shoot you when they get you there'll be a bloody song about you. Just right for Saturday nights when they're all pissed, so keep the verses short and the words not too long. What a hero. You'll want me to teach the kids the words, and all. Is that the future for us?'

She sank back on to the pillow, and holding the nearest of the two children, began to weep, in slight convulsive shudders, noiselessly.

He rose from the bed and put on his underclothes, shirt and trousers, before moving in his bare feet across the room to the door. He went down the stairs and into the front room. Checking an instinctive movement towards the light switch, he groped his way to his armchair by the grate and lowered himself gingerly down on to it. There were newspapers there, and he pushed them down on to the floor. He sat there very still, exhausted by the emotion of the last few minutes. She'd clobbered him, kicked him in the crutch, and when the pain had sped all over him come back and kicked him again. Since Danby all he had wanted was to get back here, to her, to the kids, the totalness of the family. To be safe with them. The bitch had destroyed it.

In the dark he could relive the moments of the shooting. He found the actual happenings hard to be exact about. They had faded, and he was uncertain whether the picture he put together was from his memory or his imagination. The immediate sensations were still clear. The kicking of the Kalashnikov, the force driving into his shoulder – that was as vivid as the day and the time itself, the impact feeling. So, too, was the frozen tableau of the woman on her husband. The children. That enormous, useless dog. That was all still there. He saw the incident as a series of still frames, separate episodes. Some of the pictures were in panorama, as when Danby came down the steps and was looking right for the car and waving left at the children. Others were in close up – the face of the woman he had run past. Fear, disbelief, shock and horror. He could see every wrinkle and line on the silly cow's face down to the brown mole above her right cheek. He remembered the blood, but with detachment. Inevitable. Unimportant.

He wanted congratulations for a job well done. He'd thought that out and decided he was justified in some plaudits. It had been professionally done. The movement would be proud of the effort. He knew that himself, but yearned to be told so out loud. She should have bestowed the accolade. Of course she would guess, no way she wouldn't. Dates were right, the picture. She should have been the one with a nod, and an innuendo. She had guessed. She had to. But she called him a 'stupid, daft bastard'. He was hurt and numbed by that.

They had never talked about the Provos. Right from the start that had been laid down. She didn't want to know. Wasn't interested. No word on the nights he was going out. Went and buried herself in the kitchen, played with the children, got out of his way. She accepted, though, that he needed her strength and support when he came home. That was the concession she gave him. But that was not exceptional in Ardoyne.

The women would hear the shots out in the streets where the battlefield was just beyond the front-room curtains. There would be the high crack of the Armalite, fired once, twice or perhaps three times. Within seconds would come the hard thump of the answering army rifles, a quite different and heavier noise. If the man was not home by dawn the women would listen to the first news broadcast of the day, and hear what had happened. Sometimes there would be an agony of time between hearing that the army returned fire and claimed hits and the savoured moment when the man came in untouched.

Then there would be no words, only warmth and comfort and the attempt to calm the trembling hands.

His wife had once shown him an article in a London women's magazine which told of the effect on the morale of the army wives stationed in Germany that those same early broadcasts had. He had read how fast word spread around the married quarters that the unit had been in action, and how the women then waited at their windows to see if the officer came round and which house he went to. They would know if one of the men had been killed because the chaplain or the doctor would be with the officer, and they would go to a neighbour's house first, have a quick word on the doorstep, then move next door and knock, and when the door opened go inside. The news would be round the houses and maisonettes and flats within minutes.

The man had been responsible for two of those visits. On the first occasion he had watched the funeral on television, seen the forty-five-second clip that showed the coffin with the flag on it, and a young widow clutching the arm of a relative as she walked surrounded by officers and local dignitaries. Then the staccato crack of rifle fire from the honour party. That was all. The other soldier he'd killed last week had been

353

buried without a news team there to record the event. Interest had been lost. Whether he saw it or not was of no importance to him. He extracted no satisfaction either way.

It left him unmoved. He could imagine no soldier weeping if it were he who were shot dead. He had long accepted that it could happen and, apart from the tension of the actual moments of combat and the bow-string excitement afterwards, he had learned a fatalism about the risks he took.

He had started like most others as a teenager throwing rocks and abuse in the early days at those wonderful, heaven-sent targets . . . the British army, with their yellow cards forbidding them to shoot in almost every situation, their heavy Macron shields, which ruled out effective pursuit, and their lack of knowledge of the geography of the side streets. All the boys in Ypres Avenue threw stones at the soldiers, and it would have been almost impossible to have been uninvolved. The mood had changed when a youth from the other end of the street and the opposite side of the road was shot dead in the act of lighting a petrol bomb. He had been one form above the man in secondary school. Later that night four men had arrived at the far end of Ypres Avenue to the rioting, and the word had spread fast that the kids should get off the streets. Then the shooting had started. In all, fifteen shots had been fired, echoing up the deserted street. He was eighteen then, and with other teenagers had lain in an open doorway and cheered at the urgent shouts of the soldiers who had taken cover behind the Pigs. Abruptly a hurrying, shadowy figure had crawled to the doorway, pushed towards him the long shape of a Springfield rifle, and whispered an address and street number.

He had made his way through the back of the houses, part way down the entry, and through another row of houses where a family had stared at the television, ignoring him as he padded across their living space before closing the door on to the street behind him. When he reached the address he had handed the rifle to the woman who answered his knock. She said nothing and he had made his way back to Ypres Avenue.

That had been the start.

Many of his contemporaries in the street had thrust themselves forward into the IRA. They would meet together on Saturday nights at the clubs, standing apart from the other young men to discuss in secretive voices their experiences over the previous days. Some were now dead, some in remand homes or prison, a very few had made it to junior officer rank in the IRA and after their capture had been served with the indefinite detention orders to Long Kesh. The man had kept apart from them, and been noticed by those older, shadowy figures who ran the movement. He had been marked down as someone out of the ordinary, who didn't need to run with the herd. He had been used sparingly

354

and never with the cannon fodder that carried the bombs into the town shoe shops and supermarkets, or held up the post offices for a few hundred pounds. He'd been married on his twentieth birthday when he was acting as bodyguard to a member of the Brigade staff, at a time when relations between the divided Provisionals and officials were at an all-time low. After the wedding he had not been called out for some months, as his superiors let him mature, confident that he would, like a good wine, repay well the time they gave him. They used him first shortly before the twins were born. Then he took part in an escape attempt at Long Kesh, waiting through much of the night in a stolen car on the M1 motorway for a man to come through the wire and across the fields. They had stayed seven minutes after a cacophony of barking dogs on the perimeter fence six hundred yards away had spelled out the failure of the attempt. With two others he had been used for the assassination of a policeman as he left his house in the suburb of Glengormley. It was his first command, and he was allowed to select his own ambush point, collect the firearm from the Brigade quartermaster, and lead the get-away on his own route. After that came attacks on police stations, where he was among those who gave covering fire with the Armalites to the blast of the RPG rocket launcher.

On those early occasions he had often missed with the crucial first shot, firing too hurriedly, and then had to run like a mad thing with the noise and shouting of the soldiers behind him. They were heady moments, hearing the voices of the English troops with their strange accents bellowing in pursuit as he weaved and ducked his way clear.

Amongst a small group, though, his reputation had improved, and his future value was reckoned as such that for nearly a year he had been left to lead what amounted to a normal life in the Ardoyne. Around him the army removed all but a tight hard core of activists. He was left at home, his name not figuring on the army files, his photograph absent from the wanted lists.

In their four years of marriage his wife had borne him twins, both boys, and conceived some weeks before their wedding, and two daughters. The time that he was away preparing for London, in the English capital, and then hiding in Northern Ireland before coming back to Ypres Avenue was the longest he had ever been away from his family. As he sat in the room where the light began to filter its gentle way through the thin cotton curtains he reflected on the hugeness of his disappointment at the way his wife had reacted.

He was still slumped in his chair when she came downstairs, a little after six. She came into the room on tiptoe and up behind the chair, and leaned over and kissed him on his forehead.

'We'll have to forget it all,' she said. 'The kids'll be awake soon. They've been upset, you being away so long, and the wee one has the cough. They'll be excited. There's a dance at the club on Saturday.

Let's go. Mam'll come down, and sit. We'll have some drinks, forget it ever happened.'

She kissed him again.

'We need some tea, kettle's up.'

He followed her into the kitchen.

For Davidson, in his offices up above a paint store in Covent Garden, it was to be a bad morning. He had asked for an appointment with the Permanent Under Secretary at the Ministry of Defence. The Boss. The Gaffer. Appointments with subordinates only when there was a fiasco or a potential fiasco. Davidson had to explain that their operator had gone missing and had never checked into the address that had been suggested to him.

Davidson had been hoping for a phone call, or failing that at least a letter or postcard to the office, saying, if nothing else, that Harry was installed and working. The complete silence was beginning to unnerve him. The previous day he authorized the checking of the Antrim Road guest house – discreetly, by telephone – for a Mr McEvoy, but the word had come back that no one of that name had been near the building. There was no way Davidson could find out in a hurry whether the package containing the pistol sent for collection had in fact been picked up. He told himself there was no positive foundation to his fears, but the possibility, however faint, that Harry was already blown or dead or both nagged at Davidson. Nagged enough for him to seek a rare audience in the Ministry.

By early afternoon the brandies were on the table in the restaurant of the big hotel on the outskirts of the city. Both the Brigadier and the Chief Superintendent were in their own clothes and mildly celebrating the promotion and transfer of the army officer from second in command of the Brigade with responsibilities for Belfast to a new appointment in Germany. Both knew from their own intelligence-gathering agencies in vague terms of the sending of Harry and the Prime Minister's directive – it had come in a terse, brief message from the GOC's headquarters. There was little more to it than the statement that a special team had been set up to spearhead the hunt for Danby's killer, and that all other operations in this direction should continue as before. During the serving of the food neither had spoken of it, as the waiters hovered round them. But with the coffee cups full, and the brandy glasses topped up, the subject was inevitably fielded.

'There's been nothing from that fellow the PM launched,' muttered the Brigadier. 'Long shot at the best of times. No word, I'm told, and

Frost in intelligence is still leaping about. Called it a bloody insult. See his point.'

'Sunk without trace, probably. They sniff them out, smell them a mile off. Poor devil. I feel for him. How was he supposed to solve it when SB and intelligence don't have a line in? If our trained people can't get in there, how's this chap?'

'Bloody ridiculous.'

'He'll end up dead, and it'll be another life thrown away. I hope he doesn't, but if he sticks at it they'll get him.'

'I expect your SB were the same, but intelligence weren't exactly thrilled. What really peeved them was that at first they weren't supposed to know anything, then it leaked. I think the Old Man himself put it out, then came the message, and there wasn't much to show from that. Frost stayed behind after the Old Man's conference last Friday and demanded to know what was going on. Said it was an indication of no confidence in his section. Threatened his commission and everything on it. GOC calmed him down, but took a bit of time.'

The music was loud in the dining-room, and both men needed to speak firmly to hear each other above the canned violin strings. The policeman spoke:

'I think Frost's got a case. So have we for that matter' . . . in mid-chord and without warning the tape ran out . . . 'to put a special operator in on the ground without telling . . .' Dramatically conscious of the way his voice had carried in the sudden moment of silence he cut himself short.

Awkwardly the two men waited for the half-minute or so that it took the reception staff away in the front hall to loop up the reverse side of the three-hour tape, then the talking began again.

The eighteen-year-old waiter serving the next table their courgettes had clearly heard the second half of the sentence. He repeated the words to himself as he went round the table – 'Special operator on the ground without telling.' He said it five times to himself as he circled the table, fearful that he would forget the crucial words. Then he hurried with the emptied dish to the kitchen, scribbling the words in large spidery writing on the back of his order pad.

He went off duty at 3.30, and seventy-five minutes later the message of what he had overheard and its context were on their way to the intelligence officer of the Provisionals' Third Battalion.

8

Harry spent a long time getting himself ready to go out that Saturday night. He bathed, and put on clean clothes, even changing his socks from the ones he'd been wearing through the rest of the day, took a clean shirt from the wardrobe and brushed down the one suit he'd brought with him. In the time that he'd been in Belfast he had tried to stop thinking in the terms of an army officer, even when he was on his own and relaxed. He attempted to make his first impulses those of the ex-merchant seaman or lorry driver that he hoped to become. As he straightened his tie, though, he allowed himself the luxury of thinking that this was a touch different from mess night with the rest of the regiment at base camp in Germany.

He'd spent a difficult and nearly unproductive first week. He'd visited a score of firms looking for driver's work with no success till Friday when he had come across a scrap merchant on the far side of Andersonstown. There they'd said they might be able to use him, but he should come back on Monday morning when he would get a definite answer. He had been in the pub on the corner several times, but though he was now accepted enough for him to stand and take his drink without the whole bar lapsing into a silent stare none of the locals initiated any conversation with him, and the opening remarks he made to them from time to time were generally rebutted with non-committal answers.

It had been both hard and frustrating, and he felt that the one bright spot that stood out was this Saturday night.

Taking Josephine out. Like a kid out of school and going down the disco, you silly bugger. At your age, off to a peasant hop. As he dressed himself he began to liven up. One good night out was what he needed before the tedium of next week. Nearly six days gone, and not a thing to hook on to. Davidson said three weeks and something ought to show. Must have been the pep talk chat. He came down a little after seven and sat in the chair by the fire in the front room that was available to guests. He was on his own. All the others scurried away on Friday morning with their bags packed and homes to get to after a half-day's work at the end of the week. Not hanging about up here, not in the front line.

When the door bell rang he slipped quickly out into the hall, and opened the door. Josephine stood there, breathing heavily.

'I'm sorry I'm late. Couldn't get a bus. They've cut them down a bit, I think. I'm not very late, am I?'

'I think all the buses are on the scrap yards up the road, stacks of them there, doubles and singles. I'd only just come down. I reckon you're dead on time. Let's go straight away.'

He shouted back towards the kitchen that he was on his way out, that he had his key, and not to worry if he was a bit late.

'How do we get there?' he asked. 'It's all a bit strange to me moving about the city still, especially at night.'

'No problem. We'll walk down to the hospital, get a cab there into town, and in Castle Street we'll get another cab up the Crumlin. It's just a short walk from there. It won't take long, we'll be there in forty-five minutes. It's a bit roundabout, that's all.'

In Ypres Avenue the man and his wife were making their final preparations to go out. There had been an uneasy understanding between them since their talk in the early hours after his home-coming, and no further word on the subject had been spoken. Both seemed to accept that the wounds of that night could only be healed by time and silence. She had lain in bed the first three mornings waiting for the high whine of the Saracens, expecting the troops to come breaking in to tear her man from their bed. But they didn't come, and now she began to believe what he had told her. Perhaps there was no clue, perhaps the photokit really did look as little like him as she, his wife, believed. Her mother was busying herself at the back of the house round the stove, where she kept a perpetual pot of freshened tea. All the children were now in bed, the twins complaining that it was too early. To both of them the evening was something to look forward to, a change from the oppressiveness of the atmosphere as the man sat about his house, too small for privacy or for him to absent himself from the rest of the family. It had been laid down by his superiors that he was not to try to make contact with his colleagues in the movement, or in any way expose himself to danger of arrest. It meant long hours of waiting, fiddling time uselessly away. Already he felt restless, but hurrying things was futile. That's how they all got taken, going off at half-cock when things weren't ready for them. Not like London. All the planning was there. No impatience, just when it suited and not a day earlier. Boredom was his great enemy, and the need was for discipline, discipline as befits the member of an army.

With his wife on his arm, and in her best trouser suit, he walked up his street towards the hut with the corrugated-iron roof that was the social club. He could relax here, among his own. Drain his pints. Talk to people. It was back to the ordinary. To living again.

*

359

By the time Harry and Josephine arrived at the club, it was nearly full, with most of the tables taken. The girl said she'd find somewhere to sit, and he pushed his way towards the long trestle tables at the far end from the door where three men were hard at it in their shirt sleeves taking the tops off bottles and pouring drinks. Harry forced his way through the shoulders of the men standing close to the makeshift bar, made it to the front and called for a pint of Guinness and a gin and orange.

As he was struggling back to the table where Josephine was sitting he saw a man come up to her and gesture towards him. After they'd spoken a few words he'd nodded his head, smiled at the girl and moved back towards the door.

'Someone you know?' he said when he sat down, shifting her coat on to the back of the seat.

'It's just they like to know who's who round here. Can't blame them. He wanted to know who you were, that's all.'

'What did you tell him?'

'Just who you were, that's all.'

Everything was subdued at this stage of the evening, but the effects of the drink and the belting of the four-piece band and their electrically-amplified instruments began to have a gradual livening effect. By nine some of the younger couples were ignoring the protests of the older people and had begun to pile up the tables and chairs at the far end of the room to the bar, exposing a crude, unpolished set of nail-ridden boards. That was the dance floor. The band quickened the tempo, intensified the beat. When he felt that the small talk they were making was next to impossible, Harry asked the girl if she'd like to dance.

She led the way through the jungle of tables and chairs. Near the floor Harry paused as Josephine slowed and squeezed by a girl in a bright-yellow trouser suit. It was striking enough in its colour for Harry to notice it. Then, as his eyes moved to the table where she was sitting, he saw the young man at her side.

There was intuitive, deep-based recognition for a moment, and Harry couldn't place it. He looked at the man, who stared straight back at him, challenging. Josephine was out on the floor now waiting for him to come by the girl in yellow. He looked away from the face that was still staring back at him, holding and returning his glance, mouthed an apology and was away to the floor. Once more he looked at the man, who still watched him, cold and expressionless – then Harry rejected the suspicion of the likeness. Hair wrong. Face too full. Eyes too close. Mouth was right. That was all. The mouth, and nothing else.

The floor pounded with the motion of a cattle stampede – as it seemed to Harry, who was used to more ordered dances at the base. At first he was nearly swamped, but survived after throwing off what decorum he had ever learned as he and Josephine were buffeted and shoved from one set of shoulders to another. Sweat and scent were already taking over from the beer and smoke. When the band switched to an Irish ballad he gasped his relief, and round them the frenetic movements slowed in pace. He could concentrate now on the girl close against him.

She danced with her head back, looking up at him and talking. Looking the whole time, not burying herself away from him. She was wearing a black skirt, full and flared, so that she had the freedom to swing her hips to the music. Above that a tight polka dot blouse. The top four buttons were unfastened. There were no Josephines in Aden, no Josephines taking an interest in married transport captains in Germany.

They talked dance-floor small talk, Harry launched into a series of concocted anecdotes about the ports he'd visited when he was at sea, and she laughed a lot. Twice a nagging uncertainty took his attention away from her to where the man was sitting quietly at the table with the girl in the yellow trouser suit, glasses in front of them, eyes roving, but not talking. The second time he decided the likeness was superficial. It didn't hold up. Face, eyes, hair – all wrong. Before he turned back to Josephine he saw the mouth again. That was right. It amused him. Coincidence. And his attention was diverted to the girl, her prettiness and inevitable promise.

The man too had noticed Harry's attention. It had been pronounced enough to make him fidget a little in his chair, and for him to feel the hot perspiration surge over his legs inside the thick cloth of his best suit. He had seen the door-minder talk to the girl who brought him in, and presumably clear the stranger. But his nerves had calmed when he had seen Harry on the dance floor, no longer interested, but totally involved in the girl he was with. The man could not dance, had never been taught. He and his wife would sit at the table all evening as a succession of friends and neighbours came to join them to talk for a few minutes and then move on. Along the wall to the right of the door and near the bar were a group of youths, some of them volunteers in the Provisionals, some couriers and some look-outs. These were the expendables of the movement. The teenage girls were gathered round them, attracted by the glamour of the profession of terrorism, hanging on the boys' sneers and cracks and boasts. None of the boys would rise high in the upper echelons but each was necessary as part of the supply chain that kept the planners and marksmen in the field. None knew the man except by name. None knew of his involvement.

*

First through the door was the big sergeant, a Sterling sub-machine-gun in his right hand. He'd hit the door with all the impetus of his two hundred pounds gathered in a six-foot run. Behind him came a lieutenant, clutching his Browning automatic pistol, and then eight soldiers. They came in fast and fanned out in a protective screen round the officer. Some of the soldiers carried rifles, others the large-barrelled, rubber-bullet guns.

The officer shouted in the general direction of the band.

'Cut that din. Wrap it up. I want all the men against the far wall. Facing the wall. Hands right up. Ladies, where you are please.'

From the middle of the dance floor a glass curved its way through the crowd and towards the troops. It hit high on the bridge of a nose creeping under the protective rim of a helmet. Blood was forming from the wound by the time the glass hit the floor. A rubber bullet, solid, unbending, six inches long, was fired into the crowd, and amid the screams there was a stampede away from the troops as tables and chairs were thrown aside to make way.

'Come on. No games, please. Let's get it over with. Now, the men line up at that wall – and *now*.'

More soldiers had come through the door. There were perhaps twenty of them in the hall by the time the line of men had formed up, legs wide apart and fingers and palms on the wall high above their heads. Harry and the man were close to each other, separated by three others. At her table the girl in the yellow trouser suit sat very still. She was one of the few who wasn't barracking the army with a medley of obscenities and insults. Her fingers were tight round the stem of her glass, her eyes flicking continuously from the troops to her husband.

Josephine's table had been knocked aside in the scramble to get clear from the firing of the rubber bullet, and she stood on the dance floor interested to see what the army made of her merchant-seaman escort.

Six of the soldiers, working in pairs, split up the line of men against the wall and started to quiz each man on his name, age and address. One soldier asked the questions, the other wrote down the answers. The lieutenant moved between the three groups checking the procedure, while his sergeant marshalled his other men in the room to prevent any sudden break for the exits.

Private David Jones, number 278649, eighteen months of his nine-year signing served, and Lance-Corporal James Llewellyn, 512387, were working over the group of men nearest the dance floor. The man and Harry were there. The way the line had formed itself they would come to the man first. It was very slow. Conscientious, plodding. The wife was in agony. Charade, that's all. A game of cat and mouse. They had come for him, and these were the preliminaries, the way they dressed it up. But they'd come for him. They had to know.

The lance-corporal tapped the man's shoulder.

'Come on, let's have you.' Not unkindly. It was quiet in the Ardoyne now, and the soldiers acknowledged it.

The man swung round, bringing his hands down to his sides, fists clenched tight, avoiding the pleading face of his wife a few feet away. Llewellyn was asking the questions, Jones writing the answers down.

'Name?'

'Billy Downs.'

'Age?'

'Twenty-three.'

'Address?'

'Forty-one, Ypres Avenue.'

Llewellyn paused as Jones struggled in his notebook with the blunted pencil he had brought with him. The lieutenant walked towards them. He looked hard at the man, then down into Jones's notebook, deciphering the smudged writing.

'Billy Downs?'

'That's it.'

'We were calling for you the other morning. Expected to find you home, but you weren't there.'

He stared into the young man's face. That was the question he posed. There was no reply.

'Where were you, Mr Downs? Your good wife whom I see sitting over there didn't seem too sure.'

'I went down to see my mother in the South. It's on your files. You can check that.'

'But you've been away a fair few days, Downs boy. Fond of her, are you?'

'She's not been well, and you know that. She's a heart condition. That's in your files and all. It wasn't made any better when there weren't any of you lot around when the Prods came and burned her out . . . and that's in your files too.'

'Steady, boy. What's her address?'

'Forty, Dublin Road, Cork.' He said it loud enough for his wife to hear the address given. His voice was raised now, and she listened to the message that was in it. 'She'll tell you I've been there for a month. That I was with her till four days ago.'

The lieutenant still gazed into Downs's face, searching for weakness, evasion, inconsistency. If there was fear there he betrayed none of it to the soldier a bare year older than himself.

'Put him in the truck,' the lieutenant said. Jones and Llewellyn hustled Downs across the room and towards the door. His wife rose up out of her chair and rushed across to him.

'Don't worry, girl, once the Garda have checked with Mam I'll be home. I'll see you later.' And he was out into the night to where the Saracen was parked.

363

The two soldiers came back to the line, and the lieutenant moved away to the other end where the youths, resigned to a ride back to barracks and an interrogation session at the end of it, snapped back sullen replies to the questions.

Llewellyn touched Harry's shoulder.

'Name?'

'Harry McEvoy.'

'Age?'

'Thirty-three.'

'Address?'

Jones had had his eyes down on his notebook till that moment. He glanced up to hear the answer. Harry saw an expression of astonishment take hold of him, then change to suspicion, then back to bewilderment.

'Bloody hell, what are you doing – ?'

Harry's right foot moved the seven inches into Jones's left ankle. As the private ducked forward, caught off balance by the sudden pain, Harry lurched into him.

'Shut your face,' he hissed into the soldier's ear.

Jones's face came up and met Harry's stare. Imperceptibly he saw the head move. A quick shake, left to right and twice.

'I'm sorry,' said Harry. 'Forget it. I hope you'll forget it.'

The last words were very quiet and straight into Jones's ear. The men in the line, waiting to be questioned, still faced the wall; the women, sitting at their tables, were out of earshot. The exchange between Harry and Jones seemed to have passed unnoticed.

Llewellyn had been diverted by a commotion down at the far end of the hall, where four youths were half carried and half dragged towards the doorway. He was concentrating again now.

'Come on – what's the address?'

'Delrosa Guest House, in the Broadway. Just up from Beechmount.'

Harry's eyes were fixed, snake-like, on Jones.

'Bit off course, aren't you?' said Llewellyn.

'My girl's local.'

'Which one?'

'In the polka dot, the dark-haired girl.' Harry gazed past Llewellyn, his eyes never leaving Jones. Twice the younger soldier's eyes came up from his notebook, met Harry's, and dived back to the writing.

'Lucky bastard,' said Llewellyn and moved on.

Apart from Downs, the army had taken nine youths when the officer shouted for his men to leave the club. They went out in single file, the last going out backwards with his rifle covering the crowd. As the door swung to after him a hail of empty bottles and glasses cannoned into the woodwork.

A tall man at the far end from Harry shouted a protest.

'Now come on, folks, we can do better than that. Lob things at the bastards, yes, but not so we cover *our* floor with *our* bottles and *our* glasses and *our* beer. Now, we're not going to let those swine spoil the evening for us. Let's move it all back and tidy up, and see if we can't get something out of the evening.'

It was a good effort on the part of the community leader, but doomed to failure.

Harry noticed that the girl in yellow was gone before the floor was half cleared. He shifted in his seat.

'We can't go yet. It's the principle of the thing,' said Josephine. 'You cannot let the bastards wreck everything. What did you say to that soldier?'

'I just tripped against him, that's all.'

'You're lucky. You might have got a rifle butt across your face. There's men taken to the barracks for less.'

The band had started up again, attempting to capitalize on the angry mood of those left behind.

Armoured cars and tanks and guns,
Came to take away our sons . . .

'Will it wake up again, or is this the lot for the evening?' asked Harry.

. . . Through the little streets so narrow . . .

'I doubt it,' she said, 'but it's best to give it a few minutes. Let's see, anyway.'

. . . Cromwell's men are here again . . .

'It's not that bad, is it?' said Harry, 'I heard it in the Baltic when we were working out of a Swedish port. They used to play it about every third disc. Got to quite like it. We had a mate on board who said his son was in the army here. He used to get right steamed up just listening to it.'

. . . The men behind the wire . . .

People were edging towards the door. Harry sensed there would be little more of a night out for any of them.

'Come on, let's quit. We don't want to stay for the funeral.'

'I'm going to powder my nose, then,' Josephine said.

'Looks all right to me. Don't hang about.'

She smiled, got up from the table and went out through a side door where a gaggle of girls younger than Josephine had gathered. The band was still trying, but was competing with a wave of talk particularly from a large group that had gathered round a local primary school teacher who was taking down the names of all those lifted by the military. He was promising to go round to the barracks to see what had happened to them.

It was a cold clear night as Harry, with Josephine on his arm, walked out of the hall and off towards the all-night taxi rank for the drive down to Castle Street. Then there would be another taxi, and a walk up the last part of the Falls to Mrs Duncan's.

*

365

Harry and Josephine were naked, entwined and asleep, when 275 miles to the south the Garda squad car drew up outside the stone terraced house in the Dublin Road in Cork. There was the sharp mustiness of the docks in the pre-dawn air, as the two policemen fumbled their way from the car to the front doorstep.

'It's a sod of a time, God help us, to be getting this poor dear out of her bed.'

The sergeant rang the door bell, twice and firmly, and waited. A light came on upstairs, not fast, then in the hall, and after that the noise of the bolts in the door grating open.

'From the sound of it you'd think she'd got the Bank of England in there,' muttered the sergeant into his gloves.

'Good morning, my love. I'm right sorry to be coming at such a time as this to wake you. But a message has come down over the telephone from Dublin and I'm to ask you some questions. Won't take a moment now. Shall we come on in, out of that wind?'

'We'll do what business you have here. You should be ashamed of yerselves coming at this time . . .'

'That's not our affair, my love. Now, are you ready? We want to ask you when was your boy last here.'

'Billy, you mean?'

'That's the lad, love. That's the one they want to know about.'

'He was down till the middle of the week. Been here a month, and just gone back. Why do you need to come at this time of night to ask that?'

'You're sure of that now, my dear? No mistakes?'

'Of course I'm sure. Billy was here for a month. And those are bloody silly questions to be asking at this time of night.'

She closed the door on them. The two Garda men knocked at the next-door house and again waited for the door to open. They took away the same message. Billy Downs had been there for a month.

The alibi had been passed on to the old lady and her four immediate neighbours some forty-five minutes before the police car had arrived. The wife's phone call to a friend of her man in Belfast had started the chain. Another call had been made to Dublin, another one from there to Cork, and a young man who had left his car two streets away from the Dublin Road had completed the process. The Provisionals' lines of communication were somewhat faster than the complicated and official process of liaison between North and South.

Downs had been interrogated twice, maintaining quietly and without fuss that he had been at his mother's in the South. He was kept apart from the other prisoners with the officers who had questioned him unsure whether they ought to have pulled him in or not. They heard at 5.30 the results of the checks in Cork, gave him back his coat and his tie and his shoes and told him to get away home.

9

They'd come into the house on tiptoe and holding their shoes. Both knew the prim well-scrubbed hallway and stairs well enough to estimate where the boards creaked, and where it was safe to put down their full weight. Harry held the girl's hand very tight. At first they had tried to go up the stairs together, and then, finding that impossible, he had gently led the way. There had been no talk about what they should do, where they should go when they left the taxi, no discussion whether she should come back to Delrosa with him. He had looked into her face at the doorway as he rummaged with his free hand for the latch key, seen those mocking, querying eyes turned up to his face, looking as if to challenge or dare him to take her inside. He'd squeezed her hand, and they'd gone in together. The message of silence was implicit.

Once in his back room a floorboard had erupted in protest at her foot and he had pulled her away from the place near the basin where she was standing wriggling out of her coat. That was where it would creak. That was the place where he had prised up the planks two days earlier to find a secure hiding place for his Smith and Wesson revolver.

She slung the coat across his easy chair by the window, and stood waiting for him to move towards her. He felt a tightness streaming through him. Clumsy. Gauche. Inhibited. He reached out towards the tall girl who gazed back at him, her expression one of interest, curiosity to see what he had to offer.

'You make me feel . . . a bit like someone who's forgotten most of it,' he whispered into her ear, one hand holding the back of her neck, the other flattened into the small of her back.

'You haven't made me feel anything yet.'

'Cheeky girl.'

'Try a bit of cheek yourself. Might take you a long way.'

He pulled his left hand round, drawing back from her to give himself room to unbutton the few remaining buttons on her blouse.

'Not much of an obstacle course here,' he murmured as he flicked the buttons, small and transparent, through the tautened and opened holes of the fabric.

'Who said they were supposed to be?'

His hand had moved inside her blouse, and he began to ease the soft cotton over her shoulders and down her arms.

'I was never very much one for this. Getting everything off in the right order, like a bloody production line in reverse.'

'And it takes so much more time. Let's see to it ourselves. I'll meet you under the sheets in forty-five seconds from now.'

In a welter of tights, pants, black skirt, shoes and bra she stripped herself and was away in the bed waiting for him. Harry was fighting with his right cuff link. She had started to follow the second hand of her watch with exaggerated interest before he climbed into the narrow bed alongside her.

'You took thirty seconds over the limit. Bad marks for that, sailor boy.'

'Wasn't for lack of trying.'

He had curved his arms round her, as she came close to against him. His fingers ran their course across her skin, tight, cool and firm. Beautiful girl. Her eyes closed. She moaned. Calling for him, hurrying him. That first time there were few preliminaries, few subtleties. He found her fast, deep, easy. He poured himself into her. Both engaged in a frantic, uncaring race. He sagged away. Disastrous. Bloody Belfast. Like everything else – crude and rushed. No future for tenderness or patience.

'Got a bus to catch?'

'It'll be better next time,' he said, 'it happened too quick for me. And I never got round to asking you whether . . . you know, whether you take anything . . . or what?'

'There's Catholics and good Catholics here. I'm one of the first. You don't have to worry about that.'

The second time was better. Softer, Calmer. Slower. He took a long time finding the routes and depths and contours of her body. Finding where she moved and squirmed, and when she thrust herself at him. Heat against his chest and his thighs. She called the time she was ready for him to come into her, called quietly in his ear. Her mouth open, almost soundless. He smiled down at her as he felt himself slipping away into the void. It was over and they lay together. Her hair strewn with the sweat out on the pillow, he on her softness waiting for the limpness to come. Still locked together.

'You've no worries, then?' she asked.

'What do you mean? I don't think so.'

'You can't screw if you're really worried. Did you know that?'

'Old wives. Where did you hear that? Who told you that?'

'Just what one of the girls said in the bog tonight.'

'Tell me what she said.' He lay straddled across her, her mouth an inch or so from his ear.

'She said she'd tried to do it with one of the big men, but he couldn't manage it. She said he was all so tied up he couldn't make it. She was ever so upset.'

Harry grimaced in disbelief.

'No, that's what she said. She was there tonight. She told me in the loo. She's a bit frantic at the best of times. Then the army nicked the fellow who'd have had her on the way home. Peeved her a bit. On her own on Saturday night. Not right for her. That's what she said. Big hero. Big deal. I'm all for cowards in this city.'

'I don't believe you,' said Harry, very still now. 'Which girl was it?'

'I'm not telling you the best lay in Ballymurphy!'

'I don't believe you. You're making it up.'

She pushed him back sideways. In the small bed there was hardly enough room, and he clung to her to save himself from disappearing on to the floor. She rolled over on to him, half her weight supported by his hips and waist and the other half supported by an elbow.

'It was Theresa. In pink. She had the tight skirt? Remember her? Believe me. You'll be up to Ballymurphy sniffing round now. Randy bugger.'

'I'd believe anything said by anyone as lovely as you,' said Harry.

'Bullshit,' she said.

'Who was the big man that didn't slake wee Theresa's thirst?' His hands were on the move again now, seeking the closeness between her thighs. She rolled and rose beneath him.

'Just like that. Go on. Just like that. The big man, the one they're all looking for. The London man. The one that did the politician in London. Don't stop there. Just like that. Faster! There's bugger all time. The old girl's alarm'll be off in half an hour. She's out like a flash then. Makes enough noise to wake half the folks in Milltown Cemetery.'

Minutes later she was out of bed, dressed and making her way quietly down the stairs to the front door. She refused to let Harry come and see her off, gave him a sisterly kiss on the forehead and was gone. He stood at his bedroom window and saw her some moments later walking along the main road under the street lights. When she had gone beyond the gap he lost sight of her.

After she had left Harry lay in his bed, stretching out his legs, searching out the new-found room, working over in his mind the information she had given him. No problem for the intelligence guys. A girl called Theresa, about eighteen or nineteen, in Ballymurphy. Sleeps around a bit. No problem. Should wrap up the whole thing. Not bad: one good screw in the line of duty, and the big *coup*. He could scarcely believe his luck – getting so far so quickly – all falling into his lap – and on a night out, at that. And the old woman, Davidson, who didn't rate his chances, who fussed and clucked over him, what would he be thinking when Harry called through? A moment to savour, that would be. I'd like to see his face, thought Harry.

There was still the worry over being recognized by that stupid, gawping soldier. But they should have the man within forty-eight hours, and then what the soldier saw wouldn't matter. All be academic by then. But where did the soldier come from? He turned over in his mind the military situations he'd been in over the last two years, trying to work out where he had seen the young man who had no doubts about him. Davidson would sort it out. Ring him in the morning. Let him know it's just about wrapped up.

For the first time since he had come to Belfast he felt the excitement that had been the hallmark of the Sheik Othman operation.

He used to leave little pencilled messages in English in an old fruit tin on the Sheik Othman-to-Mansoura road. Nothing as luxurious as a telephone. Sometimes he'd stay around in the afternoon heat the next day when the town was sleepy and out of gear and watch the military come bulldozing into the town in their Saladins and Saracens. He would watch the leather-faced, expressionless men hustled away into the armoured cars, resisting the show of force that came to get them only with the contempt in their eyes. That was the reward for the strange job he did – to see the clumsy boot of the army stepping into the exact footprints he had silently prepared for them.

It was a good two and a quarter hours before Davidson would be in the office. He had told Harry that for the first three weeks at least he would be there every day, Sundays included, at eight in the morning and stay till ten at night. Must be playing havoc with his marriage, thought Harry. Can't really see Davidson with a wife, though.

He'd go into town, he decided, and make the call from one of those anonymous call boxes in the city centre. Now two hours' sleep. That bloody woman. He was exhausted.

But she was a bit special.

Not like that at home. Couldn't be really. Nothing in married life vegetating round a barracks square in a line of neat, desiccated quarters that matched the drawn bow-string of the city at war. Too many bombs, too many snipers, too many mutilations for people to hang about on the preliminaries. You'd want a few memories as you bumped about in the box up the Falls to Milltown Cemetery. That was the philosophy of life for Belfast. And not a bad one, thought Harry.

Across in Germany they'd be asleep now. The wife and the kids, tucked up in their rooms, the familiar bits and pieces round them. The things, semi-junk, that they'd collected from the duty-free lounge and the market places where they went shopping when he was off duty. Knick-knacks that brightened the service furniture they lived off. Josephine didn't fit in there, was outside that world. They'd be up soon. Always had an early breakfast on Sundays. Someone would take the boys out for football. That was regular. And his wife . . . how would she spend a cold Sunday in North Germany? Harry was half asleep. Not quite dreaming but close. She'd go visiting, walk out along the line of officers' detached houses for a coffee in mid-morning, and stay for a drink before lunch, and have to make her excuses, and there'd be laughter when she'd flap about the lunch in the oven. Perhaps someone would ask her to stay and share theirs. That would be par for the course. And they'd say how sorry they were that Harry was away, and how suddenly he'd gone, and fish for an explanation. The questions would confuse her, and embarrass her, because they'd expect her at least to have an idea of why he'd vanished so quickly. And she wouldn't have an answer.

Could she comprehend it even if she did know? Could she assimilate this tatty, rotten job? Could she understand the man that was hunted, and the need to kill him? Could she accept what might happen to Harry? 'I don't know,' Harry said to himself, 'God knows how many years we've been married, and I don't know. She'd be calm enough, not throw any tantrums, but what it would all mean to her, I've not the faintest idea.'

That would all sort itself. And when the answers had to be given then Josey would be a fantasy, and over.

Billy Downs was in his bed now, and asleep. He'd come back to find his wife sobbing into her pillow, disbelieving he could be freed, still suffering from the strain of the phone call she had made hours earlier. Many times he told her it was just routine, that there was nothing for them to fear. Relax, they know nothing. It's clean. The trail is old and cold and clean. She held on to him as if uncertain that he was really there after she had mentally prepared herself for not seeing him again as a free man. The terror of losing him was a long time thawing. He put a brave face on it, but didn't know himself the significance of his arrest. But to run now would be suicide. He would stay put. Act normally. And stay very cool.

As soon as he came off duty, in the small hours of Sunday morning, Jones asked to see his commanding officer. His platoon lieutenant asked him why, and about what, but the shuffling private merely replied that it was a security matter and that he must see the colonel as soon as he woke. He was marched up the wide steps of the mill, enclosed with the dripping walls festooned with fire- and parcel-bomb warnings and urging the soldiers to be ever vigilant, and shown into the colonel's office. The colonel was shaving electrically and continued with the modern ritual as the soldier put together his report. Jones said that while searching a social club the previous night he had seen a man he definitely recognized as having been the transport officer at a base in Germany where his unit had refitted after a NATO exercise. He said that the man had given

371

his name as McEvoy, and he explained about his kicked ankle, and the instruction to forget what he had seen. There was a long pause while the officer scraped the razor round his face, doubtful what action to take, and how he should react. The minute or so that he thought about the problem seemed to the young private an eternity. Then he gave his orders. Jones was to make no further mention of the incident to any other soldier, and was confined to barracks till further notice.

'Please, sir. What do I tell sergeant-major?'

'Tell him the MO says you've a cold. That's all, and keep your mouth shut. That's important.'

When the soldier had about-turned and stamped his way out of the office the colonel asked for his second in command to come and see him. Sunday was normally the quiet morning, and the chance of a modest stay in bed. The second in command came in still wearing his dressing-gown. To the colonel the position was now clear.

'There's all these chaps running round in civvies. I think we've trampled on one. If we say we've done it, there's going to be a hell of a scene all the way round, lot of fluff flying, and problems. I'm going to ship Jones out to Germany this afternoon and have the page of his log destroyed. We can take care of this our own way and with rather less palaver than if it goes up to old Frost at HQ.'

The second in command agreed. He would ask for the log book, and deal with the offending page personally. Before his breakfast.

Early Sunday morning in Belfast is formidable. To Harry it was like the set of one of those films where there has been a nerve gas attack and no one is left alive. Nothing but grey, heavy buildings, some crazily angled from the bomb blasts, others held up at the ends by huge timber props. Outside the city hall, vast and enormous and apparently deserted, the pigeons had gathered on the lawns. They too were immobile except when they ducked their heads while searching for imaginary worms in the ground. No buses. No taxis. No cars. No people. Harry found himself scurrying to get away from so much silence and emptiness. It was almost with a sense of relief that he saw a joint RUC and Military Police patrol cruising towards him. This typified the difference for him between Aden and here. When he was on his own in Mansoura he had shut himself away from the safety of the military and accepted that the run for home would be way too long if his cover was blown or he gave himself away. Now he had the army and police all round him. He was part of their arm, an extension of their operations.

Yet he felt the very closeness of the security forces was unnerving. The agent operating in hostile territory has to be self-sufficient and self-supporting. All just as applicable to the British agent working in

Great Britain. Can't be like the little boy with the bloody nose running home to Mum. In Mansoura it had been quite conventional and therefore more acceptable.

Not only was the city centre deserted of people. It was battened down for the day. Iron railings, their tops split into sharp tridents, blocked off the shopping streets that fanned off Royal Avenue. The turnstile gates into the security precincts were padlocked. Shops inside and outside the barricades had their windows barricaded and shuttered.

Down near the post office he found a bank of empty phone boxes, with only the work of vandals to prevent him taking his pick from a choice of six. It was cold inside the booth, with the wind cutting through the gaps left where the kids had kicked out the glass in the days before the army operated in strength in the city centre.

He took from his pocket a pile of ten-pence pieces and arrayed them in formation like fish scales on the top of the money box, and dialled the London number he had memorized in Dorking. If he had gone through an operator some of his call might have been overheard. This was the safe way. The phone rang a long time before it was answered.

Davidson heard the ringing when he was at the bottom of the stairs.

Against its shrill persistence he fumbled with his key ring to release the three separate locks on the heavy door, and stumbled across the darkened room where the blinds were still down. He picked up the receiver.

'Four-seven-zero-four-six-eight-one. Can I help you?'

'It's Harry. How are the family?'

'Very well, they liked the postcards, I'm told.'

That was the routine they had agreed. Two sentences' chatter to show the other that he was a free agent and able to talk.

'How's it going, Harry boy?'

'Middling. I'll get the report over first. Then we'll talk. Going in ten from now.'

That was time enough for Davidson to get the drawer in the leg of his desk open, switch on the cassette recorder and plug in the lead to the telephone receiver.

'Going now, okay? The man is in Belfast still. I'm sure of that. He is apparently under great stress and while on the run shortly after the shooting was with a girl called Theresa. No second name. She's from the Ballymurphy area. He tried to screw her, and she's telling her friends that he couldn't make it, because he was so wound up about the shooting. She's late teens or early twenties. She was at a dance last night in a green-painted hut in Ardoyne. She was wearing pink, tight skirt. The army heifered their way in, and picked up about a dozen blokes, some

373

of them in Theresa's group. They should be holding them still, unless they work bloody fast. One of them can identify her. So she's worth a bit of chat and then I think we'll be homeward bound. Seems straight sailing from here. That's the plus side. Now the anti. In the club I was lined up for an ID check. Lance-corporal from Wales asking questions, a young boy writing down the answers. The boy recognized me. God knows from when, but he did. I'd like it sorted out. I'm going to lie low for today, but I may have a job of sorts coming up. That's about it, basically.'

'Harry, we were worried when we didn't hear anything.'

'I didn't want to call in till I had something to say.'

'But I won't mess you about. But I know you're not staying where we planned for you.'

'Too bloody right. Right little army rest house. Right out of the interesting areas, and I take a peep at the place and out comes some squaddie in plains. Shambles that was. You should crucify whoever sold you that pup.'

'Thanks, Harry. I'll kill them for it. I'll go high on it.'

'I've made it on my own. Quite snug, on the other side of town. Let's leave it that way. I'll call you if anything else shows up.'

'We'll do it your way. It's not usual, but okay. Nothing more?'

'Only tell the people who pick the girl up to go a bit quietly. Don't ask me what the source of this is, but I don't want it too obvious. If you can get her in without a razzamatazz you should have your man before anyone knows she's gone, and can link her to him.'

'I'll pass that on. Anything else?'

'Nothing more. Cheers. Good hunting.'

Davidson heard the phone click down. The call had lasted one minute and fifty-five seconds.

Harry let the receiver stay a moment in his hands after he'd pressed down the twin buttons with his fingers to end the call. He would have liked to talk with Davidson, unimportant small talk. But that would be unprofessional. Dangerous. Soft. Diverting. Pray God they would get the bastard now. He began to walk back to a lonely day at Delrosa, as the city on half-cylinder sparked to life.

Davidson had been surprised that Harry had rung off so fast. He reached down into his drawer and spun back the spools of his tape a few revolutions to check that the recording had operated correctly. He then wound the tape back to the beginning and played the tape from start to finish, taking a careful shorthand note of the conversation. He then rewound the tape back again to the start and played it once more, this time against his shorthand. Only when he was satisfied that he had correctly taken down every word spoken by Harry did he disconnect the leads between the tape and the telephone. He searched in his diary, at the back in the address and useful numbers section, for the home phone of the Permanent Under Secretary.

'I thought you'd want to know, after our talk the other day. He's surfaced. There's some quite useful stuff. Should give a good lead. He sounded a bit rough. Not having much of a joy ride, I fancy. I'll call you in the office tomorrow. I'm quite hopeful we may be on to something. Yes . . . I'm going to pass it on now.'

His next call was to an unlisted extension in the Ministry of Defence.

Minutes later Harry's message was on a coded teletype machine in the red-brick, two-storey building that housed the intelligence unit at army headquarters, Lisburn. It was of sufficient immediate importance for Colonel George Frost to be called from his breakfast. Cursing about amateurs and lack of consultation he set up an urgent and high-level conference. He summoned his own men, the 39 Brigade duty operations officer, Police Special Branch, and the army officer commanding the unit that controlled Ardoyne. The meeting was called for nine, and the unit officer was given no information as to why he was wanted at HQ, only told that on no account were any of last night's suspects to be released. Davidson had somewhat shortened Harry's message. Believing that an arrest was imminent now, he too had decided that the report of the recognition should be suppressed and should go no further. A million-to-one chance. It wouldn't happen again. Could be forgotten. Only cause a flap if it went official.

While he was waiting for the meeting Frost reflected on the punched capitals in front of him, deciphered from the code by one of the duty typists. It was detailed enough to impress him, improbable enough to sound likely, and the sort of material you didn't pick up sitting on your backside in the front lounge. When he had read his riot act at the General about being kept out of the picture he'd heard of the three weeks' crash training course, and been told the arrival date. The source was now about to start his second week. Five lines of print that might be the breakthrough – and might not.

It was the sort of operation Frost detested. Ill-conceived and, worst of all, with the need for fast results dictated by political masters. If he's working at this pace, involved enough to get his nose stuck into this sort of stuff, then Frost reckoned he had about another week to go. That would be par for the course on a job like this. That was always the way. Crash in hard while the trail is still warm. You might get something when you stir the bottom up. But not discreet. No, and not safe either.

Poor bastard.

Frost had seen the body of the Armoured Corps captain, found shot and hooded, dumped outside Belfast. He had been working with a full team behind him. All the back-up he needed. Time on his side. Now this nameless and faceless man was trying to do what the whole army and police couldn't. Stupid. Idiotic. Irresponsible. All of those things, that's how Frost rated it. And there'd be a mess. And he'd have to clear it up.

Harry was nearly at his digs by the time the meeting Frost had called was under way. He had decided this was to be his day off. Tomorrow he would chase the job and try to get a bit of permanence into his life.

But today the pubs were closed. Nothing to do but eat Mrs Duncan's mighty roast and sit in his room and read. And listen to the news bulletins.

The platoon commander briefed to go and arrest the girl deep in the network of the Ballymurphy housing estate had stood his ground when asked to take the minimum number of troops needed for the pick-up.

'We've had four patrols shot at from that street or the alleys off it in the last eighteen days. If we have to search for her we'll be in there twenty minutes or so, and I can't just leave a couple of men outside to play Aunt Sallys. If I take a Saracen and a Pig they'll carry sixteen, and that way I can have enough men round the house, and enough to search the place as well.'

'They've asked for it to be discreet,' said his company commander.

'Well, what do they want us to do, have the padre drive a Cortina up to the front door and ask her to come for a picnic with him? Who is the girl anyway, sir?'

'Don't know why they want her. We hardly know her. The CO went up to Brigade this morning about something, and then came on the net with the instruction to pick her out.'

'However we do it, the whole street will know inside five minutes. It's Sunday, so we can't take her on the way back from work, wherever that is. If we're going into those streets we ought to have a proper back-up. Can they wait till dark?'

'No, the instruction is for immediate. That's quite clear. I take your point. Have as many men as you want, but be fast in there, and don't for God's sake start a riot.'

*

Theresa and her family were at lunch when the army arrived. The armoured troop carriers outside the tiny overgrown front garden, soldiers in fire positions behind the hedge and wall that divided the grass from next door's. Four soldiers went into the house. They called her name, and when she stood up took her by the arms, the policeman at the back intoning the Special Powers Act. While the rest of the family sat motionless she was taken out to the back of the armoured car. It was moving before her mother, the first to react, had reached the front door.

None of the soldiers who surrounded the girl in the darkened steel-cased Saracen spoke to her, and none would have been able to tell her why she had been singled out for this specific army raid. From the Saracen she was taken into a fortified police station, through the back entrance, and down the stairs to the cells. A policewoman was locked in with her to prevent any attempt at communication with other prisoners in the row. An hour or so earlier the nine boys taken from the club the previous night had been freed after sleeping in identical cells on the other side of the city. One of their number, pressed to identify someone who would swear he had been in the club all evening, had unwittingly given Theresa's second name and address.

The decision had already been taken that she would be kept in custody at least until the intelligence operation that had produced the information was completed.

10

Seamus Duffryn, the latest of the intelligence officers of E Company, Third Battalion Provisional IRA, had made Sunday his main working day. It was the fourth week-end he'd been in the job, with a long list of predecessors in Long Kesh and the Crumlin Road prison. Duffryn was in work, a rarity in the movement, holding down employment as mate to a lorry driver. It took him out of town several days a week, sometimes right down to the border and occasionally into the Republic. Being out of circulation he reckoned would extend his chances of remaining undetected longer than the mean average of nine weeks that most company-level officers lasted. He encouraged those with information for him to sift through to leave it at his house during the week where his mother would put it in a plastic laundry bag under the grate of the made-up but unlit front-room fire. He kept the meagre files he had pieced together out in the coal shed. There was a fair chance if the military came and he was out that they would stop short of scattering the old lady's fuel to the four winds in an off-the-cuff search.

On Sunday afternoons his mother sat at the back of the house with her radio while Duffryn took over the front room table, and under the fading coloured print of the Madonna and Child laid out the messages that had been sent to him. They were a fair hotch-potch, and at this level the first real sorting of the relevant and irrelevant took place. They concerned the amounts of money held at the end of the week at small post offices, usually a guess and an overestimate, the occasions when a recognized man of some importance drove down the company's section of the Falls, the times that patrols came out of the barracks. Then there was the group that fell into no natural pattern, but had seemed important enough for some volunteer to write down and send in for consideration.

He kept this last group for his final work, preferring to spend the greater part of the afternoon at the detail of the job that he liked best, checking over the information from his couriers and the eyes that reported back on what was happening at street corner level. His sifted reports would then go to his company commanding officer, a year younger and three and a half years out of school. The best and most interesting would go up the chain to Battalion.

The afternoon had nearly exhausted itself by the time he came to the final group, and the one report in particular that was to take him time. He read it slowly in the bad light of the room, and then went back and reread it looking for the innuendo in the ambiguous message. It was a page and a half long, written in pencil and unsigned by name. There was a number underneath which denoted which volunteer had sent it in. He went through the report of probably only one hundred words for the third time till he was satisfied he had caught its full flavour and meaning. Then he began to weigh its importance.

Strangers were the traditional enemies in the village-sized Catholic communities of Belfast. The Short Strand, the Markets, Ardoyne, Divis, Ballymurphy . . . all were self-sufficient, integral units. Small, difficult to penetrate, because unless you belonged you had no business or reason to come. They boasted no wandering, shifting groups, no cuckoos to come and feed off them. Those who were admitted after being burned out or intimidated away from their homes came because there were relatives who would put roofs over their heads. There were no strangers. You were either known or not admitted.

What concerned Duffryn now was the report on the stranger in the Beechmount and Broadway area. He was said to be looking for a job and getting long-term rates at Delrosa with Mrs Duncan. There was a question about his speech. The scribbled writing of the report had the second name of McEvoy. First name of Harry. Merchant seaman, orphaned and brought up in Portadown. No harm in that and checkable presumably. The interest in the report came later. The flaw in the set-up, the bit that didn't ring true. Accent, something wrong with the accent. Something that had been noticed as not right. It was put crudely, the reason Duffryn read it so many times to get the flavour of the writer's opinion:

'Seems to talk okay, then loses us for a moment, or a word, or sometimes in the middle of a word, and then comes back . . . his talk's like us mostly but it comes and goes . . . it's not just as if he'd been away as he says. Then all his talk would have gone, but it only happens with odd words.'

It was enough to cause him anxiety, and it took him half an hour to make out a painstaking report for his superiors setting down all the information he had available on the man called McEvoy. The responsibility would rest higher up the chain of command as to whether or not further action was taken. He would keep up surveillance when he had the manpower.

There were difficulties of communication in the city and it would be some days before his message could be passed on.

Private Jones was on board the 15.30 Trident One back to Heathrow. He was out of uniform but conspicuous in his short hair-cut and neatly pressed flannels. He had been told he would be met by service transport at Heathrow and taken to Northolt where he would be put on the first flight to Berlin and his new posting. It had been impressed on him that he was to speak to no one of his encounter the previous night. The incident was erased.

Interrogation was an art of which Howard Rennie had made himself a master, an authority, skilled at drawing out the half-truth and capitalizing on it till the floodgates of information burst. He knew the various techniques; the bully, the friend, the quiet business-like man across the table – all the approaches that softened the different types of people who sat at the bare table opposite him. The first session with the girl had been a gentle one, polite and paternal. It had taken him nowhere. Before they went into the interview room for the second time Rennie had explained his new tactics to the officer from army intelligence. Rennie would attack, and the Englishman capitalize from it. Two men, each offering a separate tempo, and combining together to confuse the suspect.

The detective could recognize his own irritability. A bad sign. One that demonstrated the hours he'd put in that week, the sleep he had forfeited. And the girl was playing him up. They'd given her the easy

379

way. If she wanted to play it like the boyos did, then good luck to her. But she was tired now, dazed by the surroundings and the lights, and hungry, having earlier defiantly refused the sandwiches they brought her.

'We'll start at the beginning again, right? . . . You were at the dance last night?'

'Yes.'

'What were you wearing? We'll have that again.'

'My pink dress.'

That much was established again by the detective. They'd got that far before. He'd done the talking. The army captain had said nothing as he sat behind the girl. A policewoman was also in the interview room, seated to the side of the desk and taking no part in the questioning. The questions came from the big man, directly opposite Theresa, just across the table.

'Your home in Ballymurphy . . . it's a hideout?'

'No.'

'It's used as a hideout. We know that. It's more we want. But it's where the boyos lie up?'

'No.'

'We know it is, you stupid bitch. We know they stay there.'

'Why ask me, then?' she shouted back.

'It's used as a hideout?'

'You say you know it is.'

'How often?'

'Not often.'

'How many times in the last month? Ten times?'

'No, nothing like that.'

'Five times, would that be about right? In the last month, Theresa?'

'Not as often as that.'

'How about just once, Theresa? That's the one we're interested in, just the once.' It was the officer behind her who spoke. English. Soft voice, different to those RUC bastards. She sat motionless on the wooden chair, hands clenched together round the soaked and stained handkerchief from the cuff in her blouse.

'I think we know one man came.'

'How can I tell you . . . ?'

'We know he came, girl, the one man,' the big Branch man took over again. 'One man, there was one man, wasn't there? Say three weeks ago. For a night or so. One man, yes or no?'

She said nothing.

'Look, girl, one man and we know he was there.'

Her eyes stayed on her hands. The light was very bright, the tiredness was ebbing over her, swallowing her into itself.

'One man, you stupid cow, there was one man. We know it.'

No reply. Still the silence. The policewoman fidgeted in her seat.

'You agreed with us that people came, right? Not as many as five, that was agreed. Not as many as ten, we got that far. Now, understand this, we say that one man came about three weeks ago. One man. A big man. He slept in the house, yes or no? Look at me, now.'

Her head came up slowly now to look at the policeman directly in front of her. Rennie kept talking. It was about to happen, he could sense it. The poor girl had damn all left to offer. One more shove and it would all roll out.

'You don't think we sent out all those troops and pigs just for one girl if we don't have it cast iron why we want to talk to her. Give us a bit of common. Now the man. Take your time. Yes or no?'

'Yes.' It was barely audible, her lips framing the word with a fractional fluttering of the chin. The army man behind her could not hear the answer, it was so softly spoken. He read it instead on the face of the detective as he sighed with relief.

'Say it again,' Rennie said. Rub it in, make the girl hear herself coughing, squealing. That keeps the tap flowing. Once they start keep up the momentum.

'Yes.'

The detective's face lost some of its hostility. He leaned forward on the table. 'What was his name? What did you call the man?'

She laughed. Too loud, hysterically.

'What are you trying to do to me? You trying to get me done in? Don't you know I can't . . . I couldn't anyway, I don't know it.'

'We want his name.' Cut the softness. The crisis of the interrogation. She has to go on from here. But the little bitch was sticking.

'I don't know his name. He was hardly there. He just came and went. It was only about six hours, in the middle of the night.'

'He was in your house. Slept . . . where did he sleep? . . . in the back room? . . . yes, we know that. He's on the run, and you don't know his name? Don't you know anything about him? Come on, Theresa, better than that.'

'I don't know. I don't *know*. I tell you I just don't . . . that's honest to God. He came in and went upstairs. He was gone before morning. We didn't see him again. We weren't told anything. There was no need for us to know his name, and when he came we didn't talk to him. That's the truth.'

Behind the girl, and out of her sight, the army officer put up his hand for Rennie to hold his questions a moment. His voice was mellow, more reasonable and understanding to the exhausted girl in the chair four feet in front of him.

'But your father, Theresa, he'd know that man's name. We don't want to bring him in. We know what happened that night, up in this man's room. We know all about that. We'd have to mention it. They'd

381

all know at home. How would your Dad stand up to all this, at his age? There's your brother. You must think of him as well. It's a long time he's been in the Maze . . . it would go well for him.'

'I don't know. I don't. You have to believe me. He never said his name. It's because he wasn't known that he came, don't you see that? It was safe that way. Dad doesn't know who he was. None of us did.'

'You know why we want him?' the detective clipped back in, swinging her attention back into the light of the room away from the peace she found in the shadows round the soldier.

'I know.'

'You're sure. You know what he did?'

'I know.'

'Did he tell you what he'd done?'

'No.'

'How did you know?'

'It was obvious. I've never seen a man like it. He had a hand like an old man's. It was all tied up. Like a claw. I can't say how he was . . . it was horrible.'

'What was his name? We want his name.'

'You'll get me killed for what I've said. So help me, Mother of Jesus, he never said his name.'

The inspector pulled a photokit picture of the man from a brown envelope, and flipped it across the table to the girl. She look at it briefly and nodded. Then she pushed it back to him.

'Take her down,' he said to the policewoman. The two went out of the interview room and away towards the station's cells. He went on, 'Bugger it. I thought we had her. I thought it was all going to flow. I have a horrible feeling the little bitch is telling the truth. We'll have another go at her in two or three hours or so, but I don't think she knows any more than she's said. It makes sense. A strange house, strange people. They're alerted someone is coming. They stick their noses into the box, and he's a bed for the night. Come on. Let's get a nap for a bit, and then one last bash at her.'

After they had gone Theresa sat a long time in her cell. She was alone now, as the policewoman had left her. In her own eyes the position was very clear. The army had pulled her into the station to question her about the man who had stayed at the house, the man she had gone to in the middle of the night. The man who had killed in London, was on the run, hunted, and in bed couldn't screw. They had pulled her in because they thought something she knew was the key to their finding the man, arresting him, charging him, sentencing him, and locking him away to become a folk hero in the ghetto, however many years he rotted

382

in a cell like this one. If she was not vital to their case then, as they said themselves, would they have sent the troops and the pigs to collect her? when he was arrested and charged and all Ballymurphy knew she had spent two days in the station being questioned . . . what would they say? Who would listen when she denied she had ever known his name? Who would walk away satisfied when she said she had given no information that in any way led to his capture? Who would believe her?

In the legend they'd weave her name would figure. She went back again over all that she could remember of what she had said to that bastard copper. The one who shouted in the front. Nothing, she'd said nothing that helped them. She'd looked at the photograph, but they knew that he was the man. All they needed was his name, and they didn't know that, and she hadn't told them. But how had they learned of the night? She had told girls, some, a few, not many. Would they betray her? Her friends in a chatter in the bog or over coffee break at the mill, would they tout to the military?

So who was going to believe her now?

She had heard what the IRA did to informers. All Ballymurphy knew. It was part of the folklore, not just there, but all over the city where the Provos operated. The vengeance of the young men against their own people who betrayed them was vicious and complete. There'd been a girl, left at a lamp-post. Tarred and feathered, they'd called it. Black paint and the feathers from a stinking old eiderdown. Hair cut off. She'd talked to a soldier. Not loved him – not cuddled or kissed him. Just talked to him, standing with him outside the barracks in the shadows. A boy who lived on the street they'd shot him through the kneecaps. He hadn't even been an informer. 'Thief' was the word on the card they hung round the gatepost where they left him. Provo justice. She hadn't known him, just knew his face. She remembered him on the hospital crutches when he was discharged. Ostracized and frightened. They killed girls, she knew that, and men whom they reckoned were informers. They shot them and dumped their bodies, sometimes rigged with wires and batteries. Making a stiff into a bomb hoax. Then they lay a long time in the ditch waiting for the bomb disposal man to work his way through his overnight list and come and declare the body harmless. And all the reporters and photographers were there.

It was very easy to imagine. A kangaroo court in a lock-up garage. Young men with dark glasses at a table. Hurricane lamp for illumination. Arms tied behind her. Shouting her innocence, and who listens? Pulled from the garage, and the sweet smelliness of the hood going over her head, and bundled into a car for the drive to the dumping ground and the single shot.

She wanted to scream, but there was no sound. She quivered on the bed, silhouetted against the light biscuit-coloured regulation blanket with the barred-over light bulb shining down on to her. If she had

383

screamed at that moment she would probably have lived. The policewoman would have come and sat with her till the next interrogation. But in her terror she had no voice.

She knew they would come again and talk to her, perhaps in another hour, perhaps longer. They had taken her watch and she had no sense of time now. When they came again they would ask her if she had ever seen the man on any other occasion. They would ask that over and over again, however many times she maintained she'd not set eyes on him since the night at her house. They would go on asking that question till they had their answer. They would know when she was lying, especially the quiet one behind her, the Englishman. She was tired, so tired, and slipping away. Could she keep up her denials? They would know and she would say. Before morning they would know about the dance, how the man had been there with his wife. They had taken him away. So why did they still need the name? Confusion and complicated argument swayed and tossed through the girl. They had taken him but they didn't know him. Perhaps they had not made the connection, and then what she might say in her exhaustion would weave the net round him. Betray him. Play the Judas. If she told the English officer it would be treachery to her own. The pigs would be out for him, pulling him into another police station, and she would wear the brand. Tout. Informer. Despised.

She looked round the brick and tile walls of the cell till she came to the heavy metal bar attached to the cell window that moved backwards and forwards a distance of two inches to allow ventilation to the cell. As it was winter and the window tight shut, the bar protruded from the fitting. She estimated that if she stood on her bed and stretched up she could reach the bar. Very deliberately she sat up on the bed. She moved her skirt up over her hips and began to peel down the thick warm tights she was wearing.

When the policewoman came to her cell to wake her for the next round of questions Theresa was very dead. Her mouth was open, and her eyes bulged as if they were trying to escape from the agony of the contortions. The nylon had buried itself deep into her throat, leaving a reddened collar rimming the brown tights. Her feet hung between the side of the bed and the wall, some seven inches above the floor.

Frost was wakened by the duty officer in intelligence headquarters without explanation. The message was simply that he should be in headquarters, and that 'all hell is about to break loose'. By the time he reached the building there was a report from the police station waiting for him. It covered only one sheet, was slashed to a minimum and was signed by his own man who had been present at the interrogation.

Theresa . . . was interrogated twice while in police custody in the presence of myself, Detective Inspector Howard Rennie, Detective Sergeant Herbert McDonald and Policewoman Gwen Myerscough. During questioning she identified the photokit picture of a man wanted in connection with the Danby killing as a man who had stayed in her father's house around three weeks ago. After the second session of questions she was returned to her cell. She was found later hanging in the cell, and was dead by the time medical attention reached her.

Signed,
Fairclough, Arthur. Capt., Intelligence Corps.

No marks for grammar, thought Frost, as he read it through.

'Where's Fairclough?' he snapped at the duty officer.

'On his way back here, sir.' It was a time for short direct answers when the big man was in this sort of mood.

'How long?'

'Should be here in about ten minutes, sir.' Then the sparks will come. Poor old Fairclough, thought the duty officer. Rather him than me.

The colonel went to the filing cabinet behind his desk and unlocked the top drawer, pulling it out on its metal runners and rummaging around for his dog-eared Ministry of Defence extension numbers book. It was a classified document and also listed the home telephone numbers of senior staff at the Ministry, military and civilian. He found the number of the Permanent Under Secretary that Davidson worked to, and dialled the Surrey area code and then the six digits.

'My name's Frost. Army intelligence in Lisburn. It's a hell of an hour but something has come up which you should be aware of. This is not a secure line, but I'll tell you what I can. We were passed some information from a section of yours about a girl. That was yesterday morning. She was brought in yesterday afternoon and questioned twice. You know what about. She knew the man we want, identified the picture, and said he'd stayed in her house within the last month. Found her about three-quarters of an hour ago hanging in her cell. Very dead. That's all I have. But I wouldn't care to be in your man's shoes when the opposition find out about all this. Thought you ought to know. Sounds a bit of a cock-up to me. Cheers.'

The Permanent Under Secretary had thanked him for the call and rung off.

Frost locked away his directory and pocketed the keys as Fairclough came in a fraction behind his knock.

'Let's have it, Arthur.'

'We got it out of her that the man stayed at her old man's place. She said they weren't given his name, and that she never knew his name. I think she was levelling with us. We left her for a couple of hours and when they came to get her out to bring her back up she'd strung herself up with her stockings. One thing should be straight, sir. She was treated quite correctly. She wasn't touched, and there was a policewoman present the whole time.'

'Right. Put it all down on paper, and soon. I want our version on this out fast. The information from London, on which we pulled her in. It seems to have stood up? It was real stuff?'

'No doubt about that. She'd been with him, all right. No doubt.'

Fairclough went out of the colonel's office to type his report. Frost was back on the phone to army public relations, another bedside telephone waking the early morning sleeper-in. He suggested that when the press enquiries started coming the men on the information desk should treat this very much as a police matter involving a girl picked up by the army for routine interrogation. He then called the head of Special Branch, first at his home where he was told he was already at Knock Road headquarters, and then at his office there. His own people had briefed him. With the slight diplomacy that he could command he made the same suggestion about press desk treatment as he had made to his own people.

'You want our people to take the can?' said the policeman.

'Inevitable, isn't it? Your police station, your interrogation. Don't see how we can end up with it.'

'Your bloody info set the thing up.'

'And good stuff it was too. There should be an enquiry at that damned station as to how it happened.'

'The Chief Constable in his wisdom had made that point. I think we should meet for a talk about the next move, if there is one, or this trail will be dead in no time.'

'I'll call you back,' said Frost, and rang off.

Half-cock operation and the poor sod, whatever his name is, puts it right under our noses. And we drop it. Poor devil. And on top of that we let the girl kill herself, which puts a noose round his neck and a bag over his head. We've done him well today. Desertion's the least he's justified in doing.

Harry heard about the girl, with the rest of the province, on the early morning radio news bulletin. It was second story after the European Economic Community all-night talks. The item was brief and without explanation.

'In Belfast a girl has died after being taken to a police station in the Falls Road area. She was found early this morning hanging in her cell and was dead by the time she reached hospital. Police named her as nineteen-year-old Theresa McCorrigan from Ballymurphy. An investigation is being carried out to find what happened. The Northern Ireland Civil Rights Association have issued a statement calling for a full and independent enquiry into the death. They allege two armoured cars and troops were used yesterday afternoon to arrest the dead girl from her home.'

Harry switched off the radio. He felt numb. No more playing about. No more kindergarten. These were the powers of the forces at work. A simple, ordinary, decent girl. Wants to get screwed by a bloke who cannot make it. Tells the girls in the loo about it, bit of a giggle, have a laugh together. Thirty hours later she's so terrified that she puts something round her neck and steps off. Throttled. A bit randy, and talks too much . . . and now she's dead. Harry remembered her. Across the far side of the club: in with the toughies and the big kids near the bar. Rolling a little. Too much gin, and not enough chips to soak it up.

He was the cause of the fear. He was responsible for the agony of the girl, before she slung whatever it was underneath her chin, and swung off into the void. Had she even been questioned by then, he wondered? Had she been able to say anything? Or was it all a lot of boasting?

They all listen to those bulletins, Harry reflected, every last one of them, catching up on the night's disasters, funding themselves with conversation for the day. Josephine would be no different. She would hear it, making her face up, having her breakfast, washing her smalls, but the transistor would be on somewhere in her home. She'd hear it, and she'd put it together. Was she that fast, that clever? Had to be, it was there on a plate, and what then?

Harry would have to wait to find out. She wasn't doing teas this week, had a different shift at work. He'd have to wait till the week-end and their next date. Have to sit it out, Harry boy, and sweat it out, and see how bright she is, and if she is bright what she's going to do about it.

He went down the staircase, across the hall, and out on to the street. He heard Mrs Duncan calling after him about his breakfast, and ignored her as he kept on going up the pavement and turned left towards Andersonstown. It took him a good hundred yards to swallow the emotion and regain control. As he walked he set out the position, making in his mind a chess board of his job. Pawns, that's where she rated, and pawns were expendable. Bishops and knights hurt more but they could also be lost. He and the man he was hunting were the queens of his game. The superstars, and second only to the kings, who were sacred and inviolate. If, as the queens were moved round the board, the pawns toppled over, then that was the nature of the game he and the man played. There was no time to lament the loss of pawns.

The old theme song. It had been different in Aden. There had been no involvement there. Nothing personal. A clear enemy, all that was on the board was black or white but definite. Now all the squares were grey, and the figures too. Even the two queens. There would be a problem for an outsider in picking one set of pieces from another.

11

Within four hours of the first broadcast of Theresa's death a soldier had been killed and heavy rioting had broken out in the Ballymurphy, Whiterock, Turf Lodge and New Barnsley estates.

The soldier had died when he was hit by a burst of shots fired at close range from a Thompson sub-machine-gun. He was last man in a patrol in Ballymurphy, and the gunman was apparently operating from the top floor of an empty council house. Some of the photographers who had gathered outside Theresa's house to get a picture of her parents and collect a holiday snapshot of the girl herself ran in the direction of the shooting. The fleetest managed a few hurried frames as the soldiers lifted the body of their colleague into the back of a Saracen.

In the Falls and Springfield Roads, groups of youths had hi-jacked buses, driven them into the middle of the street, and set fire to them. After that the army moved in. Armoured cars and Land-Rovers were pelted with milk bottles and rocks by the crowds who had gathered on the pavements. The army responded by driving at them, firing volleys of rubber bullets from mountings beside the driver. At one building site a barricade of rocks and oil drums had been assembled by the time the Saracens arrived. They'd crashed into the flimsy wall, fracturing it and scattering the drums crazily across the street, when a lone youth, at the controls of a brilliant-yellow excavator-digger machine, charged back defiantly. The troops, who had been advancing behind the cover of the armoured cars, fell back as the mechanical dinosaur accelerated down a slight hill towards the toad-like armoured cars. A few feet from the impact the youth jumped clear, leaving his runaway digger to collide head on with the Saracens. The armoured cars, acting in strange concert for things so large, edged it against a wall, where it spent its force revving in demented futility.

The stoning went on a long time. Unit commanders made it clear in their situation reports to Brigade headquarters at Lisburn that they detected a genuine anger among people. Those who over the last months had shown disinclination to abuse and pelt the military were back with a vengeance. There were rumours, they said, sweeping the Catholic areas, that the girl who had killed herself in the police station had been tortured to a degree that she could stand no more, and that she had then killed herself. Provisional sympathizers were on the move off the main roads where the army patrolled, and behind the crowds, giving instructions.

Theresa's parents were on lunchtime television, maintaining that their daughter had never belonged to any Republican organization. They described graphically how she had been taken from the lunch table the previous day. The army press desk received scores of calls, and stalled by saying this was a police matter, that the army were not involved, and pointing out that the girl had died in a police station. At police headquarters the harassed man on the receiving end told reporters that an investigation was still going on, and that the officers who were carrying out that investigation had not called back yet.

Both at army headquarters and amongst the Secretariat that administered the Secretary of State's office at Stormont Castle there was a realization that something rather better by way of explanation was going to have to come out before the day was over.

Faced with crises the Prime Minister had a well-tried formula to fall back upon. Identify the problem. Focus all attention on it. Solve it, and then leave it alone. When he finally concentrated on any one subject his aides found he had enormous capacity to wrestle with whatever political abscess was causing the pain. But they also found that once he thought the situation dealt with then his interest faded as fast as it had risen. Northern Ireland, comparatively quiet for months, was now on the shelved list. It teetered close to what a politician had once called the 'acceptable level of violence'. So the transcripts of the lunchtime news bulletins that were brought to him he resented as an intrusion. Violence back again. Streets closed. Casualties. The distasteful death of a young girl in the police cell. It was his habit to be direct.

From the back room office overlooking the Downing Street gardens, insipid in the November light, too many leaves left around, he called the army commander in Lisburn. Without any interruption he listened to a rundown of the morning's events, and made no comment either when the General launched into the background of the girl's arrest. He was told for the first time of the intelligence reports that had been fed in from London, of her questioning, what little she had admitted to knowing, and then of the finding of the body.

'Is this the first we've had from our chap?'

'First that I've heard of. Certainly we've received nothing else we could act on.'

'And it was good stuff, accurate. Something we hadn't had before, right?'

'The information was factual. It didn't take us as far as we'd hoped it might at first. I understand, though, that this is the first positive line we've had on to the fellow we're looking for.'

'Seems we set a bit of a trap, and it's rather missed its target. We'll have to decide whether our chap's had as much out of the pot as he's going to get. Problem is at what stage to get him out, whether we've compromised him already.' He was enjoying this, just like the way it was in the war. SOE and all that. The general cut across the line.

'It's not so easy, Prime Minister. It's faintly ridiculous, but I'm told his controllers don't know where he is, don't even know where to get in touch with him. You appreciate that this chap is not being controlled from here. Your instructions were interpreted very strictly on this point. It's London's responsibility. He calls in, they don't call him. But my advice would be that he stays. For the moment, at least. When you begin this sort of thing you stick with it. There's no out, in midstream, because it's a bit too hot. He'll have to finish it, or dry up completely.'

The Prime Minister came back, 'We've no reason to believe yet that he's been compromised? But it would be difficult, very difficult, if he were to be identified in this context.'

'Those were the sort of questions I assume had been answered before the instruction was given to launch this operation, Prime Minister.'

The sarcasm bit down the line.

The Prime Minister banged the phone down, then immediately flipped the console button on his desk and asked abruptly for the Secretary of State in Stormont Castle. After forty-one years in politics he could see the storm clouds gathering long before they were upon him. He knew the time had come to pull in some sail, and close down the hatches. The combination of an agent working to the Prime Minister's orders and a teenage girl hanging herself in a cell were better ingredients than most for a political scandal of major proportions. He must start to plan his defensive lines if the worst should happen and the chap they'd sent over should be discovered. That bloody General, not much time to run over there and his next appointment already confirmed. Entrenched, which was why he was so free with the advice. But all the same, in spite of his eminence, it must have hurt him to admit that this was the best information they'd had so far . . . and for all that they'd loused it up.

'He won't have liked it. One bright thing today,' and then he turned his attention to the search for a fail-safe system. Call the Under Secretary, the man in charge of this incredible non-communication set-up. In the event of catastrophe no statement till the civil servant had cleared it, and get that away to Lisburn. No acknowledgement for the agent, of course, if all goes wrong . . . deny all knowledge of the mission.

The Secretary of State was on the line. The Prime Minister wasted no time on pleasantries.

'I've been hearing about the troubles today, and the girl. Difficult situation. I thought we were weak at lunchtime, too defensive. We need to be a lot more positive. I've a suggestion to make. It's only a suggestion, mind you, and you should bounce it off your security people and see how they react. But I think you should say something like this – get a note of it and I'll read over what I've drafted. Along these lines, now. That the girl was a known associate of the man we are hunting in connection with the killing of Danby. That she was brought in quite correctly for questioning, and had been spoken to briefly before being left in the cells for the night. You must emphasize that she was not touched. Leak it that you're prepared to offer an independent postmortem from one of the hospitals, if you think that'll help. But my thought is to bring it back to Danby. By the by, his memorial service is at St Paul's this week. You'll be there, I hope. It'll all be in the public gaze again. We'll be all right if we play a bit bold, and attack. Worst thing we can do is to get on the defensive.'

The linking of the killing of the British Cabinet Minister with the death of the teenager in the Falls Road police station was splashed across the last edition of the *Belfast Telegraph*, and extensively reported on later television and radio news bulletins. The few men in the city who knew of Harry's existence were uncertain what effect the disclosure would have on the agent's work and safety. They acknowledged an immediate lifting of the pressure on their public relations set-up for more information concerning the circumstances of the death.

Harry was not the only man in the city with pawns on the chequer board.

The scrap merchant would take Harry on to his payroll. He'd obviously liked the look of him. He said he had a brother at sea, and asked Harry if he could start there and then. There was not a word about National Insurance cards or stamps, and twenty pounds a week was offered as pay. Harry was told he'd need to spend a month or so in the yard to see the way the place was run. There was to be expansion, more lorries. When they came, if it all worked out, there would be a driving job, and more money.

On his first morning Harry prowled round the mountains of burned and rusted cars. These were the stock in trade of the scrapman, heap upon heap of rough, angled metal.

Harry said to the neat dapper little man who was his new boss, 'Is this what the business is? Just cars? You've enough of them.'

'No problems with the supplies of that. You must have seen it, though you've been away. Terrible driving here. If you take the number of cars, they say, and work it out against a percentage of all the people that own them, and the number of accidents . . . then it's worse than anywhere else in the whole of England or Ireland. Maniacs they are here. The boyos down the road do the rest. We'll have a dozen wrecks in tomorrow morning. There'll be a double-decker, as well, like as not, but they're bastards to cut up.'

He smiled. Small, chirpy, long silk scarf round his neck, choker style, hat flat on his head. They're all the same, thought Harry, likeable rogues.

The scrap merchant went on, 'It's an ill wind. Scrap men, builders, glaziers . . . we're all minting it. Shouldn't say so, but that's how it is. The military dump the cars that are burned out, up there on the open ground. We send a truck up and pull them down here. Not formal, you know. Just an understanding. They want them off the street and know if they put them there I'll shift them. We'll have a few more today, and all.'

He looked up at Harry, with the brightness evacuating his eyes. 'People are powerful angry about this girl. You'll find that. They get killed in hundreds here. Most of the time it doesn't mean a damn, however big the procession. But this girl has got them steamed again.'

Harry said, 'It's a terrible thing pulling a girl like that out of her house.'

'Poor wee thing. She must have been awful scared of something to want to do that to herself. Mother of Jesus rest her. Still, no politics in this yard, and no troubles. Those are the rules of the yard, Harry boy. No politics, and that way we get some work done.'

He walked round with Harry and introduced him to the other men in the yard, six of them, and Harry shook hands formally. They greeted him with reserve, but without hostility. When his escort went back to the office to look to the papers Harry was free to browse. At one stage as he meandered amongst the cars he was within eight feet of a Russian-made rocket launcher. It was the RPG 7 variety, complete with two missiles and wrapped in sacking and cellophane, locked into the boot of a car. There were always people coming into the yard, and the cover was good. Access was easy at night. The launcher, sealed against the wet, had been placed there after the Provisional unit to whom it had been issued had found it inaccurate and unreliable. It had been abandoned until they could come across a more up-to-date manual of operation, preferably not written in Russian or Arabic.

As the little man said, no politics, no troubles. That first day Harry abided faithfully by it, taking his cue from the other men in the yard. Slowly does it here. The high column of black smoke from a blazing Ulster bus was ignored.

The rest of the first week that Harry was there was quite uneventful.

392

He was accepted to a limited degree as far as small talk went, and nothing more. His few attempts to broaden the conversations were gently ignored and not pressed on his part. The death of Theresa and the start of the job probably meant, thought Harry, the start of the next phase. No immediate pointers for him to follow, only the long-term penetration remaining. Three weeks. What idiot said it could be done in three weeks? Three months if he was lucky. And it relaxed him. Going up the road each day and having the work to occupy his mind would ease him. Better than sitting in that bloody guest house. Claustrophobia.

And each day he was watched by Seamus Duffryn's volunteers from Delrosa to the yard, and back again.

Downs was in the kitchen swilling his face in the sink, Monday morning wash, when his wife came in white-faced, shutting the door behind her on the noise of the playing children.

'It's just been on the radio, about you. About a girl. The girl who killed herself.'

'What do you mean? What about me?'

'This girl from the Murph, it says she was linked with the man that did the London killing.'

'It didn't actually mention me?'

'Said you was linked. Connected.'

'What was her name?'

'Theresa something. I didn't catch it.'

'Well, I don't know her.'

'It said she was being questioned about him because she was a known associate. That was another word they used – "associate". God rest her, poor kid. She was just a child.'

'Well, I don't know her, and that's the truth.'

'That's what they're saying on the radio . . . loud and clear . . . where any bloody ape can hear it.'

'Well, it's all balls, bullshit.'

'When you're shouting, you're always lying. Who was she? What was she to do with it?'

'I don't know her. I tell you, I just don't know her.'

'Billy, I'm not daft. You were in town a long time before you came back here. I haven't asked you where you were, before you came home. Who is she?'

'What did you say her name was?'

'Don't play the fool with me. You heard the first time.'

'If it's Ballymurphy, I stayed there one night. I came in darkness while the family was round the box. There was a girl there. Just a kid

393

who brought me some food in the room. I was away by five-thirty.'

'Just brought some food, did she?'

''Course she did . . . don't bloody question me . . . like the fucking Branch.'

'Just on the strength of that, brought her in and questioned her, just because she brought you some grub? Didn't get her father in – he's giving interviews. Just took her in.'

'Leave it,' he snapped at her. He wanted out. Escape.

'Just tell me who the little bitch was and what she meant to you.'

'She's just a child a minute ago, now she's a little bitch. She was nothing. Nothing. Must have blabbed her mouth off. Squealed, the little cow.'

'How did she know who you were?'

She shouted the last question at him. She would have taken it back once the words were out and had crumpled against him. The noise and aggression slewed out of him. Beseeching. Pleading. Don't make me answer. The found-out child and the hollow victory.

'I'm sorry,' she said. 'Just forget it.'

She turned away, back towards the door into the living-room where the children were fighting, and one was hungry, and another crying.

'I'll tell you what happened . . .' She shook her head, but he went on, ' – This is once and for all, never ask again. If I'd wanted her I couldn't have done anything about it. I was so screwed up. I was sort of cold, frozen, shivering. I couldn't do anything for her. She asked if it was me in London. I hit her. Across the face. She went back to her room. I've only seen her once since then. She was at the dance at the club on Saturday night. I suppose she saw me.'

He walked across to his wife and put his arms round her. The children still cried, and the pitch was growing. He pulled her head against his shoulder. There was no response, but she was pliant against him, totally passive.

Downs went on, 'That's when she must have talked. Going home after the dance. Must have said that she knew the man that had been in London. Then some rat, some bastard, squealed. A fucking spy, a tout. Right there at one of our dances, some bastard who'll shop you. That's what must have happened.'

'Forget it. We have to forget all these things. There's nothing left otherwise.'

He held her for a long time in the darkened kitchen, painfully lit by the inadequate bulb hanging without a shade from the wire flex. At first she wept silently and without dramatic effect, keeping her grief private, not using it as a weapon to cudgel him with. She controlled herself, and clung to him. Nothing would be different, nothing in his way of life would change.

'You'll go back?'

'When they want me.'

'You could end it all now. You've done your share.'

'There's no way that could happen.'

He needed her now, to recharge him. When the dose was enough he would go back into his own vicious, lonely world. Of which she was no part.

She was one of the crowd. The crowd of women who had so little influence over their men that it was pointless, indecent to beg them to stay off the streets. She was still luckier than most. Her man was still with her. The bus that came each Thursday lunchtime to the top end of Ypres Avenue was well enough known. It took the women to Long Kesh to talk to their men for half an hour, across a table.

That night Billy Downs opened his door to a treble knock. He was given an envelope by a youth and saw him scurry away into the darkness. His wife stayed in the kitchen, as she too had recognized the call sign of the fist against the door. She heard him switch the hall light on, pause a few moments and then the sound of tearing paper, over and over again.

He went into the front room and threw the half-inch squares of paper that had made up the single sheet of writing into the fire. The message was from Brigade. It was short and to the point. For the moment he was to stay at home. It was believed the girl had hanged herself before identifying him.

Davidson had had a bad week. He admitted it to the young man who was drafted in to share the office with him. The fiasco of the girl had started it off. The Permanent Under Secretary had been on as well, laying the smoke screen that would be used if the operation went aground. Davidson had tried to counter-attack with complaints about the original lodgings and then the foul-up over the girl, but had been rejected out of hand. There was silence from Harry himself for six days after his first call. Davidson and the aide sat in the office reading papers, making coffee, devouring take-away fish and chips, take-away Indian, take-away Chinese. The number that had been given to Harry was kept permanently free from all other calls.

When he did call, on the Saturday afternoon, the effect was electric. Davidson started up from his easy chair, pitching it sideways, tipping a coffee beaker off his desk as he lunged for the telephone. Papers drifted to the floor.

'Hello, is that four-seven-zero-four-six-eight-one?'

'Harry?'

'How are the family?'

'Very well. They liked the postcards, I'm told.'

Davidson was on his knees, his head level with the drawer where the recording apparatus was kept. He pulled up the lead and plugged it into the telephone's body. The cassette was rolling.

'Anything for us?'

'Nothing, old chap. No, I'm just digging in a bit. I think it may go all quiet for a few days, so I'm settling into some sort of a routine.'

'We're worried about you in the wake of that bloody girl. We're wondering whether we should pull you out.'

'No way. Just getting acclimatized.'

'I think we all feel at this end that you did very well last week-end. But we want some way to get in touch with you. This may suit you, but it's ridiculous for us. Quite daft. We're sitting here like a row of virgins waiting for you to call us up.'

'It's the way I'm happiest. I've been bitten, remember. On the first house. It's going to be a touch trickier getting something further out of this, and this is the way I want it to be. Bit silly, you might say, but that's the way it is.'

Davidson backed down and switched the subject.

'Are they sniffing round you at all?'

'I don't think so. No particular sign of it yet, but I don't know. More of a problem is that I don't see where the next break is going to come from – what direction. I was very lucky last time, and look where the thing got us. It can't be on a plate like that again.'

'You're not following anything particular at the moment, then?'

'No, just entrenching. Getting ready for the siege.'

'Perhaps it is time you should come out. Like this week-end. I don't want you hanging about wasting time. Look, Harry, we know it's bloody difficult in there, but you've given the military and security people a lead that they ought to be able to do something about . . . Come out now. Get yourself up to Aldergrove and get the hell out . . .'

The phone clicked dead in his hand, before the dialling tone purred back at him. Despairingly he flicked the receiver buttons. The call was over.

Bugger. Played it wrong. Unsettled him. Just when he needs lifting. Silly, bloody fool. Should have made it an order, not a suggestion, or not mentioned it at all. The military should be following this now. The girl must have left a trail a mile wide.

Davidson could see through his uncurtained window that it was now dark outside. He thought of Harry walking back up the Falls to his digs. Past the shadows and the wreckage and the crowds and the troops, the legacy of the spluttering week-long street fighting he had been the spark to. Keep your head down, Harry boy.

12

It was acknowledged at the highest levels of the IRA's Belfast Brigade command that the campaign was at a crucial stage, the impetus of the struggle consistently harder to maintain. The leadership detected a weariness among the people on whom they relied so greatly for the success of their attacks. But the differences between the people at street level and their protectors, as the Provisionals saw themselves, were growing. Money was harder to collect for the families of those imprisoned, doors generally left unlocked for the gunman or blast bombers to escape through were now bolted, and the confidential phones at police headquarters where the informers left their anonymous messages were kept busy with tip-offs that could only come from the Catholic heartland.

As the pressure grew to a near intolerable degree on the shoulders of the Provisionals' leadership so it was understood that the days of gallantry and chivalry were gone, too. Once a British officer had stood in the turret of his armoured car, stiffly upright with his right arm in the salute position as the coffin of an IRA man was carried past him, draped in the tricolour. Once British officers after an evening's celebration and in their slacks and sports jackets found they had wandered into the Bogside, were captured and returned safely to their embarrassed seniors.

That was all over now. As the IRA fought back against the growing strength and experience of the security forces arrayed against them, so the attacks became more vicious and more calculated to shock.

It was the Brigade commander who made the reluctant decision to call Billy Downs out from Ardoyne and from inactivity. It was accepted that he was of greatest value when used sparingly, but within seventy-two hours of the earlier instruction he was given new orders.

The subject of the Brigade's death sentence was an RUC inspector. A priority was put on his death, and it was reckoned important enough to risk the exposure of one of the movement's top cards.

The policeman they wanted shot was Howard Rennie, CID, transferred to Special Branch. Their dossier reported him as coming from the hills of County Antrim, near the coast. He had been unknown in

Belfast till recently when word had begun to seep into the information system from the holding centres and prisons about a detective with sufficient ability as an interrogator that he was directly responsible for the failure of several suspects to keep their mouths shut.

It had taken a long time once they'd started for the Brigade intelligence section to identify Rennie, locate his headquarters at the holding centre in Castlereagh barracks, and put a plan into operation against him. The final decision to eliminate him was taken after a company intelligence officer reported on the list of police cars' number plates and models that had left the police station after the death of the girl in her cell. One was similar in model and colour to that driven by the detective. His association with the events of that night was sufficient to put him several places up the list of priorities, and would win the movement nothing but support when he was killed.

Billy Downs was given a dossier to read but not to keep. The caller who came to his house late, after the wife and the children had gone upstairs, was to bring it away with him when Downs had done his reading. His wife came down the stairs to see who the visitor was, paled at the sight of the long-haired youth in jeans and heavy quilted anorak coat who returned her stare and then turned away without speaking to her. She went into the kitchen, aware that the front room was no place for her. When she moved upstairs again she could hear the voices, talking hurriedly, hushed and with urgency.

Downs was shown a picture of Rennie. Taken five years ago, and one of a group. It had been gained from the copious files of a photographer in the small town where Rennie had then been stationed. It was a fair bet they'd find such a picture when they went into the photographer's shop with guns in their hands, and the competence of the filing system saw them through. The picture was of a group of policemen all celebrating their promotion to sergeant. The picture would not help Downs that much, as it suffered seriously in the enlargement, but it gave him an idea of the build, the hair and the shape of the face of the policeman that he had been ordered to kill. The car the detective would be using was a Triumph 2000 and bottle-green, but the file on Rennie carried a list of a minimum of eight number plates that he might use. He read that Rennie lived in a small, detached house in Dunmurry, down a cul-de-sac. The house right at the bottom of the 'U' of the close. Difficult for surveillance and for ambush. The dossier said he used a door direct into the garage. Wife opened the garage doors from the inside and he drove straight out in the mornings. They would be open when Rennie came home. The policeman would be armed.

The problems of the ambush were made clear to him.

'It'll not be easy to get the whore. None of them is easy. They often go together – lift each other to work. They'll be using different routes and all. They've guns, too. One of them would get a shot in if you try it then. They know how to use them. Rennie's a trained shot. And clever – won't be easy to nail the bastard. No chance of sitting down his road: all those women flappin' their curtains from not enough to do, they'd see you and be on the phone straight off. And you don't have time to set it up, next week, next month, when you like. They want it, and fast. Brigade's order. It's a special one, and they want you for it.'

His unpolished ankle-length boots were beside the chair. Jeans crumpled and not washed nor ironed since he came home. Shirt was off, white and dirty, collar frayed. The fire was small now, needing help to stay alive. He had put the light out when the courier had gone, so that he could concentrate the better on the policeman, Rennie, that they had put him against. He had memorized much of the detail of the file and now he savoured the problem they had set him, seeking out a plan of action. Like a mathematician attempting the answer to a complex formula, he stayed in the chair thinking on the method and the manner by which Rennie would be assassinated. He was surprised to have been called out, but the implication was clear. This was a vital and important operation, he was a vital and important operator.

His wife stayed upstairs, aware that this was no time for her to go down to the front room and try to break the spell her husband was weaving for himself as his mind took up attack tactics and the weapons he would use.

She drifted into an uneasy sleep that night, tossing through an immediate nightmare. She saw her man cut down by a burst of bullets, caricatures of grotesque soldiers standing over him. Life throbbing away in the gutter. Feet pushing and manœuvring him. When she reached across to see if he had come upstairs yet she found only the emptiness of the sheets beside her. Back in her half-sleep she witnessed over and over again the firing of those perpetual rifles, and the agony and throes of her man. And then exhaustion and fear took her beyond the stage of the dreams and left her in deep sleep till the morning.

That was how he found her when he came upstairs with a plan maturing well in his mind. He was impressing himself with the cleverness of what he would do. Excited and pleased with his solution to a technical problem.

He lay on his back, elbows outstretched on the pillow, his hands under his neck, going back over his plan, testing each point in it for flaws. He was tired but elated enough to find none as he checked over each aspect of the killing, each aspect bar the final one – the killing itself. He shut that out of his mind. The actuality of the killing, the pulling and squeezing of the trigger.

He seldom tried to work out the values of the killings he performed to the movement that he served. Tasks and projects set for him by his superiors. Others determined the morality. Others had the hatred. Others turned his work into victories. He did as he was told, expertise his trade mark. The soldier in his army.

There were some in the movement, men that he had met or, in other cases, heard of, who were said to relish the physical side of the killing. There were stories that they tortured the demented minds of their victims after the sentence of the kangaroo court. Demonstrate the firearm. Go right up to the moment of shooting and then fire with an empty gun. There were beatings-up, knifings and cigarette burnings. That was no part of Billy Downs. His killing was different. Clever. Organized. Against major targets. His feelings were known and respected by the top men. The ritual was for others. He belonged in the field. His mind reverted to the reconstruction and progress of the murder of Rennie, his plans racing far ahead. It was close to dawn before he slept.

In a room above a chip shop in Monaghan town, just over the border into the Republic, the Army Council met for the first time in a fortnight. Eight men round a table. Businesslike, with their pencils and notebooks round them. There was much talk of what they had seen on the earlier television news bulletins, of the film taken on the steps of St Paul's of the arrival of government ministers and Cabinet members to the memorial service for Henry Danby.

'Hardly what you'd call security. Sod-all protection.'

'They all had 'tecs with them, but by the look of it only one each. Not the big man, though. He had a couple. Little film stars, you get to know them.'

'Right open, if we wanted to put a man in again.'

'Wide open. What those bloody papermen call a wall of steel. Nothing.'

'It would only be a repetition. Took a lot of planning last time. Manpower. What do we achieve? There was good reason for that bastard Danby, but another man, what for?'

'It did a fair bit for us when we got Danby. Keeping our man on the loose, that's not done us bad.'

'There was no sympathy for Danby. There's no one else we can get who is in that crowd where we would get the same reaction. The bastard was hated. Even the Prods loathed him.'

'In London there's no way they can guard the politicos, no way at all. They have to be out and be seen to be about. They can't lock themselves away. You can do that from the White House, but not from Downing Street.'

'Let's have some talk about what we'd get from hitting them again in London.' It was the Chief of Staff who spoke, terminating the knock-about round the table.

He made only rare incursions into the talk, preferring to let it ripple round him while he weighed the ideas before coming down in support of any one in particular. He was a hard man with few feelings that did not involve the end-product. Like some cost-effectiveness expert or a time-and-motion superman, he demanded value for effort. His training in military tactics had been thorough, and he had risen to corporal in the parachute regiment of the British army. He was in his mid-thirties now and had seen active service in Aden and Borneo. He'd bought himself out at the start of the troubles and set up briefly as a painter and decorator, before going underground. When he had been voted into the number one position in the Provisionals by his colleagues it was because they knew they could guarantee he would pursue a tough, ruthless campaign. Those who believed in the continuation of the war of attrition on British public opinion had felt threatened by those they thought might compromise. The new commander was their safeguard. He was no strategist, but had learned enough of tactics on the streets of the Lower Falls where he came from. He had sanctioned the killing of Danby, and was well pleased with the dividends.

The quartermaster took it up. 'It's the trouble with all spectaculars. You launch them, and they succeed, and where do you go from there? Only upwards.'

The older man in the group, a veteran of '56, who lived now in Cork, said, 'It stirs the pot well and truly. How many bombs, how many "another soldier tonight" add up to a British Cabinet Minister?'

The quartermaster across the table was not impressed. 'But what's the reaction? If we did it again, they'd tear the bloody place apart. We'd not survive it. They'd be all over us. Down here as much as in the North.'

'That's what we have to weigh. What would happen to the whole structure? They'd go mad, knock bloody shit out of us.' The speaker was from Derry. Young, from the Creggan estate. Interned once and then released in an amnesty to mark the arrival of a new Secretary of State. He had been in the Republic's prisons as well, and now lived on the run as much in County Donegal as in the maze of streets in the Creggan housing estate. 'Our need at this moment is not to go killing Cabinet Ministers from Westminster, but winning back what we lost at Motorman when the army came into Bogside and Creggan. We have to play on the tiredness of those people across the water. There's no stomach there for this war. They're soft there, no guts. They'll get weary of hearing of another soldier, another policeman, another bomb, another tout. It's the repetition that hurts them. Not another big killing. All that does is get them going. It affronts their bloody dignity. Unites them against us. We have to bore them.'

401

'The bigger man you get the better.' It was a Belfast man. He was of the new school, and had come a long way since Long Kesh opened. He had pitiless eyes, wide apart above his ferret nose, and a thin, bloodless mouth. He chain-smoked, lighting cigarettes one after another from the butt of the one he was discarding. 'The big man himself wouldn't hurt. They never believe we mean it over there. Somehow the fucking Micks won't actually get round to it, they say. Get the old bugger, himself, that would sort them.'

That quietened it. Then the Chief of Staff chipped in, cutting through the indecision of the meeting as he brought it to heel and away from the abstract.

'We'll think about it. It has attractions. Big attractions. Total war, that's what it would mean. Davie and Sean, you'll work on it for a bit. Have something for us in a fortnight with something concrete. I don't want it done hasty . . . something in a bit of detail. Right?'

They moved on to other business.

The process of arrests went on with seeming inevitability, with frequent reunions in the Crumlin and Long Kesh. The Provisionals' intelligence officer who should have seen the report of that conversation between the army Brigadier and the policeman overheard at their hotel lunch was taken into custody before the message reached him. When there was an arrest those still in the field shifted round their weapons, explosives, equipment and files, lest their former colleague should crack under interrogation and reveal the hiding places.

That message, closely written on two sheets of notepaper, remained in a safe house in the communication chain while the Third Battalion worked round to an appointment for the vacant position. The clogging in the system lasted more than a week, and when the new man came to sort through the backlog he had a table covered with reports and documents to wade through. He was into his second day before he got to the paper written by the waiter.

He was sharp enough to sense immediately the importance of what was in front of him. He read it carefully.

The man with the thin moustache looked like an army man, and from the kitchens I could see the big Ford out in the car park with the uniformed escort sitting there in the front. The other one was talking when the music stopped. He was a policeman, I think. That's when I heard him say, 'Special operator on the ground without telling.' He must have realized I was standing there, and he just stopped and didn't say anything else until I was right away from him. He looked very bothered . . .

402

That was the guts of the message. The intelligence officer had read it once, gone slightly beyond and then rapidly coursed his eyes back over it. He could imagine the situation. Military and police, not taken in on the act, and feeding their bloody faces, weeping on each other's shoulders, stuffing the food in far away from the 'Careless Talk Costs Lives' bit. It was the sort of place you'd expect to hear a major indiscretion uttered, when they couldn't keep their big mouths shut. That was why the waiter had been introduced on to the staff of the hotel.

Undercover men working for the army or D16 were the particular dislike of the Provisionals. They believed there was a much greater secret intelligence and surveillance operation against them than in fact existed. Their traditional hatred was for the plain-clothes army squads who cruised at night round the back streets of the ghettos in unmarked cars, looking for the top men in the movement. But this had a more important ring about it to the intelligence officer than squaddies out in jeans and sweaters and armed. If a Brigadier and top copper were not in on the act, and thought they ought to have been, it meant first it was top secret, and second that they considered it important enough for them to have been briefed. Something of critical value to those English swine, so sensitive that top-ranking men had been left out in the cold.

Farther down the waiter's report was a paragraph explaining that the tone of the exchange across the lunch table had been critical.

The officer wrote a three-line covering note on a separate piece of paper, clipped it to the original report and sealed it in a plain brown envelope. A courier would take it that night to the next man up the chain, someone on the Brigade staff.

Twenty-two hours later he met Seamus Duffryn for the first time. Duffryn had originally intended that his message should go by hand, but the combination of the new appointment and the nagging worry about this man, Harry McEvoy, had led to the direct meeting, risky as it was.

They met in a pub in the heart of the broken-up and ravaged triangle of the Lower Falls. Taking their pints of beer with them, Duffryn led the other to a corner table. With their heads huddled together he spoke of the stranger that had come to the guest house farther up the Falls. Looking for work. Said he'd been away a long time. Had this strange accent that was noted by those when he first came, but which his latest reports said was not so pronounced. When Duffryn mentioned the accent, the Battalion officer looked at him intrigued, and the junior man explained the apparent lapses in speech. Duffryn said that his men who followed McEvoy and heard him talk in the pubs, said the oddness about the speech was something very much of the past. Ironed out, muttered Duffryn. He had come to the end of his patience on the matter and wanted a decision. Either the man should be cleared or there would have to be authorization for more surveillance with all its problems of manpower. Duffryn himself had personally tried to observe McEvoy by spending three successive evenings in the pub on the corner where it was reported that the stranger came to drink, but he'd stayed alone these evenings, and the man he wanted to see had not shown himself.

'I'm not that sure what it means,' said the man from Battalion. 'You never know with these things. It could mean he's a man put in to infiltrate us. It could be nothing. It counts against the bugger that his accent is improving. Would do, wouldn't it? With each day he spends here, it would improve. There's something else we have that indicated a few days ago that they could have put an undercover man in. He'll be a big bloody fish if it's right. He'll be a bloody whale if what we think about him is right.'

He hesitated as to whether he should bring the young Duffryn further into the web of reports and information that was forming in his mind. He dismissed it. The golden rule of the movement was 'need to know'. Duffryn needed to know no more than he already knew.

'That's enough. From now on – and this is important – and I want it bloody well obeyed to the letter – no more following this McEvoy. Let him ride on his own a bit. I don't want the bugger flushed before we're ready for him. We'll just leave him alone for a bit, and if we have to we'll move when it's all nice and relaxed. I want it taken gently, very gently, you see? Just log him in and out of the guest house, and that's the lot.'

Harry had not been aware of the watchers before they were called off, and therefore had no idea that he had thrown off a tail when he had gone through the city centre shopping crowds to a telephone kiosk to call Davidson. On the Friday night when he had been in the city nearly three weeks he came down past the cemetery towards Broadway with his wage packet in his hip pocket, and the knowledge that there seemed to be no sign of suspicion towards him from the men he was working with. He had a hired car booked for Saturday for his date with Josephine.

There was a Sinn Fein meeting that Friday night up on the junction of the Falls, and after he'd had his tea Harry wandered up to listen to the speeches. There were some familiar faces on the lorry that was being used as a speaker's platform. The oratory was simple and effective and the message brutally clear. Amongst the committed there would be no easing in the struggle, the war would go on till the British were gone. The crimes of the British army, the Stormont administration and the Free State government were catalogued, but the crowd of three or four hundred seemed lukewarm to it all. They'd been listening to this stuff for five years or so now, Harry reflected. He'd be a bloody good orator to give them something new at this stage. The army stayed away and after hearing the first four speeches Harry left. He'd clapped with the rest, and cheered by consensus, but no one spoke to him. He was just there, ignored. God, how do you get into this bloody mob? How does it all happen like Davidson said, in that magic three weeks? It'll take months, till the face is known and the background and every other bloody thing.

A long haul. He wouldn't call Davidson this week-end. Nothing to say. Those buggers had sent him here, they could sit and stew for a bit and wonder what was going on. The trail of the man he sought was well chilled now. It would be very slow, and his own survival would take some thinking about. But there'd be no coming out, no trotting up to Aldergrove. One-way to Heathrow please, my nerve's gone and so has that of the controller, thank you very much.

No way. You stay in for the whole way, Harry boy.

13

She was waiting at the lights at the junction of Grosvenor and the Falls when he pulled up in the hired Cortina. Tall in the brittle sunlight, her hair blown round her face, and shivering in the mock sheepskin coat over the sweaters and jeans he'd told her to wear.

'Come on, get that door open. I'm frozen out here.' A bit distant, perhaps too off-hand, but not the clamouring alarm bells Harry had steeled himself to face.

He was laughing as he reached across the passenger seat and unlocked the near-side door, and pushed the handle across to open it. She came inside, a bundle of coat and cold air, stealing the warmth he had built up since he had collected the car.

'All right then, sunshine?' He leaned over to kiss her, but she turned her head away presenting her cheek for what he hadn't intended to be the brotherly peck they ended up with.

'Enough of that. Where are we going?' she said. She straightened her back in the seat, and began to fasten her seat belt.

'You said you wanted some country. Somewhere we can stretch our-selves a bit, walk around. Where do you suggest?'

'Let's off to the Sperrins. About an hour down the Derry and Dun-given road. That's wild country, real Ulster stock. You've seen the slogans on the Proddy walls before the troubles started, "We will not

exchange the blue skies of Ulster for the grey mists of the Republic,"
well, the blue skies are over the Sperrins.'

'Well, if it's okay for the Prods it'll do for us second-class Micks.'

'I was brought up down there. My Dad had a bit of land. Not much
but enough for a living. It's a hard living down there. It's yourself and
that's all, to do the work. We cut peat down there and had some cows
and sheep. Stupid bloody creatures. We were always losing the little
buggers. There was no mains, no gas, no electricity, no water when I
was born. He's dead, now, the old man, and my Mam came to Belfast.'

'Were you involved at all, with the politics? Was the old man?'

'Not at all. Not a flicker. Most of the farmers round were Prods but
that didn't make much difference. The market was "non-sectarian", as
they'd say these days. Different schools, different dances. I couldn't
walk out with Prod boys when I lived at home. But that's years back
now. There was no politics down there, just hard work.'

He drove slowly out of town, on to the M2 motorway which runs
within minutes into the open countryside, leaving the city with its smoke
and its gibbet-like cranes and its grey slate roofs away behind the Black
Mountain that dominates the south of the city. It was the first time
Harry had seen the fields and hedgerows, farms and cottages since he
came in on the airport bus. The starkness of the contrast staggered him.
It was near-impossible to believe that this was a country ravaged by what
some called civil war. For a moment the impressions were tarnished by
the rock-filled petrol drums outside a pub, but that was a flash of the
eye, near-subliminal, and then was gone in favour of the hills and the
green of well-grassed winter fields.

Josephine slept in her seat, head back against the column dividing
the front and rear doors, her seat belt like some pompous decoration
strapped across her breasts. Harry let his eyes stray from the endless,
empty road to her.

'Just follow the Derry road, and wake me up when we get to the top
of the Glenshane,' she'd said.

The road slipped economically through the countryside till Harry
reached Toome, where the Bann came through, high and flooded from
the winter rain, forcing its strength against the medieval eel-trapping
cages that were the lifeblood of the town. He slowed almost to a halt
as he gingerly took the car over the ramps set across the road in front
of the small, whitewashed police station. Yards of bright corrugated-iron
sheeting and mounds of sandbags surrounded the buildings. It looked
deserted. No bulbs showing at the top. After Toome he began to pick
up speed. The road was straight again, and there was no other traffic.
In front was the long climb up to Glenshane in the heart of the Sperrins.
The rain gathered on the windscreen, horizontal when it came but light
and occasional.

As he came to the hills that divided the Protestant farmlands of the

Ulster hinterland from Catholic Dungiven and Derry, Harry spotted a damp, out-of-season picnic site on his right, and pulled into the car park. There was a sign marking the Pass and its altitude, a thousand feet above sea level. He stopped and shook Josephine's shoulder.

'Not so much of the blue skies and the promised land here. Looks more like it's going to tip down,' he said.

'Doesn't matter. Come on, Mr McEvoy, we're going to do some walking and talking. Walking first. Up there.' She pointed far out to the right of the road where the hill's squat summit merged towards the dark clouds.

'It's a hell of a way,' he said, pulling on a heavy anorak.

'Won't do you any harm. Come on.'

She led the way across the road and then up the bank and through the gap in the cheap wire fence where a succession of walkers had made a way.

Farther on there was a path of sorts to the top of the hill, made by the peat cutters at first and then carried on by the rabbits and the sheep. The wind picked up from the open ground and surged against them. Josephine had pushed her arm through the crook of his elbow and walked in step half a pace behind him, using him part as shelter and part as battering ram as they forced their way forward into the near gale. High above, a buzzard with an awesome dignity allowed itself to be carried on the thrusts and flows of the currents. Its huge wings moved with only a minimum of effort, holding position one hundred and fifty feet or so above the tiny runs fashioned by the creatures the bird lived off. The wind stung across Harry's face, pulling his hair back over his ears and slashing at his nose and eyes.

'I haven't been anywhere in a wind like this in years,' he shouted across the few inches that separated them.

No reply. Just the wind hitting and buffeting against him.

'I said I haven't been in a wind like this in years. It's marvellous.'

She rose on her toes, so that her mouth was in under his ear.

'Wasn't it like this at sea, sometimes? Weren't there any gales and things all those years you were at sea?'

The cutting edge of it chopped into him. Retreat. Back out.

'That was different. It's always different, sea wind, not like this.'

Poor. Stupid. Not good and not convincing. He felt the tightening deep in his balls as he went on against the wind. Up a cul-de-sac and got cornered. Slackness. The elementary error. He flashed a look down and behind to where her head nestled into his coat. He contorted his head to look into her eyes, and saw what he expected. Quizzical, half-confused, half-amused: she had spotted it. The inconsistency that he'd known the moment he'd uttered it. Phrase by phrase he went over it in his mind, seeking to undo the mistake, and evaluate its damage. The second time he'd said it, that was when she would have been sure. The

407

first time, not certain. The second time, certain. He'd semaphored it then.

There were no more words as they went on to the summit. The low jigsaw of clouds scudded above them as they clung together against the power of the gale. In spite of the heaviness of the cloud there was a clarity to the light of the day. The horizon was huge. Mountains to the north and south of them, the road leading back into the civilization of the hill farms to east and west.

A few yards beyond the cairn of stones that marked the hill top the rain running down over the years had sliced out a gully. They slid down into it, pushing against the sandy earth till they were at last sheltered. For a long time she stayed buried in his coat, pressed against his chest with only her black tossed hair for him to see. He felt the warmth from her seeping through the layers of clothes. For Harry it was a moment of beauty and isolation and complete tenderness with the girl. She broke it suddenly, crudely and fast.

'You slipped up a bit there, Harry boy. Didn't you? Not what I'd have expected from you.'

Her face was still away from his. He couldn't see into her eyes. It hit home. He said nothing.

'A bit mixed up then, weren't you, Harry? Your story was, anyway. Merchant seaman who was never in a storm like they have in the Sperrins? A bit of a cock-up, Harry.'

She'd relaxed in her voice now. Easy. In her stride. Matter-of-fact.

'Harry,' and she twisted under him to turn into his face and look at him. Big eyes, mocking and piercing at the same time, and staring at him. 'I'm saying you made something of a slip-up there. Not the first that you've had. But a good old balls-up, a right big one. Harry, it's a great bloody lie you're living. Right?'

He willed her now to let it go. Don't take it to the brink where explanation or action is necessary. Leave the loophole for the shrug and the open door.

In the town his inclination would have been to kill her, close his fingers on that white, long throat, remove the threat that jeopardized his operation. But on the mountain it was different. On the moorland of the upper hills, still crouched in the gouged-out hollow, and the wind singing its high note above and around them, it seemed to Harry ridiculous and time-wasting to deny what she had said. It wasn't in his orders to go strangling girls. That was logical as the solution, but not here. Out of context.

'It's a bad place this for strangers these days, Harry. It would be rather worse if the boyos find your story isn't quite so pat as it should be. If they find you're rather more of a handful than they took you for, then it could be a very bad place. We're not all stupid here, you know. I'm not stupid. It didn't take the world to put eight and eight together after Saturday night, or ten and ten, or whatever you thought too much for an "eejit" Mick girl who's an easy lay. It wasn't much I said to you. Just a little bit of chat. But there's half the British army round the wee girl's house for Sunday lunch. What did they find to talk to her about? God knows. Do you know, Harry? It was enough for the poor wee bitch to hang herself, God rest her. I mean, you weren't exactly covering your tracks, were you, Harry?'

The eyes that drove into him were still bright and relaxed, looking for his reaction. As he listened she grew in strength and boldness. She would close for the kill. She would make the point. Sure of her ground, she began to goad him.

'There had to be something odd about you. Obvious. No family. But you come right back into the centre of Belfast. But you've no friends. No one knows you. People might have gone to a quiet place on the outskirts if they just wanted to come back and work. You've not come to fight, not for the Provos. They don't go to war from a guest house. The voice worried me, till Theresa died. I thought about it and worked it out then. The accent. It's good now. Very polished. You're quite Belfast, but you didn't use to be. So I don't reckon your chances, Harry, not when the Provos get a hold of you. There is some who can talk their way out of it, but I don't reckon you've a chance. Not unless you run.'

Harry knew he should kill her. He looked fascinated at the soft skin, and the delicate line that searched down on either side of the little mound in her throat, saw the suspicion of a vein beneath the gentle surface. But there was no fear there, no terror in her face, no expectation of death.

They'd chosen Harry as a hard man, as a professional, able to do what was necessary, to go to the limits for his own survival. He could kill a man either in heat or from cold logic, and if the man's eyes betrayed his fear that would make it easier, remove the complications.

The endless strands of black hair were playing across her face, taken past her eyes, encircling her mouth . . . and the warmth of her body close to him . . .

There had not been women who had to die in Aden. He was now in an area beyond his experience. Harry had heard it said once that to kill in close combat you had to act instinctively, there were no second chances, the will to cause death evaporates quickly, and does not come again except to the psychopath.

His hands were numbed and useless in the big gloves, and the moment had passed. He looked out on to the moorlands where the spears of sunlight played down from the cloud gaps. He had hesitated, and that would be enough. The buzzard still hovered high above him, and she was still talking.

She was tall, but not strong, he thought. She wouldn't be able to fight him off. He could kill her now. While she yapped on. It would be a long time before they found her. Could be the spring. She'd struggle a bit but she had no chance. But she knew he wouldn't. He could see that. There was no fear in her. The moment had gone earlier when he might have put his hands to her. It was gone now.

'If I went to the bookies more often,' she went on, 'I'd say you were a real slow horse. I'd say not to put any money on you reaching the finish. I mean it, Harry. I'm not just trying to frighten you, or anything daft. That's the way it is. If I was in your shoes I'd be carrying spare knickers in my pocket. Well, don't just sit there. Say something, Harry.'

'There's not much to say, is there? What would you like to hear me say? If you go off to Portadown and see people there, they'll tell you who I am. Yes, I've been away a long time. That's why the accent was strange. I'm acclimatized. The girl – I can't explain that. How could I? I've no idea about it.'

He could not have explained why he had gone back on the resolution he'd made so few minutes earlier not to get involved in a charade of deception. There was no conviction, no belief, and he communicated it to the girl.

'Balls,' she said. She smiled at him and turned away to put her head back into the roughness of his coat. 'That won't do, Harry. I don't believe you, neither do you. You're not a good enough liar. Whoever recruited you, and for whatever, did a poor job there.'

'Let it go, then. Forget it, drop it.' Pathetic. Was that all he had to say to the girl?

'Who are you, Harry? What did you come here for? When you touted on young Theresa it was after I mentioned the man that did the killing in London. Is that why you're here? You're not just run-of-the-mill intelligence. There's more than that, I hope. I'd want to think my feller was a wee bit special. What's the handle? The Man who Tracked the Most Wanted Man in Britain?' She snorted with amusement.

'But seriously, Harry, is that what you are? A little bit special? The Danby killing?'

She gave him time now. He was not ready. As an afterthought she said, 'You don't have to worry, you know. I won't split on you or anything like that. It's the national characteristic . . . the Ulster Catholics, we don't inform. But they don't take well to spies here, Harry. If they find you, God help you. And you'll need him.'

Harry started to move.

'There's not very much to say. What do you expect me to say? Confess, dramatic revelations? Shout you down? Walk away and leave you? Strangle you? What the hell do you want me to say?'

He got up out of the ditch and moved back towards the summit of the hill, where the wind took him and fought him, coming in crude rushes that caused him to hesitate and sometimes give ground. The rain had intensified while they had been in the ditch and now it lashed across his body. He looked only at his feet, head hunched forward, with his anorak hood up as he stumbled across the gorse and the heather, slipping and falling because he would not give the attention to the ground in front of him. He'd gone a hundred and fifty yards from her when she caught him and thrust her arm into his. They went together down the hill to the car hurrying along the worn-out shape of the path.

They ran the last few yards to the car. She stood shaking by the passenger door as he looked for the keys. It was raining hard now and once they were inside he switched on the heaters. The water ran down the windows in wide streams, and they were as cocooned and private as they had been on the hill.

'What are you going to do if you find him?' she said.

'Are we serious now, or sparring still?'

'Serious now. Really serious. What will you do?'

'I'll kill him. Take him out. He's not for capturing. We pretend he is, and they mount the thing on that assumption. But he's dead if we get close enough to him.'

'Just like that.'

'Not just like that. I've got to find him first. I thought we had him after the dance. It hasn't moved from there. Up a bit of a blind alley now. Perhaps that's just talk about killing him. It should happen that way, but likely it won't. He'll be picked up, and it'll have sod-all to do with me.'

'Is that what you came for? Because a man kills a politico in England, then they send for you, and you come over here?'

'That's what I came for.'

'There's a thousand and more have died here since it all started. And you come because of one of them. He was . . . wait for it, I'm working it out . . . yes, he was a tenth of one per cent of all the people that have died here. That's not a bad statistic, is it? A tenth of a per cent. He wasn't mourned here, you know. No one gave a damn. Pompous bugger. Always on the box telling us how well he was doing flushing out the gunmen from off our backs. Why was he so special? They didn't send the big team over when they shot the Senator in Strabane, or the UDR man who had all the land down the road in Derry. So why have you come?'

'They put the glove down, didn't they? That's what shooting Danby was about. To make us react and see how effectively we would counter-attack. They killed him as a test of strength. We have to get the man and the team that did it. Either we do, or they've won. That's the game.'

'So it's not just Queen and Country? Forces of Right against Forces of Evil?'

'It's nothing to do with that. They've challenged us. Given us a bait

411

we cannot ignore. That's why we're in there kicking. We have to get the killer before the next time.'

'Who are you then, Harry? Who do you work for? Who pays your cheque?'

'You won't get that. You've too much already. Christ only knows why, I've –'

'And where does little Theresa fit into this big act? You're here to avenge a death. There's been one more already. How many more people get hurt, getting in the way, to make it still worthwhile for you?'

'Quite a lot.'

'So, even in death, some count for more than others.'

'Right.'

She shifted the ground, and softened the attack.

'What sort of fellow is he, this man you're looking for?'

'I don't know much about him. I've an idea what he looks like, but not a good description. I don't know his name. He's a cool customer, and he'll be a crack shot. One of the top men, but they'll have kept him out of the main eye of things.'

'When Theresa talked about him, do you know what it was made her say it?'

'"Course I don't know. How could I?'

'I mean, she wouldn't just bring a thing like that out of the blue, now would she? She said to me that the man that did the London killing was at that dance. He was there the whole time with his wife. She was looking such a misery that Theresa said she couldn't have been getting enough. That's how it all started. She said the cow couldn't be having it away, then she went into her own bit. That was to back her story up. She didn't know anything else.'

'That's the truth, Josephine?'

'She didn't have to die, alone like that, just with those bastard coppers round her. All she knew was what I said. I doubt she even knew the man's name.'

She had started to shout again, spitting out the unsaid accusation at Harry. The weakness had gone. The heat of her attack burst round the tiny marooned inside of the car.

'You might as well have killed her yourself, Harry. She wasn't involved in any way at all. You came here with your challenges, and the bloody games you play. And a wee girl dies who had nothing to do with it. There's enough innocent people killed here without strangers coming and putting their fingers in and digging out more shit.'

She crumpled then. Sobbing rhythmically and noiselessly. Gazing into the steamed-up window beside her. The rain was still falling.

Harry was deciding what he should do on his return to Belfast. His ego was rumpled by the way the girl had broken through him. He ought to have killed her up there on the hill, but she had said she was no

412

threat to him and he believed it. His ego was of less importance, though, than the news she had just given him. The man who he searched for had been at the caeli the previous week-end.

She shook herself, trying to shrug away her misery.

'Come on, I want a drink. There's a pub just down the road. You can't stop for the dead. Not in Ulster. Like they say, it all goes on. I should have dropped it ages ago. Come on, let's go have a couple of hot tods.'

She leaned over and kissed him lightly, again on the cheek. Then she began to adjust her face, working with deftness from her little pouch that came out of her bag, painting over the reddened and flushed valleys under her eyes.

When she had finished she said, 'Don't worry, hero boy, I won't tell the big bad Provies about you. But if you've ever taken advice, I'm telling you, don't hang about. Or whatever medal you're after will have to go in the box with you.'

They drove down the hill to where the pub and petrol station were nestled in a redoubt cut out from the stone. He ordered the drinks she wanted – Irish, with hot water and sugar and lemon.

The faint sunlight that had seen them out of Belfast was long since gone as Harry drove back on the shiny, watered road into the city. They spoke hardly a word all the way, and Harry dropped her off where he had met her in the morning, on the corner of Grosvenor and the Falls. Just before he stopped he asked her where she lived, so that he could drop her at the door. She said it would be better at the main road.

'When will I see you again?' he said, as she climbed out of the car. The traffic was hustling them.

'Next week, at Mrs Duncan's. You'll see me there.'

'And we'll go out somewhere? Have a drink?'

'Perhaps.'

She knew so much more than she had wanted to, or was equipped to handle. What had started as something of a game had become considerable enough to subdue her into a morose silence most of the way home. She darted out of the car, and without a wave disappeared into the Clonard side streets.

Harry dropped the car off at the garage and walked back to Delrosa. His mind was filled with that conversation he'd had with Davidson in the garden. The loneliness factor. Sounded so astonishing when the old chap was trying to put it over as a problem. What had he said? 'Unless you're aware of it, there will come a time when you want to tell someone.' Fumbling his way into it because it embarrassed him that his chosen man could possibly fall into so well signposted a pit, embarrassed even to suggest it. And that's the way it was, because Davidson knew what it was about, was the only one of them who knew what it was about. How many of the others could transpose themselves into the hostility of this community, live day-in, day-out with the fear and the strain and the isolation?

Don't go on with it, Harry boy, let it rest there. Don't let it infect you. The cancer of doubt spreads fast enough, Harry. Drop it.

Billy Downs decided he would go for Rennie the next day, Sunday.

The reports that were available from the minders who had been cautiously watching the policeman suggested that he made a habit of going to the interrogation centre on Sunday afternoons. He stayed a few hours and reached home around seven in the evening. It fitted with the plan that Downs had made. He discussed none of this with his wife, but as his preoccupation with the killing grew so they moved about their house, two strangers under the same roof. Life was carried on with a series of gestures and monosyllabic phrases.

Downs had been informed of the arrangement by which he would take possession of the Armalite rifle that he would use for the attack, and he had reported up the chain on the timing and the date that he would want the operation set in motion. It had been suggested to him that the Armalite was an unsuitable weapon for a close-quarters killing, but in the face of his wishes the point had not been pressed.

The huge power of the weapon excited him to such a degree that he could think of taking no other. The bullet that he intended should kill Rennie would leave the barrel at a muzzle velocity of 3250 feet per second. The statistics that he had read in a sales brochure astounded and exhilarated him. It weighed slightly less than seven pounds and would fit comfortably into the poacher-style pocket he had fashioned on the inside of his raincoat. And he would be far from his safe base area: if he were intercepted by the army or police then the sharp crack of the Armalite would be enough to send his enemy scurrying for cover for the few seconds he might need to get clear. He had asked for two thirty-round magazines for the weapon, just in case.

A brandy in his hand, Frost was sitting on his own in a corner of the Mess at Lisburn mulling over the magazines of weekly comment with which he prided himself he kept abreast. He made a point of working his way through the dog-eared *Spectator*, *Economist* and *Statesman*, and it had become sufficient of a ritual for other officers of equal rank to leave him to himself, when on any other evening they would have joined him.

The Mess waiter came over and hesitated beside the chair, before plunging in.

'Excuse me, sir. Sorry to trouble you. There's a reporter from *The*

Times on the phone. Says he needs to speak to you. Says it's urgent. He said to say he was sorry to trouble you, but he thought you'd want to hear what he had to say.'

Frost nodded, pulled himself up and followed the waiter to the phone cubicle.

'Hello, Frost here. Ah, yes, we've met. A leaving party, in the summer, right? What can I do for you?'

He listened without interruption as the reporter read over to him the story that was being prepared for Monday's editions. The Provisional IRA had tipped off one of their favoured reporters in Belfast that they believed the British had infiltrated a new secret agent into the city on a mission so sensitive that only the GOC, General Fairbairn, had been told of it. The Provos were claiming that the operation had caused great anger among British army staff officers in HQ. On Monday the story would appear in Dublin papers as well as British ones, and the IRA would be calling for special vigilance from the people to seek out the spy. The Provos, Frost was told, were saying this was a special operation and one quite different from anything mounted before.

'I'm not expecting you to comment on anything, Colonel. This is a private call, just to let you know what's going on. Good night.'

The Colonel mouthed his thanks.

He flicked the receiver's buttons up and down till the operator came on to the line.

'Evening. Frost here. GOC at home, please.' When he was connected he told the General he needed to see him immediately. There was no hint of an apology for disturbing the senior soldier in Northern Ireland at that time of night. That would not have been Frost's style. His early-warning antennae were already jangling with the possibility of a major intelligence scandal.

The General and Frost talked for an hour, and agreed to have another meeting at eight on Sunday morning with the benefit of further information. They would then, they thought, get on to the MOD and demand Harry's immediate recall before the awkward business became necessary of dragging him out of some hedgerow with an IRA bullet in the back of his head.

Across the city in Mrs Duncan's boarding house Harry was asleep. He had been somewhat unnerved by the brutality with which his cover had been stripped aside by the girl. On his return he had lifted the carpets and floorboards at the place where the revolver was hidden. The Smith and Wesson, with its six chambers loaded, was now wrapped in a towel under his pillow, in the corner over by the wall. As a day it had been a fiasco. A shambles. Back in the reality of the city with the hardness of the gun near to him he felt lunatic at what had passed between him and the girl in the wind and the rain on the hillside. Out of his tiny mind.

14

Harry was up early again that Sunday morning, and out of the house well before eight to make his way down to the city centre and the phone that he could use to talk to Davidson. This time he took the revolver with him, in his coat pocket, with the roughness of its shape shielded by the length of the covering anorak. The decision to take the gun had been an instinctive one, but now that he had it, and out on the streets and loaded, the situation that he faced was all the more clear. For the first time since they had flown him in from Germany he felt uncertain. That was the girl. Up that mountain talking a load of slop when he should have been concentrating, then letting her go last night, back into the warren that she shared with his opposition. Madness, and it aggravated him. Perhaps also there was the knowledge that the trail that had seemed so warm a week ago had now chilled.

The Smith and Wesson jarred against him as he stepped out down the Falls to the phone and communication with Davidson. There were no eyes watching him after he left Delrosa: the orders of the Battalion intelligence officer were being strictly obeyed.

He dialled the number, four-seven-zero-four-six-eight-one. After several desultory clicks he heard it ringing at the other end. It was answered.

'It's Harry here. How are the family?'

Davidson was in early too, and hoping for the call. 'Very well, they liked the postcards.'

'I've got a bit of a problem.' Pause. 'I've been blown by this girl, the one that helped me with the business I gave you last week. What a cock-up that was.' Pause. 'But anyway, putting the finger on that bird has led this girl straight back to me. She knows what I am. Not who I am, but what we're here for. I want you to take her out. Get her out of the scene for the duration. You can do that, can't you? She tells me that the man we want was at the same dance that we were at, a fortnight ago. I half-felt I remembered him. But the face wasn't quite right on the photokit. If it's the man then the army pulled him in, but that looked routine. He was just one of the ones that were rounded up. He had a

416

woman with him, presumably his wife, in a yellow trouser suit. Have you got all that?'

'I've got it on tape, Harry. Anything else?'

'Hell, what more do you want? No, that's all I have at the moment. But look, I don't want the living daylights bashed out of this girl. I just want her lifted out so she doesn't get involved any more. She's Josephine Laverty, lives with her mother in one of those little streets in Clonard, up off the Springfield on the right. You'll find her, but get to her quick, there's a good lad.'

'We'll work something out. Don't worry.'

'There's not really much else. It's a bit chill here at the moment but I think I'm settled in here okay. If you don't wrap it up on what I've just given you then it'll be a very long time. Do we have time for that?'

'We've plenty, as long as you think it worth it, Harry. But we ought, as you say, to kill it this time. It was a hell of a balls-up over the other girl. There was a lot of praise at this end for what you got. Great satisfaction. You're all right yourself, are you? No one following you about, no awkward questioning? Our assessment is that they would be right up to you by now if they were about to blow you, and that you'd probably have been aware of something. That's not just supposed to cheer you up, but if no one is sniffing around you then it should mean you're okay.'

'No, there's nothing like that,' Harry said. 'I'm working too. Job in a scrap yard in Andersonstown, and paying well. Back to the scene, then.'

'Harry, look, you ought to know this. I got well and truly chewed up over your living arrangements, us not knowing. It's not only unusual, it's unprofessional as well. Very unprofessional.'

'The whole thing's unprofessional,' Harry replied. 'Nothing's going to change. You're not going to order me, are you? I don't think it would help, and it's my neck. Thanks very much for caring. Cheers, maestro.'

''Bye, Harry, I understand. No one else does. Take care, and listen to the news. As soon as you hear we've got him, come whistling out. Give me a call first if you can, but head on up to the airport like you've got a bomb up your backside. Take care.'

Harry put the phone down, and hurried out into the cold and the long walk back up the Falls. He was concerned that they should get the girl out of the quagmire, and fast, before her involvement became too great for her to extricate herself . . . before she followed the other girl he'd brought into the game.

But things did not move fast that Sunday.

*

417

Twenty minutes after Harry had rung off Davidson called the Permanent Under Secretary. He caught the civil servant on the point of going to early morning service. The bad news first. Always play it that way, Davidson liked to say. Kick them a bit, then produce the magic sponge. They like it better. The agent was still declining to name a contact point. Not refusing, but declining. Don't want to make an order of it. Told him it's stupid, but can't do more than that. As he says, it's his neck. Our scandal if he catches it, mind, but his neck for all that. Now the bonus. Good information out of our chap. He'll like that.

'Keep that for a moment,' snapped the civil servant. 'I've had calls in the night. GOC has been on, and that man of his, Frost of intelligence. Bloody misnomer that. They want our fellow out, and kicking up a hell of a scene. They think he's blown.'

Davidson bit at his tongue. He heard at the end of the line the call for the rest of the family to go on.

'There's been some sort of leak. Like a sieve, that place. The papers have got a story from the opposition that they know a big man has been put in. There's panic stations over there. Anyway the order is get the chap out or the General says he'll go to the PM. Consolation is that the men over there say they don't think the IRA have a name. But that'll come soon enough. And you haven't an idea where we could go and just take hold of him?'

'All I have is that he works in a scrap merchant's in Andersonstown. Nothing more.'

'That won't do us much good till Monday morning.'

'He's done well again, our chap. The man we want was actually at the dance where Harry was the other night. The military had him, and must have let him go, or are holding him on something else . . .'

'Look, for God's sake, Davidson, I'm at home. I'm going to church. There's no point feeding me that sort of material over the phone. Talk to Frost direct. He'll be in his office, prancing about. He's having a field day. But if this Harry man should call again, get him out. That now is an instruction.'

Davidson had always had to admit that he enjoyed the complicated paraphernalia of introducing the agent into the operations theatre. He could reflect on it now, with the phone quiet, and his superior racing down the country lanes late for his communion. Davidson had been on the old Albania team. There had been the months with the undercover Greeks and Turks in Cyprus. Three years' secondment to the Singapore government to train bright-faced little policemen in the techniques of urban infiltration and maintaining men in a hostile environment. There was a gap in his wide experience. He recognized it. The men he sent into the field or discussed sending were all, as Davidson saw them, foreigners. The involvement with the men who listened to his lectures or acted under his orders was loose, and in no way binding.

With Harry it had become quite different. The danger that he now knew his agent to be facing numbed Davidson to a degree that almost shamed him. He had long seen himself as a tough, near-ruthless figure, the man in charge who put his agents on to the ground without sentiment or personal feeling. His defensive walls were being breached, he realized, as he thought of his man across the water, with the enemy closing on him.

And Harry didn't just not know of it: he'd just been told that all was well and looked good. That made him vulnerable.

Davidson had a growing feeling of nausea when he remembered how Harry had been brought to Dorking. Damn-all chance he'd had of backing out of the operation. The Prime Minister personally authorized the setting up of the team, and we've chosen you as the most suitable man. What chance did he have of side-stepping that little lot? He'd been belted off on the plane on a wild-goose chase. If he's not out of there soon he'll be number a thousand and bloody something pushing up daisies.

He picked up his phone and called Frost direct, in his office where he'd been told he'd be. At the other end of the line the serving colonel in intelligence left the London-based civilian with no illusions as to what he thought of armchair administrators organizing undercover work without consultation or know-how. Davidson resigned himself to it, letting it blaze over him. Between the interruptions he read over the transcript of Harry's message. He ended on a high note.

'He did pretty well with the first lot of stuff we gave you. We were disappointed in our team it didn't come to much. You should have it sewn up this time, don't you think, old boy?'

Frost didn't rise. It was a juicy and wriggling bait, but the office was crowded, and it was not the day for telephone brawling. That would come after this merry little show was wrapped up and in mothballs – what was left of it. He called the Springfield Road police to request the locating and picking up of the girl Josephine Laverty of Clonard, and then turned his attention to the matter of the man having been in and presumably out of military hands on Saturday night two weeks back. Cool bastard he must be, appraised the colonel. In between the calls he cancelled his Sunday-morning nine holes with G2 Ops.

Other operations had gone wrong before, Davidson recalled. There were those endless nights when they parachuted Albanians into the marshlands between the sea and Tirana and waited in vain with their CIA colleagues for the chatter of radio signals that would let them know all was well. When the Cypriot agents he had controlled had disappeared there had been days of nagging uncertainty until the bodies showed up – generally tortured, and always shot through the back of the head. But they were only aliens, so that the recriminations were short-lived, the kick-backs muted. But if they lost Harry then the ramifications would be huge, and public. The round-up of scapegoats would be spectacular, Davidson had no doubt of that. The Permanent Under Secretary would have faded from the picture by then, would have fetched his sliding carpet out. The old hack would be left holding the baby.

He called his assistant in from the outer office where, thank God, the man spent most of his time, and told him to watch the phones. He was to tape all calls, regardless, on the cassette recorder, whichever phone they came through on. He slipped out of the building. Sunday morning in Covent Garden. Some sunlight about on the upper reaches of the big buildings. Piles of fruit and vegetable boxes. No people. Davidson walked to the small grocer, that he knew would be open to serve the flats, big and grey-smeared, to the north of the market square. He bought bread, and cartons of milk, coffee and biscuits, some butter, and lemon curd. He'd liked that ever since boarding school thirty-five years ago. The total was about all his cooking facilities would cope with.

There had been no calls when he returned. He phoned his wife, told her he would be in town for a day or so, and not to worry. She didn't sound as if she was. There was an army-issue camp bed kept in the wardrobe behind his desk, excruciatingly uncomfortable but better than nothing. It would be a long wait, and no one to spend it with but the boring young man they'd sent along to give him a hand. Davidson had realized soon that they had not fully briefed his assistant on what was happening. He had no intention himself of enlightening him. They were on stand-by now, operational twenty-four hours.

The boys ran intricately between the towering regimented lines of the pine trunks, hurtling their way over the bending carpet of needles and cones in perpetual games of chase and hide and seek. Their voices were shrill, loud as if to fight off the cold attacking wind that heralded the real winter of the great plain east of Hanover. This was where Harry liked to bring them, to search for trout in the streams in high summer and spend week-ends in a wooden chalet, to run round to keep warm in the early winter, and then, when the snow came, to bring their tobog- gans. Sometimes they would set up a fox that had hidden in the sparse, stunted undergrowth under the pine umbrella hoping to avoid detection, then when its nerve went and it bounded clear there would be the noisy, clumsy chase, the ground giving under their boots before the quarry made its escape. It would take them deep into the forest, and when the brown flash was well lost they would stop and ponder and think of the direction of the fire-break path where they had left their mother, Mary Brown.

She had brought sandwiches full of sausage and a Thermos of tomato

420

soup today, and they would have that later sitting at a wooden table in the picnic area beside the car park.

From the wide path she could hear the distant noise of their voices, as she walked with a taller, older woman, her mother. A week after Harry had gone she had written to her home in the English midlands countryside. There the three-page letter had been recognized as a distress flare, a call for help. Arrangements had been made. Father could look after himself for a week, cook his own meals, get the garden into shape for the long winter lay-off.

When the children were in bed the conversation often, and hardly accidentally, strayed to Harry's abrupt departure, and now that they were again out of earshot it continued.

'It's just so difficult to understand,' said Mary's mother, 'that no one should be able to tell you anything about it. You'd have thought someone could have had the gumption, even the courtesy, to say something to you.'

'There's been nothing,' said Mary, 'not a word from anyone since they came and packed his case. Rummaged around in the wardrobe, right down the bottom where his old things are – half of them should have gone this week to the sergeants' wives' Jumble Sale – things he'd only wear if he was gardening or painting or cleaning out the cellar, or something like that. We've had two postcards from somewhere down the Gulf, and otherwise nothing.'

The postcards had shown a camel corps contingent of the Sultan, and a gold-domed mosque. The messages had been brief and facetious. 'Having a wonderful time, got a very red nose from the heat, don't think there'll be snow here this Christmas, love to the boys and to you, my darling, Harry,' and 'Giving church parade a miss this week. Missing you all. Sorry about the nonsense but it will all seem clear when I'm home. Love you all, Harry.' They'd taken a long time to arrive, and now they decorated the mantelpiece above the fire in their front room.

'But tell me again, dear, exactly what they said when you asked the people in the office.' Mother had the infuriating habit of demanding endless, word-by-word repetitions of conversations she'd already heard umpteen times.

'Just what I told you. That it was as a result of a signal from London, that everyone here was as much in the dark as I was. That Harry would be away six weeks' minimum, probably not more than eight. And that if I were short of anything or having problems not to hesitate to call the Families Officer. He's an awful old bore – a passed-over major. I'd really be on my last legs if I called him. I just don't think they know.'

'It must be to do with the Aden business, I suppose. The thing he was awarded the Military Cross for. Your father and I were very proud for you . . .'

Mary cut in, 'I cannot believe it's anything to do with that. It was years ago, and Harry was really knocked out by that. He had weeks of sick leave. He doesn't talk much about it. But it must have been awful from what I was told. He just lived in amongst them then, wasn't even fluent in Arabic. Passable but not even fluent.'

'Well, it has to be something secret.'

'Has to be.' She was wearing her hair up, and the wind was pulling it away from the big tortoiseshell clip at the back of her head. It was wisping away – she hadn't taken enough time to settle it properly in the hurry to get the food ready and the kids dressed for the expedition. She had little make-up on, lipstick untidy. Not how she'd want Harry to see her. 'But I don't think he'd volunteer for anything like this now, and I cannot for the life of me see why anyone would just pick him out over all the people they've got and rush him down to the Gulf. It just doesn't make sense. I thought he'd burned all the spook stuff out of him.'

'Still, it's not long now, only a fortnight or so,' comforted her mother.

'That's what they said. We've no option but to believe them.'

Mary Brown could not confide the depth of her unhappiness to her mother. Too many years of marriage and before that secretarial college in London had dulled the relationship. Their marriage was too confidential to gossip about. What hurt most was that she had thought she had understood the man she had been living with for so long, and now she had discovered that there was a different compartment in his make-up.

'Well, at least we know he can look after himself,' said her mother, sensing the barriers going up.

'Let's hope he doesn't have to. We'll get the kids back and have lunch.'

She called for them, and when they emerged filthy from the forest they all walked back to the car.

That same lunchtime Seamus Duffryn was summoned to a house in Beechmount and told by the Battalion intelligence officer to resume close surveillance on McEvoy. Duffryn was told a squad was going out in the afternoon to find a friend of McEvoy, a girl who had been out with him. Josephine Laverty from Clonard.

A few hundred yards away in the Springfield Road the British army unit that had been asked to find the girl was puzzled that it had no record of her or her mother living in the area. There was no reason why they should have done, as the house was in the name of Josephine's uncle, Michael O'Leary. A little after three o'clock the unit reported in that it had been unable to locate the girl. By then a critical amount of the available time had run out.

*

422

It took more than two hours from the time Frost called the army head-quarters dominating Ardoyne and told them of the tip to the moment Billy Downs was identified. First the troops who had taken part in the search operation at the caeli had to be located. The lieutenant who had led the raid was in Norfolk on week-end leave, and there was no answer to his telephone. The sergeant, the next senior man out, recalled that he had busied himself near the door on security, but he was able to name the six soldiers who had carried out the split-up question-and-answer work. Private Jones was now in Berlin, but Lance-Corporal James Llewellyn was picked up by a Saracen from a foot patrol on the far side of the Battalion area. There was no written record, of course. That, along with Jones, were the only two pieces of evidence of the confrontation, and both had now disappeared. Llewellyn stared at the photokit issued in London that had been brought up from the guard room.

'That's the one it's like, if it's any of them. It's Downs. It's not a great likeness. It's not easy to pick him on that picture. But if he was there that's the one it was. There was his woman there, in yellow. She ran out across to him.'

With the name they attacked the filing system. Billy Downs. Ypres Avenue, number 41. There'd been a spot-check on his story about being down in Cork with his mother. The Garda had been fast for a change, and had cleared him of involvement. They said he'd been there through that period. There'd been a query about him because he was away from home. Otherwise, clean with nothing known. The net inside the headquarters spread wider, to include the policeman who had seen him that night in the small hours.

'He was very cool. Not even a sweat on his palms. I know, as I looked.'

It was into the afternoon that they called Frost back.

'We think we've located the man you want. He's Billy Downs, without an "e" on the end. Ypres Avenue, wife and kids. Very quiet, from what we've seen of him. Unemployed. His story stuck after the Garda ran a check on the alibi he gave us to account for his long absence from the area. There was no other reason to hold him. Like to point out that the chaps that have actually seen this fellow say that he's not that like the pics you put out. Much fatter in the face, I'm told. Perhaps you'll let us know what you want done. We've a platoon on immediate. We can see pretty much down that street: I've an OP in the roof of a mill, right up the top.'

Frost growled back into the phone, 'I'd be interested in knowing if Mr Downs is currently at home.'

'Wait one.' As he held on for the answer Frost could hear the distant sounds of the unit operations room as they called up the OP on a field telephone. 'Not quite so hot, I'm afraid. They log comings and goings.

We think Downs left his home, that's number forty-one, around twenty-five minutes ago. That's fifteen-o-five hours precisely that he went out. But he goes in and out pretty regularly. No reason to think he won't be back in a bit.'

'I'd like it watched,' said Frost, 'but don't move in yet, please. This number will be manned through the evening and the night. Call me as soon as you see him.'

Downs was on his way by car up the Lisburn Road at the time that the observation post overlooking Ypres Avenue was warned to look out for him. There were several subsequent entries in the exercise book the two soldiers kept for logging the comings and goings in the street. They had noted him as soon as he came from his front door and began the walk up the hill away from them to one of the decreed exits from Ardoyne. When the message came through on the radio telephone to the troops, Downs was just out of his heartland, standing in the no-man's ground at the top of the Crumlin waiting for his pick-up. This was neither Protestant nor Catholic territory. Side streets on either side of the road shut off with great daubed sheets of corrugated iron. Two worlds split by a four-lane road with barricades to keep people from each other's throats. Scrawled on one side was 'Up the Provos', and 'British Army Out', and beyond the opposite pavement the messages of 'Fuck the Pope' and 'UVF'.

He was edgy waiting there in daylight beside such a busy road, one used heavily by military traffic, and the relief showed in his face when the Cortina pulled up alongside him, and the driver bent sideways to open the passenger door. The car had been hi-jacked in the Falls thirty-five minutes earlier.

A moment later they moved off, weaving their way through the city. By the crossroads in the centre of the sprawling, middle-class suburb the car turned left and up one of the lanes that lead to the Down countryside through a small belt of woods. They turned off among the trees.

The driver unlocked the boot and handed over the Armalite rifle. It was wrapped in a transparent plastic bag. Downs checked the firing mechanism. It was a different weapon to the one that he had used before in his attack on the patrol, and was issued by a quite unconnected quartermaster. But the rifle came from the same original source – Howa Industries, of Nagoya in Japan. It had been designed as a hunting weapon, and that astonished him. What sort of animal did you take a killing machine of this proven performance to hunt? He released the catch on the stock to check that the folding hinge was in working order. That reduced the length of the weapon by eleven inches, bringing it down to less than two-and-a-half feet, so that it would comfortably fit into the padded inside pocket of his coat. He was passed the two magazines, glanced them over and fitted one deep into the attachment slot under the belly of the gun. He activated a bullet up into the breech, and flicked with his thumb at the safety catch to ensure it was engaged. The volunteer at the wheel watched the preparations with fascination.

With the stock folded, Downs pushed the rifle down into the hidden pocket.

'I don't know how long I'll be,' he said. 'For God's sake don't suddenly clear off or anything smart. Stick here. At least till midnight.'

They were the only words Downs spoke before he disappeared into the growing darkness to walk the half-mile towards Rennie's house. The only words of the whole journey. The teenager left behind with the car amongst the trees subsided, shivering, into the driver's seat to wait for his return.

The regular Sunday afternoon visit to the office to clear the accumulation of paper work off his desk was no longer a source of controversy between the policeman and Janet Rennie. It had been at first, with accusations of 'putting the family into second place' being levelled. The increasing depression of the security situation in the province had caused her to relent.

It was now understood that she and the two girls, Margaret and Fiona, would have their tea, watch some television and then wait for him to get home before bedtime.

Over the last four years Janet Rennie had become used to the problems of being a policeman's wife. A familiar sight now was the shoulder holster slung over the bedside chair when he had an extra hour in bed on Saturday mornings, before the weekly trip to the out-of-town supermarket. So too were the registration plates in the garage, which he alternated on the car, and around the house the mortise locks on all the doors, inside and out. At night all these were locked with a formal ritual of order and precedence, lest one should be forgotten, and the detective's personal firearm lay in the half-opened drawer of the bedside table, on which rested the telephone which, as often as not, would ring deep into the night.

Promotion and transfer to Belfast had been hard at first. The frequency of the police funerals they attended along with the general level of danger in the city had intimidated her. But out of the fear had come a fierce-rooted hatred of the IRA enemy.

Janet Rennie had long since accepted that her husband might not last through the troubles, might be assassinated by one of those wild-eyed, cold-faced young men whose photographs she saw attached to the outside of the files he brought home in the evenings and at week-ends. She didn't shrink from the possibility that she might ride in the black Austin Princess behind the flag and the band to a grey, country church-yard. When he was late home she attacked her way through the knitting, her therapy along with the television set. He was often out late, seldom in before eight or nine – and that was a good evening. But she felt pride for the work he did, and shared something of his commitment.

The girls, seven and five, were in the bright, warm living-room of the bungalow, kneeling together on the treated sheepskin rug in front of the open fire, watching the television, when the door bell rang.

'Mama! Mama! Front-door bell!' Margaret shouted to her mother at the back, too absorbed to drag herself away from the set.

Janet Rennie was making sandwiches for tea, her mind taken by fish-paste fillings and the neatness of the arrangement of the little bread triangles. They had become a treat, these Sunday teas, the girls and their mother playing at gentility with enthusiasm. With annoyance she wondered who it could be. Which of the girls from the close was calling right at tea time?

The bell rang again.

'Come on, Mama. It's the front door.' Margaret resigned herself. 'Do you want me to go?'

'No, I'll do it. You stay inside, and you're not going out to play on your bikes at this time of night.'

She wiped her hands on the cloth hanging beside the sink. Right from the start she ignored the basic rule of procedure that her husband had laid down. As her hand came up towards the Yale lock that was always on, she noticed that the chain had been left off since the children came back from playing with their friends of three doors down. It should have been fastened. She should have fastened it before she opened the door. But she ignored the rules and pulled the door back.

'Excuse me, is it Mrs Rennie?'

She looked at the shortish man standing there on her front doorstep, hands in his coat pockets, an open smile round his face, dark hair nicely parted.

'Yes, that's right.'

Very quietly he said, 'Put your hands behind your head, keep them there and don't shout. Don't make any move. I know the kids are here.'

She watched helplessly as through his coat, unbuttoned and open, he drew out the ugly squat black shape of the Armalite. Holding it in one hand, with the stock still folded, he prodded her with the barrel back into the hallway. She felt strange, detached from what was happening, as if it were a scenario. She had no control over the situation, she knew that. He came across the carpet past the stairs towards her, flicking the door closed with his heel. It clattered as it swung to, the lock engaging behind him.

'Who is it, Mama?' From behind the closed door of the lounge Fiona called out.

'We'll go in there now. Just remember this. If you try anything I'll kill you. You, and the children. Don't forget it when you want to play the bloody heroine. We're going to sit in there, and wait for that bastard husband of yours. Right? Is the message all plain and clear and understood?'

The narrow barrel of the Armalite dug into her flesh just above the hip as he pushed past her to the door and opened it. Their mother was half into the room before Fiona turned, words part out of her mouth but frozen when she saw the man with the rifle. Even to a child three months off her fifth birthday the message was brilliantly obvious. The girl rose up on her knees, her face clouding from astonishment to terror. As if in slow motion her elder sister registered the new mood. Wide-eyed, and with the brightness fading from her, she saw first her sister's face then her mother standing hunched, as if bowed down by some great weight, and behind her Downs with the small shiny rifle in his right hand.

Too frightened to scream the elder girl remained stock still till her mother reached her, gathered the children to her, and took them to the sofa.

The three of them held tightly to each other as on the other side of the room Downs eased himself down into Rennie's chair. From there he was directly facing the family, who were huddled away in the front corner of the sofa to be as far as possible from him. He also had a clear view of the door into the room, and of the window beyond it at the far edge of the lounge. It was there that he expected the first sign of Rennie's return, the headlights of the policeman's car.

'I'll warn you for the last time, missus. Any moves, anything clever, and you'll be dead, the lot of you. Don't think, Mrs Rennie, when it comes to it, that you're the only one at risk. That would be getting it very wrong, a bad miscalculation. If I shoot you I do the kids as well. We'll leave the TV on, and you'll sit there. And just remember I'm watching you. Watching you all the time. So be very careful. Right, missus?'

Billy Downs paused and let the effect of his words sink in on the small room.

'We're just going to wait,' he said.

15

The four men sent to question Josephine Laverty had none of the problems finding her that the British army unit in the Springfield Road had encountered. Smiling broadly, the oldest in the group, and the leader, suggested that old Mrs Laverty might care to go into the kitchen and take herself a good long cup of tea.

They took Josephine up to her bedroom far from the mother's ears. One of the younger men drew the curtains, cutting out the frail shafts of sunlight, and took up his position by the window. Another stood at the door. The third of the volunteers stood behind the chair they cursorily suggested Josephine should sit in. The older man they called Frank, and they treated him with respect and with caution.

The girl was poorly equipped to handle an interrogation. Frank's opening question had been harmless enough, and he was as astonished as the other three boys in the room at the way she collapsed.

Perhaps it was because she was one of the uninvolved, those few in the city who tried to weave a life outside the troubles. Her lack of commitment had built up a fear of violence, second nature to so many, and therefore not so terrifying. Without loyalties there was only self-preservation, and there was little anyone could do now to help her in the face of the unspoken brutality of the men who had crowded round her. Cold, cruel faces, pallid, expressionless, used and trained in begetting pain. There was only one reason they would come to her . . . because of Harry, sweet and beautiful and chatty Harry. She looked at their hands, big, dirty, broken fingernails, roughened with usage. Their boots, hard and bruised from wear, drab from the rain outside. Men who would hurt her, punch her, kick her. And for what? For a few minutes' delay in the inevitable. She would tell them what they had come to find out. They were far outside her experience, the men who stood around her, moving among her possessions as if there by right. They did have the right, she thought. Yesterday on the Sperrins she had become involved in their territory, and that was why they had come.

'This fellow McEvoy, that you've been going with. Who is he?'

There had been no reply, only a dissolve as her head went down to her lap and she buried her cheeks and her eyes and ears into the palms of her hands.

'Who is he?' Frank was insistent. 'Who is he, where does he come from?'

'You know who he is. Why come to me for it? You know well enough.'

Frank paced up and down, short steps, continually twisting round towards the girl when he lost sight of her, moving back and forward between the window and the door, skirting the single bed littered with the girl's clothes.

'I want you to tell me.' He emphasized it. Like an owl with a scarce-whelped mouse, a stoat with a rabbit, he dominated the cringing girl at the wooden chair before him.

'I want it from you. D'yer hear? I've not much time.'

Josephine shook her head, partly from the convulsion of her collapse, and reeled away from him as he swung his clenched fist back-handed across her face. Her knuckles took much of the force of the blow, but through the splayed fingers across her eyes she saw the blood welling close and then breaking the skin at the back of her hands.

Frank could see that what had been put to him as somewhat of a routine questioning had become rather more complex. The fear and hesitation of the girl had alerted him. Her inability to answer a simple explicit question. Frank knew McEvoy only as a lodger at the girl's employer's guest house . . . been out with him once or twice. A fair-looking piece, he'd probably knocked her off, but that wouldn't be enough to put her there doubled up and sniffling.

'I'm getting impatient, girl. To him you owe none of the loyalty you should give to us.'

He weighed up whether he would need to hit her again.

She nodded her head, very slightly at first, then merging into the positive move of acquiescence and surrender. Frank held back. He would not have to hit her again.

She straightened up, steadying herself as she prepared the words.

'He's with the British, isn't he? You knew that. He's British. I don't know what he does, but he's been sent to live amongst us. He's looking for the man that killed the politico. Over in London. That's his job. To find that man. He said when he found him he'd exterminate him.'

She stopped, leaving the shadowy little room quiet. Below she could hear her mother about the kitchen, picking things up and putting them down.

Josephine saw the enormity of what she had said. She'd told him, hadn't she, that his truth was safe with her. One backhander and she spilled it all. She remembered it, outside the pub on the hill at Glenshane. She'd promised it then, when she'd told him to quit.

Frank stared intently at her.

'His job was as an agent in here? He's a British agent? Sent to infiltrate us? . . . Holy Jesus!'

'You knew? You knew, didn't you? You wouldn't have come if you hadn't known.'

429

The room was near-dark now. Josephine could barely make out the men in the room – only the one silhouetted at the window by the early street light. Her mother called up for tea for her visitors. No one answered. The old lady lingered at the bottom of the stairs waiting for the reply, then went back to the kitchen, accepting and perhaps understanding the situation and unable to intervene.

The girl wavered one last time in her loyalties and her allegiance. Upbringing, tradition, community all came down heavily on the scales against the balance of the laugh and adulthood and bed of Harry. But there was the wee girl with the tossing feet and the tightening stocking, and the obscenity and the misery of death in the police cell, and that wiped Harry from the slate. She spoke again.

'He was the one that shopped Theresa, the girl that hung herself. She said she'd been with the man that did the London killing, but he couldn't perform. Harry tipped the army about it. He said the killing was a challenge to the British, and they had to get the man who did it, and kill him. Something like that, just to show who ran things. He told me this yesterday.'

The volunteers said nothing, their imagination stretched by what the girl said. Frank spoke. 'Was he close to the man he was looking for? Did he know his name? Where he lived? What he looked like? Just how much did the bastard know?'

'He said he thought he knew what he looked like.' She saw Theresa again in her mind, heard her giggling in the small space round the basin outside the lock-up closet. That was the justification, that was enough . . . to see the girl's face. Hear her choking. 'He said he was a good shot, and a cool bugger, that's what he called him. And, yes, they were looking, he said, for a man who would be out of the main eye of things. That was the exact phrase he used.'

'And you, how did you spot this highly-trained British assassin, little girl?'

'I spotted him because of a silly thing. You have to believe me, but we were on the Sperrins yesterday. He said he'd been in the Merchant Navy, and sailed all over, but the gale on the mountain seemed to shake him a bit. I said to him it wasn't very good if he'd been to sea as much as he said. Then he didn't hide it any more. He seemed to want to talk about it.'

Clever little bitch, thought Frank.

'Is he in regular touch, communication, with his controller?'

'I don't know.'

'Is he armed?'

'I don't know that either. I never saw a gun. I've told you all I know. That's God's truth.'

'There's one little problem for you, Miss Josephine.' Frank's voice had a cutting edge to it now, something metallic, cold and smooth. 'You haven't explained to me yet how this British agent came to hear about Theresa and what she was saying about the London man. You may need a bit of time for that, you bastard whore. Treacherous little bitch.'

He came very close to her now. She could smell the tobacco and beer on his breath and the staleness of sweat on his clothes. He hadn't shaved that day, and his face was a prickled, lumpy mass.

'Just work it out,' he said. 'Then tell the lads, because they'll be waiting for an answer. To us you're nothing, dirt, scum, shit. You've shopped one of your own . . . a wee girl who hanged herself rather than talk to the fucking British. You betrayed her. You betrayed your lover boy as well. We'll put it about, you know, and we'll let the military know as well. You'll find somewhere to run, but there'll be sod-all people to help you get there, you little cow. But then, when these lads have finished with you, you'll be thinking twice before you go drop your knickers to another Britisher.'

Frank turned away and walked to the door. He said to the man who was standing there, 'It's just a lesson this time, Jamie. Nothing permanent and nothing that shows. Something just for her to remember, to think about for a long time. Then lose yourselves. If we need you later we know where you'll be, so split from here. And, little girl, if you've half an inch of sense in your double-dealing painted head you'll not mention what's happened here tonight, nor what's going to.'

He went out of the door and down the steep staircase. In the hall the old woman saw him, as she turned in her chair by the fire and looked at him. He smiled at her.

'Don't worry, lady,' he said, 'I can find my way out. You just stay where you are.'

The three younger men followed him through the door fifteen minutes later. They left Josephine doubled up on the bed wheezing for air and holding the soft solar plexus of her stomach. She lay a long time in the room, fighting the pain and willing it away. Her clothes lay scattered in the corner of the room where the men had ripped them from her.

'Right on your bloody flesh, you little bitch, where it hurts, and where it'll last.'

She'd thought they were going to rape her, but instead they simply beat her. She curled herself up, foetal position, her arms protecting her breasts and lower stomach, thighs clamped together. That was how she stayed after they'd gone. Her breath came back to her soon, and after that there was the long, deep aching of the muscles, and, mingled with it, the agony of the betrayal. Betrayal of Theresa. Betrayal of Harry.

Perhaps the men had been sensitive about beating up a girl, perhaps it was the sight of her nakedness, but the job was not thoroughly done. The effect soon faded. There was time to think then. Frank would have gone straight to the house to find Harry. He'd be taken, tortured, and shot, that would come later, or tomorrow morning. Her reasoning made any thought of warning Harry irrelevant. They would have him already, but did she want to warn him? One good screw, and what had he done? Lifted her bedroom tattle from pillow confidence to military intelligence information. Let him rot with it.

When her mother came up the stairs late in the evening she was still doubled up, still holding her stomach, and cold now on her skin. The old lady looped the girl's nightdress over her head, and twisted her feet under the clothes. She spent some minutes picking the clothes up from the floor, showing no more interest in those that were torn than in those that formed the general muddle on the floor.

Twice during the Sunday evening Davidson phoned through to Frost. The first-floor office had with the coming of darkness taken on the appearance of a bunker. The telephone that was specified for outgoing outside calls was on the floor beside the canvas camp bed, now erected.

Davidson was curtly told there was no information, and reminded that he'd already been told that he would be notified as soon as anything was known. The earlier elation had left him, and he allowed Frost the last word on an operation so inefficient that you cannot even get in touch with your man when you need to get him out.

But for all his bark Frost was now sufficiently involved in the operation to call Springfield Road, wait while the commanding officer was brought to speak to him, and stress the urgency with which the girl Laverty should be found.

In their eyrie high above Ardoyne two soldiers looked down on Ypres Avenue. There were no street lights, old casualties of the conflict, but they watched the front door of No. 41 from the image intensifier, a sophisticated visual aid that washed everything with a greenish haze and which enabled them to see the doorway with great clarity. On the hour they whispered the same message into their field telephone. No one had used the front door of the house.

Frank did not go near Delrosa that night. On his bicycle he had ridden up to Andersonstown in search of his Battalion commander. It was arranged that at midnight he would be taken to meet the Belfast Brigade commander. Frank knew his name, but had never met him.

*

From his home the Permanent Under Secretary had authorized the sending of a photograph of Harry to Belfast. The next morning, Monday, it was to be issued to troops who would raid the various Andersonstown scrap merchants. Less than half a dozen people in the province would know the reason for the swoops but each search party would have several three-inch-by-four pictures of Harry. It had originally shown him in uniform, but that had been painted out.

The big television in the corner of the room droned on, its Sunday message of hope and charity, goodwill and universal kindness expounded by ranks of singers and earnest balding parsons. The family sat quite still on the sofa watching the man with the Armalite rifle.

The pictures claimed no part of the attention of Janet Rennie as she stared, minute after minute, at the man with the rifle across his knee, but for long moments the children's concentration was taken by the images on the screen before being jerked to the nightmare facing them across the carpet. It was a new degree of fear that the children felt, one they were not able to cope with or assimilate. They held fast to their mother, waiting to see what would happen, what she would do. To the two girls the man opposite represented something quite apart from anything they had experienced before, but they recognized him as their father's enemy. Their eyes seldom left his face, held with fascination by the greyness of his skin, its lack of colour, its deadness. This was where they saw the difference between the intruder and their world. There was none of the ruddiness and weight, the life and colour that they knew from their friends' fathers and the men that came home with their father.

In the first twenty minutes that Downs had been in the room, Fiona, who traded on her ability to charm, had attempted to win the stranger with a smile. He looked right through her, gap-toothed grin and all. She'd tried just once, then subsided against her mother.

He's never come out into the light, the elder girl, Margaret, told herself. He's been locked up, and like a creature he's escaped from wherever they've kept him. This man was across the wall, but she knew little of the causes of the separation and the walling-off. She studied the deepness of his eyes, intent and careful, uninvolved as they took in the room, traversing it like the light on a prison camp watchtower, without order or reason but hovering, moving, perpetually expecting the unpredictable. She saw his clothes too. A coat with a darned tear in the sleeve, the buttons off the cuffs, trousers without creases and shiny in the knees, frayed at the turn-ups and with mud inside the lower leg. To children suits were for best, for work, not for getting dirty and shabby. His shoes were strange to them, too. Cleaned after a fashion

433

by the rain on the winter pavements, but like his face without lustre, misused.

Margaret understood that the gun on Downs's lap was to kill her father. Her sister, twenty months younger, was unable to finish off the equation and so was left in a limbo of expectancy, aware only of an incomprehensible awfulness. Margaret had enough contact with the boys at school who played their war games in the school yard to recognize the weapon as an Armalite rifle.

He'll be a hard bastard, Janet Rennie had decided. One of the big men sent in for a killing like this. Won't be able to distract him with argument or discussion enough to unsettle him. He's hard enough to carry out his threat. She saw the wedding ring on his finger. Would have his own kids, breed like rats the Catholics, have his own at home. But he'd still shoot hers. She felt the fingers of her daughters gripping through her blouse. But she kept her head straight, and her gaze fastened on Downs. There was no response to her stare, only the indifference of the professional, the craftsman who has been set a task and time limit and who has arrived early and therefore must wait to begin. Faster than her children she had taken in the man, searched him for weakness, but the gun across his knees now held her attention. If he were nervous or under great strain then she would notice the fidgeting of the hands or the reflection of perspiration on the stock or barrel of the gun. But there was no movement, no reflection.

He held the gun lightly, his left hand half-way along the shaft and his fingers loose round the black plastic that cradled the hard rifled steel of the barrel. His hand was just above the magazine and her eyes wandered to the engineered emplacement where the capsule of ammunition nestled into the base of the gun. Just after he had sat down, Downs had eased the safety catch off with his right index finger, which now lay spanning the half-moon of the trigger guard. Like a man come to give an estimate on the plumbing, or the life insurance, she thought. None of the tensions she would have expected on display. Thirty minutes or so before she thought her husband might be arriving home she decided to talk.

'We have no quarrel with you. You've none with us. We've done nothing to you. If you go now you'll be clean away. You know that. You'll be right out of here and gone before my husband gets back.' That was her start. Poor, she told herself, it wouldn't divert a flea.

He looked back with amused detachment.

'If you go through with this they'll get you. They always get them now. It's a fact. You'll be in the Kesh for the rest of your life. Is that what you want?'

'Save it, Mrs Rennie. Save it and listen to the hymns.'

She persisted. 'It'll get you nowhere. It's the Provisionals, isn't it? You're beaten. One more cruel killing, senseless. It won't do any good.'

'Shut up.' He said it quietly. 'Just shut up and sit still.'

She came again. 'Why do you come here? Why to this house? Who are you?'

'It's a pity your man never told you what he did when he went to work of a morning. That's late in the day now, though. Quiet yourself and stay where you are.'

He motioned at her with the rifle, still gently, still in control. The movement was definitive. Stay on the sofa with the children. He sensed that the crisis was coming for her, and that she knew it. With growing desperation she took up the same theme.

'But you're beaten now. It'll soon be all over. All your big men are gone. There'll have to be a cease-fire soon, then talking. More killing won't help anything.' Keep it calm, don't grovel to him, talk as an equal with something on your side. There's nothing to counter-balance that Armalite but you have to make believe he doesn't hold everything.

'We're not beaten. It's not over. We've more men than we can handle. There'll be no talks, and no cease-fire. Got the message? Nothing. Not while there are pigs like your man running round free and live.'

The children beside her started up at the way the crouched stranger spoke of their father. Janet Rennie was an intelligent woman and hardened by her country upbringing. That she would fight for her husband's life was obvious: the problem had been in finding the medium. For the first time in nearly two hours she believed she stood a chance. She still watched the hands and the rifle. The hands were in a new position on the Armalite. From resting against the gun they were now gripping it. Attack, and how can he hit back before Rennie comes home?

'There's no future for you boys. Your best men are all locked up. The people are sick and tired of you. You know that. Even in your own rat holes they've had enough of you . . .'

'You don't know a bloody thing about what goes on. Not a bloody thing. You know nothing. Nothing. Shut up. Shut your bloody face . . .'

She taunted him, trying to act it with her voice to overcome the fear. 'They don't want you any more. You're outnumbered, living off the backs of people. Without your guns you're nothing . . .'

He shouted back across to her. 'What do you know of the way we live? What do you know of what support we have? All you see is what's on the bloody television. You don't know what life is like in the Falls, with murdering bastards like your husband to beat the shit out of boys and girls. We're doing people a service when we kill fucking swine like that husband of yours.'

'My husband never killed anyone.' She said it as a statement of fact. Safe.

'He told you that, did he?' Very precise, low and hissing the words out. 'Pity you never asked him what sort of little chat he had with the wee girl that hanged herself in the cells at Springfield.'

435

She had built herself towards the climax. Now he watched with relish the demolition. She remembered reading about the girl, though it had not been mentioned at home. Work rarely was. The rebuttal caught her hard, draining her. The hands. Hold on to the hands, and concentrate on them. The only lifeline is the hands. The left knuckle was white on the barrel, blood drained out from round the bones. He was holding the rifle with both hands as he brought it up across his face to wipe his forehead with the sleeve on his right arm. He was sweating.

'You're nothing, are you? That's all you're fit for. Sitting in people's homes with guns, guarding women and wee bairns. You're a rat, a creeping, disease-ridden little rat. Is that what the great movement is about? Killing people in their homes?'

Her voice was battering it out now, watching the anger rise first in his neck and spreading through the lower jaw, tension, veins hardening and protruding. Safe. What can the gun do now that would not rouse the neighbours who lived through the thin brick-and-cement walls of the estate just a few feet from her own bungalow?

'You've made it all out wrong, Mrs Rennie. Whatever your bloody man says you don't kill the Provos just by locking a few up. We are of the people. Don't you know that? The people are with us. You've lost, you are the losers. Your way of life, God-given superiority, is over and finished, not us . . . We're winning. We're winning because the people support us. Go into Andytown, or the Murph or Ardoyne or Turf Lodge. Go in there and ask them about Provo rule. Then ask them what they think of RUC scum.'

He was shouting, half-rising out of the flower-covered seat of the chair. The rifle was now only in the right hand, but with the finger still close to the trigger. His left arm was waving above his head.

The hatred between the two was total. His fury was fanned by the calmness she showed in face of the rifle, and the way she had made him shout and the speed with which he had lost his control. Her loathing for the Republicans, bred into her from the cradle, gave her strength. With something near detachment she weighed the pluses and minuses of rushing him there and then. He was gripping the gun, but it was pointed away from the family. There was no possibility that she could succeed. She felt the children's grip on her arms. If she surged suddenly across the room she would carry them like two anchors half-way with her.

He was not so calm now, and she saw the hint in his eye that he felt the claustrophobia of the room, that the time he had sat in the chair had sapped that sense of initiative and control that were so important to him. She remembered a young Catholic boy who had come round her father's store, idling or loitering or just with nothing to do, and how her father had pulled him up by the front of his collar, and shaken him like an animal to find what he was doing there, on the corner outside the shop. And there had been then the trapped-rodent fear of the youth, of the second-grade boy, who accepted that this would happen, and ran when released, feeling himself lucky not to be thrashed. In the eyes of the man across from her was the hint that he knew he no longer dominated the situation.

When Rennie turned into the cul-de-sac he noted immediately that the garage interior light was not switched on. He stopped his car forty yards from the bottom of the road, and turned off his engine and lights. The bungalow seemed quite normal. The curtains were drawn, but there was a slice of light through the gap where they had been pulled not quite together, from the hall light filtering through the patterned and coloured glass. Everything as it should be.

But no light in the garage. For months now it had been a set routine that an hour or so before he was expected Janet would go into the kitchen and switch on the light in the garage. They kept the garage empty, without the clutter that their neighbours stored there. That way there was no hiding place for an assassin.

The detective sat in the car watching, allowing himself some minutes just to look at the house and search in front of him in detail for any flaw other than the unlit garage. There was no light upstairs. Perhaps there should have been, perhaps not. Usually Fiona would be having her bath by now, but only darkness there. That was another cautionary factor.

Over the years Howard Rennie had been to enough full-dress police funerals to wonder how it could happen to himself. There was only one way. The epitaphs of the dead men were clear enough. Carelessness. Somewhere, for some time, usually minuscule, they had slackened. Not all, but most, grew over-confident and fell into the convenience of routine, began to believe in their own safety. A few were killed in closely-planned attacks, but most as Rennie knew well presented themselves as casual targets.

This was why he had a light fitted for the garage that should now be on, and why he noticed it was not lit.

His wife was a meticulous and careful person. Not one to make a silly mistake about the garage. It was the dilemma of the life they led that he wondered constantly how far as a family they should take their personal security. On the one hand there could be something drastically wrong that had prevented his wife from switching on a light as agreed. On the other she could be next door for sugar or milk, and stayed to gossip while the children played or watched television.

But it was quite out of character for her to forget.

He eased out of the car, pushing the door to but not engaging the

437

lock, and reached to the PPK Walther in his shoulder-holster. He had loaded and checked it before starting his drive home from Castlereagh, but he again looked for the safety-catch mechanism to see it was in the 'on' position. On the balls of his feet he went towards the front gate. The gate was wrought-iron and had never hung well – it rattled and needed a lifting, forcing movement to open it. Rennie instead went to the far side of the gatepost before the hedge thickened, through a gap, past the roses and on to the grass. The run up to the front door was gravel and he kept to the grass, fearful of any noise his feet might make. Though the window showed the light from inside the gap between the curtains it was not enough for him to see through.

There were no voices at the moment he reached the window, just the hymn-singing on the television. Rennie came off the grass and stepped on to the tiled step of the doorway. The Walther was in his right hand, as with the left he found his Yale key and inserted it gently into the opening. Steady now, boy. This is the crucial time. If you're noisy now it's blown – if there's anything to blow. For a fraction he felt sheepish at the stupidity of tiptoeing across his own front lawn. Had the neighbours seen? The door opened, just enough to get him inside. To the lounge door. It was off the latch, and the aperture of an inch or so acted as a funnel to the final crescendo of the programme, and the choir's lusty singing. As the sound tailed away he heard his wife speak. 'Great hero, aren't you? With your bloody rifle. Need it to make a man of you . . .'

The voice, shrill and aggressive, was enough to deaden the tiny amount of sound Rennie made as he leaned into the door, and the man in his chair was aware of nothing till the door started swinging on its hinges towards him.

Downs saw the door moving long before the woman and her children.

His body stiffened as he fought to take hold of himself, and for concentration after seeing his control debilitated long before by the argument across the room. He was still raising his rifle into the fire position when Rennie came in, low and fast, to hit the carpet and roll in one continuous action towards the heavy armchair between the fireplace and the window.

The movement was too fast for Billy Downs, who fired three times into the space by the door before checking to realize that the policeman was no longer there. He struggled up from the sitting position in the deep soft armchair, flooded with the sudden panic that he had fired and missed, and didn't know where his target was.

The metallic click of Rennie's safety catch, and the single shot that howled by his ear and into the french windows behind, located the target.

Rennie was not a marksman. He had been on pistol-shooting courses, most of which simulated a street situation. Only once they'd practised storming a room. When you go in, they'd said, dive and roll as soon as you hit the floor, and keep rolling till you find cover. You're difficult to hit while you're moving. The first shot came as he balanced momentarily on his left side, his right arm free to fire in the general direction of the dark shape across the carpet. But his momentum carried him on till he cannoned into the solid bulk of the big chair. He was on his right side, the Walther driving into the softness of his thigh when he realized his impetus had wedged him between the wall and the chair. He twisted his head, seeing for the first time with agonizing clarity the man, his wife and the children, as he struggled helplessly to swivel his body round. His survival depended on that movement.

The rifle was against Downs's shoulder now, eye down the barrel, not bothering with the complicated sight device, just using the barrel itself to give him a line. He poised himself to fire. Wait for it, you bastard copper, wait for it, now. The triumph of the mission was there now, the bloody slug of the copper on the deck, soft, fat and vulnerable. And dead.

Rennie was screaming. 'No, no. Keep away.'

For the two children the room had disintegrated in speed and noise. When Fiona saw her father some four seconds after he had come through the door she fled from the sofa across the middle of the room towards him.

It was the moment that the man had chosen to fire.

Fractionally his vision, misted and unclear, of the man that he had come to kill was blocked by the chequered dress and the long golden hair.

He hesitated. Staring at the body feverishly trying to get the child behind it and away. It was the time to shoot, a perfect target. Still he hesitated.

He saw the child with pin-point clarity, as sharp as the mummified kids back in the street in London. Not part of the bloody war. He couldn't see the face of the girl as she writhed closer to her father, only the brightness of her dress, the freshness of the white socks, the pink health of the moving skin on the small legs. Couldn't destroy it. Rennie was struggling to pull the child under him to protect her. Downs could see that, and when he'd done so the big policeman would be free to fire himself. Downs knew that. It had no effect. Not shoot a child, no way he could do it. He felt himself drifting away from the reality of the room, concentrating now on his wife. Kids at home, not as clean, scrubbed as these, but the same. If his wife knew he'd slaughtered a small one . . . He saw the slight body fade under the shape of the detective, and the other man's firing arm come up to aim.

Behind the man were the french windows and the light framework of wood. He spun and dived at the centre of one of the glass panels. The wall of wood and glass squares gave way. Rennie, the child spread-eagled under him, emptied the pistol in the direction of the window.

It was the fifth or sixth shot that caught Downs in the muscle of the left arm, just above the elbow. The impact heaved him forward through the obstacle of wood and glass splinters and across the neat patio towards the well-cut back lawn.

The pain was searing hot as Downs ran across the lawn. At the bottom, among the vegetables still in the ground, he crooked the rifle under his injured arm and with his right levered himself over the fence and into a cut-through lane.

Struggling for breath he ran down the lane and then across a field to get to the road where the car was parked. Pushing him forward was the fear of capture, and the knowledge that the failed shooting would bring massive retaliation down on him. Like the fox discovered at work in the chicken coop who flees empty-handed, the sense of survival dominated. The experience in the house, coupled with the exhaustion of the running and the pain in his arm combined to create a confusion of images all returning to the looming blonde head of the child thrust into his line of fire as the detective lay on the ground. It merged with the memory of the muted stunned children in London as he fired at their father. Again and again, though, as with a film loop, came the face of the child across the room, throwing herself at her prone father. And after that, as he neared the car, was the knowledge that if he had fired he would have killed the policeman. He might have hit the child, that was the area of doubt, he would have killed the policeman, that was certainty. He had hesitated, and through his hesitation his target was alive. It was weakness, and he had thought himself above that.

The young driver was asleep when he felt his shoulder shaken violently and above him the frantic and blood-etched face of the man.

'Come on. Get the fucking thing moving. Don't hang about. Get it out of this bloody place.'

'Aren't you going to do something about that . . . ?' the youth pointed to the still-assembled Armalite, but cut off when he saw the blood on the arm that was holding the rifle.

'Just get moving. Mind your own bloody business and drive.'

The boy surged the car forward and out on to the road in the direction of Andersonstown.

'Did it go okay?' he asked.

440

16

The Belfast Brigade staff met in a semi-detached corporation house in the centre of the conglomeration of avenues, crescents, walks and terraces that make up the huge housing estate of Andersonstown. It was very different country to the Falls and Ardoyne. Landscaped roads, and flanking them a jig-saw of neat red-brick homes. Ostensibly the war had not come here with the same force as in the older battlegrounds closer to the city centre, but such an impression would be false. This was the Provo redoubt, where the Brigade officers and top bomb-makers had their hideouts, where the master snipers lay up between operations, where five thousand people voted for a Provisional supporter in a Westminster election. Cups of tea were rare for the troops here, and it was the tough and experienced battalions who were asked to hold the ring with the most dedicated and intransigent of the enemy.

The particular house where the Brigade met had been chosen with care. It had been noticed that the combination of a twist in the road and a slight lip shielded both the front and rear doors of the house from the army camp some three hundred yards away. The house could be approached from the rear with virtual impunity.

The Brigade commanders were key figures in the campaign in the main urban area of Northern Ireland. Some, like Joe Cahill and Seamus Twomey, had become household names round the world, famous as the man who had converted the guerilla wars of South-East Asia and the Middle East and Latin America into West European terms. Promotion had exposed younger men to the job, none of them any the less hardliners for their youth . . . Adams, Bell, Convery. All had learned assiduously the arts of concealment and disguise. Their capture called for rounds of drinks and celebration toasts in the Mess of the army unit concerned, and articles in the national press maintaining that the Provos were about to fold up. But within a week of the one-time commander being carried off to Long Kesh so another young man moved forward into the scene to take over. During their reign in office, however short, they would set the tone of the administration. One would favour car bombs, another would limit attacks only to military and police targets, or direct operations towards spectaculars such as big fires, major shootouts and prison escapes.

Each left his imprint on the situation, and all went into the mythology of the movement. The one common factor was their ability to move, almost at will, round the rambling Andersonstown estate. Their names were well known to the troops, but their faces were blurs taken for the most part from out-of-date photographs. One had ordered his wife to destroy all family pictures that included him, and given all his briefings from behind curtains and drapes, so that under the rigours of cross-examination his lieutenants would not be able to give an accurate description of him. The most famous of all had sufficient mastery of impersonation to be able to win an apology for inconvenience from a young officer who had led a search party through the house where the Brigade commander was giving an interview to a reporter from a London Sunday.

To a portion of the community their names provoked unchecked admiration, while to those less well disposed they sowed an atmosphere of fear. There were enough youths with 'kneecap jobs' and daubed slogans of 'Touts will be shot dead' for the message not to have to be repeated that often.

That there were a few prepared to risk the automatic hooding and assassination was a constant source of surprise to the army intelligence officers. Money was mostly the reason that men would whisper a message into a telephone booth, but not even then big sums. There was seldom the wish to rid the community of the Provisionals . . . Men who felt that way stayed silent, kept their peace, and went about their lives. It was because the Brigade commander and his principal lieutenants could never be totally certain of the loyalty of the men and women who lived in Andersonstown that they delayed their meeting till midnight, though their arrival at the house had been staggered over the previous seventy minutes.

None was armed. All were of sufficient importance to face sentences of up to a dozen years if caught in possession of a firearm. If arrested without a specific criminal offence proveable against them they could only be detained in the Kesh – with the constant likelihood of amnesties.

They took over a back bedroom while below the lady of the house made them a pot of tea. She took it up the stairs on a tray with beakers and milk and sugar. They had stopped talking when she came in and said nothing till she had placed the tray on the flat top of a clothes chest, and turned to the door.

'Thanks, mam,' the Brigade commander spoke, the others nodding and murmuring in agreement. She was away down the stairs to busy herself with her sewing and late-night television. When that was over she would sleep in her chair, waiting for the last man to leave the house to tell her the talking was over. The woman asked no questions and received no explanations other than the obvious one that the positioning of the house made it necessary that the men should use it.

There were six men in the room when the meeting started. The Brigade commander sat on the bed with two others, and one more stood.

Frank and Seamus Duffryn were on the wooden chairs that, apart from the bed and the chest, represented the only furniture in the room. The present commander had been in office more than six months, and his general features were better known than was common. He scorned the flamboyance of masks. From the pocket of his dark anorak he brought a small transistor radio of the sort with a corded loop to be slipped over the wrist so that he could walk along the pavement with it pressed to his ear. This was how he kept abreast of the activities of the ASUs, the Active Service Units.

The crucial listening times of the day for him were 7.50 a.m., the 12.55 lunchtime summary, and then five to midnight. Each day the BBC's Northern Ireland news listed with minute detail the successes and failures of his men. Shootings, hi-jackings, blast bombs, arms finds, stone-throwing incidents, all were listed and chronicled for him. The lead story that night was of the shooting at a policeman's house in Dunmurry.

The men in the room listened absorbed to the firm English accent of the announcer.

The gunman had apparently held Mrs Rennie and her two children at gunpoint in their house for some hours while he waited for her husband to return from duty. A police spokesman said that when Mr Rennie entered the living-room of his home the gunman fired at him. Mr Rennie dived for shelter behind an armchair just as his younger daughter ran towards him. It seems the child ran into the field of fire of the terrorist, who then stopped shooting and ran from the house. Mr Rennie told detectives that when the girl moved he thought she was going to be killed as the gunman was on the point of firing at him. The family are said to be suffering from shock and are staying the night with friends.

  In the Shantallow district of Londonderry a blast bomb slightly wounded . . .

The commander switched off the set.

'That's not like bloody Downs from Ardoyne. Not like him to lose his nerve. Why should he do that?'

'Stupid bastard. We needed Rennie killed. Put a lot of planning in and a deal of work to have him rubbed. Then it's screwed. Could be they're just feeding us this crap.' It was the Brigade quartermaster who came in.

'Doesn't sound like that. Sounds like Downs just threw it. Hardly going to fool us, are they? The bugger Rennie, he's alive or he's dead. We sent for him to be killed, he's not. So that means it's failure, can't be any other answer. What matters is that our man couldn't finish it.'

He pondered on the decision he was about to take as the other men

443

waited for him. He alone knew of the link between Danby in London and the man Downs from Ardoyne. Later perhaps he would include the others in the knowledge, he decided, but not now. At this stage, he felt the fewer the better. Some of the commanders ran the office by committee, but not the man who now spoke again.

'On from there. What about the man they've put in? What do we have?'

'I think it's watertight.' Frank had taken the cue and come in. Frank had been with the Provisionals since the split with the Officials, the 'Stickies' as they called them, but this was the first time he had been in such élite company. It slightly unnerved him. 'The girl he was laying spills it all. It's incredible, what he told her. She was saying that he says to her that he was sent over to get the man that shot Danby in London. She told him about the girl, the one that was picked up and taken to Springfield, the one that hanged herself. It was because he shopped her that she was taken in. She says she challenged him about it yesterday afternoon. He admitted it.'

The Brigade intelligence officer was sitting on the bed beside the commander. Hard face, tight pencil lips, and darting, piglike eyes.

'What's his name, the Englishman?'

'The name he's using is Harry McEvoy. I doubt if it's real or –'

"Course it isn't. Doesn't matter that. They must be a bit touched up then over there, if they send a man over on his own, to find us just like that.'

Duffryn spoke.

'But it all fits with what we had from the hotel. The army man and the RUC. The bit we had about them putting a man in and then not telling the brass. We thought we'd caught the buggers griping about it. It has to be some nonsense drawn up by one of them bastards sat behind a desk in London, in the Ministry.'

Duffryn was little more than a name to the commander. He looked at him with interest.

'You had a line on the man first, right? Through his accent? Where is he now? What's covering him?'

'He's at the guest house, where he has his lodgings. It's called "Delrosa", run by Mrs Duncan, off the Broadway. She's all right. He's there in a back room that he rents. The front and back are watched at the moment and the lads have been told in the last hour or so that if he goes out he's to be tailed. But they must stay right back.'

'And the girl you've talked to, won't she warn him?'

'We told her not to. I think she understood. She won't do anything,' Frank said.

The commander lit his fourth cigarette in less than half an hour, pulled at it, forcing the smoke down into his throat.

'I think we want him before we hood him. We would like to talk to him for a bit first. Pick him up and bring him in for a talk. Does he work?'

'In a scrap yard. He leaves to walk there about eight, just a few minutes after perhaps.'

'Take him when he's walking. On the main road, get him into a car and take him up the Whiterock, into the Crescent, the house there we've used. I don't want him killed unless it's that or he's away. Remember that, I want him chatted with.'

For Frank and Seamus it seemed the end of their part in the evening. They rose out of the chairs, but were waved down by the commander.

'Where's Downs now?'

The Brigade quartermaster said, 'The message came through just before I left to come here. The wound he got, it's a light one, in the arm. Flesh. It's being fixed up now by the quack in the Murph. He's okay, but he hasn't gone home yet. The quack will want to keep an eye on him for the next few hours.'

The Brigade commander talked to no one in particular.

'What do they say when a driver's been in a crash? A lorry driver, bus, heavy truck? That sort of thing. What do they say? Send him straight back out again. Don't hang about fidgeting and mumbling about it. Get stuck in again. Downs can go on this one. His nerve wasn't too good last night. He'll need this to get him back into scratch again. He'll want to retrieve himself a bit. Get him here in an hour. Downs can finish him after the talking to.'

It amused him: the fox turning back on the hound.

For Frank and Seamus the briefing was finished. They went out through the back of the house to where a car was parked some three hundred yards away, keys in the dash. Frank would drive on to the doctor and drop Seamus near his home.

Seamus Duffryn was frightened for the first time since he had become involved with the movement. He'd been present three months earlier at an interrogation. A kid from up in Lenadoon. The charge was that he had betrayed colleagues in the movement to the military. The muffled screaming of the youth was still in his ears, bouncing and ricocheting about. They'd burned his naked stomach with cigarette ends while he was strapped in a chair, with a blanket over his head folded several times to deaden the noise. He'd screamed each time the glowing ash met his skin, from a deep animal desperation and not with hope of release. Seamus Duffryn had become involved that night, and would become involved again tomorrow. The paper stuff he did, that was unimportant. This is when it mattered and you were either in the movement or you were out of it. There had been an awful, shaming thrill through his entire body when he saw the light grey material of the boy's trousers turn to heavy charcoal. As the urine ran down the kid's leg there'd been the steam rising through the trousers, and the hood had gone on, and the gun had been cocked. At the moment they shot him the kid was still screaming but uncontrolled.

If McEvoy was British army, how would he take it? Duffryn wondered. That was a nothing from Lenadoon. McEvoy would be different. How would he stand up to their interrogation and the ritual end?

He would find out by tomorrow night. He hurried on his way through the night to his home and his mother.

After he'd made his phone call to London Harry had spent the rest of the day in his room. Before dark he gazed mindlessly into the abstract of roofs and walls that was the view from his window. He had not gone down to Sunday high tea, and to Mrs Duncan's enquiries only replied that he thought he had something of a chill coming on. He was going to have an early night, he shouted through the door. She had wanted to bring him a hot drink in his room, but through the closed door he managed to persuade her that there was no need.

He wanted to be alone, shutting out the perpetual tension of moving in company and living the falsehood that had been planned for him. That girl. It had upset him. Created imbalance in the delicate poise he had taken up. Blown by a silly girl who couldn't stop talking. Up on a mountain, wind and rain, like some cigarette advertisement, and he'd chucked the whole operation. Ridiculous and, worse, so bloody unprofessional. He brooded away the hours. He'd put faith down on the line of a girl whose address he didn't even know. What in Christ's name would they be thinking in London when he put the request in for the special treatment for Harry's bit of tail? Go raving mad, wouldn't they? And reckon he'd twisted. No way they wouldn't. And they'd want to get him out.

He'd heard all the radio broadcasts, searching for the formula announcement that would end it all. Arrest . . . Man wanted for questioning . . . London murder . . . Big operation . . . Tip off . . . Appear in court. That would be the jargon. There had been nothing.

He had steeled himself to what he would do if he heard of the capture of the man. He'd be out of the front door, straight out, with no farewells or packing of luggage, on to the Falls, and turn right along the main road, and then right again before the hospital and on down to the Broadway barracks, and in through the front door . . . But without the news he couldn't end it. He had to stay, finish the job. No arrest and it was all a failure, abject and complete. Not worth going back for, just to report how it all got boobed. Didn't really matter what Davidson said. No arrest, no return.

But where was the bloody army? Why wasn't it all wrapped up? Big enough, weren't they? Got enough men, and guns, and trucks. He's out there just waiting for you to go and get him. The National bulletins traced their way round the news; there was nothing from Northern Ireland.

The frustration mounted in Harry, welling up against his reason and his training. How much information had he pushed at them in London over the last two, three weeks? How much did they *want*? All sewn up, it should be, cut and dried, taped and parcelled – and now more delay. Through Josephine, streak of bloody luck there, about as much information had come out as he was ever likely to get his hands on. The long-term adrenalin was fading . . . he wanted out . . . he wanted it over . . . but when it was finished.

As the dusk came he unwrapped the Smith and Wesson. After locking the door he took the weapon to pieces and laid it out on a handkerchief on the bed. With a second, dirtied handkerchief from his pocket he cleaned the firing mechanism, then reassembled the gun. He would take it with him next morning to the yard. Put it in the bag where the sandwich box went. It was a sort of therapy, the gun, the instant pick-me-up. It had gone wrong. Nothing on the radio when there should have been. The girl, that was where it had gone wrong, with that bloody girl. Lovely face, lovely body, lovely girl, but that was where it all loused up. Nothing else, that's the only point where it's gone wrong, but that's enough. Gossip, don't they, and she won't keep her mouth shut any more than the rest of them. Like she talked about Theresa, so she'll talk about me. A lonely man in a back-room bed-sitter. The gun was insurance, the disaster was less distinct.

When he went to bed he lay a long time in the dark of the room thinking about Germany, the family, home and the people with whom he worked. The other officers, easy and relaxed, none of them knowing where Harry was, and few caring. He envied them, yet felt his dislike of that easy way of life. His distrust of the others not committed to the front, as he was now, was all-consuming. It was only rarely that he turned his mind to his wife and the children. It took him time, and with difficulty he re-created them and home on the NATO base. The chasm between their environment and Harry's was too difficult for him to bridge. Too tired, too exhausted.

His final thought was salvation and made sleep possible. Of course the man was in custody, but they'd be questioning him. It would take thirty-six hours at least. They wouldn't rush it, they'd want to get it right. Tomorrow evening they would be announcing it, and then home, and out of the hole, another forty-eight hours perhaps, and then out.

*

447

In the early hours of that Monday morning, while Harry alternately dozed and dreamed in his bed, and while the Brigade nucleus sat up in Andersonstown waiting for Downs to come, Davidson in the Covent Garden office was scanning the first London editions of the papers.

Both *The Times* and the *Guardian* carried reports from Northern Ireland that the Provisional IRA were claiming that British intelligence had launched a special agent into the Catholic areas, and that people in those areas had been warned to be especially vigilant. Both the writers under whose byline the stories appeared emphasized that, whether true or false, the claim would have the effect of further reducing the minimal trust between the people of the minority areas, the front-line housing estates of the city and the security forces. There was much other news competing for space – on the diplomatic front, the state of the economy, and the general 'human interest clap trap' that Davidson raged about. The Belfast copy was not prominently displayed, but to the man propped up on his camp bed it presented a shattering blow. He lay deep in newsprint and pondered his telephone, wondering whether there were calls he should make, anything he could usefully do.

Those bungling idiots had still failed to pick up the chap Downs and the girl Josephine. Near a day to get them, and nothing to show for it. He was astonished, too long after the war, too long after the organization had run down, too many civilians who'd never been up the sharp end. Without the arrest the scheme of which he was an integral part would collapse, and at a rate of knots. In all conscience he could not ring that man Frost again, supercilious bastard, and once more expose himself to that sarcasm. On the wall by the door the clock showed after two. For a moment he comforted himself that Harry might see the report for himself and do a bunk on his own.

No, that wouldn't fit, scrap men don't take *The Times* or the *Guardian*, that wouldn't match the cover.

Davidson tried to shut the problem out of his mind, and closed his eyes. He fumbled unseeing above him till his fingers caught at the string that hung down from the light switch. By the time he drifted into sleep he had worked out his immediate future. The early retirement and professional disgrace, and all because that hoof-footed army couldn't pick one man up. The unfairness of it all.

Frost had gone to bed a little after midnight, and lain half awake expecting the phone to ring, and unwilling to commit himself to the task of sleeping. It had to come, the message that either the man or the girl had been found. The bell's shrill insistence eventually woke him. The army in Ardoyne reported no known entries or departures at the house in Ypres Avenue. He authorized the unit to move in and search at 05.30 hours.

After that he slept, safe in the knowledge that Monday would be a real day, a real bugger.

The doctor had cleaned the wound. He'd found the damage slight, lessened further as the cotton wool and spirit cleaned away the caked blood that had smeared itself on the upper part of the left arm. A small portion of flesh had been ripped clear close by the smallpox vaccination scar. There was an entry and exit wound, almost together and one, and after he had cleaned it thoroughly the doctor put a light lint dressing over the pale numbed skin.

'You can move yourself around a bit. If you need to, that is. But if possible you should stay still, take it quiet. Go put yourself in the easy chair out the back, and get a rest or something.'

'Is it serious? Will I be left with anything?' asked Downs.

'If you look after it you'll be okay, nothing to worry about, nothing at all. But you must go easy to start with. The only problem is if it gets infected at this early stage. But we'll see that doesn't happen – yes?'

The doctor had been associated with the fringes of the movement since the start of the violence. He asked no questions, and needed few answers. Once every fortnight or so he would hear the square of gravel flick once, twice, against his bedroom window, and in his dressing-gown he would open the door to a casualty too sensitive to face ordinary hospital treatment. He had made his attitude clear at least three years earlier, that there was no point them bringing men to him who were already close to death. Take them to the RVH, he'd said. If their wounds were that bad they'd be out of it for months anyway, so better for them to get top medical treatment in the best hospital than the hand-to-mouth service he could provide. He handled a succession of minor gunshot wounds, was able to remove bullets, clean wounds and prevent sepsis setting in.

He was sympathetic to the Provisionals but he gave them no material support other than the late-night *ex officio* surgery. Perhaps if he had been born into the ghetto he would have been one of them, but he came from off the hill, and went to medical school after sixth-form secondary education. Though they had his sympathy he reflected he was a very different person from the hard, wild-eyed men who came to him for treatment.

Downs was very white in the chair, his shirt ripped away on the left side and his coat, holed and bloody, draped over the back. He heard the faint knock at the door down the corridor at the front of the house. There was a whispered dispute in the hall. He heard that distinctly and twisted himself round in the chair to see two men push their way past the doctor and into the room.

There was a tall man, in jeans and a roll-neck sweater. 'The Chief wants you. He's waiting in Andytown now. Said he wants to see you straight away.'

The doctor remonstrated, 'Look at the state he's in. You can see that for yourself. He should be here all night, then go and rest. He's in shock.'

'No chance. He's wanted at a meeting. There'll be no permanent damage if we take him?'

'You're setting back recovery time, and adding to the risk of infection.'

'We'll see you get a look at him tomorrow. Right now we have to go. Come on.'

This last was to Downs. Twice he looked backwards and forwards from the messenger to the doctor, willing the doctor to be more insistent. The doctor didn't meet him, avoiding the pleading in the man's eyes. The tall man and his colleague took hold of Downs under his armpits and gently but decisively lifted him towards the door.

The doctor said, 'You may need these to pull him up a bit, if there's something that he has to do. Not more than a couple at a time, after that he has to sleep. If he takes them they'll help him for a few hours, then it's doubly important that he rests.'

From the high wall cabinet in the back room he took down a brown pill bottle, half filled with tablets, half with a wad of cotton wool.

They always said they'd come back, but few did. If they needed further treatment they headed south, where they could lie up more easily away from the daily tensions of the perpetual hunt by the military for men on the wanted list. The doctor watched them carry the man to the car and ease him into the back, propped up against the arm-rest in the centre of the seat. He wagered himself the pills would be in use before lunchtime.

The drive between the doctor's house and the meeting place in Andersonstown took twenty minutes. They helped the wounded man out of the car and in through the back entrance the way the night's other visitors had come. Irritably he shrugged them off him once he was inside the scullery, and independently followed their instructions up the stairs and in through the second door on the left of the landing.

Only the Brigade commander had remained to see him.

'How are you, Billy? Have they fixed you up all right?'

'Not so bad. It's only in the flesh. Not much more than a graze, the thing went straight on through. It's bandaged up now and the doc says it's clean.'

'I heard a bit about it on the radio. Said you didn't get a shot into

450

the bastard, you didn't hit him. Said his brat got in the way and you didn't fire. Is that right?'

'It's not as simple as that.' Oh, Christ, not an inquest now. Not why, wherefore, how and when at this time of night. 'I fired once and missed, then when I had a clear shot at him the kid came right across. She was right in front of his body and his head. I couldn't see him so I didn't fire.'

The Brigade commander was still smoking, in front of him the clear glass ashtray mounted with a score of filtered ends steeped in the grey powder he flicked continuously into the bowl. The debris was left in a circle round the ashtray where it balanced on the blanket over the bed.

'If you'd just fired, child and all . . . then you would have got him, yes? If you'd just gone right on through with it Rennie would be dead, right?'

'Is that what they said on the radio?' Downs was peeved by the reception, not used to being challenged and questioned. 'Is that what Rennie is saying, on the radio? If I had fired through the kid then I would have killed him?'

Who did this bugger think he was, thought Downs. When was this miserable sod out with an ASU? When did he expose himself? All right for those who give orders and send kids out to carry bombs into tuppenny-ha'penny supermarkets. Get out on the streets at night, know the silence of waiting, the terrible noise of action, feel a nine-millimetre slug hit you. Then come quizzing me. Anger rose in him, but not sufficient for him to shout, to release him from the discipline inculcated into him. Can't shout at the Brigade commander. That's mutiny.

'I don't know what Rennie is saying,' said the commander. 'The radio said the child was in the way and that you didn't fire. That's all. There's no criticism of you. I know of no cause for criticism.'

Cunning sod. 'There shouldn't be. Rennie was no soft one. He moved bloody well.'

'One or two people, who don't know the facts as we do, might feel if they only had half the story that Billy Downs had ballsed it up, gone soft on the job. If they hadn't the big picture, and knew it all, they might say Billy Downs was sent on a job, and when one of the copper's brats got in the way that then he held his fire.' Downs didn't really know the commander, he was from a different part of the city. They had had no real dealings before, but rank separated them, and dictated that he must let him have his say. 'These people, they might recall that when we shot Sean Russell, of the UDR, in New Barnsley, that he had his kids draped all over him. Now two of them were wounded, but Russell was still shot dead. The order had been to shoot him. Now we all know that it wouldn't be fair to put your escapade tonight in the same category. And we know that your nerve is as good as ever. That you are one of the top soldiers we have. We know that, don't we, Billy?'

451

'You know it's balls,' said Downs. 'I'm not soft. My nerve hasn't gone. We're not fighting five-year-olds. Is that what you're saying, that we kill wee girls? Are you saying that I should have fired straight through the girl? Is that what you think I ought to have done?'

'Don't get ratty, Billy. It's just we have to be careful that people who don't know the circumstances might think that. They might point out that getting you that close to Rennie took a deal of time, and that then the front runner botched the whole bloody thing . . . because a kiddie got in the way. That's nonsense, Billy.' The voice droned on, repetition of failure dragging itself through Downs. He had to sleep, to rest, to escape from this room with this boring and nagging whore of a man.

'We know it's not true, Billy. We know there was a good reason for you not to shoot. We know you couldn't see the target. We know Rennie wasn't straightforward. I don't know how many other people feel the same way. But that's enough of that. Nobody will have a leg to stand on by tomorrow night. Right, Billy? We have a little job tomorrow, and by the time that's done they'll be silenced.'

Downs looked away, broken by the twisting of the screw. Self-doubt rampant. The commander crushed the ego out of him.

'I'm the only one of Brigade group that knows about London. We've kept it tight for your protection. It's worked pretty well . . . up to now. There's a difficulty come up. The Brits have put a man in to find you. An agent. McEvoy. Harry McEvoy. Lodging down in Broadway. There's a split in their top ranks about him. We think London wanted him but Lisburn didn't.'

He let it sink in, watched the colour return to the man's face, watched the fear come back to his eyes and saw the hands begin to clasp and activate.

'His job, the agent's job, is to find you. Perhaps to kill you, perhaps to take you in, or just tell them where to go. We fancy he wants to kill you. He's been near to you already. He tipped the troops that picked up the girl that hanged herself. We think she did that rather than tell about you. Rennie was the one that questioned her. He chatted to that girl till she was ready to hang herself. You couldn't kill him when his brat jumped in the way. You had no cause to be soft with Rennie. You'll have a chance to let people know what you're made of, Billy. Tomorrow we're going to lift this fellow that's come for you, and we'll talk to him, then we'll hood him. That's where you come in. You'll shoot him, like you shot Danby, like you should have shot Rennie.'

Downs felt faint now, exhausted by the sarcasm of the top man. He nodded, sweat rising from his crotch across his body.

'When it's over we'll send you down to Donegal. Sleep it all off, and get fit again. Tonight you'll stay in Andytown. You'll be taken there now, and they'll pick you up at six-fifteen. They'll have the guns when they meet you. This will sort it out, I think. Be just the right answer to those who say that Billy Downs has gone soft.'

452

He wanted out, and this was the chance. They were showing him the way. The way to do it properly, not so as you were looking over your shoulder for half a lifetime, and running. The official way, that was how it was done. One more day, one more job. Then out. Leave it to the cowboys. The heroes who didn't hold their fire, who shot wee kids. Squeeze the trigger right through the scream of a five-year-old. Was that Pearse's revolution, or Connolly's or Plunkett's? Was it, hell. Leave it to the cowboys after one more day.

17

The long night was coming to its close when B Company swarmed into Ypres Avenue. The column of armoured cars had split up some hundreds of yards from the street, and guided by co-ordinated radio messages had arrived at each end of the row of bleak terraced houses simultaneously. The first troops out sprinted down the back entrances behind the houses, taking up positions every fifteen yards or so of the debris-strewn pathways. From the tops of the Land-Rovers searchlights played across the fronts of the houses as the noise and banging in the street brought the upstairs lights flickering on.

The major who commanded the company had received only a short briefing. He had been told the man they were looking for was named Billy Downs, the address of his house, and that he was expected to search several houses. He was thirty-three years old, on his fourth tour to Northern Ireland, and as a company commander in South Armagh on his last visit had witnessed four of his men killed in a culvert bomb explosion. His hatred of the Provisionals was deep-rooted and lasting. Unlike some of his brother officers who respected the expertise of the opposition he felt only consuming contempt.

What Downs was wanted for he hadn't been told, nor what his status was in the IRA. He'd only guessed the reason for the raid when they unpinned the picture from the guardroom wall and given it him. It was the photokit that had gone up five weeks earlier after the London shooting and remained top of the soldiers' priority list. The intelligence officer down from Lisburn noticed the flash of recognition spread across his face as he looked down at the picture.

*

Once the street was sealed there was time to work carefully and slowly along the road. No. 41 was the third house they came to. The soldiers banged on the door with their rifle butts. The few who had seen the picture of the man they wanted were hanging on the moment of anticipation, wondering who would come and open the door.

From upstairs came the noise of crying, steadily increasing to screaming pitch as the family woke to the battering at the wooden panels. Downs's wife came to the door, thin and frail in her nightdress and cotton dressing-gown. A tiny figure became silhouetted against the light from the top of the stairs when she drew back the bolts, turned the key and stood against the soldiers. The troops in the search party pushed past her, huge in their boots and helmets and flak jackets. They raced up the stairs, equipment catching and bouncing off the banisters. A lieutenant and two sergeants. All had seen the picture, all knew what they were there for. The officer, his Browning pistol cocked and fastened to his body by a lanyard, swung his left shoulder into the front bedroom door, and bullocked his way to the window. The man behind switched on the light, covering the bed with his automatic rifle.

Two faces peered back at the intruders. Saucer-eyed, mouths open, and motionless. The troops patted the bodies of the children and pressed down in the bedclothes round them, isolating the little humps they made with the blankets. They looked under the bed and in the wardrobe. There were no other hiding places in the room, and that effectively exhausted the possible hiding places.

They had come in hard and fast, and now they stopped, halted by the anti-climax of the moment.

The lieutenant went to the top of the stairs and shouted down.

'Not here, sir.'

'Wait there, I'll come up.'

The major came in and looked slowly round the room.

'Right, not here now. But he has been, or she's a dirty little bitch round the house. There, his pants, vest, socks. I wouldn't imagine they lie round the house too long.'

By the window was the crumpled pile of dirty clothes underneath the chair that Downs used to hang his coat and trousers on at night.

'Get her up here,' said the major. 'And get the floorboard chaps. He's been here pretty recently. May still be in the house. If he's about I want him found, wherever he is, roof, basement if there is one, wherever.'

She came into the room, her two youngest children hanging like monkeys over her shoulders, thumbs in mouths. Like their mother they were white-faced, and shivering in the cold away from their bedclothes.

'We were wondering where we might find your husband, Mrs Downs.'

'He's not here. You've poked your bloody noses in, and you can see that. Now get out of here.'

454

'His clothes are here, Mrs Downs, you and I can both see that. I wouldn't expect a nice girl like you to leave his dirty pants lying on the floor that many days.'

'Don't be bloody clever with me,' she snarled back at him. 'He's not here, and you can see that, now get your soldiers out of here.'

'The problem, Mrs Downs, is that we think your husband could still be here. That would be the explanation for his clothes being on the floor. I'm afraid we're going to have to search round a bit. We'll cause as little disruption as possible. I assure you of that.'

'Big heroes, aren't you, when you have your tanks and guns. Big and bloody brave.'

The soldier with the crowbar mouthed an apology as he came past her. He flipped up a corner of the threadworn carpet and with a rending scrape pulled up the board at the end of the room. In four separate places he took the planks up before disappearing to his hips down the holes he had made. The major and the soldiers waited above for him to emerge with his torch for the last time and announce with an air of professional disappointment that the floor space was clear. Using ladders they went up into the loft shaking the beams above the major and the man's wife, and swinging the light fitting.

'Nothing up there either, sir.'

The ground floor was of stone and tile, so that stayed put, while the expert banged on the walls with his hammer in search of cavities. The coal bunker out in the yard was cleared out, the wooden framework under the sink taken down.

'It's clean, sir.'

That was the cue for her to return to the attack.

'Are you through now, you bastards? All these men and one little house, and one wee girl alone with her kids, and it takes all of you and your bloody guns and Saracens . . .'

'You know why we want him?' The major lashed out. 'You know what he did? We'll go on till we get him. If we have to rip this house to pieces each week till we get him, we'll do that. Doesn't he tell you where he's going at night? Doesn't he tell you what he did last month? Try asking him one day.'

He strode out through the house, followed by his search team. It was three minutes after six o'clock. Failure and frustration was how the majority of these raids ended. He knew that, and he'd never lost his temper before, never gone overboard as he'd done with the woman in No. 41. He comforted himself on two points. It needed saying; and the intelligence officer who had tagged along hadn't heard it.

Once the army had gone a clutch of neighbours moved into the house to gather round the woman and commiserate on the damage left behind. None knew of the importance of Billy Downs amongst the Provisionals and so news of the army outrage at the house would travel fast through the community. Yet those that came to dress the children and help in the clearing up and the making of tea and breakfast noted how subdued was their friend. Cowed by what had happened. That was not the usual way. The familiar reaction was to greet the going of the soldiers with a hail of insults and obscenities at their backs. But not this woman.

Once the friends and neighbours had left her to get their own families ready for work or school or just dressed and fed, the words of the officer returned to ring in her ears. Quietly she padded about the house, her children in a crocodile procession behind her, checking to see which of her few possessions were damaged or tarnished or moved.

This was the confirmation. God, this was what she had feared. Right back to the first night back home after London, she had been waiting. So much wind this confidence he had, that no one knew him. Like a rat he was, waiting in a barn with the door shut for the farmer to come in the morning with his gun and his dogs. The big, fresh-faced officer, with the smears on his cheeks, with his suspicion of a moustache and posh accent, who hated her, he had laid down the future. He had mirrored her nightmares and hallucinations while she lay sleepless beside her man. They would come, and come again for him, and keep on till they found him.

Last night he had not slept beside her. On the radio in the back room she heard the early news. A policeman shot at . . . an intruder hit . . . in the middle evening. That was the top story. Whoever had been involved should have been home now. Her man was usually home by now, or he would have said something.

Around the passage and stairs and landing of the house she thought of her man. Wounded, maimed, alone in the dawn of the city. What hurt most was that she was so unable to influence events.

News carried across the city. With the efficiency of tribal tom-toms word passed over the sprawling urban conglomeration that the terraced house in Ypres Avenue had been raided. Less than an hour after the major had walked through the front door and to his armoured Land-Rover Billy Downs would hear of it. Brigade staff had decided that he should know. They felt it could only enhance his motivation for the job at hand.

Harry's alarm clock dragged him from the comfort of his dreaming, and woke him to the blackness of his room. His dreams had been of home, wife and children, makeshift garden behind his quarters, holidays in timber forest chalets, fishing out in the cool before the sun came up, trout barbecued for breakfast. With consciousness came the knowledge of another Monday morning. It was three weeks to the day that he had left the house at Dorking with the view of the hills and vegetable garden.

456

Twenty-one days exactly. 'Must have been out my mind,' he muttered to the emptiness of the room.

Over the week-end he had thought of what Josephine had said to him. She'd accused him of interfering in something that was basically none of his concern, of causing death when he should have stayed uninvolved. Stupid bitch should have passed the same message to the man who came to London with the Kalashnikov.

He examined his position and its natural courses. He wanted to finish it. End it properly. End it with a shooting, with the man in the picture with his black and white-lined face, dead. That was not emotional, there was no wild spirit of revenge, just that such an ending was the only finite one, otherwise the job was incomplete.

In Aden, good old Aden, it had been so much more simple. British lives at stake, the justification of everything, with the enemy clearly defined – Arabs, gollies. But here, who was the enemy? Why was he the enemy? Did you have to know why to take his life? It churned over and over, unanswered, like pebbles in a coffee machine, grating, ill-fitting and indigestible.

In spite of the fact that Harry came originally from the country town an hour or so's drive from Belfast the army's mould had been the real fashioning influence over-reaching his childhood. Like his brother officers in the mess he was still perplexed at the staying power of the opposition. But here he parted company. To the others they were the enemy, to Harry they were still the opposition. You could kill them if it was necessary, or if that was demanded for operational reasons, but they remained the opposition. They didn't have to be the enemy to make them worth killing.

But how did they keep it up? What made them prepared to risk their lives on the streets when they took on the power of a British army infantry section? What led them to sacrifice most of the creature-comforts of life to go on the run? What made them feel the God-given right to take life, and torture a man in front of his family?

They're not heroes. Bloody lunatics, he said to himself as he pulled his sweater over his head. They rejected all the ordinary things that ordinary people search for, and chose to go on against these massive odds. It didn't involve Harry. The man he was searching for was quite straightforward. He was a killer. He was a challenge. Simple and clean. Harry could focus on that.

'A cup of tea, Mr McEvoy?' Mrs Duncan at the door cut short his thoughts. 'What would you be wanting for breakfast? There's the lot if you can manage it. Sausages, bacon, tomatoes, eggs, and I've some soda bread? –'

'Just toast and coffee, thanks. I'll be away down in a moment.'

'That won't get you far. It's a raw day, right enough.'

457

'Nothing more, thank you, Mrs Duncan. Really, that's all I want. I'll be right down.'

'Please yourself then. Bathroom's clear. Coffee's made, and remember to wrap up well. It's a cold one.'

After he'd shaved there was not much to the dressing. Sweater already on and damp from the soap and flannel, faded jeans, his socks and boots and his anorak. He took the face towel from the rail in the bathroom, brought it back into his room and when he had finished dressing laid it out on the bed. About two feet by one and a half, it was bigger than the one the Smith and Wesson was already wrapped in, and he changed them over, putting the revolver in the new towel.

'Silly bugger,' he thought, 'clean towels just to wrap a gun in.' He needed a towel to disguise the outline of the weapon when it sat in the deep pocket of his anorak on the way to work. But he didn't need a clean towel. That's the army for you: everything clean on a Monday morning. Funny if he got stopped at a road block. He thought of that and a whole band of disappointed squaddies having to hand him over. Wouldn't have cried overmuch either. Last night, late, he'd decided to put the gun in his coat, easier access than the food bag slung over his shoulder, and the bag with the sandwiches and flask would be lying about in the rest hut through the day, and God knows who could be rummaging around in there. When the revolver was wrapped it was light and blunt, though still bulky and hard to ignore, bigger than a spectacle case, bigger than twenty cigarettes and the large box of matches that most men carried.

He breezed into the kitchen.

'Morning, Mrs Duncan, all right then?'

'Not so bad, little enough to complain about. You're sure about the toast and coffee?' Disappointment clouded her face when he nodded. Harry had been in the bathroom during the seven o'clock news bulletins, and through the closed door he had heard her radio playing faintly downstairs, loud enough to be aware of it, but too indistinct to hear the actual words.

'Anything on the news, then?'

'Nothing to note, just the usual. It goes on. A policeman chased a man out of his house and shot him. That's his version, anyway, up Dunmurry way, more trouble in the Unionists. Never change their spots, that crowd. They've given nothing to us without it being wrung out . . .'

Harry laughed. 'They haven't caught the big man yet then, top of the Provos?'

'Well, Mr McEvoy, if they have, they didn't say so, which means they haven't. They'd be trumpeting it if they had, but that's all the news is, the troubles. Makes you wonder what they used to put in before it all started. I can hardly remember. There must have been something else for them to talk about, but they've forgotten it now, right enough.'

'Well, then, no big man in the net –'

'They don't get the real big men, only the shrimps.'

'No, it's just that I read in one of the papers I saw up at the yard that they were mounting an effort to rake in the big fish.'

'They say they're doing that each week, and nothing comes of it.'

Harry had banked a lot on the man being in custody. It was twenty-one hours after the call to London, to Davidson. Couldn't be that difficult to pick the bastard up. Shouldn't be taxing the might of the British army. They must have him, but they weren't saying yet, had to be that way. They wouldn't say yet, too early, of course it was. The explanation was facile but enough to tide him over his breakfast.

It was Monday morning and he was the only guest. Tonight, round tea time, the travellers and the others would be back in the front room. The place then was not quite his own as on Saturdays and Sundays. Lord and master of the household was how he felt over the weekend. Delusions of grandeur.

'Will Josephine be in this afternoon?' He sounded casual, matter-of-fact.

'Should be, Mr McEvoy. Should be here in time to help me with the teas and a bit of tidying up that I haven't got round to. She's back on early shift this week. You wanted to see her?'

Shrewd old goat, thought Harry. Beautiful throw-away, real after-thought.

'I'd said I'd lend her a book,' he lied gracefully.

'She'll be here when you get back. I'll need her today, and all. We're full tonight. It's the way it should be, but work all the same.'

'And money, Mrs Duncan.' It was as much familiarity as was permitted.

'Your sandwiches are there on the sideboard.' She wasn't drawn. 'Bovril as you like them, horrid stuff, and some coffee in the flask. I put a boiled egg in, too, and an apple.'

'Very naughty, Mrs Duncan, you'll make me into an elephant.'

She liked the banter and was still laughing with him as he walked into the hall and to the front door.

'You've got enough clothes on, then? We don't want you with a cold and that.'

'Don't you fuss, Mrs Duncan.'

The Prime Minister liked to start the day with his papers, a cup of tea and the first radio news bulletin. He amused himself by making that first news the commercial one, maintaining to all those who expressed surprise that he was not locked on to the BBC, that he was a capitalist,

459

and as head of a capitalist government he should hear the capitalist-funded station. The radio acted as window dressing to his reading, the spoken version of canned music. He could not do without it, hated silence, but it took an almighty news story to distract his attention away from the newspapers. Like all politicians he had a consummate appetite for newsprint, able to take in, extract, cross-reference or ignore the thousands of words that made up his daily diet. Included in the pile that rested on his lap in the middle of the bed were the *Western Mail* and the *Scotsman*. He would have liked the *Belfast News Letter*, but the printing times and transportation problems across the Irish Sea made it impossible, so he compromised by having the previous afternoon's *Telegraph* sent over. He waded through the politics, diplomatic, economic, pausing fractionally longer on the gossip columns than he would have wanted others to know, and through sport where he delayed no longer than it took him to turn the pages. The pace was enormous, nothing read twice unless it had major impact.

The frown began deep between the overbearing bushiness of the eyebrows. The degree of concentration extended. The mixture written on his stubbly face was of puzzlement and anger.

The Times had put it on page two, and not given it much. Eight paragraphs. No byline.

He found the same story in the *Guardian*, a little longer, and above it the resident staff reporter's name. The length of the copy had relatively little importance or significance to the Prime Minister. The content flabbergasted him. He read three, four times that a British agent had been identified by the Provisional IRA, and the population in the ghetto areas alerted so that they might be on their guard against him.

For Christ's sake. Five weeks since Danby was killed. Outcry and outrage over, gone with the memorial service. Whole wretched business faded, and just as well, no leak that Danby himself had asked for his detective to be taken off. And now the prospect of it all back again, supercharged, and with what drifting out? Heaven only knows. With a surge he swept the bedclothes from him and leaned across the bed. He never had been able to make a telephone call lying on his side. He slung the dressing-gown over his shoulders and sat on the edge of the single bed he had occupied since his wife died, feet dangling, and picked up the telephone.

'Morning, Jennifer, first of the day.' Always something friendly to the girls on the switchboard, worked wonders with them. 'Secretary of State for Northern Ireland. Quick as you can, there's a good girl.'

He sat for two-and-a-half minutes, reading other papers but unable to turn his full attention to them till the telephone buzzed angrily in its console.

'The Secretary of State, sir. Seems he's in the air at the moment. Left Northolt about eight minutes ago. He'll be down at Aldergrove in forty-one minutes. He's early this morning because he's going straight down to an industrial estate in Londonderry, opening something. There's a helicopter waiting to lift him down there. That's his immediate programme.'

'Get him to phone me as soon as he reaches Aldergrove. Let them know I'd like it on a secure line.'

He considered calling Ministry of Defence or Fairbairn in Lisburn, and then dismissed it. Protocol up the spout if he did. If they were to be dropped in a monumental balls-up then the Secretary of State should do some of the lifting, and take a bit of the weight. Time to play things straight down the middle, the Prime Minister reflected.

Across London Davidson was shaving. Wet. With a brush and new blade. He had read his papers again in the daylight. He knew, since he had not been woken from his sleep by the telephone, that in Belfast Billy Downs and the girl were still at large. He could not be certain at this stage to what level of danger Harry was exposed. When he ditched his logical appraisal the only conclusion was that the situation must be slightly worse than critical. He said that out loud; the aide was in the other half of the office and would not hear him. The words rolled off his tongue, giving him that almost sexual pleasure that excitement and tension carry in their wake. He stood there in his trousers, socks and vest, with the bowl of tepid water in front of him . . . all so much like the war. The Albania operation, Cyprus. But how to reconcile that when advanced base headquarters, ABHQ, they used to call it, was in Covent Garden, West One, Central London?

He patted his face, reddened by the sharpness of the blade and the cool water. Putting on his shirt, he dialled Lisburn military direct. When the WRAC operator came on the line he asked for Frost. The intelligence colonel was already in his office.

'Morning, Colonel. I wanted to ring you to find the up-to-date situation. I fancy there'll be various meetings in the morning. People will want to know. I take it there's been no positive news or you would have called me.'

'Right, Mr Davidson.' Had to be the 'Mister', didn't it? Doesn't miss them. Not a chance of twisting it. 'There is no news. We haven't found the girl. We did Downs's home, and the report an hour ago said he wasn't there, but had been a few hours earlier. There's an off-chance he's in trouble. A man of his description attacked a policeman's home late yesterday and botched it up. The policeman thinks he hit him with a single revolver shot as he was escaping. There are one or two blood spots on the escape trail, but we won't get much from them for a bit till the follow-up report is in. It doesn't seem enough to indicate a

461

serious wound. As for your man, well, we're taking out the Andersonstown scrap merchants in about forty minutes. I've nothing else.'

'Are you putting it that there's a good chance Downs was out on this shooting last night, or not?'

'There are similarities, but it's not a positive identification. Hair's not the same as the picture, so the policeman's wife says. She was a long time with him. Face is similar. The policeman himself is not able to be very helpful as he was moving most of the time and getting his gun out and being shot at. He didn't get much of a look. We have the picture you sent us, it's with the unit now that's going to try to round your fellow up.'

'Thank you very much, Colonel.'

'That's all right, Mr Davidson. I'm sure we'll never have the opportunity again of providing a similar service to your organization.'

Davidson put the phone down.

'Stupid, pompous bugger. Bloody man, does he think we're having a picnic at this end?'

He said it with enough ferocity to wake his assistant in the armchair by the door on the other side of the partition. The younger man shrugged himself out of his sleep.

'Any news?'

'Not a bloody dicky bird that matters.'

The men on duty in the intelligence section moved quietly round the room, unwilling to attract Frost's attention. He was slumped ungracefully in his chair, his eyes half closed, half focused on the ceiling. He was a man of method and neatness, following his own individual rule book, but following it closely, and expecting others to ape him. Harry McEvoy violated the rule book. The theory, the preparation and the execution of the McEvoy operation all contravened the requirements of this sort of business. His subordinates had detected the inner anger and knew enough to keep their distance.

Frost could see the weakness in the whole affair. This lunatic fighting between departments and services. Point-scoring at a grand level and at the expense of the man out there on the streets. He was as guilty as any. But the issue had to be settled so there would be no repetition. That was where it was all so amateurish. The Prime Minister and the GOC . . . They should have their heads knocked together. But rivalries don't come from a victory march, they don't surface when the show's going well, they're the product of long-drawn-out failure.

The chatter of the teletype machines and the noise of men shuffling round the room, doors opening, muted talk were insufficient to disturb his train of thought.

It's because we're all lashing around, stranded by the tide, looking for the way out when there isn't one, that a damn-fool thing like this gets launched. And after five endless years of it, and the promise of how many more to come, the inevitability that the professionals are going to be cold-shouldered, that the outsiders will want to have their say. Inevitable. And the price we pay for it is having that poor devil McEvoy or whatever his real name is out there on the streets, working for God knows who.

Frost straightened up in his chair. 'Get me some coffee, please. Black, and make sure there's plenty there this morning.' He was tired, exhausted by it all. They all were.

The postcard was lying on the mat, colour side down, when Mary Brown responded to the flap of the letterbox in the front door.

'There's a card from Daddy, darlings,' she called into the back of the house where the boys were having their breakfast.

'Not a letter, Mum?' her elder boy shouted back.

'No, just a card. You know how awful your father is about letters.'

There was a market scene on the card. Men in kaffiyehs and futahs staring blankly from the gold market that stood in the middle distance.

'Hope to see you all soon. Still very hot, and not much to do. Love you all, Harry.' That was all there was on the card, written in Biro and in Harry's large hand.

Josephine Laverty was late, and hurried in a frantic mixture of a run and a walk down the Falls to the mill where she worked. She couldn't go fast as the pain still bit into her ribs. She too had heard the early radio news, half expecting in an uninvolved sort of way to hear that Harry McEvoy had been found face down, hooded and dead. It had surprised her that there was no mention of him. This morning she had wondered for a wild moment whether to go to see if he was still at Delrosa, but there was no will power and the emotion he had created was now drained from her.

Perhaps she would go to Mrs Duncan's tonight to help with the teas. Perhaps not, but that could be a later decision. There was now an irrelevance about Harry McEvoy. Forget him. The pillow eavesdropper who had a girl killed. Forget the sod.

With their photographs of Harry the troops from Fort Monagh raided the five scrap yards in Andersonstown. No one in the operation had been told why they were to pick up the smiling man in the picture who

463

wore his hair shorter than their more general customers. The orders were that if the man was found he was to be taken straight to Battalion headquarters and handed over. Amongst those NCOs who were the foremen of the military factory floor and who knew most of what mattered there was surprise that so many men were occupied in looking for a man whose picture was not on the operations room wall, whose name was completely fresh. They had their regular batch of photographs, top ten for the week, top thirty for the month, four for each day of the week. Made up on little cards and issued to the troops to study before they went out on patrol. But this face had never been among them.

At the scrap yards the employees who had arrived before the troops stood sullenly against the walls of the huts, hands above their heads, as they were searched and then matched with the photograph. From the five locations the initial report was that a blank had been drawn. But the troops would lie up in the yards till nine at least in the hope that the man they wanted would still come – was just late. At the yard where Harry in fact worked there was disbelief when they were shown the picture. Never involved, never talking politics, just an ordinary man, too old to be with the cowboys. The little man who ran the yard looked round the armoured cars, and the soldiers, reckoned Harry must be important and determined to say nothing. He confirmed the picture, that he employed a man called Harry McEvoy, that he had started work recently, that was all. Let them find the rest out for themselves.

'Where does he live?' the lieutenant who led the raid asked him.

'Don't know. He never said. Just down the road somewhere, that's all he said.'

'He must have given some impression where he lived?'

'Nothing.'

'What about his stamps, his insurance?'

The little man looked embarrassed. The answer was clear enough.

The lieutenant was new to Northern Ireland. The man opposite him seemed of substance, a cut above the yobbos, respectable even.

'Look, we need this man rather badly.' He said it quietly out of earshot of the other men.

'Well, you'll have to wait for him, won't you.'

But time was ticking on its way, and as the soldiers crouched behind the wrecked cars and buses and waited there was no sign of the face in the photograph. Even the little man became worried by Harry's non-arrival. His first reaction had been that it was a case of mistaken identity, but that Harry should be absent at the same time that the military launched this reception led him to suppose that his newest hand was a rather more complex figure than he had believed.

The soldiers radioed in, hung about a few more minutes and drove back, empty-handed, to Fort Monagh.

464

18

The Secretary of State spoke to Downing Street from the single-storey red-brick building that was the RAF Reception at Aldergrove. They'd offered him a car to take him to the officers' quarters and the use of the group captain's phone, but he'd declined. The message waiting for him was of the sort the Prime Minister rarely burdened him with, must be important and should be returned at speed.

It took several minutes for the connection to come through. The delay came from the need to patch in the speech distortion apparatus that would safeguard the security of the call and prevent any casual telephone user listening in on the conversation. When the instrument rang out in the partitioned office indicating that the call was ready the service aides discreetly backed out through the door. The Secretary of State's men stayed with him.

'Morning, Prime Minister. I'm returning your call.'

'I won't keep you long. I wondered how thoroughly you'd read your papers this morning. *Guardian* and *Times*. Provisionals claiming they've identified an agent of ours, warning the population. All a bit melodramatic but enough to cause anxiety.'

'I haven't seen it, I'm afraid.'

The Prime Minister replied, 'We're a little anxious at this end that it could be the fellow we sent over for Danby. Could be difficult if they nabbed him, and he talked.'

'Trifle awkward, no doubt about that. Well, we'll get the people who run him to move him out right away. Get him back to UK and snappy. That's the simple answer.'

'The problem lies right there,' said the Prime Minister. 'It's a bit incredible, but the chaps controlling him in London cannot contact him. Seems he just calls in when he has something to say.'

The Secretary of State winced. 'Bit unusual that, isn't it? Bit unique. Not standard procedure. What you are saying is that he may not know he's blown if in fact he is. That we may not be hearing too much from him in the future.'

'You're not a million miles away from it.'

'And what do we do . . . ? Sorry, I'll rephrase that one. What do you want done about it?'

'I'm just letting you know the situation. There's not very much we can do about it beyond the obvious. Stand by to catch the cradle.'

'If it comes, it'll be from a fair altitude.' The Secretary of State played a slow smile round his lips at the head of government's discomfiture.

'Could be a bit tricky.' The Prime Minister was sounding old, tired, and a long way away.

'I'm glad it wasn't down to me, this one,' he paused, to let it sink home. 'Still, we'll see what comes out of it. It may be just a kite they're flying. They often do that. I'll keep a weather eye out for the storm clouds. Goodbye, Prime Minister.'

There were no confidences with his staff as the group left the building and walked to the big Puma helicopter for the ride to Londonderry. He asked his army liaison officer to keep him informed if there should be any assassination victims during the day.

His remark of 'hare-brained scheme at the best of times' was heard only by the Scotland Yard detective, his bodyguard, sitting next to him as he adjusted his safety harness while the rotor blades gathered their impetus.

The ambush was in position.

It was a proven, brutally simple piece of organization. A stolen Ford Escort was parked sixty yards up from Delrosa just before the junction with the Falls Road. The car was empty and unlikely to cause suspicion. The number plates had been changed. Harry would walk along on the opposite side of the pavement and turn into the main road. He would be watched by three men who had placed themselves behind the lace curtains of the house in front of which the car was parked. With Harry safely round the corner the men could come out of the house, start up the car, and cruise up from behind him to surprise their target. It was a fast and effective method and over the years had come to be considered fail-safe. The three men in the room, back from the lace curtains, were Downs, Frank and Duffryn. All were at this stage without their guns, but in the Escort's glove was a Luger, and underneath the driver's seat a folded-down Armalite, placed in position, ready loaded and cocked.

To both Frank and Duffryn this was a novel situation. Neither had ever been entrusted with a mission of such importance before, and the tension they felt was reflected in the frequency with which both of them came forward and tugged at the flimsiness of the curtain to view the other side of the road. They talked quietly in staccato style to each other, avoiding the eyes and attention of Downs, who stayed at the back behind them. Neither Frank nor Duffryn knew the third man's name, only vaguely his reputation as a marksman. That was something both had reflected on overnight to comfort themselves, as the few hours slipped away before the rendezvous.

Since he had been told of the operation Downs had had little to say.

He burned up his anger and frustration inside himself till he was as taut as a stretched catapult. The pain of his injury told on him, too, and though that was slightly compensated for by the tablets he had taken he felt weak and, above all, disorganized.

Both Frank and Duffryn looked to the third man for leadership, but he buried himself away from them, not communicating the confidence and expertise they were looking for. He wore a loose overall sweater, with his left arm in a sling underneath it, with the sleeve hanging free at his side. He knew he was not fit enough to get into a fire-fight like that, but for a pick-up and at close range he'd see it through. To back him up he had the strength and fitness of the other two men. He would sit in the front with Duffryn to drive, and Frank in the back with the Englishman for the short ride from Broadway to Whiterock.

Frank said, 'He's late now. He can't be much longer. He's a big fellow. We'll not miss him. He's the only visitor at the house.'

'How long do we leave him after he's away round the corner?' Duffryn asked. He'd been told the answer three times but kept on asking with the insecurity of a small boy who needs to quiz his teacher in class so that she won't forget his presence.

'Hardly at all,' said Frank. 'Just a few yards. We want to pick him on the bend near the cemetery, so we need him to move about a hundred yards, not much more.'

'Hope the bloody car starts,' Duffryn giggled weakly, and looked at Downs. 'You done this sort of thing before?'

Duffryn saw the pale, pinched, hating face. Sensed the quality of his anger and hostility.

'Yes,' said Downs.

'It works like they plan it, does it? I mean, it all seems so straightforward when you put it on paper and work out a timetable and that. But does it really happen as easily as that?'

'Sometimes. Other times it doesn't.'

'The thing that worries me –' like a bloody tap, drip, drip, drip, thought Downs as Duffryn chattered on – 'is if they have a Pig going by as we jump him. Christ knows what we do then.'

He said the last to himself, as the anxiety built up in him about the calibre of the morose and injured man that he and Frank were depending on for success. Just as Duffryn put it out of his mind, Frank stiffened and edged forward again towards the window.

'He's coming. Here comes the English bastard.'

Duffryn pushed his friend to the side to see for himself. The tall figure in the distance, blurred and in soft focus, closing the wicket gate at the front of Delrosa behind him, that was their enemy. He'd thought about him most of the night, about the killing of him, now he came, walking straight without a sideways glance. Looks as if he owns the place, thought Duffryn.

467

'Keep back from the window, you stupid buggers,' the man behind them hissed.

Harry was stepping out, aware of his slow start to the morning, and conscious that whatever speed he walked to the yard he would still be late. The combination of Mrs Duncan's chatter and her insistence on the fresh coffee that percolated interminably had delayed him. He came up the familiar pavement fast, with his sandwiches and flask in the bag bouncing on his shoulder and the weight of the wrapped revolver thudding against his right hip.

He saw the car, one of several parked on the other side of the road. It was small, neat and well kept, but slightly different, something strange . . . the keys left in the ignition. Daft idiot, who leaves keys in his car down the Falls. People didn't leave the keys in the ignition round here unless they'd gone inside for something shorter than a quick crap.

Harry moved on past the car and up to the junction of the side street and the Falls, where the Catholic community came into town, and where the traffic snarl-ups were beginning.

The side of the road that Harry walked on, though, was virtually clear, with just an occasional car speeding past him. He was a punctual man. The army and his aunt's upbringing had disciplined him in this, and his lateness this Monday morning annoyed him. He checked with his left wrist to see how far behind the morning schedule he was, and realized with a suppressed oath that he had left his watch behind . . . Where? . . . Not in his room, not at breakfast . . . in the bathroom after shaving. He was thirty yards into the Falls, the guest house some seventy-five back round the corner. Damn and blast it. Only a hundred yards back to get it. He wavered. And then, a hundred yards back to where he was now. Two hundred yards. Nothing. It's a naked feeling without a watch. Not as bad as leaving glasses behind, or your fly unzipped, but an irritation. Harry swung on his heel and walked back towards Delrosa.

As he turned the corner Duffryn was beside the driver's door of the car, at the handle and in the process of opening it. Frank was already in the back seat, and the man coming out of the house last was half-way between the front door and the car.

For a moment all four men froze.

Harry, mind racing like a flywheel, trying to put a situation and background to the familiarity of the face in front of him.

Where? Where did that face come from? Find it.

It was fractional, the lapse of doubt before the image slotted. The dance, the woman in yellow, the army crashing in, and as the concentration lasted so the face confronting him across the street suffused into

468

the detail of the photokit picture. Outline of cheek-bone structure, that matched. More so than when the man had been at the club, the contours of the flesh on the face merged with the painstaking impression built up in London. Perhaps it was the strain Downs had been under these last hours, or the pain from the wound, but the features at last resembled those the old lady had seen in the park, that the girl in the Underground station had stared at as she fought to keep her balance.

The first movement. Harry reached into his anorak pocket, thrust deep with both hands to pull out the pistol. He dragged at the sharp white towelling, and ripped it from the blackness of the gun, tearing a ladder of bright cotton on the foresight. Thirty feet away Duffryn flung himself face down behind the car, his mind clouded by the sight of the gun in his enemy's hand. Frank jack-knifed his body over the front passenger seat to open the glove compartment where the Luger lay, stretching himself over the obstacle of the head rest. Downs bent low, ducking forward towards the back of the car. Out of sight and to the rear right door beyond which his beloved Armalite was resting.

Aimed shots, Harry boy. Don't blaze. Aim and you'll hit the buggers. He shrugged the duffel bag from his shoulder on to the paving stones, and, legs squat and apart, brought the revolver up to the aim position. Knees slightly bent, body weight forward, both arms extended and coming together with the gun at eye level. The classic killing position. Hands and gun as one complete sighting apparatus. Squeeze, don't jerk the trigger. Take it gently. The thumb of the right hand fumbled forward, rested on the safety catch in the 'on' position, and eased it forward.

In the big 'V' of the arms, reaching to the barrel of the revolver, was the contorted shape of Frank, still stretching for the Luger. Harry steadied as the man lurched back into the rear seat with the gun in his hand, and fired his first shot. The left side of the rear window disintegrated, and Frank jolted as the bullet hit him in the throat. The effort of getting at the Luger had denied him a clear look at Harry. Bewilderment was spread over his face as he subsided on to the back seat with a rivulet of crimson flooding down on to the collar of his shirt. Not in itself a fatal shot, but it would become one if Frank did not get immediate hospital treatment. He was out of Harry's sight now. The Englishman stood stock-still, looking for the next target. Come out, you bastards. Show yourselves. Where's the bloody man we want? Which of you has the next gun? Who shoots next? Steady, Harry boy. You're like a big lamp-post up there, you berk, right in the open. Get some cover.

Harry knelt on the pavement.

'Come out with your hands above your heads. Any attempt to escape and I'll shoot.'

Good control, Harry, dominate the buggers.

Downs whispered to Duffryn as they huddled on the reverse side of the car.

'Make a run down the hill. He'll not hit you with a hand gun. But for God's sake run – and now!'

He pulled Duffryn past him and shoved him out into the open and away from the sanctuary of the car. Downs shouted after him, 'Run, you little bastard, and weave . . .'

Duffryn, in deep terror, bolted from the cover. Out of control and conscious only of the empty space around him he sprinted down the street in the direction of Delrosa. His intention was to shift direction from right to left and to change his speed at the same time. The effect was to slow him down and make him the easier target. Harry fired four times. By the time he pulled the trigger for the second time he had sensed that he was after a man who had never faced this type of situation before. He heard Duffryn sob out as he ran, pleading, merging with his shout as the third shot caught him between the shoulder blades. Duffryn cannoned forward into the lamp-post, leant spread-eagled against it for a few seconds, and then slid down to become a shapeless mass at its base. The fourth bullet, unnecessary, jolted into his sluggish body. Duffryn would live; neither of the hitting bullets had found a critical resting place.

Now that he was down and stationary the confusion ebbed, and clarity came to the young intelligence officer. The enemy would kill him. No doubt – certainty. It seemed not to matter. There was hurt but not so much as Duffryn had expected. He was puzzled he could barely picture the face of the Englishman who had shot him. The clothes he could see, and the gun resting between the hands and the kick as it rocked back when Frank was shot. But there had been no face. The gun obscured it. He had not even seen his enemy. He never would now.

The moment that Duffryn had run Downs eased open the front door of the Escort, forced himself upwards into the driving seat and started the engine. The four shots that Harry had fired at the decoy – the hare with the job of distracting him – had given Downs sufficient time to get the car rolling in the direction of the Falls.

Harry swung the revolver round tracking his attention away from the fallen boy to the moving car. He saw Downs's head low over the wheel before it swung lower still, below the dashboard. That was the moment he fired, knowing instinctively as he did so that he was going too high. The bullet struck the angle of the roof of the car, exited and thudded into the wall of the house opposite. Count your shots, they always drilled that. He had done, and he was out, chamber empty, finished, exhausted. Three more cartridges in the picnic bag, down at the bottom below the plastic food box and the coffee flask. Frantically he broke the gun and pushed the used cases out so that they clattered and shone

470

on the pavement. He slid in the three replacements, copper-plated ends and grey snub-nosed tips.

Downs was out in the traffic of the Falls, desperate to avoid the cars round him, but unable to escape from the conformity of the Catholic route into town. As a reflex Harry ran after him, revolver still in hand. He saw cars shy away from him as he came out into the traffic lanes, heard the grind of acceleration and scraping of brakes as men tried to put space between him and themselves. It was as though he had some plague or disease and could kill by contact. His man was edging away when Harry worked out the equation. Nine cars back was a Cortina Estate, crawling with the others and unwilling to come past the man waving his revolver. Harry ran to the passenger door. It was unlocked. As he looked into the driver's eyes he shouted at him.

'This is loaded. You're to follow that car. The white Escort in front and follow it close. For your own safety don't bugger about. I'm army, but that won't help you if you mess me.'

Donal McKeogh, aged twenty-seven, a plastics salesman living outside Dungannon, forty miles down the motorway, gave a mechanical, numbed response. The car trickled forward, its driver's mind still blank. Harry saw the Escort drawing away.

'Don't mess me, you clever bugger,' he screamed at the face a few inches away, and to reinforce the effect of his intentions fired a single shot through the roof of the car. McKeogh surged forward towards the Springfield Road lights. The message was understood now, and would not need repeating. He might have seen me coming out into the traffic, reckoned Harry, but he's unlikely to have seen which car is following him. Little chance of that. McKeogh swerving through on the inside, crossing the double lines in the centre and drawing angry shouts from other drivers, had closed the gap to five cars by the time they reached the lights.

Two bullets remained in the Smith and Wesson.

It had taken Billy Downs little time to work out where he was going. The failure to kill the Englishman dictated the decision. He was going home. Blown, finished, out.

He was tired. Needing a corner to sleep away the stabbing pains and biting disappointments of the last few hours, he needed quiet, and silence. Away from the guns, and the firing, and the blood. Above all he wanted to get away from the noise of the weapons that blasted out close to his ears, screwing up his guts with tension, then releasing them like an unplugged bladder, flat and winded.

Away from it all, and the only place he could go was home. To his wife. To his children. To his house. To Ypres Avenue. The logic and will power and control that had caused him to be chosen for London were drained from him. No emotion, no sensitivity left. Even the slight bubbling coughs of Frank in the back seat could not disturb him.

Failure. Failure from the man considered so valuable that only the most important work was ear-marked for him. Failure from the élitist. More important, failure against the enemy who was working to kill, eliminate, exterminate, execute *him*. The words kept tempo with the throbbing of the arm wound. Christ, how it hurt. A bad, dangerous pain that dug at him, then went, but came again with renewed force, chewing at his strength and resolve.

The Armalite was still in the car, untouched under his seat, but useless now. It had no further part to play. The Armalite days were over, they didn't settle things. It was over. Concluded, done with, half a lifetime ago.

Driving was hard. He had to stretch his left arm to the gear handle every few seconds, and even the movement from the second to third aggravated the injury. He mapped out a route for himself. Down to Divis, then across the top fringe of town to Unity flats, and then on to Carlyle Circus. Could park there, on the roundabout. It was a walk to Ardoyne then, and the car and Frank would be close to the Mater, their own people's hospital. Frank would be found quickly there, and would get the treatment he needed. There were no road blocks and he moved with the traffic, Frank too low down to be seen and the bullet holes failing to draw people into involvement. It was nine minutes to the Circus where the Crumlin and the Antrim Road come together, and where cars could be left unattended. He drove on to the space and stopped the car. To get out he had to lever himself up with his right hand, then he looked behind and into the back. Frank was very white, with much of his blood pooled beside his face on the plastic seating. In his eyes was just enough light to signal recognition.

'Don't worry, Frank boy. You're close to the Mater. You'll be there in five minutes. I'm going to call them. I'm going now, and don't worry. God bless. It's all okay, you'll be safe. A few minutes, that's all.'

Frank could say nothing.

Downs left the engine running and the driver's door open as he ran away from the car. It was enough to ensure that someone would look inside. The broken window would clinch it. The Armalite was still under the driver's seat, and the Luger lay beneath Frank's body. He ran up the Crumlin, Mater hospital on his right, huge and red and cleansed, giving way to the prison. High walls, coils of barbed wire, reinforced stone sentry towers and, dominating it all, the great gatehouse. Downs went on by them, and past the soldiers on guard duty, and the policemen guarding the court house opposite with their flak jackets and Sterlings. None spared him a glance as he ran.

The sprint gave way to a jog, then to little more than a stumble as

472

he neared the safety of Ardoyne at the top of the long hill. The weight of his legs seemed to pin him back as he forced his feet forward, separating himself from the chaos and disaster behind him. His breath came in great sobs and gulps as he struggled to keep up momentum. The only demand he made of himself now was to get to his home, to his wife, and bury himself in her warmth. The Circus and the hospital and the prison were far behind down the road when he reached the iron sheeting that divided Shankhill from Ardoyne, where he had stood the previous afternoon waiting for the lift that took him to Rennie's home. God-rot that bastard copper and his bloody children. That was where it had all collapsed. The child in the way, smack in the way, never a clear sight at the copper, only the kid's head. Panting and wrenching for air he slowed up to walk the last few yards.

They were right. He'd lost his nerve. Billy Downs, the one selected by the Chief of Staff, had slipped it because of a child's head.

And then, this morning . . . Frank with his voice shot out, and the young bugger they'd sent him, down on the pavement shredded. And you, you clever sod, you told him to run to make room for yourself, and he did, and he bloody bought it.

In the race across the city McKeogh had several times fallen back in the traffic stream, losing completely the sight of the white Escort before spotting it again far to the front manœuvring among the lorries and vans and cars. Then Harry screamed and threatened McKeogh, and the salesman would speed up. He doubted his hi-jacker was a member of the British army but was undecided whether he was IRA or UVF. That he would be killed if he didn't follow the bellowed instructions, he was certain. As they came out of the town and reached the circus the Escort was gone. Four major routes come together there, including the Crumlin leading up to Ardoyne and the Antrim Road running up to the nearer equally hard-line New Lodge. New Lodge offered the quicker refuge, and Harry aimed his arm that way, as McKeogh swung round the Circus and then up the wide road. They drove a mile and fast up beyond the scorched entrance to the ghetto before Harry indicated they should turn back.

'Try the Crumlin, it has to be that way.'

'He could have got away from us and still be in this road. If he went up the Crumlin he'll be out of the city by now, up in Ligoniel, half-way to the airport,' said McKeogh.

'I know where he can be. Just drive and close your attention on that,' Harry snapped back. He would be lucky now to find him again. He knew that, but didn't need any bloody driver to tell him. Neither saw the Escort still parked among the other cars on the Circus, and they

473

turned up the long haul of the Crumlin. Harry was forward in his seat now, peering right and left as McKeogh swept up the road. At the top he shouted. The exultation of a master of hounds throwing off the frustration of a lost quarry.

'There he is, at the tin wall.'

McKeogh slowed the car in against the near pavement.

'Who is he?' he said.

Harry looked at him, didn't reply and bolted from the car. He ran across the road and disappeared from McKeogh's view through the gap in the silver corrugated fence. Downs had a start of less than a hundred yards.

Talk of the initial shooting straddled the city. The first officer into the road was taken by a lance-corporal to meet the tear-swamped Mrs Duncan. Between gulps and pauses to blow her nose she told the immediate story that formed the basis of the situation report.

'He'd just left for work, Mr McEvoy, and I heard the shooting, and I ran to the door. Up the end of the street was Mr McEvoy with a gun, and one man seemed to run down the street towards this end, and he was shot. Mr McEvoy just aimed and shot him. Then another man got into the car and started to drive away, and Mr McEvoy fired at him too, and I don't know whether he was hit or not. It was so fast. Then Mr McEvoy ran into the road waving and shouting at people in cars. Then I came indoors.'

'Who is this Mr McEvoy?' the bemused subaltern asked automatically.

'He's my lodger, been here three weeks. Quiet as a mouse, and a gentleman, a real proper man. Never spoke to anyone, and then there he was crouched behind his gun and shooting it over and over.'

The ambulance took Duffryn to hospital, and bulletins later in the day spoke of his condition as 'critical'.

Frost, still in the 39 Brigade Operations Room at Lisburn, saw the reports coming in over the teletype. In rapid succession he spoke to the GOC, the Brigade commander in Londonderry – in order that the Secretary of State could be briefed when he arrived there – and finally to Davidson in London. In each case the message was substantially the same.

'At first sight it looks as though they mounted some sort of ambush for McEvoy this morning. There was a balls-up on the job, and our fellow ended up shooting at least one of theirs. He's in hospital injured. Another chap escaped in a car, and when last seen McEvoy was standing out in the Falls trying the old tack of waving down a spot of transport, civilian, for hot pursuit. It gets a bit more droll each stage. He'd holed up in a small guest house just off the Falls in the Broadway section. So he's on the loose again, and it's my wager that by lunchtime the place will be buzzing a bit.'

Four minutes later the teletype was chattering again. A shot-up car had been discovered in Carlyle Circus, and a man had been taken from the back with serious gunshot wounds.

'This McEvoy, he's one of ours,' said Frost to the major from his department who stood beside him.

'Working for us?' said the other man in astonishment. The clerks and corporals and duty officers strained to listen.

'Not as simple. Working for our side, but not working for us, not for this department. It's involved and complicated and a cock-up. The guts are that the Prime Minister wanted an outsider with good cover and uncompromised, to move in and operate while controlled from London. He had a specific task, to locate the man that killed Danby. I think he did it and all the trimmings as well. It's a boy called Billy Downs, from Ardoyne. The place is watched now, and we did a raid this morning but that was negative. But the whole thing went sour. This man, McEvoy, had little faith in his controller and not much more in us. Can't blame him for that. The talk I've had with his controller shows him as stupid as they come. So we had a ludicrous situation, lunatic, with McEvoy phoning his controller and passing over information but not saying where he could be contacted. In between his weekly messages not a word from him. Revolutionary tactics, okay. Then it leaked to the opposition – how they got hold of it I don't know – complete secrecy was supposed to be the strength of the whole enterprise, and the Provos still heard about it. There was the bit in the papers this morning, that was the tip of it.'

The major nodded. He'd seen the cutting already, snipped out and noted.

Frost went on.

'Well, it seems the boyos went for McEvoy this morning to try to get him on the way to a job he'd picked up. He's cool enough, this lad. There's been quite a shoot-out. McEvoy shot at least one of them. Maybe more, there's another half stiff turned up beside the Mater in a car with guns in it. It may be something to do with it. Could well be.'

One of the desk sergeants came towards the colonel pushing a telephone trolley across the floor of the ops room, a light set in the handle flashed brilliantly.

'Call for you, sir.'

Frost took the phone, identified himself, and listened rather more than a minute. Then he thanked the caller, asked him quietly not to move anything, and said he would be on his way.

'There's been shooting in Ypres Avenue, that's Billy Downs's street. Looks a bit like *High Noon* apparently, bodies and plenty all over the place.' Frost rattled it out, hard and composed. 'I think I'll go down there, so hold the fort, please. And call RUC HQ, Special Branch. Ask for Rennie, Howard Rennie. He might want to come up there. It'll take me about fifteen minutes to get there. But if there's any word of McEvoy let me know right away.'

And he was gone before the major could stand on any of his dignity and complain about being kept in the dark. That Frost traditionally kept things close to his chest was small consolation. Suddenly the operations room was alive. It was seldom the staff on the first floor of headquarters were able to feel the tension of street-level operations. Frost had brought them into it, though at the expense of his famous discretion. The sergeant brought the trolley over once more.

'It's a call for Colonel Frost, sir. They say it's London and personal and urgent. A Mr Davidson. The colonel called him a few minutes ago. Will you take it?'

The major took the phone. 'It's his deputy here.' He waited while the question was framed at the other end, then went on, 'We have another wounded man, and a shooting in Downs's street in Ardoyne. Bodies but no names to match them with is the order of the morning so far. You'll have to wait half an hour or so, and then we might have the answers. Sorry, old chap, but that's the way it is.'

19

Feverish in the torment of her uncertainty, Billy Downs's wife had sent two of her children to the community infant crèche, and dumped the others with her neighbours. In her threadbare green coat and with her bag and purse she had taken herself to the shops at the top of Ardoyne. The screw had been well twisted on her exhausted nerves.

The news programme less than two hours earlier had carried reports of the shooting at the policeman's house, amplified by eye-witness accounts. The BBC had sent a man to the house, and his story made much of the gunman who hesitated, the intervention of the child, and the wounding of the gunman. There had been a trail of blood and the policeman was a trained marksman, the report said. The *Irish News*, which she had seen when she took the young ones three doors down, had shown a floodlit picture of the neat bungalow and white-faced detectives working with their fingerprint kits by the front door. The paper had also spoken of the wounding of the would-be assassin.

Men from the community association would come in later in the day to help repair the boards pulled up at dawn by the army, but for now the debris and confusion in the house and the noise of the children coupled with the danger to her husband to defeat her.

But the single factor that weighed most with her was the knowledge that the military knew of her husband, had identified him, and that their life together was effectively over. If he had survived last night then he would be on the run and go underground, otherwise the future held only the prospect of years in the Kesh or the Crumlin.

And for what?

She was not one of the militant women of the streets who blew the whistles and beat the dustbins, and marched down the Falls, and screamed at the soldiers and sent food parcels to the prisons. At the start the cause had not interested her, till parallel with the growing involvement of her husband she had become passively hostile to the movement. That a Cabinet minister should die in London, a soldier in Broadway or a policeman in Dunmurry was not the fuel that fired her. Her conviction was of far too low a grade to sustain her in her present misery.

Her purse had been full from the social security last Thursday. Now most of it was spent, with only enough for the basics of bread and milk bolstered by sausages and baked beans and tins. At the shops as she queued many eyes were on her. Word had passed in the streets that the army had raided her house, that they were looking for her man, that he had been out all night. Over the years it had become a familiar enough situation in the little community, but that it was this family that was at the centre of the morning's swoop caused the stares, the muttered comments and the pulling aside of the front window curtains.

She glared back at them, embarrassing the lookers enough to deflect their eyes. She paid for her food, pecking in her purse for the exact money, and swung out of the door and back on to the street. She had forty yards to walk to the top of Ypres Avenue.

When she turned into the narrow long street the observation post spotted her. The soldiers were concealed in the roof of the mill, disused and now converted into warehouse space. They came and went by the back stairs, and where the boards were too rotten hauled themselves up by rope ladder. Once in position they put a heavy padlock on the door behind them, locking themselves in the roughly-fashioned cubicle, constructed out of sandbags, blankets and sacking. They had some protection and some warmth: that was all. To see down the Avenue they lay on their stomachs with their heads forward into the angle of the roof with a missing tile providing the vantage point. The two men in the post did twelve hours there at a stretch, and with three other teams

477

would rotate in the position, familiarizing themselves enough with the street so that eventually they would know each man and woman and child who lived there. The comings and goings were logged, laboriously, in a notebook in pencil, then sifted each evening by their battalion's intelligence officer. A synopsis of life in the street was sent each week to headquarters for evaluation. It was a process repeated in scores of streets in the Catholic areas of Belfast, as the security forces built up their enormous and comprehensive dossiers on the minority community.

Lance-Corporal David Burns and Private George Smith had been in the mill since six that morning. They arrived in darkness and would leave long after the few street lights had come back on. They had been in Belfast eleven weeks on this tour, five more to go. Thirty-four days to be exact.

To the OP they'd brought sandwiches and a flask of sugared tea plus the powerful German binoculars they used, a folded card that expanded to show a montage of the faces of wanted men, the rifles with daytime telescopic sights and also the bulging image intensifier for night work. They carried everything they needed for the day up the rope ladder to the roof. Only the radio telephone and the bulk treacle tin for emergency nature calls were permanent fixtures.

Burns, face intent behind the glasses, called out the details on the slight woman walking towards him.

'The bird from forty-one. Must have been shopping. Didn't go for long. Can't be ten minutes since she went. Looks a bit rough. Didn't find her husband, did they?'

The soldier squirmed closer to the aperture, pressing the glasses against his eyebrows, face contorted with concentration.

'Hey, Smithie, behind her. I think he's coming. Right up the top there. Sort of running. That is her old man, isn't it? Looks like him. Have a squint yourself.'

'I'm not sure, not at this range. We'll be definite when he gets down the road a bit.' Smith had taken over the hole. 'Is he a shoot-on-sight, or what?'

'Don't know. They didn't say nothing about that. I'm sure enough now it's him. Get HQ on the radio. Looks like he's run a bloody marathon. Knackered, he is.'

It was the pounding of his feet that first broke through her preoccupations. The urgency of footsteps dragged the woman away from the images of her wounded husband and the breaking of her home. She turned towards the noise, and stopped still at the sight.

Downs was struggling to run now, head rolling from side to side and the rhythm of his arm movements lost. His legs flailed forward over the last few paces to her, unco-ordinated and wild. The stitch in his right side bit into the stomach wall. The pallor of his face was slug-like, excavated from under something of permanence. His face was hollow at the cheeks as he pulled the air inside his lungs, eyes fearful and vivid, and round them the skin glistened with a sheen of sweat. He was shapeless, the big sweater worn over the left shoulder and arm giving him a grotesque breadth. But as he came towards her it was the eyes that held her. Their desperation, loneliness and dependence.

She put down her shopping bag on the paving, careful that it should not topple over, and held out her arms for her man. He fell against her, stumbling, and she reeled with the sudden weight as she took the strain. Against her he convulsed as his lungs forced down the air they needed. There were words, but she could not understand them as they buried themselves in the shoulder of her coat. Far distant, on the top street corner a knot of women had gathered.

'They came for you, you know, this morning.'

'I know.'

'They searched all over, and they said they'd come again. Again and again till they got you.' He nodded, numbed and shocked by the pain of the running and the throbbing in his arm. 'They know, don't they? They know it all. They're not so daft as you said.'

'I was told.' The voice, the speaking, was a little easier now. The air was there, coming more naturally, and the legs steadied.

As she twisted herself against him, working away from the sharpness of his collar-bone against her cheek, she felt him wince and tear away his left arm.

'Is that where they hit you? Last night it was you. At the policeman's home. Did he hit you?' The pain came and went, surging and then sagging. 'Has it been looked at? Have you seen a doctor?' Again he nodded.

'Where are you going now? What are you going to do?'

'I'm going home. It's over, finished. I just want to go home.'

'But they came this morning for you,' she screamed, her voice high, hysterical that he could not understand something so simple. 'They'll be back as soon as you walk through the door. They'll take you. They were crawling all through, under the floorboards and into the roof, looking for you. They took the place apart trying to find you.'

He wasn't listening. 'They put a man in, just to find me.' He said it with wonder, as if surprised that the enemy would classify him of such importance that they would take a step so great. 'We found him first. We went to get him this morning, and it just ballsed up. There's two boys shot by him, by the Englishman. And last night that was another cock-up. That bloody copper, he . . .'

'I heard it on the radio.'

479

'Well, there's no point in running now. I'm finished with it. There'd be a reason to run if I was going on, but I'm not.'

'You mean all this? It's not just because you're hurt? We can get you away from here, the boys will shift you.'

'It's definite,' he said. He was very tired now, deeply tired and needing to sit down, to take the great weight from his legs. He picked up her shopping bag with his right hand, and draped the injured left arm over the small woman's shoulder. They began to walk by the terraced doors and the chipped and daubed red brick of the street. It was a grey Belfast morning, rain threatening, wind cold and from the east, coming in over the Lough. The two threaded a path over the fractured paving stones, past the endless heaps of dogs' mess towards the house that had become Downs's goal.

The moment the two had created for each other was broken by the footsteps behind. Instinctively both knew the noise of pursuit. In Ardoyne the knack of recognizing it was inbred.

The women on the corner were silent as Harry ran by them down the gentle incline towards where the man and his wife were walking away from him. He held the revolver close to him, reassured by the hardness of the wooden handle, roughened with age and usage. He pulled up twenty feet short of them. The pair swung round to face him.

'Don't move. Don't try to run or get your firearm. If you do I'll shoot.'

Harry barked the instructions. The harshness of his tone and its assurance surprised him. He felt almost detached from the orders he was shouting.

'Put the bag down and begin to walk towards me, and slowly. Your hands on your head. The woman – she stays where she is.'

Be strong. Don't mess about with him. You'll be a long time before you shift the bastard. Don't let him dominate you. Keep the gun on him, look at his hands the whole time. Watch the hands, and keep the gun in line. Keep it so it's only got to come straight up to fire, and the catch off. Check with the thumb that the catch is off. It is, certain. Now separate them, don't let them be together so she can shield him. She'll do that, they all will, throw themselves at you to give him a yard. And shoot. If he moves shoot him. Don't hesitate. Stay still yourself. Don't march about. That disorganizes the shot you may make. Two bullets only. One up the spout, and the other in the next chamber, that's all.

Harry studied him hard. The other man, the opposition. Dirty, cowed and frightened – is that the terrorist? Is that all he is? Is that the killer in all his glory? Not much to look at, not much without his Kalashnikov.

'Start walking now, and remember: keep it very cool, or I shoot. What's your name?'

'Billy Downs. You're the Englishman they sent for me? The one that had the girl killed?' They'd told him the Britisher hadn't come to take

480

him, not to put him in the Kesh, but to kill him. The fight of survival was returning, steadily and surely. 'You won't get out of here, you know. Not with me on the end of your pistol, you won't.'

He looked past Harry and seemed to nod his head into the middle distance. It was cleverly done. Good try, Billy boy. But you're with the professionals now, lad. A squaddie might have turned and given you the third of a second you needed to jump him. Not Harry. Pivot round. Get your back to the wall. Keep going till you feel the brickwork. But watch the bastard. All the time keep your eyes on his hands.

Faced with troops in uniform, Downs would probably have submitted without a struggle and climbed into the armoured car to start whatever segment of his lifetime in captivity they intended for him. But not this way. No surrender to a single hack sent from London to kill him watched by his wife and in his own road. For a year it would be talked about – the day when a lone Englishman came into Ardoyne and shot down meek little Billy Downs. The day the boy's nerve went.

He was formidable, this Englishman, in his old jeans and dark anorak, with the clear-cut face, softer than those fashioned in the bitterness of Belfast. He had not been reared through the anguish of the troubles, and it showed in the freshness of his features. But he was hard, Downs had no doubt on that. They'd trained him and sent him from London for this moment, and Downs knew his life rested on his capacity to read the expressionless mouth of his enemy. When he made his break all would depend on how well the Englishman could shoot, and, when he fired, how straight. Downs made his assessment . . . he'll fire, but fire late, and he'll miss. He turned himself now from the waist only, and very slowly, towards his wife. He was close to her, much closer than Harry, and with his face in profile he mouthed from the far side of his lips, the one word.

'Scream.'

She read it in the shape of his mouth, the way the lips and gums twisted out the message. Harry didn't see the instruction, and was still concentrating on the man's hands when she yelled. It came from deep down. A fierce noise from so small a woman. Harry jerked from his preoccupation with Downs as he searched for the source of the noise, his eyes shifting direction.

Downs had made his decision. Now or not at all, either now or the bastard has you in his own time, to shoot like a rat in a cage. He pushed his wife violently towards Harry and started for the freedom of the open street down the hill. His first two strides took him to the edge of the pavement. A flood of adrenalin . . . anticipating the shot, head down, shoulders crouched. This was the moment. Either he fires now or I make it, three, four more paces then the range and accuracy of the revolver is stretched. His eyes half closed, he saw nothing in front of him as his left foot hit hard on the steep edge of the pavement. For his

481

heel there was support, for his sole there was nothing, only the gap between the flagstones and the gutter eight inches below. His weight was all there, all concentrated on that foot, as he catapulted himself forward, the momentum taking over.

. He realized the way he was falling, and tried to twist round on to his back, but there was no time, no room. He hit the rough gravel of the road on his left arm, right on the spot where the flesh had been twice torn open by Rennie's bullet. The frail lint bandage gave no protection. With his right arm he clawed at the road surface trying to push himself up and away from Harry, who was coming to him, revolver outstretched . . .

Harry saw the pain reach over and cover the man's face. He saw the hand scruffing under the body. If the man had a gun that was where it would be, down by the waist, where the hand was fumbling now. It wasn't a difficult decision any more. He raised the revolver so that the line went down from his right eye, down his right arm to the 'V' of the back sight and along the black barrel to the sharp foresight, and then on to the man's upper chest. He held the aim just long enough for his hand to steady, then squeezed the trigger gently into the cup of his forefinger. The noise was not great. The revolver gave only a slight kick, jolting down the rigid arm to Harry's shoulder. Below him Downs's body began to twitch, giving way to spasmodic convulsions. The blood found its own pathway from the side of his mouth out on to the greyness of the road. Like water tracking across dry earth it kept its course, faster, thicker, wider as the road discoloured with its brightness.

There was no need for the second bullet, Harry could see that.

'Why did you shoot him? He had no gun. Why did you kill him?' She was moving towards Downs, looking at Harry as she spoke. 'You didn't have to shoot. You could have run after him, and caught him. You know he was shot last night, and hit. He wasn't much opposition to you, you Britisher sod.'

She knelt down beside her husband, her stocking dragging on the harsh surface of the road. He lay on his side, and she could not cradle him as she would have wanted. Both her hands touched the face of her man, unmarked in his death, fingering his nose and ears and eyes.

Harry felt no part of the scene; but something was demanded of him, and painstakingly he began to explain.

'He knew the rules. He knew the game he was playing. He came to London and murdered the Cabinet Minister. In cold blood. Shot him down in front of his house. Then he went to ground. It was a challenge to us. He must have known we had to get him – you must have known that. It was a test of will. There was no way we could lose – we couldn't afford to.'

Harry had wondered how this moment would be. How he would feel if the man were dead, destroyed. There was no hatred, no loathing for

482

the slight body that lay on the grit of the tarmac. There was no elation, either, that his world and his system had beaten that of the young man who they had told him was the enemy, evil, vermin. Harry felt only emptiness. All the training, all the fear, all the agony, directed to killing this awkward, shapeless nonentity. And now nothingness. He looked again at the wife as she stayed bent over her lifeless man, and began his walk up the hill out of Ardoyne.

She was watching him, hands still on the man's body, when the shot came. Simultaneously with the crack she saw Harry stagger, appear to regain his balance, and then career backwards, before thudding against the front wall of a house. His arms were pressed against the middle of his chest. Then he toppled in slow motion over on to the pavement.

In the OP it was Smith who was at the aperture, giving a continuous description to the lance-corporal who relayed the message back to headquarters over the radio telephone.

'There's a man running up behind Downs. With a shooter. A revolver, looks like, a little one. Tell 'em to shift 'emselves back at HQ. Downs has his hands up, and they're talking. Not much, but saying something.'

From the telephone set Burns called, 'What about the other bloke, they want to know, what's he look like?'

'Civvies, anorak and jeans. It's a short-barrel revolver he's got, not Downs . . . the other man. Scruffy-looking. He's making a run for it, Downs is. Bloody hell, he's down, tripped himself. Fuck me, he's going to shoot him, he's going to shoot him!'

High in the hidden observation post Burns heard the single shot.

'I can get the bugger, can't I, Dave? He just shot the other bastard. Waving a gun about and all that, it's enough.'

Smith was manœuvring his rifle into position. The old Lee Enfield with the big telescopic sight, the sniper's weapon, the marksman's choice.

'I've a good line on him from here. No problem.' Smith was talking to himself, whispering into the butt of the rifle. Burns was motionless and watched from the back of the OP nestled among the blankets and sacking as Smith drew back the bolt action, and settled himself, shifting his hips from side to side to get comfortable for the shot. He was a long time aiming, wanting to be certain the first time. The firing echoed round under the roof of the mill.

'Did you get him?' urged Burns.

'A real bloody peach.'

*

The sharpness of the pain numbed Harry. As he lay, stomach down on the pavement, he could feel nothing, his head was facing the walls of the houses away from the street. Green moss rubbed close to his nose, and beyond that lay the jagged edge of a milk bottle, and, huge and high, a front doorstep. There was no understanding of what had happened. Just the noise, and the helpless collapse, the blows that had carried him from his feet.

He worked his right hand slowly from under him where it had gripped his chest. The fingers were scarlet and shiny. The effort was so great. No strength left, no power, and endless labour just to move an arm. The action of all the muscles, all working in his biceps, his heavy shoulders, and deep behind the ravaged rib cage, combined to bring on the first stabs of agony. Bruised from his fall, his face contorted with pain, the upper teeth clamping on the softness of his lip, he struggled to control the spasms.

And with the pain came the realization of what had happened. They've had you, Harry. As you stood there like a big idiot, consumed in your inviolability, they took you. So silly. Just standing there, in the heart of Ardoyne, standing and waiting, and they obliged. His mind was clearing as the flesh and tissue round the great wound torn by the bullet throbbed out its protest. This is the way it ends, he knew that. Here against the dampened pavings, by the weeds and the fractured glass, among hatred and loathing. Some little swine out there with a rifle, taking a long time, waiting for the moment, not hurrying. That was the way death comes, Harry. Billy Downs already dead, the woman beside him; that was somewhere in the greater distance, away beyond.

Other faces were closer, sharp-etched now . . . Davidson, in the garden near Dorking – it'll be dangerous, he had said. Hadn't wanted to say it, thought it might frighten . . . Mary came closer to him, and the boys, big faces happy with laughter, all noise and running to him. Take hold, Harry, fight it.

The impact of the shot had flung Harry several feet back before it felled him. His hands with animal instinct had closed on his stricken body, the revolver careering from his fist and bouncing into the roadway where it rested.

Harry forced himself upwards, using his right hand to provide the lever till he could jack-knife his lower body under him and spread the great weight from the arm on to his knees. The first time he failed, collapsing back into the pool of blood. Again he attempted it, this time with greater success, till, like a pantomime dog, he began to work his way up the hill. There were people at the doorways now, but none moved or spoke as the Englishman dragged his way past. A single child screamed as his opened coat slipped from his left hand fingers, and permitted a flow of blood down on to the ground and over the hardness of the pavement before his knees smeared its ordered passage.

A hundred pairs of eyes watched Harry move away, aware that this was the effort of a man already doomed but unable to accept it. These people knew the inevitability of death, knew how a man fought to stave off its coming, and knew from the signs when he would win, and when lose. The Englishman they knew would lose, the blood told them that, the whiteness of his face, the breathing, irregular and bubbling. And then they saw Billy Downs's wife rise up from the road where her man lay and walk with quick, neat steps towards Harry. They saw that in her path was the revolver.

She bent down and picked it up. It was heavy, cumbersome in her small hand. Her index finger had to strain forward to find by feel the metal coldness of the trigger arm. She didn't look at the gun, or check it as a man used to handling firearms would have done. Those people at their doors who saw themselves in line with her and Harry backed away, seeking the safety of their front doors, but the uninvolved stayed to see what would happen.

Eighteen inches from his head a door slammed, its noise breaking into Harry's thought, diverting his attention from his sole preoccupation of taking himself beyond the pain of Ypres Avenue, and then he heard the brush of her feet, scurrying closer to him. She walked on past him and then spun round, blocking his way till his face was close to her legs. Harry subsided backwards, his hand still holding his body up, but his weight down on his hips. He could see all of her from there, not just the legs and the feet, but her coat that was old and tired, her face once pretty and now hideous from the grief and shock of the last few minutes, and her short narrow arm, and the tight, pale-skinned clenched fist. And the revolver, too big for her, grotesque.

The barrel of the gun was steady, so were her eyes, nothing distracting her from the man near-prone in front of her.

She said, 'You didn't have to shoot my man. What was Billy to you? What did it matter to you, what happened to him? He was finished, broken, and you cut him down like a rat in the gutter. And you talk about rules and challenges. What rule was that, to kill Billy, hurt and unarmed?'

There was no fear in Harry now. It had all evaporated a long time back. The words came hard to him. 'You know why he died, what he did. He was against us. Each was determined to destroy the other. He understood that.'

'You never knew anything of him – what sort of man he was, how good he was to us. And yet you come to our street, and shoot him down, defenceless.'

Harry struggled to speak again to her. So difficult, so exhausting, this twisted, shattered face above him, not understanding the world of her man, not understanding the war that was being fought out on her own streets. It was all so simple, so easy, but Harry felt the waves of tiredness

485

pouring over him, and no longer had the strength to reason with the woman.

She went on: 'You think we're all animals over here. But what's it to you if Danby gets killed, or a soldier, or a policeman, what's it to you, over from England? Do you think you're any better than our people?'

Harry stayed silent a long time as he struggled to concentrate his thoughts.

'He deserved to die. He was an evil little bastard. He's better off . . .'

The fingers wrenched at the trigger. The noise mingled with her sobs as Harry rolled slowly and with precision over on to his back. At the top of Ypres Avenue the first two Saracens were arriving.

The soldiers looked over the two bodies, made the decision that both were beyond medical help, and left them where they had fallen. Both Harry Brown and Billy Downs were in the awkward, sack-like form that the troops could recognize as death. Downs lay a few feet from the kerb, out in the road. The blood had run from him to create a lake, dammed from escaping farther by the debris of the gutter. His wife was beside him again, and still holding the revolver loosely and without interest. The sergeant of the platoon walked towards her and, with nervousness showing in his voice, asked her to hand over the gun. She opened her fingers and it clattered noisily on the road. When the soldier spoke again to her there was no reply. She stood, quite still, swamped by her emotions.

Harry was sprawled face up close to the wall of a house, his head beneath the front room window from which a face, old but without the softness of compassion, looked down on him. The women of the street edged their way closer to Billy Downs's wife, the men gathered in clumps, leaving the business of comforting and abusing to their women.

In their shawls and head scarves and short skirts they shouted at the officer who came with the platoon. 'He's one of yours. That bastard dead over there.'

'He's a fucking Englishman.'

'Shot a man without a gun.'

'SAS killer squads.'

'Killed an unarmed man. In front of his wife, and he never in trouble before.'

The crescendo gathered round the young man. In a few moments his Company commander and Battalion commander would be there, and he would be spared, but till then he would take the brunt of their fury. Faced with the accusation that Harry was one of theirs the soldiers looked curiously at the body of the big man. They knew a certain amount about the undercover operations of the army, particularly the Mobile Reconnaissance Force (MRF), but to the men in uniform it was a different and basically distasteful world. The soldiers had their rules and regulations to abide by. The book was near to God.

In exasperation the lieutenant shouted above the babble.

'Well, if you say the chap who shot Downs is one of ours, who shot him then?' He'd phrased it clumsily, said it in anger and expected no answer.

The chorus came back, gloating, satisfied. 'The Provies got him. A Provie gunman. One shot. From the bottom of the street.'

The far end of the street down the hill was deserted, dominated only by the massive red-brick wall and grey-slate roof of the old mill. The lieutenant looked up at it, and winced.

'Bloody hell,' he said.

His sergeant who had been examining Harry came over to him. 'The chap on the pavement, sir. He's been hit twice. First I would say was high velocity, there is an entry and exit wound and a big blood marker, looks as if he tried to get away, you can follow the trail, about fifteen yards to where he is now. He was shot again then, right in the head, no exit, and it must have been a hand gun or something, that killed him.'

'Thank you, sergeant. The woman who was holding the pistol, you'd better put her in the Saracen. Go easy with her, she's in shock, and I don't want a riot here.'

'It's just as we found it, as you requested,' they told Frost when he arrived.

The Battalion commander briefed him. 'The chap by the wall shoots Downs and then is shot himself. I'm not a hundred per cent sure where the second shot comes from. Still waiting for all the reports. Indications are that it's my OP in the mill roof. We're rather quiet about that position, but I haven't spoken to the men up there yet. Seems they wounded the fellow, then Downs's wife, she's in the Saracen now, came in and finished him off.'

There was no reaction on Frost's face. His eyes travelled round the street taking in the faces and the scene. He walked over from one body to another, his bodyguards hovering at each shoulder. He recognized Harry from the photograph that had been sent the previous evening from England. It should never have worked, but it had. And now right at the end was all loused up. Poor devil.

He paused where Downs lay, looking into the profile of the face and running a check against the picture they'd issued. We'd have been lucky to spot him from that, the colonel thought, not really good enough, something to be learned from that. He went past the open door of the Saracen. Mrs Downs sat huddled deep in the shadow of the interior. She sat totally still staring at the armour-plated sides, festooned with pick-axes, CS gas-grenade canisters, ammunition boxes. Two soldiers guarded her.

'It's not for general release,' he said to the Battalion commander, 'but you'll hear about it soon enough anyway. The Prime Minister ordered a special man put in, with the sole job of finding Danby's killer, right? The Cabinet Minister shot in London, what is it? six or so weeks ago. Downs was the assassin. By something of a miracle, and a quite unaccountable amount of good luck, the agent tracked him down. That's not a generous assessment, but that's how I evaluate it. He tracked him and shot him dead about fifteen minutes ago. I think your OP has just shot the Prime Minister's man.'

Frost knew how to play his moment. He stopped there, let it sink, then went on.

'We'll deflect it as much as we can, but I suggest you leave it to Lisburn to make the statements. It may be some consolation to you, but I didn't know much about the agent either. He wasn't working to me. I wouldn't worry about the role of the OP in all this.'

'I wasn't worrying –'

Frost cut across him.

'It's happened before, it'll happen again. Marines shot their own crowd in the New Lodge. RUC have shot our people, we've killed theirs. Bound to happen.'

The other man considered. They stood alone in the street away from the people of Ypres Avenue, with the bodyguards and troops giving them room to talk. He remembered now the soldier they had sent to Berlin; what he had seen in the green-topped social club less than three hundred yards from where they stood. There was nothing to say, nothing that would help the prone figure by the wall, nothing that would achieve anything beyond unnecessary involvement. Businesslike, brisk as always, he said to Frost:

'Is there any reason for us not to clean this lot up now? Our photographer has done his stuff, and the RUC people won't want to come in here.'

'No reason at all. Get it out of the way before the press and cameras start showing up.'

'Will there be much aggro, the fact that this fellow Downs wasn't armed when he was killed?'

'I wouldn't have thought so,' said Frost, 'there isn't usually when we get one of the real ones. They seem to accept that, part of the game. Right at the beginning there used to be mayhem. But they've become tired of saying it. They're all unarmed men – that's the charm. Doesn't work them up any more. Be interesting to see what sort of show he gets in the death notices in the press tomorrow morning. We'll see how highly they regarded him then. A big man can get three or four columns. Be interesting. Come from the Brigade command, their Battalions, Companies and a good number from the Kesh. Costs them a fortune – and keeps the papers going.'

They walked together back towards Frost's Land-Rover.

Frost was gone by the time Rennie was brought to Ypres Avenue in a Saracen from Battalion headquarters. He climbed gingerly out of the protection of the personnel carrier and jumped down on to the road. First time in Ardoyne for sixteen months. The Special Branch had no love for parading their faces on the streets of the Provisional heartland. He was conspicuous, he knew that. Anyone in civilian clothes who needed five soldiers and a three-ton armoured car to take him in and out would attract attention. He was conscious of the eyes at the doors, blank and subdued but watching him.

'Are the bodies still here?' he asked the Battalion commander.

'We've shifted them, I'm afraid. My people have taken the necessary pictures. There's not much to see now. That's where Downs died, the blood on the road. The other fellow, McEvoy, he was shot on the pavement by number twenty-nine. There's a small blood pool there.'

'Who's McEvoy?' said the detective.

'I fancy you'll hear more of him from your own office. But he's a rather sensitive creature right now. One of ours, they tell me. Trailed Downs back here and shot him. I'm still waiting for the details on the rest. Looks a bit black, though. I think one of my OPs shot him. McEvoy was waving a gun round, in civilian clothes. It's pretty definite.'

He had no need to ask about Downs. The wild, staring face that had confronted him fourteen hours earlier across the width of his bright living-room remained vivid in his mind.

But Downs was dead now. Rennie thanked the officer and hurried back to the Saracen.

The press statement from Lisburn was short and took something more than two hours to prepare. It was the result of a series of compromises but owed most of its drafting to the civilian deputy head of the army public relations department who had recently transferred from the Treasury, and had experience of the art of communiqué writing.

Billy Downs, a known IRA gunman, was shot dead at 09.10 hours in Ypres Avenue where he lived. He was involved in an exchange of shots with a member of the security forces, an officer engaged in plain-clothes surveillance duties. The officer, who will not be named

489

till his next of kin have been informed, was hit by a single shot in the chest and died before medical treatment reached him. Downs was high on the army's wanted list in Northern Ireland, and was also wanted in London for questioning by detectives investigating the murder of Mr Henry Danby.

The main object was to keep it short, pack it with information and deflect the press away from the sensitive bit. There was, he said when he had finished typing it, more than enough for the scribes to bite on without them needing to go digging round any more.

A solitary journalist moved towards the delicate area that first day, but without knowing it, and was easily put off.

'Then this man Downs was carrying a gun?' he asked the duty press officer.

'Obviously, old man, it says in our statement that there was an exchange of shots. Have to be armed, wouldn't he?'

There were no other questions to be asked. Amongst the resident reporters in McGlade's pub that night interest was warm but not exceptional, and the treatment of the story was straight and factual.

Locally it was denied that Downs had been armed, and three hours of rock-throwing followed the news bulletin that contained the army statement. By then it had started to rain.

20

The Prime Minister learned the news at lunchtime. The message had been framed by the Under Secretary, Ministry of Defence, with an eye to the political master's taste, and the order in which he would read of the events in Ypres Avenue had been carefully thought out. First, Billy Downs identified as the killer of Henry Danby had been shot dead. Second, he had been identified by the agent specifically sent to Northern Ireland by the Prime Minister. Third, and unfortunately, the agent had been shot in the chest during the incident and had died.

As he read the message that the aide gave him his attentive smile had switched to a frown of public concern, studied by the bankers round the table with him in the first-floor salon of No. 10. They looked for a clue as to the contents and information that was important enough to intercede in discussions on the progress of the floating pound, albeit the end of the discussions. The Prime Minister noted their anticipation and was anxious to satisfy it.

'Just on a final note, gentlemen.' He refolded the typewritten sheet. 'You will all be reading it in the papers tomorrow morning, but you might be interested to hear that we have caught and killed the man that assassinated Henry Danby. He was shot in Belfast this morning after being hunted down as part of a special investigation that was launched from this building a few hours after our colleague was murdered.'

There was a murmur of applause round the table and a banging of the palms of hands on the paper-strewn mahogany surface.

'But you will be sorry to hear, as I am, that the man we sent to find this terrorist was himself killed in the shooting exchange. He'd been operating under cover there for some weeks, and obviously carried out a difficult task extremely successfully and with great bravery. The whole concept of this intelligence operation really goes back to the last war. My family were involved in Special Operations – you know, the crowd that put agents into the occupied countries. I had a hell of a job getting the military and police to agree to it. But it just shows, you sometimes need a fresh approach at these things. Perhaps we should get that general over there, who always seems to be wanting more troops, to have a try at banking and running a budget!'

There was general and polite laughter.

'He'll get a medal, won't he? The man you sent over there? They look after the families and all that sort of thing, I suppose?' the elegantly-dressed deputy chairman of the Bank of England spoke.

'Oh, I'm sure he will. Well, I think we can adjourn now. Perhaps you would care to join me for a drink. I have a luncheon, but I'm not off to that till I've had a drop of something.'

Later in the day he called the Under Secretary to express his appreciation of the way the operation had been handled.

'It'll get a good show in the papers, I trust,' said the Prime Minister. 'We ought to blow our own trumpets a bit when we chalk one up.'

'I don't think there will be too much of that, sir.' The civil servant replied decisively. 'MOD have put out a short statement only. I think their feeling is that undercover is bad news in Ulster, and that apart from anything else it was a damn close thing whether our man got theirs first or vice versa. They're playing it rather low key I'm afraid, sir.'

'As you like. Though I sometimes feel we don't give ourselves the pat on the back we deserve. I'll concede that. One more thing. The man we sent over there, I'd like a medal for him now it's over. What sort of chap was he, by the way?'

'I'll see to that. He already had an MC from Aden. We could make it a bar to that, but perhaps that's a bit on the short side. I personally would favour the OBE. The George Cross is a bit more than we usually go for in these circumstances, and it would obviously provoke a deal of talk. You asked what sort of chap. Pretty straightforward, not too

bright. Dedicated, conscientious, and a lot of guts. He was the right
man.'

The Prime Minister thanked him and rang off. He hurried from his
study to the Humber waiting outside the front door of the official residence. He was late for the House.

The Army Council of the Provisional IRA, the top planning wing of
the military side of the movement, had noted the killing of Downs. The
Chief of Staff had received a letter from the Brigade commander in
Belfast relaying the collapse of their man's morale and his failure in the
last two missions assigned to him.

The two members of the Council who had been asked to report on
the practicality and desirability of further assassinations in the political
arena, particularly the plan involving the British Prime Minister,
delivered their assessment at the first meeting of all members after the
Ardoyne shoot-out.

They advised against the continuation of attacks on the style of the
Danby assassination. It had, they said, been disastrous for fund-raising
in the United States: the picture of Mrs Danby and her children at the
funeral had been flashed across the Atlantic and coast to coast by the
wire syndication services. The Provisionals' supporters in the States
reported that November's fund-raising and on into December would
show a marked drop. They said that if there were a repeat or a stepping-
up of the tactics the results could prove fatal. And money was always
a key factor for the movement: RPG7s and their rockets did not come
cheap, not from Czechoslovakia or Libya nor from anywhere else.

The Chief of Staff summed up that in the foreseeable future they
would not consider a repetition of the Danby attack, but he finished: 'I
still defend the attack we carried out against Danby. That bastard
deserved to go. He was a straight, legitimate target, and it was well
done, well carried out. They acknowledge that on their side, too.
There's been no trumpeting on their side even though they've shot our
lad. They've been keeping their heads down for more than a week.'

There was criticism in the Council, that had not been voiced while
Downs was still on the run, of the way the Chief of Staff had monopol-
ized the planning of the attack. That would stand against him in the
future, being one of the factors in his eventual replacement and conse-
quent demotion.

Little of the credit for the killing of Billy Downs landed on Davidson's
desk. It jumped with no little agility to the posthumous name of Harry
McEvoy via the desk of the Permanent Under Secretary.

492

Frost put in a long and detailed complaint about the amount of work the independent and, for so many days, unidentified agent had meant for the security services. He logged the man-hours involved in the search for Harry at the scrap yards, and for the girl round the Clonard, and described them as wasteful and unprofessional. The control of the agent received scathing criticism, particularly the inability of London to reach their man when they wanted to draw him out. The paper concluded with the demand that such an operation should not be repeated during the following eighteen months that Frost would be on the staff of Northern Ireland headquarters.

The Under Secretary who had a copy of the document forwarded to him read it over the phone to Davidson. The response was predictably angry.

'He forgets it was over there and on his side of the fence that some big mouth let the cat out of the bag.' Davidson already had the transcript of the interrogation of the stricken Duffryn. Still suffering from shock, the young man had given Special Branch all of his limited knowledge of the Provisional IRA and its affairs relating to Harry McEvoy.

'He forgets that our man got the fellow, not all their troops and police and Special Branch and SIB, and whatever they call themselves, SAS and the others.' Davidson roared it into the receiver.

The Under Secretary soothed. 'They have a point, you know. This bit how you couldn't reach him, and he didn't stay where he was supposed to, that was a bit irregular.'

'The way they clod about over there, I'm not surprised he didn't go to the house they fixed for him. The fact is we were set a mission, and carried it out, with success. Is that cause for a bloody inquest?'

Davidson had not been told how Harry had died. That was to be kept very close in London. 'Need to Know' was being applied with rigour. The Under Secretary decided that if the PM wasn't on the list then Davidson ranked no greater priority.

'Of course the mission was a success, but it's put a great strain on inter-service and inter-department co-operation. The feeling at MOD is that a similar operation would not be mounted again. That means, I greatly regret to say, that the team we set up to direct our man will have to be dismantled.' There was no change in his voice as he delivered the hammer blow. It gave him no pleasure, but Davidson was so excitable that one really did have to spell it out in simple words and get it over with. He went on: 'I did have hopes at one stage that if this went off without a hitch we might have had something a bit more regular going through Dorking. Make a habit out of the place. But that's not to be.'

Davidson could recognize the shut-out. The shouting was over. He asked, 'And what now? What happens to me?'

'It's recognized here, Davidson, that in fact you did very well on this one, particularly in the preparation of our man. You made him ready for a difficult and dangerous task, which was subsequently carried out with great expertise. You must not take all that Frost says too seriously. You've a great deal of experience to offer, and this showed in the way you got the fellow ready. I want you to think about it carefully, and not come to any hasty decision, but the feeling is that there's a good opening abroad for you.'

Here it comes, the old pay off, reckoned Davidson. What would they have for him, sewing blankets in the Aleutians?

'You've built up great experience of counter-terrorist operations.' The civil servant kept going – don't lose pace, don't let him interrupt – 'I won't beat about the bush. Hong Kong wants a man who can advise them on the posture they should be in. Now don't say anything hasty, the terms are first class. You'd get more than I'm getting. Good allowances, good accommodation, and pretty much of a free hand. Probably live off expenses and bank the rest, I'd say. Don't give me an answer now, but sleep on it and call me in the morning. Cheers, and we all think you did well.'

The conversation was over.

Davidson ranged round the office, fumbling at his papers, diving into the drawers of the old wooden desk. He aimed a kick at the folded camp bed away in the corner, not used since the last Sunday night of his vigil. It took around an hour to find the will and inclination to exert some order to the anger of his feelings. The documents and maps of the operation filled two briefcases. The rest was government property. Some bloody man could clear that up. Sort it out themselves.

He made a call to his wife. Didn't speak much, just said he'd be home early, that he had some news, they would be going out for a meal. Then he locked up. He'd thought about Harry considerably since the shooting, and by the time he had reached his commuter train his rage had subsided and he brooded in a corner over the evening paper about the young man who had died in Belfast . . . sent away across the water with all that damn-fool optimism coursing through him.

For days Mrs Duncan talked of little more than the strange events that preceded the death of her favourite lodger.

That the man who shared her bathroom, her front room and occasionally her kitchen, who lived in her best back bedroom should have turned out to be an English agent was rather too much for her to serve out in a single session of conversation. Her neighbours came several times to hear the full saga, culminating in the eye-witness description of the final shoot-out beyond the front garden gate.

She was to remain unaware of her full role in the death of Harry and

Billy Downs. She never discovered that it was her chatter over the back fence about the strange accent of the man who lived under her roof that was to start the process that led, near-directly, to the gunfire in the street (interrupting her late Monday morning breakfast). She told those who came to listen to her that the thing she found the strangest was the confidence and authority with which Harry was holding the gun as he shot down Duffryn against the lamp-post (a few feet from where she stood at the door). The cold methodical power with which that quiet man, a man she had grown to like but knew little about, executed the youngster, had shaken her more than any of the other horrors of five years of living on the Falls.

The army had come mid-morning and backed a Saracen right up to the gate. Two men in civilian clothes had waited till the doors were opened and screened them from casual view from the pavements, then hurried into the house. They had searched Harry's room slowly and carefully while soldiers hovered round the house and the street was sealed to all cars. When the men left it was with all Harry's possessions slung together into big transparent plastic bags.

Later that same day Josephine arrived to help with the teas. It was a wasted visit, as the guests had cried off. There were no takers for the lodging used by British intelligence. Some telephoned their apologies and listed excuses, others simply failed to turn up. Instead Josephine was told the events of the day. She listened without comment, and sat on a straight chair in the kitchen, sipping her tea, and smoking a cigarette. She was another who would never learn her full part in the affair. She went home that night believing her information alone had led the Provisionals to Harry. In the months ahead she was to stay distant from any connection with politics and with violence. Left alone by the IRA, she took to remaining at home in the evenings with her mother, shutting out the memories of the few hours she had spent with Harry, of how he had betrayed her, and of how she had betrayed him.

Billy Downs's funeral was a bigger day than any in his young life. A huge and winding crocodile of relatives and friends marched behind his tricolour-draped coffin up the Falls Road. It had been the army's intention to prevent the firing of the traditional volley over the body, but the procession diverted into the back streets of the Lower Falls and before it emerged again the shots had been fired. Photographers were icily warned of the consequences of taking pictures.

Eight men from Ypres Avenue took the weight of the coffin on their shoulders for the first part of the journey to Milltown Cemetery. Grim, set faces, they marched at the head of a crowd estimated by police at around three thousand. Behind them came the display of force, youths and girls in semi-uniform, the green motif dominating, polished Sam Brownes, shouted commands and the tramping of feet.

At the bleak, over-ornate, Milltown gates faces in the crowd were recorded by the Asahi cameras of the military from behind the sandbags on top of the walls of the Andersonstown bus station. Inside the cemetery the Chief of Staff of the movement, who arrived and departed unseen by those who were hunting him, delivered the graveside oration. They played the 'Last Post' while small children in their best clothes played and skipped among the stones that marked the last resting place of other heroes of the Cause.

As weeks and months passed by, so increased the adulation and estimation in which Billy Downs was held. They named a club after him, and wove his picture into a big, wide banner. It was some eight feet across, with slots for two poles, one at each end, so that it could be carried high in procession on the marches the Provisionals organized.

The songs followed, sung with the nasal lament in the bars of Andersonstown and Ardoyne to drinkers who sat silent and rapt. They were heavy with sentiment, helping to cement the legend that in Ulster solidifies so quickly. The brave soldier of the songs had been gunned down by the British killer squads while his woman and bairns were round him. It was as his wife had said it would be.

The Secretary of State had refused the request by Billy Downs's wife that she be allowed to attend the funeral of her husband.

Early on the morning of her husband's burial she was transferred from the police station where she had initially been held to Armagh women's prison. She was declared an 'A' category prisoner, an automatic classification that took into account what she was accused of, not her potential as an escape risk. They flew her, with a prison escort, by Wessex helicopter from Belfast to the parade square of Gough barracks in the old cathedral town. When she stepped out on to the tarmac, half deafened by the rotor blades, and dominated by the armed men round her, she seemed to some who watched a pitiful and harmless creature. She still wore the green coat that she had put on the previous Monday morning to go and get her groceries from the shop on the corner in Ypres Avenue. By the time they had hustled her from the helicopter to the armoured car that waited on the edge of the square, she was shivering. It would be warmer when they reached the cells just down the road, and she would get a mug of tea then.

*

The Royal Air Force flew Harry out on a Hercules transporter, along with a cargo of freight and two private soldiers going home on compassionate leave.

The two boys, both in their teens and only just old enough to serve in the province, huddled in their canvas seats away from the tin box wrapped in sacking and strapped down with webbing to the floor of the aircraft. There was a brown label attached to the box, filled in with neat handwriting.

'Says he's a captain.'

'It's the one that did that shooting on Monday morning, and got it himself.'

'Says on here he's got an MC and all.'

'Took one of their big men with him, didn't he?'

'He tracked this joker for weeks. The officers were talking about it. I heard it when I was on dinner-waiting. Lived right in amongst them.'

'This is the first time I've been over, but I've nearly had a full tour, done three and a half months, but I've never seen an IRA man, or anything like one. All we do is patrol, patrol, patrol, but we never find much.'

'Undercover agent, they called him in the paper.'

'Didn't do him much good, whatever he was.'

That terminated it. They spoke no more of Harry as the plane brought them down to Northolt, where it had all started six weeks earlier.

They buried Harry Brown in the village churchyard close to where his wife's parents lived. By army standards it was a conventional funeral. There was an honour party, immaculate and creased. A staccato volley was fired over the grave. An army chaplain gave a short address by arrangement with the local vicar. In the event it was not much different from the funeral accorded to Billy Downs. Smaller, less stylized, less sentimental, but with all the same ingredients.

There were few civilians present. Mostly soldiers in uniform, stiffly upright as the bugler played the final haunting farewell. There was a wreath from the Prime Minister, and Davidson took time from his packing to attend. Frost was there too. Both stayed back from the graveside, and neither introduced themselves to the family.

Mary walked away supported by her mother and father. She had had two large brandies before coming, and could tell herself she had borne herself well. As she climbed into the large black car the public side was over. She could weep, leaning heavily on her mother's shoulder.

And she could say, 'Why in heaven's name did they choose Harry? He was lovely, precious to me, nothing special to them. They could have chosen a thousand men in front of him. Why did it have to be Harry?'

By the time they had gone, dispersing in their different directions and leaving the covering of flowers over the heaped-up earth, the evening was bearing down on the day. And across the water the truce that runs to heel with the daylight was coming to an end. A few more minutes and the darkness would have engulfed the Falls, the Murph, Andytown and the New Lodge. The young men were preparing to draw their rifles, receive their orders, move out on to the streets. Later a policeman would be killed, and a pub be destroyed by explosives. The life and the death of Billy Downs changed none of that, nor the brief entry into his world of Harry Brown.

Red Fox

To Gillian and Nicholas and James

1

An hour now they had been in position. The car was nestled off the road under a blanket of high mushroomed pine branches. It was back from the main route and on a parking space that later would be used by those who came to play tennis on the courts behind. The place was quiet and unobserved as they wanted it.

Not that the car was here by chance, nothing in these matters was casual and unplanned and spontaneous. For a clear fortnight the men had toured this discreet web of sidestreets, watching and eyeing and considering the location that would afford them the greatest advantage, accepting and rejecting the alternatives and the options, weighing the chances of attack and escape. They had not chosen this place till all were satisfied, and then they had reported back and another had come on the morning of the previous day and had heard from them their description of what would happen and nodded his head, slapping them lightly on the shoulders to affirm his agreement and accolade.

So the ambush was set, the trap was sprung, the wires taut, and the men could scrutinize their wristwatches, bright with chrome and status, and wonder whether the prey would be punctual or tardy.

In front of their car the road ran down a gentle hill towards the main six-lane route into and from the city, which it joined at an intersection two hundred and fifty yards from them. Under the pines the road was shadowed and grey, the potholes and rainwater tracks in dark relief. There was no chance that when he came in his car he would be speeding. He'd be doing thirty kilometres at most, because he would be safeguarding the expensive framework of his Mercedes, creeping between the ruts, avoiding the hazards, and as unaware and unsuspicious as they all were.

The car in which the men sat had been stolen three weeks earlier from outside a hotel in the centre of Anzio away to the south of Rome. By the time the loss had been reported, written in the ledger book by the polizia, the Alfetta had already been fitted with new number plates, likewise stolen, but from a car owned in Arezzo to the north. The number plates had originally belonged to a Mirafiori Fiat. The calculation was that the marriage of the stolen car and the stolen number plates would be too complex for any casual check by the Polizia Stradale. The paperwork of insurance and tax had been matched to the vehicle's new identity by men who specialized in such work.

Three men were in the car, all sharing the lank, coarse hair and mahogany-sheened faces of the deep south, of the toe of Italy. Men of Calabria, of the rugged and daunting Aspromonte mountains. This was their game, their playtime. Their experience qualified them for such occasions. Men who travelled from the lofty villages down to the big city to effect the grab and then fled back to the safety of their families, their community, where they lived uncharted and unknown to the police computers. The smell in the car was of the crudely packed MS cigarettes that they smoked incessantly, drawn to their mouths by roughened fingers that carried the blister scars of work in the fields, and mingling with the tobacco was the night-old stench of the Perroni beer they had consumed the evening before. Men close to middle age. The one who sat in front of the steering-wheel had the proud hair on his forehead receding in spite of the many and varied ways he combed it, and the one who sat beside him carried traces of grey at his temples highlighted by the grease he anointed himself with, and the lone one in the back wore a wide belly strapped beneath his leather belt.

There was little talk in the car as the minute hands of the watches moved on towards seven-thirty. They had nothing to communicate, conversation was futile, and wasted breath. The man in the back drew from a grip bag that rested on the floor between his legs the stocking masks that they would wear, purchased the previous afternoon in the Standa supermarket and pierced with a knife for eye and mouth vents. Without a word, he passed two forward to his companions, then dived again into the bag. A snub-barrelled Beretta pistol for the driver, who probably had no need for a gun at all as his work was to drive. For himself and the front passenger there were squat submachine-guns made angular as he fitted the magazine sticks. The quiet in the car was fractured by the heavy metallic clacking of the weapons being armed. Last to be taken from the bag was the hammer, a shiny varnished handle of new wood weighted with its grey-painted iron head.

They had a man to lift this time. A man of their own age, their own fitness, their own skill. It would be harder than the last one, because that had been a child. Just a child toddling to kindergarten in Aventino with the Eritrean maid. She'd screamed at the sight of them, the black whore, and collapsed in a dead faint on the pavement and the dog shit by the time they'd reached the child, and the brat hadn't struggled, had almost run with them to the car. The car had been stationary no more than fifteen seconds before they were moving again with the kid on the floor and out of sight and only the noise of the keening wail of the maid to let anyone know that anything had happened. Two hundred and fifty million they'd paid out, the parents. Good as gold, placid as sheep, shut the door on the investigations of the polizia and the carabinieri, co-operated as they'd been told to, sold the shares, went and tapped the grandfather up in Genova just as it had been planned they would.

504

Nice and clean and organized. Good quick payout, used 50,000-lire notes, and not a uniform in sight. Just the way it should always be. But how this one would react, there was no way of knowing, whether he'd fight, whether he'd struggle, whether he'd be a fool . . . The man in the back fingered the hammer-head, stroking its smoothness with his fingers. And in all their minds was the thought of the welcome the big men would provide if there was failure, if the car came back empty, if the cash investment were not repaid . . . no room for failure, no possibility . . . the big bastard would skin them. From behind his ample bottom, muffled by his trousers, came the screech of static noise, and then the call sign. He wriggled round, heaved his bulk so that it no longer suffocated the transmitter/receiver radio, pulled the device clear and to his face. They hadn't used the system before, but this was advancement, this was progress.

'Yes. Yes.'

'Number Two?'

'Yes.'

There had been a code, an agreed one, but the suddenness of the transmission had seemed to surprise him and he was aware of the frustration of the men in front at his fumbling. They'd practised the link often enough in the last week, assured themselves that the receiver would pick up from behind the first block a hundred metres up the hill. He saw the anger on the driver's face.

'Yes, this is Number One.'

'He is coming . . . it is the Mercedes and he is alone. Only the one.'

For each man in the car the distorted and distant voice brought a syringe of excitement. Each felt the tension rise and writhe through his intestines, felt the snap of stiffness come to the legs, clasped at the security of the guns. Never able to escape it, however many times they were involved, never a familiarity with the moment when the bridge was crossed and spanned, when the only road was forward. He'd skin them if they failed, the big man would.

'Did you hear me, Number One? Did you receive?'

'We hear you, Number Two.' Spoken with the grey lips against the built-in microphone.

Big and large and fat and juicy, that was what the big man called it, the capo. A foreigner, and with a renowned company behind him, a multinational, and they'd pay up well, pay fast and pay deep. A billion lire in this one, that for minimum . . . could be two billion. Spirals of noughts filling the minds. What was two billion to a multinational? Nothing. A million and a half dollars, nothing.

The man in the back switched off the radio, its work completed.

Burdening silence filled the car again. All ears strained for the drive of the heavy Mercedes engine. And when it came there was the whine of the low gear, the careful negotiation of the pitfalls of the road.

Creeping forward, cutting distance. The growing thunder of the wasp wings as the insect closes on the web the spider has set.

The driver, Vanni, half turned, winked and grimaced, muttered something inaudible and indistinct, gave Mario in the front, Claudio in the back, the curl of a smile.

'Come on.' Nerves building in the back.

'Time to go get the package.' Vanni raised his voice. 'Time to go pluck the rooster.'

He thrust the gear lever forward, eased his foot on to the accelerator, nudged the car out into the narrowness of the road as all three peered left and upwards to the bend.

A black monster of a machine. The Mercedes, sleek and washed. A machine that justified its existence only on the autostrada but which was now confined and crippled on the broken surfaces. Clawing towards them.

Ear-splitting in the confines of the car, Claudio shouted.

'Go, Vanni. Go.'

The Alfetta surged forward. Swinging right with the tyres protesting across the loose roadside gravel. The wrench of the brakes took Mario and Claudio unawares, punching them in their seats. Thirty metres in front of the Mercedes, the Alfetta bucked to a stop across the road, blocking it, closing it. The drumroll of action as the passengers dragged the stockings over their heads, reducing their features to nondescript contours. This was a moment for Vanni to savour – the visible anger of the driver as he closed in on them. He knew the man's background, knew he had been nineteen months in the country, and saw framed in his overhead mirror the caricature of the Italian gesture of annoyance. The flick of the wrist, the point of the fingers, as if this were a sufficient protest, as if this were a common drivers' altercation.

Vanni heard the door beside him and the one behind crash open. As he spun in his seat to see the scene better there was the impact of splintering glass, vicious and vulgar. He saw Claudio, hammer in one hand, machine-pistol in the other, at the driver's door, and Mario beside him and wrenching it open. A moment of pathetic struggle and Mario had the collar of his jacket and was pulling him irresistibly clear. Making it hard for himself, wriggling, the stupid bastard, but then the men usually did. Vanni felt a shiver in his seat, involuntary and unwelcome, as he saw a car turn on the bend of the hill, begin its descent. Unseen by Mario and Claudio, both wrestling with the idiot and on the point of victory. He reached for the pistol from his lap, heart pumping, the cry of warning gorging his throat.

Just a woman. Just a signora from the hill in her little car, hair neatly coiffed, who would be on her way to the Condotti for early morning shopping before the sun was up. He eased his fingers from the gun and back to their places on the gear stick and the wheel. She'd sit there till

506

it was over. A woman wouldn't hurt them. Hear nothing, see nothing, know nothing.

The man still struggled as if the shrill of the brakes behind him had provided the faint hope of salvation, and then Mario's fist caught him flush on the jutting chin, and the light, the resistance, died.

All finished.

The man spreadeagled over the back seat and floor of the Alfetta, Mario and Claudio towering over him, and there was a shout for Vanni to be on his way. Critical to get clear before the polizia blocked the roads, stifled their escape. First fifteen minutes critical and vital. Vanni wrenched at the wheel, muscles rising in his forearms as he spun left at the junction, flicked his fingers to the traffic horn, dared another to cut him out, and won through with his bravado. From the back came first a grovelling whimper and then nothing but the movement of his friends and the breathing of their prey as the stench of the chloroform drifted forward.

The crisis for Vanni would soon be over. Clear of the immediate scene, the principal hazards would disperse. A few hundred metres on the narrow Tor di Quinto, then faster for two kilometres on the two-lane Foro Olympico, before he slowed at the lights at the Salaria junction and then left on the main road leading to the north and the autostrada away from the city. He could have driven it with his eyes covered. There was no necessity now for speed, no need for haste, just steady distance. He must not attract attention, nor invite notice, and there was no reason why he should if he did not fall into the panic pit. He felt Claudio's fingers tighten on the collar of his shirt and press against the flesh of his shoulder; ignoring him, he kept his attention for the road as he pulled out behind a lorry, passed it, slotted back into the slower lane.

Claudio could not sense his mood. He was a big man, heavy in weight and grip and with a dulled speed of thought unable to judge the moment when he should speak, when he should bide his time. Past the lorry safe, and clear and cruising. Claudio did not look down at the prone body, easy in its sleep, the head resting on his lap, the torso and legs on the carpet floor enmeshed between Mario's shins.

'Brave boy, Vanni. You took us clear and did it well. How long till the garage?'

He should have known the answer himself; they had made the journey four times in the previous week; they knew to within three minutes the time it would take to cover the distance. But Claudio wanted to talk, always wanted to talk, a man to whom silence was a punishment. He could be removed from his cigarettes, his beer and his women, but he would die if he were left to the cruelty of his own company. Vanni appreciated the loneliness of a man who must be spoken to and talked with at all times.

507

'Four or five minutes. Past the BMW depot and the Bank sports place . . . just past there.'

'He fought us, you know. When we had to take him from the car.'

'You took him well, Claudio. You gave him no chance.'

'If he had gone on then I would have hit him with the hammer.'

'You don't know the sap in your arm,' Vanni chuckled. 'They'd pay little for a corpse.'

'How long did you say to the garage?'

'Three more minutes, a little less than when you last asked. Idiot of Calabria, are you frightened of losing us? You would like to come with us on the train this afternoon? Poor Claudio, you must endure a night of the boredom and the tedium of Rome. You must be patient, as the capo said. A bad night for the whores, eh Claudio?'

'We could all have travelled together.'

'Not what the capo said. Travel separately, break the group. Give Claudio his night between the thighs. Don't you go hurting those girls, big boy.' Vanni laughed softly; it was part of the game, the prowess of Claudio the lover. If a girl spoke to the buffoon he'd fall on his arse in fright.

'I would like to be back in Palmi,' Claudio said simply.

'Calabria can wait for you just one day more. Calabria will survive without you.'

'It's a bastard strain – on your own.'

'You will find someone to talk to, you'll find some fat cow who thinks you're a great man. But don't go flashing her, not your money anyway, not five million.' And the laughter faded. 'That's how they get you, Claudio, how the polizia take you, when you have the money running free in your palm.'

'Perhaps Claudio should put his money in the bank,' murmured Mario.

'And have some criminal bastard walk in with a shooter and take it? Never! Don't do that, Claudio.'

They laughed together, heaving their bodies in the seats. Exaggerated, childish humour because through that came a relaxation from the tension that had taken three weeks to build since the outline of the plan was first put to them.

Beyond the Rieti turn-off they went right and drove on a rough track skirting a recently completed four-floor block of flats and towards the garages that lay to the rear, partly shielded from the upper windows by a line of vigorous conifers. There was a van waiting there, old and with its paintwork scratched from frequent scarrings and the rust showing at the mudguards and road dirt coating the small window set in the rear doors. Two men lounged, elbows on the bonnet, waiting for the arrival of the Alfetta. Vanni did not hear what was said as Mario and Claudio carried the crumpled, drugged form of their prisoner from the back seat to the opened rear doors of the van. It would be of little interest, the passing of a moment between men hitherto unknown to each other who would not meet again. When the doors were closed an envelope passed between fingers, and Claudio slapped the men on their backs and kissed their cheeks, and his face was wreathed in happiness, and Mario handed the grip bag to new owners.

Mario led the way back to the car, then paused by the open door to watch the men fasten the back of their van with a padlock and drive away. There was a certain wistfulness on his features as if he regretted that his own part in the matter was now completed. When Claudio joined him, he looked away from the retreating vehicle, and slid back into his seat. Then the vultures were at the envelope, ripping at it, tearing it apart till the bundles in the pretty coloured plastic bands were falling on their knees. One hundred notes for each. Some hardly used in transactions, others elderly and spoiled from passage of time and frequency of handling. Silence reigned while each counted his bounty, flicking the tops of the notes to a rhythm of counting.

Vanni loaded his money into the folds of his wallet, pulled a small key from his pocket, climbed from the car and walked to one of the garage doors. He unlocked it, then returned to the car and motioned for Mario and Claudio to leave. He drove the car into the garage, satisfied himself that the doors prevented a casual glance from the building seeing his work, and spent five slow minutes wiping clean the plastic and wood surfaces of the interior with his handkerchief, and then, when he was satisfied, the outer doors. When he was finished he came out into the warmth and slammed the garage doors shut. The garage had been rented by telephone, a letter with a bogus address containing cash had provided the deposit and confirmation. He threw the key far on to the flat roof, where it clattered momentarily. The rent had six weeks to run, time enough for the Alfetta to rest there, and by the time an irate landlord prised open the doors all other traces of the group would have been covered.

Together the three men walked out past the flats and to the main road and then along the pavement to the green-painted bus stop sign. It was the safest way into the city and ultimately to the railway station.

On that morning, in a flat across two Roman hills, the first of the occupants to wake was the boy Giancarlo.

Lithe on his bare feet, he padded across the carpet of the living-room, sleep still heavy and confusing to his eyes, blurring the shapes and images of the furnishings. He avoided the low tables and velvet-seated chairs, stumbling on a light flex as he pulled a shirt over his young, undeveloped shoulders. He had shaken Franca gently and with the care

509

and wonderment and awe of a boy who wakes for the first time in a woman's bed and is frightened that the tumult and emotion of the night will be relegated by dawn to a fantasy and dream. He had scratched his fingers across her collar-bone and pulled quietly at the lobe of her ear, and whispered her name, and that it was time. He had looked down on her face, gazed intoxicated on the shoulder skin and the contour of the drawn-up sheet, and left her.

A small flat they lived in. The one living-room. The bathroom that was a box which crammed in a toilet, a bidet and a shower unit. The kitchen with a sink buried under abandoned plates and a cooker that had not seen a damp cloth round the burners for more than a week. The bedroom where Enrico still slept noisily and where there was the unused bed that till last night had been Giancarlo's. And there was Franca's room with the single narrow divan, her clothes draped as haphazard carpeting across the woodblock floor. A small hallway and a door with three locks and a spyhole, and a metal bar with chain that enabled the door to be opened an inch for additional checking of a visitor. It was a good flat for their needs.

The requirements of Franca Tantardini, Enrico Panicucci and Giancarlo Battestini were not great, not complex. It was determined that they should live among the borghese, in a middle-class area, where there was wealth, prosperity, where lives were shuttered, self-reliant affairs and closed to the inquisitive. Vigna Clara hill suited them well, left them secure and unnoticed in the heart of enemy territory. They were anonymous in a land of Ferraris and Mercedes and Jaguars, among the servants and the spoiled children and the long holidays through the summer, and the formidable foreign bank accounts. There was a basement garage and a lift that could carry them out of sight to their own door in the attic of the building, affording them the possibility of cloaking their movements, coming and going without observation. Not that they went out much; they did not roam the streets because that was dangerous and put them at risk. Better that they should spend their hours cooped between the walls, profiting from seclusion, reducing the threat of casual recognition by the polizia. Expensive, of course, to live there. Four hundred and seventy-five thousand a month they paid, but there was money in the movement. Enough money was available to meet the basic precautions of survival, and they settled in cash on the first day of the month and did not ask for the contract to be registered and witnessed and the sum to figure on their landlord's tax return. There was no difficulty finding premises that were private and discreet.

Giancarlo was a boy with two terms of psychology study at the University of Rome behind him, and nine more months in the Regina Coeli gaol locked in a damp cell low down by the Tiber river. Still a boy, little more than a child, but bedded now, bedded by a woman in every way his senior. She was eight years older than he was, so that he had

510

seen in the first creeping light of the bedroom the needle lines at her neck and mouth and the faint trembling of the weight at her buttocks as she had turned in her sleep, resting on his arm, uncovered and uncaring till he had pulled the sheet about her. Eight years of seniority in the movement, and that he knew of too, because her picture was in the mind of every car load of the Squadra Mobile, and her name was on the lips of the capo of the Squadra Anti-Terrorismo when he called his conferences at the Viminale. Eight years of importance to the movement; that too Giancarlo knew of, because the assignment of Enrico and himself was to guard and protect her, to maintain her freedom.

The bright, expansive heat drove through the slatted shutters, bathing the furniture in zebra shades of colour, illuminating the filled ashtrays and the empty supermarket wine bottles and the uncleared plates with the pasta sauce still clinging to them, and the spreadeagled newspapers. The light flickered on the glass of the pictures with which the room was hung, expensive and modern and rectangular in their motifs, not of their choosing but provided with the premises, and which hurt their sensitivities as they whiled away the cramped hours waiting for instructions and orders of reconnaissance and planning and ultimately of attack. All of it, all of the surroundings grated on the boy, disturbed him, nurturing his distrust for the flat in which they lived. They should not have been in a place like this, not with the plumage and trappings of the enemy, and the comforts and ornaments of those they fought against. But Giancarlo was nineteen years old and new to the movement, and he was quick to learn to keep his silence at the contradictions.

He heard the noise of her feet tripping to the bedroom door, swung round and in haste dragged his shirt tails into the waist of his trousers and fastened the top button and heaved at the zip. She stood in the open doorway and there was the look of a cat about her mouth and her slow, distant smile. A towel was draped uselessly around her waist, and above its line were the drooping bronzed breasts where Giancarlo's curls had rested; they hung heavily because she forswore the use of a brassiere under her daily uniform of a straining blouse. Wonderful to the boy, a dream image. His hands were still on the zip-fastener.

'Put it away, little boy, before you run dry.' She rippled with her laughter.

Giancarlo blushed. Tore his eyes from her to the silent, unmoving door to Enrico's room.

'Don't be jealous, little fox.' She read him, and there was the trace of mocking, the suspicion of scorn. 'Enrico won't take my little fox away, Enrico won't supplant him.'

She came across the room to Giancarlo, straight and direct, and circled her arms around his neck and nuzzled at his ear, pecked and bit at it, and he stayed motionless because he thought that if he moved the towel would fall, and it was morning and the room was bright.

'Now we've made a man of you, Giancarlo, don't behave like a man. Don't be tedious and possessive and middle-aged . . . not after just once.'

He kissed her almost curtly on the forehead where it rested against his mouth, and she giggled.

'I worship you, Franca.'

She laughed again. 'Then make some coffee, and heat the bread if it's stale, and get that pig Enrico out of his bed, and don't go boasting to him. Those can be the first labours of your worship.'

She disentangled herself, and he felt a trembling in his legs and the tightness in his arms, and close to his nostrils was the damp, lived-with scent of her hair. He watched her glide to the bathroom, flouncing and swinging her hips, her hair rippling on her shoulder muscles. An officer of the Nuclei Armati Proletaria, organizer and undisputed leader of a cell, a symbol of resistance, her liberty was a hammered nail in the cross of the State. She gave him a little wave with a small and delicate fist as the towel fell from her waist, and there was the flash of whitened skin and the moment of darkened hair and the tinkle of her laugh before the door closed on her. A sweet and gentle little fist that he had known for its softness and persuasion, divorced from the clamped grip of a week ago as it held the Beretta P38 and pumped the shells into the legs of the falling, screaming personnel officer outside the factory gate.

Giancarlo hammered at Enrico's door. He battered on through the stream of obscenities and protest till he heard the muffled voice cleared of sleep and the tread lumbering for the door.

Enrico's face appeared, the leer spreading. 'Keep you warm, boy, did she? Ready to go back to your Mama now? Going to sleep all afternoon . . .'

Giancarlo dragged the door closed, flushed and hurried for the kitchen to fill the kettle, rinse the mugs, and test with his hands the state of the two-day-old bread.

He went next to Franca's bedroom, walking with care to avoid stepping on her clothes, staring at the indented mattress and the stripped sheets. He slid to his knees and dragged from the hiding-place under the bed the cheap plastic suitcase that always rested there, unfastened the straps and pulled the lid back. This was the arsenal of the covo – three machine-guns of Czech manufacture, two pistols, magazines, loose cartridges, batteries, wires of red and blue flex, the little plastic bag which held the detonators. He moved aside the metal-cased box with its dials and telescopic aerial that was marketed openly for radio-controlled aeroplanes and boats and which they utilized for the triggering of remote explosions. Buried at the bottom was his own P38. The rallying cry of the young people of anger and dispute – P trent' otto – available, reliable, the symbol of the fight with the spreading tentacles of fascism. P38, I love you. The token of manhood, of the coming of age. P38, we fight together. And when Franca ordered him he would be ready. He squinted his eyes down the gunsight. P38, my friend. Enrico could get his own, bastard. He fastened the straps again and pushed the bag away under the bed, brushing his hand against her pants, clenching them in his fingers, carrying them to his lips. A whole day to wait before he would be back there, lying like a dog on his back in surrender, feeling the pressures on his body.

Time to get the rosetti out of the oven and find the instant coffee.

She was standing at the doorway.

'Impatient, little fox?'

'I had been at the case,' Giancarlo floundered. 'If we are to be at the Post when it opens . . .'

Her smile faded. 'Right. We should not be late there. Enrico is ready?'

'He will not be long. We have time for coffee.'

It was an abomination, an ordeal, to drink the manufactured 'instant brand' but the bars where they could drink the real, the special, the habitual, were too dangerous. She used to joke that the absence of bar coffee in the mornings was the ultimate sacrifice of her life.

'Get him moving. He has enough time to sleep in the rest of the day, all the hours of the day.' The kindness, the motherliness, had fled from her, the authority had taken over, the softness and the warmth and the smell washed away with the shower water.

They must go to the Post to pay the quarterly telephone bill. Bills should always be paid promptly, she said. If there are delays there is suspicion, and checks are made and investigations are instituted. If they went early, were there when the Post opened, then they would head the queue at the Conti Correnti counter where the bills must be met in cash, and they would hang around for the least time, minimize the vulnerability. There was no need for her to go with Enrico and Giancarlo but the flat bred its own culture of claustrophobia, wearing and nagging at her patience.

'Hurry him up,' she snapped, wriggling the jeans up the length of her thighs.

Stretching herself in the bed, arching her body under the silk of the pink nightgown, irritation and annoyance surfacing on her cream-whitened face, Violet Harrison attempted to identify the source of the noise. She had wanted to sleep another hour at least, a minimum of another hour. She rolled over in the double bed seeking to press her face into the depth of the pillows, looking for an escape from the penetration of the sound that enveloped and cascaded round the room. Geoffrey had gone out quietly enough, put his shoes on in the hall, hadn't disturbed her. She had barely felt the snap of his quick kiss on her cheek before he left for the office, and the sprinkling of toast crumbs from his mouth.

She did not have to wake yet, not till Maria came and cleared the kitchen and washed up the plates from last night, and the lazy cow didn't appear before nine. God, it was hot! Not eight o'clock and already there was a sweat on her forehead and at her neck and under her arms. Bloody Geoffrey, too mean to fit air-conditioning in the flat. She'd asked for it enough times, and he'd hedged and delayed and said the summer was too short and prattled about the expense and how long would they be there anyway. He didn't spend his day in a Turkish bath, he didn't have to walk around with stain in the armpit and an itch in his pants. Air-conditioning at the office, but not at home. No, that wasn't necessary. Bloody Geoffrey . . .

And the noise was still there.

. . . She'd go to the beach that morning. At least there was a wind at the beach. Not much of it, precious little. But some sort of cool from off the sea, and the boy might be there. He'd said he would be. Cheeky little devil, little blighter. Old enough to be his . . . Enough problems without the clichés, Violet. All sinews and flat stomach and those ridiculous little curly hairs on his shins and thighs, chattering his compliments, encroaching on her towel. Enough to get his face slapped on an English summer beach. And going off and buying ice-cream, three bloody flavours, my dear, and licking his own in that way. Dirty little boy. But she was a big girl now. Big enough, Violet Harrison, to take care of herself, and have a dash of amusement too. Needed something to liven things, stuck in this bloody flat. Geoffrey out all day and coming home and moaning how tired he was and what a boring day he'd had, and the Italians didn't know the way to run an office, and why hadn't she learned to cook pasta the way it was in the ristorante at lunchtime, and couldn't she use less electricity and save a bit on the petrol for her car. Why shouldn't she have a little taste of the fun, a little nibble?

Still that bloody noise down in the road. Couldn't erase it, not without getting out of bed and closing the window.

It took her a full minute to identify the source of the intrusion that had broken her rest. Sirens baying out their immediacy.

In response to a woman's emergency call the first police cars were arriving at the scene of the kidnapping of Geoffrey Harrison.

514

2

The cars were Enrico's responsibility.

This week it was a Fiat 128, the fortnight before a 500 that was hardly large enough for the three of them, before that a Mirafiori, before that an Alfasud. Enrico's speciality. He would drift away from the flat, be gone three or four hours, and then open the front door smiling away his success and urging Franca to come to the basement garage to inspect his handiwork. Usually it was night when he made the switches, with no preference between the city centre and the distant southern suburbs. Good and clean and quick, and Franca would nod in appreciation and squeeze his arm and even the gorilla, even Enrico, would weaken and allow a trace of pleasure.

He was well satisfied with the 128, lucky to have found a car with a painstaking owner and an overhauled engine. Fast in acceleration, lively to the touch of his feet at the controls. Coming down off Vigna Clara, heading for the Corso Francia, they seemed like three affluent young people, the right image, the right camouflage, blending into their surroundings. And if Giancarlo sitting hunched in the back was unshaven, poorly dressed, it was not conspicuous because few of the sons of the borghese who had their flats on the hill would have bothered with a razor in high summer; and if Franca sitting in the front passenger seat had her hair tied with a creased scarf, neither was that of importance because the daughters of the rich did not require their finery so early in the morning. Enrico drove fast and with ease and confidence, understanding the mechanism of the car, rejoicing in the freedom of escape from the confines of the flat. Too fast for Franca. She slapped her hand on his wrist, shouted for him to be more careful as he overtook on the inside, weaved among the traffic, hooted his way past the more sedate drivers.

'Don't be a fool, Enrico. If we touch something . . .'

'We never have, we won't now.'

Enrico's familiar uncurbed response to correction. As always, Giancarlo was perplexed that he treated Franca with such small deference. Wouldn't grovel, wouldn't dip his head in apology. Always ready with a rejoinder. Brooding and generally uncommunicative, as if breeding a private, secret hatred that he would not share. His moments of humanity and humour were rare, fleeting, paced out. Giancarlo wondered what Enrico had thought of the unmade bed, his absence in the night hours,

515

wondered if it stirred the pulse, kicked at the indifference that Enrico presented to all around him. He doubted if it would. Self-sufficient, self-reliant, an emotional eunuch with his shoulders rounded over the wheel. Three weeks Giancarlo had been at the covo, three weeks as guard at the safe house of the prize of the movement, but Enrico had been with her many months. There must be a trust and understanding between him and Franca, a tolerance between her and this strange padding animal who left her side only when she slept. It was beyond Giancarlo to unravel it; this was a relationship too complex, too eccentric for his comprehension.

The three young people in a car that carried a licence plate and a valid tax disc on the windscreen merged without effort into the soft, flatulent society with which they were at war. Two days earlier Franca had exclaimed with triumph, shouted for Giancarlo and Enrico to come to the side of her chair and read to them a statistic from the newspaper. In Italy, she had declaimed, the increase of political violence on the previous year's figures was greater than in any country in the world.

'Even Argentina we lead, even the people of the Monteneros. So we're wounding the pigs, hurting them. And this year we wound them more, we hurt them harder.'

She had played her part in the compilation of those figures, had not been backward in advancing herself and had earned the accolade bestowed on her by the magazines and tabloids of 'Public Enemy Number One (Women)', and shrieked with laughter when she read it the first time.

'Chauvinist bastards. Typical of them that whatever I do I cannot be labelled as the greatest threat, because I am a woman. They would choke rather than admit that a woman can do them the greatest damage. My title has to be embroidered with a category.'

Eight times in the past twelve months she had led the strike squads, the action commandos. Target ambushes. Bullets blasted into the lower limbs because the sentence of maiming was thought more psychologically devastating than death. Eight times, and still no sign that many beyond the hierarchy of the colossus knew of her existence, or cared. Eight times, and still no indication that the uprising of the proletariat forces was imminent. It was as if she was teased, mocked to do her worst, undo herself in the very audacity she was taunted towards. When she thought like that, in the late evening when the flat was subdued, when Enrico was sleeping, then she came for the boys who were Enrico's constant but changing companions. That was when she demanded the pawing, clumsy association with the juvenile, that her mood might be broken, her despair smashed under the weight of a young body.

These were hard and dangerous times for the movement. The odour of risk was in the air, constant after the kidnapping and execution of Aldo Moro, the mobilization of the forces of the State, the harrying of the groups. The gesture on the grand scale by the Brigatisti had been the taking of Moro and the People's Court to try him and pass sentence. But there were many who disputed that this was the way to fight, who counselled caution, argued against the massive strike and favoured instead the process of wearing erosion. More men were rallied against them now; there was more awareness, more sophistication. It was a time for the groups to burrow deeper, and when they surfaced on the street it was in the knowledge that the risks were greater, the possibility of failure increased.

Swerving across the traffic lanes, Enrico brought the car to rest spanning the gutter, half on the pavement, half in the road. Franca wore a watch on her wrist, but still asked with a flow of irritation in her voice:

'How long till it opens?'

Enrico, accustomed to her, did not reply.

'Two minutes, perhaps three, if they begin on time,' Giancarlo said.

'Well, we can't sit here all morning. Let's get there.'

She slipped the door open, swung her feet out and stretched on the pavement, leaving the boy to fiddle at getting her seat forward so that he could follow her. As she started to walk away Enrico went hurrying after her because his place was at her side and she should not walk without him. To Giancarlo, her stride was light and perfect, shivering in the taut and faded jeans. And she should walk well, thought the boy, because she does not carry the cold clear shape of the P38 against her flesh buried beneath a shirt and trouser belt. Not that Giancarlo would have been without his gun. It was more than a tube of chewing gum, more than a packet of Marlboro. It was something he could no longer live without, something that had become an extension of his personality. It owned a divinity to Giancarlo, the P38 with its simple mechanism, its gas routes and magazines, its hair-trigger, its power.

'No need for us all to be in there,' Franca said when Giancarlo was at her side, Enrico on the other flank, and they were close to the Post doorway. 'Get yourself across the road to the papers. And get plenty if we're to be stuck in the flat for the rest of the day.'

He didn't wish to leave her side, but it was an instruction, a dismissal.

Giancarlo turned away. He faced the wide and scurrying lanes of early morning traffic, looked for the opening that would enable him to reach the raised centre bank of the Corso Francia. There was a newspaper stall on the far side nearly opposite the Post. There was no hurry for him because however early you came to the Post there was always a man there before you; the pathetic fools who were paid to take the bills and the money for gas and telephone and electricity because it was beneath the dignity of the borghese to stand and wait in a line. He saw the opening, a slowing in the traffic and launched himself through the welter of bonnets and bumpers and spirited horns and spinning wheels. A hesitation in the centre. Another delay before the passage was clear and he was off again, skipping, young-footed, across the remaining roadway to the stand with its gaudy decoration of magazine covers and paperbacks. He had not looked back at Franca and did not see the slowly cruising car of the Squadra Mobile far out in the traffic flow of the road behind him. Giancarlo was unaware of the moment of surging danger, the startled gape of recognition on the face of the vice brigadiere as he riveted on the features of the woman, half in profile at the entrance to the Post and waiting for the lifting of the steel shutter. Giancarlo did not know as he took his place in the queue to be served that the policeman had savagely urged his driver to maintain speed, create no warning, as he rifled through the folder of photographs kept permanently in the glove box of the car.

The boy was still shuffling forward as the first radio message was beamed to the Questura in central Rome.

Giancarlo stood, hands in pockets, mind on a woman as the radio transmissions hit the air. While cars were scrambling, accelerating, guns being armed and cocked, Giancarlo searched his memories, finding again the breasts and thighs of Franca.

He did not protest as the woman in the cream coat pushed past him without ceremony, passing up the opportunity to sneer and laugh so that she should be discomfited. He knew the newspapers he should buy. *L'Unità* of the PCI, the communists; *La Stampa* of Turin, the paper of Fiat and Agnelli; *Repubblica* of the Socialists; *Popolo* of the right, *Il Messaggero* of the left. Necessary always, Franca said, to have *Il Messaggero* so that they could browse through the 'Cronaca di Roma' section and read of the successes of their colleagues in different and separated cells, learn where the Molotovs had landed in the night, what enemy had been hit, what friend taken. Five papers, a thousand lire. Giancarlo scratched in the hip pocket of his trousers for the dribble of coins and the crumpled notes he would need, counting out the money, standing his ground against the pushing of the man behind him. He would ask Franca to replace it, it was she who kept the cell's money, in the small wall safe in her room with the combination lock and the documents for identity changes, and the files on targets of future attacks. She should replace the money – a thousand lire, three bottles of beer if he went to the bar in the evening. It was all right for him to go out after dark, it was only Franca who should not. But he would not be drinking beer that evening, he would be sitting on the rug at the feet of the woman and close to her, rubbing his shoulder against her knee, resting his elbow on her thigh, waiting for the indications of her tiredness, her willingness for bed. He had been to the bar the night before, after their meal, and come back to find her drooped in the chair and Enrico sprawled and sleeping opposite her on the sofa with his feet on the cushions. She had said nothing, just taken his hand and turned off the lights and led him like a lamb to her room, and still she had not spoken as her hands slipped down the length of his shirt to his waist.

The agony of waiting for her would be unendurable.

Giancarlo paid his money, stepped back from the counter with the folded newspapers and scanned the front page of *Il Messaggero*. Carillo of Spain and Berlinguer of Italy were meeting in Rome, a Eurocommunist summit, middle-class, middle-aged, a betrayal of the true proletariat. A former Minister of Shipping was accused of having his hand in the till, what you'd expect from the bastard Democrazia Cristiana. The steering committee of the Socialists was sitting down with the DC, games being played, circles of words. A banker arrested for tax evasion. All the sickness, all the foetid corruption was here, all the cancer of the world they struggled to usurp. And then he found the headlines that would bring the smile and the cold mirth to Franca; the successes and the triumphs. One of their own, Antonio de Laurentis of Napoli, missing inside the maximum security gaol on Favignana island, described as 'most dangerous', a leader of the NAP, inside the prison and they'd lost him. An executive of Fiat shot in the legs in Turin, the thirty-seventh that year to have the people's sentence inflicted and the year not eight months old.

He tucked the papers under his arm and looked out across the road to the Post. Franca would be furious, icy, if he kept her waiting. It was heavily parked now around their 128. Two yellow Alfettas there and a grey Alfasud, close to their own car. He wondered whether they'd be able to get out. God, she'd be angry if they were boxed. Over the top of the traffic, solid and unpassable to him, Giancarlo saw Enrico emerge from the doorway, cautious and wary. Two paces behind him, Franca, cool, commanding. His woman. Christ, she walked well, with the loping stride, never an eye left nor right.

And the blur of movement. Shatteringly fast. Too quick for the boy to retain. Franca and Enrico were five, six metres from the entrance to the Post. The doors of the three intruding cars bulged and split open. Men running, shouting. The moment of clarity for Giancarlo, he saw the guns in their hands. The two at the front sprinted forward, then dived for the crouch with the automatics held straight arm to the front. Enrico twisted his arm back for the hanging flap of the shirt tail and the concealed Beretta.

Across the traffic and tarmac void Giancarlo heard the shriek of the doomed Enrico. The cry for the woman to run. The scream of the stag that will stand against the dogs to give time for the hind to hasten to the thickets. But her eyes were faster than his, her mind quicker and better able to assess the realities of the moment. As his gun came up to face the aggressors she made the quicksilver decision of survival. The boy saw her head duck and disappear behind the roofs of the passing cars, and then there was the vision of her, prone on the stomach, hands on her head.

Enrico would not see her, would believe in his last sand-running moments that his sacrifice had achieved its purpose. Even as he fired, he was cut down by the swarm of bullets aimed at him in a thunderclap of gunfire, and lay writhing on the pavement as if trying to shake away a great agony, rolling and rolling from his back to his belly. The men ran forward, still suspicious that their enemy might bite, might hurt. There was a trail of blood from Enrico's mouth, another two from his chest that meandered together and then separated, and more crimson paths etching from his shattered legs. But his life lingered and a hand scrabbled at the dirt for the gun that had been dropped, that had fallen beyond reach. The men who towered above him wore jeans and casual slacks and sweatshirts, and some were unshaven or bearded or carried their hair long on their shoulders. Nothing to tell them from Enrico and Giancarlo. These were the men of the Squadra Anti-Terrorismo, undercover, dedicated, as hard and ruthless as those they opposed. A single shot destroyed the frenzy of Enrico's groping hands.

An execution bullet. Just as it had been said it was when the carabinieri dropped La Muscio on the church steps near the Colosseo. Bastards, bastard pigs.

A man beside Giancarlo crossed himself in haste, a private gesture in the glare of a public moment. Down the road a woman bent in sickness. A priest in long cassock abandoned his car in the road and ran forward. Two of the men covered the figure of Franca, their guns roaming close to her head.

A terrible pain coursed through the boy as his hands stayed clamped on the folded newspapers and would not waver towards the gun buried in the flesh of his buttock. He watched, part of the gathering crowd, terrified of risking the intervention that Enrico had affected. He willed himself to run forward and shoot because that was the job the movement had chosen for him, protector and bodyguard of Franca Tantardini. But if he did his blood would run in the deep gutter, company for Enrico's. There was no thrust in his legs, no jolt in his arms; he was a part of those who stayed and waited for the show to end.

They pulled the woman, unresisting and limp, to her feet and dragged her to a car. Two had their hands on her upper arms, another walked in front with his fist caught in the long blonde strands of her hair. There was a kick that missed at her shins. He could see that her eyes were open but bewildered, unrecognizing as she went to the opened car door.

Would she have seen the boy she had opened herself to a short night before?

Would she have seen him?

He wanted to wave, give a sign, shout out that he had not abandoned her. How to show that, Giancarlo? Enrico dead, and Giancarlo alive

520

and breathing, because he had stepped back, had dissociated. How to show it, Giancarlo? The car revved its engine and its horn was raucous as it pulled out into the open road, another Alfetta close in escort behind. The cars swung across the central reservation, lurching and shaken, and completed their turn in front of where Giancarlo stood. The crowd around him pressed forward to see better the face of the woman, and the boy was among them. And then they were gone and one of the men held a machine-gun at the car window. A fanfare of sirens, an explosion of engine power. For a few moments only he was able to follow the passage of the cars in the growing traffic before they were lost to him, and the sight of Enrico was taken from him by a moving bus.

Deep in a gathering shame at the scope of his failure, Giancarlo began slowly to walk away along the pavement. Twice he bumped into men who hurried towards him, fearful that they had missed the excitement and that there was nothing remaining for them to see. Giancarlo was careful not to run, just walked away, not thinking where he should go, where he should hide. Too logical, such thoughts for his fractured mind to cope with. He saw only the stunned deep golden eyes of Franca, who was handcuffed and for whom a boy had not stepped forward.

She had called him her little fox and scratched with her nails at his body, had kissed him far down on the flatness of his stomach, had governed and tutored him, and he drifted from the place, feet leaden, unseeing with the moisture in his eyelids.

The British Embassy in Rome occupies a prime site set back from high railings and lawns and a stone-skirted artificial lake at 80a Via XX Settembre. The building itself, unlikely and original, supported by pillars of grey cement and with narrow arrow-slit windows, was conceived by a noted English architect after the previous occupant of the grounds had been destroyed by the gelignite of Jewish terrorists . . . or guerrillas . . . or freedom fighters, a stop-over in their search for a homeland. The architect had fashioned his designs at a time when the representatives of the Queen in this city were numerous and influential. Expense and expediency had whittled down the staff list. Many diplomats now doubled on two separate jobs.

The First Secretary, who handled matters of political importance in Italian affairs had also taken under his umbrella the area of liaison with the Questura and the Viminale. Politics and security, the aesthetic and the earthy, strange bed partners. That Michael Charlesworth's two previous foreign postings had been in Vientiane and Reykjavik was a source of astonishment neither to himself nor his colleagues. He was expected to master the local intricacies of a situation inside three years, and this accomplished, he could correctly anticipate that he would be sent to a country about which he had only the most superficial knowledge. After Iceland and the tangled arguments of the Cod War, with the island's fishing interests ranged against the need of his countrymen to eat northern water fish from old newspapers, Roman politics and police had a certain charm. He was not dissatisfied.

Charlesworth had demanded and won a rise in rent allowance from his Ambassador and had been able to set up home with his wife in a high-roofed flat within earshot, but not sight, of the Piazza del Popolo in the centro storico. The garaging of a car there was next to impossible and while his wife's veteran 500 was parked beneath the condescending eyes of the Vigili Urbani in the piazza, he himself cycled to work on the machine he had first used twenty years earlier as a Cambridge undergraduate. The sight of the dark-stripe-suited Englishman pedalling hard along the Corso d'Italia and the Via Piave with collapsible umbrella and attaché case clamped to the carrier over the rear wheel was a pleasing sight to Italian motorists, who from respect for his efforts afforded him unusual circumspection. Once the slopes of the Borghese Gardens had been surmounted, the bicycle provided Charlesworth with fast and intrepid transport, and often he was the first of the senior diplomatic staff to reach his desk.

A salute from the gatekeeper, the parking and padlocking of the machine, the shaking free of trouser turn-ups from the clips, a wave to security in the ground-floor hall, a gallop up two flights of stairs, and he was striding along the back second-floor corridor. Fully three doors away he heard the telephone ringing from his office. Fast with the key into the lock, swinging the door open to confront the noise, abandoning the briefcase and umbrella to the floor, he lunged for the receiver.

'*Pronto*.' Panting a little, not the way he liked to be.

'*Signor Charlesworth?*'

'Yes.'

'*La Questura. Dottore Giuseppe Carboni . . . momento.*'

Delay. First a crossed line. Apology, rampant clicking and interruption before Charlesworth heard the Questura switchboard announce with pride to Carboni that the task was accomplished, the connection successful. They were not friends, the policeman and Michael Charlesworth, but known to each other, acquainted. Carboni would know that Charlesworth was happier in English, that language courses were not always victorious. With a faint American accent Carboni spoke.

'Charlesworth, that is you?'

'Yes.' Caution. No man is happy talking to the police, least of all to foreign police at fourteen minutes past eight in the morning.

'I have bad news for you, my friend. Bad news to give you for which I am sorry. You have a businessman in the city, a resident, a man called Harrison. He is the financial controller of ICH in EUR, International

Chemical Holdings. They are at Viale Pasteur in EUR, many of the multinationals favour that area . . .' What's the silly blighter done, thought Charlesworth resigned. Socked a copper? Drunk himself stupid? No, couldn't be that, not if Carboni was calling, not if it was at that level. '. . . I regret very much, Charlesworth, to have to tell you that Geoffrey Harrison was kidnapped this morning. Armed men, forced from his car near his home.'

'Christ,' muttered Charlesworth, low but audible.

'I understand your feelings. He is the first of the foreign residents, the first of the foreign commercials to be affected by this plague.'

'I know.'

'We are doing everything we can. There are road blocks . . .' The distant voice tailed and died, as if Carboni knew the futility of boasting to this man. He came again. 'But you know, Charlesworth, these people are very organized, very sophisticated. It is unlikely, and you will understand me, it is unlikely that what we can do will be sufficient.'

'I know,' said Charlesworth. An honest man he was talking to, and what to say that wouldn't be churlish. 'I am confident you will exercise all your agencies in this matter, completely confident.'

'You can help me, Charlesworth. I have called you early, it is not half an hour since the attack, and we have not yet been to the family. We have not spoken to his wife. Perhaps she does not speak Italian, perhaps she speaks only English, we thought it better if someone from the Embassy should be with her first, to give her the news.'

The dose prescribed for diplomats seeking nightmares was purveying ill-tidings to their own nationals far from home. A stinking, lousy job and indefinite involvement. 'That was very considerate of you.'

'It is better also that you have a doctor go to her this morning. In many cases we find that necessary in the first hours. It is a shock . . . you will understand.'

'Yes.'

'I do not want to lecture you at this stage, because soon you will be busy, and I am busy myself in this matter, but you should make a contact with Harrison's employer. It is a London-based company, I believe. If they have taken the employee of a multinational they will be asking for more than poor Harrison's bank balance can provide. They will believe they are ransoming the company. It could be expensive, Charlesworth.'

'You would like me to alert the company to this situation?' Charlesworth scribbled hard on his memo pad.

'They must make their attitude clear, and quickly. When the contact is made they must know what attitude they will take.'

'What a way to start the bloody day. Well, they'll ask me this, and it may colour their judgement: you would presume that this is the work of a professional, an experienced gang?'

523

There was a faint laugh, quavering over the telephone line before Carboni replied. 'How can I say, Charlesworth? You read our newspapers, you watch the Telegiornale in the evening. You know what we are up against. You know how many times the gangs are successful, how many times we beat them. We do not hide the figures, you know that too. If you look at the results you will see that a few of the gangs are amateur – you English, always you want to reduce everything to sport – and we catch those ones. Does that give us a winning score? I would like to say so, but I cannot. It is very hard to beat the professionals. And you should tell to Harrison's firm when you speak with them that the greater the police efforts to release him, the greater the risk to his life. They should not forget that.'

Charlesworth sucked at his pencil top. 'You would expect the company to pay what they are asked to?'

'We should talk of that later. Perhaps it is premature at this moment.' A gentle correction, made with kindness, but a correction nevertheless. Not manners to talk of the will and the beneficiaries while the corpse is still warm. 'But I do not think that we would expect the family or the company of a foreigner to adopt a differing procedure to that taken by our own families when they are faced with identical problems.'

The invitation to pay. It wouldn't be made clearer than that. The invitation not to be stubborn and principled. Pragmatism winning through, and a bloody awful scene for a policeman to have to get his nose into.

'There may be some difficulty. We don't do it like that in England.'

'But you are not in England, Charlesworth.' The taint of impatience from Carboni. 'And in England you have not always been successful. I remember two cases, two ransom demands unmet, two victims found, two deaths. It is not a straightforward area of decision, and not one which we can debate. Later perhaps, but now I think there are other things that you wish to do.'

'I appreciate greatly what you have done, Dottore.'

'It is nothing.' Carboni rang off.

Five minutes later Charlesworth was in the ground-floor hall of the Embassy waiting for the arrival of the Ambassador, still shrill in his ears the piercing protests of the woman he had telephoned.

Who was going to pay?

Didn't they know they hadn't any money?

Nothing in the bank, just a few savings.

Who was going to take responsibility?

Not a conversation that Charlesworth had relished and his calming noises had been shouted out till he'd said he had to go because he must see the Ambassador. No more blustering after that; just a deep sobbing, a pain echoing down the wire to him, as if some dam of control and inhibition had been broken.

524

Where was he, the poor sod? What were they doing to him? Must be a terrible loneliness. Mind-bending, horrific. And damn-all for comfort. Didn't even know that idiots like Michael Charlesworth and Giuseppe Carboni were flapping their wings and running in circles. Better he didn't know it; it might make him turn over and give up. And what chance the Ambassador being in before nine? What bloody chance?

They'd tied him expertly as they would have done a lively bullock going to slaughter. Not a casual job, not just a length of rope round his legs.

Geoffrey Harrison had lain perhaps twenty minutes on the coarse sacking on the van floor before he had tried to move his ankles and wrists. The effects of the chloroform were dissipating, the shock of capture and the numbness of disorientation sliding. The nobbled bones on the inside of his ankles wrapped in cord caught hard against each other, digging at the flesh. The metal handcuffs on his wrists, set too tight for him, pressed on the veins and arteries. Tape, adhesive and broad, was across his mouth, forcing him to breath through his nose, reducing any sounds he could make to a jumbled, incomprehensible moan. One man had trussed him swiftly before the chloroform had gone to be replaced by the desperate passiveness of terror in an alien surrounding. And they'd hooded him, reducing his horizons to the limited things he could touch and smell. The hood was cool and damp as if it had spent the night in the grass, been subject to the light dew and retrieved before the coming of the drying warmth of the early sun. Because of the handcuffs behind his back he lay on his right side where the undulations of the road surface caused his shoulder to impact through the sacking against the ribbed metal floor.

They seemed to move at a constant speed as if far from the reach of traffic lights and road junctions, and many times Harrison heard the whine of overtaking engines, and occasionally the van shuddered as if under strain and pulled out to the left. Just once they stopped, for a short time, and he heard voices, a rapid exchange, before the van was moving again, riding through its gears, getting under way and back to the undisturbed progress. He thought about and conjured a route along the Raccordo Annulare with its festoons of white and pink oleander between the central crash barrier, and imagined the halt must have been at the toll gate for entry to an autostrada. Could be north on the Florence road, or west for L'Aquila and the Adriatic coast, or south for Naples. Could be any bloody direction, any road the animals wanted to use. He'd thought he'd been clever and superior in his intellect to make the calculations, and then came the wave of antipathy, carried on the wing. What did it matter which direction they took? It was a futile and petty exercise, because the control of his destiny was removed, turning him into a bloody vegetable. Anger surfaced for the first time, and spent itself straining against the ankle cords, striving to bite with his teeth against the tape across his mouth. It created a force and a power that struggled even as the tears rose and welled. In one convulsion, one final effort to win even the minimum of freedom for any of his limbs, he arched his back, forced his muscles.

Couldn't shift. Couldn't move. Couldn't change anything.

Pack it in, Geoffrey, you're being bloody pathetic.

Once more?

Forget it. They don't come with machine-guns and chloroform and then find, surprise, surprise, that they don't know how to tie knots.

As he sagged back his head thumped on the floor above the reach and slight protection of the sacking and he lay still with the ache and the throb in his temples and the smell of the hood in his nose. Lay still because he could do nothing else.

3

The immediate sense of survival was uppermost now in the mind of Giancarlo.

It was the instinct of the stoat or the weasel that has lost its mate and must abandon its den, move on, but has no notion of where to go, only that it must creep stealthily away from the scene of its enemies' vengeance. He wanted to run, to outstrip the pedestrians who cluttered and barred the pavements, but his training won out. He did not hurry. He strolled, because he must blend, must forsake the identity bestowed on him by the P38.

The noise and confusion and shouting of the beginning of a new day swamped him. The hooting of impatient motorists. The crashing intrusion of the alimentari shutters rising in their doorways and windows to display the cheese and hams and tins and bottles. The arguments that spilled from the bars. Confident, secure sounds, belonging and with a right to be there, swarming around Giancarlo. The boy tried to shut inside himself his concentration and avoid the cancer of these people that swept and surged past him. He belonged to no part of them.

Since the NAP had drifted into existence in the early nineteen-seventies, coalesced from a meeting of minds and aspirations to an organization, it had derived its principal security from the cell system. Nothing new, nothing revolutionary in that; laid down by Mao and Ho and Guevara. Standard in the theoretical treatises. Separated in their

526

cells the members had no need for the identity of other names, for the location of other safe houses. It was essential procedure, and when one was taken, then the wound to the movement could be swiftly cauterized. Franca was their cell leader. She alone knew the hidden places where ammunitions and materials were stored, the telephone numbers of the policy committee, and the lists of addresses. She had not shared with Enrico, much less with the boy, the probationer, because neither required such information.

He could not go back to his previous flat where he had lived with a girl and two boys as that had been closed and abandoned. He could not tour the cars and streets of Pietralata behind the Tiburtina station and ask for them by name; he wouldn't know where to begin, and who to ask. It made him shudder as he walked, the depths of the isolation in which the movement had so successfully cloaked him.

Where among the streaming, scrambling crowds that passed on either side of him did he find the nod and handshake of recognition? It was frightening to the boy because without Franca he was truly alone. Storm clouds rising, sails full, rudder flapping, and the rocks high and sharp and waiting.

Giancarlo Battestini, nineteen years old.

Short and without weight, a physical nonentity. A body that looked perpetually starved, a face that seemed for ever hungry, a boy that a woman would want to take in and fatten because she would fear that unless she hurried he might wither and fade. Dark hair above the growth of his cheeks that was curled and untidy. A sallow, wan complexion as if the sun had not sought him out, had avoided the lustreless skin. Acne spots at his chin and the sides of his mouth that were red and angry against the surrounding flesh and to which his fingers moved with embarrassed frequency. The pale and puckered line across the bridge of his nose that deviated on across the upper cheekbone under his right eye was his major distinguishing mark. He had the polizia of the Primo Celere to thank for the scar, the baton charge across the Ponte Garibaldi when the boy had slipped in headlong flight and turned his ankle. He had been a student then, enrolled two terms at the University of Rome, choosing the study of psychology for no better reason than that the course was a long one and his father could pay for four years of education. And what else was there to do?

The University with its bulging inefficiency had seemed to Giancarlo a paradise of liberation. Lectures too clogged to attend unless you took a seat or standing place a full hour before the professor came. Tutorials that were late or cancelled. Exams that were postponed. A hostel within

527

walking distance in the Viale Regina Elena where the talk was long and bold and brave.

Heady battles they had fought around the University that winter. The Autonomia in the van, they had driven the polizia back from the front façade of arches and across the street to their trucks. They had expelled by force Luciano Lama, the big union man of the PCI, who had come to talk to them on moderation and conformity and responsibility; thrown him out, the turncoat communist in his suit and polished shoes. Six hundred formed the core of the Autonomia, the separatists, and Giancarlo had first hung round their fringe, then attended their meetings and finally sidled towards the leaders and stammered his pledge of support. Warm acceptance had followed. A paradise indeed to the boy from the seaside at Pescara where his father owned a shop and carried a stock of fine cotton dresses and blouses and skirts in summer, and wool and leather and suede in winter.

Hit and run. Strike and retreat. The tactical battles of the Autonomia were in the name of repression in Argentina, the deaths in Stamheim of comrades Baader and Raspe and Enselin, the changing of the curriculum. No long searches for cause and justification. Hurt the polizia and the carabinieri, the forces of the new fascism. Goad them into retaliatory dashes from the wide streets that were safe to the narrow maze of centro storico where the Molotovs and the P38s could score and wound. Formidable the polizia looked, with their white bullet-proof tunics lolling to their knees and their stovepipe face masks behind which they felt a false invulnerability. But they could not run in their new and expensive equipment, could only fire the gas and beat the clubs on the plastic shields. They were loath to follow the kids, the Pied Pipers, when the range of the pistols and the petrol diminished.

A scarf tight across his face for protection both from press photographs and the gas, Giancarlo had never before experienced such orgasmic, pained excitement as when he had sprinted forward on the bridge and launched the bottle with its litre of petrol and smouldering rag at the Primo Celere huddled behind their armoured jeep. A shriek of noise had erupted as the bottle splintered. The flames scattered. There was a roar of approval from behind as the boy stood his ground in defiance while the gas shells flourished about him. Then the retaliation. Twenty of them running, and Giancarlo had turned for his escape. The desperate, terrifying moment when the ground was rising, space under his feet, control lost, and in his ears the drumming of the boots that were in pursuit. His hands covering his head were pulled away as they put the baton in, and there was blood cool across his face and sweet in his mouth, and blows to the leg, kicks to the belly. Voices from the south, from the peasant south, from the servants of the Democrazia Cristiana, from the workers who had been bought and were too stupid to know it.

Two months in the Regina Coeli gaol awaiting his court appearance. Seven months' imprisonment for throwing the Molotov to be served in the Queen of Heaven.

A whore of a place, that gaol. Intolerable heat and stench through that first summer when he had bunked in a cell with two others. Devoid of draught and privacy, assimilated into a world of homosexuality, thieving, deprivation. Food inedible, boredom impossible, company illiterate. Hatred and loathing bit deep in the boy when he was the guest of the Queen of Heaven. Hatred and loathing of those who had put him there, of the polizia who had clubbed him and spat in his face in the truck and laughed in their dialect at the little, humbled *intellettuale*.

Giancarlo sought his counterstrike and found the potential for revenge in the top-floor cells of the 'B' Wing where the men of the Nuclei Armati Proletaria were incarcerated, some on remand, some sentenced. They could read in the boy's eyes and in the twist of his lower lip that here was a progeny that could be useful and exploited. He learned in those heated, sweating cells the theory and the practice, the expertise and the strategy of urban guerrilla conflict. A new recruit, a new volunteer. The men gave him diagrams to memorize of the mechanism of weapons, lectured him in the study of concealment and ambush, droned at him of the politics of their struggle, hectored him with the case histories of corruption and malpractice in government and capitalist business. These men would not see the fruits of their work but took comfort that they had found one so malleable, so supple to their will. They were pleased with what they saw. Word of his friendship spread along the landings of his own wing. The homosexuals did not sidle close and flash their hands at his genitals, the thieves left undisturbed the bag under his bunk where he kept his few personal possessions, the Agenti did not bully.

In the months in gaol he passed from the student of casual and fashionable protest to the political militant.

His parents never visited him in the Queen of Heaven. He had not seen them since they had stood at the back of the court, half masked from his sight by the guard's shoulders. Anger on his father's face, tears making the mascara run on his mother's cheeks. His father wore a Sunday suit, his mother dressed in a black coat as if that would impress the magistrate. The chains on his wrists had been long and loose, and they gave him the opportunity to raise his right arm, clenched fist, the salute of the left, the gesture of the fighter. Screw them. Give them something to think on when they took the autostrada back across the mountains to Pescara. And his picture would be in the Adriatic paper and would be seen by the ladies who came to buy from the shop and they would whisper and titter behind their hands. In all his time in the gaol he received only one letter, written in the spider hand of his brother Fabrizio, a graduate lawyer and five years his elder. There was a room

529

for him at home, Mama still kept his bedroom as it had been before he had gone to Rome. Papa would find work for him. There could be a new start, he would be forgiven. Methodically Giancarlo had torn the single sheet of notepaper into many pieces that flaked to the cell floor.

When the time came for Giancarlo's release he was clear on the instructions that had been given him from the men in 'B' Wing. He had walked out through the steel gates and on to the Lungotevere and not looked back at the crumbling plaster of the high ochre-stained walls. The car was waiting as he had been told it would be and a girl had moved across the back seat to make room for him. First names they called themselves by, and they took him for a coffee and poured a measure of Scotch whisky into the foaming milk of the cappuccino and brought him cigarettes that were imported and expensive.

Half a year now of being hunted, half a year of running and caution and care, and he had wondered what was the life expectancy of freedom, thought of how long his wings would stay unclipped by cell bars and locked doors.

Once he had been in the same flat as the one they called the Chief, had seen his profile through an opened door, bushy-bearded, short, vital in the eyes and mouth – the Chief who stayed now on the island prison of Asinara and who they said had been betrayed.

Once he had strayed into the bedroom of a covo carrying the cigarettes he had been sent to buy, looking for the man who had dispatched him, and recognized the sleeping form of the one they said was expert with explosives. He too, they said, had been betrayed to a life sentence on the island.

Once he had been taken to stand for a moment on the steps of a church where Antonio La Muscio and Mia Vianale had sat and eaten plums on a summer evening, and he now in his grave with half a carabinieri magazine to put him there, and the fruit unfinished, and La Vianale rotting in the gaol at Messina.

Hard and dangerous times, only recently made safer by the skill and calm of Franca.

But as the net grew closer, shrinking around the group, Franca had disowned the safety of inactivity.

'Two hundred and fifty political prisoners of the left in the gaols, and they believe we are close to the moment of our destruction, that is what they say on the RAI, that is what they say at the DC congress. So we must fight, demonstrate beyond their concealment that we are not crushed, not neutered.'

Franca did not talk in the slogans of the kids of his first covo. She had no use for the parrot words of 'enemies of the proletariat', the 'forces of repression', 'capitalist exploitation'. It confused the boy because they had become a part of his life, a habit of his tongue, cemented to his vocabulary. Franca vented her anger without words, displayed her dedication with the squeezed, arctic index finger of her right hand. Three bedridden victims in the Policlinico, another in a private room of the nursing home on the Trionfale, they were her vengeance – men who might never walk again with freedom, would not run with their children, and one among them who would not sleep with and satisfy his wife.

Inevitable that it must end. The risks were too great, the pace too heady, the struggle unequal.

Giancarlo crossed a road, not looking for the cars, nor for the green-lit 'Avanti' sign, not hearing the shriek of the brakes, ignorant of the bellowed insult. Perhaps he would have brought her flowers that evening. Perhaps he would have gone to the piazza and bought from the gypsy woman some violets, or a sprig of pansies. Nothing gaudy, nothing that would win a sneer from her. Simple flowers from the fields to make her smile and her face soften, to erase the harshness of her mouth that he had first seen as she walked from the shooting of the personnel officer.

But flowers would not help her now, not from the boy who had declined to step forward, who had walked away.

There was a hunger already in his stomach and little chance to appease it. His wallet still lay in the flat on the small table beside his unused bed. There was some loose change in his hip pocket and the mini-assegni notes that were worth not more than a hundred and a hundred and fifty lire apiece. In all he had enough for a bowl of pasta or a sandwich, and a coffee or a beer, and after that – nothing. He must keep two hundred lire for an afternoon paper when they came on the news stands – *Paese Sera* or *Momento Sera*. Meanwhile his wallet was in the flat. His wallet that he touched and handled through the day, held with his finger-tips, the contour whorls that were only his own and that the police fingerprint dust would find and feed to the files. They had taken his fingerprints months back in the police station after his arrest.

They will have your name by the afternoon, Giancarlo, and your photograph. All they want about you they will have.

Time to begin to think again, to throw off the weight of depression and self-examination. Stupid bastard, take a hold. Behave like a man of the NAP. Save yourself and survive.

Where to start?

The University.

In the vacation, in the summer? When there is no one there?

Where else? Where else do you go to, Giancarlo? Home to Mama, to tell her it was all a mistake, that you met bad people . . . ?

Perhaps there would be someone at the University.

531

The University offered him the best chance of a bed with no questions asked among the students of the Autonomia whom he had known many months before. He had not been there since his release and he would have to exercise the utmost care as he approached the faculties. The campus was heavy with informers and policemen who carried books and mingled. But if he could find the right boys, then they would hide him, and they would respect him because he had graduated from the sit-ins and the lock-ins and the Molotovs to the real war of the fully fledged, of the men. They would look after him at the University.

A long walk it would be, across the wide Ponte Flaminio, through the Parioli, along the tree-lined ribbon of the Viale Regina Margherita. With the decision taken and his mind clearing he quickened his step. It was a risk to go that far and his name and description and his clothing would soon be radioed to the polizia who cruised and watched over the city, but there were no alternatives.

Because he worked directly to the Minister of the Interior, Francesco Vellosi's office was on the second floor of the lowering grey stonework of the Viminale. His subordinates were found either a kilometre away at the Questura, or far to the west in the Criminalpol building at EUR. But the capo of the Squadra Anti-Terrorismo was required to be close to the seat of power, just down the corridor from it, which served to emphasize the recognition of the threat to the country posed by the rash of urban guerrilla groups. A fine room he occupied, reached through high double doors of polished wood, with an ornate ceiling from which hung electric bulbs set in a shivering chandelier of light, oil paintings on the walls, a wide desk with an inlaid leather top, easy chairs for the visitors, a coffee table for magazines and ashtrays, and a signed photograph of the President between the tall twin windows. Francesco Vellosi, thirty years in the police, detested the room, and would have given much to have exchanged the brilliance of the surroundings for a shirtsleeves working area. The room got the sun in the afternoons but on this July morning the brightness had not yet reached it.

The radio telephone in his armour-plated car had warned Vellosi when mid-way between his bachelor flat and place of work that his men had met with a major and significant success that morning, and waiting for him when he bustled into the office had been the initial incident report and photostats of the files held on Franca Tantardini and Enrico Panicucci.

Vellosi gutted the paperwork with enthusiasm. A bad winter and spring they had had, built on the depressive foundation of the loss the previous year of Aldo Moro. There had been arrests, some significant, some worthless, but the plague of bombings and shootings had kept up its headlong pace, prompting the disquiet of the Deputies in the Chamber of the Democrazia Cristiana, the ridicule of the newspapers, and the perpetual demand of his Minister for solutions. Always they came to Vellosi, hurrying in pursuit of the news of a fresh outrage. He was long tired of trying to find the politician or the senior civil servant who would take responsibility for what he called the necessary methods, the hard and ruthless crackdown that he believed essential; he was still looking for his man.

Here at last was good news, and he would issue his own order that the photographers should have a good look at the Tantardini woman. The national habit of self-denigration went too deep, and it was good when the opportunity presented itself to boast a little and swagger with success.

A tall, heavily built boar of a man, the roughness of his figure softened by the cut of his jacket, the elegance of his silk tie, Vellosi shouted acknowledgement across the room of the light tap at his door. The men who entered the presence were from a different caste. Two in tattered suede boots. Two in canvas training shoes. Faded jeans. A variety of T-shirt colours. An absence of razors. Hard men whose faces seemed relaxed while the eyes were ever alert and alive and bright. Vellosi's lions, the men who fought the war far below the surface of the city's life. The sewer rats, because that was where they had to exist if they were to find the rodent pests.

The four eased a careful way across the thick carpet, and when he gestured to them, sat with care on the deep, comfortable chairs. They were the officers of the squad that had taken the woman, destroyed the animal Panicucci, and they had come to receive their plaudits, tell at first hand of the exploit, and bring a little solace to the days of Vellosi in the Viminale.

He wriggled with pleasure in his seat as the work of the morning was recounted. Nothing omitted, nothing spared, so that he could savour and live in his mind the moment when Panicucci and the woman had emerged from the Post. As it should be, and he'd wheel them in to shake the hand of the Minister and blunt the back-stab knives that were always honing for him. He limited himself to the briefest of interruptions, preferring to let the steady flow of the story bathe him in the triumph of his squad.

The telephone broke into the recital.

Vellosi's face showed his annoyance at the interference – the annoyance of a man who hopes to make it and is on the couch with his girl when the doorbell sounds. He waved his hand to halt the flow; he would return to it as soon as the business of the call was dispatched. It was the Questura.

Had Vellosi's men been certain when they took the woman that there was not another boy with her? Had they missed one?

533

The covo had been found, the address taken from the telephone slip just paid by the Tantardini woman. The polizia had visited the flat and found there the clothes of another boy, far too small to be those of Panicucci. There was a woman on the ground floor of the block, sick, and from the moment she was dressed in the morning she would sit and watch from her window the passing street; when the ragazzi drove their car from the garage there were always three, and there were three that morning. Fingerprinting had begun, there was another set and fresh, not to be confused with Tantardini's and Panicucci's. The polizia had been careful to check with the woman at the window the time of the departure of the car from the block and compare it with the timing of the incident at the Post. It was their opinion that there had been no time for a substantial deviation to drop off a second male.

A cold sponge was squeezed over Vellosi.

'Have you a description of this second man?'

'The woman says he is not a man, just a boy really. There are many identity cards in the flat, one of the photographs may be genuine, but we are working on a photo-fit now. Your own people are there now, no doubt they will brief you. We think the boy is eighteen, perhaps nineteen. We thought you would like to know.'

'You are very kind,' Vellosi said quietly, then hammered the telephone down.

He ran his eyes over the men in front of him, brought them sitting upright and awkward on the edge of their seats.

'We missed one.' Spoken with coldness, the pleasure eroded from the session.

'There was no one else at the Post. The car had no driver waiting in it, and only the two came out. They were well clear of the doorway when we moved.' The defensive, bridling argument came from a man who an hour earlier had faced the barrel of a Beretta, who had out-thought, out-manoeuvred his opponent and fired for his own survival.

'Three came from the flat. The car went straight to the Post.'

The inquisition was resented. 'He was not there when we came. And after the shooting some of our people watched the crowd, as is standard. Nobody ran from the scene.'

Vellosi shrugged, resigned. Like eels, these people. Always one of them wriggled away, slipped through the finest meshes. Always one of a group escaped, so that you could never cut off the head and know that the body was beyond another spawning. 'He is very young, this one that we have lost.'

Three of the men stayed silent, peeved that the moment of accolade had turned to recrimination. The fourth spoke up, undaunted by his superior's grimness. 'If it is a boy, then it will have been her runner, there to fetch and carry for her, and to serve in the whore's bed. Always

534

she has one like that. Panicucci she did not use, only the young ones she liked. It is well known in the NAP.'

'If you are right, it is not a great loss.'

'It is an irritation, nothing more. The fat cat we have, the gorilla we have killed; that the flea is out is only a nuisance.'

It was not yet ten o'clock and there were smiles as Vellosi produced the bottle from the lower drawer of his desk, and then reached again for the small cut-glass tumblers. It was too early for champagne but Scotch was right. The brat had broken the pattern of perfection, like a summer picnic when it rains and the tablecloth must be scooped up, but the best of the day had gone before.

Only a nuisance, only an irritation, the missing of the boy.

He knew they had been travelling many hours because the van floor on which he lay was warmed by the outside sun even through the layer of sacking. The air around Geoffrey Harrison was thick, tasting of petrol fumes, pricking against his skin as if all the cool and freshness of the morning's start had been expelled, thrust out. It was painfully hot, and under the weight of the hood over his head he had sometimes begun to pant for air, with accompanying hallucinations that his lungs might not cope, that he might suffocate in the dark around him. Occasionally he heard two slight voices in conversation but the words, even had he been able to understand them, were muffled by the engine noise. Two different tones, that was all he could distinguish. And they talked infrequently, the two men riding in the seats in front. There were long periods of quiet between them and then a brief flurry of chatter as if something they passed took their fancy, attracted their eyes.

The motion of the van was constant, its progress uneventful, releasing him to his thoughts. It was as if he were a package of freight being transported to a far destination by two men who had neither interest nor concern in him and thought only of their delivery time.

In the *Daily News* and the *Daily American* and the Italian papers that he struggled with in the office Harrison had read many times of the techniques practised by the flourishing Italian kidnap gangs. In the bar of the Olgiata Golf Club, little America, little Mid-West, where there were Tom Collins and Bourbon mixes, he had joined the drift of conversation when the foreigners had talked of the Italian disease. Different setting, different values; easy then to relate all sickness to the bloody inefficiency of Italians, and what else could you expect when you were half way to the Middle East. Well down the road to Damascus here, right? Wasn't it a scandal, the transatlantic executives would say, that a fellow could get picked off the street and have to cough up a million dollars, however many noughts that was in lire, to get himself back to his wife and kids? And wasn't it about time that something was done about it? Couldn't happen at home, of course – not in London, not in Los Angeles . . . not in Birmingham, not in Boston. And there'd always be one there, elbow at the bar and face pulled with authority, to drop his voice beneath the reach of the Italian members, and lean forward and whisper, 'Wouldn't happen if old Musso was running the place. And it's what they need again. A damn great shock up the ass, and someone like Musso to give it to them. Not exactly Musso, because he was an idiot, but someone with a damn great stick.' Simple answers, more drinks, and none of them had an idea. He wondered whether they'd remember him: young Harrison, quite a junior fellow, didn't make it up this way that often, always hanging on the edge of a chat, and a wife with bright lipstick. Just a drinking member.

Perhaps you're lucky, Geoffrey, perhaps you're lucky you didn't struggle. You put up a bit of a show, but not much. Just enough for vague self-respect. Remember the picture in the paper of the man from Milan, the man who'd fought back and mixed it. Stone dead in a box, with the wife in black and the kids holding her hands walking behind. At least you're bloody alive. Because they don't muck about, these people; they're not governed by Queensberry or any other set of rules. Hard, vicious bastards. Remember the black-and-white images on the television in the living-room; the body of little Christina, eighteen years old, being dragged out of the rubbish tip and the ransom had been paid. Remember the race-course king; he made the front pages, trussed like a chicken and a hood on him, just like you are now except that he had a hunk of cement to weight him down in the lake near Como. Remember the boy in the village in Calabria with his ear sliced away to encourage his father to dig deeper into the family savings . . .

Horrible bastards.

Not like anything those stupid sods in the bar would know about when they came off their nine holes. All a bit of a joke over a pre-lunch gin, a bit of a chuckle. Something local that didn't affect foreigners. They should have seen them for themselves, those bloody faces under the stockings, the way the guns came, and the hammer. That would have splashed the tonic round a bit, would have stifled all the rectitude, the platitudes. They'd never bloody laugh again, those sods in the bar, not if they saw that crowd coming at them. Remember the Telegiornale, Geoffrey, what happens to the Italian families. Drawn curtains, shuttered windows, people hurrying by on the pavement below, not wishing to look in as if that would somehow involve them with a family that flew the yellow flag of quarantine. The face of a child or a mother in the doorway who looked for support and sympathy and found none; the humble car of the priest pulling up on the pavement and scattering the waiting photographers. Geoffrey knew the pictures, knew the way the story was chronicled on the first day and never mentioned again afterwards until the moment of conclusion. Stale in twenty-four hours.

Pray God there isn't some pompous fool in there.

What do you mean?

Well, some stupid ass with a good lunch inside him and letters after his name who wants to talk about the principle of paying.

What do you mean?

Well, if some ape says it's not right to pay, that you have to stand up to these people, that if you give way now what do you do next time.

They wouldn't say that, would they, not really say that?

They're not where you are, Geoffrey. They're in a boardroom, not in handcuffs. They may have cut themselves shaving, but they haven't had a bloody great fist slammed in. Some of them are bloody geriatric. All they know about the sodding country is what they see on a balance sheet.

They wouldn't be so stupid, they couldn't. Don't they know people get chopped if there's no payola, don't they know that?

Calm it, kid. Not bloody helping, is it? They'll know it, and if they don't there'll be someone there to tell them.

You're sure?

I'm sure, I'm certain.

How can you know?

I'm certain because I have to believe that, otherwise we go stark bloody mad, straight insane.

With the sun playing on its roof without remorse or hindrance, baking the closed interior, the van headed at a steady and unremarkable one hundred and ten kilometres per hour southwards along the Autostrada del Sol.

4

His Excellency the Ambassador of Her Britannic Majesty, who had known the tap of her sword on his right shoulder and had kissed her hand and valued his audience, was a man who admired discipline of action, and protocol of approach. He had not disguised his distaste at what he regarded as the breathy intervention of young Charlesworth when he was only one foot out of his official burnished transport. He had been short with his First Secretary, had permitted only the briefest of résumés and failed to raise his eyebrows in either shock or astonishment. And as he had marched away, smiling at the doorman, with Charlesworth snapping like a lap dog at his heels, he had suggested that something on paper by lunchtime would satisfy his requirements for information.

As he strode down the drive to the security lodge, Charlesworth cursed himself for his flustered account, for his failure to interest his superior, regretting that he had allowed himself to be put down as a bubbling child is by an overburdened parent. He recalled that the Ambassador was hosting a luncheon-party that day; the newly appointed Foreign Minister would be at his right hand, the guest of honour. Present would be the senior members of the diplomatic corps, a smattering of ranking civil servants, the best bone china and the silverware out from the cupboard. The Ambassador had his priorities, Charlesworth growled to himself. The soup shouldn't be too salted, the plates must be warm, the wine chilled, the conversation clever. He had too much on his mind to worry about the fears of a hysterical woman, and a man trussed and perhaps half dead who was experiencing the greatest degree of terror he had known in his life. He'd be far too busy for such sordidness, and a piece of paper with some aptly chosen words presented before the sherry flowed would be sufficient.

Charlesworth dived out into the road beyond the regimented railings of the Embassy, scanning the traffic that burst through the arches of the ancient reddened brick city wall. Getting a taxi would need the luck of old Jupiter. But luck was with him, the yellow Fiat snaking to the pavement, and he waved frantically and hurried towards its stopping point. He saw the face in the back, equal shades of mauve and pink. 'Buster' Henderson; Military Cross in Korea God knows how many years ago and for doing something nobody sane would have dreamed of; military attaché; half-colonel; always took a cab in, and one home in the afternoon. Charlesworth didn't know how he could afford it, not that and the gin as well.

'In a hurry, young man?' Charlesworth detested the way the older staff regarded him as a juvenile. 'Flap on, is there? Eyeties declared war on us . . . ?' A boom of laughter. Must have been the life and soul of some gory cavalry mess east of the Rhine.

'One of our people has been kidnapped this morning.'

'One of the Embassy chaps?' Henderson was waiting for the change from his 10,000-lire note.

'No, it's not the end of the world, not one of ours. It's a businessman, a fellow who works out here. I've to get up to his wife.'

'Poor bastard,' said Henderson quietly. His wallet was open, the notes being carefully put away in order of value, damn-all of a tip. 'Poor devil, rather him . . .'

'Could be rather a shambles for us. It's the first time a foreigner has been lifted. Well, only the Getty boy, and that was different, I suppose.'

Henderson held the door open for Charlesworth. 'You'll be handling our end, eh? Well, if you get a bit overwhelmed, give us a shout.

Damn-all I have to worry about at the moment, diary's empty as a larder these next three days. Don't hang about if you want a hand, if you want to talk it over.'

'Thank you . . . thank you very much. It's most kind . . . Buster.'

Charlesworth had never called him that before, never really had a conversation with the army officer on any more substantive subject than whether it would rain on QBP day, whether they'd have to retire to the marquee for the annual Queen's Birthday Party celebrations. Silly little thing, the offer of help, but he was grateful, grateful because he was stepping on stones that he did not know.

'Poor devil, rather him . . .' Charlesworth heard half-colonel 'Buster' Henderson mutter again as he closed the taxi-door on himself.

He walked in what shade he could find, seeking out the places where the sun was denied sight of the pavements by the towering blocks of flats flanking the Regina Margherita. Unable now to control the speed of his legs as they pumped a way along the uneven flagstones, hurrying when he knew he should be calm, because the coolness he had first sought to impose on himself was disappearing, slipping from his grasp. Giancarlo was feeling the stress and lead weight of the fugitive.

Not that the shade offered him solace. The stinking, brutalizing heat of the morning penetrated the air, broke open his white skin and thrust out the carousing sweat rivers that saturated his few clothes, soaking and irritating him. No wind down at street level. Just the furnace and the car exhausts, nothing to bluster across his face and limbs. He tramped on for the sanctuary of the University, where a face might be familiar, where the environs would be known, where there would be an end to the perpetual swinging of his head for a first glimpse of the coasting police cars. It was a new experience for Giancarlo. Never before had he known the feeling of being hunted, of being loose and adrift from the companionship of the group, of being cast outside the protective womb of the NAP.

When Giancarlo had walked at the side of Franca Tantardini, the NAP had seemed to him a great and powerful organization. Limitless authority and potential gushed when he had been close to her, and the words of victory and success and triumph had cascaded from her tongue. Now the sheen of safety was stripped from him and Enrico was dead, washing his face in his own blood, and Franca taken. He fled towards the reassurance of the nursery, the safety of the crèche, to the University.

Tired legs, sore feet, a heaving chest, the classic symptoms of flight. He turned left towards the Piazza Giorgio Fabrizio, then right into the Viale del Policlinico. He stumbled from tiredness as he passed the huge, drawn-out complex of the hospital. The signs of PRONTO SOCCORSO that

539

guided the racing, siren-loud ambulances to where they should bring their emergencies were on his right. Where they brought Franca's victims. Where they deposited the men with the gunshot wounds for the first immediate life-saving operation to counter the work of the P38. The boy saw the men who waited in their short white coats and the nurses in their belted dresses who lounged under the trees alert for the screaming of the ambulance approach that would send them scurrying in preparation to Casualty Reception.

Going past the Policlinico, Giancarlo knew with the sureness of the first lightning flash in a storm why they would hate him, track him, spend a lifetime edging towards his back. No forgiveness, no charity, not while men lay in pain on the metal bed-frames of the Policlinico, and shouted in the night for their wives. A great army they would bring against him, and a mind with a limitless and unbroken memory.

A boy who was as nothing. Devoid of possessions, importance, status. Armed with a P38 and a magazine of eight shells.

Devoid of plan and programme and blueprint.

Armed with a detestation of cruel force against the system that rallied now to crush him.

Bereft of friendship and accomplices and the strength of a leader to guide.

Armed with the love of a girl who had taken him into herself. Armed with the love of Franca Tantardini. For she must have loved him, she must have wanted him, Giancarlo Battestini, or he would not have known her bed and her warmth and her murmurs and her fingers. If it took a week or a month or a year, he would take her from them. Repossess her freedom, the freedom of the bird to escape the cage. Because she had loved him.

Dwarfing the boy were the great white stone walls and archway of the University. Designed for immortality, designed to stand for a thousand years as proof to a grateful worker class of the power wielded by the black shirt and the leather boot. Giancarlo took in the daubed slogans of the paint spray aerosols, bright colours of graffiti that disfigured the impression of omnipotence, but only as high as a student's arm could rise. Above the reach of the protestor was the clean-cut stone of the rejected regime. The slogans of the Autonomia were here at shoulder height. The painted outline of the closed fist with the first and second fingers extended – the P trent' otto. Here were daubed the cries of hate against the Ministers of government, the parties of democracy, the polizia, the carabinieri, the borghese. He had arrived at the place where succour might be found.

Stretching away in front of him was the wide avenue between the Science and Medical Faculties and the Administration buildings. Many doors were closed, many windows shuttered, because the academic year and examinations had terminated six weeks earlier. But there would be some students here, those who had taken a cause and rejected the cloying parental hand over the family holiday, they would have stayed. Giancarlo broke into a run. He lifted the weariness from his legs, lengthened his stride, till he was sprinting down the gentle hill.

The taxi, its driver displaying caution rare in his vocation, nudged up the hill at a crawl and rounded the three police cars straddled in front of the Mercedes. Charlesworth saw the driver's side window breached and shattered, frozen glass glittering in the gravel surface of the road.

The polizia, in blue and mauve trousers with the thin maroon cord astride their thighs and open blue shirts and caps pushed back on their foreheads, were working round the smitten vehicle. They dabbed on fingerprint dust and a tin was beside them in which plaster glistened wetly and which would be used if the impression of a tyre grip needed recording. It was too warm for the polizia to move with energy and their inertia was augmented by the very familiarity of the scene. There was nothing new, the scene of crime procedures for a kidnap. As the taxi circumvented the blockage, Charlesworth saw two men in civilian suits, and they were the only ones that mattered. Only two. Not the young boys in their crumpled uniforms recruited from the Mezzo Giorno who knew less of crime than a Neapolitan pickpocket or a Milanese burglar and wore the uniform because it was the only escape from the region of unemployment. Just two, the trained ones who took the privilege of wearing their own clothes, enough to make him heave and throw up. Dear old Carboni, with his courtesy and his compromise, who had promised nothing, he knew the limitations of his force. And why should they bust a gut – because the man who'd been lifted had a blue passport with a lion rampant and English scroll inside the front flap? Carboni had marked Charlesworth's card, said there should be a payout, that they should get the misery over, forget the games. So what's in it for a policeman, standing on his big flat feet, when more money will be paid than he'll see in a lifetime, and it won't be missed, won't be noticed, and his own chief says that's the way to do business?

He paid the driver, stepped out of the taxi and looked around him.

A wide street on a sloping hill. Flats which owned areas of neat lawn in front and flower-bushes that had been tended and cropped and watered that morning by the porters. Blocks of five floors with deep terraces and canvas awnings and jungles of foliage. The ladies' cars parked bumper to bumper; the little runabout city motors. Dust floated softly down on to Charlesworth's jacket and the maid in the starched apron stared him out as she shook her mop. Not much poverty here, not much malaise from the economic crisis, not up here on the hill. And there was the reaction to the affluence for him to see, provided by

541

those who crept up the slope under cover of night: paint-sprayed swastikas, the daubed MORTE AL FASCISTI that could never be scrubbed from the marble veneer surfaces.

Didn't do badly for their people, the old multinationals. If International Chemical Holdings had put their man in here, then they were solvent, they had no liquidity problems. And the bastards would have known that, or Geoffrey Harrison would be sitting at his desk right now, clobbering his secretary for the lateness of the post, straightening his tie for his next appointment. Money here, and plenty of it, and these people knew where to sniff the air for it, where to strike, where the dividend was assured.

Charlesworth walked into the hallway of the block, paused at the porter's nook where a man with a saddened and troubled face sat, mentioned the name and was told which floor. A slow lift creaked and swayed upwards. Two policemen lolled against the wall beside the door of the flat. They straightened when they saw the diplomat, not dramatically but enough to swing the holstered pistols that hung from waistbelts. Charlesworth said nothing, merely nodded, and pressed the bell.

Soft, slippered feet shuffled to the door. An age passed while four sets of locks were unfastened. The door opened an inch and a half, as far as a chain would allow. Like a bloody fortress, he thought. But they all lived like that on the hill and damn-all good it did them when the vultures began to circle. It was dark inside and he could see nothing through the gap.

'Who is it?' A small voice, invisible and inanimate.

'It's Charlesworth, Michael Charlesworth. From the Embassy.'

A pause, and then the door was closed. He heard the button on the end of the chain being withdrawn from its socket. The door opened again, not extravagantly, but sufficient to admit him.

'I'm Violet Harrison. Thank you for coming.'

He turned almost startled, two steps inside the hall, as if he had not expected the voice to materialize from behind – a quick movement that betrayed his unease. She came out of the shadows and her hand took his elbow and manoeuvred him towards the living-room where the blinds were drawn and the low table lights lit. He followed meekly behind the tented swirl of her trailing cotton dressing-gown with the big flowers embroidered across the shapes of her back and her buttocks and legs. He stole a glance at the silhouette against a light and dug his nails into the palm of a hand. You'd have thought she'd have dressed by now, on a morning like this, with a bloody deluge of visitors about to come tripping in. You'd have thought the woman would put some clothes on.

He saw her the first time when she reached her chair and angled her face at him. She might not have dressed but she'd made her face, had worked at it long enough to give the tears scope to smudge and spoil her efforts. She would have been crying from the time he telephoned.

542

The eyelids were puffy and bulging, red above the dark broad painted eye shadow. A small tight-turned nose that had taken the sun and the freckles offset her cheeks that were smooth and bronzed. Attractive but not remarkable. Well shaped but not beautiful. His eyes flickered over her, unwilling but compelled, and she gazed back at him, no hint of embarrassment. Charlesworth looked away, the blush rising in him. Been caught like a schoolboy hadn't he? Been seen peering in the Soho bookshop windows during school holidays. Been noticed ogling a woman who wore a sheer nightdress and a light cotton wrap.

'I'm very sorry for what has happened, Mrs Harrison,' he said.

'Would you like some coffee . . . there's only instant.'

'You're very kind, but no. Thank you.'

'There's tea, I can make a cup.' A small, far voice.

'No, thanks. Thank you again, but I won't. Would you like me to put the kettle on for you? Can I make you some tea?'

'I don't want any tea. Would you like a cigarette?' Still staring at his eyes, raking and examining them.

'It's very nice of you, but I don't. I don't smoke.' He felt he should apologize because he didn't want Nescafé, didn't want teabags, didn't want a cigarette.

She sat down in an armchair, flanked by the tables that carried last night's glasses and last night's coffee cups, with a flurry of shin and knee glimpsing out. He followed into a chair across the central rug, felt himself going down, slipping away, falling into far-settling cushions, the sort that you drown in and then for ever feel ill at ease with because you're too low and can't dominate the conversation, and your nose is half way to the carpet. She was still looking into him boring and penetrating.

'Mrs Harrison, first I should tell you who I am. I have responsibility for political affairs at the Embassy, but I also double on matters affecting the police, relations between the British community in Rome and the Italian police. Those, that is, that aren't covered by the Consular Department . . .' Come on, Charlesworth, you're not doing your own testimonial; not applying for a job either. '. . . So I was called this morning by a fellow called Carboni, he's one of the bigger men at the Questura. There wasn't very much known then, it was just a few minutes after your husband had been seized. Doctor Carboni gave me a solemn assurance that everything possible was being done to secure your husband's early release.'

'And that's bugger all,' she said slowly and with deliberation.

Charlesworth rocked back, rode it, but the blow had done damage, confused and deflected what was building in his mind. 'I can only repeat . . .' He hesitated. They didn't use that sort of language, the Embassy secretaries and his wife's friends. First Secretary at the British Embassy he was, and she should be listening to him, and grateful that he'd taken the time to come out and see her. 'What Doctor Carboni said was that everything would be done . . .'

'And what's everything? Half of nothing, if that much.'

Charlesworth bridled. 'It's not a very sensible attitude to take in the circumstances, Mrs Harrison. You'd be better . . .'

'I've had my cry, Mr Charlesworth. I got that over before you came. It won't happen again. You know you don't have to come here with platitudes and a bottle of Librium. I'm pleased you came, grateful to you, but I don't need a shoulder to weep on, and I want to know what's going to happen. What's going to happen, not what a crummy Italian policeman says he's doing. And I want to know who's going to pay.'

Bit early, wasn't it? Knots hardly settled on the old man's wrists and she was chattering about money. God Almighty. 'I can advise you on procedures,' Charlesworth ploughed on, coldness undisguised, 'I can tell you what has happened in the past, to Italians. I can suggest what I think that you should do, and I can indicate the areas where I think the Embassy can be of service.'

'That's what I want to hear.'

'When they write about kidnapping in the Italian papers they call it a successful growth industry. That's a fair enough description. Since 1970 there have been more than three hundred cases. What you'd expect, of course, but the people responsible vary enormously. There are the big gangs, big organizations, well led, well funded, well briefed, probably originating from the real south, probably with what we'd call the Mafia at their roots. I never quite know what's meant by the Mafia, it's an overused word, something simplistic to cover whatever you want it to. In my book the Mafia means skill and ruthlessness and power and patience. If your husband has been taken by these people, then there will be an initial contact followed by a drawn-out haggle over money, and it will end with a business transaction. Very clinical and quite slow because they will want to know that their tracks are well covered.'

'And if it's such a group how will they treat my husband?'

A long time coming, that question, thought Charlesworth. 'Probably quite well. They'd keep him fed and dry and marginally comfortable, enough to sustain his health . . . in a basement, perhaps a farmhouse . . .'

'That's as long as they think we're going to pay?'

'Yes.'

'And if they aren't sure we're going to pay?'

Charlesworth looked hard at her, slipped behind the swollen eyes, delved beyond the mascara. He wondered how his own wife would react in these circumstances, loved her and knew for all that she'd be a disaster. Helpless as a bloody ship on the rocks and thrashing around for someone to blame. She was different, this woman. Different because she didn't wear her concern and her care on her shoulders. Hadn't even put her knickers on for the great day. Didn't sound as if it meant a damn to her beyond the inconvenience.

'Then they'll kill him.'

She didn't react beyond a flutter of the eyebrows, a slight and fractional quiver at the mouth, but nothing that he would have noticed if he hadn't been watching her, absorbing her face.

'And if we go to the police and throw it all into their lap, give it to your Mr Carboni, what then?'

'If they see through an indiscretion or a clumsiness that we have offered full co-operation with the police, and if they feel that endangers their security, then too they will kill him.' He turned the knife because the realization of how much he disliked the woman, how alien she was to his background, seeped through him. 'I put it to you, Mrs Harrison, that the people who have your husband will not hesitate to murder him if that serves their purpose better than keeping him alive.'

He paused, allowed the message to sink and spread, find its own water level. He found his advantage growing. The signs of fear were shown by the slight pant in her chest, the motion of the fingers.

'And even if we pay, if the company pays, we still have no guarantee . . .'

He anticipated her. 'There are never guarantees in these matters.' That was about as strongly as he had the stomach to put it. He couldn't bring himself to tell her of Luisa di Capua whose husband had been dead two months before the body was found, and who had received the last ransom note the day before the discovery. 'No guarantees, we would just have to hope.'

He won a shrill, short laugh from her.

'How much will they ask, Mr Charlesworth? How much is my Geoffrey worth on the Italian market?'

'They'll ask for more than they'll be happy to end up with. Starters would probably be around five million dollars, and they'll settle for perhaps two. Not less than one million.'

'Which I don't have.' She was faster now, and louder and the control was fracturing. 'I don't have it, do you understand that? Geoffrey doesn't, his parents don't. We don't own that sort of money.'

'It's not really your husband that's being ransomed, it's his company. The group will expect the company to pay.'

'And they're tight bastards,' she spat across at him. 'Tight and mean and penny-pinching.'

He remembered the exterior of the block, allowed himself to glance across the interior fittings of the flat.

'I'm sure they will look favourably when they have had the situation explained to them. I had intended to speak to them after I had seen you. I thought that might be valuable to them.'

'So what happens now? What do I do?'

545

The questions rolled from her, as if Charlesworth were some all-knowing guru on the subject of kidnap reaction. 'We have to await the first contact, probably by telephone. Then it can take quite a time for them to decide what arrangements they want to make for payment.'

'So what do I do, sit by the bloody telephone all day? And I don't even speak the bloody language, just what I need round the shops in the morning. I don't speak their bloody language. I won't know what they're bloody well saying.' Shouting for the first time, dipping into hysteria. Charlesworth fidgeted in the deep chair, willed the session to end.

'We can have it said in the papers that your husband's office is standing by to receive a message.'

'But they're all bloody Italians . . . what the hell do they know about it?'

'A damn sight more than we do, because they live with it every day of the year. Because every one of your husband's senior colleagues knows this can happen to him any time, and a fair few of them will ring their wives each morning as soon as they've sat down at their desks, just so that the woman will know they've made it safely. They know more about this than you or I do, or your husband's company in London. If your husband is to come out of this alive you'll need the help of all his friends in that office. All of those "bloody Italians", you'll need all of their help.'

He was out of the chair, backside clear of the cushions, fingers gripping for leverage into the upholstered arm rests. Poor old show, Charlesworth. A stupid, ignorant cow she may be, but not your job to pass judgement. Lost your rag and you shouldn't have done. He sagged back, ashamed that he had battered the remnants of the calm, destroyed the very thing that he had come to maintain. The colour had fled from her face, which had taken a pallid glow in the shock of his counter-attack. Not a whimper from her, not a choke. Only the eyes to give the message, those of someone who has just stepped from a car accident in which driver or passenger has died and who knows dimly of catastrophe but does not have the power to identify and evaluate the debris.

'Mrs Harrison, you mustn't think yourself alone. Many people will now be working for your husband's release. You must believe in that.'

He stood up, shuffled a little, edged towards the door.

She looked up at him from her chair, cheeks very pale below the saucer eyes, knees apart and the gown gaping. 'I hate this bloody place,' she said. 'I've hated it from the day we arrived. I've hated every hour of it. He'd told me we wouldn't have to stay here, not more than another year, he'd promised me we'd go home. And now you want to go, Mr Charlesworth, well, don't hang about because of me. Thank you again for coming, thank you for your advice, thank you for your help, and thanks to bloody everybody.'

'I'll get a doctor to come round. He'll have something for you. It's a very great shock, what has happened.'

'Don't bother, don't inconvenience anyone.'

'I'll send a doctor round.'

'Don't bother, I'll be a good girl. I'll sit beside the telephone and wait.'

'Haven't you got a friend who could come and stay with you?'

The old laugh back again, high and clear and tinkling. 'Friends in this bloody hole? You're joking, of course.'

Charlesworth hurried to the door, mumbled over his shoulder, 'I'll be in touch and don't hesitate to call me at the Embassy, the number's in the book.'

Trying to master the different locks delayed his flight sufficiently for him to hear her call from the remoteness of the living-room, 'You'll come again, Mr Charlesworth? You'll come again and see me?'

He pulled the door brutally shut behind him, erasing from his ears the trickle of her laughter.

Some five minutes the colonnello spent attempting to marshal the moving waves of photographers and reporters into a straight line. He threatened, pleaded, negotiated the issue of how many paces the prisoner should walk in front of the lenses and microphones before he was finally satisfied with his arrangements in the square internal courtyard of the Questura.

'And remember, no interviews. Interviews are absolutely forbidden.'

He shouted the last exhortation for discipline before the wave of his arm to the polizia who stood shaded in a distant doorway.

When she emerged Franca Tantardini held her head high, jutted her chin, thrust her eyes unwaveringly into the sun. The chains at her wrists dangled against her knees as she walked. Her jeans and blouse were smeared with the street dirt of the pavement outside the Post. To her right the polizia linked arms to hold back the press of cameramen. An officer gripped tightly at each of her elbows; they were not the men who had taken her, not the men who had killed Enrico Panicucci, because those were anonymous and undercover and would not be photographed. These were men in uniform, spruced, with combed and greased hair and polished shoes, who preened themselves and swelled with importance. She ignored the babble of shouted questions and walked on until she was level with the place where the crowd was densest, the pushing at the police shoulders most acute, the cameras closest. A glance she spared for the scrummaging, then ripped her right arm clear of her escort's hold, swung it aloft into the air, clenched her fist in salute, seemed to hover a smile at the chatter of the camera shutters. The policeman regained his hold, dragged her arm down, she was pulled through a doorway, lost from sight. Show completed. Police taking their kudos, cameramen their pictures. Satisfaction of all parties. A triumphal procession of victor and vanquished, and smoothly done.

From an upper window, unnoticed by the journalists, Francesco Vellosi had watched the courtyard parade. At his side stood an Under-Secretary of the Interior Ministry.

'Still defiant, la leonessa. Magnificent even in defeat,' the Under-Secretary murmured.

'A year in Messina, perhaps two, then she'll be tamed,' responded Vellosi.

'Magnificent, quite magnificent. Such hate, such pride.'

'We should have shot her on the street.' There was a cold and bitter snarl on Vellosi's lips.

The computer trace on the third set of fingerprints found by police in the covo was fast and efficient. But then the equipment was German, modern and expensive, the sort of item on which government, harassed and defensive, was prepared to lavish its money in the fight against the urban activist. The print-out on the teleprinter was clear and concise.

CRIMINALPOL EUR ROMA
XXXXXXX 25 7 80 XXXXX REF: A419/B78
BATTESTINI GIANCARLO MARCO BORN 12 3 60
82C VIA PESARO PESCARA
RIOTOUS ASSEMBLY SENTENCED 7 MONTHS 11 5 79
PHOTOGRAPHED FINGERPRINTED 9 3 79

More information would follow later, but a name and a picture would be waiting on Francesco Vellosi's desk when he returned from the Questura. Another identity, another set of features, another case history to settle on the top of his mountain of files of wanted persons.

5

It had taken many minutes of the new motion of the van before Geoffrey Harrison was sufficiently aroused to realize that they were no longer travelling on the smooth worn surface of the autostrada.

The tang of the chloroform was just a memory now, one receding aspect of the morning nightmare. The smell of the moisture across his limbs and torso had become acceptable with familiarity. The breathing through the hood became more possible as time went on, the harsh smell of the carbon monoxide from the engine could be ignored. It was a long time since he had tried to struggle with his bonds and he had abandoned the ambition to loosen the tapes. With the greater calmness came a greater comfort. No tears, no fight, no desperation. No reason for him to compete any more, just a need to lie back and let it all float across him, to obliterate the more vicious fantasies that hovered near his imagination. There was nothing he could do to change his situation, and so he lay there feeling the jar and jolt and shift of the van wheels, and gaining from the bruising impacts the knowledge that they had moved to a slower, indirect road.

He thought of Violet, poor old Violet. She'd know by now, she'd have heard and the police would be swarming round the flat and she'd be shouting at them and crying, and unless someone came who spoke English she wouldn't have a clue what they were talking about. Poor old Violet, who'd wrung it out of him that they wouldn't stay past next summer – two and a half years she'd have existed then, and she'd said that was her limit, that was enough. She should have adjusted, shouldn't she? Should have compromised, made something of it.

Of course it was different to England, but people go abroad and people cope. She should have been able to find some friends to coffee-morning with, go walk-about the ruins with. Didn't seem to make the effort, though, did she? And didn't seem interested, not in anything, not in his job, not in his business colleagues, not in the few foreigners who lived within walking distance of the flat. She'd never accepted living in a flat and not having neighbours she could lean over a fence and gossip with, never accepted that people who spoke a different language were still human beings and intelligent and kindly and funny, and that if they weren't British it didn't mean they wiped their backsides with their hands.

Bloody ridiculous it was, old Violet locked up in her castle on the hill and not letting the drawbridge down. Tried hard enough, hadn't he? Yes, Geoffrey. Well, what the hell else could be done? Couldn't throw her out of the front door with a street map and shout down the terraces that she mustn't be back before six. He remembered when her parents had come to visit from Stoke-on-Trent. Never been out of England before. Didn't know whether they should put their teeth in the water at night. Didn't hold with all the wine at meals. Didn't master the coils of spaghetti falling off their forks when he took them all out to dinner. Set them back, the pair of them, that visit, they'd argued about it endlessly after the old people had gone; he telling her she should make more effort and not live like a bloody mole and what an advantage and opportunity she had; she telling him she hated it, wanted out and to England. He telling her to get interested in the city, get off her bottom and visit the Vatican and the Foro Italico; she telling him she was buggered if she'd be ordered to tramp round museums. Poor old Violet. Must have been out of her mind with boredom. And she didn't even hit the bottle, because he looked each night when he came home, checked the gin level and the Martini Bianco level and the Tio Pepe level. She didn't even drink the time away.

Only thing she seemed to like was getting down to the beach and that was bloody ridiculous too. There was a nice quiet pool just down the road for her to use, and some very decent families using it. But she preferred the beach and a hell of a drive down to Ostia and all the filth and the oil to sit on, pressed in close by those Italians burning themselves nigger brown. A total bloody mystery. Getting the sand in her hair, not speaking to anyone. Poor old Violet, poor bored old Violet. Hadn't thought about her for a long time, had he? Not like this, not examining her day. Well, he didn't have time, did he? Someone had to put the clothes on her back, the food in her fridge. A damn good job he had in Rome. Better prospects, better pay than he could have hoped for in London. He wished she'd see that. Working damned hard he was, and he could do without the abuse when he flopped home in the evenings.

They were slow rambling thoughts, indulgent and close, lulling him from the crisis, until there was another change in the engine pitch and he felt the movement of the gears, the slowing of the engine, the application of brakes. The van bumped crazily on rough ground. A dead stop. Voices that were clearer with the motor cut. The complacency vanished, the trembling began again, because this was frightening to the man who was bound and gagged and hooded and who had no horizons of sight. A way of existence that had become settled, achieved tranquillity, was ruptured.

The van had left the autostrada half way between Cassino and Capua, bypassed the small town of Vairano Scalo, avoiding the single wide street and central piazza. They had turned east on a winding open hill road that would eventually reach the village of Pietramelara, the home of just over a thousand people with shuttered minds and uninquisitive tongues who would not question the presence of a strange vehicle with distant number plates that might rest for half an hour among the trees and off the road short of their community.

Harrison felt himself bracing his muscles as if trying to push his way further back into the interior of the van, crawl on his buttocks away from the rear door. He heard the slamming at the front and the gouging scratch of feet on the ground that walked along the length of the side walls and then the noise of a lock being turned and a handle being tugged. When the door opened there was a slight smudge of light filtering through the weave of the hood and the floor of the van bucked under a new weight. He felt the shape, alien and revolting to him, brush against his knees and thighs, and then there were hands at the hood, scrabbling close to his chin, at the back of his neck, as the cloth was drawn back across his face. He wanted to scream, wanted to vomit, to expel the fear. Taut, tensed, terrorized. The smell of garlic was close to his nose, and the odour of a farm.

The light, brilliant, blinding, flooded over him, hurting so that he screwed up his face and tried to twist away. But he was not just turning from the intrusive sun, but also from the man who was bent double under the low roof and now loomed above him. Boots close to his head, hard, roughened, unpolished, cracked with wear. Trousers that were old and patched and shapeless, grease-stained. A shirt of red check material, sleeves turned high on muscled forearms. And dominating, compelling his eyes, was the hood, black cloth with eye slits and the crudely cut hole that simulated the position of the mouth. Nowhere for Harrison to writhe to. Nowhere for him to find refuge. The hands, coarse and blistered, thrust to the tapes across his mouth. One savage pull ripped them clear and left the skin as a vast, single abrasion. He coughed hard, spluttered with his face smarting, eyes heavy with tears at the sharpness of the pain.

No word from the man above who screwed up and tossed away the jumble of adhesive tape. There was another silhouetted against the light of the doorway, and Harrison saw him pass forward a roll of bread that bulged with lettuce and tomato and ham. Big and fat and filling it would have been if he were hungry. The bread was placed against his mouth. He bit and swallowed. Bit again, swallowed again. Around him an awareness of the surroundings grew. The tastes were of the far country-side, distant and removed from the city that was his home. The air was closed to urban sounds, open only to the calls of the birds that were free and roaming at their will. Harrison ate half the roll, could stomach no more and shook his head, and the man threw it casually behind him, successful in his aim avoiding his friend. They let him swig from a bottle of water; aqua minerale, lively with gas and bubbles from the movement of the van. One drink and then the bottle was withdrawn. He lay numbly still, unresisting, as his face was again taped. Instinctively he pleaded with his eyes because they were the only vehicle of argument left to him, but the hood was returned to its place. Back in his realm of darkness, his stomach ground on the food it had taken down, his bowels were loose and confused by the content of what he had eaten. He heard the back door close, the lock being fastened, the men walking back to the front of the van. The engine started.

No threat, no kindness. No cruelty, no comfort.

Men without any minuscule, foetal sensitivity. Vicious bastards, without emotion, without charity. To take a blindfold off a man who was terrorized, holding his muscles to keep his pants clean; to rip the gag from his mouth and offer him nothing, nothing in communication, nothing as one human being to another. The one who had fed him had worn on the third finger of his left hand, the hand that held the bread, the wide gold band of a wedding-ring. He had a wife whom he would hold close to him and sweat and grunt his passion against, and children who would call to him and laugh. The bastard, the fucking bastard, who could extinguish compassion, drown it, say not a word, give not a sign to a fellow creature who was in pain and suffering and alone.

So help me God, if ever I have the chance I'll kill that bastard. Beat his head with a stone, smash and pound and break it. While he pleads, while he cries, while the blood spatters. So help me God, I want to kill him, I want to hear him scream.

You've never hit anyone in your life, Geoffrey, you wouldn't know how.

The van moved off.

They drove slowly into the village of Pietramelara. The driver found what he was looking for without difficulty. A bar with the circular sign of a telephone dial that heralded the presence of a coin-box machine. He left his passenger in the seat, nodded respectfully to the village priest hurrying home for his lunch, accepted the smile of greeting. Conversation in the bar was not interrupted. The driver pulled from his pocket a clutch of gettoni, the tokens necessary for the call. He took from the breast pocket of his shirt a packet of cigarettes, and deciphered the number written on the inside of the cardboard lining. Six gettoni he required for Rome. He remembered the zero six prefix, then carefully repeated the seven figure number from the packet. When the answer came he spoke quickly, gave only his first name and that of the village and his estimation that the journey would be completed in eight hours.

Had there been difficulties?

There had been none.

The call was terminated by the other party. The driver did not know to whom he was speaking. He walked back to the van anxious to be on his way. He faced a long drive, far into the very toes of the Italian boot, into the mountain country of Calabria. And tonight he would sleep in his own cottage, sleep against the cool stomach of his woman.

The driver's contact would permit the organization in the group that had kidnapped Geoffrey Harrison to make their first contact with the Englishman's home. They now knew that their merchandise was far beyond the reach of rescue by the polizia, that the cordons and road blocks were way outstripped.

Claudio stood with his hands in his pockets among the little groups of waving Romans. A varied sadness painted all those who watched the train, the anaconda, snake away from the long platform of the Termini, bending at the first far curve, engine already lost. Mario and Vanni gone, settled into their seats in the grey carriage that carried the sign of Reggio Calabria, nine hundred kilometres to the south. Their going left Claudio without a companion, condemned to wait away the night, contain his resentment that he was not with his friends. Time to be killed and frittered as a man does when he is in a strange city that has no heart, no belonging for him.

Once he waved, simply and without demonstration, lifting his arm and waggling his fingers at the train as it diminished and blended with the softness of the heat haze that distorted and tricked.

As Mario and Vanni walked along the platform he had been tempted to follow and join them, but fear of the men of the organization was enough to cast the apple from big Claudio's mouth. Some before had discarded the instructions of the organization, trifled with their orders. All had been awarded a fine funeral, two or more priests to celebrate the Mass, many boys to sing in the choir, enough flowers to cover all the stones in the cemetery, enough tears to make a dead man believe he was mourned. Claudio had stayed behind and waved; he would catch tomorrow's train.

He swung his eyes away from the converging, empty tracks and headed for the bar and the first of a new session of Perroni beers that would help him watch the hour and minute hands of his watch.

Later he would find a room near the station.

Sometimes hurrying, sometimes slowly when the lethargy bred from failure was on him, Giancarlo searched among the familiar places, the rooms and corridors where he expected to find his friends. He had gone to the Faculty of Letters where the walls were bright in a technicolour of protest paint and wandered the high plaster-coated corridors, past the stripped notice-boards, past the locked lecture theatres, into the quiet of the library. To some who were relaxed and lounging in chairs he had spoken. Not with confidence but sidling towards them. He had mentioned a name and seen a head shaken; moved on, another name, shoulders shrugged in response. On from the Faculty of Letters to the Faculty of Social Sciences and further echoing and deserted corridors

553

that rang with his thin-soled shoes and in which reverberated the laughter of those who belonged and knew their place.

Hopeless for him to ask the question directly.

Where are the people of the Autonomia? Where can I find any member of the Autonomia? It was not information that would be given to a stranger, not in a casual conversation. He plodded on, wet and constricted in his clothes, dampened and caught in his unhappiness. On from the Faculty of Social Sciences, heading for the Faculty of Physics. Two hours Giancarlo paced the University complex. There was no one he knew among the students who sat and talked in the sunshine, or walked with their bundles of books, or crouched over the printed words of their study texts. No one who could send him with a smile and a gabble of directions to where he might discover the people of the Autonomia.

Still careful, still watchful, he hesitated by the great opened doors of the Faculty of Physics, pausing in the shadow short of the sun-bright steps that led down into the central yard of the University, traversed with his eyes, as a fox will when it sniffs the early air before leaving its den. Giancarlo quivered, stiffened, focused on the grey gunmetal Alfa-sud parked back and out of the light, far into the shade of the trees. The car was distinctive because of its radio aerial, high and set above the right rear wheel, and because of the three men sprawled in the seats. Bearded two of them, clean-shaven the third, but all of them too old to be students. He watched the car for many minutes, hidden by shadow as it was, observing the men fidget and shift in response to the comfort of their seats, assimilating their mood, their state of preparedness. There was nothing exceptional about the police being there, he told himself, the place crawled with the pigs and their informers, and there was no urgency about these men as they watched the young people move across their vision. Dumb bastards, because even if they had his name and his picture they telegraphed their presence by their age, by their location.

Had they his name yet?

Not so quickly, surely, not within a few hours. Confidence and depression, ebullience and fear, competed in the boy's mind as he scurried for a side entrance and cover among the parked buses at the Tiburtina termini. Rampant in his imagination was the sight of the three men low in the seats of their car. The one with his newspaper, the one with his arm trailing through the open window with the dangled cigarette, the one with the barely opened eyes. They had made him run, hastened the end of his fruitless, wasted search, and that was how it would always be, till the gutter time, till the shooting time, till he no longer needed to scan the cars and the faces for the polizia.

Pig bastards. There would be a moment when he stood his ground. A moment when they would know of him. When, Giancarlo? The moment

554

when he would take Franca Tantardini from them. By yourself, Giancarlo? There was a pain at the boy's eyes, and agony behind the lids, because this was a public place among the buses and the people who waited and they must not see him weep.

He climbed on to a bus. Chose it not for its route but because it was one that did not have a conductor to collect money and hand out tickets, and relied instead on a machine and the honesty of passengers.

Heart pumping, blood coursing fast, the little boy who had lost his protection and was running.

The girl in faded jeans and a flowing, wrist-buttoned blouse came quickly to the top of the high steps at the entrance to the Faculty of Social Sciences. She paused there, raking the open ground in front of her, then jogged down the steps and across the car park towards the grey Alfasud. It was not remarkable that she could identify the unmarked police car, any student could have done that. As she approached the car she saw the interest of the occupants quicken, the cigarette stubbed, the newspaper dropped, the backs straightened. At the driver's open window she hesitated as the men's eyes soaked into her, for this was a public place for an informant to work.

'You are looking for a boy?'

The cool smile from the front passenger in response, the lighting of another cigarette.

'Dark curly hair – jeans and a shirt – not tall, thin.'

The man in the back seat flipped casually at a notepad in which were scribbled words.

'A boy like that came into the library, it was just a few minutes ago. He was nervous, you could see that, in his voice, in his hands . . .'

The notebook was passed to the front, examined with a secrecy as if the knowledge written there were to be denied to the girl.

'. . . he asked a friend if two boys were in the University. The boys are both of the Autonomia, both were arrested after the last fight, more than three months ago.'

She was answered. The front passenger drew his Beretta pistol from the glove drawer and armed it, the man in the back groped to the floor for a short-barrelled machine-gun. The driver snapped a question: 'Where did he go?'

'I don't know. There is the students' lounge, he went in that direction . . .'

The girl had to step back as the car doors whipped open. Hand-guns pocketed, the machine-gun closed to view under a light jacket, the three policemen ran for the Faculty entrance.

They searched methodically for an hour in the public places of the

University, while more men of the anti-terrorist squad arrived to augment their efforts. There were curses of frustration at the failure of the hunt, but satisfaction could be drawn from the knowledge that the identification if it were genuine showed that the kid was short of a covo. It would not be long before the boy was taken, not if he were scouting the University for friends more than twelve weeks in the cells.

That night the University and its hostels would be watched. Men would be detailed to stand in their silence in the shadows and doorways. Pray God, the bastard returns.

By telephone the message from Pietramelara was relayed to the capo. That the initial moments of the kidnapping of the Englishman had met with success he knew from the radio beside his desk. The communiqué bearing the fruits of his enterprise had been broadcast with commendable speed by the RAI networks.

How they help us, he thought, how they facilitate our business. And now the cargo was moving beyond the scope of the road checks. Soon he would authorize the initial approaches to the family and the company, and set in motion the financial procedures in the matter laid down by his specialist accountant. A fat, choice haul, and the lifting sharp and surgical.

It was not for a man of the prominence of the capo to consider and burden himself with the machinery of the extortion of ransom; a team he paid did that; he paid them well so that tracks should be smothered and hidden. He let himself out of his office, locked his door from a wide ring of keys and crossed the pavement to his car. For the long journey to the south and the hill village where his wife and children lived, he used the Dino Ferrari that would eat into the kilometres to the Golfo di Policastro, where he would break the journey back to his family. Beside the sea, in the sprouting coastal resorts, his business was fuelled by the new and flourishing source of revenue. He cut a good figure as he climbed athletically into the low-slung sports car. To the superficial watcher there was nothing in his bearing or his dress to link him with profitable crime, painstakingly organized, ruthlessly executed. He would be at the resort area by early evening, in time to take a functionary of the regional planning office to dinner, and when the man was drunk and grateful for the attention the capo would leave him and motor on to his villa in the Aspromonte.

He drove aggressively from the kerbside, attracting notice. To those who saw him go there was a feeling that this was a man on whom the sun shone.

*

Violet Harrison had no clear intention of going to the beach at Ostia that afternoon. Nothing definite in her mind, no commitment to escape from the funereal movements of her maid, but there had to be an alternative to sitting and smoking and drinking coffee and straining for the telephone's first ecstatic ring. She had taken the three newest bikinis from the drawer of the chest in her bedroom, one in yellow, one in black, the third in pink with white dots, and laid them with a neatness that was not usually hers out on the bedspread, and looked at their flimsy defiance.

'Bit on the small side isn't it?' Geoffrey had laughed. 'Bit of a risk running round in that in these parts.' That was last week and he'd slapped her bottom, kissed her on the cheek and never mentioned it again. But written all over his bloody face, What's an Old Girl like you wanting a Teenager's fripperies for? He'd settled in his chair with a drink in his hand and a folder of accounts on his lap. 'Bit on the small side . . .' and he'd held her most recent purchase, pink with white dots, between his fingers, dangling. She'd found it in the boutique window down past the market, wanted it, urged herself to buy it. She'd ignored the superciliousness of the stare of the shop girl, tall and manicured and straight-backed; haughty bitch who said with her eyes what her husband had spoken five hours later.

Violet Harrison had only worn the pink and white bikini once. Just the one time, the day before, while she lay on the beach at Ostia and listened to the virulent run of conversation around her. Couldn't understand a word they said, to her it was a medley of silly chatter and giggling and exuberance. But it made a state of independence for her, a secret hideout. Among the people and litter from the ice-cream wrappers and the beer bottles and Pepsi cartons, it was her place, unknown to the cool and monied world of the inhabitants of Collina Fleming. Marvellous she felt there, bloody marvellous, and the sun burned into her skin, and the sand flicked across her face and went unnoticed. The nearest thing to happiness and guiltless pleasure. And then the silly kid had started talking to her. All part of the game, wasn't it? All part of the scenario of escape and freedom. A silly little kid trying to pick up an English matron, old enough to be . . . his aunt anyway. Trying to pick her off as if she were an au pair on an afternoon out. And he'd said he'd be there that afternoon.

It's not my bloody fault, Geoffrey.

What am I supposed to do? Dress in black tights and put Polaroid specs on so that people can't see that I haven't cried for four hours? Put flowers round the living-room and wear soft shoes so I'll make no noise when I pace up and down, and keep the bloody place looking like a laying-out parlour?

What do you want me to do? Sit here all day, sit here and weep, and ask Mummy to come out and hold my hand and make mugs of tea? I don't mean that, Geoffrey, not like that. I don't mean you any harm. I can't just sit here, you understand that, I can't just eke it all out. I'm not strong enough, that's what I mean . . . I'm not a public person's wife.

But I'm not going to go, anyway. I mean it, I'm not going to the beach. I'm going to stay here and wait for the telephone, that's what I have to do, isn't it? I have to suffer with you because you're out there, somewhere. Are you frightened, Geoffrey? . . . A man came to see me, some idiot from the Embassy, and he said they wouldn't hurt you. Well, he didn't quite say that, but they won't actually hurt you if everything goes well, if nothing is wrong. That's what he said.

She grabbed the bikini from the bedcover, the little cotton triangles, the linking cords, the fastening straps. Crushed them in her fist and hurled the pieces towards the corner that housed the neat formation of Geoffrey's shoes.

She started to run from the bedroom, drawn always faster by the piercing, siren call of the telephone. Crashing through doors, slipping on the smooth floor surface. The caller was patient, allowed the bell to ring out its summons, let the persistence of the noise swamp the flat, cutting the walls, floating to the crannies.

Again the air-conditioning was not working.

Michael Charlesworth sat in his office, jacket draped over his chair, tie loosened, top three shirt buttons undone. No surprise, the air-conditioning, had to be phlegmatic about it. What chance of finding a maintenance man who wouldn't carve half the wall off pulling at the pipes, and who wasn't like the rest of the city, prostrate with the heat or on holiday?

Sweat coated the paper in front of him, running the ink where he'd written with his ballpoint, and beside his elbow the telephone was still wet from his palm print. A great quiet in a building usually leaking with noise; the Ambassador and his guests at lunch, attachés and First and Second Secretaries disappeared to the shaded restaurants near the Porta Pia and the Via Nomentana. The typists had covered their machines, the clerks locked their filing cabinets. Charlesworth scribbled on fiercely.

He had started with a list of his immediates. A call to Carboni at the Questura, to ensure the message was discreetly fed to the afternoon newspapers that Harrison's office was standing ready to receive contact. He had barely put the phone down when Violet Harrison rang; she had seemed detached, distant. Enough for him to wonder if a doctor had called with sedatives. She had spoken of a message and a man who talked only in Italian and she had shouted and he had shouted, each obliterating the words of the other. There was a great calmness about her, as if a narcotic were at work, and a politeness as she had told Charlesworth that she was going out for a few hours.

'I can't just sit here,' she'd said, matter of fact, untroubled by crisis. 'I can't just hang about. I think you understand.'

He had tried to reach the Ambassador, sent a spiritless message through to the Personal Secretary, and received the reply he anticipated.

'If nothing has changed the Old Man would be happy to see you about five. He wouldn't want to be disturbed before that. At least, not unless it's a case of life and death, you know.'

A nice girl, the Personal Secretary, long and leggy and combed and sweet, projecting out of cotton print dresses, but fierce and loyal in her protectiveness. And what was a case of life and death? A guy on his back, crapping himself and bound so that he lay in his filth, and savage bastards round him who'd kill if it was to their advantage. Life and death? Not in the Old Man's terms, not enough reason to spoil a good lunch. And there wasn't anything new, not if he were honest about it. Just that a woman was having a plucky try and likely to succeed at a nice and public nervous breakdown, not a special woman who knew an MP back home with clout, or who'd figure on the Embassy scones-and-tea invitation list. But Michael Charlesworth hadn't provided the granite pillar for Violet Harrison to support herself against, nor the shoulder, nor the handkerchief. A dreadful woman, awful manners, disastrous sense of occasion, but worthy of some small charity – yes, Michael Charlesworth? His teeth played on his lower lip as he heaved in his chair and grabbed again for the telephone.

'It's ten minutes since I asked for that London call, sweetheart. Ten minutes, and that's too long.' He called her Miss Foreman normally.

'I can't help it, Mr Charlesworth. The operator on International won't answer. You know how it is.' The syrup voice of a lady who knitted and took holidays in Welsh hotels off-season, and thought of Italians as dirty, and wished she was twenty years younger, not too old to be loved.

'Can't you just dial it for me, darling . . . ?'

'You know that's not allowed, Mr Charlesworth.'

'You can dial it for me.' Wearying of the game.

'You'll have to sign for it. One of the girls will have to come up to Second when she's free and get your signature . . .'

'Just get me the call.' Charlesworth's temper fraying, ragged.

'As soon as we've looked out a Priority form and a girl's available I'll send her up.'

'Get me that bloody call, get it now. Dial it. A man's bloody life may depend . . .'

'You don't have to swear, there's no need for offensiveness.'

'Just get me the call, darling. I'll sign the Priority later, but it's important that I speak to London and that cretins like you don't waste any more of my time.'

The earpiece exploded in the sounds of switchboard mechanics. Plugs extracted, plugs inserted. Numbers dialled and whirring on their arcs. The ringing tone. He'd never spoken to Miss Gladys Foreman MBE like that. Doubted if anyone ever had, not in three decades anyway. Like urinating right across the lounge carpet at a stand-up buffet at the Residence.

Two rings and the plastic, automated voice of a faraway girl.

'International Chemical Holdings. Can I help you, please?'

'It's the British Embassy in Rome. Michael Charlesworth speaking. I need to talk with the Managing Director.'

Delays, re-routings, a false start and the call retrieved. Charlesworth sat at his desk, soaking the sunlight, telling a secretary that he was damned if he was going to précis his message and that he wanted her master, and she should pull her bloody finger and get off the line. Yes, he could wait a moment, he could wait all day, why not? Different whether the other blighter could, whether Geoffrey Harrison could.

'Adams speaking. What can I do for you, Mr Charlesworth?' Sir David Adams, captain of industry, clipped voice, a brusqueness that demanded information and warned against wasted time.

'It's good of you to speak to me. I have to tell you that your representative in Rome, Mr Geoffrey Harrison, was kidnapped this morning on his way to your office.' Charlesworth paused, cleared his throat, a guttural clatter, then launched into the few available facts, recounted his conversations with the Questura. Not a great deal to say, and the inadequacy hurt.

'I've read in the newspapers of these happenings, but I confess I was under the impression this was an Italian problem, a domestic one.' A sharp voice distorted to a high pitch by the static of the communication.

'Your man is the first of the foreign business community.'

'And it could be expensive?'

'Very expensive, Sir David.' Lurched to the heart of the issue, hadn't he? Charlesworth contained himself from laughing. Get the priorities right, lad. Get the balance sheets organized and the rest follows.

'To get him back, what sort of figure might we be talking about?'

'The asking price might be anything up to four or five million dollars.' That'll set him swinging in his black leather chair, that'll start him gawping out over the City skyline. 'There might be a possibility of negotiation, but it won't be easy for a company like yours to plead poverty.'

'And if we don't pay?'

'Then you are in for a long widow's pension. Mrs Harrison is a young woman.'

'Well, that's a Board decision. And in the meantime, what action should we take?'

'The only thing you have to do is to get that decision taken, and fast. It could go very hard for Mr Harrison if the group that hold him thought you were prevaricating. As you probably realize, in this country there is a tradition of paying up, they would not respond well to the breaking of that custom.'

Don't ever say I didn't root for you, Geoffrey Harrison. Don't ever say I didn't go in there with two feet kicking. A silence on the line, the big man chewing on it, deliberating. A slow smile winning across Michael Charlesworth's face.

When Sir David Adams spoke again, the chisel had blunted in his voice. 'It's a great deal of money, Mr Charlesworth. My Board would have be very certain that it's totally necessary to pay the sort of sum you mention. They won't like it. And there's a question of principle too; there's a tradition in this country that we don't crumble to blackmail.'

'Then you would have to make the decision that on a point of principle you were prepared to sacrifice the life of Mr Harrison. Of course, it might not come to that, but the possibility, perhaps the probability, exists.'

'You are very frank, Mr Charlesworth.' There was the trace of disapproval in the scraped gravel tones. 'If we suppose, and only suppose, that we were to pay a very considerable sum, then who would control the arrangements?'

'It would be best done by your office in Rome. The Embassy couldn't get involved.'

Charlesworth heard the low laugh in response. Ten minutes they'd been talking, ten minutes in querying the profit and loss columns, and whether a ransom should be paid. Principle or expediency. A martyr for the greater good of the majority or a shame-laden deal for the return of one man. Perhaps, Charlesworth thought, he'd minimized the issues at stake. Perhaps a line had to be drawn. No deals, no bargains, no compromise, there would be many willing to shout that clarion call. If you gave in once, if you slipped one time into the shadows with a suitcase of used banknotes and a string of Zürich bank account numbers, then how many other poor bastards were going to follow the road of Geoffrey Harrison? Not his business, though, not his concern, because as he'd said most clearly, the Embassy couldn't be involved, would stand detached within its glass walls and watch and murmur occasional interest. That was why Sir David Adams, Managing Director of International Chemical Holdings in the City of London, could laugh lightly at him, without humour, without rancour, at the moment of dismissal.

'You've been very kind, Mr Charlesworth. I'll get one of my people on the plane this evening. I'd like him to be in touch with you.'

The call was terminated.

Michael Charlesworth flopped back into the small comforts offered by the plastic padding of his chair. A time for reflection. He must call

Miss Foreman, he must apologize, and there would be some flowers for her basement bunker tomorrow in the morning. And then the bell again, the bloody telephone.

The Questura had been informed from the offices of ICH in Viale Pasteur that a demand of two million dollars for the return of Geoffrey Harrison had been received. There should be no contact with the police, further details of arrangement for payment would follow through intermediaries. Dottore Carboni was not in his office at present but he had requested that the information be passed to Signor Charlesworth. There were mutual thanks and politeness.

Two million dollars. More than a million in sterling at whatever the fluctuating rate. Four million Swiss francs. Cascades of figures. And less than he'd thought it would be, as if those who had taken Harrison had settled for a bargain basement price and would not haggle and barter, but expect settlement without delay.

Michael Charlesworth changed his mind. He would apologize in person to Gladys Foreman. He fastened his shirt buttons, straightened his tie, slipped on his jacket and walked slowly out of his office. He wondered what the man looked like, Geoffrey Harrison, how his voice sounded, whether he'd be good company for dinner, if he told a good joke. He felt himself inextricably involved with a man he did not know, could not picture and might never meet unless a company on the other side of the continent jettisoned an issue of principle and made available more money than he could decently imagine.

6

The Termini was a good place for Giancarlo to come to.

A great extended white stone frontage before which the buses parked, the taxis queued, the traders hawked gaudy toys and shiny shoes and polished belts, and where thousands streamed each morning and afternoon on their way to and from the business of the city. Shops and bars and restaurants and even a subterranean aquarium catered for those who had time to pass. Vast, sprawling, a dinosaur dedicated to the days before the private car and the growth of the autostrada. Businessmen were there, neat and watching the departure board for the evening expresses for Torino and Milano and Napoli. Families of impatient mothers and fretful children waited for connections to the resorts of Rimini and Ricci and the towns south of Bari. Soldiers and sailors and airmen looked for the trains that would carry them to far distant barracks or back to their homes, the routine of conscription broken for a few short days. Gypsy girls in ankle-length wraparound skirts and painful faces of destitution held out paper cups for money. Noise and movement and blurred features, and the mingling of accents of Lombardia, Piemonte, Umbria and Lazio and Toscana.

Tired, famished, with a throat desert dried, he stalked slowly and still with care and watchfulness on to the main concourse. It was a good place for Giancarlo because there were many here. Too many people, too many scuffling feet for the polizia to notice one small boy. The training of the NAP was well etched in the youth so that the places of concealment were second nature as he sought camouflage to his presence. With his weariness had come no sense of defeat, no will to cringe and concede, only a confusion as to how he might best strike back at those who had taken Franca Tantardini. A white scabbed face, bristle on his cheeks, hair hanging, eyes sunken. Past the stalls for the children's toys, past the stands of newspapers and magazines and books, oblivious of the broadcast news of platform changes and delays, he walked the wide length of the concourse.

The second time he passed the big bar, the one that faced the platforms, he saw the man and stirred the response of recognition.

It took Giancarlo many more dragging steps as he racked his memory to identify the fatted face, threatening body, dropped shoulders of the man who leaned on his elbows with a glass in his hand and gazed out of the bar. The boy had to examine a host of recent experiences, sift through them and reject the failures before there was satisfaction and confirmation.

The one they called *gigante* – the huge one, that was the man in the bar. He saw him on the iron steps that led between the landings, his great strides that echoed down the yawning corridors, men stepping back from his path and skirting his strength. All had conceded precedence to the gigante, all except the NAP men on 'B' Wing. Claudio – he could even place his name. Not his other name, only the first one, the given one. Claudio – treated with respect in the Regina Coeli because his fist was the width of a pizza portion and his temper short and his sensitivity slight. To the boy he seemed gross in his stomach, looked to have taken his food, and from the tilt of the glass his beer was not the early one of the day.

Giancarlo turned on his heel, retraced his way till he came and stood at the doorway of the bar that was open to lure the faint breeze into the heated interior. Stood stationary waiting for the head to rise and the gaze to fasten. The boy stood statue still until the sleep-lost, narrow eyes of the big man rolled across the doorway and past him, and then swept backwards as if awakened. Giancarlo smiled and slipped forward.

'Ciao, Claudio,' the boy said quietly, close to him.

563

The big man stiffened, the prodded bullock, as if recognition ruffled and unsettled him.

'It's a long time, Claudio, but I think you remember me.'

He read the uncertainty in the other's face, watched the war going on between the frown lines of his shallow forehead, the fight to put a name and a place to the boy who had accosted him. Giancarlo prompted.

'At the Queen of Heaven, Claudio. Do you not remember me, do you not remember my friends? My friends were in the political wing, and I was under their protection.'

'I've not seen you before.' Something in the denial that was weak and furtive, and the big man looked round, peering about him.

'But I know your name. And I could tell you the number on the cell door, perhaps even I could tell you the names of those that slept there with you.' A half smile played on Giancarlo's lips, and an ebb tide of relaxation was running in him. It was the first time in the day, through the long hours since the Post, that he felt an intuition of advantage. 'If we had coffee and we talked then you might remember more of me and of my friends. My friends were in the political wing, they were people of influence in the Queen of Heaven, they still hold that influence.' His voice died away, the message of menace inherent in the boast of his pedigree.

Claudio laughed with a ripple of nervousness and looked past the boy as if to be certain that he was alone, that a trap was not set for him. He walked away without explanation to the girl at the cash desk, shouldered his way past others. Giancarlo saw a thickened wad of notes emerge from the hip pocket, saw the hands that trembled and scuffed at the notes before the 1000-lire note was produced. Money, endless rolls of it, enough to quicken the attention of the boy. As a pilot fish clings to a shark that he may feed from the droppings at its jaws, so Giancarlo stayed close to the reluctant Claudio.

'You will have a beer with me,' said Claudio when he was back from the bar.

Slowly and stilted, the man and the boy circled each other in sporadic conversation over the first beer. Claudio seeking to determine what the other wanted of him, Giancarlo working at the crannies of information and looking for advantage and the area of profit. A second beer, and a third, and Claudio's head was rolling from the intake, his words sluggish and with a creeping edge of confidence leading him forward. By the fourth bottle of tight, gassed Perroni, Claudio's arm was across Giancarlo's bent shoulder, and together they scanned the front page of the afternoon paper. A pudgy, scarred finger, grime to the quick of the nail, stabbed at the report on the front page of the kidnapping of a British businessman as he had left his home that morning.

When Giancarlo looked sharply into the big man's face there was a dissolve of giggles.

The boy struggled to stay alert, to hose out the beer that flowed in him, seeking the information that might lead to power over his drinking companion. Claudio was from the south, Giancarlo's memory told him, the fact confirmed by the thickened accent of Calabria, and he was waiting for a train from Rome and there was the music of his laughter and his attention to a kidnapping. Here was a source of money, a source of protection, because the big man was running too, was also a fugitive and had betrayed himself.

'But we are not the most important news today,' muttered Claudio with a tinge of disappointment, an actor denied limelight. 'Because they have taken one of yours. They have taken a whore of the NAP. They took her this morning and that is what excites the polizia.' Giancarlo kept his peace, and the finger was moving again, dabbing down and smudging with dirt the picture of Franca Tantardini. 'A leader of the NAP they call her, and the one that guarded her dead. Silly bitch, to have been out in the open. Silly cow. Did you know her, boy? She looks worth knowing.'

'I had met her.' Giancarlo kept the casualness in his words. 'But there are many like her and she will be avenged. They will not hold her in prison, her friends will release her. They cannot hold our people.' In the picture Franca's head was high and her blouse tight, and the camera had caught the sting of the nipple and the clasp of the manacles at her wrists.

'That's shit, boy. When they have her, they hold her. Good-looking bitch,' mouthed Claudio. And then it was as if a clarity had come to him and the beer vapour was dispersed and the interest crawled like a spider's path across his face. 'That is why you are running. Why you are here without food, without money, sponging from an old peasant. It is because they have taken her.'

Giancarlo looked back at him, unwavering, deep into the bloodstreams of his eyes. 'It is why I seek the help of a friend.'

'You were with the girl?'

'I need the help of a friend.'

'Because they have taken her you have no place?'

'I have no place to go.'

'In a city, in Rome, you have nowhere to cover yourself?'

'I am alone,' said Giancarlo.

'But there are friends, there are others.'

'We do not have that structure. We have the cell grouping. We are separated because that is the rule of the NAP.'

Around their ears the noise and chaos of the bar was rampant. Arms pressing against them, orders shouted to the white-shirted men behind the bar. Humour, rancour, impatience buffeting at their ears. But they had created their island, were immune to disturbance.

'Perhaps you should go home.' Something softer from the big man. 'You should go back to your family. Bury yourself away, let the thing pass.'

'I am hunted. I was with her when she was taken, and the other who was with her was killed by the pigs. They are searching for me.' The supremacy over Claudio was lost, frittered away. Giancarlo was searching for comfort, and turning for it to a hardened, brute-fashioned animal. 'I have walked all day. I have nowhere to go.'

'I remember you, boy, because you were the one that went always to their cells. You had their protection.' The arm was tight on Giancarlo's shoulders and the breath of garlic bread and sausage and beer was close to his nostrils. 'So you became a man in the movement, something of substance, and now you turn to a Calabrian idiot for help, a man from the farms, one you would have dismissed as an ignorant and stupid pig.'

'I would not dismiss you as an ignorant and stupid one. You have money in your pocket. You are not the victim of exploitation and oppression.'

'You have eyes then, my little lost one.' Something cold and bovine in Claudio's face. 'You watch a man when he has too much beer.'

Giancarlo smiled with richness and warmth and cracked the frozen stare. More beers, and Claudio spoke of a hotel room, but of a meal first. Playing the grand host, he would be provider, he said, for a few hours of shelter and safety. Giancarlo wondered why, laid the reasoning of the other man at the bottles of beer he had drunk, and acquiesced.

The Mafia and its tentacles were hated and despised by the politicized groups such as the NAP. To the organizations of the extreme left, organized crime represented the total and complete control of the working classes, its survival dependent on fear and repression inflicted on the lesser and weaker, and its helpers were the senior and corrupt officials in administration. In the revolutionary war of Giancarlo, high on the list of enemies would be the gangs that operated for money and chattels. Venality was despicable. So Claudio was Giancarlo's opponent, but the boy would be patient because he had need of the other man and because he would use him for his purposes. If Claudio had been sober, if his limited wits had been alerted, he would not have countenanced the liaison, but he was well oiled now and had lost his native and naive cunning for self-preservation.

In the boy's mind was the first budding of a plan. Something that needed to be cultivated and pruned if it were to show a bloom. A way to win back from the bastards his Franca. A desperate, deep yearning for her, for her body and the cavities and the bright laugh and the brazen love. He wanted it so that his shape quivered and glowed and

566

his belly ached. Franca, Franca, a muted shout. And they went into the humid night air.

The political activist and the kidnap gorilla, arms unequally around each other, bloated by beer, headed together from the Termini in search of a plate of spaghetti.

Caught now in a static turmoil of traffic on the Raccordo Annulare, both lanes blocked, the possibility of advancement denied, Violet Harrison cursed and shouted her abuse at the unhearing, uncaring audience. One hundred metres she had crawled in the last eight minutes. On the back seat of the car was the plastic bag with the towel thrown angrily inside so that on her return it would be creased and untidy, and beneath it the pink polka dot bikini, buried and unworn.

She had willed herself to stand her ground in the flat, to sit beside the telephone because that was the proper and right thing for her to do, the proper and right place for her to be. But the desire for self-preservation had won the field. She had turned her back, abandoned the apartment, driven to the beach.

A ludicrous sight she must have seemed, that much she knew. A woman, a foreigner, pacing the length of the sand, her feet slipping and stumbling in its insecurity. Scanning with her eyes, peering at the boys with the golden torsos and bare legs and muscled shoulders. Seeking to keep an assignation, and showing to all who cared to watch, the torment and humiliation of not finding him whom she had chosen to meet. A grown woman with a fertile womb, and thighs that were thickening, and a waist no longer slender, and a throat that showed the time ravages, and she had succumbed and come back to the beach to talk to a boy whose name she did not know. Salted, angry tears ran without hindrance on her cheeks by the time she had climbed back into the car and surged away in the glowering dusk.

Perhaps if she had come at the time she was always at the beach, perhaps he would have been there. Bloody boy, as if he had no knowledge of what she had sacrificed to come to find him. He couldn't have known the pain he inflicted or he would have been there. Bloody child.

I'm sorry, Geoffrey. As God is my witness, I can't help myself. I even ironed the bikini.

Michael Charlesworth cycled home without enthusiasm, taking no pleasure from the ease with which he skirted the piled, slow-moving cars and ignored the impatient defiles. Normally he revelled in the freedom of the bicycle, but not this evening.

His meeting with the Ambassador had been predictable. The

aftermath of the lunch and flowing hospitality had left His Excellency with scant reserves of attention for matters outside the strict protocol of functions exercised by the Embassy.

'In a criminal kidnapping there can be no area of responsibility for us,' the Ambassador had remarked, his cigar tapering between his fingers. 'It's a matter for this poor devil's company. It's their decision whether to pay, and how to conduct their negotiations. Personally I don't think they've any option in the matter, local conditions being what they are. The company can afford it, and let's hope they get it over as quickly as is decently possible. And don't forget the legal problems. If they're not discreet they can run into all sorts of internal problems with the law here. It's not that I'm unsympathetic, just that it's a fraught area, and not one for us. So I see no need for our feet to go in any deeper, and we should let the matter rest in the hands of those directly involved.'

So the bowl of water had been brought to the throne and the hands had been rinsed. Charlesworth returned to analysis of the newly announced power structure in the Central Committee of the PCI. The Old Man was right, of course; he invariably was. Paying out ransom money could be assessed as aiding and abetting a felony; thin ice for diplomatic boots to step on. But the ice wasn't thick under Geoffrey Harrison, and he was without his woollies and a life-jacket. Poor bastard. Geoffrey Harrison could scratch Michael Charlesworth off his list of angels.

He flung out his left arm, failed to turn his head, swerved across two traffic lanes, ignored the hurt scream of tyres and brakes. Their country, so do it their way. Local conditions, he thought. Local conditions, the catchphrase of the day.

Through the afternoon and early evening Francesco Vellosi had wrestled with the temptation, until at the time he would normally have left the Viminale for his home he had finally asked his private secretary to warn the Questura that he was coming to their offices and that he wanted to sit in on the interrogation of Franca Tantardini. There was no place on such an occasion for a man in his position, nothing that he could usefully learn by being present that could not as satisfactorily be taken from the transcripts that would await him in the morning. But the admiration of the Under-Secretary, the reverence in which the civil servant had clothed the distant chained figure as she had been paraded for the photographers, had haunted and disturbed him through the day. Most of those taken were humbled figures by the time their photographs had been executed in the basement cells, bravery leaking, the struggle and fervour of the revolution drained. It was the same with both factions, with the red fascists and the black fascists, the maniacs of the extreme left and the extreme right. But to Vellosi this girl had been particular, unique. Haughty and proud, as if beaten in only a skirmish, not a battle. As an experienced and dedicated policeman who had learned his trade in the hard schools of Milano and Reggio, his favour was sought after, his presence was the delight of a dinner-party hostess. He was a man regarded with envy by his colleagues because of his competence and single-minded determination. Yet the sight of the woman in the warm Questura yard had unsettled Vellosi. Two years they had hunted her, countless man-hours had been expended in the following of scrappy particles of information, the watching of buildings, the frustration and the disappointment. Two years of the treadmill, and now that they had her there was an absence of the satisfaction that the capture should have brought.

In the back of his car, mindful of the escort vehicle behind him without which it was deemed unsafe for him to travel, Vellosi pondered the equation he had set himself. What made the Tantardini woman turn aside from the world that the majority were grateful to accept? Where did the web of conformity break? Where did the grotesque mutation spawn? There were more than five hundred of them, red and black, in the gaols. Mostly minnows, mostly idiots, mostly the cruel oddities of life who saw in violence and maiming the only outlet they might capture in their desire to be heard of, shouted about.

But not this woman. Too intelligent, too trained, too vicious to be classified with the herd. From a good family in Bergamo. From a convent school. From money and opportunity . . . The real and worthy opponent, the one that taxed and exhausted Francesco Vellosi. A woman who could make a man bend and crawl and suffer. She could grind me, this one, he thought, could squeeze and suck me dry between her legs, between her brain. And there was little to confront her with, nothing to frighten her with, no instrument with which to break her.

'Mauro, I've said it before today and I say it again. We should have shot the bitch on the pavement.' He spoke quietly to his driver, the trusted dustbin for his musings. 'More people have been killed or crippled in the name of Renato Curcio than ever were attacked while he was at liberty. More of these bastard kids are motivated by the name of La Vianale than ever were before we took her. We shall build another rallying-point when we lock up Franca Tantardini. We can put her down in Messina, throw the key away and it will change nothing. If we segregate her from other prisoners then it's called inhuman treatment, mental torture. If we put her with the pack it's too easy for her, she'll be over the wall. Each month she's in Messina the Radicali will be yelling her name in the Camera. All ways we approach it, we lose. Eh, Mauro?'

It was not the driver's place to reply. He nodded agreement. His attention was on the road, always watchful for a car closing too fast on the open side, looking to his mirror that the escort should not have become separated.

'They have called for a demonstration tonight,' Vellosi continued his monologue. 'The students, the unemployed, the men of the Democrazia Proletaria, the children of the Autonomia. A medley of the discontented. The Questura has banned it, no march, no meeting is permitted, but the rats will be out once they have the night to hide them. The murder of Enrico Panicucci is the rallying cry. They will break some limbs and smash some shops and burn some cars and scream about the violence of the State. And Tantardini's name will be heard in the centro storico and the ones that shout it would not have heard of her before this morning's radio. Mauro, I feel I should weep for Italy.'

The driver, sensing the discourse was exhausted, again nodded, decisively and with agreement. Perhaps if the Dottore had a wife and children then he would be changed, not bleed himself so copiously. But Vellosi was alone, and his home was his office and his furniture was his filing cabinet, and his family were the young men he sent on to the streets at darkness to fight his war. The cars swept into the back entrance of the Questura, recognized and saluted by the officer on the barrier.

Francesco Vellosi was not a man to be kept waiting. A greeting party of three inclined their heads as he emerged from his car. If the Dottore would follow them they would lead to the interrogation room. Tantardini was eating in the cell block. She had been questioned once; a shrug of the shoulders and a grimace to demonstrate how much had been learned. The session was about to be resumed. Vellosi followed his guides through pale lit corridors, down steps, past guards. Down into the bowels of the building. There were more handshakes at the entrance to the designated room and then Vellosi's escort abandoned him. He was left with his own people, the ones prepared to dirty their hands, while those who had brought him this far could retreat from the subterranean world of violence and counter-violence and breathe again the real air that was not conducted by ageing generators and fans. There were two men in the room, both known to Vellosi because they were his appointees; hard men, and efficient and devoid of soul. Skilful in interrogation, impatient of prevarication, these were their credentials. And what other criteria could be used in recruitment? What other men could be found to muddy their fingers in defence of a gross and obese society? The excitement was running for Vellosi because these were his colleagues, and in their company he was content and at ease.

He gestured his readiness and sat himself on a bare wooden chair in the shadow of the door where he would face the interrogators. The prisoner would not see him as the lights shone in her eyes, where she would be confronted by her questioners; her back would be to him. Vellosi heard the far distant, the approaching tramp of weighted shoes, and he found himself arched and taut as the woman, eclipsing the lights, was brought through the door. She blazoned her indifference, casually flopped down in a chair in front of the lone table. This was the enemy, the opponent of menace and hazard, and all he could see were the angular shoulder-blades of a good-looking woman with her hair circled by a cheap cotton scarf. Dirty jeans and unwashed blouse, no lipstick and a sneer to substantiate the threat. Where were her tanks, and her ADCs? Where was her army and her regiments and platoons? Where was her serial number and her rank? Dead still Vellosi stayed, because that way she had no reason to turn and face him. That way he was the voyeur, the intruder at a private party.

One interrogator lounged across the table from her. The second man was further back behind him with the file and the notepad on his knees. There was no paper laid out on the table because the man who would ask questions and seek to find flaws in her defiance must demonstrate his knowledge, must have no need for typed reports, must dominate if he were to succeed.

'You have had your food, Tantardini?' He spoke conversationally, without rancour.

Vellosi heard her snort, the derision that communicated tension.

'You have no complaints about the food?'

No response.

'And you have not been hurt, you have not been tortured?'

Vellosi saw her shrug. Non-committal, as if the question were unimportant. But then the woman had no audience; she would be a changed person in the cockpit of the public courtroom.

'We have not treated you in any way that violates the constitution? We have behaved, Tantardini, is that right?' He mocked her gently, feeling his way forward, amused.

Again the shrug.

'And that is not as you would have expected? Am I correct? That is not what the communiqués will state, am I correct?'

No response.

'But then we play by different rules from yours.'

She drove back at him, seeking to destroy the smugness and complacency that he had fashioned on his face. 'If you do not hurt me it is because you are afraid. There is no compassion in lackeys like yourself. There is no kindness among you pigs. Fear governs you. Fear of the reach of our arm. The society that you are servile to cannot protect you. If you lay a hand on me, a finger, a nail, then we will strike you down. That is why you give me food. That is why you do not touch me.'

'We are afraid of no one, Tantardini. Least of all the little ones, like yourself. Perhaps we are cautious of the strength of the Brigate Rosse, cautious only, perhaps we treat them with care. But the NAP does not

571

match the Brigate Rosse, the NAP is trivial and without muscle.'

'You hunt us hard. If we have no muscle you spend much time on us.'

The interrogator smiled, still sparring, still dancing far apart, as if unwilling yet to clash with the gloves. Then he leaned forward and the grin was erased.

'In twenty-five years' time, Tantardini, how old will you be?'

Vellosi could see the outline of the woman's neck, could see the smooth bright skin of youth.

'You have the files, you have the information,' she replied.

'You will be old, Tantardini. Old and withered and barren. In twenty-five years there will be new generations. Young men and women will grow and take their places in society and they will never have heard of La Tantardini. You will be a dinosaur to them. An ancient creature, verging on extinction.'

Perhaps he has hurt her, perhaps that is the way to her. Vellosi sat very still, breathing quietly, satisfied she was unaware of his presence. There was no response from her.

'That is the future, that is what you have to consider, Tantardini. Twenty-five years to brood on your revolution.' The interrogator droned on. 'You'll be a senile hag, a dowager of anarchy, when you are released. A tedious symbol of a phase in our history, courted by a few sociologists, dug out for documentaries by the RAI. And all will marvel at your stupidity. That is the future, Tantardini.'

'Will you say that when the bullets strike your legs?' she hissed, the cobra at bay. 'When the comrades are at you, when there are no chains at their wrists? Will you make speeches to me then?'

'There will be no bullets. Because you and your kind will be buried behind the walls of Messina and Asinara and Favignana. Removed from the reach of ordinary and decent people . . .'

'You will die in your own blood. It will not be in the legs, it will be to kill.' She shouted now, her voice dinning across the room. Vellosi saw the veins leaping at her neck, straining down into the collar of her blouse. Fierce and untamed, the magnificent savage. La Leonessa, as the civil servant had christened her.

'La Vianale cursed her judge, but I think he is well and with his family tonight, and it is now two years that her threat has been empty and hollow.' The interrogator spoke quietly.

'Be careful, my friend. Do not look for paper victories, for victories that you can boast of. We have an arm of strength. We will follow you, we will find you.'

'And where will you find your army? Where will you recruit your children, from which kindergarten?'

'You will find the answer. You will find it one morning as you kiss your wife. As you walk back from school from setting the children down. You will see the power of the proletarian masses.'

'That's shit, Tantardini. Proletarian masses, it means nothing. Revolutionary warfare, nothing. Struggle of the workers, nothing. It's gibberish, boring and rejected gibberish.'

'You will see.' Her voice was a whisper and there was a cold in the room that clutched at the man who wrote the notes behind the interrogator and which made him thankful that he was far from the front line, a non-combatant, obscure and unrecognized.

'It's shit, Tantardini, because you have no army. You go to war with sick children. What have you to throw against me? Giancarlo Battestini, is that the hero who will strike –'

The pain fled her face. She shrieked with laughter, pealed it round the faces of the watching men. 'Giancarlo? Is that what you think we are made of? Little Giancarlo?'

'We have his name, we have his fingerprints, his photograph. Where will he go, Tantardini?'

'What do you want with him, little Giancarlo? His capture won't win you a war.'

Angered for the first time, resenting the dismissal of a situation he had worked towards with care and precision, the interrogator slammed his fist to the table. 'We want the boy. Tantardini, Panicucci, Battestini, we want the package.'

She jeered back at him. 'He is nothing, not to us, not to you. A little bed-wetter, looking for a mother. A thrower of Molotovs. Good for demonstrations.'

'Good enough for your bed,' he chanced.

'Even you might be good enough for my bed. Even you, little pig, if there was darkness, if you washed your mouth.'

'He was with you at the shooting of Cesare Fulni, at the factory.'

'Sitting in the car, watching, messing his pants, masturbating most likely.' She laughed again, as if in enjoyment.

Vellosi smiled, deep and safe in his privacy. She was a worthy enemy. Unique, styled, irreplaceable as an opponent.

'Where will he go?' The interrogator was flustered and unsettled.

'If you want Giancarlo go and stand outside his mother's door, wait till it is cold, wait till he is hungry.'

The interrogator shook his shoulders, closed his eyes, seemed to mutter an obscenity. His fingers were clamped together, knuckles showing white. 'Twenty-five years, Franca. For a man or a woman it is a lifetime. You know you can help us, and we can help you.'

'You begin to bore me.'

Vellosi saw the hate summoned to the man's narrowed lips.

'I will come one day each year and stand over the exercise yard and I will watch you, and then you will tell me whether I bore you.'

573

'I will look for you. And on the day that you have broken the rendez-vous then I will laugh. You will hear me, pig, however deep you are buried, however far is your grave. You will hear me. You do not frighten me because already you are running.'

'You stupid little whore.'

She waved her hand carelessly at him. 'I am tired. You do not interest me and I would like to go now. I would like to go back to my room.'

She stood up, proud and erect, and seemed to Vellosi to mesmerize her questioner because he came round the table and opened the door for her. She was gone without a backward glance, leaving the room abandoned and without a presence.

The interrogator looked sheepishly at his chief. 'The boy, sweet little Giancarlo, she would have eaten him, bitten him down to the bone.'

'A very serious lady,' replied Francesco Vellosi with as composed a face as he could muster. 'She will have given her little bed-wetter and Molotov-thrower a night he will not quickly forget.'

7

For four undemanding years Archie Carpenter had been on the sprawl-ing staff list of International Chemical Holdings. Four years in which his life revolved around negotiated office hours, a stipulated lunch break, five weeks' annual holiday, and days off for working public holi-days. A 'soft old number, Archie', his one-time friends in the Special Branch of the Metropolitan Police called it when the old ties proved too strong and he hunted them out in the pub behind the Yard for a grouse and a gossip. He had settled for a predictable backwater in an unremarkable current. So, it had been a traumatic evening. First, he had been summoned to the Managing Director's suite of offices. He'd stood with a puzzlement on his face through a briefing on the kidnapping of Geoffrey Harrison and its company implications. The Personnel Director had handed him an open-dated return ticket to Rome on the way out. In a fluster he'd been ushered to the front entrance where a company car waited to speed him to Heathrow. Last on to the plane.

But he wasn't in Rome. Hadn't arrived at his destination. Archie Carpenter was in front of the departure board at Linate, Milan's inter-national airport. Strike in Rome, he'd been told. Cockpit crew, and he was lucky to have reached this far. There might be a flight later and he must wait as everybody else was waiting. He'd asked repeatedly whether he would have a ticket for the first flight to leave for Fiumicino. He was smiled at and had learned in twenty minutes that the shaken shoulder of a man in uniform meant everything or nothing, the interpretation was free. All done up for the party, and nowhere to go. He paced, cursing, through the ant-scurrying crowds of fellow travellers, always returning to the crush around the board. Four years ago he wouldn't have been flapping, would have made his assessment and either sat back and let the tide take him or jumped off his backside and done something about it, like a self-drive hire car, or a taxi down to the Central Station and an express to the capital. But the improvisation was on the way out, the mechanics of initiative were rusty, and so he tramped the concourse and breathed his abuse.

A Detective Chief Inspector in Special Branch had been Archie Carpenter's lofty ranking in the Metropolitan Police when he had moved over into 'industry', as his wife liked to spell it out to the neighbours. All the big firms in the City had been frantic for security-trained personnel to advise them on protection from the rash of Provisional IRA bombings in London. Frightened half to death they'd been at the prospect of letter bombs in the mailbags, of explosive devices in the corridors and the underground car park, looking for chaps with a confident jargon who seemed to know what they were at. ICH, a multinational colossus, offices and factories half way round the world, had one small plant outside Ballymena, County Antrim in Northern Ireland. The Board of Directors had determined that this put the vast conglomerate at risk and was sufficient reason to lure Archie Carpenter from sixteen hours a day five days a week of plodding with the Branch. They had popped him into a nice, clean, air-conditioned office with a secretary to write his letters, a pension when he was senile and nine thousand a year for his bank account. It had seemed like one long holiday. No more surveillance on winter evenings, no more meetings of the political loonies to drift into, no more Irish pubs to swill Guinness in, no more tetchy Arabs to stand alongside with a Smith and Wesson rammed in his belt. It had taken him a month to seal Chemical House, to put a system into operation that reduced the always faint threat to a minimum, and after that it had been more than comfortable, with little to worry him beyond the occasional pilfering from the typists' lockers, and the one great drama of the loss of a set of board-room minutes. He didn't complain, didn't want it to change.

He wasn't a small man. Had a good set of shoulders on him, and a stomach to go with it from four years of canteen lunches. But they availed him nothing when the herd of would-be passengers responded to the loudspeaker announcement and surged for the nominated check-in counter. Slight little girls bouncing him aside, chaps with concave chests pushing him half off his feet. Never seen anything like it.

'Wait a minute. Excuse me, won't you. You don't have to push like that, you know.' Helped him not at all.

Archie Carpenter's anger rose, the tired flush driving up his cheeks, and he thrust with the best of them and was almost ashamed at his progress. The gaps opened for his sharp, driving kneecaps and the heave of his elbows, and there were pained stares. Bit heavy, perhaps, but I didn't start it, darling, did I? So don't curl your bloody lip and flick your fingers. A little victory it had been, and one worth winning if there wasn't anything else about to compete for.

Ticket and boarding card in his hand, step a little lighter, Archie Carpenter headed for the security gates dividing the concourse from the departure lounges. His face twisted in distaste at the sight of the polizia, slacks that looked as if they'd been sat in for a week, dowdy pointed shoes, and those bloody great machine-pistols. What were they going to do with them? In a crowded space like an airport lounge, what was going to happen if they let one of those things off? Be a massacre, a Bloody Sunday, a St Valentine's Day job. Needed marksmen, didn't they? Chaps who'd be selective, not wall-paper merchants. First impressions, Archie, and they're the worst. Fair enough, sunshine, but if that's the mob that has to bust out Harrison, then draw the curtain and forget it. He'd carried a gun a dozen times in eight years with the Branch, always under a jacket, and it hurt him, professionally, to see these kids with their hardware lolling against their chests.

With no moon and a heavy darkness round them, the Alitalia DC9 lifted off. Hours late they'd be into Rome, and then all the joke of the money change queue and finding whether he'd been met and if the hotel had a booking. Stop bloody moaning, Archie. Off on your holidays, aren't you? Remember what the wife said. Her mum had brought back from Viareggio some nice leather purses, be good for Christmas presents for the family, mustn't forget to bring something like that. I'm not going for my health, for a saunter round, darling. But you'll have some time off. Not for a shopping spree. Well, what are you going for? Haven't time to tell you now, darling, but it's all a bit messy and the plane's leaving five minutes ago. And he hadn't any clean underwear. He'd rung off, gently put down the telephone in the Chemical House hallway. Would have shaken the poor old sweetheart. Weren't many fellows in Churchill Avenue, Motspur Park who charged off abroad without so much as a toothbrush to hold on to.

All a bit messy, Archie Carpenter.

No drinks on the flight. Cockpit crew strike ended. Cabin crew strike continuing.

The Managing Director had been explicit enough. They'd pay up and pay quickly. Head Office didn't want it lingering. The locals would set it up and he was there to oversee the arrangements and report back. Going to cause a bit of pain, paying out that sort of cash. Surprised him really, that they'd made up their minds so fast and hadn't thought of brazening it out.

576

Fifty minutes of sitting cramped in his seat and nothing to read but Personnel's photostat file on Geoffrey Harrison with a six digit number stamped on the outside. In the file was a blown-up passport photograph of the man, dated eighteen months earlier. He looked to be a reasonable enough chap, pleasant nondescript sort of face, the sort people always had problems describing afterwards. But then, Archie Carpenter thought, that's what he probably is, pleasant and nondescript. Why should he be anything else?

They had stripped the hood from him before he was brought from the van, affording a vast relief at the freedom from the musk of the material that had strained and scratched at his throat. The plaster too had been pulled away from his mouth, just as they had done hours earlier when they had fed him. The tape around his legs had been loosened and the blood flowed, quick and tingling, to his feet.

All that Geoffrey Harrison had seen of his new prison had been from the beam of the torch that one of the masked men had carried as they pushed him along a way between small stones and across sun-dried earth, until they had come after a few metres to the shadowed outline of a farmer's shed. The beam had played vaguely on a small sturdy building, where the mortar was crumbling from between the rough-hewn stones and replaced by dangling grass weed. Windowless and with twin doors at each end and a shallow sloping corrugated tin roof. They had hurried him through the door and the light had discovered a ladder set against piled hay bales. No words from his captors, only the instruction of the jabbed fist that he should climb, and immediately he started to move there was the weight and shudder of another man on the rungs below him, steadying and supporting because his hands were still fastened at his back.

Between the roof and the upper level of the hay bed was a space some four feet in height. The man in the darkness behind shoved Harrison forward with a lurch and he crawled ahead along the noisy shifting floor of bales. Then there was a hand at his shoulder to halt him. His wrist was taken in a vice grip. One ring of the handcuffs was unlocked. He looked upwards as the man worked in haste by torchlight. His hand that was still held was jerked high and the ratchet action of the handcuff closed on a steel chain that hung from a beam to which the roofing iron was nailed. A chain of the width and strength to subdue a farmyard Alsatian dog.

Geoffrey Harrison had been brought to the safe house. He had been hidden in a distant barn long disused for anything except the storage of winter fodder for cattle. The barn lay a hundred metres off a dirt track that in turn was a tributary of the high-banked tarmac road a kilometre away that linked the town of Palmi with the village of Castellace in the pimpled foothills of the Aspromonte. Through the day and the greater part of the night the van had travelled more than nine hundred kilometres.

To the north-east of the barn was the village of San Martino, to the south-east the village of Castellace. To the north-west were Melicucca and San Procopio, to the south-west the community of Cosoleto. From the rooftop of the barn it would have been possible to identify the separated lights of the villages, bandaged tightly by the darkness, lonely and glowing places of habitation. This was the country of lightly rolling rockstrewn hills decorated with the cover of olive groves, the territory of shepherds who minded small sheep flocks and herds of goats and who carried shotguns and shunned the company of strangers. These were the wild hill lands of Calabria that claimed a fierce independence, the highest crime rate per capita in the Republic, the lowest incidence of arrest. A primitive, feudal, battened-down society.

The low voices of two men were Harrison's company as he lay on the bales, the talk of men who are well known to each other and who speak merely because they have time on their hands and long hours to pass.

As a formality he ran his left hand over the handcuff, then tested with his fingers the route of the chain over the bar, and groped without hope at the padlock that held it there. No possibility of movement, no prospect of loosening either his wrist or the chain attachment. But it had been a cursory examination, that of a man numbed with exhaustion who had burned deep into the core of his emotion.

On the warm softness of the hay he was soon asleep, curled on his side with his knees pressed up against his chest. His mind closed to all around him, permitting neither dream nor nightmare, he found a peace, stirring hardly at all, his breathing calm and regular.

The clashes spread far through the centro storico of the capital city. Under cover of darkness the gangs of young people, small and co-ordinated, smashed a trail of broken shop windows and burned-out cars. The night air echoed with the crack of Molotovs on the cobbles, the howl of police sirens and the reports of carabinieri rifles that threw gas shells into the narrow streets. A night full of the noise of street battle and the cries of 'Death to the fascists', 'Death to the assassins of Panicucci' and 'Freedom for Tantardini'.

Twenty-nine arrests, five polizia injured, eleven shops damaged and eighteen cars. And the name of Franca Tantardini had been heard and would be seen when morning came to the city written large on the walls in dripping paint.

His guests gone, the dinner table of the executive suite in ICH House cleared, Sir David Adams retreated to his office. In midweek he frequently worked late, his justification for prohibiting business interference during weekends at his country retreat. The principal officers of the company had learned to expect his staccato tones on the telephone at any hour before he cleared his desk and walked across to his Barbican flat for the trifle of sleep that he needed.

His target this evening was his Personnel Director, who took the call on a bedside extension line. The conversation was typically to the point.

'The man we sent to Rome, he got away all right?'

'Yes, Sir David. I checked with Alitalia, he was diverted to Milan, but he managed an onward to Rome.'

'Have you called Harrison's wife?'

'Couldn't get through. I tried before I left the office, but this fellow Carpenter will do that.'

'He'll be in touch with her?'

'First thing in the morning.'

'How's Harrison going to stand up to all this? The man from the Embassy who called me was pretty blunt in his scenario.'

'I've been through Harrison's file, Sir David. Doesn't tell us much. He's a damn good record with the company . . . well, that's obvious for him to have had the posting. He's a figures man . . .'

'I know all that. What's he going to be like under this sort of pressure, how's he going to take it?'

'He's fine under business pressure . . .'

The Personnel Director heard a sigh of annoyance whistle at his ear.

'Is he an outdoor type, does he have any outdoor hobbies listed on his file?'

'Not really, Sir David. He listed "reading" . . .'

There was a snort on the line. 'You know what that means. That he comes home, switches on television, drinks three gins and gets to his bed and his sleep. A man who offers reading as a hobby is a recreational eunuch in my book.'

'What are you implying?'

'That the poor blighter is totally unfitted for the hoop he's going to be put through. I'll see you in the morning.' Sir David Adams rang off.

*

In a restaurant in the northern outskirts of Rome, secure and far from the running street fight, Giuseppe Carboni shuffled his ample wife around the cleared dance floor. The tables and chairs had been pushed back against the walls to make space for the entertainment. A gypsy fiddler, a young man with a bright accordion and his father with a guitar, provided the music for the assortment of guests. It was a gathering of friends, an annual occasion and one valued by Carboni. The kidnapping of Geoffrey Harrison provided no reason for him to stay away from the evening of fancy dress enjoyment.

He had come dressed as a ghost, his wife and her sewing-machine concocting from an old white sheet and a pillowslip with eye slits the costume that had caused loud acclamation on his entry. She was robed in the costume of a Sardinian peasant girl. They had eaten well and drunk deep of the Friuli wine and the night would serve as a brief escape from the dreary piling of reports on his desk at the Questura. And there was advantage for Carboni in such company. An Under-Secretary of the Ministry of the Interior in a mouse's habit with tail hanging from his rump, was dancing close to his shoulder. Across the floor a deputy of the Democrazia Cristiana, and one spoken of as ambitious and well-connected, clutched at the hips of a girl both blonde and beautiful and attired solely in a toga created from the Stars and Stripes. Good company for Carboni to be keeping; and what good would be achieved sitting in his flat with an ear cocked for the telephone? It was too early in the Harrison matter for intervention. Always it was easier to work when the money had been paid, when there were not tearful wives and stone-faced legal men complaining in high places that the life of their dear one and their client was being endangered by police investigation.

He bobbed his head at the Under-Secretary, smirked beneath his pillowcase at the deputy, and propelled his wife forward. There were few enough of these evenings when he was safe from disturbance and aggravation. He bowed to the man in property who wore the fading theatrical uniform of a Napoleonic dragoon and who was said to be a holiday companion at the villa of the President of the Council of Ministers. Diamonds catching brightly in the guttering candlelight, the crisp cackle of laughter, the sweet ring of the violin chords. Movement and life and pleasure, and the white-coated waiters weaved among the guests dispensing brandy tumblers and glasses of sambucca and amaro. The man in property was beside him, more smiles and a hand released from his wife's waist so that Carboni could greet the interloper.

'Please forgive me, Signora Carboni, please excuse me. May I take your husband for a moment . . . ?'

'He dances badly,' she tinkled.

The man in property kissed her hand, laughed with her. 'It is the cross of marrying a policeman, always there is someone to take him aside and whisper in his ear. My extreme apologies for the interruption.'

'You have the gratitude of my feet.'

The ghost and the dragoon huddled together in a corner, far from earshot, achieving among the sounds of talk and music a certain privacy.

'Dottore Carboni, first my apologies.'

'For nothing.'

'You are busy at this time with the new plague, the blight over us all. You are involved in enquiries into the kidnappings.'

'It is the principal aspect of our work, though less intense here than in the north.'

'And always the problem is to find the major figures, am I right? They are the hard ones.'

'They protect themselves well, they cover their activities with care.'

'Perhaps it is nothing, perhaps it is not my business . . .' It was how they all began when they wished to pour poison in a policeman's ear . . . 'but something has been brought to my attention. It has come from the legal section of my firm, we have some bright young men there and it was something that aroused their interest, and that involved a competitor.' That was predictable too, thought Carboni, but the man must be heard out if it were not to reach the head of government that a policeman had not reacted to the advice of a friend.

'A year ago I was in competition for a site for chalets on the Golfo di Policastro, near to Sapri, and the man against me was called Mazzotti, Antonio Mazzotti. Around two hundred millions were needed to settle the matter, and Mazzotti outbid me. He took the site, I took my money elsewhere. But then Mazzotti could not fulfil his commitments, it was said he could not raise the capital, that he was over-extended, and I am assured he sold at a loss. It is a difficult game, property, Dottore, many burn their fingers. We thought nothing more of him, another amateur. Then two weeks ago I was in competition for a place to the south of Sapri, at the Marina de Maratea. There was another location where it was possible to build some chalets . . . but my money was insufficient. Then yesterday my boys in the legal section told me that the purchaser was Mazzotti. Well, it is possible in business to make a fast recovery but he paid in bank draft the greater proportion of the sum. From an outside bank, outside Italy. The money has run back sharply to the hands of this Mazzotti. I set my people to find out more and they tell me this afternoon that he is from the village of Cosoleto in Calabria. He is from the bandit land. I ask myself, is there anything wrong with a man from the hills having brains and working hard and advancing himself. Nothing, I tell myself. Nothing. But it was in foreign draft that he paid, Dottore. That, you will agree, is not usual.'

'It is not usual,' Carboni agreed. He hoped the man had finished, wished only to get back to the music. 'And I would have thought it a matter for the Guardia di Finanze if there have been irregularities of transfer.'

581

'You do not follow me. I do not care where the fellow salts his money, I am interested in where he acquires it, and how its source springs up so quickly.'

'You are very kind to have taken so much trouble.'

'I have told no one else of my detective work.' A light laugh.

'In the morning I will make some enquiries, but you understand I have a great preoccupation with the kidnapping of the Englishman.'

'I would not wish my name to be mentioned in this matter.'

'You have my word,' said Carboni, and was gone to the side of his wife. Something or nothing, and time in the morning to run a check on Antonio Mazzotti. Time in the morning to discover whether there were grounds for suspicion or whether a disgruntled businessman was using the influence of the network of privilege to hinder an opponent who had twice outwitted him.

Giuseppe Carboni scooped the pillowslip over his head and downed a cooled glass of Stock brandy, wiped his face, dropped again his disguise and resumed with his wife a circuit of the dance floor.

When they reached the second-floor room, puffing because they came by the turning staircase as there was no lift in a pensione such as this, Giancarlo stood back, witnessing the drunken effort of Claudio to fit the room key to the door lock. They had taken a room in a small and private place between the Piazza Vittorio Emanuele and the Piazza Dante, with a barren front hall and a chipped reception desk that carried signs demanding prepayment of money and the decree that rooms could not be rented by the hour. The portiere asked no questions, explained that the room must be vacated by noon, pocketed the eight thousand lire handed him by Claudio and presumed them to be from the growing homosexual clan.

On the landing, waiting behind the fumbling Claudio, Giancarlo looked down at his sodden jeans, dark and stained below the knees, and his canvas shoes that oozed the wine he had poured away under the table in the pizzeria. He had eaten hugely, drunk next to nothing, was now sobered and alert and ready for the confrontation that he had chosen. The Calabrian needed a full minute, interspersed with oaths, to unfasten the door and reveal the room. It was bare and functional. A wooden table with chair. A wooden single-door wardrobe. A thin-framed print of old Rome. Two single beds separated by a low table on which rested a closed Bible and a small lamp. Claudio pitched forward, as if it were immaterial to him that the door was still open, and began pulling with a ferocious clumsiness at his clothes, dragging them from his back and arms and legs before sinking heavily in his underpants on to the grey bedspread. Giancarlo extracted the key from the outside lock, closed the door behind him and then locked it again before pocketing the key.

Cold and detached, no longer running, no longer in flight, Giancarlo looked down with contempt at the sprawled figure on the bed, ranged his eyes over the hair-encased legs, the stomach of rolled fat and on up to the opened mouth that sucked hard for air. He stood for a long time to be certain in his mind that the building was at peace and the other residents asleep. An animal, he seemed to Giancarlo, an illiterate animal. The pig had called his Franca a whore, the pig would suffer. With a deliberation he had not owned before, as if sudden age and manhood had fallen to him, he reached under his shirt tail and pulled the P38 from his belt. On the balls of his feet and keeping his silence he moved across the linoleum and stopped two metres from the bed. Close enough to Claudio, and beyond the reach of his arms.

'Claudio, can you hear me?' A strained whisper.

In response only the convulsed breathing.

'Claudio, I want to talk to you.'

A belly-deep grunted protest of irritation.

'Claudio, you must wake up. I have questions for you, pig.'

A little louder now. Insufficient to turn the face of Claudio, enough to annoy and to cause him to wriggle his shoulders in anger as if trying to rid himself of the presence of a flea.

'Claudio, wake yourself.'

The eyes opened and were wide and staring and confused because close to them was the outstretched hand that held the pistol, and the message in the boy's gaze was clear even through the mist of station beer and pizzeria wine.

'Claudio, you should know that you are very close to death. I am near to killing you, there as you lie on your back. You save yourself only if you tell me what I want to know. You understand, Claudio?'

The voice droned at the dulled mind of the prostrate man, dripping its message, spoken by a parent who has an ultimatum on behaviour to deliver to a child. The bedsprings whined as the bulk of the man began to shift and stir, moving backwards towards the head rest, creating distance from the pistol. Giancarlo watched him trying for focus and comprehension, substituting the vague dream for the reality of the P38 and the slight figure that held it. The boy pressed on, dominating, sensing the moment was right.

'There is nowhere to go, no one to save you. I will kill you, Claudio, if you do not tell me what I ask you. Kill you so that the blood runs from you.'

The boy felt detached from his words, separated from the sounds that his ears could hear. No word from the pig.

'It is the P38, Claudio. The weapon of the fighters of the NAP. It is loaded and I have only to draw back the trigger. Only to do that and

583

you are dead, and rotting and fly-infested. Am I clear, Claudio?'

The boy could not recognize himself, could not recognize the strength of his grip upon the gun.

'It is the P38. Many have died by this gun. There would be no hesitation, not in sending a Calabrian pig to his earth hole.'

'What do you want?'

'I want an answer.'

'Don't play with me, boy.'

'If I want to play with you, Claudio, then I will do so. If I want to tease you, then I will. If I want to hurt you, then you cannot protect yourself. You have nothing but the information that I want from you. Give it me and you live. It is that or the P38.'

The boy watched the man strain in the night stillness for a vibration of life from the building, ears cocked for something that might give him hope of rescue, and saw the dumb collapse at the realization that the pensione slept cloaked in night. The big body crumbled back flat on to the bed as if defeated and the coiled springs tolled under the mattress.

'What do you want?'

He is ready, thought Giancarlo, as ready as he will ever be.

'I want to know where the man is hidden that was taken this morning.' The message came in a flurry, as a transitory shower of snow falls on the high places of the Apennines, quick and brisk and blanketing. 'If you want to live, Claudio, you must tell me where to find him.'

Easier now for Claudio. Easier because there was something that he could bite at. Half a smile on his face, because the drink was still with him and he lacked the control to hide the first, frail amusement.

'How would I know that?'

'You will know it. Because if you do not you will die.'

'I am not told such things.'

'Then you are dead, Claudio. Dead because you are stupid, dead because you did not know.'

From the toes of his feet, moving with the swaying speed of the snake, Giancarlo rocked forward, never losing the balance that was perfect and symmetrical. His right arm lunged, blurred in its aggression till the foresight of the gun was against the man's ear. Momentarily it rested there, then raked back across the fear-driven, quivering face and the sharp needle of the sight gouged a ribbon welt through the jungle of bristle and hair. Claudio snatched at the gun, and grasped only at the air and was late and defeated while the blood welled and spilled from the road hewn across his cheek.

'Do not die from stupidity and idiocy, Claudio. Do not die because you failed to understand that I am no longer the child who was protected in the Queen of Heaven. Tell me where they took the man. Tell me.' The demand for an answer, harsh and compelling, winning through the exhaustion and the drink, abetted by the blood trickle beneath the man's hand.

'They do not tell me such things.'

'Inadequate, Claudio . . . to save yourself.'

'I don't know. In God's name I don't know.'

Giancarlo saw the struggle for survival, the two extremes of the pendulum. If he spoke now the immediate risk to the pig's life would be removed, to be replaced in the fullness of time by the threat of the retribution that the organization would bring down on his dulled head should betrayal be his temporary salvation. The boy sensed the conflict, the alternating fortunes of the two armies waging war in the man's mind.

'Then in your ignorance you die.'

Noisily because it was not a refined mechanism, Giancarlo drew back with his thumb the hammer of the pistol. It reverberated around the room, a sound that was sinister, irretrievable. Claudio was half up on the bed, pushed from his elbows, his hand flown from the wound. Eyes, saucer-large and peering into the dimness, perspiration in bright rivers on his forehead. Dismal and pathetic and beaten, his attention committed to the rigid, unmoving barrel aimed at the centre of his ribcage.

'They will have taken him to the Mezzo Giorno,' Claudio whispered his response, the man who is behind the velvet curtain of the confessional and who has much to tell the Father and is afraid lest any other should hear his words.

'The Mezzo Giorno is half the country. Where in the south has he gone?'

Giancarlo pickaxed into the strata of the man. Domineering. Holding in his cage the trapped rat, and offering it as yet no escape.

'They will have gone to the Aspromonte . . .'

'The Aspromonte stretch a hundred kilometres across Calabria. What will you have me do? Walk the length of them and shout and call and search in each farmhouse, each barn, each cave? You do not satisfy me, Claudio.' Spoken with the chill and deep cold of the ice on the hills in winter.

'We are a family in the Aspromonte. There are many of us. Some do one part of it, others take different work in the business. They sent me to Rome to take him. There was a cousin and a nephew of the cousin that were to drive him to the Aspromonte where he would be held. There is another who will guard him . . .'

'Where will they guard him?' The gun, hammer arched, inched closer to Claudio's head.

'God's truth, on the Soul of the Virgin, I do not know where they will hold him.'

The boy saw the despair written boldly, sensed that he was prising open the area of truth. 'Who is the man that will guard him?' The first minimal trace of kindness in the boy's voice.

585

'He is the brother of my wife. He is Alberto Sammartino.'

'Where does he live?'

'On the Acquaro road and near to Cosoleto.'

'I do not know those names.'

'It is the big road that comes into the mountains from Sinopli and that runs on towards Delianuova. Between Acquaro and Cosoleto is one kilometre. There is an olive orchard on the left side, about four hundred metres from Cosoleto, where the road begins to climb to the village. You will see the house set back from the road, there are many dogs there and some sheep. Once the house was white. His car is yellow, an Alfa. If you go there you will find him.'

'And he will be guarding the Englishman?'

'That was what had been arranged.'

'Perhaps you try only to trick me.'

'On the Virgin, I swear it.'

'You are a pig, Claudio. A snivelling coward pig. You swear on the Virgin and you betray the family of your wife, and you tell all to a boy. In the NAP we would die rather than leave our friends.'

'What will you do with me now?' A whipped dog, one that does not know whether its punishment is completed, whether it is still possible to regain affection. On a lower floor a lavatory flushed.

'I will tie you up and I will leave you here.' The automatic response. 'Turn over to your face on the pillow. Your hands behind your back.'

Giancarlo watched the man curl himself to his stomach. In his vision for a moment was the shamed grin of self-preservation on Claudio's face because he had won through with nothing more than a scratch across his cheek. Gone then, lost in the pillow and its grease coat.

When the man was still, Giancarlo moved quickly forward. Poised himself, stiffened his muscles. He swung down the handle of the pistol with all his resources of strength on to the sun-darkened balding patch at the apex of Claudio's skull. One desperate rearing convulsion that caused the boy to adjust his aim. The breaking of eggs, the shrieking of the bedsprings and the tremor of breathing that has lost its pattern and will fade.

Giancarlo stepped back. An aching silence encircled him as he listened. Not the creak of a floorboard, not the pressure of a foot on a staircase step. All in their beds and tangled with their whores and boys. Blood on the wall behind the bed, spattered as if the molecules had parted on an explosive impact, was running from drops in downward lines across the painted plaster, and above their furthest orbit, untainted, was the smiling and restful face of the Madonna in her plastic frame with the cherubic child. The boy did not look at Claudio again.

He cleared the hip pocket from the strewn trousers on the floor and went on tiptoe to the door. He turned the key, carried outside with him the 'non disturbare' sign, attached it to the outer door handle, locked

586

the door again and slipped away down the stairs. To the portiere he said that his friend would sleep late, that he himself was taking an early coach to Milano. The man nodded, scarce aroused from his dozing sleep at the desk.

Far into the night and with little traffic to impede him as he crossed the streets, the wraith, Giancarlo Battestini, headed for the Termini.

8

What in Christ's name am I doing here?

The first thoughts of Archie Carpenter. He was naked under a sheet, illuminated by the light that pierced the plastic blind slats. He flailed his arms at the hanging cloud of cigarette smoke, spat out the reek of brandy from the glasses that littered the dressing-table and window-sill.

Archie Carpenter sat up in bed, putting his memory together, slotting the evidence into place. Half the bloody night he'd spent with the men from ICH. All the way from the airport in the limousine he'd listened and they'd talked, he'd asked and they'd briefed. Convincing the big man from Chemical House of their competence, that's how he saw it. They'd taken care of his bags at the hotel with a finger snap and tramped into his room, rung down for a bottle of cognac and kept up the barrage till past three. He'd slept less than four hours and he had to show for it a headache and the clear knowledge that the intervention of Archie Carpenter had no chance of affecting Geoffrey Harrison's problems. He climbed out of bed and felt the weakness in his legs and the mind-bending pain behind his temples. Half midnight, at the latest, they wound things up in Motspur Park. Had to, didn't they? With babysitters at a pound an hour there wasn't much time after the ice-cream and fruit salad to sit on your arse and chat about the rate of income tax. And the brandy didn't flow, not out there in the suburbs, not at seven pounds a bottle. A quick splash after coffee and the Mums and Dads were on their way. Not that the Carpenters had kids . . . that's another trial, Archie. Not for now, old sunshine.

He'd need a shower to flush it out of him.

Beside his bed, under a filled ashtray, was his diary. He thumbed through for the number the Managing Director had given him. A chap called Charlesworth, from the Embassy and said to be helpful. He dialled, listened to the telephone ringing out, took a time to answer. What you'd expect at this time in the morning.

'Pronto, Charlesworth.'

'My name's Carpenter. Archie Carpenter of ICH. I'm the company's Security Director . . .' Since when had he had a title like that? But it sounded right, just sort of slipped out like a palmed visiting card. 'They've asked me to come out here and see what's going on. With this fellow Harrison, I mean.'

'It's nice of you to ring, but I'm a bit out of touch since yesterday evening.'

'They said in London you'd put yourself out in this business. I was asked to pass on the thanks of the company.'

'That's very kind of you, it was nothing.'

'They thought it was. I have to go out to this EUR place wherever that is, and I have to visit Harrison's missus, so I'd like to meet you before that. First thing.'

Carpenter was aware of a hesitation on the line. A natural request, but it had sparked prevarication.

'I don't think there's very much that I can tell you.'

'I'd like to hear views other than from the company people. They're Italians, every last one of them. I'd like your views.'

'There really isn't much that I can tell you.'

'Not in the line of duty?' Carpenter clipped in, cold, awake, the brandy disgorged.

'I double between political and security. Security doesn't warrant a great deal of time, and the desk is pretty loaded with the political stuff at the moment. My plate's more than full.'

'So is Harrison's.' A flare of anger from Carpenter. What was the bloody fool at? 'He's British isn't he? Entitled to a bit of help from the Embassy.'

'He is,' came the cautious reply. 'But there's debate in the shop about how much help.'

'You've lost me.'

'I'm sorry, then.'

Carpenter closed his eyes, grimaced. Begin again, Archie boy. Start all over again.

'Mr Charlesworth, let's not waste each other's time. I'm not a moron, and I've kidnapping coming out of my ears after last night with the locals. I know it's not straightforward. I understand the threat that exists, that Harrison's on the edge. I know it's not just a matter of sitting in the front parlour and waiting for the shareholders to cough up so Harrison can come back and kiss his sweet wife hello. I know the risks for Harrison. They told me about Ambrosio, shot because a mask slipped and he saw his captors. I heard how they chopped Michelangelo Ambrosio. They told me about de Capua. Now on to the other side of things. I did eight years in Special Branch before I moved to ICH. My rank at Scotland Yard was Chief Inspector. This isn't the time for a "need to know" show.'

A laugh on the line. 'Thanks for the speech, Mr Carpenter.'

'What's the problem, then?'

'I wouldn't want what I say repeated.'

'I've signed the bloody Official Secrets Act, Mr Charlesworth, just like you have.'

'It's a tedious matter of keeping our hands clean. Theoretically it's a criminal offence to pay ransom money, and it would be damaging to us if we could be linked with such a felony. In the Ambassador's view this is a private matter between ICH and a gang of Italian criminals. He doesn't want us to be seen to be condoning the extortion of money, and he feels that any public involvement could give the impression that we're bending the knee to criminal action. If Harrison worked for Whitehall we wouldn't be paying, it's as simple as that.'

'And a chat in your office . . .'

'That's involvement in the Ambassador's eyes.'

'That's bloody ridiculous,' Carpenter barked into the telephone.

'I agree, particularly in a country where ransom payment is the normal way of extrication. If you're that well briefed you'll have heard of a man called Pommarici in Milano. He's a prosecutor and has tried to freeze kidnap victims' assets, to prevent payment. He lost . . . the families said he was endangering the lives of their loved ones. It all went back to the jungle. So what it adds up to is that the Embassy has no role to play. Off the record we can help, but not if it's visible. Do you read me?'

Carpenter slopped back on to his bed. 'I read you, Mr Charlesworth.'

'Give me a ring this afternoon. We'll have an early bite in town.'

'I'd like that,' Carpenter said and rang off. Poor bloody Harrison, but how inconsiderate of him. To get himself kidnapped and embarrass HMG. Not a very good show, my old love.

The wooden shutters, bent and paint-peeled but still capable of restricting light, stayed late across the upper window of the narrow terraced home of Vanni, the driver. The noises made by children and cars in the cobbled street behind the main road through Cosoleto merely lulled the man as he lay in the drowsy pleasure of his bed.

It had been close to midnight when he had returned to his home, and there was the radiance in his worn face to tell his wife that the journey had been profitable. She had not asked what the work had been, what the danger, what the stake, but had busied herself first in the kitchen, then against the muscles of his stomach in the great bed that had been her mother's. And when he had slept she had slid from the sheets and looked with a glowing excitement at the hard roll of banknotes before replacing them in the hip pocket of the trousers thrown with abandon on a chair. A good man he was to her, and a kind man.

While she worked in the kitchen beneath, Vanni was content to idle the early morning hours. Not time yet for him to dress, throw on a freshly ironed shirt, put a sheen on his shoes and drive his car into Palmi for a coffee and a talk with Mario who would make a similar journey if ever he woke – she was an animal, Mario's woman, consumed in the brute passion of the Sicilians. A coffee with Mario if he had satisfied his woman, if he had the sap to leave his bed.

And when Claudio had returned on the morning rapido, then perhaps they all would be summoned to the villa of the capo to take a glass of Campari and talk of the olive trees, the goat herds and the death of an old man of the village. They would not speak of anything that was immediate and close to them, but they would smile at their mutual knowledge, and each in his own way reflect a peculiar glory.

At least another hour Vanni could keep to his bed.

At Criminalpol, where the Rome police forensic effort is mounted, the first particles of evidence were being gathered in the scientific analysis section. Brought from the central telephone exchange were recordings of all calls received by ICH in EUR and of those directed to the private number of the Harrisons. One of the most far-reaching advances in the hunt for the kidnappers had been the development of a voice bank programmed for the computer to match similarities. The same man, the electronics decided, who had called ICH with the ransom demand had also made the abortive call to Mrs Harrison. Nothing particular in that. The stir of interest among the technicians came when they fed to the brain scores of recordings made from previous interceptions, and sought a similarity with their latest material. On the read-out screens the file on the Marchetti case was flashed. Eight and a half months earlier. A four-year-old boy. Taken from a foreign national nanny in the Aventino district of Rome. No arrests. No clues left on site. A ransom payment of 250 million paid. Marked notes. No sign of ransom money. The Marchetti communication and the calls on the Harrison case had been made by the same man. Vocal interpretation located an accent from the extreme south.

The night work of machines. The recordings were sent by line to the Questura to await the arrival of Giuseppe Carboni.

The Agente di Custodie hurried from the prison officers' mess to the main gate of the Asinara gaol. He had not eaten the breakfast provided for the men coming off night shift after they had supervised the first feeding of the prisoners. The weight of the message that he must telephone to the contact number bore down on him, spiriting up the fear waves of nausea.

His recruitment as a pigeon for the leading members of the NAP held on Asinara when they wished to communicate with the outside world had been a long-drawn-out affair. As a badger will sniff and dig for choice roots, so members of the group at liberty had discovered the turmoil that the Agente and his family lived with as they devoted themselves to the care of their ailing spina bifida baby. Reports had come back of crippling doctors' bills in the town of Sassari on the Sardinian mainland to the south of the prison island. There had been word of the inability of the father to pay for visits to Roma or Milano for consultation with specialists.

The Agente had been ripe for plucking. There was money for his wife, used notes in envelopes. He was no longer in debt and muttered instead and without conviction to the medical men of the help of a distant relative. Not that the child could improve, only that the conscience of the parents might be easier. The numbers that he must telephone changed frequently, and the cryptic messages that he must pass on became a deluge.

On Asinara is the maximum security cage of the Italian forces of justice, escape deemed impossible. It is the resting-place of the most dedicated of the male urban guerrilla community, the receptacle for those found guilty of armed insurrection against the State. Originally a prison colony, then a gaol for the liberal few who opposed Mussolini's fascism, the gaol drifted into disrepair before the refurbishment that was necessary for the incarceration of the new enemy. The renovation had been from the drawing-board of the magistrate Riccardo Palma; he had done his work well, and died for it. But through the Agente the words of the Chief of Staff of the NAP could pass beyond the locked cell doors, along the watched corridors with their high closed-circuit cameras, through the puny exercise yards, piercing the lattice of the electrically controlled double gates and their dynamite-proof bars. The message had been given to the Agente as he lined the prisoners in a queue for their food, slipped into his hand, drowned in the sweat sea of his palm.

Beyond the gates and heading for his home, the free house of the prison service where only anxiety and pain awaited him, he had read the message on the scrap of sharply torn paper.

Per La Tantardini. Rappresaglia. Numero quattro.

For Tantardini. Reprisal. Number Four.

The Agente, held in the clutch of compromise, walked in a tortured daze that vanished as the pale broken face of his wife greeted his arrival at the front door. His child was dying, his wife was failing, and who cared, who helped? He kissed her perfunctorily, went to their room to

591

change out of uniform, and then looked in silence through the half-open door at the child asleep in her cot. In his own clothes and without explanation he strode down into the hamlet to telephone to the number he had been given at Porto Torres across the narrow channel on Sardinia. Within one day, perhaps two, he would witness on the little black and white television screen in the corner of the living-room the results of his courier work.

The swollen pressure of his bladder finally awoke Geoffrey Harrison. He stretched himself, jerking at the handcuff, wrenching at his wrist, aware immediately of the inhibitions of his slept-in clothes. Still the suit that he had dressed in for the drive to the office, still with the tie at his neck, and only the top button undone as a concession to the circumstances. The sun had not yet played on the roof of the barn and he was cold, shivering. His socks smelt, pervading the limited space between the rafters and the bales; the nylon ones that he always wore in the summer and that he changed when he came home in the early evening.

Didn't speak the language, did he? Had never taken a Berlitz. He could only order a meal and greet his office colleagues at the start of the day. So what to shout to the men in the other half of the barn? He wanted to urinate, wanted to squat and relieve himself, and didn't know how to say it. Basic human function, basic human language. He couldn't mess his trousers. That was revulsion, and so from necessity came the shout. Couldn't have an accident.

'Hey. Down there. Come here.' In English as if because of his urgency they would understand him. They'll come, Geoffrey, they'll want to know why the prisoner shouts. 'Come here.'

He heard the sudden movement, and the voices of two men that were closer. A creaking from the swing of the barn door that was hidden from him by the bales, and the ladder-top slid into position and shook from a man's weight. A gun first, black and ugly, held in a firm grip, and following it the contortion of a hood with eye slits. Eerie and awful in the half light before it gave way to the recognizable shape of shoulders and a man's trunk. The gesture of the gun was unmistakable. He obeyed the order of the waved barrel and stumbled back as far as the chain would allow. He pointed down to his zip, then across with his free hand to his buttocks. A grotesque mime. And the hooded head shook and was gone, lost below the lip of the hay.

There were noisy chuckles from below and then a farm bucket arched up, from an unseen hand. Old and rusted and once of galvanized steel. A folded wad of newspaper pages followed. He was left to a slight privacy as he pulled the bucket towards him, turned his back on the ladder and fingered at his belt. Humiliated and hurt, one arm aloft and fastened, he contorted his body over the bucket. He speeded his

592

functions, willing his bladder and bowels to be emptied, before the slitted eyes returned to laugh at his dropped pants and his bared thighs and genitals. How half the world does it, Geoffrey, so get used to it. Don't think I can bloody well take it, not every day, not like this. God, what a bloody stink. The sandwich . . . all stink and wind. Remember the sandwich, back sometime yesterday, that the men in the van gave you, the curse in the guts. He groped down for the paper; damp with the morning dew, must have been outside through the night, and it tore soggily in his hands. He wanted to cry, wanted to weep and be pitied. Harrison cleaned himself as best he could, tears smarting, pulled at his underwear and trousers, zipped himself and fastened the belt.

'I've finished. You can come and take it.'

Movement and repetition. The ladder moved as before and the gun and the hood reappeared. He pointed to the bucket.

'I've used it. You can take it away.'

Just a belly laugh from the covered face and a jumping in merriment of the shoulders, and the hood sinking and going, and the muffled call of fun and entertainment. A bloody great joke, Geoffrey. Do you see it, do you see why he's splitting himself? You asked for the bucket, they've given it to you, given it for keeps. They've given you a little present. It's going to sit there, a couple of yards away. Stinking and rotten and foul. Own pee, own shit, own waste. You've given them a bloody good laugh.

'Come here. Come back.' All the command that he could summon. The tone of an order, unmistakable, and enough to arrest the disappearance of the hood. The laugh was cut.

'Come here.'

The head came upwards, revealed again the shoulders. Geoffrey Harrison leaned back on his left foot, then swung himself forward as far as the chain permitted. He drove his right instep against the bucket, saw it rise and explode, career against the shoulder of the man, spill its load across his mask and faded cotton shirt. Stained, dripping, and spread.

'You can have it back,' Harrison giggled. 'You can have it again now.'

What in God's name did you do that for?

Don't know. Just sort of happened.

They'll bloody murder you, Geoffrey Harrison, they'll half tear you apart for that.

It's what they're for, those bastards, to be crapped and peed on.

Right, dead right. When you've a bloody army at your back. You're an idiot, Geoffrey Harrison.

I don't know why I did it.

You won't do it again.

They came together for him. The other man leading, the one with the smears on his shirt and hood a rung on the ladder behind. No words, no consultation, no verbal reproach. Nothing but the beat of their fists and the drumming of their boots against his face and chest, and the softness of his lower belly and his thighs and shins. They worked on him as if he were a suspended punchbag, hanging from the beam. They spent their strength against him till they panted and gasped from their effort, and he was limp and defenceless and no longer capable of even minimal self-protection. Vicious, angered creatures, because the act of defiance was unfamiliar and the bully had risen in them, sweet and safe. Harrison crumpled down on to the hay floor, feeling the pain that echoed in his body, yearning for release, wishing for death. The worst was at his ribcage, covered now in slow funnels of agony. When did you ever do anything like that in your life before, Geoffrey? Never before, never stood up, not to be counted. And no bastard here this morning with his calculator. No one there to see him, to cheer and applaud. Just some mice under his feet, and the stink of his body, and the knowledge that there was a man close by who loathed him and would cut off his life with as little ceremony as picking the muck from his nostrils.

He worked a smile over the pain of his jaw and gazed at the emptied bucket. He'd tell Violet about it, tell her it blow by blow. Not what they did to him afterwards, but up till then, and his foot still ached.

He struggled upright, knees shaking, stomach in torment.

'You're animals,' he shouted. 'Slobbering, miserable swine. Fit to shovel shit, you know that.' The scream wobbled under the low cut of the rafters. 'Get down in your shit and wash yourselves, you pigs. Rub your faces in it, because that's what makes pigs happy. Pig shit, pig thick.'

And then he listened, braced for a new onslaught, and heard the murmur of their voices. They took no notice of him, ignored him. He knew that he could shout till he lifted the roof and that they had no fear of it. He was separated from every civilization that he knew of.

Without hunger, without thirst, numbed by the annihilation of the big Calabresi, Giancarlo sat on a bench in the Termini, waiting the hours away. Close to exhaustion, near to drifting to fitful sleep, hands masking his face, elbows digging at his legs, he thought of Franca.

There had been girls in Pescara, the daughters of the friends of Father and Mother. Flowing skirts, starched blouses and knee boots, and the clucking approval of Mother as she brought the cream cakes out. The ones that giggled and knew nothing, existed with emptied minds. Crucifixes of gold at their necks and anger in their mouths if he reached for buttons or zips or eye-fasteners.

There had been girls at the University. Brighter and more adult stars

594

who regarded him as an adolescent. There he was someone who could make up the numbers for the cinema or the beach, but who was shunned when it was dark, when the clinching began. The spots, the acne, and the titter behind the hand. It should have been different with the Autonomia, but the girls would not grovel for a novice, for a recruit, and Giancarlo had to prove himself and win the acclamation. Far out in the front of the crowd, running forward with the fire eating into the rag at the hilt of the milk bottle, arcing the Molotov into the air. The battle for approval, and his ankle had turned. Would they even remember him now, the girls of the Autonomia? Giancarlo Battestini had no experience other than in the arms, between the thighs, wrapped warm by Franca. It was the crucible of his knowledge. A long time he thought of her.

Franca with the breasts golden and devoid of the rim of suntan, Franca with the cherry-pip nipples, with the flattened belly holed by a single crater, Franca with the wild forest that had tangled and caught his fingers. The one who had chosen him. Darling, darling, sweet Franca. In his ears was the sound of her breathing, the beat of her movement on the bed, her cry as she had spent herself.

I am coming, Franca. I am coming to take you from them, he whispered to himself.

I am coming, Franca. Believe it, know it. Thinking of Franca as the station began to live again, to move and function, participate in a new day. Thinking of Franca as he walked to the ticket counter and paid the single fare on the rapido to Reggio. Thinking of Franca as he climbed up to a first-class carriage. Away from the herd of Neapolitans and Sicilians with their bundles and salads and children and hallucinating noises of discussion and counter-discussion. No other passengers in the compartment. Thinking of Franca as the train pulled away from the low platform, and crawled between the sidings and junctions and high flats draped in the day's first washing. The boy slumped back, slid his heels on to the seat in front and felt the pressure power of the P38 against his back.

Out across the flatlands to the south of the city, carving through the grass fields and the close-packed vineyards, skirting the small towns of Cisterna di Latina and Sezze away on the hills, and Terracina at the coast, the train quickened its pace. Blurring the telegraph poles, homing and seeking out the dust-dry mountains and the bright skies of the Aspromonte.

'Believe in me, Franca. Believe in me because I am coming.' The boy spoke aloud above the crash of wheels on the welded track. 'Tomorrow they will know of me. Tomorrow they will know my name. Tomorrow you will be proud of your little fox.'

9

At the Questura there were barely disguised smiles from the uniformed men who watched Dottore Giuseppe Carboni disgorged from his car. The evidence of the night before was plain and clear-cut. Bulldog bagged eyes, blotched cheeks, a razor-nicked chin, a tie not hoisted. He swept uneasily through the door, searching straight ahead of him as if wary of impediments and took the lift instead of risking the flight of stairs. Carboni had greetings for none of those who saluted and welcomed him along the second-floor passage. Ignoring them all, he was thankful to make the haven of his desk without public humiliation. They would think he had been drinking all night, would not know as they whispered and clucked in disapproval that he had left the party before two, and back at his flat had collapsed in a chair with a tumbler of whisky that he might better search his memory for patterns and procedures in his latest kidnap burden. Never time for thought, for analysis, once he was at work with the telephone ringing and the stream of visitors, humble and distinguished. And a tumbler had become two, and merged into half a bottle as he had picked into the recesses of the problem before him. He had stayed up till his wife, magnificent in her flowing nightdress, had dragged him to her bed, and little enough chance of sleep then.

He sat heavily in his chair and buzzed the connecting speaker for his aide. A moment and the man was there, sleek and oiled and ready with an armful of files, battered brown folders encasing a hillock of typed paperwork. What did the Dottore intend the priority of the day to be?

Carboni winced, the stab of pain ringing in his head. 'The Harrison case. There is nothing else.'

'We have the tapings of the calls to Mrs Harrison and to ICH. The one to Harrison's wife was futile. She couldn't understand what she was being told and rang off.' There was a sneer at the mouth of Carboni's assistant. 'The first tangible steps towards extortion were made in a message to his company. Also from Criminalpol there is voice analysis. They believe there is similarity here with the communication at the Marchetti kidnapping, the child.'

'Just the one message to the company?'

'A single message, the establishment of lines of approach.'

'Leave me with the tapes,' said Carboni, eyes closed, head spinning, wishing deliverance from intelligent and confident young men.

When he was alone he played the cassette many times. Hands over his face, shutting out the noise through the open windows of the traffic below, concentrating his effort on the brief and staccato message. A callow, rasping voice he heard, and the policeman did not need the help of the memorandum that was attached to the package to know that this voice came from the toe of the country, from Calabria, from the land of the Mafiosi chieftains. Where else? A humble, inarticulate voice, reading a message that had been written for him, which was normal. Then there was the tape of the first call to the Marchetti family to be heard. A match; it didn't take a computer to tell him that.

Time now for work on the telephone. He mopped at his neck with his handkerchief. Half an hour in his office and his shirt was soaked. Calls to his subordinates drew a blank. No further eye-witnesses had been produced since he had left for home the previous evening. There was nothing to feed into the machines beyond the very basics of description supplied by the single woman on Collina Fleming: bulk and height and generality of clothing. No faces, no fingerprints, no escape car yet traced. No information had emerged from the tenuous links with the Underworld maintained by the discreeter elements of the anti-kidnap squad. No word and none expected, because to inform in these matters was the sure and fast way to a wooden box. Not for the first time since he had reached his lofty eminence Giuseppe Carboni pondered the value of his work. The servant of a society which stepped back from commitment and involvement. The servant, neither trusted nor appreciated, and struggling for standards that those who lodged even in the higher places renounced. Lockheed, Friuli, Esso Italiana, Belice, even the Quirinale, even the Presidency. Scandals; nasty and deceitful, and the guilty were from the chief echelons of the great Mama Italia. So, who wanted law, who wanted order? The ache was back at his head, the throb of a hungover man, wetted with disillusion. He could take his pension. He could go on his way, and the President would hang a medal round his neck, and his parting would be unseen, unimportant.

Carboni smacked his pudgy hand down on to the desk, felt the shockwaves vibrate back up to his elbow, enjoyed the affliction. There was time for a few more of the great ones to go behind bars, time for a few more handcuffs to be wrapped on the wrists of those who at last would show shame as the doors of the Regina Coeli closed on them. Abruptly he pressed the intercom button, and heard the silked voice of his assistant.

'A man called Antonio Mazzotti, originally from Cosoleto in Calabria.' He had slipped away from the priority of the day because he did not know how to harness the energy he wished to exude for Harrison's freedom. 'He has an office in Rome and deals in property speculation. He has made some development deals in the Golfo di Policastro. I want the telephone number of his office. Just the number and I will call it myself.'

'It will be attended to, Dottore.'

'And not this evening, not this afternoon,' Carboni growled. 'I want it this morning.'

'Of course, Dottore. And the firm of Harrison rang. They would like an Archibald Carpenter to see you. He is the Security Director of ICH head office, from London . . .'

'Around twelve I could see him.'

'I will let the company know.'

'And the number of this man, Mazzotti, no delay.'

'Of course not, Dottore.' The voice dripped. Carboni hated him, would have him shifted. 'Dottore, the news is coming of another kidnapping. From Parioli.'

'I cannot handle it. Someone else will have to.'

'They have taken the nephew of a considerable industrialist . . .'

'I told you, I have enough to concern me.'

'. . . an industrialist who is generous to the Democrazia Cristiana with funds.'

Carboni sighed in annoyance and resignation. 'Get my car to the door, and when I am back I want that number on my desk, and I want this Carpenter here at twelve.'

'Of course, Dottore.'

Vengefully Carboni slapped the intercom button to the 'off' position, locked his desk and headed for the corridor.

Far out on the Nomentana Nuova, set among the high-rise flats that the planners had dubbed 'popular', shadowed by them, was a simple row of garages of precast concrete with swinging, warped doors. The garages were skirted by waste ground, stray dogs and discarded rubbish. Few were in use as the occupants of the flats found them too far from their front doors and out of sight of their windows, and therefore unsafe from the work of thieves and vandals. The garages were generally deserted and distant from the motion and life of the flats. One was a chosen burrow of an NAP cell, rented through an intermediary not to house a car but to provide storage and meeting space. There were guns here. Pistols and automatic weapons from the factories of countries with widely disparate political creeds. Quarry explosives stolen by sympathizers. Boxes full of car number plates. Sleeping-bags and a camping stove, and the Roneo machine on which the communiqués were run off. None of the possessions of the cell would have been visible if the doors had been carelessly opened because time had been lavished on the garage. If the dirt on the floor were brushed away the outline of a trap door

598

became apparent. They had carved through the cement and underneath had dug out a tomb some two metres wide, two and a half metres long and a metre and a half high. A narrow plumbing pipe to the surface brought air to them. This was the hideaway in times of great danger, and this was where three young men sheltered because it was just a day since La Tantardini had been taken and they had abandoned their safe house. Though she was a leader, who could say whether she would talk to her interrogators? Dark and closed, the pit provided a lair for the men who breathed the damp and must-laden air. There was the son of a banker, the son of a landowner, the son of a Professor of Economics at the University of Trento.

Above them, and muffled through the thickness of the cement, came four sharp raps at the closed wooden doors of the garage. It was a sign they recognized, the signal that a courier had visited them. An envelope had been pushed far from sight under the cover of the doorway, the message it held dispatched four hours earlier from the island of Asinara.

For Tantardini. Reprisal. Number Four.

In the pit among the cell's papers would be the code sheet that would identify Number Four, the target the young men must reach for. They would wait several minutes in the calm of the darkness before levering aside the entrance and crawling upwards to find and read the communication.

Through the morning as the sun rose and blazed with its full force on the tin roof above him they left Harrison to himself. No food, no water, and he hadn't the stomach and courage to call for either. Preferring not to risk another beating, he kept his peace, chained in the oven space that they had chosen for him.

There were pains in many parts of his body, slow and creeping and twisting at the bruised muscle layers. And there was the heat, combining with the welts and bruises to empty his mind, leave his imagination as an unused void.

Deep in sweat, heavy in self-pity, slumped on the hay and straw, conscious of his own rising smells, he ebbed away the hours without hope, without anticipation.

Giancarlo was half asleep, meandering in the demi-state between dream and consciousness, relaxed and settled, the plan in his mind evaluated and approved. Small and lone and hungry for the action he had decided upon, he was sprawled indifferently between the padded seat back and the hard face of the window's glass. The sights beyond the comfort of the speeding train were ignored.

It would be hot that day in Pescara, hot and shrouded in a sea-top mist, and noisy and dusty from the car wheels and the tramping of the thousands who would have come to roast themselves on the thin sand line between promenade and water. The shop would be open and his father wheedling the lady customers. Perhaps his father would know by now, would know of his boy. Perhaps the polizia would have come, pained and apologetic because this was a respectable citizen. His father would curse him, his mother cry in her handkerchief. Would he shut the shop if the polizia came and announced with due solemnity that little Giancarlo was with the NAP and living in a covo with a feared terrorist, the most dangerous woman in the land and their lad cohabiting? They would hate him. Hate him for what he had done to them. And the base rock of their hatred would be their majestic, colossal absence of understanding of why he had taken his road.

Stupid, pathetic, insignificant, little crawling fleas. Giancarlo rolled the words round his tongue. Grovelling servants, in perpetual obeisance to a system that was rotten and outworn. Cowering behind the façade of phoniness. Savagely he recalled the wedding of his elder brother. Hair oil and incense, an intoning doddering priest, a hotel reception on the sea front that neither the groom's nor the bride's father could afford. New suits and hair trims for the men, new dresses for the ladies and jewellery out from the wall safes. An exhibition of waste and deception, and Giancarlo had left early, walked across the evening town and locked himself in his room and lain in the darkness till his father, much later, hammered at the door and shouted of the offence given to aunts and cousins and friends. The boy had despised his father for it, despised him for the chastity-belt of conformity. Governing them was the necessity of normality; the mayor must come to the flat each year, the bishop to the shop, and after Mass in April the shining new BMW must be blessed by the priest and a fee given. They buckled their knees, ran their hands together damp with nervousness when a town hall official visited to safeguard his votes; a rotten little creep with his hand in the till, and they treated him like Christ Almighty. The relationship was past repair. Past patching and bandaging.

The boy mouthed his insults, sometimes aloud, sometimes without sound, working off, as an athlete sheds weight in roadwork, the relaxed rest that had held him during the early hours of the journey. The society of clientilismo; who his father knew in business, had been to school with, was owed a favour by, the way towards a job for a growing boy. The society of the bustarelle; the little envelopes of old banknotes that smoothed and purred their way around the town hall. The society of evasione; avoidance of commitment to the weak, the ethic of selfishness and personal preservation. That was their society and he had vowed that the break was final, and the adhesive quality of family blood was inadequate to change his determination.

600

The train rolled on, Napoli left behind.

A boy who had killed and found it no special experience, who sometimes smiled and sometimes laughed and who had no companion, Giancarlo Battestini on the rapido to Reggio.

The screams of the cleaning woman carried far down the column of the staircase well.

The shrieks brought the day porter of the pensione as fast up the steps as his age and infirmity would permit, and when he arrived panting at the upper landing the woman was still bent to the door keyhole, the clean folded sheets on the floor beneath her feet, her bucket in one hand, her sweeping broom in the other. He had fished the pass key from his pocket, opened the door, taken a cursory look, mouthed a prayer and pushed the woman back from the door. He had locked the room again and without explanation scrambled back down the stairs to raise management and authority.

With sirens and gusto the carabinieri arrived, running from the car, leaving the winking blue light revolving, pacing through the hall in a clatter of heavy boots and pounding on the stairs past the opened rooms of those who had been roused and wondered at the intrusion.

The barest glance at the battered head and the accompanying bloodstains was sufficient to convince the maresciallo that hope of life and survival had long expired. One man he sent to the car to radio for the necessary assistance, another he detailed to stand by the door and prevent entry by the gathering crowd on the landing – salesmen, servicemen on leave and waiting for later trains in the day, and the prostitutes who had kept them company during the night. By the time the maresciallo had found the dead man's identity card there were more sirens in the air, warning all those who heard of further misery, the reckoning time for an unfortunate.

Below on the street, another gathering, few of their faces betraying sympathy. The day porter stood among them, a man much in demand at this time, with the story to tell of what he had seen.

A blue Fiat 132 limousine brought Archie Carpenter from International Chemical Holdings through the old battered dignity of central Rome to the formidable front archway of the Questura. Like a bloody great museum, he'd thought. More churches per square yard than any place he knew, cupolas and domes by the dozen. The history, the markets, the shops, the women, bloody fantastic the whole place. Oozing chic steady class, he'd felt; dirty and sophisticated, filthy and smart. Women with a couple of hundred pounds' worth of summer dress picking their way between the rubbish bags, dogs crapping on the pavements of the High Street; never seen anything like it. And now this place, police headquarters for the city – a great grey stone heap, coated in pigeon dirt. Flag limp and refusing to stir on the pole above him.

He gave Carboni's name at the front desk and showed the official the name written on paper. Had to do that because they'd looked blank when he opened his mouth. But the name seemed to mean something because heels clicked together and there were bows and ushering arms towards the lift.

Archie Carpenter laughed behind his hand. Wouldn't be like this if one of their lot came over to the Yard. Be made to sit down for half an hour while they sorted out his accreditation, checked through to his appointment, made him fill out a form with three carbons. And no chance of getting called 'Dottore', no bloody chance. All a bit strange, but then it had been strange all morning – from the Embassy man who wouldn't talk to the time when he'd gone into an empty office at ICH and dialled the number they'd given him for Violet Harrison.

Yes, he could come round if he wanted to. If there was something that he had to say to her, then he should come round, otherwise she'd be going out. Carpenter had stuck at it. He had to see her, Head Office was particularly keen that he should personally make sure everything possible was being done for her. Well, in that case, she'd said, he'd better come and she wouldn't go out. She'd stay at home. Like she was doing him a favour, and would about six o'clock be right, and they could have a drink.

Well, not what you'd expect, was it, Archie?

Down the corridors they went, Carpenter a pace behind his escort, bisecting the endless central carpet, worn and faded, hearing all about him the slow crack of typewriters, turning his eyes away when two men came out of an office in front and gave each other a big smacker on the cheeks. Round a corner, down another corridor, like a charity hike.

And then he was there. A young man was shaking his hand and prattling in the local and Carpenter was smiling and nodding, catching on with the manners. The inner door of the office burst open.

The man who came through the door was short, grossly overweight but moving with the speed of a crocodile on the scent of fresh meat. Papers and a cassette recorder were gripped in his left hand, the other remained free for waving as a stage prop to the waterfall of words. Carpenter understood not a phrase, stood rooted to the carpet. Both of them hammering away, and at the body work, arms round the shoulders, heads close enough to recognize the toothpaste. Something had gone well. He was acting as if he'd drawn the favourite in the Irish Sweepstake, the little fellow with the big belly.

A change of gear, an effortless switch to English, and, the recorder and paperwork passed to his subordinate, Giuseppe Carboni introduced himself.

'I am Carboni. And you are Carpenter? Good. You come from London, from ICH? Excellent. You come at the right moment. Everything is well. Come into my room.'

Can't be bad, thought Carpenter, and followed the disappearing figure into the inner office, where he looked round him, swayed a bit. Massive and tasteful, furnished and carpeted. Prints on the wall of old Rome, velvet drapes on the windows, a framed portrait of the President on a desk half submerged in an Everest of files. He sat himself down opposite the desk.

'Carpenter, this morning I am proud. This morning I am very happy and I will tell you why . . .'

Carpenter inclined his head, had the routine straight, gave him a flash of teeth. Roll on, let the dam break.

'. . . Let me tell you that from yesterday morning when I first heard of what happened to your Mr Harrison, from the time I first telephoned to the Embassy, this has been a case that has worried and disturbed me. To be frank, there are not many of these kidnappings that greatly affect me. Most of the people who are taken are excessively rich and you will have read of how much money they can pay for their release. And after they have been freed many are investigated with enthusiasm by the Guardia di Finanze, our fiscal police. One wonders how it is, in a modern society, that individuals can legally accumulate such funds, hundreds of thousands of dollars are necessary to win freedom. They give us little help, these people, neither the families during the imprisonment, nor the victim after return. They shut us out so that we must work from the side, from the edge. When our record of arrests is decried, then I sweat, Carpenter, because we work with only one hand free.'

'I understand,' said Carpenter. He had heard this, and it stank and ran against all his police training. Intolerable.

'When it is children, or teenage girls, the innocent parties, then it hurts more. But your Mr Harrison, he is an ordinary businessman, I do not seek to denigrate him, but an ordinary fellow. Not important, not rich, not prepared. The shock for him, the ordeal, may be psychologically catastrophic. You know, Carpenter, I was up half the night worrying about this man . . .'

'Why?' Carpenter cut in, partly from impatience at having the news that provoked the ebullience withheld from him, partly because the syrup was too thick. Benedictine, when he wanted Scotch.

'You laugh at me, you laugh at me because you do not believe I am serious. You have not been a policeman for twenty-eight years in Italy. Had you been, then you would know my feelings. Harrison is clean, Harrison is not tainted, Harrison observes legality. He is in our country

603

as a baby, a baby without clothes, without malice, and he deserves our protection, which is why I work to bring him back.'

'Thank you,' Carpenter spoke with simplicity. He believed he understood and warmed all the time to the barely shaven, perspiring man across the desk from him.

'You have come to supervise the payment of an extraordinary sum for Harrison's release. Why else would you come? . . .'

Carpenter flushed.

'. . . It does not embarrass me, it was my own advice to your Embassy. What I have to tell you is that it may not be necessary. It may not be required.'

The jolt shuddered through Archie Carpenter, straight-backed in his chair, peering forward.

'We try to use modern methods here. We try not to justify the image that you have of us. We do not sleep through the afternoon, we are not lazy and stupid. We have a certain skill, Carpenter. We have the tapes of the telephone calls to Mrs Harrison and to ICH. The computer gobbles them. Then we feed other calls into the machine, from other events. And we have made a match. We have two cases where the contact was from the same man. You understand police work?'

'I did eight years with Special Branch in London, with the Metropolitan Police. What you'd see as the political wing.' Carpenter spoke with a certain pride.

'I know what is Special Branch.'

Carpenter flashed his molars, creased his cheeks.

Carboni acknowledged, then launched himself again. 'So I have a match and that tells me that I am not dealing with a first time out group. I am working against an organization that has been in the field. It tells me a little, it tells me something. Just now I am talking to a man from the office of a business fellow that I have been asked to investigate. You know the situation. Many times when you have my position people come with a whisper for the ear. Look at this man, they say, look at him and think about him. Is everything correct about him? And if he is a Calabrese, if he is from the south and has much cash, then you look closely. I rang the office of a property speculator in Rome this morning, but he is not available, he is away on business. I must speak to his junior.'

Carboni paused, master of theatre, paused and waited while Carpenter willed him on. Seemed to fill his lungs as if the ten minutes of near continuous talk had vacuumed them.

'Carpenter, we need fortune in this business. You know that, we need luck. This morning we have been blessed. You saw me in the office when I hugged that little prig – I detest the man, arrogant and sneering – and I hugged him because to my ear the voice of the man that says his master is in Calabria is the same as that of the man who called the office of Harrison.'

Carpenter bobbed his head in praise. 'Congratulations, sincerely, Mr Carboni, my congratulations. You have a wrap-up.'

'It is not definite, of course. I await the confirmation of the machines.' A coyness across the desk.

'But you have no doubts.'

'In my own mind there are none.'

'I say again, congratulations.'

'But we must move with care and discretion, Carpenter. You understand that we go into surveillance and tapping. Caution is required if we want your Harrison returned . . .'

Sharply, an intrusion on the men's concentration, the telephone rang. Carboni reached for it and even where Carpenter sat he could hear the strident talk. Carboni scribbled on his notepad as the Englishman's excitement dissipated and waned. He had not wanted the spell of success broken and now had to endure interruption of the sweet flow. Carboni had written on and covered two sheets of paper before, without courtesies, he put the telephone down.

'Don't look worried, Carpenter. Complications, yes. But those that thicken the mixture. A man has been found dead in a small hotel close to the railway station. He had been clubbed to death. We have the teleprint of his history. He was held briefly on a kidnapping charge, but the principal witness declined to testify at his trial, the prosecution was lost. He comes from the village of Cosoleto, in the far south, in Calabria. The man that I tried to telephone this morning, he is from that village too. There is a web forming, Carpenter. A web is sticky and difficult to extract from, even for those who have made it.'

'I think you'd prefer that nobody's hopes were raised yet. Not in London, not with the family.'

Carboni shrugged, sending a quiver through his body and eased his fingers through the rare strands of his forehead hair. 'I have given you much in confidence.'

'I'm grateful to you because you've wasted much of your time. If I could see you tomorrow I'd be more than pleased.' Archie rose out of his chair, would love to have stayed because the atmosphere of investigation was infectious, and for too long he had been away from it.

'Come tomorrow at the same time,' said Carboni and laughed, deep and satisfied. The man who has enjoyed a lively whore, spent his money and regretted nothing. 'Come tomorrow and I will have something to tell you.'

'We should put some champagne on ice.' Carpenter trying to match the mood.

'From this morning I don't drink.' Carboni laughed again and gripped Carpenter's hand with the damp warmth of friendship.

*

For two and a half years Francesco Vellosi had accepted the escort of a loaded Alfetta, three men of his own squad always in place behind him as he made the four daily journeys to and from the Viminale and his flat. Sun and frost, summer and winter, they dogged his movements. He had people coming for drinks that evening at home, he told Mauro, with his clipped, even voice. But he would be returning to his desk later. Would Mauro fix the movements and co-ordination of the escort? A flicker of the eyes went with the request.

For Vellosi there was now time for a brief rest before his guests arrived. He would not permit them to stay late, not with the papers piling on his desk. When he was inside his front door and passed to the responsibility of the guard who lived with him, the motor escort withdrew. Because he would later return to his office, there were curses from the men who accompanied him, and who would again suffer a broken evening.

10

The shadows had gone now, called away by the sun that had groped beyond the orange orchard over to his right. The lines had lengthened, reached their extremity and disappeared, leaving in their wake the haze of the first darkness. With their going there was a cold settling fast among the trees and bushes that Giancarlo had taken for his watching place. The building in front of him was no more than a blackened outline, indistinct in shape, difficult to focus on. Around him the noises of the night were mustering, swelling in their competition. The barking of a far distant farm dog, the droning of the bees frantic for a last feed from the wild honeysuckle, the engine drive of the skeleton mosquitoes, the croak of an owl unseen in a high tree. The boy did not move, as if any motion of his body might alert those who he knew stayed unaware and unsuspicious in the barn that was less than a hundred metres from him. This was not the moment to rush forward. Better to let the darkness cling more tightly to the land, throw its blanket more finally across the fields and olive patches and the rock outcrops that were submerging in the dusk. The ideas of Giancarlo convoluted and hesitant when conceived in the rocking pace of the rapido were now near to fulfilment. Wild and ill-thought at their birth, they now seemed to him to own a pattern and a value. Worth a smile, little fox, worth a grin.

*

Unchallenged, he had walked out of the small station with its wide platforms on the Reggio esplanade, gulped at a waft of sea-blown air, and mingled with the stream of descending passengers. If there were watching polizia at the barrier, Giancarlo had not seen them, and there had been no shouted command to halt. He had walked from the station, among the people laden with suitcases and string bags. The snakes of humanity had slithered in their differing directions, splintering again and again till he was alone. In a tabacchi he purchased a map of Calabria. The names were clear and well remembered. Sinopli . . . Delianuova . . . Acquaro . . . Cosoleto. He found them where the red ribbons of the roads began to twist into the uplands of the Aspromonte, beyond the green-shaded coastal strip, far into the deeper sand and brown of the rising ground.

In early afternoon with the time of siesta weighty on the empty streets, Giancarlo found his car. Among the white-washed houses, with the light battering back at his unprotected eyes, parked haphazardly as if the owner were late for an important meeting, not just restless for his lunch. The life of the Mezzo Giorno ruled, the land of the half day. Washing hung down, bleached and stiffened, from the balcony of a house under which was abandoned a red Fiat 127. Right outside the front door, keys in the ignition. Shutters fastened to protect the cool in the interior, not a child crying, not a grandmother complaining, not a radio tuned to music. He slipped into the driving seat, eased off the handbrake and coasted slowly down the incline, waiting till he was clear of the corner before firing the engine.

He headed north for the long viaduct, where the Mafiosi had made their fortunes in extortion from those who needed to move in materials and equipment and found it cheaper to concede the dues than to fight. He drove slowly because that was the style of the Calabrian after lunch and his need to avoid drawing attention was as acute as ever. His face was sufficient of a problem, white with the pallor of prison and confinement in the covo; not the complexion of the south, not the burned and dark wood tan of those who owned this country. He drifted past the turn-off signs to Gallico and Carnitello, and climbed high with the road above the sea channel that separated the Sicilian island from the mainland. For a moment he slowed and stared hard away to his left, his gaze held on the sprawl of Messina away across the azure of the water.

Messina, blurred and indistinct, lay white in the sun among the spreading green and rust of parks and waste ground. Messina, where they had built the gaol for the girls. This was where they had taken La Vianale, where Curcio's Nadia had waited for her trial, where if he did not succeed his Franca would decay and crumble. He could not see the prison, not across eight kilometres of reflecting sea, but it was there, a spur and a goad.

The car increased speed. Past the road on the left to Scilla, and on the right to Gambarie. Through the booming length of rock-cut tunnels, and on into the interior. Sinopli and Delianuova were signed to the right and he pulled the little Fiat off the dual carriageway and started the winding negotiation of the hill road. Through Santa Eufemia d'Aspromonte, a barren and meagre community where his coming scattered only the chickens feeding in the road gravel, and his going raised barely an eyebrow of attention from the elderly who sat in black skirts and suits in front of their homes. Through Sinopli where he hooted for the right to pass a bus that struggled in an exhaust cloud on the main street, and where the shops were still padlocked, and it was too hot, too sickly clammy for the ragazzi to have brought out their plastic footballs.

Bitter country now. Laden with rock and precipice, covered with the toughened scrub and trees that grew from little earth. In low gear, rising and descending, Giancarlo drove on, till he was over the old and narrow stone bridge across the Vasi, and into Acquaro. Perhaps some saw him go through the village but he was unaware of them, studying by turns the map laid out on the front passenger seat, and the perils of the curving route. A half-kilometre further, he stopped. There was a lay-by, and a heap of gravel where the workmen would come in the winter when there was ice to make the road safe for motorists. Further back was a turn-in among the trees where perhaps the hunting parties parked their cars on Sundays or the young men took the virgins when they could no longer suffer the claustrophobia of the family in the front room and the watch of the Madonna above the fireplace. Giancarlo grinned to himself. Wrong day for hunters, too early in the evening for virgins. This was a place for him to park hidden from the road. He drove as far between the trees as the track permitted.

From habit, in the quiet of his seat, Giancarlo checked over the P38, stroked its silk barrel length, and wiped on his shirt waist the faint stains on the handle. Eight bullets only, eight to do so much with. He climbed lightly from the car, eased the pistol back into his belt and was lost in the close foliage.

He skirted the road, leaving it what he judged to be a hundred metres on his left, seeking the thickness of the wood, easing on to the toes of his canvas shoes, thankful for the cover. It took him only a few minutes before he found the vantage point for the once-white house from which paint and plaster alike peeled, served by a rutted track. A hovel to Giancarlo, a place for sheep and cows. Medieval, had it not been for the car parked outside the only door. This was the home of a contadino, a peasant; and his wife moved beside the building with a bucket, and his half-clothed children played with a spar of wood. The boy settled himself comfortably on the mould of generations of fallen leaves and watched and waited for the brother of the wife of Claudio.

Not long. Not long enough to try him.

A big man, balding above a flat weatherbeaten forehead. Cheeks that were not shaved, trousers that were held at the waist with string, a shirt that was torn at the armpit. Contadino, Giancarlo spat the word. But of the proletariat, surely? He smiled mirthlessly. A servant of the bosses . . . ? The boy agreed, satisfied in the ideology equation. The man carried a plastic bag and walked down the track from his house to the road, paused there and his eyes traversed a sweep that covered the boy's hide. The man had passed close to where Giancarlo lay before his sounds subsided. Like a stoat, Giancarlo was after him, ears cocked and attuned to the distant noises in front, eyes fastened on the dried twigs and oak leaves that he must not break nor displace.

The tree line covered the rim of a slight hill, beyond it was a roughened field indented from the cattle's wet spring grazing. On the far side of the open ground Giancarlo saw the stone-built barn with its rain-reddened tin roof and two doors facing him. The man he had followed was met by one who had come from the right-hand door and who carried a single-barrelled shotgun, the weapon of the country people. They talked a brief discourse, before the bag was handed over and a gust of laughter carried to the boy. As the man retraced his steps, Giancarlo melted among the trees and undergrowth, unseen, unheard.

When it was safe he came slowly forward to the dry stone wall that skirted the field, and picked his watching place. A boundless pride swept through him. He wanted to stand up and shout defiance and exultation. Giancarlo Battestini, remember the name, because he had found the Englishman of the multinationals, and would exploit him, as the foreign companies exploited the proletariat.

Later Giancarlo would begin his advance, edge closer to the building. Later. Now was the time for him to rest, and to relax if that were possible. And to dream . . . and the images of the thighs, warm and muscled in moisture, and of the curling growth and the breasts where his head had lain blasted and echoed through his mind. Alone on the ground, the myriad earth creatures converging on him, he shuddered and knew he would not sleep.

Archie Carpenter had been shown round the flat. He'd made the right noises and stood hesitantly at the bedroom door casting a quick eye over the wide pink coverlet, studied the wall pictures, paced the corridors with his hands joined behind his back in the pose of Royal males factory-visiting, and expressed his opinion as to what a fine place it was. She was a queer one, this Violet Harrison, making it all seem so natural as she marched him over the marble floors, pointing to this and that, offering the limited history of the furniture. She'd poured him a drink. Gin with hardly enough tonic to notice, and splashed some ice cubes in. And he'd seen her hand shaking, rocking like a sick man's and he'd known it was all a damn great sham. All the poise, all the silly chat, just a counterfeit. That's when the sympathy had started to roll, watching the trembling fist and the way the finger talons clutched at the bottle.

Loose and slim in the full flow of her dress, she sat on a sofa, the shape and form projecting without angular emphasis. The sort of woman you could take to your chest, Archie, sort of nuzzle against, and it would be all soft and wouldn't hurt anywhere. He wasn't looking at her eyes when he started to speak, just at the cleavage, where the freckles ran down. His suit was tight and hot and too thick for Roman summer. Bloody strange dress she'd put on for a time like this.

'You have to know, Mrs Harrison, that the company are doing all they can to get Geoffrey back to you. As quickly as humanly possible he'll be home again.'

'That's very kind,' she said, and her words were not easy to follow; it wasn't the first drink she'd had that day. You don't have to stand up like a preacher, Archie, and tell people how to behave and conduct themselves, not when their whole world's falling in.

'Everything possible,' Carpenter hurtled on. 'The Board will rubber-stamp the Managing Director's decision to pay. He wants you to know that the company will pay whatever is required to get your husband back. There's nothing on that count for you to worry about.'

'Thank you,' she said. Raised her eyebrows at him as if trying to show how impressed she was that the Board should make such a commitment.

Bloody marvellous, he thought. What a pair, and not a trace of sweat on her where the neckline cut down and him dripping wet like a horse at the Derby finish. 'There's not a great deal that we can do at the moment, but your husband's colleagues at ICH in Rome are geared to take calls, and make the financial arrangements. It'll probably all be outside the country, which makes it smoother.' He paused, drank it all in, watched the shift of the material as she crossed her legs. 'But you have to soldier on for a bit, Mrs Harrison, for quite a few days. It takes time, this sort of thing, we cannot settle it in a matter of hours.'

'I understand that, Mr Carpenter.'

'You're taking it very well.'

'I'm just trying to go on as I usually would, as if Geoffrey were away on a business trip, something like that.' She leaned forward slightly in her chair.

What to say now, what ground to stumble over? Carpenter swallowed. 'Was there anything you wanted, anything I could help with?'

'I doubt it, Mr Carpenter.'

'It may take a few days, but we're working on two fronts. We can pay, that's no problem. At the same time the police are co-operating and have a major and discreet recovery effort underway, they have their best men on the case and . . .'

'I don't really need to know that, do I?' she asked quietly.

Carpenter bridled. 'I thought you'd want to hear what was happening.' Cool it, Archie, she's under stress. A brave front and damn-all underneath.

'So what you're offering me is that after a week or two I'll know whether Geoffrey is going to walk through the door, or whether I'm never going to see him again.'

'I think we should look on the bright side of things, Mrs Harrison.' Out of training, Archie. Bloody years since he'd been a beat copper in uniform and knocking on doors with a solemn face to tell the wife that her old man's come off his motor-bike and if she doesn't hurry she'll see him in the hospital chapel.

She seemed to sag, and the tears came, and then the deeper sobs, and the protest in the choked voice. 'You don't know anything. Nothing at all . . . Mister bloody Carpenter. You treat me like a bloody child . . . Let's all have a drink, let's believe it isn't for real . . . What do you know about this place, sweet fuck-all of nothing . . . You don't know where my husband is, you don't know how to get him back. All you talk about is "everything possible", and "major effort", "best men on the case". It's just bloody bromide, Mister bloody Carpenter . . .'

'That's not fair, Mrs Harrison, and don't swear at me . . .'

'And don't you come marching in here oozing your platitudes, telling me everything is going to be marvellous . . .'

'Too bloody right I won't. There's people that don't know when someone's trying to help them.' Carpenter's voice rose, his neck flushed. He pushed himself up from the seat, gulping at the remains of his drink. 'When someone comes and tries to give a hand there's no call for foul language.' He couldn't get smoothly out of his chair, couldn't make a quick and decent exit with dignity. By the time he was on his feet she was between him and the door and the tears were wet on her face, gleaming in the sheen of her make-up.

'I think I'd better go,' he said, mumbling his words, conscious of his failure to complete his task.

She stood very close to him, barring his way, a frail little thing for all the bravura of her language and looked straight into his face. Her head was turned up towards him, with a small, neat mouth, and her arms hung inert down to her hips.

'I think I'd better go . . . don't you? I don't think I can help any more.'

'If you think you ought to.' Brown hazel eyes, deep-set and misted, and around them the morass of freckles that he followed the patterns of, followed where they led.

'Geoffrey's bloody useless, you know.' Her hand came up, wiping hastily across her face, smudged the cosmetic grease, and the smile was there again. Curtained herself from him, just as she had done when she showed him round the flat, taken a public stance. There was a little

611

laugh, bright in his ear. 'I'm not shocking you, am I, Mr Carpenter? Quite bloody useless, to me anyway. I don't mean to shock you, but people ought to understand each other. Don't you think so?'

One hand was sliding under his jacket, fingers rifling at the damp texture of his shirt, the other played at the uppermost buttons of her dress.

'Don't let's mess about, Mr Carpenter. You know the geography of this flat, you know where my room is. Oughtn't you be taking me there now?' Her nails dug into the small of his back, a small bone button slipped from its hole, the spirals of excitement climbed at his spine. 'Come on, Mr Carpenter. You can't do anything for Geoffrey, I can't do anything for Geoffrey, so let's not pretend. Let's pass the time.' There was pressure on his back ribs, drawing him closer, the mouth and the pink painted lips mesmerizing him. He could smell her breath, could smell that she smoked, but she must have used toothpaste just before he came, peppermint toothpaste.

'I can't stay,' Carpenter said, a hoarseness at his throat. Out of his depth, wallowing in deep water, and not a life-raft in bloody miles. 'I can't stay, I have to go.'

The hands abandoned his back and the buttons and she stepped aside to leave him space to pass into the hall.

'No hesitations, Mr Carpenter?' she murmured behind him. He was fiddling with the door locks, anxious to be on his way and therefore hurrying and in the process slowing himself; the man who is impatient and cannot unfasten a brassiere strap. 'No second thoughts?'

Teased, bowed by a shame that he could not recognize as coming from either inadequacy or morality, Archie Carpenter, nine-to-fiver, opt-out from the grown-up world, finally opened the door.

'You're a boring bastard, Mr Carpenter,' she called after him. 'A proper little bore. If you're the best they can send to get my husband out, then God help the poor darling.'

The door slammed. He didn't wait for the lift, but took the stairs two at a time.

In pre-war Rome the fascist administration sometimes ordered the lights of the principal government offices to be left burning long after the bureaucracy had gone to their trams and buses; a grateful population would believe that the State was working late and be impressed. The spirit of such deception had long since passed and the prevailing dictates of austerity decreed that unnecessary lights should be extinguished. Giuseppe Carboni was one of only a very few who worked late into that night in the shadowed sepulchre of the Questura. By telephone he had indefinitely postponed his dinner at home as he put off and avoided the anathema of communication with the force that he saw as his principal rival, the para-military carabinieri. The polizia and carabinieri existed, at best, as uneasy bedfellows between the communal sheets of law and order. Competition was fierce and jealous; the success of either was trumpeted by its senior officers, and a weak executive power was satisfied that neither should become overpowerful. A recipe for inefficiency, and a safeguard against the all-encompassing police state power that Italy had laboured under for twenty-one years.

Carboni's problem, and it had taken him many hours to resolve it in his mind, was whether or not he should place in the lap of the opposition his information on the speculator Mazzotti. The man was in the far south, apparently at the village of Cosoleto and beyond the striking and administrative range of the polizia at the Calabrian capital of Reggio. Cosoleto would come under the jurisdiction of the carabinieri at the small town of Palmi, his maps showed him that. His option was to allow the man Mazzotti to return from Calabria to the Roman district, where he would again be liable to police investigation. But if the gorilla Claudio were linked to the kidnapping of the Englishman Harrison, then the report of his killing in Rome would serve only to alert those involved. For another few hours, perhaps, the name of the dead man could be suppressed, but not beyond the dawn of the next day. It was immaterial at whose hand the strong man had met his death; sufficient for Carboni that it would be enough to set into play the fall-back plans of the kidnap group. It was not possible for him to delay in his action, but if he acted now, made a request for help that were successful, then what credit would be laid at the door of Giuseppe Carboni? Trivial plaudits, and victim and criminals in the hands of the black-uniformed carabinieri.

Enough to make a man weep.

He broke the pledge of the morning and poured himself a Scotch from his cabinet, the bottle reserved for times of celebration and black depression, then placed the call to Palmi. Just this once he would do the right deed, he promised himself, just this once break the habit of a professional lifetime.

When the call came the static was heavy on the line, and Carboni's voice boomed through the quiet offices and out through the opened doors into the emptied corridors of the second floor of the Questura. Many times he was obliged to repeat himself to the carabinieri capitano, as he was urged to great explanation. He stressed the importance of the Harrison affair, the concern in the matter of high administrative circles in Rome. Twice the capitano had demurred; the action suggested was too delicate for his personal intervention, the Mazzotti family were of local importance, should there not be authorization from the examining magistrate? Carboni had shouted louder, bellowed bull-like into the telephone. The matter could not wait for authorization, the situation was too fluid to be left till the morning appearance of the magistrate in his office. Perhaps the very vehemence impressed the carabinieri officer, perhaps the dream of glory that might be his. He acquiesced. The home of Antonio Mazzotti would be placed under surveillance from three o'clock in the morning. He would be arrested at eight.

'And be careful. I want no suspicions, I want no warnings given to this bastard,' Carboni yelled. 'A little mistake and my head is hanging. You understand? Hanging on my belly. You have the man Mazzotti in the cells at Palmi and I'll be with the magistrate by nine, and have him brought to Rome. You will reap full praise for your initiative and flexibility and co-operation; it won't be forgotten.'

The capitano expressed his gratitude to the Dottore.

'Nothing, my son, nothing. Good luck.'

Carboni put the telephone down. There was a black sheen on the handpiece and with his shirt cuff he smeared the moisture from his forehead. Rome in high summer, an impossible place to work. He locked his desk, switched off his desk light and headed for the corridor. For a man so gross in stomach and thighs there was something of a spring in his step. The scent sharp in the nose of the professional police-man. The old one, the one above pride and expediency. Time to go home to his supper and his bed.

Uncomfortable, irritated by the sharpness of the hay strands, impeded by the wrist manacle, Geoffrey Harrison had been denied the relief of sleep. They left no light for him, and the darkness had come once the slanting sun shafts no longer bored through the old nail holes of the roof. A long darkness, aggravated by the absence of food. A punishment, he thought, a punishment for kicking the bucket over them. As if the beating wasn't enough. His belly ached and groaned out loud in its deprivation.

He lay full length on his back, the chain allowing his right arm to drop loosely on the hay beside his body. Still and inert, occasionally dozing, eking out minutes and hours and not knowing nor caring of their passage.

The voices of his guards were occasional and faint through the thick-ness of the dividing wall of the barn. Indistinct at best and punctuated by laughter and then loud silence. Little he heard of them, and since one had walked heavily outside the building and urinated with force there had been nothing. His concentration was sharpened by the whisper of the scurrying feet of rats and mice who had made their nests in the gaps between the hay bales under him. Little bastards, eating and crap-ping and copulating and spewing out their litters, performing their func-tions of limited life a few feet below his backside. He wondered what they made of the smell and presence close to their heartland, whether they'd summon the courage or curiosity to investigate the intruder. Each movement of the rodents he heard; the vibrations of the small feet, frantic as they went about their business. Perhaps there would be bats tonight; there might have been last night but the sleep had been too great, too thick for him to have noticed. All the phobias, all the hates and fears of bats rushed past him so that he could examine and analyse the folklore – the scratchers, the tanglers, the disease-carriers . . .

And there was a new sound.

Harrison stiffened where he lay. Rigid now on his back. Fingers clenched. Eyes peering upward into the unbroken darkness.

A footfall beyond the side wall away from where his guards rested.

Frightened to move, frightened to breathe, Harrison listened.

A soft-soled shoe eased on to the dirt and mess beyond the wall. A step taken slowly as if the ground were being tested before the weight of a man was committed.

A tree brushing with a laden branch against the coarse granite stone, sweeping across it with the gentle motion of the night wind – that Harrison could identify, that was not what he had heard. An outside man, a stranger was coming silently and in stealth to the barn, without warning, without announcement. A person had come before the sun had set and had called from some way off and there had been greetings and conversation. This was not as then.

Another footstep.

Clearer this time, as if nerve and caution were failing, as if impetuosity and impatience were rising. Harrison willed him forward. Anyone who came with the hush of feet on the tinder grass and the scraping stones, anyone who came with such secrecy had no love nor friendship for the men who waited in the far room of the barn.

Cruel and mocking came the long void of silence unbroken to Harrison's alert ears.

Each noise of the night available to him he rejected because the sounds he searched for were lost. The last footstep had been clear, and perhaps the man had taken fright and would stay still and listen before he came on. The perspiration invaded Harrison's body, floating to the crevices of his body. Who was it who had come? Who would travel to this place?

A shatter of noise, a warning shout, a blasting pistol shot, ripped an echo through the space under Harrison's low ceiling.

In the half light from the storm lamp set low, Giancarlo saw the man nearest him pitch forward, the cry in his throat destroyed. For a moment he caught the reflection of the eyes of a second man, a rabbit's in headlights, and then a stool careered in the air towards him and his

615

ducking weave was enough to take the force of the blow on his shoulder, and to distort his gathering aim. Like a huge shadow the man dived against the wall, but his movements were sluggish and terrorized and without hope. Giancarlo had time before the man reached the shortened shotgun. He held the P38 close with his two fists, cursed as the barrel wavered and the ache sagged in his upper arm. The man stole a last glance at him, without hope of salvation and reached the last inches for the shotgun. Giancarlo fired, two shots for certainty into the target that sank to the earth floor.

Harrison heard the answering whimper, a moan of supplication, perhaps a prayer, before a choked sob sliced it to silence.

He was frozen still, unmoving, uncomprehending.

The leaning door, old and protesting on its hinges, was opened beneath him; the chain was tight between his arm and the roof denying him escape. What in God's name happens now? This was not the noise the police would have made. Not the way it would have been if they were here. There would have been voices all round and shouts and commands and organization. Only the door below him, deep in the darkness, being prised open.

His name was called.

''Arrison, 'Arrison.'

Difficult for him to register it at first. Slow and tentative, almost a request.

'Where are you, 'Arrison?'

A young voice, nervous. A young Italian. They could never get their tongues round his name, not in the office, not at business meetings, not in the shops when he was out with Violet. The fear swelled inside him, the child that lies in the blackness and hears a stranger come. To answer or not, to identify or to remain silent. Pulsing through him, the dangers of the unknown.

'Where are you, 'Arrison? Speak, tell me where you are, 'Arrison.'

His reply was involuntary, blurted out, made not because he had worked out the answers but because there was a plea for response and he had no longer the strength to resist.

'Up here. I am up here.'

'I am coming, 'Arrison.' Heavy in the stumbled English was the tinge of pride. The door scraped across the floor, the caution of the footsteps was abandoned. 'There are more of them, 'Arrison? There were two. Are there more?'

'Just two, there were only two.'

He heard the sound of the ladder thudding into position against the hay wall, and the noise was fierce as the feet came against the rungs.

'Come down quickly, we should not stay here.'

'They have me by a chain, I cannot move.' Would the stranger understand, would his English be competent? 'I am a prisoner here.' Harrison slid into the staccato language of the foreigner, believing that was how his own tongue was best understood.

Two hands clawed at his feet and he could make out the slight silhouette of a man rising towards him. He cringed backwards.

'Don't fear me. Don't be afraid, 'Arrison.' A soft little voice, barely out of school, with the grammar fresh from the reading primers. The fingers, cruising and exploratory, reached along the length of his body. Across Harrison's thigh, scratching at his waist, onwards and upwards to the pit of his arm and then away out past his elbow to the wrist and the steel grip of the handcuff. A cigarette lighter flicked on, wavering and scarcely effective. But from the kernel of light Geoffrey Harrison could distinguish the face and features of the boy beneath the short-thrown shadows. Unshaven, pallid, eyes that were alive and burned bright. A shape to marry to the garlic smell of bread and salad sandwiches.

'Take it.'

An order and the lighter was directed towards Harrison's free hand.

'Turn your face away.'

Harrison saw the shadowed pistol drawn, squat and revolting, a macabre toy. He bucked his head away as the gun was raised and held steady. Squinted his eyes shut, forced them closed. Tearing at his ears was the noise of the gun, wrenching at his wrist the drag of the chain. The pain burned in the muscle socket of his shoulder, but when his arm swung back to his side it was free.

'It is done,' the boy said, and there was the trace of a smile, sparse and cold in the flame of the lighter. He pulled at Harrison's hand, led him towards the ladder. It was a cumbersome descent because Harrison nursed his shoulder, and the boy's hands were occupied with the gun and the flick lighter. The pressed earth of the floor was under Harrison's feet and the grip on his arm constant as he was led towards the opaque moon haze of the doorway. They stopped there and the fingers slipped to his wrist and there was a sharp heave at the bullet-broken handcuff ring. A light clatter on the ground.

'The men, those who were watching me . . . ?'

'I killed them.' The face invisible, the information inconsequential.

'Both of them?'

'I killed the two of them.'

Out in the night air, Harrison shuddered as if the damp loose on his forehead were frozen. The waft of fresh wind caught at his hair and flipped it from his eyes. He stumbled on a rock.

'Who are you?'

'It is not of concern to you.'

617

The grip on his wrist was tight and decisive. Harrison remembered the fleeting sight of the pistol. He allowed himself to be dragged away across the uneven, thistled grass of the field.

The eyewitnesses to the attack melted and died from the pavement with the wailing approach of the ambulance sirens. Few would stay to offer their account and their names and addresses to the investigating police. Out in the middle of the road, slewed at right angles to the two traffic flows, was the ambushed Alfa of Francesco Vellosi. Mauro, the driver, lay, death pale across his steering-wheel, his head close to the holed and frosted windscreen. Alone in the back, half down on the floor was Vellosi, both hands clamped on his pistol and unable to stifle the trembling that invaded his body. The door of reinforced armour plate had saved him. Above his scalp the back passenger windows, for all their strengthening, were a kaleidoscope of reflected colours amid the fractured glass splinters. So fast, so vivid, so terrifying, had been the moment of assault. After eight years in the Squadro Anti-Terrorismo, eight years of standing and looking at cars such as his, at bodies such as Mauro's, yet no real knowledge had accrued of how the moment would find him. Everything he could previously have imagined of the experience was inadequate. Not even in the war, in the sand dunes of Sidi Barrani under the artillery of the English, had there been anything as overwhelming as the trapped rat feeling in the closed car with the sprays of automatic fire beating over his head.

The escort car had locked its bonnet under the rear bumper of Vellosi's vehicle. Here they had all survived and now they were scattered with their machine-pistols. One in cover behind the opened front passenger door. One away in a shop doorway. The third man in Vellosi's guard stood erect in the middle of the street, lit by the high lights, his gun cradled and ready and pointing to the tarmac lest the prone figures should rise and defy the blood trails and the gaping intestinal wounds and offer again a challenge.

Only when the street was busy with police did Vellosi unlock his door and emerge. He seemed old, almost senile, his steps laboured and heavy.

'How many of them do we have?' he called across the street to the man who had been his shadow and guard these three years, whose wife cooked for him, to whose children he was a godfather.

'There were three, capo. All dead. They stayed beyond their time. When they should have run they stayed to make certain of you.'

He walked into the lit centre of the street and his men hurried to close around him, wanting him gone, but reading his mood and unwilling to confront it. He stared down into the faces of the boys, the ragazzi,

618

grotesque in their angles with the killing weapons close to their fists, only the agony left in their eyes, the hate fled and gone. His eyes closed and his cheek muscles hardened as if he summoned strength from a distant force.

'The one there –' he pointed to a shape of denim jeans and a blood-flawed shirt. 'I have met that boy. I have eaten at his father's house. The boy came in before we sat down at dinner. His father is a banker, the Director of the Contrazzioni Finanziarie of one of the banks in the Via del Corso. I know that boy.'

He turned reluctantly from the scene, dawdling, and his voice was raised and carried over the street and the pavement and to the few who had gathered and watched him. 'The bitch Tantardini, spitting her poison over these children. The wicked, contaminating bitch.'

Hemmed in on the back seat of his escort car, Francesco Vellosi left for his desk at the Viminale.

11

With the headlight beams flashing back from the roadside pine trees, hurling aside the startled shadows, the little two-door Fiat ground its way into the inky night leaving behind the cluster of the Cosoleto lights. Giancarlo forced the motor hard, regardless of the howling tyres, the crack of the fast-changed gears and the drift of Harrison's shoulders against his own. His purpose now was to be rid of the vacuum of the darkened roads and fields, the silhouetted trees, and the lonely farm-houses. He was a town boy and nurtured the urban fear of the wide spaces of the country where familiarity was no longer governed by a known street corner, a local shop, or a towering cement landmark.

He drove on the narrow road to Seminara scarcely aware of the silent man beside him, contemplating perhaps the gun that rested on the shelf of the open glove compartment. The P38, ready and willing even though its magazine had been rifled in the barn, still with sufficient cartridges in its bowels to remain lethal. Through Melicucca where the town was asleep, where men and women had taken to their early beds heavy with the wine of the region, the weight of the food and the condemnation of the priest for late hours. Through Melicucca and beyond before even the lightest sleepers could have turned and wondered at the speed of the car that violated the quiet of their night. He turned sharp left at Santa Anna because that was the route to the coast and the main road.

And the task was only begun. Believe that, Giancarlo. The starting

619

of a journey. The pits, the swamps, all ahead, all gathering, all conglomerating. They are nothing, the boy said soundlessly to himself. Nothing. He slowed as they came to Seminara. A town where people might still be alert, where his caution must be exercised. He'd studied the map in the field near the barn, knew the town had one street; the mayor's office would be there.

A formidable building it was, but decayed and in need of money for repair. Heavy doors tight shut. Sandwiched between lesser constructions and close to the central piazza. Illuminated by the street lights. He braked, and the man beside him lunged forward with his hands to break an impact.

'Get out of the car,' Giancarlo said. 'Get out of the car and put your hands on the roof. And stand still, because the gun watches you.'

Harrison climbed out, his shoulder still paining, did what he was told to do.

Giancarlo watched him straighten, flex himself, and shake his head as if internal dispute had been resolved. He wondered whether Harrison would run, or whether he was too confused to act. He held the gun in his hand, not with aggression but with the warning implicit. He would see the P38 and he would not play the idiot. The movements on the pavement of the Englishman were sluggish, those of a netted carp after a protracted struggle. He would have few problems with this man. From the shelf he took a pencil and a scrap of paper on which had been written on one side the petrol purchases and additions of the car's owner.

'We will not be long, 'Arrison. Stand still because it is not sensible that you move. Afterwards it will all be explained.'

There was no response from the sagging trousers that he could see against the opened door. He began to write with the bold flourished hand that had been taught him by a teacher at the Secondary School of Pescara who prided herself on copperplate neatness. The words came quickly to the paper. There had been time enough on the train to formulate the demand that he would make.

Communiqué 1 of the Nuclei Armati Proletaria.

We hold prisoner the English multinational criminal, Geoffrey Harrison. All those who work for the multinational conspiracy, whether Italian or foreigners, are exploiters of the proletarian revolution, and are the opponents of the aspirations of the workers. The enemy Harrison is now held in a People's Prison. He will be executed at 09.00 CET, the 27th of this month, the day after tomorrow, unless the prisoner of war held in the regime concentration camp, Franca Tantardini, has been freed and flown out of Italy. There will be no further communiqués, no further warnings. Unless Tantardini is freed from her torture the sentence will be carried out without mercy.

620

In memory of Panicucci.
Victory to the proletariat. Victory to the workers. Death and defeat to the borghese, the capitalists and the multinationalists.
Nuclei Armati Proletaria.

Giancarlo read over his words, screwing his eyes at the paper in the dim light. As Franca would have wanted it. She would be satisfied with him, well satisfied.

"Arrison, do you have any paper, something that identifies you? An envelope, a driving licence?' He thrust the gun forward so that the weight of his message would be augmented, and accepted the thin hip wallet in return. Money there, but he ignored it, and drew out the plastic folder of credit cards. Eurocard, American Express, Diners Club. American Express was the one he coveted.

'Perhaps you will get it back at sometime, 'Arrison. With this paper push it under the door. It is important for you that it is found early in the morning. Push it carefully and the card with it, that too is important.'

Giancarlo folded the sheet of paper and wrote on the outside leaf in large capitals the letters of the symbol of the Nappisti. He handed the paper and the credit card to his prisoner and watched him bend to slide the two under the main door to the office of the mayor of Seminara.

'You will drive now, 'Arrison, and you will be careful because I am watching you, and because I have the gun. I have killed three men to come this far, you should know that.'

Giancarlo Battestini slid across into the passenger seat, vacating the driver's place for Geoffrey Harrison. Their stop in the centre of Seminara had delayed them little more than three minutes.

In the rhythm of driving, the numbing shock wore away, chipped from the mind of Geoffrey Harrison.

Neither attempted conversation, leaving Harrison free to absorb himself in the driving while in the darkness beside him the boy wrestled with the map folds and plotted their route and turnings. As the minutes went by the doldrums cleared from Harrison's thoughts. No explanation yet from the boy, everything left unsaid, unamplified. But he felt that he understood everything, had been given the signs which he now used as the text book of his assessment. The way the hand had gripped his wrist, that told him much, told him he was incarcerated and under guard. The pistol told him more, evidence of lightning attack, of a ferocity of purpose. There was the warning too, the warning in Seminara, spoken as if it were meant kindly. 'I have killed three men to come this far.' Three men dead that Harrison should drive in the warm night past signposts to towns he had not heard of, along the light-constricted visions of a road he had never before travelled on. A prisoner a second time. A hostage with a dropped note setting out terms of release.

Yet he felt no fear of the gun and the youth with the bowed head beside him, because the capacity for terror had been exhausted. Devoid of impatience, he would wait for the promised explanation. Out beyond Laureana, racing alongside the dried-out river bed, Harrison forced the Fiat 127 away from the memories of the barn at Cosoleto and the men with their hoods and kicking boots and fouled shirts. Hours more till dawn, he reckoned. He had no complaint, only a dulled brain that was exerted by the need to hold the car on the road, the dipped lights on the verge. Only rarely did his attention waver, and when he turned he saw that the boy sat with his arms folded and that the pistol was cupped by an elbow and the barrel faced the space beneath his armpit.

An hour down the road from Seminara, past the sign to Pizzo, the silence broke. 'You don't have a cigarette, do you?' Harrison asked.

'I have only a very few.'

Frank enough, thought Harrison, marking the bloody card. 'I haven't had one for a couple of days you know. I'd really like one.'

'I have only a very few,' the boy repeated.

Harrison kept his eyes on the road. 'I don't ask what the hell's going on, I don't throw a fit. I wait to be told all about it in your own good sweet time. All I do is ask for a cigarette . . .'

'You speak too fast for me, I do not understand.'

Hiding, the little bastard, behind the language.

'I just said that perhaps we could share a cigarette.'

'What do you mean?'

'I mean I could smoke it, and you could smoke it, and as we were doing that you could talk to me.'

'We could both smoke the cigarette?'

'I've no known disease.'

The boy reached into the breast pocket of his shirt, reluctant as a bloody Fagin, and from the corner of his eye Harrison saw the red packet emerge. Tight, wasn't he? Not what you'd call the generous type, not like you've hit one of the big spenders of whatever creepy scene this kid owned. Inside the car there was the flash of the igniting lighter, then the slow glow of the cigarette burning, tantalizing and close to him.

'Thank you.' Harrison spoke out clearly.

The boy passed the cigarette. First contact, first humanity. Harrison wrapped his lips on the filter end, pulled hard into his lungs and eased his foot on the accelerator.

'Thank you.' Harrison spoke with feeling and nicotine smoke eddied inside the car's confines. 'Now it's your turn. There'll be nothing funny, I'll keep going, but it's you for the talking. Right?'

Harrison looked quickly away from the road's illuminated markers and the direction lines, gave himself time to absorb the furrow of frown and concentration on the boy's face.

'You should just drive,' and there was the first simmering of hostility.

'Give me the cigarette again, please.' It was passed to him; one desperate intake, like the swill minutes in the pub back in England when the beers are on the counter and the landlord's calling for empty glasses. 'What's your name?'

'Giancarlo.'

'And your other name, what's that, Giancarlo?' Harrison spoke as if the question were pure conversation, as if the answer carried only trivial importance.

'You have no need to know that.'

'Please yourself. I'll call you Giancarlo. I'm Geoffrey . . .'

'I know what your name is. It is 'Arrison. I know your name.'

Brutal going. Like running up a bloody sandhill. Remember the shooter, if you don't want the ketchup running out of your armpit.

'How far are you going to want me to drive, Giancarlo?'

'You must drive to Rome.' Uncertainty in the boy's voice. Unwilling to be pulled through the wet clothes wringer with his plan.

'How far's Rome?'

'Perhaps eight hundred kilometres.'

'Jesus . . .'

'You will drive all the time. We will only stop when the day comes.'

'It's a hell of a way. Aren't you taking a turn?'

'I watch you, and the gun watches you. Eh, 'Arrison.' The boy mocked him.

'I'm not forgetting the gun, Giancarlo. Believe me, I'm not forgetting it.' Start again, try another route, Geoffrey. 'But you're going to have to talk to me, otherwise I'll be asleep. If that happens it's the ditch for all of us. Harrison, Giancarlo and his pistol, all going to be wrapped round the ditch. We're going to have to find something to talk about.'

'You are tired?' A query. Anxiety. Something not considered.

'Not exactly fresh.' Harrison allowed a flicker of sarcasm. 'We should talk, about yourself for starters.'

The car bounced and veered on the uneven road surface. Even the autostrada, the pride of a motoring society, was in a creeping state of disrepair. The last time the section had been resurfaced the contractor had paid heavily in contributions to the men in smart suits who interested themselves in such projects. For the privilege of moving machines and men into the district he had cut hard into his profit margins. Economies had been made in the depth of the newly laid tarmac which the winter rains had bitten. Harrison clung to the wheel.

'I told you my name is Giancarlo.'

'Right.' Harrison did not turn from the windscreen and the road in

623

front. The smells of the two mingled closely till they were inseparable, unifying them.

'I am nineteen years old.'

'Right.'

'I am not from these parts, nor from Rome.'

No need any more for Harrison to respond. The flood-gates were breaking and the atmosphere in the little car ensured it.

'I am a fighter, 'Arrison. I am a fighter for the rights and aspirations of the proletariat revolution. In our group we fight against the corruption and rottenness of our society. You live here and you know what you see with your eyes, you are a part of the scum, 'Arrison. You come from the multinational, you control workers here, but you have no commitment to the Italian workers. You are a leech to them.'

Try and comprehend him, Geoffrey, because it's not the time for argument.

'We have seen the oppression of the gangsters of the Democrazia Cristiana and we fight to destroy them. The communists who should be the voice of the workers are in the DC pockets.' The boy shook as he spoke, as if the very words caused him pain.

'I understand what you say, Giancarlo.'

'On the day that you were taken in Rome by those Calabresi pigs, I was with the leader of our cell. We were ambushed by the polizia. They took our leader, took her away in their chains and with their guns round her. There was another man with us – Panicucci. Not of our ideology at first, but recruited and loyal, loyal as a fighting lion. They shot Panicucci like a dog.'

'Where were you, Giancarlo?'

'Far across the street. She had told me to bring the newspapers. I was too far from her. I could not help . . .'

'I understand.' Harrison spoke softly, tuned to the failure of the boy. He should not humiliate him.

'I could not help, I could do nothing.'

And soon the little bastard will be crying, thought Harrison. If the gun wasn't at his ribcage, Geoffrey Harrison would have been laughing fit to bust. Saga of bloody heroism. Away across the road buying newspapers, what sort of medal do you get for that one? Driving hard past the road to Vibo Valentia, hammering over the bridge and the low reflected waters of the drought-starved Mesima river.

'The one you call the leader, tell me about her.'

'She is Franca. She is a lovely woman, 'Arrison. She is a lady. Franca Tantardini. She is our leader. She hates them and she fights them. They will torture her in the name of their shitty democratic state. They are bastards and they will hurt her.'

'And you love this girl, Giancarlo?'

That deflated the boy, seemed to prick him where the gas was densest.

624

'I love her,' Giancarlo whispered. 'I love her, and she loves me too. We have been together in the bed.'

'I know how you feel, Giancarlo. I understand you.'

Bloody liar, Geoffrey. When did you last love a woman? How long? Not that recently, not last week. Bloody liar. In the early days with Violet, that was something like love, wasn't it? Something like it . . .

'She is beautiful. She is a real woman. Very beautiful, very strong.'

'I understand, Giancarlo.'

'I will liberate her from them.'

The car swerved on the road, swung out into the fast lane towards the crash barriers. Harrison's hands had tightened on the wheel, his arms had stiffened and were unresponsive, clumsy.

'You are going to liberate her?'

'Together we are going to liberate her, 'Arrison.'

Harrison stared, eyes gimlet clear, out on to the ever-diminishing road in his lights. Pinch yourself, kick your arse. Push the bedclothes off and get dressed. Just a bloody nightmare. It has to be.

He knew the answer, but he asked the question.

'How are we going to do it, Giancarlo?'

'You sit with me, 'Arrison. We sit together. They will give me back my Franca and I will give you back to them.'

'It doesn't work like that. Not any more . . . not after Moro . . .'

'You have to hope it is like that.' The cold back in his voice, the ice chill that the boy could summon from the high ground.

'Not after the Moro business. They showed it then . . . they don't bend. No negotiation.'

'Then it is bad for you, 'Arrison.'

'Where were you when Moro was done?'

'At the University of Rome.'

'. . . and weren't there any bloody newspapers there?'

'I know what happened.'

Harrison felt his control sliding, and fought it. His eyes were no longer on the road, his head was swung towards the boy. Noses, faces, unshaven cheeks, mouth breath, all barely separated.

'If that's your plan it's lunatic.'

'That is my plan.'

'They won't give in, a child can see that.'

'They will surrender because they are weak and soft, fattened by their excesses. They cannot win against the might of the proletariat. They cannot resist the revolution of the workers. When we have destroyed the system they will talk of this day.'

God, how do you tell him? Harrison said quietly, chopping his words with emphasis. 'They won't give in . . .'

The boy screamed, 'If they do not return her to me then I kill you.'

The wail of the cornered mountain cat, and the spittle flecked Giancarlo's chin.

'Please yourself then.'

Wasn't true, wasn't real, not happening to Geoffrey Harrison. He had to escape from it, had to find a freedom from the snarling hatred.

Harrison swung the car hard to the right, stamped his foot on the brake, whistled to himself in tune with the tyre screech, and wrenched the car to a halt. The pistol was at his neck, nestled against the vein that ran behind his ear lobe.

'Start again,' Giancarlo hissed.

'Drive yourself,' Harrison muttered, sliding back in his seat, folding his arms across his chest.

'Drive or I will shoot you . . .'

'That's your choice.'

'Listen, 'Arrison. Listen to what I say.' The mouth was close to his ear, competing for proximity with the gun barrel, and the breath was hot and gusting in the boy's anger. 'At Seminara, at the town hall, I left a message. It was a communiqué in the name of the Nuclei Armati Proletaria. It will be read with care when it is found, when the first people come in the morning. With the message is your card. They will know that I have you, and later in the morning the barn will be found. It will confirm also that I have taken you when they find the bodies. I have no more need of you, 'Arrison. I have no more need of you while they think that I hold you. Am I clear?'

So why doesn't he do? Harrison wondered. Not scruple, not compassion. Didn't know and didn't ask. The gun was harder against his skin and the defiance sagged. Not going to call the bluff, are you, Geoffrey? Harrison engaged the gears, flicked the ignition key, and coasted away.

They would talk again later, but not now, not for many minutes. Giancarlo lit another cigarette and did not share it.

Where the carabinieri lay close to the two-storey villa of Antonio Mazzotti they could hear without difficulty the stumbling account of the woman close to hysteria at the front door of the house. She wore a cotton shift dress and a cardigan round her shoulders and rubber boots on her feet as if she had dressed in haste, and the man she spoke with displayed his pyjama trousers beneath his dressing-gown. There had been a brief pause when Mazzotti disappeared inside leaving the woman alone with her face bathed in light, so that the carabinieri who knew the district and its people could recognize her. When Mazzotti came again to the door he was dressed and carried a double-barrelled shotgun.

As they hurried down the road and on to the wood path the woman

626

had clung to Mazzotti's arm and the volume of her tale in his ear had covered the following footsteps of the men in camouflage uniforms. She had heard shots from the barn and knew her husband had work there that night, she knew he stayed at the barn for Signor Mazzotti. Of what she had seen there she could not speak and her wailing roused the village dogs. Mazzotti made no attempt to silence her, as if the enormity of what she described had stunned and shaken him.

When the carabinieri entered the barn the woman was prostrate on the body of her husband, her arms cradling the viciously wounded head, her face pressed to the coin-sized exit wound in his temple. Mazzotti, isolated by the flashlights, had dropped his shotgun to the earth floor. More light poured into the musty room and searched out the second body owning a face contorted by surprise and terror. Men had been left to guard the building till dawn while the capitano hurried with his prisoners to their jeeps.

Within minutes of arriving at the Palmi barracks, the officer had telephoned to Rome, prised the home number of Giuseppe Carboni from an argumentative night clerk, and was speaking to the policeman in his suburban flat.

Twice Carboni asked the same question, twice he received the same deadening answer.

'There was a chain from a roof beam with part of a handcuff attached. That is the place the Englishman could have been held, but he was not there when we came.'

A solitary car, lonely on the road, fast and free on the Auto del Sol. Closing on the ankle of Italy, the heel and toe left in its wake. Coming at speed. Geoffrey Harrison and Giancarlo Battestini headed towards Rome. Geoffrey and Giancarlo and a P38.

Archie Carpenter was at last asleep. His hotel room was cruelly hot but he had lost the spirit to complain to the management about his reverberating air-conditioner. He'd drunk more than he'd intended in the restaurant.

Michael Charlesworth had been purging his guilt at the Embassy's stance by maintaining a high level in Carpenter's glass. Gin first, followed by wine, and after that the acid of the local brandy. The talk had been of strings that could not be tugged, of restrictions on action and initiative. And they had talked late and long on the extraordinary Mrs Harrison. Violet, known to them both, who behaved as no one else would that they could imagine in those captured circumstances.

627

'She's impossible, quite impossible. I just couldn't talk to her. All I got for the trouble of going up there was a mouthful of abuse.'

'You didn't do as well as I did,' Carpenter grinned. 'She bloody near raped me.'

'That would have been a diversion. She's off her rocker.'

'I'm not going back there, not till we march old Harrison through the door, shove him at her, and run.'

'I wonder why she didn't fancy me,' Charlesworth had said, and worked again on the brandy bottle.

Violet Harrison, too, was deep in sleep. Still and calm in the bed that she shared with her husband, week after week, month after month. She had gone to bed early, stripping her clothes off after the flight of the man from Head Office. Had dressed in a new nightgown, silky and lace-trimmed, that rode high round her thighs. She wanted to sleep, wanted to rest, so that her face might not be lined with tiredness in the morning, so that the crow's feet would not be at her eyes.

Geoffrey would understand, Geoffrey would not condemn her. Geoffrey, wherever he was, would not blame her, would not pick up and cast the stone. She would not be late again at the beach.

Her legs wide and sprawled, she slept on a clear, bright star night.

With a small torch to guide them, their bodies heaving, their feet stumbling, Vanni and Mario charged along the trail in the forest towards the rock face above the tree line.

Word of what had happened at the barn and the villa of the capo raced in a community as small as Cosoleto, travelled by a spider's web of gently tapped doors; calls from upper windows across the streets, by telephone among those houses that possessed the instrument. Vanni had flung his clothes on his back, snapped to his wife where he was going and run from the back door to the home of Mario.

It was a path known to them since their childhood, but the pace of the flight ensured bruised shins, torn arms, and guttural obscenities. Beyond the trees the way narrowed to little more than a goat track, necessitating that they use their hands to pull them higher.

'Who could have been there?'

Vanni struggled on, out of condition, seeing no reason to reply.

'Who knew of the barn?' The persistence of shock and surprise consuming Mario. 'It's certain it's not the carabinieri . . . ?'

Vanni drew the air down into his lungs, paused. 'Certain.'

'Who could have been there?' Mario wrung advantage from the rest, spattered his questions. 'No one from the villages here would have dared. They would face the vendetta . . .'

'No one from these parts, no one who knew the capo . . .'

'Who could it have been?'

'Cretino, how do I know?'

The climb was resumed, slower and subdued, towards a cave beneath an escarpment, the bolt-hole of Vanni.

Past five in the morning the discreet banging at his door woke Francesco Vellosi. In the attics of the Viminale were the angled ceiling closets where men in haste who coveted the clock could sleep. He had worked late after the attack, calming himself with his papers, and neither he nor his guards were happy that he should drive back to his home. And the death of his driver, the killing of Mauro, had rid him of his desire for the comforts of his flat. At the second persistence of the knocking he had called on the man to enter. Sitting on his bed, naked but for a pale blue vest, his hair ragged, his chin alive with the growth of the small hours, he had focused on the messenger who brought blinding light into the room and a buff folder of papers. The man excused himself, was full of apologies for disturbing the Dottore. The file had been given him by the men in Operations, in the basements of the building. He knew nothing of the contents, had simply been dismissed on an errand. Vellosi reached from his bed, took the folder and waved that the messenger should leave. When the door was closed he began to read.

There was a note of explanation, handwritten and stapled to the long telex screed, signed by the night duty officer, a man known to Vellosi, not one who would waste the capo's time. Workmen had come at four in the morning to the offices of the mayor of the town of Seminara in Calabria. The message reproduced on the telex was the text of what they had found, along with an American Express credit card in the name of Geoffrey Harrison.

It was the work of a few seconds for him to absorb the contents of the communiqué. God, how many more of these things? How much longer the agony of these irrelevances in the lifespan of poor, tottering, broken-nosed Italia? After the pain and division of the last one, after the affair of Moro, was all this to be inflicted again? Dressing with one hand, shaving with the battery razor provided thoughtfully beside the washbasin, Vellosi hurried towards the premature day.

The fools must know there could be no concessions. If they had not weakened for the elder statesman of the Republic, how could they crumble now for a businessman, for a foreigner, for a life whose passing would hold no lasting climax? Idiots, fools, lunatics, these people.

Why?

629

Because they must know there cannot be surrender.

What if they have judged right? What if their analysis of the malaise and sickness of Italia were more perceptive than that of Francesco Vellosi? What if they had discerned that the country could not again endure the strained preoccupation of sitting out ultimatums, deadlines, and photographs of prospective widows?

Was he confident in the sinew of the State?

Over his body they would free Franca Tantardini. Let the bitch out to Fiumicino, bend the constitution for her . . . not as long as he held his job, not as long as he headed the anti-terrorist squad. Badly shaven, temper rising, he headed for the stairs that would lead him to his office. His aides would be at home in their beds. The dawn meetings with the Minister, with the Procurator, with the carabinieri generals, with the men handling the Harrison affair at the Questura, would have to be scheduled by himself.

The route to a coronary, Vellosi told himself, the sure and steady road. He tripped on the narrow steps and cursed aloud in his frustration.

12

The first spars of light pushed across the inland foothills greying the road in front of Harrison and Giancarlo. A watercolour brush dabbed on the land, softening with pastel the darkness. The grim hour of the day when men who have not slept dread the hours of withering brightness that will follow. They wound down from the hills, running from the mountains as if the sniff of the sea had excited them, towards the beaches of Salerno.

For more than an hour they had not spoken, each wrapped in his committed hostile silence. A fearful quiet lulled only by the throb of the small engine.

Harrison wondered whether the boy slept, but the breathing was never regular, and there were the sudden movements beside him that meant lack of comfort, lack of calm. Perhaps, he thought, it would be simple to disarm him. Perhaps. A soldier, a man of action, would risk all on a sudden swerve, a quick braking and a fast grapple for the P38. But you're neither of those, Geoffrey. The most violent thing he'd ever accomplished in his adult life was to kick that bucket at the guerrillas in the barn. And a smack at Violet once. Just once, not hard. That's all, Geoffrey, all your offensive experience. Not the stuff of heroes, but it isn't in your chemistry, and for heroes read bloody idiots.

Geoffrey Harrison had never in his life met the dedicated activist, the political attack weapon. It was something new to him, of which he had only limited understanding. Newspaper photographs, yes, plenty of those. Wanted men, captured and chained men, dead men on the pavement. But all inadequate and failing, those images, when it came to this boy.

They're not stupid, not this one anyway. He worked out a plan and he executed it. Found you when half the police in the country were on the same job and late at the post. This isn't a gutter kid from the shanties down on the Tevere banks. A gutter kid wouldn't argue, he'd have killed for the stopping of the car.

'Giancarlo, I'm very tired. We have to talk about something. If I don't talk we'll go off the road.'

There was no sudden start, no stirring at the breaking of the quiet. The boy had not been asleep. The possibility of action had not been there. Harrison felt better for that.

'You are driving very well, we have covered more than half the distance now. Much more than half.' The boy sounded alert, and prepared for conversation.

Harrison blundered in. 'Are you a student, Giancarlo?'

'I was. Some years ago I was a student.' Sufficient as a reply, giving nothing.

'What did you study?' Humour the little pig, humour and amuse him.

'I studied psychology at the University of Rome. I did not complete my first year. When the students of my class were taking their first year examinations I was held a political prisoner in the Regina Coeli gaol. I was a part of a struggle group. I was fighting against the borghese administration when the fascist police imprisoned me.'

Can't they speak another language, Harrison thought. Are they reduced only to the compilation of slogans and manifestos? 'Where do you come from, Giancarlo? Where is your home?'

'My home was in the covo with Franca. Before that my home was in the "B" Wing of the Regina Coeli, where my friends were.'

Harrison spoke without thought. He was too tired to pick his words, and his throat was hoarse and sore even from this slight effort. 'Where your parents were, where you spent your childhood, that was what I meant by home.'

'We use different words, 'Arrison. I do not call that my home. I was in chains . . .' Again the warm spittle spread on Harrison's face.

'I'm very tired, Giancarlo. I want to talk so that we don't crash, and I want to understand you. But you don't have to give me that jargon.' Harrison yawned, not for effect, not as a gesture.

Giancarlo laughed out loud, the first time Harrison had heard the rich little treble chime. 'You pretend to be a fool, 'Arrison. I ask you a question. Answer me the truth and I will know you. Answer me, if you were a boy who lived in Italy – if you were from privilege of the DC, if you had seen the children in the "popular" quarter in their rags, if you had seen the hospitals, if you had seen the rich playing at the villas and with their yachts, if you had seen those things, would you not fight? That is my question, 'Arrison, would you not fight?'

The dawn came faster now, the probes of sunlight spearing across the road, and there were other cars on the autostrada, passing or being passed.

'I would not fight, Giancarlo,' Harrison said slowly with the crushing weariness surging again and his eyes cluttered with headlights. 'I would not have the courage to say that I am right, that my word is law. I would need greater authority than a bloody pistol.'

'Drive on, and be careful on the road.' The attack of the angered wasp. As if a stick had penetrated the nest and thrashed about and roused the ferocity of the swarm. 'You will learn my courage, 'Arrison. You will learn it at nine o'clock if the pigs that you slave for have not met –'

'Nine tomorrow morning.' Harrison spoke distantly, his attention on the tail lights in front and the dazzled centre mirror above him. 'You give them little time.'

'Time only for them to express your value.'

Away to the left were the lights daubed on the Bay of Naples. Harrison veered to the right and followed the white arrows on the road to the north and Rome.

Another dawn, another bright fresh morning and Giuseppe Carboni, alive with the lemon juice in his mouth, arrived at the Viminale by taxi.

It was a long time since he had been to the Ministry. For many months there had been no reason for him to desert the unprepossessing Questura for the eminence of the 'top table', the building that housed the Minister of the Interior and his attendant apparatus. His chin was down on his tie, his eyes on his shoes as he paid off the driver. This was a place where only the idiot felt safe, where the knives were sharp and the criticism cutting. Here the sociologists and the criminologists and the penologists held court and rule was by university diploma and qualification by breeding and connection, because this was close to power, the real power that the Questura did not know.

Carboni was led up the stairs, a debutante introduced at a dance. His humour was poor, his mind only slightly receptive when he reached the door of Francesco Vellosi who had summoned him.

He knew of Vellosi by title and reputation. A well-known name in the Pubblica Sicurezza with a history of clean firmness to embellish it, the one who had made a start at cleaning the drains of crime in Reggio

Calabria, ordered significant arrests, and not bowed to intimidation. But the corridor gossip had it that he delighted in public acclamation and sought out the cameras and microphones and the journalists' notebooks. Carboni himself shunned publicity and was suspicious of fast won plaudits.

But the man across the desk appealed to him.

Vellosi was in his shirtsleeves, glasses down on his nose, cigarette limp between his lips in the gesture of the tired lover, tie loosened, and his jacket away on a chair across the room. No reek of after-shave, no scent of armpit lotion, and already a well-filled ashtray in front of him. Vellosi was studying the papers that piled up on the desk. Carboni waited, then coughed, the obligatory indication of his presence.

Vellosi's eyes fixed on him. 'Dottore Carboni, thank you for coming, and so soon. I had not expected you for another hour.'

'I came immediately I had dressed.'

'As you know, Carboni, from this office I manage the affairs of the anti-terrorist unit.' The rapid patter had begun. 'If one can make such a distinction, I am concerned with affairs political rather than criminal.'

It was to be expected that time would be consumed before they arrived at the reason for the meeting. Carboni was not disturbed. 'Obviously, I know the work that is done from this office.'

'And now it seems that our paths cross, which is rare. Seldom do criminal activities link with those of terrorism.'

'It has happened,' Carboni replied. Non-committal, watchful, the bird high on its perch.

'An Englishman has been kidnapped. It happened two mornings ago. I am correct?' Vellosi's chin was buried in his hands as he gazed hard across the desk. 'An Englishman from one of the big multinational companies that have an operation in Italy. Tell me, please, Carboni, what was your opinion of that case?'

There was something to be wary of. Carboni paused before speaking. 'I have no reason to believe that the kidnapping was not the work of criminals. The style of the attack was similar to that previously used. The limited descriptions of the men who took part indicated an age that is not usually common among the political people; they were in their thirties or more. A ransom demand was made that we have linked with a previous abduction, a further connection has been found with the office of a speculator in Calabria. There is nothing to make me doubt that it was a criminal affair.'

'You have been fortunate, you have come far.'

Carboni loosened. The man opposite him talked like a human being, playing down the superiority of his rank. The man from the Questura felt a freedom to express himself. 'Last night I was able to ask the carabinieri of Palmi near Reggio to keep a watch on this speculator. His name is Mazzotti, from the village of Cosoleto, he has connections in local politics. I acted without a warrant from the magistrate but the time would not allow. If I might digress, a man was found yesterday in a Roman pensione battered to death . . . he had a record for kidnapping, his family is from Cosoleto. I return to the point. The carabinieri behaved faultlessly.' Carboni permitted himself a slow smile, one policeman to another, histories of rivalry with the para-military force, mutual understanding on the scale of the compliment. 'The carabinieri followed Mazzotti to a barn, he was taken there by a woman who had heard sounds in the night. The woman's husband was dead there, shot at close range, another man also had been killed. There were signs of a temporary holding place, flattened down hay bales, and there was a chain with a manacle. A pistol, Vellosi, had been used to break the lock of the handcuff. It had been broken by gunshot. We did not find Harrison, nor any trace of him.'

Vellosi nodded his head, the picture unveiled, the drape drawn back. 'What conclusion, Carboni, did you draw from this information?'

'Someone came to the barn and killed the two men that he might have Harrison for himself. It was not a rescue, since there have been no messages from the south of Harrison's arrival at a police station or a carabinieri barracks. I checked before I left my home. I cannot draw an ultimate conclusion.'

The head of the anti-terrorist squad hunched forward, voice lowered and conspiratorial, as if in a room such as his there were listening places. 'Last night I was attacked. Ambushed as I left my home, and my driver killed.' Vellosi understood from the stunned frowns building and edging across Carboni's forehead that he knew nothing of the evening's horror. 'I survived unhurt. We have identified the swine who killed my driver. They are Nappisti, Carboni. They were young, they were inefficient, and they died for it.'

'I congratulate you on your escape,' Carboni whispered.

'I mourn my driver, he was a friend of many years. I believe I was attacked as a reprisal for the capture of the woman Franca Tantardini, taken by my squad in the Corso Francia. She is an evil bitch, Carboni, a poisoned, evil woman.'

Carboni recovered composure. 'It was a fine effort by your people.'

'I have told you nothing yet. Hear me out before you praise me. There is a town, Seminara, in Calabria. I have no map but we will find, I am sure, that it is close to your Cosoleto. Under the mayor's door an hour ago was found a scribbled statement, not typed, not neat, from the NAP. A credit card of Harrison was with the paper. They will kill him tomorrow morning at nine o'clock if Tantardini has not been freed.'

Carboni whistled, an expiry of wind from his lungs. His pen fumbled between the fingers of his two hands, his notebook was virgin clean.

'I make an assumption, Carboni. The Nappisti reached your man Claudio. They extracted information. They have taken Harrison from the custody of Mazzotti. The danger now confronting the Englishman is infinitely greater.'

With his head bowed, Carboni sat very still in his chair as if a heavy blow had struck him. 'What has been done this morning to prevent an escape . . .'

'Nothing has been done.' A snarl from Vellosi's mouth, and above it the cauterized cheeks, the whitened skin at the temples. 'Nothing has been done because until we sat together there was no dialogue on this issue. I have no army, I have no authority over the polizia and the carabinieri. I do not have the numbers to stifle an escape. I have given you the Nappisti, and you have given me a location, and now we can begin.'

Carboni spoke sadly, unwilling to stamp on the energy of his superior. 'They have five hours' start on us, and they were close to the autostrada and at night the road is free.' His head shook as he multiplied kilometres and minutes in his mind. 'They could travel hundreds of kilometres in a fast car. The whole of the Mezzo Giorno is open to them . . .' He tailed away, awed by the hopelessness of what he said.

'Bluster the local carabinieri, the polizia, breathe some fire under their backsides. Get back to your office now and hunt the facts.' Shouting now, consumed by his mission, Vellosi banged on his desk to emphasize each point.

'It is outside my jurisdiction . . .'

'What do you want? A rule book and Harrison dead in a ditch at five minutes past nine tomorrow? Get yourself on to the fifth floor at the Questura. All the computers, all the Honeywell machines there, get them moving, let them earn their keep.'

Resistance failing, Carboni subsided. 'May I make a telephone call, Dottore?'

'Make it and be on your way. You're not the only one to be busy this morning. The Minister will be here in forty minutes . . .'

Carboni was on his feet, galvanized into activity. With quick, sweaty fingers he flicked in his diary of telephone numbers for that of Michael Charlesworth of the British Embassy.

The early sun was denied entry to the reception lounge of the Villa Wolkonsky by the drawn drapes. The more fancied of the room's collection of rare porcelain had been put away the night before because there had been a small reception and the Ambassador's wife was ever wary of light fingers among her guests. There remained enough to satisfy the curiosity of Charlesworth and Carpenter as they stood close to each other in the gloom. They had come unannounced to the Ambassador's residence, spurred by Giuseppe Carboni's call to Charlesworth sketching the night's developments. The diplomat had collected Carpenter from his hotel. A servant in a white coat, not hiding his disapproval of the hour, had admitted them. If we broadcast we're on our way, Charlesworth had said in the car, then the barricades go up, he'll stall till office hours.

The irritation of the Ambassador was undisguised as he entered the room. A puckered forehead and a jutting chin sandwiched the hawk eyes of annoyance. He wore his familiar dark striped trousers, but no jacket to drape over the braces that held them firm. His collar was unfastened. The opening was abrupt.

'Good morning, Charlesworth. I understand from the message sent upstairs that you wished to see me on a matter of direct and pressing importance. Let's not waste each other's time.'

In the face of this salvo Charlesworth did not falter. 'I've brought with me Archie Carpenter. He's the Security Officer of International Chemical Holdings in London . . .'

His Excellency's eyes glinted, a bare greeting.

'. . . I have just been telephoned by Dottore Carboni of the Questura. There have been disturbing and unpleasant developments in the Harrison case . . .'

Carpenter said quietly, 'We judged that you should know of these – whatever the inconvenience of the hour.'

The Ambassador threw him a glance, then turned back to Charlesworth. 'Let's have it, then.'

'The police have always believed Harrison was kidnapped by a criminal organization. During the night it seems this organization was relieved of Harrison, who is now in the hands of the Nuclei Armati Proletaria.'

'What do you mean – "relieved"?'

'It seems that the NAP have forcibly taken Harrison from his original kidnappers,' said Charlesworth with patience.

'The police are offering this as a theory? We are to believe this?' Spoken with the killer chop of sarcasm.

'Yes, sir,' Carpenter again interjected, 'we believe it because there are three men on their backs in the morgue to convince us. Two have died of gunshot wounds, the third of a dented skull.'

The Ambassador retreated, coughed, wiped his head with a handkerchief and waved his visitors to chairs. 'What's the motive?' he said simply.

Charlesworth took his cue. 'The NAP demand that by nine tomorrow morning, Central European Time, the Italian government shall release the captured terrorist Franca Tantardini . . .'

The Ambassador, sitting far to the front of the intricately carved chair, reeled forward. 'Oh my God . . . Go on, Charlesworth. Don't spare the rod.'

'. . . the Italian government shall release Franca Tantardini or Geoffrey Harrison will be killed. In a few minutes the Minister of the Interior will get his first briefing. I imagine that within twenty you will be called to the Viminale.'

Rock still, his head in his tired, aged hands, the Ambassador contemplated. Neither Charlesworth nor Carpenter interrupted. The buck had been passed. For a full minute the silence burgeoned, causing Charlesworth to feel for the straightness of his tie knot, Carpenter to look at his unpolished shoes and the lace that was loose.

The Ambassador shook himself as if to dislodge the burden. 'It is a decision for the Italian government to make. Any interference, any pressure on our part, would be quite unwarranted. Indeed, any suggestion of action would be quite uncalled for.'

'So you wash your hands of Harrison?' Carpenter was flushed as he spoke, temper surging.

'I don't think that's what the Ambassador meant . . .' Charlesworth cut in unhappily.

'Thank you, Charlesworth, but I can justify my own statements,' the Ambassador said. 'We don't wash our hands of the fate of Mr Harrison, as you put it, Mr Carpenter. We face the reality of local conditions.'

'When this was a criminal matter, when there was only money at issue, then we were prepared to deal . . .'

'Your company was prepared to negotiate, Mr Carpenter. The British Foreign Office remained uninvolved.'

'What's so bloody different between a couple of million dollars and freedom for one woman?' Thanks to all that bloody brandy that Charlesworth had plied him with, he couldn't marshal his sentences, couldn't hit at the smug little sober bastard opposite him. The frustration welled in his mind.

'Don't shout at me, Mr Carpenter.' The Ambassador was cold, aloof on his pedestal. 'The situation is indeed different. Before, as you rightly say, only money was involved. Now we add principle, and with that the sovereign dignity of the Republic of Italy. It is inconceivable that the government here can bow to so crude a threat and release a public enemy of the stature of the Tantardini woman. It is equally inconceivable that the government of Great Britain should urge such a course.'

'I say again, you wash your hands of Geoffrey Harrison. You're prepared to see him sacrificed for the "dignity of Italy", whatever bloody nonsense that is . . .' Carpenter looked across to Charlesworth for an ally, but he had been anticipated and the gaze was averted.

'Well, thank you, gentlemen, thank you for your time. I'm sorry you were disturbed, that the day started badly, and early.'

Carpenter stood up, a little pencil of froth at the sides of his mouth. 'You're putting our man down the bloody bog, and you're pulling the bloody chain on him, and I think it's bloody marvellous.'

There was a passionless mask across the Ambassador's features and he stayed far back in his chair. 'We merely face reality, Mr Carpenter, and reality will dictate that if the losers in this matter are to be either Geoffrey Harrison or the Republic of Italy, then it will be Harrison who loses. If that is the conclusion, then the life of one man is of lesser importance than the lasting damage to the social and political fabric of a great and democratic country. That is how I see it, Mr Carpenter.'

'It's a load of bullshit . . .'

'Your rudeness neither offends me nor helps Harrison.'

'I think we should be on our way, Archie.' Charlesworth too was standing. 'I'll see you later in the office, sir.'

When they were out in the sunshine and walking towards the car, Charlesworth saw that there were tears streaming down Archie Carpenter's face.

For several minutes Harrison had been watching the jumping needle of the fuel dial that bounced against the left corner of the display arc bringing him the knowledge that the tank was drying, emptying. He wondered how the boy would react to the idea that the car would soon be static and useless, considered whether he should alert him to the impending halt of their progress, or whether he should simply drive on till the engine coughed and died, barren of petrol. It depended what he wanted from it, whether it was a fight, or whether it was the easy way and safety, however temporary. Tell him now that they were about to stop on the hard shoulder and perhaps the boy wouldn't panic, would work at his options. Allow it to happen and the boy might crumble under a crisis, and that was dangerous because of the ready presence of the P38.

Same old question, Geoffrey, same old situation. To confront or to bend, and no middle road.

Same old answer, Geoffrey. Don't shake it, don't rock it. Don't kick the bucket of muck in his face because that's the short way to pain, and the gun's close and armed.

'We won't be going much further, Giancarlo.'

Harrison's softly spoken words boomed in the quiet of the car. Beside him the boy straightened from his low-slung sitting posture. The gun barrel dug at Harrison's ribs as if demanding explanation.

'We're almost out of petrol.'

The boy's head in its curled and tangled hair darted across Harrison's chest to study the dial. Harrison eased back in his seat, gave him more room, and heard his breathing speed and rise.

'There's not much more in the old girl, Giancarlo. Perhaps a few more kilometres.'

The boy lifted his head, and the hand that did not hold the gun scraped at his chin as if this were a way to summon inspiration and clarity of decision.

'It's not my fault, Giancarlo.'

'Silence,' the boy snapped back.

Just the breathing to mingle with the steady purr of the little engine, and time too for Harrison to think and consider. Behind their different walls the man and the boy entertained the same thoughts. What would a stoppage mean to the security of the journey? What risk would it offer Giancarlo of identification and subsequent pursuit? What possibility of escape would it present to his prisoner? And it's not only the boy with decisions to make, Geoffrey, it's you as well. He couldn't be as vigilant, could he, if they were stopped on the roadside, pulled into a toll gate, going in search of a petrol station? Opportunities were going to loom, opportunities for flight, for a struggle.

Then he'll shoot.

Sure?

Can't be sure but likely.

Worth a try, whether he'll shoot or not?

Perhaps, if the opportunity's there.

That's the crawling way out, that's the gutless way.

For Christ's sake, it's not a bloody virility contest. It's my bloody life, it's my bloody stomach with the P38 stuck into it. It's my neck with the axe hanging over it. It's not gesture time. I said perhaps, that should bloody be enough.

You won't do it, you won't take him on, you won't fight.

Perhaps, but only if it presents itself.

'We take the Monte Cassino turn-off.' Giancarlo was out of his dream, breaking Harrison's debate.

High above them to the right of the autostrada perched the triumphant monastery. It loomed on the mountain top, a widow's shrine for women of many far countries whose men had staggered and fallen distant years back under the rain of shrapnel and explosive, and bullet swathes. The car plunged past the signs for the turn-off.

Giancarlo raised himself in his seat and pulled from a hip pocket a wad of notes and the autostrada toll ticket taken hundreds of kilometres back from a machine.

'I had not thought of the petrol,' he laughed with a quick nervousness. A drip of weakness before the tap was turned tighter. ''Arrison, you will not be silly. You will pay the ticket. The gun will be at you all the time. You are not concerned with what will happen to me, you are concerned with what will happen to yourself. If you are silly then you are dead; whether I am too does not help you. You understand, 'Arrison?'

'Yes, Giancarlo.'

Harrison pulled the wheel hard to the right, felt the tyres bite beneath him, heard their squeal, and the pace of the autostrada diminished from his windscreen mirror. He had slowed the car as they wound on the tight bend towards the toll gate. Giancarlo reached back to the seat behind and grabbed at his light anorak, arranged it over his lower arm and his fist and the gun and again pressured the barrel into the softness at Harrison's waist.

'You don't speak.'

'What if he talks to me?' Harrison stammered, the tension exuding from the boy spread contagiously.

'I will talk to him, if it is necessary . . . If I fire the pistol from here I kill you, 'Arrison.'

'I know, Giancarlo.'

Perhaps, but only if it presents itself. You know the answer, Geoffrey. He pressed the brake as the cabins of the toll gate loomed in front of him. He stopped the car as the bonnet edged against the narrow barrier, carefully wound down the window and without looking passed the ticket and a banknote out into the cool dawn air.

'*Grazie.*'

The voice startled Harrison. Contact again with the real and the permanent life, contact with the clean and the familiar. His eyes followed his arm but there was no face in his vision, only a hand that was dark and hair-covered with a worn greasy palm that took his money, and was gone before snaking back with a fist full of coins. It had not presented itself. The gun gouged at his flesh, and the man would not even have seen their faces. The voice beside him was shrill.

'*Una stazione de servizio, per benzina?*'

'*Cinquen cento metri.*'

'*Grazie.*'

'*Prego.*'

The barrier was raised, Harrison edged the car into gear. Shouldn't he have crashed the gears, stalled the engine, dropped the change in the roadway? Shouldn't he have done something? But the gun was there, round and penetrating at the skin. All right for those who don't know, all right for those without experience. Let them come and sit here, let them find their own answers to cowardice. Within moments the lights of a petrol station shone at them in the half light, diffused with the growing sun.

'You follow my instructions exactly.'

'Yes, Giancarlo.'

'Go to the far pumps.'

Where it was darkest, where the light was masked by the building, Harrison stopped. Giancarlo waited till the handbrake was applied, the gear in neutral, before his hand snaked out at speed to rip the keys from the ignition. He snapped open his door, thrust it shut behind him and jogged around the back of the car till he was at Harrison's door.

He held his anorak across his waist, with an innocence that was above suspicion.

Harrison saw a man in the blue overalls of Agip stroll without urgency towards the car.

'*Venti mila lire di benzina, per favore.*'

'*Sì.*'

Would he look into the car, would the curiosity bred from the long night hours cause him to turn from the boy who stood beside the driver's door, and wish to examine the occupant? Why should it? Why should he care who drives a car? This has to be the moment, Geoffrey. Now, right now, not next time, not next week.

How?

Fling the door open, crash it into Giancarlo's body. You'd knock him back with it, he'd fall, he'd slip. For how long? Long enough to run. Sure? Well, not sure . . . but it's a chance. And how far do you run before he's on his feet, five metres . . . ? It's the opportunity. Then he shoots, and he doesn't miss, not this kid, and who else is here other than a half-asleep idiot with his eyes closed, who'll have to play the hero?

Giancarlo passed the man the notes and waited as he walked away, then hissed through the window, 'I am going to walk round the car. If you move I will shoot, it is no problem through the glass. Do not move, 'Arrison.'

Only if it presents itself. Geoffrey Harrison felt the great weakness creeping into his knees and shins, lapping in his stomach. His tongue smeared a dampness across his lips. You'd have been dead, Geoffrey, if you'd tried anything, you know that, don't you? He supposed he did, supposed he had been sensible, behaved in the intelligent, responsible way that came from education and experience. Wouldn't have lasted long on that mountainside in 1944, Geoffrey; wouldn't have lasted five bloody minutes.

Beneath the triumphant monastery on Monte Cassino, Giancarlo ordered Harrison to turn off the autostrada.

He held the pistol hidden between his legs as Harrison paid the sleepy toll attendant at the barrier with the money the boy had given him. They drove sharply through the small town, rebuilt from the ravages of bombardment into a characterless warren of flat blocks and factories, and headed north on a narrow road among the rock defiles, ever watched by the great whitestone eye on the mountain top. They bypassed the sombre war cemetery for the German dead of a battle fought before the birth of Giancarlo and Harrison, and then the road's turns became more vicious, and the high banks more intrusive.

Three kilometres beyond the rugged message of the graveyard cross, Giancarlo indicated an open field gate through which they should turn. The car lurched over the bare grass covering the hardened ground and was lost to sight behind a gorse hedge of brilliant yellow flowers. Shepherds might come here, or the men who watched the goat flocks, but the chance was reasonable in Giancarlo's mind. Among the grass and weed and climbing thistle and the bushes of the hillside they would rest. Rome lay just one hundred and twenty-five kilometres away. They had done well, they had made good time.

With the car stationary, Giancarlo moved briskly. The flex that he had found in the glove compartment in one hand, the pistol in the other, he followed Harrison between the gorse clumps. He ordered him down, pushed him without unkindness on to his stomach, and then, kneeling with the gun between his thighs, bound Harrison's hands across the small of his back. The legs next, working at the ankles, wrapping the flex around them, weaving it tight, binding the knot. He walked a few paces away and urinated noisily in the grass and was watching the rivulets when he realized he had not offered the Englishman the same chance. He shrugged and put it from his mind. He had no feelings for his prisoner; the man was just a vehicle, just a machine for bringing him closer to his Franca.

Harrison's eyes were already closed, the breathing deep and regular as the sleep sped to him. Giancarlo watched the slow rise and fall of his shoulders and the gaping mouth that was not irritated by the nibbling attendance of a fly. He put the gun on the grass and scrabbled with his fingers at the buckle of his belt and at the elastic waist of his underpants.

Franca. Darling, sweet, lovely Franca. I am coming, Franca. And we will be together, always together, Franca, and you will love me for what I have done for you. Love me, too, my beautiful. Love me.

Giancarlo subsided on the grass and the sun played on his face and there was a light wind and the sound of the flying creatures. The P38 was close to his hand, and the boy lay still.

13

Giancarlo asleep seemed little more than a child, hurt by exhaustion and dragged nerves, coiled gently. His real age was betrayed by the premature haggardness of his face, the witness to his participation in the affairs of men. His left forearm acted as a shield to the climbing sun, and his right hand was buried in the grass, fingers among the leaves and stalks and across the handle of the P38.

He was dreaming.

The fantasy was of success, the images were of achievement. Tossed and tumbling through his febrile mind were the pictures of the moment of triumph he would win. An indulgent masturbation of excitement. Sharp pictures, and vivid. Men in blue Fiat saloons hurrying with escorts of outriders to the public buildings of the capital, men who pushed their way past avalanches of cameras and microphones with anger at their mouths. Rooms that were heavy in smoke and argument where the talk was of Giancarlo Battestini and Franca Tantardini and the NAP. Crisis in the air. Crisis that was the embryo of chaos. Crisis that was spawned and conceived from the sperm of the little fox. Papers would be set in front of the men and pens made ready by the acolytes at their shoulders. Official stamps, weighty and embossed with eagles, would clamp down on the scrawl of the signatures. The order would be made, Franca would be freed, plucked clear from the enemy by the hand of her boy and her lover. The order would be made, in Giancarlo's dreaming and restless mind there was no doubt. Because he had done so much . . . he had come so far.

He had done so much, and they could not deny him the pleasure of his prize. There was one more element among the images of the boy sleeping in the field. There was a prison gate, dominating the skyline and shadowing the street beneath, and doors that would swing slowly open, dragged apart against their will by the hands of Giancarlo. There was a column of police cars, sirens and lights bright on a July morning, bringing his Franca free; she sat like a queen among them, contempt in her eyes for the truncheons and Beretta pistols and machine-guns. Franca coming to freedom.

It would be the greatest victory ever achieved by the NAP. Loving himself, loving his dream, Giancarlo groped downwards with his right hand, urging his thoughts to the diminishing memory of his Franca, conjuring again her body and the sunswept skin.

And the spell was broken. The mirror cracked. The dream was gone with the speed of a disturbed tiger at a waterhole; a blur of light, a memory and a ripple. Lost and wrecked, vanished and destroyed. Trembling in his anger, Giancarlo sat up.

'Giancarlo, Giancarlo,' Geoffrey Harrison had called. 'I want to pee, and I can't the way I'm tied.'

Harrison saw the fury in the boy's face, the neck veins in relief. The intensity of the little swine frightened him, the loathing that was communicated across the few metres of stone and burned field flowers.

He wormed back from confrontation. 'I have to pee, Giancarlo. It's not much to ask.'

The boy stood up, uncertain for a moment on his feet, then collected himself. He scanned all the surroundings as if they were unfamiliar to him and in need of further checks to establish his security. He examined the long depth to the horizon, breaking the fields and low stone walls and distant farm buildings into sectors to vet them more thoroughly. Harrison could see that the boy was rested, that sleep had alerted and revived him. He used a bush of gorse with yellow-petalled flowers to screen himself from the road as he looked around. There was something slow and workmanlike and hugely sinister about his calm. Better to have tied a knot in it or soaked his trousers, Harrison thought, than to have woken him.

Giancarlo walked towards him, feet light on the springy grass, avoiding the stones set deep in the earth, the hand with the gun extended, aimed at Harrison's chest.

'Don't worry, don't point it, I'm not playing heroes, Giancarlo.'

The boy moved behind Harrison, and he heard the scuff of his feet.

'There's a good lad, Giancarlo, you know how it is. I'm fit to bloody burst, you know . . .'

The blow was fierce, agonizing and without warning. The full force of the canvas toe-cap of Giancarlo's right shoe digging into the flesh that formed the protective wall for the kidneys. The pain was instant, blending with the next stab as the following kick came in fast and sharp. Three in all and Harrison slid on to his side.

'You little pig. Vicious . . . bullying . . . little pig . . .' The words were gasped out, strained and hoarse, and the breath was hard to find. More pain, more hurt, because the wounds of the men in the barn were aroused again and mingled with the new bruising. Harrison looked up into the boy's eyes and they bounced his gaze back with something animal, something primitive. Where do they make them, these bloody creatures? Where's the production line? Where's the factory? Deadened and unresponsive and cruel. Where's the bloody stone they're bred under?

Slowly and with deliberation the boy bent down behind Harrison, the barrel of the pistol indenting the skin where it was smooth and hairless behind the ear. With his free hand Giancarlo untied the flex. It was the work of a few moments and then Harrison felt the freedom come again to his wrists and ankles, the shock surge of the blood running free. He didn't wait to be told but rose unsteadily to his feet. He walked a half-dozen paces with a drunken gait, and flicked at his zip-fastener. The spurting, draining relief. That's what it had come down to; ten minutes of negotiation, a kicking, a gun at the back of his head – all that because he wanted to pee, to spend a penny, as Violet would have said. Being pulled down into the cesspool, being animalized. He looked down into the clear, reflecting pool in front of his feet and in a moment of hesitation between surges saw the traces of his own concerned and wrung-out face.

Geoffrey, we want to go home. We're not fighters, old lad, we're not like those who can just sit in a limbo and be pushed and tugged by the wind. We're just a poor little bloody businessman who doesn't give a stuff about exploitation and revolution and the rights of the proletariat; a poor little bloody businessman who wants to wrestle with output and production and raw materials, the things that pay for summer holidays and the clothes on Violet's back, and a few quid to go on top of a widowed mother's pension. It's not our war, Geoffrey, not our bloody fight. Harrison shook himself, swayed on his feet, pulled up the zip and turned his hips so that he could see behind him. His movements were careful, designed to cause no alarm. The boy was watching him, impassive and with as much emotion as a whitewashed wall. The two of them, devoid of relationship, without mutual sympathy, stared at each other. He'd kill you as he'd stamp on a dragonfly, Geoffrey, and it wouldn't move him, wouldn't halt his sleep afterwards. That's why he doesn't communicate, because the bastard doesn't need to.

'What are we going to do now?' Harrison asked in a small voice.

The boy stood out of arm's reach but close. Another gesture from the arm that held the pistol and they walked the few metres towards the car.

'Where are we going?' Harrison said.

Giancarlo laughed, opening his mouth so that Harrison saw the fillings of his teeth and felt the stench of his breath. This is the way the Jews went to the cattle trucks in the railway sidings, without a struggle, making obeisance to their guards, thought Harrison. Understand, Geoffrey, how they forsook resistance? You're gutless, lad. And you know it, that's what hurts.

He opened the door of the car, climbed in and watched Giancarlo walk round the front of the engine. The keys were exchanged, the P38 took up position by his ribcage, the brake was eased off, the gears engaged.

Harrison headed the car back towards the road.

Its headlights shining vainly in the morning brilliance, a white Alfetta swept down the sloping crescent of the driveway outside the Viminale. An identical car with the smoked, half-inch-thick windows and reinforced bodywork had latched itself close behind, the worrying terrier that must not leave its quarry. Alone among the members of the Italian government, the Minister of the Interior had discarded the midnight blue fleet of Fiat 132s after the kidnapping of the President of his party. For him and his bodyguards bulletproof transport was decreed. The Minister had said in public that he detested the hermetically sealed capsule in which he was ferried in high summer from one quarter of the city to another, but after the chorus of inter-service recrimination that followed the attack on the vulnerable Moro car and the massacre of his five-man escort, the Minister's preferences mattered little.

With siren blaring and driving the motorists on Quattro Fontane languidly aside, the Alfetta plied through the mounting traffic. The driver was hunched in his concentration, left hand steady on the wheel, the right resting loosely on the gear stick. Beside the driver, the Minister's senior guard cradled a short-barrelled machine-gun on his lap, one magazine attached, two more on the floor between his feet.

For the Minister and his guest, the British Ambassador, conversation was difficult, each clinging to the thong straps above the darkened side windows. The Ambassador was travelling at the Minister's invitation, his presence hurriedly requested. Would he care to be briefed on the situation concerning the businessman Harrison while the Minister was in transit between his offices and those of the Prime Minister? Somewhere lost behind them in the dash and verve of the Roman streets was the Embassy Rolls that would collect the Ambassador from Palazzo Chigi.

Public men both of them, and so they were jacketed. The Italian sported a red silk tie above his blue shirt. The Ambassador favoured the broad colour bands of his wartime cavalry unit. The two men were stifled near to suffocation with the heat in the closed car, and the Minister showed his irritation that he should be the cause of his guest's discomfort. His apologies were waved aside, and there was the little clucking of the tongue that meant the problem was inconsequential.

Unlike many of his colleagues, the Minister spoke English, fluently and with little of the Mediterranean accent. An educated and lucid man, a professor of Law, an author of books, he explained the night's events to the Ambassador.

'And so, sir, we have at our doors another nightmare. We have another journey into the abyss of despair that after the murder of our friend, Aldo Moro, we hoped never to see again. For all of us then, in the Council of Ministers and in the Directorate of the Democrazia Cristiana, the decision to turn our backs on our friend provoked a bitter and horrible moment. We all prayed hard for guidance, then. All of us, sir. We walked across to church from the deliberations at the Piazza Gesù, and as one we went on our knees and prayed for God's guidance. If He gave it to us He manifested Himself in His own and peculiar way. His message bearer was Berlinguer, it was the Secretary-General of our Communist party who informed us that the infant understanding between his party and ours could not survive vacillation. The PCI dictated that there could be no concession to the Brigate Rosse. The demand that we release thirteen of their nominees from gaol was rejected. The chance to save one of the great men of our country was lost. Who can apportion victory and defeat between ourselves and the Brigatisti?'

The Minister mopped a smear of sweat from his neck with a handkerchief scented with cologne sufficiently to offend the Ambassador's nostrils. The monologue, the exposition of the day's business, continued.

'Now we must make more decisions, and first we must decide whether we follow the same rules as before or whether we offer a different response. The hostage on this occasion is not an Italian, nor is he a public figure who could by some be held accountable for the society in which we live. The hostage now is a guest, and totally without responsibility for the conditions that unhappily prevail in our country . . . I won't elaborate. I turn to the nature of the ransom demanded. One prisoner, one only. Thirteen we could not countenance, but one we might swallow, though the bone would stick. But swallow it we could if we had to.'

The Ambassador rocked pensively in his seat. They had cut down the curved hill from the Quirinale and surged with noise and power across the Piazza Venezia scattering the locust swarms of jeaned and T-shirted tourists. Not for him to reply at this stage, not till his specific opinion was required.

The Minister sighed, as if he had hoped for the load to be shared, and realized with regret that he must soldier on.

'We would be very loath to lose your Mr Harrison, and very loath to lose the Tantardini woman. We believe we should do everything within our power to save Mr Harrison. The dilemma is whether "everything in our power" constitutes interference in the judicial process against Tantardini.'

The Ambassador peered down at the hands in his lap. 'With respect, Minister, that is a decision the Italian government must take.'

'You would pass it all to us?'

The Ambassador recited, 'Anything else would be the grossest interference in the internal affairs of a long-standing and respected friend.'

The Minister smiled, grimly, without enjoyment. 'We have very little time, Ambassador. So my questions to you will be concise. There should be no misunderstandings.'

'I agree.'

The Minister savoured his question before speaking. The critical one, the reason that he had invited the Ambassador to travel with him. 'Is it likely that Her Majesty's Government will make an appeal to us to barter the woman Tantardini with the intention of saving Harrison's life?'

'Most unlikely.' The Ambassador was sure and decisive.

'We would not wish to take a course of action and afterwards receive a request from Whitehall for a different approach.'

'I repeat, Minister, it is most unlikely that we would ask for the freeing of Tantardini.'

The Minister looked with his jaded blue eyes at the Ambassador, a dab of surprise at his mouth. 'You are a hard people . . . you value principle highly. It does not have much merit in our society.'

'My government does not believe in bowing to the coercion of terrorism.'

'I put another hypothesis to you. If we refuse to negotiate with the Nappisti for the freedom of Tantardini and if as a consequence Harrison dies, would we be much criticized in Britain for the hard line, *la linea dura*, as we would say?'

'Most unlikely.' The Ambassador held the Minister's questioning glance, unswerving and without deviation, the reply clear as a pistol shot.

'We are not a strong country, Ambassador, we prefer to circumvent obstacles that fall across our path. We do not have the mentality of your cavalry, we do not raise our sabres and charge our enemy. We seek to avoid him . . .'

The car came fast to a halt and the driver and bodyguard leaned back to unfasten the locks on the rear doors. Out on the cobbled courtyard of the Palazzo Chigi the Ambassador breathed in the clean, freshened air and dried his hands on his trouser crease.

The Minister had not finished, busily he led the Ambassador into the centre of the yard where the sun was bright and where there was none who could overhear their words.

The Minister held the Ambassador's elbow tightly. 'Without a request from your government, there is no reason for our cabinet even to consider the options over Tantardini. You know what I am saying to you?'

'Of course.'

'You value the point of principle?'

'We value that consideration,' the Ambassador said quietly and with no relish.

The Minister pressed. 'Principle . . . even when the only beneficiary could be the Republic of Italy . . .'

'Still it would be important to us.' The Ambassador pulled at his tie, wanting relief from its grip. 'A man came to see me earlier this morning, he is a representative of Harrison's firm, and I told him what I have told you. He called me Pilate, he said I was washing my hands of his man. Perhaps he is right. I can only give my opinion, but I think it will be ratified by London.'

The Minister, still sombre, still clinging to the Ambassador's arm as if unwilling to break away for his cabinet colleagues waiting upstairs, said, 'If we refuse to release Tantardini, I do not think we will see Harrison again.'

The Ambassador accepted his opinion, nodded gravely.

'I will relay your view to Whitehall.'

The two men stood together, the Ambassador disproportionately taller. High frescoes in centuries-old paint leered down at them, mocking their transitory plans for history. Both perspired, both were too preoccupied to wash away the moisture beads. 'We understand each other, my friend. I will tell my colleagues that the British ask for no deal, no barter, no negotiation . . . and whatever happens we win the victory of principle . . .'

The Ambassador interrupted his short choked laugh. 'I am sure that Defence would send the Special Air Service, the close-quarter attack squad, as they did for Moro. They could be here this afternoon, if it were helpful.'

The Minister seemed to snort, give his judgement on an irrelevance, and walked away towards the wide staircase of the Palazzo.

Those who came late that morning to their desks in the Viminale on the second floor found that already the corridors and offices were nests of harsh and total activity. Vellosi paced among rooms, querying the necessity of bureaucrats and policemen alike to occupy their premises and their precious telephones, and where he found no satisfaction he commandeered and installed in their place his own subordinates. By ten he had secured an additional five rooms, all within shouting distance of his own. Technicians from the basements were kept busy hoisting the mess of cables and wires, attaching the transmitters and receivers that would secure him instant access to the control centre of the Questura and the office of Carboni. Some of the dispossessed hung about in the corridors, sleek in their suits and clean shirts, and smiled sweetly at the pace and moment of the working men around them and vowed they would have Vellosi's head served up on a charger were he not to deliver Geoffrey Harrison, free and unharmed, by the next morning. It was not the way that things were done in the Viminale. Noise, rising voices, the ringing of telephone bells, the pleas of radio static all mingled and coalesced in the corridor. Vellosi bounced between the sources of the confusion. He had told an examining magistrate that he was a hindrance and an obstruction, a carabinieri general that if he didn't push reinforcements into the Cosoleto area he would face speedy retirement, the persistent editor of the largest Socialist newspaper in the city that his head should be down the lavatory pan and would he clear the line, and sent out for more cigarettes, more coffee, more sandwiches.

At a hectic pace, bewildering to all those who were not central to the knot of the enquiry, the operation and investigation was launched. Those who participated and those who were idle and smirking behind their hands could agree on the one common point. The mood on the second floor of the Viminale was unique. Very few, though, were privy to the telephone conversation between Vellosi and the Minister, who spoke from an anteroom outside the cabinet deliberations at the Palazzo Chigi; only the inner court, the hard men on whom Vellosi leaned for succour and advice.

He had slammed the telephone down, barely a grunt of thanks to the Minister and confided to those in the room near him.

'They're standing firm, our masters. The men of deviation and compromise are holding a line. The bitch stays with us. Tantardini stays in her cell and rots there.'

The four who heard him understood the importance of the political decision, and they smiled to each other in a grim satisfaction and dropped their shoulders and raised their eyebrows and returned to their notepads and their internal telephone directories.

The information began to flow as the team hustled, begged and screamed into the telephones; shapes and patterns emerging from the kaleidoscope of mystery and dead alleys with which the day had started. Photographs of the known Nappisti at liberty had been spread out on a table for the portiere of the pensione where Claudio's body had been found. He had not wished to be involved, this elderly man whose job required a short tongue and shorter memory. He had turned over many pictures, showing little interest, muttering repeatedly of the failure of his recollection. One flicker of curiosity nullified his reluctance and a detective had seen the betrayal of recognition that the portiere had tried to hide. It was the work of a police photographer, and the typed message on the back of the picture gave the name of Giancarlo Battestini.

What name had he used? What identity card had he shown? What had he been wearing? What time had he arrived? What time had he left? The questions battered at the old man in his fading uniform till he had broken the reticence born of the sense of survival and told the story the police wanted to hear. The information breathed a new activity into the squad of men around Vellosi, whipped up their flagging morale and drove them on.

'It's beside the station,' Vellosi stormed down his telephone to a maggiore of the Pubblica Sicurezza. 'Right beside the station, this pensione, so get the photograph of Battestini down to the ticket counters, get it among the platform workers. Check him through all the trains to Reggio yesterday morning. Find the ticket inspectors on those trains, find their names, where they are now, and get that picture under their noses.'

There was so much commitment, so much cajoling and abuse that for a full minute Giuseppe Carboni stood ignored in the doorway of Vellosi's office. He bided his time; he would have his moment. And it would be choice, he thought, choice enough for it to have been worth his while to abandon his desk at the Questura and come unannounced to the Viminale. Vellosi was on his way for another prowl along the corridor to chase and jockey his men when he careered into the solid flesh wall of the policeman.

'Carboni, my apologies.' Vellosi laughed. 'We have been very busy here, we have been going hard . . .'

'Excellent, Vellosi, excellent.' A measured reply, tolerant and calm.

'. . . you will forgive my hurry, but we have discovered an important connection . . .'

'Excellent.'

'The boy of the NAP, Battestini . . . the one we missed when we took Tantardini, this is the kernel of this matter, it was he who killed the gorilla in the hotel. We have established that, and this Claudio was from those who took your Harrison . . . we have not been idle.'

'Excellent.'

Vellosi saw the smile on Carboni's face, as though the man had picked up a book and found it already familiar. His revelation won no recognition of achievement.

'And are you prospering too, Carboni?' Subdued already, Vellosi braced himself. 'Tell me.'

Carboni led the head of the anti-terrorist squad back to his desk. With his heavy rounded fingers he produced from a neat briefcase two facsimile documents. He laid them on the desk, carelessly pushing aside the piles of handwritten notes that had accumulated there through the morning. With his forefinger, Carboni stabbed at the upper sheet.

'This is the statement taken from Battestini by the polizia more than eighteen months ago . . . after his arrest for some student fracas. It carried his handwriting at the bottom.'

'I have seen it,' Vellosi said curtly.

Carboni pulled clear the under sheet. 'This is the statement from the Nappisti found at Seminara along with Harrison's card. Observe the writing, Vellosi, observe it closely.'

Vellosi's nose was a few inches from the papers as he held them to the light.

'It has been checked. At Criminalpol they ran it through the machines for me. The scientists have no doubt that they match.' Carboni savoured the moment. It was perhaps the finest of his professional life. He stood among the gods, the princes of the elite force, the cream of the anti-subversion fighters, and he told them something they had not seen for themselves. 'Giancarlo Battestini, nineteen years old, born in Pescara, university drop-out, probationer of the NAP, he is the one who has taken Geoffrey Harrison. Harrison is in Battestini's hands, and I venture to suggest that is the limit and extent of the conspiracy.'

Vellosi dropped back to his chair. A hush spread across the room and on into the corridor and further offices. Men in shirtsleeves holding cigarettes and plastic coffee beakers crowded to the doorway. 'Is it possible for one man – a mere boy – to have achieved all this?'

'Vellosi, it has happened.' The pleasure shone on Carboni's face. 'I won't detain you, but you should know we are sifting the reports of stolen vehicles from the area of the city of Reggio – there are not many, not at the times that fit. Two cinquencentos, but they would be too small for the purpose. There was a BMW but that is a conspicuous car. Close to the main station at Reggio, a few minutes' walk away, there is reported missing within ninety minutes of the arrival of the rapido from Roma a one-two-seven. It is red, and the registration is going out now. There is the same problem as always with the road blocks because we do not know where to set them, but if it is on the radio and the lunchtime television, then perhaps . . .'

'Shut up, Carboni.' Vellosi spoke quietly. He reached up with both arms, put them round Carboni's neck and pulled the ill-shaven face towards him. Their cheeks met, the kiss of friends and equals. 'You're a genius, Carboni, nothing but a genius.'

Carboni blushed, swung on his heel and left with a little wave of his fingers for farewell. He had stirred Vellosi's ant hole, changed its direction, shifted the whole basis of the enquiry.

'Well, don't stand about,' Vellosi snapped at his audience. 'We've let an amateur show us what's happening, point to what's been staring at us for hours. We have more in a day than we had in a month with Moro. Use it.'

But for Moro he had had time. For Harrison he had less than twenty-four hours till the expiry of the ultimatum.

Vellosi scuffed among his papers till he found the photograph of Battestini. He searched the mouth and the jaw line and the set of the eyes for information, scrabbling to catch up, scratching to make do with diminishing hours, the tools of a policeman's trade.

'The little bastard could be anywhere.' And Vellosi swore and reached for his coffee that was cold.

He must go back to the basics, back to deep and quiet thought in the midst of the noise surrounding him, back to analysis of the minimal factual evidence available.

Start again, start from the beginning. Return to the face of Battestini, drag from those features the response that should be made.

Giancarlo Battestini, imprisoned in Rome after studying in the capital's university, and a member of a NAP cell in that city. Could the boy have links with the far countryside? Likely or unlikely? Vellosi flexed his fingers. The answer was obvious. The boy would know nothing of Calabria. A city boy, a town boy, a foreigner in the Mezzo Giorno.

He turned and called to a colleague, who stubbed his cigarette, drained his coffee and came to him.

'Battestini would not believe he could survive in the countryside, it is beyond his experience. Correct?'

'Correct.'

'He would try to return to the city?'

'Possible.'

'In the files he is linked only with Rome: would he try to get back here?'

'Perhaps.'

'He is divorced from Pescara. He has nothing there. And if he comes back towards Rome he must come by car because he cannot take a prisoner by train.'

'Probable.'

The momentum carried Vellosi on. 'If he comes by road he must decide for himself whether he will attempt speed on the autostrada, or whether he will go for the safer and slower old roads.'

'I think he would choose the autostrada.'

Vellosi slapped his fist into the palm of his other hand. 'And he must stop . . .'

'For petrol.'

'He has to stop.'

'Certain.'

'Either at a station on the autostrada or he must come off and use a toll gate and a station off the main route.'

'If he is coming to Rome, if he is coming by car, if he is on the autostrada, then that is correct.'

Vellosi thrust his chair behind him, rose to his full height and shouted, 'Work on the petrol stations and the autostrada tolls. Each side of Naples. Call Carboni, tell him that too.'

His colleague was no longer beside him.

Vellosi slumped back into his seat. There was no one to praise him, no one to smile and slap his back and offer congratulations. To himself he muttered, over and over again, 'The boy will come back to the city, the boy will return to Rome.'

14

While the disparate arms and commands of security forces strove to drag themselves into a state of intervention, the small red Fiat slipped unremarked through the toll gate marking the terminal of the autostrada at Roma Sud and away towards the Raccordo Annulare, the ring road skirting the capital. With the passing of the mass-produced common car through the toll check, the chances of its detection, always remote, were reduced to the minimal.

The two men had exchanged only desultory conversation, preferring to brood to themselves in the confined space. Geoffrey Harrison, the pain gone from his back, drove in a careless and detached way as if concern and anxiety were no longer with him. His mind numbed, his brain deadened, he performed the automatic tasks of keeping the car in the centre lane of traffic, the speed constant. At two places, the petrol station and the toll gate, he told himself there had been the possibility of a break-out from the car. But the will to seek his freedom was reduced. He had sat meekly in the driving seat, neither looking at nor avoiding the man who secured the fuel tank cap and wiped wetly over the windscreen. He had held his silence as the young man at the toll had handed the change through the open window.

Manipulated and broken, too destroyed to weep, too cudgelled to fight, Harrison guided the car around the east side of the city.

For Violet Harrison the mood of the morning alternated between remorse and defiance.

She had lain in bed, curling slowly over, switching the images of a prisoner husband with those of a dark-chested boy with a flat stomach and sinewed hair-covered legs. Both caused her pain.

If she could again find the boy at the beach and forge her liaison, then it would not be the first time, nor the second, nor the third. It was the usual way she found relief when the strain became too much for her. It had nothing to do with loving Geoffrey, whatever that meant, nothing to do with being his wife, sharing his life. All that was irrelevant. But there had to be a valve somewhere when the steam built up, and this was her release: writhing under a stranger, without obligation, without attachment.

There had been an Irish barman from Evesham in Worcestershire, sought out on the day after Geoffrey, the young industrial trainee, had told her there was a discrepancy in the books and that the branch Chief Accountant believed him responsible. He had been cleared of suspicion, but only after Violet had spent an afternoon in an autumn field with a man whose name she had never known.

There had been a West Indian bus driver from Dalston in East London after a Friday night when Geoffrey had come home to report that he had drunk too much that lunchtime and told the head of his department to stuff his job where it would hurt and smell. Geoffrey had apologized on the Monday morning, been accepted back with hand-shakes and smiles and had never known of Violet's two hours on a

Sunday morning in a railway hotel close to King's Cross ridden hard by a muscled lad who called her 'darlin'' and bit her shoulders.

Other crises had come, some greater, some lesser. Same palliative, same escape; and Geoffrey had remained unaware of them, of that she was sure and grateful. She remembered once watching on television the wife of the British governor of an island colony, just widowed after her husband had been terribly murdered while taking a late evening stroll in the gardens of the Residence. The woman had worn white and sat on a sofa with her daughters and talked to the cameras with composure and dignity. Had it been Violet, she thought, she would have been in the chauffeur's bed. She knew it, hated it, and told herself she did not have the strength to resist. And if Geoffrey did not know, if Geoffrey were not wounded, then what did it matter? Who else's business was it?

There had been no boy in Rome. God knows there were times when she would have wished for one, hoped for the release from an arched back and a driving thrust. But there had been none. Until she had been to the beach she had not given herself even the opportunity. Isolated and cocooned in a flat where the telephone never rang, the doorbell never sounded, she had been protected from the predators.

She dressed with studied care as if anxious not to crease the bikini and the covering dress, as if forgetful that she would be sitting in her car for the hour-long drive to Ostia or Fregene or Santa Marinella. A peahen jealous of her scant plumage. The bikini was new, and the dress a month old had not been worn. Adornment for the fall. Her hair she combed loosely, sitting at her dressing-table mirror and aware of the excitement and the tremble that came with the narcotic, with the contemplation of the unmentionable. It was the only gesture of independence that Violet Harrison was capable of, to climb into her little car, drive away down the road and spend and punish herself of her own volition, in her own time, in her own panting scenario. Would Geoffrey have cared if he had known . . . ? Perhaps. Perhaps not. But it didn't matter because Geoffrey did not know, Geoffrey was away, bound like a chicken with the stubble on his face and a gun at his head. Geoffrey would be thinking of her, hers would be the face in his mind, as clear and sharp as it was in the mirror before her. Geoffrey would be leaning on her, conjuring in his mind only the good times. That was when the remorse always won through from the defiance. That was when it hurt, when the urge was strongest, when she was weakest, least able to struggle.

Smudges of tears were summoned below the neatly careened blonde hair.

She was aware of the telephone bell. Long, brilliant calls, summoning her to the kitchen. Perhaps it was Mother from London announcing which flight she was taking, and was her little poppet all right, and did she know that it was all over the papers. Perhaps it was those miserable bastards who had called before and jabbered in an alien language. The ringing would not abandon her, would not leave her, and pulled her off the low chair and dragged her through the doorway towards it. Every step and she prayed that it would cease its siren call. Her entreaties were ignored, the telephone rang on.

'Violet Harrison. Who's that?'

It was Carpenter. Archie Carpenter of ICH.

'Good morning, Mr Carpenter.' A cool voice, the confidence coming fast, because this was the little man who had run from her, the little suburban man.

Had she heard the latest information on her husband?

'I've heard nothing since last night. I don't read the Italian papers. The Embassy haven't called me.'

She should know that her husband was now thought to be in the hands of an extremist political group. She should know that demands had been made to the government for the release of a prisoner before nine the next morning. She should know that if the condition was not met the threat had been made that her husband would be murdered.

Violet rocked on the balls of her feet. Eyes closed, two hands clutching at the telephone. The pain seemed to gather at her temples, then sear through deep behind.

Was she still there?

A faint, small voice. 'I'm here, Mr Carpenter. I'm listening.'

And it was a damned scandal, the whole thing. The Embassy wouldn't lift a finger. Did she know that, could she credit it? Geoffrey had been relegated in importance, dismissed and left to the incompetence of an Italian police investigation.

Fear now, and her voice shriller. 'But it was all agreed. It was agreed, wasn't it, that the company would pay? It was all out of the Italians' hands.'

Different now. Money was one thing. Easy, plenty of it, no problem. Different now, because it was said to be a point of principle. Said to be giving in to terrorism if the prisoner were to be released.

'Well, what's a fucking principle got to do with Geoffrey? Do they want him dead or what?' She shrieked into the telephone, voice raucous and rising.

They'd say it was the same as in the Schleyer case in Germany, the same as in the Moro case locally. They'd say they couldn't surrender. They'd use words like blackmail, and phrases like 'dignity of the State'. Those were the things they'd say, and the Embassy would support them, every damned inch.

'But it will mean Geoffrey's killed . . .' The hysteria was rampant, and with it the laughter and the breaking of flimsy control. '. . . They can't just sacrifice him. This bloody place hasn't had a principle in years,

656

it's not a word in the bloody language. They couldn't even spell it here.'

Carpenter was going to call Head Office in London. They wouldn't take this lying down. She could rely on that. He'd call back within an hour, she should stay by the telephone.

Her voice had risen to its summit, to its highest pitch, and was now the product of crouched and humiliated shoulders.

'Could you come and see me, Mr Carpenter?'

Did she want him to come to the flat?

'Could you come and tell me what's happening? Yes, to the flat.'

Carpenter was sorry, very sorry indeed. But he had an appointment, an urgent appointment. She would understand, but he had a fair amount on his plate, didn't he? But Carpenter would telephone her as soon as he had something to say, and that would be, he thought, within an hour.

The cycle of her changing mood swung on. The screaming past, the whimpering gone. Cold again with the veneer of assurance. 'Don't call again, Mr Carpenter, because I won't be here. Perhaps I'll be back this evening. Thank you for telling me what's going on. Thank you for telling me what's going to happen to Geoffrey.'

Before he could speak again she had cut Carpenter off the line.

Violet Harrison strode into her bedroom, swept a swimming towel off a bedside chair, and the underclothes that she had discarded the previous evening to the floor. She dropped them into her Via Condotti shopping-bag and headed for the lift and the basement garage.

Forty minutes after the red Fiat had moved on to the Raccordo with its centre reservation of pink and white oleanders, Giancarlo gestured to Harrison to turn off to his right. It was the Via Cassia junction and within five miles of his home. Strange to Harrison to be in the midst of tried and trusted surroundings. But the disorientation won through and he obeyed the instruction without question. The silence, which for both of them was now safe and losing its awkwardness, remained unbroken.

They had made good time. Giancarlo could reflect that the stamina of the driver had been remarkable.

They had given up the speed of the Raccordo for a slow, winding road, heavy with lorries and impatient cars, flanked by the speculative flats that overburdened the facilities. Several times they stopped in the bumper to bumper jams. Harrison sat passively, not knowing where he was being led, declining to ask.

*

657

Along the length of the Reggio Calabria to Rome autostrada patrol cars of the Polizia Stradale and carabinieri had begun the pin and haystack game of searching for a red Fiat car of the most popular model in use. Scores of motorists found themselves pitched out of 127s, covered by aimed machine-guns as they were searched, ordered to produce identity papers while their faces were examined against the photostated likenesses of Battestini and Harrison. The road blocks were large and impressive, each utilizing a minimum of a dozen armed men, and were comprehensive enough to warrant coverage by the RAI electronic camera teams.

The concentration of effort and manpower was blessed. From the toll gate at Monte Cassino a Fiat of the right size and colour was remembered. A young man had asked for petrol. A small success and one sufficient to whet the appetite as the police concentration built up in the community of Monte Cassino. The garage owner was quizzed in his office.

Yes, he could tell them who had been manning the pumps at that time. Yes, he could tell them the address of that man's home. Yes, and also he could tell them that this man had said the previous evening when he came on duty that after he finished the night shift it was his intention to take his grandchildren into the central mountains. No, he did not know where they would go, and he had waved expansively at the big hazed skyline, and shrugged.

The helicopters were ordered from Rome. The military twin-engined troop carriers were loaded with armed men, sweating in the confined spaces on the baked, makeshift landing-pad outside the town. Four-seater spotter machines were dispatched to fly low over the high ranges and valleys, brushing the contours. Lorryloads of polizia were slowly given the co-ordinates on large-scale maps that the whole rugged area might be sealed.

The white walls of the mountain monastery looked down upon the hopeless task, while the shouting and irritation of the flustered staff officers in the commandeered school reflected the feeling that the terrain, rugged and vast, would mock their efforts to find a boy and his captive and his car.

But the element of chance born from the routine moved the chase on, gave it a new impetus, a new urgency. The chance without which the police cannot hope for success in a manhunt and which had forsaken them when the centre of the country was scoured for the ill-fated President of the Democrazia Cristiana.

A young man had gone off duty from his work at a gate on the Roma Sud toll. He had taken the bus home after a six-hour shift, had doused himself under the shower, and dressed and sat down at the kitchen table for cheese and fruit before lying on his bed to rest. His daughter, just a baby, had been crying, and therefore he could not be certain he had heard correctly the description of the two men that had been broadcast on the radio. The detail, rigidly held to, from which he would not deviate, caused the men in uniform and suits to paw at the air in their frustration, but Giuseppe Carboni was master of his own office, was at pains to thank the young man for his gesture in calling his nearest police station. Past eleven in the morning, time hurtling on its way, and Carboni demanded the patience of those around him. The photograph was produced, the picture of Geoffrey Harrison, and the young man nodded and smiled and looked for praise. It was strange, he said to Carboni, that a man who wore an expensive shirt should be unshaven, with grime at his neck and his hair untended.

Carboni's room had disintegrated into movement, leaving the witness to gaze long and hard at the picture.

Telephones, telexes, radios, all into play now to seal the city of Rome. Close it up, was the order, block the routes to L'Aquila to the east, to Firenze in the north. Tighten a net on the autostradas and damn the queues. Pull off the men beginning the search of the Monte Cassino hills, bring them back to the capital. Carboni set it all in motion, then came back to the young man.

'And there was a boy, just a ragazzo, with this man?'

'I think so . . .'

'It is the older man that you are clear on?'

'That was the one that gave me the money. It is difficult to see across the interior of a car from where we sit in the cabins.'

A good witness, would not admit to that which he was not certain of. Carboni replaced the photograph of Harrison with that of Giancarlo Battestini. 'Could it be this boy? Could this be the passenger?'

'I am sorry, Dottore, but really I did not see the passenger's face.'

Carboni persisted. 'Anything at all that you can remember of the passenger?'

'He wore jeans . . . and they were tight, that I remember. And his legs were thin. He would have been young . . .' The toll attendant stopped, head low, frowning in concentration. He was tired and his thoughts came slowly. Unseen to him Carboni held up his hand to prevent any interruption from those who were now filtering back into the room. '. . . He paid, the driver that is, and he paid with a big note and when I gave him the change he passed it to the passenger, but the other's hands were beneath a light coat that was between them, I could see that from my cabin, the driver dropped the change on to the top of the coat. They did not say anything, and then he drove away.'

Pain on Carboni's face. To the general audience he announced, 'That is where the gun was, that is why Harrison drives, because the boy Battestini has the pistol to his body.'

The young man from Roma Sud was sent home.

Fuel for the computer, for the dispersal system of information, and with each piece of typed paper that slipped from his office, Carboni fussed and plotted. 'And tell them to be careful, for God's sake to be careful. Tell them that the boy has killed three times in forty-eight hours and will kill again.'

There was no smirk on the features of Giuseppe Carboni, no expression of euphoria. Geographically they had run their quarry to a ground comprising a trivial number of square kilometres, but the ground, he could consider ruefully, was not favourable. One man and a prisoner to hunt for in a conurbation that housed four million citizens.

Chance had taken the sad, worn-down policeman up a road of promise, and had left him at a great crossroads which boasted no signposts.

He reached for his telephone to ring Francesco Vellosi.

At noon the men held in maximum security on the island of Asinara were unlocked from their cells and permitted under heavy supervision to queue together in the communal canteen for their pasta and meat lunch. Conversation was not forbidden.

The long-term prisoners, those serving from twenty years to the ultimate maximum of ergastolo, the natural end of life, all had radio sets in their cells. Behind the heavy doors and barred windows news had been carried of the kidnapping of Geoffrey Harrison, the ultimatum for the freedom of Franca Tantardini, the failed reprisal against Francesco Vellosi.

Several men sidled close to the leader of the NAP. Who was the boy Battestini, they asked, a name blasted from every news bulletin in the previous hour? How big was the infra-structure organization from which he worked? The capo, the movement's spiritual leader in intellect and violence, had shrugged his shoulders, opened his hands and said quietly that he had never heard of the boy nor sanctioned the action.

A few had felt he was being obsessively secretive, but there were those who waited and shuffled forward with their steel trays who understood the bafflement of the man who claimed absolute domination of the NAP from his island cell.

It was one thing to give orders, another to have them implemented. Many men in the Questura and the Viminale had lent their names and authority to instructions for the sealing of the city. Contingency plans

660

for such measures were to hand, but it was not easy to mount a police and para-military effort of the scale required. Which were the vital routes, which were the areas for the greatest concentration of man-power, where in the streets of the city should the maximum vigilance be observed? They were questions that demanded time for answers, and time was a lost commodity.

The Fiat had turned off the main Cassia road at the village of La Storta, travelled fifteen more kilometres and then turned again, choosing a narrower route that would skirt the hill town of Bracciano and lead towards the deep, blue-tinted volcanic lake beneath the collection of straggling grey stone houses. The car was forty kilometres now from the heart of the capital and here the country was at peace, and the bombs and killings and kidnappings were matters delivered only by the newspapers and television bulletins. This was a place of small farmers, small shopkeepers, small businessmen, people who valued their tran-quillity, drank their wine and drew their curtains against the wind of brutality, chaos and graft that blew from across the fields and the main road.

Abruptly Giancarlo pointed to an open field gate that was set in a wall of stone and blackthorn to the left of the road and some four hundred metres short of the water's edge. The field into which they drove, jerking over the thick grass, was skirted on two sides by a wood of heavy-leafed oaks and sycamores. Tall, shade-bearing trees. Gian-carlo had taken a great risk, to travel this far in daylight, but he was sufficiently secure in himself, sufficiently buoyant after coming so far, to believe that he had outstripped the apparati of the nation. Far up the side of the field, where it was shielded from the road, he waved for Harrison to stop, glanced around him and then motioned towards a place close by where the grazing of the field merged with the trees, a place where the cattle would come in winter to escape the ferocity of the rain-storms.

There was a darkness and shadow in the interior of the car as Harrison finally pulled at the brake handle and switched off the ignition. The place was well chosen. Hidden from the air, hidden from the road, perfect in its safety and loneliness. Giancarlo grabbed decisively at the keys, smiled with contempt at his driver, and watching him all the time with the gun cocked, climbed out. He stretched himself, flexed his barely developed chest, enjoyed the sun that filtered and dappled between the leaf ceiling.

'Are you going to kill me here?' Harrison asked.

'Only if by nine o'clock tomorrow morning they have not given me Franca.'

It was the first time that Giancarlo had spoken since they had left the autostrada.

International Chemical Holdings with representation in thirty-two countries of the First and Third Worlds maintained close links with the Foreign and Commonwealth Office and the Ministry of Overseas Development. Its Board members and principal executives were frequent guests at the black tie dinners given by government to visiting delegations, they figured cautiously in the New Year's and Birthday Honours lists, and to some the workings of the company were regarded as an extension of British foreign policy. An aid package to a newly independent member of the Commonwealth often contained the loan necessary to launch an ICH plant.

Sir David Adams was well known to the Minister both as a businessman aloof from party politics and as a social guest to be valued for his ease and humour in difficult company. On the telephone pad of Sir David's desk in the City tower block was the Foreign Secretary's direct number. He had spent a few brief moments pondering Archie Carpenter's call from Rome before scanning the pad for the number. He had been connected with a private secretary, had requested, and been granted, a few minutes of the Foreign Secretary's time before lunch.

A desolate sort of room, the Minister's working office seemed to Sir David. Not the sort of quarters he'd ever have tolerated for himself. Wretched velvet drapes, the furniture out of a museum, and a desk large enough for snooker. He'd have had one of those young interior decorator chaps in with a bucket of white paint and some new pictures and something on the floor that represented the nineteen-eighties, not the days of dropping tigers at Amritsar. He was not kept waiting sufficiently long for the completion of his refurbishment plans for the office.

They sat opposite each other in lush, high-backed armchairs. There was a Campari soda for the Minister, a gin and French for the Managing Director. No aides, no stenographers.

'Not to beat about the bush, Minister, the message from my chap out there came as a bit of a shock. My chap, and he's no fool, got his feet on the ground, says your Ambassador has just about told the Italians that so far as Whitehall is concerned they should run this new phase in the Harrison business as if our man was any Italian businessman. I find that a bit heavy.' Sir David sipped at his glass, enough to dampen his tongue, little more.

'Bit of an oversimplification, David. Not quite the full story.' The Foreign Secretary smiled over the bulldog lapping folds of his cheeks. 'The actual situation is that a senior member of the Italian cabinet, and this is of course confidential, asked HMG via the Ambassador and at a time when the Italians were having to make early but very important decisions of approach in this matter, whether HMG would be requesting the release of a terrorist to safeguard your fellow. That's not quite the same thing, is it?'

'With respect, it's the germ of the same thing. I'll put it another way and ask you what initiative the British government are taking to secure the release, unharmed, of Geoffrey Harrison?' Another sip, another faint trembling of the liquid line in the glass.

'You should know there can only be one answer. There is no initiative that I can take with regard to the internal politics of Italy . . .'

'You can suggest that it is desirable to get my man back, whether or not that requires unlocking a door for this woman they're holding.'

'David, I have a full programme of meetings.' There was a sternness in the rebuke. 'I should have been at one now but I've relegated it to a junior. When I make that gesture, please do me the courtesy of hearing me out.'

'Accepted. Apologies, and sincerely meant.' An inclined head acknowledged the ministerial rap.

'Italy isn't a business competitor, David. It's not a rival company. If it collapses, if it goes bankrupt, morally or financially, if it's greatly weakened, the Members of the Commons won't stand up and cheer and wave their Order papers as your shareholders would. It's not just a place of funny foreigners, David, of spaghetti and gigolos and bottom-pinchers. It's a major power in the West, it's a NATO ally, it's the seventh industrial power in the world. You know all that better than I do. When things are difficult there we draw no pleasure from it. We do our damnedest to support them, and a friend needs support when she's on her knees. The Moro affair nearly crippled them. The State was held to ransom, the very system of democracy was threatened, but they held firm, and in doing so they lost – they sacrificed – a leader of great standing.'

'It's a fine speech, Minister, and it will do you credit in the House on the day my company buries Geoffrey Harrison. You'll send a wreath, I trust?' The two men eyed each other. The counter-punches had bloodied the noses and the eyes were puffing and there were many rounds to go.

'Not worthy of you, David, and you know better than to taunt me. When the German was missing in Northern Ireland, the one we never found, the Minister of the day didn't have Bonn snapping at him. When Herrema, the Dutchman, was kidnapped in Eire, The Hague was quick to express support for all the measures that Dublin was taking.'

'You're still hiding, Minister.' Sir David Adams was not one to be easily deflected. He pushed his adversary towards the ropes, leading with his chin, a lifetime's habit. 'You're hiding behind a screen of meaningless protocol. I want a young and innocent man back, I want him

663

back with his wife. I don't give a damn for Italian terrorism, nor do I give a damn for Italian democracy. I've done business there and I know the place. I know how much of our payments go to the bank in Milan, how much goes to Zürich. I know about the yachts and the bribes and the villas. I understand why they've an urban guerrilla problem on their doorstep. It's a nasty, clannish society that can't look after itself, and it's not for you to abandon an Englishman in the sewer there in order to start giving those people lessons in principle, or whatever.'

'You haven't been listening to me, David.' Ice cold, the Foreign Secretary, but the temper concealed beneath the frozen smile. 'They sacrificed one of their principal post-war leaders, wrote him off, and on a point of principle.'

'We're going in circles.'

'We are indeed, but I suggest you are leading.'

Sir David gulped at his glass, the impatience winning, half drained it. 'I put it to you, Minister, that there is something you can do that doesn't infringe on the question of "principle" . . .' He rolled over the word, gutting it of all feeling. 'You can find out from your friends in Rome the exact importance of this woman. You can find out her importance to the guerrilla movement. And let's not stand on too high a pedestal. I know my recent history. Northern Ireland, right? . . . We emptied Long Kesh when we were after a political initiative, chucked the Provisionals out on to the streets to get on again with their bombing and maiming. What happened to principle, then? We've given their leaders safe-conduct. We sent the Palestinian girl, Leila Khaled, home from Ealing courtesy of an RAF jet. We're not lily-white. We can bend when it suits us . . .'

'Who's making speeches, David?'

'Don't be flippant, Minister. My fellow has little more than twenty hours to live.' The gimlet eyes of Sir David Adams offered no concessions. 'Italy can live without this woman in a gaol, Italy can survive . . .'

He broke off in response to a light knock on the door behind him. Irritation at the interruption registered on both men's faces. The Foreign Secretary glanced at his watch. A young man, shirtsleeves and club tie, glided across the room with a telex flimsy in his hand. He gave it without explanation to the Minister and withdrew as silently as he had come. There was quiet in the room as the message was read, the Minister's forehead lined, his lips pursed.

'It's the Harrison business, that's why they interrupted.' No emotion in the voice, just an ageing and a sadness. 'He's held by a young psychopath responsible for three killings in two days. The assessment of the Italians is that he will kill your man without hesitation or compassion should the deadline expire. The woman involved is called Franca Tantardini. She is classified in Rome as a major activist and will face charges of murder, attempted murder, armed insurrection, they're putting the book on her. Our Embassy records the observation that several of the senior and most respected officers of the Italian public security forces would resign should she be released. In addition the Italian Communist Party have endorsed in a statement the government's no deal approach.'

The Foreign Secretary looked across the room to the shadowed face of the industrialist.

'It's not in our hands, David. It is beyond the British government to offer intervention. I am very sorry.'

Sir David Adams rose from his chair. A little over six feet in height, a dominating and handsome man, and one unused to failure.

'You won't forget the wreath, Minister?'

And he was gone, leaving his glass half filled on the small table beside the chair.

Michael Charlesworth from his office and Archie Carpenter from his hotel room had spoken by telephone. These two men of differing backgrounds, drawn from divergent social groups, seemed to want to talk to each other because their feeling of helplessness was overpowering. Both were eunuchs with little to do but listen to the radio, as Charlesworth did, and scan the newspapers and gaze at the staring photographs of Battestini plastered in the afternoon editions, as Carpenter did.

'Shouldn't you be with Violet Harrison?' Charlesworth had asked.

'I called her this morning, said I'd call her back – she said not to bother . . .'

'It's not my job, thank God, holding her hand.'

'Not mine either,' Carpenter had snapped.

'Perhaps.' Charlesworth had let it sink, let the thought drown. He sensed the desperation of the man who had been sent to take decisions, to move mountains, and who was failing. 'You'd better come up to my place tonight and have a bite with us.'

'I'd like that.'

Charlesworth had returned to his radio, moodily flitting between the three RAI services. They portrayed activity and haste and effort, and nothing of substance.

It had taken Giancarlo fully thirty minutes to find the place that satisfied him. He had prodded Geoffrey Harrison through the deeper recesses of the wood, using him as a plough to clear a way between the whippy saplings that sprang back at the eyes and ears and forearms. But the place that pleased him was close to a slight path, where once a giant oak had grown before the wind had pulled it down, tearing open a great gouge in the earth beneath its raised roots. A shallow pit had been left that would only be found if the searcher stumbled to its very rim.

Giancarlo methodically repeated the drill of earlier in the morning. He bound Harrison's ankles with the flex, and then again tied his wrists behind his back. The spare lengths he used to loop around the stronger roots exposed under the earth roof. If Harrison lay still he could rest on his side in some attitude of comfort. If he moved, if he struggled, then the wire would bite at his flesh and cut and slash it. The boy had thought of this, introducing knots that dictated that the reward for movement was pain. There was one refinement from the morning, the handkerchief from Harrison's trouser pocket, twisted like a rope, was inserted between his teeth, knotted behind his ears. Giancarlo was careful in tying the handkerchief, as if he had no wish to suffocate his prisoner.

When the work was finished he stepped back and admired it. He was going to get some food. Harrison should not worry, he would not be away long.

Within moments he was lost among the lines of trees and shadows and the slanting columns of light.

15

Geoffrey Harrison's field of vision was minimal. It comprised only a slight arc encompassing a score of rising tree-trunks, heavy with lime and flaking bark, that soared above the rim of the small crater in which he lay. Above and around him was the motion of the isolated wood; a pair of woodpeckers in pursuit of a jay, cackling protest at the intrusion of the nest-hunting bird; a tiny pettirosso, its reddened breast thrust forward proudly as it dug and chipped for grubs and insects; a young rabbit that darted in terror among the trees after a brief encounter with a skilful stoat; the wind in the upper branches that collided with one another high up and beyond the limit of his vision. Action and activity. Those that were free and liberated going about the business of their day while he lay helpless and in fear beneath them.

But his brain was no longer stifled. The very solitude of the wood had roused him, made him aware of each miniature footfall, keened and sharpened his senses. The drug effect of the endless miles of autostrada driving was drifting from his system and with the withdrawal from the approaching headlights and the perpetual traffic lanes came the increasing awareness of his situation. That something was stirring in him, some desire once again to affect his future, was clear from the way he tested the skill with which he had been bound. He tried to move his arms apart, seeing how tightly the knots were tied, whether there was stretch in the plastic-coated flex. The sweat crawled again on his chest. Several minutes the effort lasted before the realization came that the binding had been done well, that it was beyond his capabilities to loosen the wires.

So what are you going to do, Geoffrey? Going to sit there like a bloody turkey in its coop, waiting for Christmas Eve and the oven to heat up? Are you going to lie on your side and wait for it, and hope it's quick and doesn't hurt? Should have done something in the car, or at the petrol stations, or at the toll gates, or when the traffic stopped them on the Cassia. When you had the chance, when you were body to body, close in the seats of the car.

And what would he have done about it, precious Giancarlo?

Might have fired, might not, can't be sure.

But it would have been better than this, better than sitting the hours out.

Would it have been that easy in the car? He'd kept the door locked because that way there was one more movement required before it could have been opened, and more delay, more confusion, more chance for him to shoot.

Idiot, Geoffrey Harrison, bloody idiot. It wouldn't have mattered how long it took to get the door open because he'd have been flattened by then, squashed half out of existence, you're damn near double his bloody weight, starved little scarecrow.

But you didn't do it, Geoffrey, and there's no thanks in dreaming, no thanks in playing the bloody hero in the mind. The time was there and you bucked it, preferred to sit in the car and wait and see what happened.

You can see it now, lad, can't you? Half scared to bloody death already, and there's a pain in your balls and an ache in your chest and you want to cry for yourself. Scared out of your mind.

Too bloody right, and who wouldn't be? Because it's curtains, isn't it? Curtains and finish and they'll be getting the bloody box ready for you and cutting the flowers and choosing the plot, and the chaps in Head Office will have sent their black ties to the dry-cleaner's. Through his mind the misery was fuelled. No chance in a hundred bloody light years that Franca would get her marching orders. All in the imagination of the little prig. Couldn't let her out, not a hard line girl that it had taken months to get the manacles on. But that doesn't leave room, Geoffrey. Leaves you on a prayer and a hope . . . And what had Geoffrey bloody Harrison done, how come his number was spinning with the lottery balls?

God, he was going to cry again, could feel the tears coming, thirty-six years old and fit to wet himself, and no stake in the place, no commitment.

Wrong again, Geoffrey, you're bleeding the masses, crucifying the workers.

That's lunacy, bloody madness.

Not to this kid, not to little Mister Giancarlo Battestini, and he's going to blow the side of your bloody head off just to prove it's real.

Harrison lay with his eyes tight shut, fighting the welling moisture. The foul taste of the cotton handkerchief suppurated around his back teeth. Nausea rising and with it the terror that he would be unable to be sick and choke in his own vomit. What a bloody way to go, choking in your own filth. Eyes so tight closed, lids squeezed so that they hurt, so that they were bruised.

Violet, darling bloody Violet, my bloody wife, I want to be with you darling, I want you to take me away from here. Violet, please, please, don't leave me here to them.

Near to his head a small branch cracked.

Harrison flashed open his eyes, swung his body up and blinked away the tears.

Ten feet from him was a pair of child's knee-high boots, their sheen broken by smears of dried mud and bramble scratches, the miniature replicas of an adult's farm wear, and rising out of them were little baggy trousers with the knees holed and the material faded with usage and washing. He twisted his head slowly higher and gulped in the salvation of a check sports shirt with the buttons haphazardly fastened and the sleeves floppily rolled. There was a sparse and skinny bronzed neck and a young clean face that was of the country and exposed to wind. Harrison sagged back, dropped himself hard against the earth. Thank God. A bloody ministering angel. White sheets, wings and a halo. Thank God. He felt a shiver, the spasm of relief, running hard in him . . . but not to hang about, not with Giancarlo gone only for food. Come on, kid. God, I love you. Come on, but don't hang about. You're a bloody darling, you know that. But there's not all day. He looked up again into the child's face, and wondered why the little one just stood, stationary and still. Like a Pan statue, three paces away, not speaking, demonstrating a graveness at the cheeks, a caution in the eyes. Come on, kid, don't be frightened. He tried to wriggle his body so that the bound wrists would be visible – waste of time, the child could see the gag and the trussed legs. The little feet backed away, as if the movement disconcerted him. What's the bloody matter with the kid? Well, what do you expect, Geoffrey? What did your mother tell you when you were small and went out into the fields and woods to play, and along the street and out of sight of the row of houses that belonged in their

668 ,

road? Don't talk to strangers, there's funny people about, don't take sweets from them.

Harrison stared at the boy, stared and tried to understand. Six, perhaps seven years old, deep and serious eyes, a puzzled and concerned mouth, hands that tugged and pulled the cloth of his trousers. Not an idiot, not a daft one, this child, but hesitant in coming forward as if the man who lay in this contorted posture was a forbidden apple. As best he could through the impediment of the gag Geoffrey Harrison tried to smile at the child and beckon with his head for the boy to come closer, but he won no response. Be a loner, wouldn't he, a self-contained tiny entity? Won't take chewing gum from a man he doesn't know. It can't bloody happen to me. Please, not now, God. Please, God, not a trick like this on me. It was going to take time. But time wasn't available, not with Giancarlo gone only for food. What would the mean bastard do with the child? Think on that, Geoffrey, think on that as you try to win him forward, try to bring him closer. What does Giancarlo do with the kid if he finds him here, all bright eyes and a witness? That's an obscenity, that's foul. But that's truth, Geoffrey . . . Hurry up, kid, come closer quickly. Not just my life, your life is hanging on a cotton thread.

Geoffrey Harrison knew that he had no call on the child, that this was a private matter between himself and the boy Giancarlo. But he beckoned again with his head and above the cloth at his mouth his cheeks creased in what he thought of as a welcome greeting.

The child watched him with neither a smile nor fear, and the small boots stayed rooted, neither slipping forward nor back. It would take a long time and Giancarlo might return before the work was finished.

There were many young campers on the wooded hills and beside the lake at Bracciano and the stubble-cheeked boy in the alimentari on the waterfront aroused no comment. High summer holiday season, and for many the cool, shaded slopes and the deep lake in its volcanic crater represented a more welcome resting ground than the scrum pack of the beaches. For those who had abandoned the city, however temporarily, the news bulletins went unheard, the newspapers unread. In the alimentari Giancarlo attracted no attention as he bought a plastic razor, an aerosol of shaving soap, and six rosetti filled with cheese and tomato slices.

From the alimentari he headed for the back lavatory of one of the small trattorie that stretched out on precarious stilts over the grey beach dust. With the cold water and the thickness of his cheek growth and the sharpness of the new blade he had to exercise care that he did not lacerate his face. It would not be a clean shave but sufficient to change his appearance and tidy him in the minds of any who looked at and examined him. He had once read that the art of successful evasion was a dark suit and a tie; he believed it. Who searches for the fanatic among the closely groomed? He grinned to himself, as if enjoying the self-bestowed title. The fanatic. Many labels they would be handing down from the top table of the Directorate of Democrazia Cristiana, and the Central Committee of the PCI, and they had seen nothing yet.

His humour was further improved by the wash, and there were more shops to visit. He bought socks, and a light T-shirt that carried a cheaply stencilled rendering of the fifteenth-century castle of Bracciano that dominated the village. His former clothes he stuffed into a rubbish bin. Further along the pavement he stopped and bought with coins from the newspaper stand the day's edition of *Il Messaggero*. He looked into Geoffrey Harrison's picture, holding the page hard in front of his face. The company portrait, serene and sleek, harmless and smug, beaming success. On an inside page was the information that had led him to need a newspaper, the full story of the hunt with the facts available till two o'clock that morning and the name of the policeman who controlled the search. Dottore Giuseppe Carboni, working from the Questura. Giancarlo's mouth twisted with his innate contempt for his adversary. Among the clatter of loose change in his pocket were four gettoni, enough for his task. He hunted now for a bar or trattoria that had a closed phone booth, not willing to be overhead when he made his telephone call. At a bar he passed there were two coin telephones for the public, but both open and fastened to the wall where there would be no privacy. He walked on till he reached the ristorante attached to the sailing club at the end of the half-kilometre esplanade. There was a closed telephone booth in the hallway leading from the street door to the inner eating sanctum. He had to wait some minutes for two giggling girls to finish. Neither bothered to glance at the frail built boy as they plunged out, loud in their shared noise.

This near to the capital the telephone booths were equipped with Rome directories. He flicked through the first pages of the scruffed edition of the Yellow Pages, running down the addresses and numbers listed under Commissariati PS with his cleaned fingernail. At the bottom of the page he found the answer. Questura Centrale – v. di S Vitale 15 (46 86).

This would stir the bastards.

He would carry the fight to them, as Franca would have wished, carry it right to the doors of the Questura where they sat with their files and their minions and their computers. They would hear of Giancarlo, the hacks and lackeys would hear his name. He was trembling, taut as a whiplash at the moment it cracks on a horse's back. The shaking convulsed his palms and the gettoni rattled dully in his fist.

*

670

No nearer, no further from Harrison, the child had sat down. He was cross-legged, his elbows resting on his knees and his hands supporting his chin, the kindergarten pose, listening to a teacher's story.

Like you're a bloody animal, Geoffrey, like he's found a fox half dead in a gin-trap, and he has the patience to wait and see what happens. All the hours in the world the child had to be patient, too young for a watch, for a sense of fleeting time. Harrison's attempts to draw him closer, to engage those small sharp fingers in the binding knots had failed. All the nodding and gesturing with his head had been ignored except for the few times when his most violent contortions had gathered a flash of fear to his face and the child's slim muscles had stiffened and prepared for escape. Don't get excited, Harrison had learned, and for God's sake, even with the eyes, don't threaten him. The child has to be kept there, his confidence has to be conserved, he has to be wooed.

You want to keep him there, Geoffrey, with Giancarlo coming back? Giancarlo and the P38 coming back with the food, and you're trying to keep the child there?

God, I don't know, and the moments were marching, the hands would be sliding on the watch face on his wrist.

There was almost a sadness on the child's face as Harrison peered into its shallow depths. He would be a kid from a farmhouse, self-sufficient, self-reliant in his entertainment, a creature of the woods, and owing loyalty and softness only to his parents. A pleasant child. You'd find one like this on the Yorkshire uplands or the Devon moors, or on the far west shoreline of Ireland's Donegal. God knows how to communicate with the blighter. Can't frighten him, can't please him. If there had been a child of his own, but Violet had said that her figure . . . Can't blame bloody Violet, not her fault you don't know how to talk to a child.

Hope was fleeing from Harrison. His head movements became less frequent, and he noticed that when he subsided into inertia then the start of boredom glazed the child's eyes. That way he would leave, pick himself off the earth and wander on his way. That's what he should do, lie still, bore the kid out, and hope that he was gone before Giancarlo was back; that was saving the kid. That was the proper way, that was diving clothed into an icy pool to pluck a baby out.

God, I don't want him to go. The fear came again, the horror of being abandoned by this child mind, and he nodded again with his head and wore the pantomime face of the clown in his urgency.

Hating himself, with the fever in his eyes as he called mutely for the child to come forward, Harrison strained to hear the footfall of the returning Giancarlo.

*

671

'Pronto, Questura.'

Giancarlo stabbed with his finger at the button that would release a gettone to fall into the caverns of the machine.

'Questura . . .'

'Please, the office of Dottore Giuseppe Carboni?'

'A moment . . .'

'Thank you.'

'For nothing, sir . . .'

A hesitation, the sounds of connection. Perspiration dribbled down Giancarlo's chest.

'Yes . . .'

'May I speak to Dottore Giuseppe Carboni.'

'He is very busy at the moment. In what connection . . . ?'

'In connection with the Englishman, 'Arrison.'

'Can I help myself? I work in Dottore Carboni's office.'

'I must speak with him directly. It is important.'

There would be a taping of all incoming calls for Carboni. Giancarlo assumed that, but unless suspicions were aroused the trace procedures would not be automatic. He kept his voice calm, regulated.

'A moment . . . who is it calling?'

Giancarlo flushed. 'It does not matter . . .'

'A moment.'

More delays and he fed another gettone. He smiled mirthlessly. Not the time to lose the call for lack of coins. His last two rested in his hand. More than sufficient . . . He started, clenched at the receiver.

'Carboni speaking. What can I do for you?'

The voice seemed to come from a great distance, a whispering on the line as if there were a great tiredness and the resignation was heavy.

'Listen carefully, Carboni. Do not interrupt. This is the spokesman of the Nuclei Armati Proletaria . . .'

Don't gabble, Giancarlo. Remember that you are kicking them. Remember that you are hurting them as surely as the P38 in Franca's hand.

'. . . We hold the Englishman, 'Arrison. If Franca Tantardini has not been released and flown out of Italy to the territory of a friendly Socialist nation by nine o'clock tomorrow morning, then the multinationalist 'Arrison will be executed for his crimes against the proletariat. There is more, Carboni. We will telephone again this evening, and when your name is asked for then the call must be put through to you immediately, and in your room must be Franca Tantardini. We will speak to her ourselves. If the connection is not made, if Comrade Tantardini is not there to talk to us, then 'Arrison will be killed. The call this evening will come at twenty hours . . .'

Forty seconds on the revolving hand of his watch since he had announced the source of the communication. And the trace system would be in operation. Mad, Giancarlo, mad. It's the behaviour of a fool.

'. . . Is that understood?'

'Thank you, Giancarlo.'

The boy's head jolted forward, fingers white and bloodless on the plastic telephone. A breathy whisper. 'How did you know?'

'We know so much, Giancarlo. Giancarlo Battestini. Born Pescara. Father, a clothes shop there. One metre sixty-eight tall. Weight on release from Regina Coeli, sixty-one kilos. Call again, Giancarlo . . .'

Another twenty seconds departed on his watch, lost. Giancarlo snapped, 'You will have her there. You will have Comrade Tantardini on this telephone?'

'If it pleases you.'

'Do not doubt us. When we say we will kill the man 'Arrison, do not doubt us.'

'I believe you will kill him, Giancarlo. It would not be clever, but I believe that you are capable . . .'

With his forefinger Giancarlo pulled down the hook beside the telephone box, felt the moment of sliding pressure before the sound that told him the call was terminated. Franca had told him they needed two minutes for a trace. He had not exposed himself to their reach. Time in hand. He walked out of the ristorante and into the lively afternoon sun, knees weak, breath summoned fast, his mind a confusion of spattered images. They should have grovelled and they had not. They should have bent and they had held the mast erect. Perhaps in the sinking pit of his stomach there was an alien and unholy presentiment of the imminence of failure.

But the mood was soon discarded. The chin jutted and the eyes glowed and he hurried back on the dust-covered road, retracing his way towards the wood.

It was more than an hour now since the child had come, and the crease lines of interest still wrapped his face.

Harrison no longer moved, no longer attempted to wheedle the small boy closer. Tried, you poor bastard, tried all you knew. The ants were at him. Virile swine, monsters with a swingeing bite, hitting and retreating and returning, calling for their friends because the mountain of food was defenceless and amusing. And the kid hadn't spoken one bloody word.

Go away, you little blighter, get lost, get back to your mama and your tea. You're no bloody use to me. A pretty face the child had, and the frown lines were worn as if by a martyred infant in the colours of a church window. Violet would notice a face like this child's, and she'd enthuse on it and want to tousle his hair and coo to him. Why didn't

673

the child respond? God knows, and he's not caring. He'll be in church, this brat, on Sunday morning, with his hair combed and his face washed with a red cassock down to shined sandals and white socks, probably be singing his bloody heart out in the choir stall, and he won't even remember the strange shape of the man in the woods with the wild gaze and the body twist of fear. He'll be in church . . . if Giancarlo isn't back soon.

The child started up, the rabbit alerted, slid fast to his feet, easily and with the suppleness of youth.

For Harrison there was nothing beyond the lethargic motion of the wood.

The child began to move away and Harrison watched fascinated for there was a silence under the boots that glided over the dry minefield of leaves and sticks. His place, thought Harrison, here among the animals and birds and the familiar; he probably didn't know what the inside of a schoolroom looked like, because this was his playground. He watched the child go, his slight body merging with the pale grey lines of the tree-trunks. When he was at the murky edge of vision, Harrison saw him drop to his knees and ease the fronds of a sapling across his face and shoulders. The child had covered less than twenty yards but when he was settled Harrison had to strain and search with his eyes to find his hiding-place.

Into view, trying to move with caution but failing to find quiet places for his feet, came Giancarlo, source of the disturbance.

He closed quickly, gun in hand, and the brown paper bag held between the crook of his arm and his body. He was alert, hunting between the trees with his eyes, but finding nothing to caution nor alarm him. He dropped to his knee and slipped the pistol into the waist of his trousers. The cleaned face and the bright T-shirt gave him a youth and innocence that Harrison had not seen before.

'Food, and I haven't had mine either. We are both equally starved.' There was a little laugh and Giancarlo leaned forward and put his arms behind Harrison's head and unknotted the handkerchief, pulled it clear and dropped it beside him. 'Better, yes?'

Harrison spat from the side of his mouth, cleared the spittle. Still bent low, Giancarlo bounced on his toes down into the earth crater and worked quickly and expertly at the wrist flex.

'Still better, yes? Even better?'

Harrison looked deep into his face and struggled to comprehend the volatile changes of atmosphere. After hours of silence in the car, after the kicking of the early morning, the new direction of the wind was too complex for him to comprehend. 'What did you get for us to eat?' he asked lamely, rubbing his wrists and restoring the glow of circulation. And what the hell did it matter? What importance did it hold?

'Not much. Some bread, with cheese and salad. It will fill us.'

'Very good.'

'And I spoke to the man who is trying to find you. A fool at the Questura, I called him by telephone. I told him what would happen if Franca were not freed by tomorrow morning.' Giancarlo took a bulging bread roll from the bag, ignored the cheese spillage, and passed it to Harrison. He spoke proudly. 'He tried to keep me talking to give them time for a trace but that's an old trick, you won't hear sirens tonight, 'Arrison. I told him also that I would talk direct to Franca this evening and that they should bring her to his office.'

A chatty, banal conversation. That of two men who have been buried for too long and for whom the quiet has proved oppressive.

'What did you say would happen if Franca were not freed?' Harrison's words were mumbled through the sea of bread and salad.

'I told them you would be executed.'

'That's what you told them?'

'I said that I would kill you.'

'And what did they say?' Harrison ate on, the words of both of them too unreal to be of value.

'Carboni is the name of the man who is hunting for you. He was the only one that I spoke to. He said nothing.'

'Did he say if Franca would be freed?'

'He did not answer that.' Giancarlo smiled. There was a certain warmth, a certain charm in the scrubbed, shaved features. 'He did not answer any of my questions. You know, he knew my name, he knew who it was that he was speaking to. He was pleased with that, the man Carboni. I mean it, I mean it very deeply, 'Arrison, I would be sorry to kill you. It would not be what I want.'

It was too much for Geoffrey Harrison to assimilate. Once in the yard behind his father's house they had watched the chickens prowling beside the fence and decided which one would make their meal and which should survive, and he had tried to communicate to the chosen fowl that there was nothing personal in the choice, no malice.

'It doesn't help you if you shoot me.' Harrison trying to be calm, trying to soften and mollify through dialogue.

'Only that each time you make a threat you must carry it out if you are to be believed. You understand that, 'Arrison. If I say that I will kill you unless I am given something, then I must do it if I am denied. It is credibility. You understand that, 'Arrison?'

'Why do you tell me this?'

'Because you have the right to know.'

Harrison turned his head, a slow, casual movement, traversed across the tree-front and caught like a flash that was there and then gone the blue and white of the check shirt of the idiot child who had sat where Giancarlo now squatted.

'Will they give you back your Franca, Giancarlo?'

'No . . .' he said simply, and his hand dived again in the bag and he passed another roll across to Harrison. An afterthought: 'Well, I do not think so. But I must try, right, 'Arrison? You would agree that I should try?'

With the arrival of Francesco Vellosi from the Viminale, the summit meeting in Carboni's office could begin. Just preceding the head of the anti-terrorist unit had been the Minister of the Interior and before him the examining magistrate who had successfully jockeyed among his profession for the nominal role of heading the investigation.

Tired men, all of them. Harassed and without small talk. At the outset there was argument over priorities around the bowed figure of the Minister, who knew the penalty for failure to arrest terrorist outrage was resignation and could not find in the bearing of the men about him the stimulus for a new initiative.

There were many points for dispute.

Should any new advice be presented to the Council of Ministers regarding the decision to refuse consideration of the freeing of Franca Tantardini?

Should Franca Tantardini be permitted to speak by telephone to the boy Battestini?

At least two gettoni had been used on the telephone communication, the call had come from outside the Rome city limits, and in the countryside the principal enforcers of the law were the carabinieri; should they now control any further search operation, or should the overall direction remain with the polizia?

Was it useful to contact the Vatican Secretariat to explore the possibility of His Holiness issuing a similar appeal to the rejected call of Pope Paul VI for Aldo Moro's life?

Should the President of the Council of Ministers broadcast to the nation?

Why had it not been possible to extract greater information from the location of the telephone message?

Much of it was unnecessary, much of it time-wasting, sapping the concentration of the men in the room. But then, many had to clear themselves if there was a chance of failure to be found in tomorrow's dawn. Reputations could be damaged, perhaps destroyed. Backs must be protected. As one of the most junior men in the hierarchy present, Giuseppe Carboni was finally given what amounted to a free hand. He would be provided with a liaison team to link him with Criminalpol, the carabinieri force, and the armed forces. If he succeeded, then those who had set in motion the search operation would be well to the fore. If he failed, then shoulders would droop, heads turn away, and Carboni would stand alone. When they rose from the meeting the room emptied quickly. It was as if the paint daubs of disaster already swept across the walls. As he stood beside his desk smiling weakly at the Minister's departing back, Carboni reflected that little had been gained, only time frittered and disposed of.

'Look at it another way,' said Vellosi, his arm around Carboni's short shoulder. 'There is little likelihood of us saving Harrison, and perhaps that is not even the first priority. What matters is that we find this scum . . .'

'You talk as if we have reached a state of war,' Carboni murmured.

'What matters is that we find this scum, whether tomorrow, or in a month, or a year, and we kick the shit out of him . . . He never reaches Asinara.'

'They are dragging us down, Vellosi.'

'That is the ground where we meet them, where we fight them, and where we win.'

'If in such times victory is available . . . I am less certain.'

'Concern yourself with the present, Carboni. Find me the boy Battestini.' Vellosi squeezed his arm and walked on out through the door.

In the front parking area of a small trattoria Violet Harrison parked her car. Not tidily, not quietly, but with a splash of movement and rising dust and the protest of an over-extended engine. The parking area was for patrons, but she would take a cup of coffee and perhaps half a carafe of white wine, and that would satisfy the white-shirted waiters of her right to a table. The verandah of the trattoria was at the back, and she walked through the small construction of timber and corrugated iron roofing and past the kitchen where the fires were being stoked for the lamb and the veal. She would sit beneath a screen of interlaced bamboo, and from there she could watch, across some scrub grass and shallow shifting hills of sand, the boys who walked on the beach.

She seemed relaxed, at peace, but the Polaroids on her face hid reddened eyes. She showed a calm pose to the world, obliterated her inner self, sat at the table and waited. Occasionally she swung her head and gazed away down the beach, a searchlight roving, hunting all the time, haunting and punishing.

677

16

Early afternoon in the great slumbering capital.

A wicked heat, clamping on the bodies of the few Romans who moved listlessly on the steaming, paper-strewn streets. Little protection for walkers, even from the high buildings of nineteenth-century finery on the Corso. The pavements, abandoned by their own citizens, were given over to the perspiring, grumbling tourists. The map-clutchers, guide-book-scanners, ice-cream-suckers, groped from ruin to ruin expressing their admiration for what they saw in shrill Japanese, blaring American, dominant German.

Like a stranger in his own community, Giuseppe Carboni threaded an impatient way between the loiterers. He crossed the small square in front of the colonnaded church and hurried up the six shallow steps to the central entrance of the church of San Pietro in Vincoli. The visitors were thick, shoulder to shoulder, huddled close to their guides, serious and solemn-faced as they mopped up the culture and the dampness of their armpits. Here Carboni had been told he would find Francesco Vellosi. The church of Saint Peter in Chains is where the bonds of the saint are reverently kept, shining and coated in dark paint inside a gold and glass-faced cabinet. The central nave was occupied by the groups, soaking up the required information: the age of the construction, the dates of renovation, the history of the tomb of Julius II, the smooth sculpture of the bearded and muscled Moses that was the work of Michelangelo. But in the aisles, in the narrower naves, where the tourists gave ground to the worshippers, Carboni would find his man. Where the shadows were thicker, where the tall candles burned in flickering insecurity, where the women in black came in from the streets to pray.

In the right-hand nave he saw Vellosi, three rows from the front, kneeling hunched on a red hassock. The hard man of the anti-terrorist squad was now bent in prayer because his driver was slain and would be buried in the morning. It was no surprise that Vellosi chose this church. On the same steps that Carboni had climbed the carabinieri had shot to death Antonio La Muscio and captured the girls La Vianale and Salerno. The place acted as a symbol to those who fought the underground of subversion and anarchy, it was their place of triumph and riposte.

Carboni did not intrude. He crossed to the small side altar and waited with hands joined across his stomach. The voices of the guides seemed

678

distant, the brush of scores of feet was near eliminated. A place of tranquil value. A place to shed, for precious moments, the fearsome and desperate load that the two men carried. Watching and waiting, curling his toes, ignoring the passage of time that could not be recouped, Carboni curbed himself. He could be thankful that, if nothing else, he had escaped from his desk, his aides, his telephone and the endless computer print-outs.

Abruptly, Vellosi jack-knifed himself from his knees and back on to his chair. Carboni darted forward and eased himself down beside him. When their eyes met Carboni could see that the man was rested, that the purgative of prayer had refreshed him.

'You forgive me, capo, for coming here to find you?'

'Nothing, Carboni. I came to say some words for my Mauro . . .'

'A good place to come to.' Carbon spoke softly, with approval.

'Here we killed the rat, exterminated La Muscio . . . It is a good place to come to speak with my friend.'

'It is right to remember the success. Catastrophe is burdening, deadening.'

There was a wry smile at Vellosi's lips. 'Catastrophe we are familiar with, success is the star we seek.'

'And too often the cloud obscures the star . . . it is seldom visible.'

The two men spoke in church whispers, Vellosi content to idle till Carboni was ready to unveil the purpose of his visit.

A deep sigh from Carboni. The man who will jump into a winter sea from a breakwater, and must strip off his robe and discard his towel.

'We talked long enough at the meeting,' Carboni plunged. 'Long enough to have settled every matter that was outstanding, but at the end we had decided nothing, nothing beyond the fact that Giuseppe Carboni should take responsibility . . .'

'You had expected something different?'

'Perhaps yes, perhaps no.' Carboni stared in front of him as he spoke, over the shoulder of the wizened sparrow woman with her bones angular under the black blouse who mouthed quiet words to the altar. 'A gathering like that is a farce, a babble of men seeking with one voice to disclaim ultimate responsibility, prepared only to pile it on my shoulders.'

'They are broad enough,' chuckled Vellosi. 'You should work at the Viminale, you would quickly learn then what is normal, what is acceptable.'

'Do we let the woman Tantardini speak to the boy?' Carboni sharper now, play-acting completed.

Vellosi too responded, the smile draining, a savagery in his voice. 'I hate that bitch. Believe me, dear friend, I hate her. I wish to dear Jesus that we had slaughtered her in the street.'

'Understandable and unhelpful.'

679

Vellosi snatched back at him. 'What do you need most?'

'Now I have nothing. I know only that Battestini was early this morning in the area of Rome. I know that he has travelled on. I have a car number, but that could have been changed. I have no hope of intervention before tomorrow morning.' The ebbing of the bravura.

'So you must have a trace, you must have a location. If the bitch is there and talks to him, then you give your engineers the possibility . . .'

'She has to speak to him?'

'You have to make her.' There was a snarl in Vellosi's voice, as if the discussion had reached obscenity. 'If I were to ask her she would spit in my face.'

Carboni looked around him in response to the protest coughs of those who objected to the interference of raised voices in their worship. He stood up, Vellosi following, and together they walked down the aisle between the colonnade and the chairs. 'What would you tell her?'

'That you have to decide for yourself.'

'I came for help, Vellosi.'

'I cannot aid you. You must read her when you see her. When you meet her you will know why I cannot help you.' The inhibitions of the church quiet were lost on Vellosi. 'She is poison, and you must think of the consequences for yourself if you involve her.'

Carboni stared back at Vellosi as they stopped at the great opened doors. A small and pudgy figure dwarfed by his colleague of the open and strong face. He weighed his words for a moment. 'You are nervous of her. Even from her cell in the Rebibbia she frightens you.'

No denials, no stuttered protests. Vellosi said simply, 'Be careful, Carboni, remember what I say. Be careful of the bitch.'

Through the afternoon little had passed between Geoffrey Harrison and Giancarlo Battestini. Harrison's arms had not been tied again since the food and he lay on his side on the earth of the bunker, his only movements to swat the flies from his face and brush the ants and insects from his body and legs. He might have slept, had certainly dozed in the twilight area. All the while Giancarlo watched him with a casual and intermittent observation and with the gun resting on the leaves close to his hand. The summer sun was high, burning even now through the ceiling of foliage, sufficient to shrivel any wind that might have infiltrated earlier. Sticky, hot and defeated, Harrison slipped into a vegetable sloth, his mind devoid of ideas and expectations. No longer did the presence of the check shirt in the undergrowth a few yards beyond and behind Giancarlo offer any hope of salvation. Just another witness to his helplessness, another voyeur.

The body functions drove Harrison to speak again.

'It's the call of nature, Giancarlo.' Ridiculous that he was embarrassed. Couldn't use the language of the dressing-room, of the men's club. Couldn't say . . . I want to have a crap, Giancarlo . . . I want to have a shit, Giancarlo. Didn't want to say it any other way and feared to foul his trousers. 'It's been a long time.'

Giancarlo looked at him curiously as if experiencing some new buttress of his power. The great man of the multinational must ask Giancarlo's permission again, because otherwise he would smell and lose his dignity, and no more be a person of stature and importance. The cat with the mouse. The boy and the butterfly with the broken wing. Giancarlo teased in mock disbelief. 'Perhaps you are trying to trick me, 'Arrison.'

'Really, Giancarlo, I have to go. I'm not tricking you.'

The boy warmed to the hint of desperation. 'Perhaps you would try to escape from me.'

'I promise there is no trick . . . but quickly.'

'What do you say then, 'Arrison? What were you taught to say when you wanted something?'

'Please, Giancarlo . . .'

The boy grinned, a sneer playing over his lips. 'And you want to go in the trees where you cannot be seen. You think many are watching you?'

'Please, Giancarlo.'

The boy was satisfied. Another victory, another demonstration of strength. Enough, and the pleasure was satiated. He left the P38 on the ground and slowly, taking his time, manoeuvred himself behind Harrison. It was the work of a few seconds to detach the flex that fastened the ankles to the tree roots. 'Four or five metres only, 'Arrison, no more.'

'Aren't you going to loosen my legs?'

Giancarlo was further amused. 'Crawl, 'Arrison, and watch where your hands move, that they do not go close to my knots.'

Once more Harrison gazed away past Giancarlo and towards the hiding-place of the child. Still visible were the flecks of the shirt between leaves and branches. Anger was rising out of the frustration. The little bastard. Like a bloody puppy that's too young to have been trained, that stays and mocks and will not come. On his hands and knees, Harrison crawled, the performing pet, towards a cluster of birch trunks.

'Not too far, 'Arrison.' The mocking call of derision.

His knees scuffed a trail through the leaves and surface earth before he was partially hidden by the trees. He lowered his trousers, squatted using his hands to support himself and felt the constriction and pain gush away. God, the bloody relief of it. Bloody freedom. And the bloody smell too.

'Please, Giancarlo, do you have any paper?'

681

There was a ripple of laughter from past the trees. 'I have no bidet for you, I have no aerosol for you to spray under your armpits. But paper I have for you.'

Subdued, Harrison thanked him and then repeated himself when the bag that had carried the rolls landed close to his feet, thrown with accuracy. He cleaned himself, retrieved his trousers, scuffed some dirt over the soiled paper and dragged himself back to his captor and his prison. He crawled to the flattened earth in the cavity and lay down, resuming his familiar position, pliant and non-resistant, and curled his arms behind his back.

'Close your eyes.' A command, and with his legs trussed, what chance? Nothing, just pain, nothing. He clenched his eyes shut, and heard only the slight sounds of Giancarlo's feet, and then the hands were cruelly at his wrists and the flex was wound tight and brutally across his flesh, and there was the pressure of a knee on the small of his back.

The weight slid from him and with its going there was again the mocking voice. 'You can open your eyes.'

Above the horizon of the crater rim, Harrison saw Giancarlo standing, observing, hands on hips. Something mindless, something vacuous about the smile and the mouth and the dulled glare of the eyes.

'You're enjoying yourself, Giancarlo. It's sick to be that way. It means that you are ill . . .'

'Now we have a grand speech.' Derision from the boy, the void unbridged by the contact.

'To treat anyone like this, it means you're deranged. You're a bloody lunatic. You know what that means . . . you're mad, Giancarlo, you've flipped your bloody lid.' Why say it? Why bother? What bloody difference does it make?

'I understand what you say.' But the boy was not roused.

'You've become an animal, Giancarlo. A vicious, infected, little –'

Giancarlo with studied care turned his back. 'I do not listen to speeches. I am not obliged to hear you.'

'Why don't you do it now?' The whisper, without fervour, without passion. The words of a second in the boxer's ring when he has seen enough blood, when he is ready to throw in the towel.

'Because it is not time. Because I am not ready.'

'I say it again, Giancarlo, you enjoy it. You must have felt like a kid giving yourself a wrist job when you killed the men back in the barn, jerking yourself. What are you going to do when you kill me, take your bloody trousers down . . . ?'

Giancarlo narrowed his eyes, and on his slight forehead the frown deepened in its ruts. His voice came as a rush of breeze among the trees. 'You know nothing of us. Nothing. You cannot know why a man goes sotto-terra, why a man discards all the trappings so sought after by your stinking breed, why a man fights to destroy a system that is rotten. You were smug and safe and fat, and you were blind. You know nothing of the struggle of the proletariat.'

Half into the dirt, Harrison shouted back, 'Bloody clichés. Parrot talk you learned in the drains.'

'You do not make it easier for yourself.'

Attempting an order and a sternness, Harrison called, 'Get it over with.'

'I have said to them that it will be at nine o'clock if I have not my Franca. I will wait till nine. That was my word. Keeping you till then does not threaten me.'

Giancarlo walked away a few paces, discarded the conversation, withdrew to his inner recesses, gone from Harrison's reach.

And he's right, Geoffrey, you know nothing of them, nothing at all of the new and embryo species. Nothing of the hate squashed into that mind. And there's no help, no succour, the cavalry don't come this time. Just a bloody carcase already, that's all, Geoffrey. Harrison looked into the green grey mist of the trellis of sapling branches and leaves, and felt the falling of a greater loneliness. He could not see the child. Perhaps it was his eyes, perhaps he looked in the wrong place, but he could not find the checked shirt though he peered till his eyes ached and hurt him.

A second carafe now stood emptied on the table.

The Bo-Peep act and the boy not to be found. The waiters had served the lunches, waved their patrons away and stripped the cloths from the chipboard tables. Violet Harrison seemed not to notice and with their studied politeness they waited on her pleasure as she toyed and sipped at the last glass of wine. On the big circus wheel she alternated between hope and despair as the young men of the beach sauntered by. Straight-backed, tanned from wind and sun and the flailing blows of the fine grains, cocky assured eyes, combed-down hair. Any would have served her purpose. She saw the boy a long way off on the beach, walking between two companions.

Recognized him instantly.

'Could I have my bill, please.' She rummaged in her bag for the notes, gestured to the waiter that she required no change, and was on her feet and smiling sweetly.

She walked out from the eating verandah, taking what she hoped was a casual saunter and following a line that would intercept the boy's path. She did not look to her right, the direction from which he was coming, but held her head high and straight and focused on the blue sea's depths and its breaking flecks of spume. She strode on, waiting for the greeting, consumed with a growing, creeping nervousness.

'The English lady, good afternoon.'

She spun round, gouging at the warm sand beneath her sandals. Not that she could claim surprise, but when his voice came, almost behind her, it cut and burned at her consciousness.

'Oh, it's you.' How else did you do it? How to flick up a clever answer when all you were confronting was the stud required for half an hour's brisk anonymous work?

'I did not expect to see you here again.'

'It's a public beach.' Don't frighten him off. Too trite, Violet. God, you'd kick and curse yourself. 'I come here quite a lot.'

She saw the boy's little gesture with his hands, the clipping of his forefinger against his thumb, the message to the other two that the principal wished to be left to his opportunities. Close together but untouching, no bridging contact of fingers, no brushing of thighs, they moved together towards the sea.

'You would like to swim, Signora?'

How he'd speak to a friend of his bloody mother, thought Violet. 'Not yet. I thought I'd just lie on the beach for a bit.'

'Give me your towel.'

She dived into her bag and produced it for him. He spread it out on the sand, gestured with his hand for her to sit and followed her down. There was little room for both of them if they were to share it. His swimming costume was brief and bulging grotesquely. You understand, Geoffrey. Their hips touched. You won't cast a rock, Geoffrey.

'My name is Marco.'

And Geoffrey wouldn't know. That was the rule. No blows below the belt for Geoffrey. No knowledge and therefore no hurt.

'I am Violet.'

'That is the name of a flower in English, yes? A very beautiful flower, I think.'

I know you are alone, Geoffrey. I too am alone. You cannot move, you cannot help yourself. I too, Geoffrey.

'I said it the last time we met, and I was right. You are a very cheeky boy, Marco.'

He smiled across the inches of towel at her. The toothpaste advertisement, the smile of a child taken to a shop, who knows it is his birthday, knows if he is patient he will receive his present.

'What time is it, Giancarlo?'

'Past five.'

The boy returned to his own chasm of silence.

684

He had much to think of, much to concern himself with. Less than three hours to the schedule that he had set himself, had insisted on. Less than three hours till he spoke once more with his Franca. Problems and options bombarded his limited intellect. If they met his demand, if they agreed to the exchange, where should he fly to? Algiers, Libya, Iraq, the People's Republic of South Yemen. Would any of those places take them? And how to choose, a boy who had never been out of Italy. How would he guarantee their safety if an airport rendezvous were permitted? What was the capability of the anti-terrorist pigs? Would they seek a shooting gallery, regardless of the prisoner? It was too much for him to assimilate. Too great the difficulties, too encompassing. A great team the Brigatisti had for the Moro operation, and they now sat in Asinara, locked in their cells, the failed men. As he weighed each trick in the card pack, so too grew the realization of the sheer mountainface he must scale. Start with the haven, start there, because with nowhere to go they were lost. A country to welcome them and harbour them, start there. An Arab country? What else? But even their own people were now shunned and ignored; he had seen the pictures of the lorries blocking the runways in Algiers and Benghazi and Tripoli. If they would do that when an Arab brother was seeking refuge . . . Late for the answers to the questions. The time was ripe for answers before Claudio walked to his room in the pensione, before the rapido sped towards Reggio, before the Calabresi whimpered in their terror.

Perhaps it was all irrelevant.

Did he know in his heart there would be no exchange? And if there were to be no exchange, what then would the leadership want of him? He wrestled in the growing purgatory of the dilemma. Where lay the victory in this skirmish? The body of his 'Arrison in a ditch, the head blasted with the shell of the P38, that or his prisoner released to walk away on a road with a communiqué in his pocket to be printed the next morning in *Paese Sera* and *Il Messaggero*? Where lay the victory for the proletariat's revolution? How had the Brigatisti advanced when they took the life of Aldo Moro on the slime-covered beach at Focene?

He was old enough only for questions, too young for their responses. If he could not conjure the answers then he would not see his Franca again. Not for twenty years and that was for ever. Three days since his hands had travelled her skin, since her golden head had passed across the softness of his belly. To be denied that for a lifetime. The boy felt a gust of pain. There was nothing that was simple, facile, and that was why there was a steel in the comrades who fought, in Franca Tantardini and the men in the island gaol. And what was the sinew of Giancarlo Battestini, in his twentieth year, lover of Tantardini, son of a borghese, member of the NAP? A dozen hours, slow and tardy hours, and he would have the answer.

His hands clutched together, white to the knuckles, Giancarlo waited

685

for the time when he should leave Harrison and make his way again to the lakeside of Bracciano.

In his hotel room Archie Carpenter listened to Michael Charlesworth's clipped and exact résumé.

A voice far away on a bad connection. The situation if anything had deteriorated. Reuters and UPI carried on their wires that a boy, Giancarlo Battestini, categorized as little more than a probationer of the NAP, had telephoned the Questura to emphasize the terms of his ultimatum.

'I don't know how it is that the Italians allow this sort of information out, but nothing stays secure here. It seems Battestini was full of his threats. There's a fair depression about the way it's going,' Charlesworth had said.

Holding himself, the diver conserving his oxygen, Carpenter had heard him out. Then the explosion.

'So what are you all doing about it?'

'What we were doing about it earlier, Archie. It has not changed.'

'Sweet damn-all.'

'You can put it that way,' Charlesworth placated. 'That way if you want to.'

'What other bloody way is there?'

'Abuse doesn't help, Archie. You've spoken to the Ambassador yourself, he's explained our situation. I've heard since that London have called him. They back him.'

'He's written off my man.'

'Histrionics don't help either. I'm sorry, you're sorry, we're all sorry . . . But you'll come and have that meal tonight.'

'If you want me to.'

'Come on up and help us through a bottle. Did you get in touch with the wife?'

'I rang again, took a bloody effort to, but I tried. There's no answer.'

'It's a filthy business, Archie, but don't think you're alone with the hair shirt. It's shared about a bit, you know.'

Charlesworth rang off.

Archie Carpenter straightened his bed, brushed his hair, raised his tie knot and drew on his jacket. He took the lift downstairs and walked out through the front foyer of the hotel, stepping irritably over the piled suitcases of an arriving tour. He summoned a taxi and asked for the Questura. Early summer evening, the traffic rushing for home and guaranteeing him an exciting and lively journey among the pedestrians and across the traffic lanes. Carpenter barely noticed. A telephone call from the enquiry desk had promptly led to his being ushered up the stairs to the offices of Giuseppe Carboni, now transformed into a tactical crisis centre.

Shirtsleeves, tobacco smoke, coffee beakers, a three-quarters emptied Scotch bottle, faces lined with weariness, the howl of electric fans, the chatter of teletype machines, and, radiating energy, Carboni in the midst, rotund and active.

Carpenter hesitated by the door, was spied out, waved forward.

'Come in, Carpenter. Come and see our humble efforts,' Carboni shouted at him.

This was the old world, the known scents. An emergency room under pressure. This was something for Carpenter to feel and absorb. He felt an interloper, yet at home, among the men he could find sympathy for. The clock was turned back as he came diffidently past the desks where the paper mountained, past the photographs stuck with tape to the walls that showed shocked and staring faces, past the telephones that demanded response.

'I don't want to be in the way . . .'

'But you cannot sit in the hotel room any longer?'

'Something like that, Mister Carboni.'

'And you come here because everyone you speak to gives you bad news or no news, and from me you hope for a difference?'

Something lovable about him, Carpenter thought. Overweight, ugly as sin, dirty fingernails, a shirt that should have seen the wash, and a bloody good man.

'It was getting at me, just sitting about . . . you know how it is?'

'I will educate you, Carpenter.' Carboni was sliding on his coat, then turning away to bellow what seemed to Carpenter a score of differing instructions to varied recipients, and simultaneously. 'I will show you our enemy. You will witness what we fight against. I know you policemen from England, detailed and organized men, who have believed that you are the best in the world . . .'

'I'm not a policeman any more.'

'You retain the mentality. It has stayed with you.' Carboni laughed without a smile, a nervous tic. 'The rest of the world are idiots, second-class people. I understand. Well, come with me, my friend. We go across the city to the Rebibbia gaol. That is where we hold the Tantardini woman and I must play the taxi-driver and bring her here, because that is what little Giancarlo wants and we must please him . . .'

Carpenter sensed the swollen anger in the man, wondered where it could find an outlet. The laugh came again, raising and suspending the flesh rolls of the jaw.

'. . . I must please him, because if he does not talk to Tantardini, then your Harrison is dead. I am here to save him, I will do my humble best to save him.'

'I hadn't really doubted that, sir.' Carpenter let the respect run in his voice, because this was a professional man, this was a caring man.

'So, come and see her. Know your enemy. That is what you say in England? The better you know him, the better you fight him.' Carboni caught Carpenter's arm and propelled him back towards the door. 'You will see that we risk much at this stage. But don't tell me that it was never like that in London. Don't tell me that always you were supreme.'

'We had the black times.'

'We have experience, we know the black times. Tonight it is that but darker.'

His arm still clamped by Carboni's fist, Carpenter surged down the corridor.

Across the bonnet of the little red Fiat, the child drew with a pliant finger the letters of his name in the dirt covering the paintwork. It had perplexed him at first to find a car edged from the field into the shelter of the trees, and he had skirted it twice before gaining the courage to approach it. He had gazed inside, admired the shiny newness of the seat leather and let his hand flit to the bright chrome door handle and felt it slide down under pressure. But he did not dare to climb into the car and sit in the driver's seat and hold the steering-wheel as he would dearly like to have done. His compensation was the writing of his name in big and bold and shaking letters.

That task completed, his interest moved on and he walked away as the sun slipped, delaying his journey home to the farm only for the time it took to pluck some hedgerow flowers for his mother. He had little sense of the hour but the chill that was rising from the grass, carried by the freshening wind was enough to dictate his going. He ambled between the chewing cows, holding tightly to the stems of the flowers, admiring their colours. That his mother and father might be cruelly anxious for him was beyond the comprehension of his young mind.

17

Together Archie Carpenter and Giuseppe Carboni stood in the courtyard of the gaol, far on the inside from the high swinging gates, ringed by walls and watch-towers and men who patrolled catwalks with the guns ready in their hands. The Rebibbia prison, Carboni said, was the maximum security holding centre for the capital city. A fearsome and odious place it seemed to Carpenter, where even in the open, where the wind could blow, there was the smell of kitchens and lavatories, and a community in confinement.

'She will be here one more day,' Carboni intoned. 'Then we transfer her to Messina to await the courts. God willing, it will be months before they drag her into the light again.'

'This is not your work, these are not the people you are normally with?' A gentle query from Carpenter.

'I am a criminal policeman, I do not have a political background. That is the can of worms for a policeman. But everyone is very willing that I should be the man who takes the weight of this action. There are others better fitted than I, but they did not raise their hands.' There was a tight, resigned sadness on Carboni's face. 'But that is how we live here, that is our society. We do not fall down and wag our tails and demand to be given the hardest task because there lies the way to honour and promotion, when the risk of failure is greatest. We are survivors, Carpenter. You will learn that.'

He broke off, his attention directed to the side door of a small building that fronted a towering five-storey cell block. Carabinieri with light machine-guns led the way, officers with medal ribbons followed and then the prisoner. It was the sound of the chains, intrusive and strange to Carpenter, that alerted him to the presence of Franca Tantardini, diminutive when surrounded by so many taller men. A flower choked by weeds. Carpenter shrugged. Stop the bloody politicizing, Archie. She's not a bad-looker either. Good pair of hips on her.

There was no fear on the woman's face. A battleship under steam, proud and devastating and intimidating. The face that launched Giancarlo, chucked him far out to sea.

'An impressive bit of woman, Mister Carboni.'

'If you find a psychopath impressive, Carpenter, then this one would meet your definition.'

You've overstepped the line, Archie. Taking the guided tour for granted, as of right. You're the workhouse boy here, out on a charity ride and taking favours. And remember what they brought you here to see. The bloody enemy, Archie, the enemy of the State. They watched as Franca Tantardini was led into the windowless grey van with her gaolers, and around them there was running and movement and the revving of engines from the escort cars; four of them, back windows lowered, machine-guns protruding.

The rear of the van was held open and Carboni moved rapidly inside, Carpenter following and chastened.

'We are sensitive at this moment . . . about these people.'

'Take my apology, it was the remark of an idiot.'

'Thank you.' A half smile, fast and then obliterated, replaced by the set, hard features of a man about his work. Carboni offered a hand to help Carpenter climb inside. There were two lines of benches in the interior, running against the sides, and the woman rested in a corner far from the door. Illumination came from a single bulb protected by steel mesh. Carboni felt in his waist and produced his short-barrelled pistol and handed it without comment to an escort who would sit at a distance from the prisoner.

'You are armed, Carpenter?'

'No.' A blush, as if he had displayed an inadequacy.

The van drew away, slowly at first, then speeding forward and the echo of the sirens in front and behind bathed the shallow interior.

'Come and join me.'

Carboni, a hand against the ceiling to preserve his balance, had struggled across the heaving floor and subsided on to the bench beside the woman. Carpenter took a place opposite her. Tantardini eyed them indifferently.

'Franca.' The policeman spoke as if it hurt to use her first name, as if afterwards he would soap-rinse his mouth. 'I am Carboni of the Questura. I am in charge of the investigation into the kidnapping of an English businessman, Geoffrey Harrison . . .'

'Am I to be accused of that too?' She laughed clearly. 'Is every crime in Rome to be set against the terrible, the fearsome Tantardini?'

'Listen to me, Franca. Listen and do not interrupt . . .' The talk was fast and in Italian, leaving Carpenter uncomprehending, his attention held only by the calm, bright face of the woman. '. . . Hear me out. He was taken, this Englishman, by a Calabresi group. Now he has been removed from them, and he is in the hands of your boy, your Giancarlo.'

Again the laugh, and the rich, diamond smile. 'Battestini could not deliver a letter . . .'

'He has killed three men, he has moved Harrison half across the country.' Carboni pierced her with his small pig eyes. The heat in the van was intolerable, and he mopped at his face with a stained handkerchief. 'Battestini holds the Englishman in Rome and demands your freedom against his prisoner's life.'

There was a trickle of wonderment and surprise. 'Battestini has done all this?'

'On his own, that is what we believe.'

Almost a chuckle. 'So why do you come to me?'

'You are going now to my office. In little more than an hour, in eighty minutes, Battestini will telephone that office. He has demanded to talk to you. We have agreed . . .'

Carpenter, the eyewitness, watched the tightening of the woman's body, saw the muscles ripple against the cloth of her jeans.

'. . . He is very young, this boy. Too young. I tell you something very honestly, Franca: if any harm should come to Harrison, then Giancarlo will die where we find him.'

690

'Why tell this to me?'

'You bedded him, Franca.' The words ripped in distaste from Carboni's mouth. 'You poured the paraffin on his calf-love. He does this for you.'

The van had lost its speed, telling the occupants that the built-up sprawl of north-east Rome had been reached, and the sirens bellowed for passage with a greater ferocity. Carpenter watched the woman as she lapsed into silence, as if pondering what she had been told. The blanket of warm air wrapped all of them, and there was a drop of sweat eking from her hairline across the fine chiselled nose.

'What do you offer me?'

'I offer you the chance to save the boy's life. He is not of your sort, Franca. He is not a man of the Nappisti, he is a boy. You will go to gaol for many years, not less than twenty. Help us now and it would be taken into account at your trial, there would be clemency.'

As if from instinct her mouth curled scornfully, before the softness of the woman's lips reappeared. 'You ask me to secure the release of the Englishman?'

'That is what we ask of you.'

'And I will talk with Giancarlo?'

'You will talk with him.'

Carboni looked hard into her, waiting for the response, conscious that he had committed much of his future to the conversation of a few minutes. Whitened skin, pale as the flesh of an underground creature, hair that was not greased and ordered, tired to exhaustion.

'He is very young,' the woman murmured. 'Just a boy, just a pair of clumsy little hands . . .'

'Thank you, Franca. Your action will be rewarded.'

What had been settled Carpenter could not know. Carboni had leaned back against the discomfort of the rolling metal wall, and Tantardini sat very still except that her fingers played on the links of the chains that fastened her wrists. And she wasn't wearing a bra either. Bloody marvellous sight, and the blouse must have shrunk in the last wash. Wrap it, Archie. Carboni seemed happy enough, something would have been sorted.

The van travelled at steady speed towards the inner city.

Only when the last of them had retreated noisily through the low yellow gorse clump beneath the pines did Violet Harrison open again her eyes. It was too dark under the trees for her to see his fleeing back, but there were the sounds for a long time of his blundering feet and his calls for his friends. The pain in her body was intense, bitter and vivid, and there was a chill seeping against her skin. But the cold was nothing, set against the agony of the wounds provided by the boy Marco and his friends. The worst was at the gentle summit of her thighs, on the line where the tan and the whiteness split, where the bruises would be forming. She did not cry out, was beyond tears and remorse, her horizon set only on controlling the violence of the aching. The scratches on her face were alive, where the nails had ripped at her cheeks as she had writhed and sought to escape from them, and the harshness of the ground dug deep into the weak slackness of her buttocks that had been pounded, battered, into the earth surface.

At first it had been right, as she had prepared it, as her fantasies had dictated.

She and the boy Marco had gone together from the heat of the beach to the shade of the pine canopy. A tight path that flicked the gorse against her bared legs below the hem of the loose beach dress had led them to a place that was hidden, where the scrub formed a fortress wall of privacy. Swimming to the ground she had slipped the dress over her head, an absence of words and invitation because everything was implicit and unspoken. First the bikini top, loosened by herself because his hands were jumping with nervousness, and then the cupping of her breasts till the boy was panting, frantic. Fingers leaping over her, and Violet Harrison lying back, willing him on, exposed. Fingers on the smoothness of her belly and reaching down and feeling for her and hunting for her, and she clutching at the dark curled hair of his head. That was when she had heard the giggles of the watchers, and she had started up, arms crossing her chest, and they had come like hyenas to a prey. One on each arm and Marco pulling her knees apart, cutting at her with the sharpness of his nails, and tugging at the slight cotton fabric of the bikini bottom. The sweet smile of respect lost from Marco's face, replaced by the bared teeth of the rampant rat. First Marco, penetrating and deep and hard and hurting her because she was not ready. And when he was spent then the first friend came, and there was a hand across her mouth and her arms were spread for crucifixion. After the first friend, the second, and then again Marco, and nothing said among them. Just the driving of the hips and the gush of their excitement at the forbidden. Too good to miss, Marco's fortune. Right that it should be shared among his friends. The last had not even managed, and when she spat in his face and his friends jeered encouragement he had raked her cheek and she had felt the warm blood sprinkle her skin. He had rolled away leaving only his eyes and those of the other two boys to perpetuate the violation.

The tears would come later, back in the flat, back at their home, when she thought again of Geoffrey.

She stood up on her weakened legs, said aloud: 'God help me that he should ever know.'

What if this were the time that he was preparing to die, what if this was the moment that he clutched at an image of Violet? What if it were

692

now that he looked for her as she was walking on a path in strange woods, her clothes devastated, her modesty wrecked and laughed over and splintered?

'Never let him find out, please God. Never.'

She had not even spoken to him when he left the house that morning. She had lain in the bed, her nightdress tight around her, aware of his movements in the flat, but she had not called him, because she never did, because they had only banalities to speak of.

'Forgive me, Geoffrey. Please, please.'

Only if Geoffrey died would he never know. Only then would she be safe in her secret. And he must live, because she had betrayed him and was not fit for the weeds of the widow, for the hypocrisy of condolence. She must will him to live. A terminal patient of catastrophic internal illness sometimes comes back; always there is hope, always there is chance. And then he will know, if the miracle is enacted he will know.

Violet Harrison ran on the pine needle rug. The pain of the wounds was subsidiary to the greater hurt of shame and humiliation. She skirted the trattoria, darkened and shuttered, and sprinted for the car park. Her hand plunged in her bag, wrenched at the cosmetics in the search for the car keys. When she sat in the driving seat and the ignition fired, she trembled with the tears that had been stifled.

'Come home, Geoffrey. Even if no one is there. Come home, my brave darling, come home.'

'Goodbye, 'Arrison.'

Giancarlo could barely see his prisoner against the dirt black of the earth pit.

'Goodbye, Giancarlo.' A faint voice, devoid of hope.

'I will be back soon.' As if Harrison needed to be reassured, as if all his ordeal was a fear of being alone with darkness. A slight stirring of warmth and the nudge of communication. Was the confidence of the boy failing, was the certainty sliding?

Giancarlo slipped away along the path, feeling with his arms outstretched in front of him for the low branches. There was plenty of time.

He had come so far, and yet where was the measure of his achievement? A bramble stem caught with its spikes at the material of his trousers. He tore himself clear. Had he advanced his claim to Franca's freedom? His ankle turned under a protruding root. The P38 dug at the skin of his waist, the acknowledgement that this was his sole power of persuasion, his only right to be heard and known in the great city basking in its summer evening to the south.

*

The breath of darkness had eddied into the great courtyard of the Questura. The headlights and roof lamps of the convoy from the Rebibbia gleamed out their urgency as they swung through the archway from the outside street into the parking area. More shouting, more running men, more guns as the van was backed towards an opened door that led directly to the cell corridor. Among those who worked late in the city's police headquarters there were many who hurried down the internal staircases and craned from the upper windows that they might catch a brief glimpse of 'La Tantardini'. They were rewarded sparsely, a flash of the colour of her blouse as she was manhandled the few feet from the van steps to the entrance of the building, and disappearance.

Carboni did not follow her, but stood in the centre of the courtyard among the reversing, straightening cars that jockeyed for the last parking places. Archie Carpenter stood a few feet from him, sensing that the policeman preferred his own thoughts for company.

She had been long gone from their sight when Carboni threw off the spell, turned to look for Carpenter. 'You would not have understood what passed between us.'

'Not a word, I'm sorry.'

'I have to be brief . . .' Carboni began to walk towards the principal entrance to the building, ignoring the many who watched him as a related secondary object of interest now that the woman was gone. 'The boy will telephone at eight. I have to trace that call. I must know the location from where he telephones. To trace the call I must have time. Only when he talks to Tantardini will he gabble on. He will talk to her.' Carboni's face was etched with anxiety. 'I have told her also that if Harrison is harmed, then we will kill Battestini wherever we find him, but that if she co-operates then clemency will be shown her in the courts.'

'Which you have no power to guarantee.'

'Right, Carpenter, no power at all. But now they have plenty to talk of, and they will use quickly the time that the engineers need. I have no other option but reliance on the trace procedure.'

Carpenter spoke quietly, 'You have one other option. To free Tantardini for Harrison's life.'

'Don't joke with me, Carpenter, not now. Later when it is finished.'

They stopped at the outer door of Carboni's office. The retort was rising in Carpenter's throat, and he suppressed it and thought for the first time how ludicrous to these people was the proposition that seemed straight and clear and common sense.

'I wish you luck, Mister Carboni.'

'Only luck . . . you are mean with your favours, Englishman.'

They entered the office, and Carpenter was quick to appraise the mood, sensitive to the atmosphere of downed heads, flattened feet, gloom and frustration. This was Carboni's own team and if they were not believing in success, then who was he to imagine in his mind the incredible. Carpenter watched as Carboni moved among the impromptu desks and tables and the teleprinters in the outer room, speaking softly to his men. He saw the queue of shaken heads, the mournful mutters of the negative. Like he's going round a cancer ward, and nobody's carrying the good news, nobody's lost his pains, nobody thinks he's coming through. Poor bastard, thought Carpenter.

Carboni expended a long, powered sigh, and slumped to the chair behind his desk. With the sense of theatre, of tragedy, he slapped a hand on to the cream telephone receiver in front of him.

'Call Vellosi. Get him to come here. Not the same room as this . . . but ask him to be close.' He rubbed at the weariness in his eyes. 'Bring her up now, bring Tantardini.'

The child fled from the raw, opened hand of his mother.

Neat and nimble on his feet, he dodged the swinging blow, scattered the posy of hedge flowers on to the stone slabs of the kitchen floor, and scampered for the corridor that led to his bedroom.

'All afternoon I've been calling you from the house . . .'

'I was only in the wood, Mama.' He called shrilly in his fright from the sanctuary of his room.

'I even went and bothered your father in the field . . . he called too . . . he wasted his time when he was busy . . .'

She did not follow him, he had achieved safety.

'Mama, in the wood, I saw . . .'

His mother's voice boomed back, surging to him, as in falsetto she mimicked his small voice. 'I saw a fox . . . I saw a rabbit . . . I followed the flight of a hawk. You'll have no supper tonight. Into your night clothes . . . sick with worry you had me.'

He waited, trying to gauge the scale of her anger, the enormity of his fault, then wheedled in justification. 'Mama, in the wood I saw . . .'

She snapped her interruption back at him.

'Silence your chatter, silence it and get yourself to bed. And you'll not sit with your father after his supper. Not another sound from you, or I'll be in and after you.'

'But, Mama . . .'

'I'll be in and after you.'

'Good night, Mama, may the Virgin watch over you and Papa tonight.'

The voice was small, the fluency broken by the first tears on the child's smooth-downed cheeks. His mother bit her lower lip. It was not right to shout at a small child, and he had so few to play with, and where else was there for him to go but to the woods or to the fields with his father? It would be better when he started school in the autumn.

695

But she had been frightened by his absence, and she consoled herself that her punishment of her only little one was for his own good. She returned to the preparation of her man's supper.

Throughout the city and its suburbs the security net was poised. More than five hundred cars and trucks and riot vans were on the streets. They wore the colours of the Primo Celere, and the Squadra Volante and the Squadra Mobile; others were decorated in the royal blue of the carabinieri. There were the unmarked cars of the undercover men, and of SISDE, the secret service. The agencies of government were poised to spring should the engineers of the Questura basement provide the map reference from which Giancarlo Battestini telephoned. Engines ticking idly, watches and clocks repeatedly examined, machine-guns on the back seats of cars, on the metalled floors of vans. A great army, but one which rested till the arrival of the orders and instructions without which it was a helpless, useless force.

On the fifth floor of the Questura, in the control centre, the technicians had exhausted the lights available on their wall map for marking the position of their interception vehicles. A clock creeping up to twenty hours had silenced conversation and movement, leaving only the mindless hum of an air-conditioning system.

Grim-faced, wearing his years, Francesco Vellosi strode from the central doors of the Viminale to his car that waited at the apex of the half-moon drive. The men who were to escort him to the Questura fidgeted in the seats of the car that would follow. As he settled in the back seat he was aware of the clatter of the arming of weapons. From an upper room the Minister watched him go, then resumed his tiger pacing of the carpet. He would hear by telephone of the night's developments.

Nothing impeded Giancarlo, a fierce moonlight guided his way. There was a stream of cars on the road, but of course there would be cars, for this was a resort of the Roman summer, and no driver would see anything extraordinary in a youth with the long hair of a student, the T-shirt and jeans uniform of the unemployed. On the road he did not flinch from the blinding beams of the headlights. On down the hill he walked till he could see the still reflection of the lights of the trattorie and bars playing on the distance of smooth water. On down the hill, with only occasional stolen glimpses at the slow-moving hands of his watch. The fools with their wives and girls, they would know of Giancarlo Battestini. Those who rushed past him impatiently in their cars would know of him tomorrow. Tomorrow they would know his name and roll it on their tongues and savour it, and try to ask how, and try to ask why.

The pavements beside the lake were filled with those who drifted in aimless procession. They did not glance at the boy. Safe in their own lives, safe in their own business, they ignored him.

At the ristorante the kiosk with the telephone was empty. He darted his eyes again to his watch. Patience, Giancarlo, a few more minutes only. He collected the gettoni from the knot in his handkerchief where they had been segregated. Noise and money-purchased happiness crept from the interior. Where he stood, hemmed in by the glass walls of the cubicle he could see the mouths that burst with pasta, the hands grasping at the wine bottles, the bellies that rocked over the table-tops. Tomorrow they would not shriek in their gusts of laughter. Tomorrow they would talk of Giancarlo Battestini till it consumed them, till it burned them, the very repetition of the name. His name.

The child's father came to the stone-walled, tin-roofed farmhouse when there was no longer light for him to work his fields. A tired, sleep-ridden man, looking for his food and his chair and his television and his rest.

His wife chided him for the late hour, played the scolder, till she kissed him light and pecking, on a hair-roughened cheek; to her he was a good man, full of work, heavy in responsibility, a loyal man to his family, who depended on the long-drawn-out power of his muscles to make a living from the coarse hillside fields. His food would soon be ready and she would bring it on a tray to their living parlour where the old television set, provider of black and white pictures, sat proudly on a coarse wood table. Perhaps later the boy could sit with him because her anger had evaporated with the passing of her fear at his absence, but only if he had not already drifted to sleep.

He had not replied when she had told her man of the time their child had returned and the punishment imposed, just shrugged and turned to the sink to wash away the day's grime. She held sway over the domestic routine and it was not for him to challenge her authority. Hearing him safely settled, she hurried to her stove, lifted the big grey metal saucepan down and drained the steaming water from the pasta, while through the opened doorway blazoned the music of the opening of the evening's news programme. She did not go to watch beside her husband; all day the radio channels had been obsessed with an event from the city.

City people, city troubles. Not relevant to a woman with stone floors to be scrubbed daily, a never-filled purse, and a distant, difficult child to rear. She set the pasta on a plate, doused it in the brilliant red of the tomato sauce, flecked it with the grated cheese, and carried it to

697

her man, flopped in his chair. She could draw satisfaction from the happy and contented smile on her husband's face, and the way that he shook off his weariness, sat himself upright, and the speed with which his fork drove down into the eel lengths of the brilliant butter-coated spaghetti.

On the screen were photographs of a man with combed hair and a knotted tie and the smile that read responsibility and success, replaced by those of a boy whose face showed confrontation and fight, and the trapped gaze of a prisoner. There was a picture of a car, and a map of the Mezzo Giorno . . . She stayed no longer.

'Animals,' she said, and returned to her kitchen and her work.

At one hundred and forty kilometres an hour, Violet Harrison careered along the dual carriageway of the Raccordo.

Her handbag lay on the seat beside her, but she did not bother to winkle out the square lace handkerchief with which she might have dabbed her puffed, tear-heavy eyes. Only Geoffrey in her thoughts, only the man with whom she lived a rotten, neutered life, and who now, in her fear, she loved more than she had ever before been capable. Commitment to Geoffrey, the boring little man who had shared her home and her bed for a dozen years. Geoffrey, who polished the heels of his shoes, brought home work from the office, thought marriage was a girl with a gin waiting at the front door for the return of the frontiersman husband. Geoffrey, who didn't know how to laugh. Poor little Geoffrey. In the hands of the pigs as she had warmed and nestled close to a stranger on a crowded beach, and watched the front of his costume and believed that prayers were answered.

Beyond the grass and crash barriers of the central reservation cars rushed past her, swallowed in the night, blazing headlights lost as fast as they had reared in front of her. The lights played on her eyes, flashed and reflected in the moisture of her tears, cavorted in her vision as tumbling cascades and aerosols of lights and stars.

That was why, beyond the Aurelia turn-off from the Raccordo, she did not see the signs beside the road that warned of the approaching end of the dual carriageway, did not read the great painted arrows on the tarmac. That was why she was heedless of the closing headlights of the fruit lorry bound for Naples.

The impact was immense, searing in noise and speed, the agony howl of the ripped bodywork metal of the car. A fractional moment of collision, and then the car was tossed away, as if its weight were trifling. The car rose high in the air before crashing down, destroyed and unrecognizable, in the centre of the road.

The face of Geoffrey Harrison, its lines and contours, was frozen to his wife's mind in the final broken seconds of her life. The sound of herself speaking his name was bolted to her tongue.

There was much traffic returning at that time from the coast. Many sitting behind their wheels would curse the unseen source of the queues that built on either side of the accident, and then shudder and avert their faces as they witnessed in their lights the reason for their delay.

In front of Carboni's desk, Franca Tantardini sat on a hard, unprepossessing chair. She was upright, taking little notice of the men who bustled around her, gazing only at the window with its dark abyss and undrawn curtains. The fingers of her hands were entwined on her lap, the chains removed. More like a waiting bride than a prisoner. She had not replied when she had first come into the room and Carboni had taken her to a corner and spoken in his best bedside hush beyond the ears of his subordinates.

Archie Carpenter's eyes never left her. Not the sort of creature that he had handled when he was with Special Branch in London. His career spanned the years before the Irish watch, before the bombers came in earnest. Not much colour in those days for Carpenter who was concerned with the machinations of the far-out shop stewards, the Marxist militants and that old source of inspiration, the Soviet Trade Delegation from Highgate. His had been the old Branch, the archaeological specimen that withered and died in its ice age before learning the new techniques of the war against urban terrorism. The guerrilla fighter was a new phenomenon for Archie Carpenter, something only experienced through newspapers and television screens. But there seemed to be nothing special about the woman, nothing to put her on the pedestal. Well, what do you expect, Archie? A Che Guevara T-shirt, the hammer and sickle tattooed on her forehead?

The telephone on Carboni's desk rang.

Difficult really to know what to expect. Criminals the world over, all the same. Whether it's political, whether it's material. Big fat bouncy kids when they've the air of freedom to breathe. Miserable little bastards when the door closes behind them, when they've twenty years of sitting on a blanket.

Carboni grabbed at the receiver, snatching it from the cradle.

Thought she'd have more fight in her, from the way they cracked her up. Belt it, Archie, for Christ's sake.

'Carboni.'

'The call that you have been waiting for, Dottore.'

'Connect it.'

*

699

The light bulb had been removed from the telephone kiosk. In the half dark Giancarlo watched the second hand of his watch moving slowly on its path. He knew the available time, was aware of the ultimate danger. With one hand he held the telephone pressed hard against his right ear, the noise of the ristorante stifled.

'Pronto, Carboni.' A voice fused in metallic interference.

'Battestini.' He had used his own name, chipped at the pretence.

'Good evening, Giancarlo.'

'I have little time . . .'

'You have as much time as you want, Giancarlo.'

The sweat rivers ran on the boy's face. 'Will you meet the demands of the Nuclei Armati Proletaria . . . ?'

The voice cut back at him, smothering his words. 'The demands of Giancarlo Battestini, not of the Nappisti.'

'We stand together as a movement, we . . .' He broke off, absorbed in the motion of his watch ticking on its way, edging towards fiasco.

'You are there, Giancarlo?'

The boy hesitated. Forty seconds gone, forty seconds of the two minutes that was required for a trace.

'I have demanded the freedom of Franca . . . that is what must happen if 'Arrison is to live . . .'

'It is a very complicated matter, Giancarlo. There are many things to be considered.' There was an awful, deadening calmness in the responses. A sponge that he hit at but could not corner and pinion.

Close to a minute gone.

'There is one question only, Carboni. Yes or no?'

The first hint of anxiety broke in the distorted voice, the noise of breathing mingled with the atmospherics. 'We have Franca here for you to talk to, Giancarlo.'

'Yes or no, that was my question.'

More than a minute gone, the hand on its second arc.

'Franca will talk to you.'

All eyes in the room on the face of Franca Tantardini.

Carboni held the telephone mouthpiece against his shirt, looked deep and far into the woman, saw only the blank, proud, composed eyes, and knew that this was the ultimate moment of risk. Nothing to be read from her mouth and from her hands that did not fidget, showed no impatience. Total silence, and an atmosphere lead-laden that even Carpenter without the Italian language could sense and be fearful of.

'I trust you, Franca.' Barely audible the words as Carboni's hand with the telephone stretched out towards the responding arm of La Tantardini.

There was a carelessness now in her smile. Almost human. Long slender fingers exchanged for the fatty, stumpy grip of Carboni's fist. When she spoke it was with a clear and educated voice, no roughened edges, no slang of the gutter. The daughter of a well-set family of Bergamo.

'It is Franca, my little fox . . . do not interrupt me. Hear me to the finish . . . and, little fox, do as I instruct you, exactly as I instruct you. They have asked me to tell you to surrender. They have asked me to tell you that you should release the Englishman . . .'

Carboni permitted his eyes, in secrecy, to float to his watch. One minute and twenty seconds since the call was initiated. He saw the image of activity in the Questura basement. The isolation of the communication, the evaluation of the digital dialling process, the routing of the connection back towards its source. He strained forward to hear better her words.

'You have asked for my release, little fox. Listen to me. There will be no freedom. So I say this to you, Giancarlo. This is the last –'

It was the action of a moment. Franca Tantardini on her feet. Right arm high above her head, the fist in clenched salute. A face riven with hatred. Muscles of the neck bulged like sewer pipes.

'– kill him, Giancarlo. Kill the pig. *Forza la proletaria. Forza la rivoluzione. Giancarlo, la lotta continua* . . .'

Even as they were rising to their feet, the men about her, struggling to reach her, she had moved whiplash fast towards the receiver on Carboni's desk. As she wrenched at the telephone, tearing its flex from the wall fitting, they pounded her to the ground. The little men of the room kicked and punched at the unresisting body of the woman while Carboni and Carpenter, separated by the mêlée and on their different sides of the office, sat stock still and assessed the scope of the catastrophe.

'Take her back to the Rebibbia, and I want no marks on her . . . none that can be seen.' A terrible ice cold in his voice, as if the shock wave of betrayal had broken Giuseppe Carboni.

Another telephone ringing. He picked it up, placed it to his ear and dropped his weight on to an elbow. As he listened he watched Franca Tantardini half carried, half dragged, take her leave of him. Carboni nodded as information was given him, offered no gratitude for the service.

'They say, from the basement, that I had told them they would have a minimum of two minutes to find the trace. They say that I gave them one minute and forty seconds. They say that was not sufficient. I have failed your man, Carpenter. I have failed your man.'

Carpenter spat back at him. 'They gave you nothing?'

'Just that it was from the north of the city . . .'

Carpenter stood up and walked towards the door. He wanted to say something vicious, wanted to let the frustration go, and couldn't find it in himself. You couldn't kick a dog, not one that was already limping, that had the mange at its collar. There was nothing he could say. Grown men, weren't they? Not kids who could bully. All adults, all trying, all confronted by the same cancer that was eating deep and ravenously.

'I'm going round to Charlesworth's place. The Embassy fellow. You can reach me there . . . till late.'

'I will be here.'

Of course he would be. Where else for him? No Embassy duty-free Scotch for Giuseppe Carboni, no shutting out of the problem with seventy per cent proof. Carpenter let himself out, didn't look back at Carboni, and walked down the corridor to the staircase.

Through the connecting door and into the inner sanctum marched Francesco Vellosi. There was uninhibited hatred on his face, brutal and devastating, informing Carboni that he had heard the words of Tantardini.

'I told you to be careful, Carboni, I told you.'

'You told me . . .'

A strand of sympathy shone. 'Anything?'

'With the time available, nothing of substance, nothing that matters.'

Their arms around each other's waists, in mutual consolation, the two men walked from the room to the wire-caged lift for the fifth floor.

They would saturate an area of slightly more than three thousand five hundred square kilometres, from Viterbo in the north to La Storta in the south, while the western limit would be the coastal town of Civitavecchia and the eastern line would be the Roma–Firenze autostrada. Formality, the task provided by the basement technicians. Too great an area for a manhunt, too great an area to lift the men's bowed shoulders.

As they emerged from the lift Vellosi said softly, 'They will crucify you, they will say she should never have spoken to the boy.'

'It was the best chance to make him talk for longer.'

'Who will say that? You will be torn apart, Carboni, the entertainment of the wild dogs.'

Arms still round each other, faces close, Carboni looking up and Vellosi down, eyes meeting. 'But you will be with me, Vellosi.'

Only a smile, only a tightening of the fist in the material of Carboni's shirt, as they came to the operations centre.

The child's head, wearing a winning smile, drifted around the kitchen door.

'Mama . . .' the plaintive call. 'Can I sit with Papa?'

'You were a bad boy today.'

'I'm sorry, Mama . . .'

She had no stomach for the fight, was pleased the child had come from his room, exorcizing her shame that she had lost her temper and tried to strike him. God knows they both worshipped their lone son.

'Papa is tired.' She heard the distant steady snore from her man's throat, the warm food cosseted in him, the burned energy of the day seeking replacement. 'You can sit with him, but don't you bother him, don't you wake him . . .'

The child waited for no more hesitation from his mother. He raced in his light bare feet, his loose pyjamas flowing, through the kitchen and into the living-room.

His mother listened.

'Papa, are you asleep? Papa, can I tell you what I saw in the wood? Please, Papa . . .'

She slapped the towel across her hands, summoned herself across the room in a cloak of annoyance and hissed through the doorway at the sofa where the child snuggled against his sleeping father.

'What did I say to you? That you were not to wake him. Another word from you and you go to your bed. Leave Papa alone. You talk to Papa in the morning.'

'Yes, Mama, can I watch the programme?'

A concert flickered on the aged screen, the harmony of the notes suffering from the distortion of the set. She nodded her head. That was permitted, and it was good for the boy to sit with his father.

'But don't you wake Papa . . . and don't you argue when I call you for bed.'

18

The sounds of the returning Giancarlo carried from far away to Geoffrey Harrison. The arrival was blundering and clumsy as if silence and stealth were no longer of importance. The noise spread through the quiet of the wood, where there was nothing to compete with the snapping of branches, the crushing of fallen leaves. He would not be able to see the boy's face when he came, would not be able to recognize the mood and the danger. A blessing or an additional wound? Better to know when the boy was still far from him, better his news while the creature was still distant.

They say some men die well, and others die badly. Harrison remembered when he was a kid and he'd read in a magazine stories of executions by law in a gaol. They said some had screamed and some walked with a high head, and some were carried, and some went unaided and thanked the men around them for their courtesy. What bloody difference did it make? Who looks at a skinned pig hanging from a butcher's hook and says, 'That pig would have died well, you can see it on his face, brave bugger, well done'; who looks at the carcase and thinks of its going?

You'll crawl, Geoffrey, grovel on your knees, because that's the way you are. The bender and the compromiser. Have to be, don't you? Because that's the way you do business, and you're good at business, Geoffrey. That's why International Chemical Holdings sent you here, sent you to lie on your side with the hair growing on your face and the smell from your socks and pants, and the hunger in your belly, and the pain at your wrists, and a kid coming to kill you. Crawl, Geoffrey, play the lizard on his stomach, scuffing through the deadwood. That's the way of commerce. Know when you can fight and when you can lose, and if it's defeat, then turn the cheek and summon the sweet words and save something for the shareholders. Bloody shareholders. Fat women in Hampstead, poodles and jewels, apartments with lifts, and deceased husbands. For you, you bitches, for you I'm lying here, listening to him coming.

There were the escape moments, Geoffrey. In the car, plenty of them, each time you stopped . . . God, do we go through all that again? It's a big grown-up world, Geoffrey. Nanny isn't here any more. No one to save you but yourself. Why isn't little Giancarlo messing his knickers, why isn't he frightened that his time is coming? Because he believes in something, idiot. It's a faith, it has a meaning to him.

And Geoffrey Harrison has no creed.

Who does Geoffrey Harrison fight for? What principle?

Where is his army of companions who will weep if one of their number falls?

Another bloody casualty, Geoffrey, and there will be a public sadness in Head Office, and a few will scratch their heads and try and remember the chap who went abroad because it paid more. But don't expect there's going to be any wet on the blotting-paper, any stains on the ledgers, any flags pulled down.

Remember the bar at the Olgiata Golf Club. Red faces and long gins. Men who were always right, always knew. Certainty of opinion. Remember the bar of the Gold Club when Aldo Moro was cringing for the world to see and urging in letters to his friends for government weakness to preserve his life from the Red Brigades.

Despicable behaviour. The man's no dignity.

What you'd expect from these people.

Only have to go back to the war, in North Africa, show 'em a bayonet and you've more prisoners on your hands than you can feed.

What a wonderful wallowing security, membership of the Golf Club.

They'll make hay of you, Geoffrey. The man who came back for nine holes after he'd been on his knees with the tears on his cheeks and the sobbing in his throat, and pleaded and held the legs of a boy half his age.

Got to fight 'em, show 'em there's going to be no nonsense. That's the way to beat the scum.

Giancarlo was very close, and his voice pierced the darkness.

'They want you dead, 'Arrison.'

Harrison wriggled and dragged at the wires, tried to turn to face the boy. Managed a few inches.

'What do you mean?'

'They do nothing to save you.'

'What did they say?'

'They tried only to use up time so that they could trace the call.'

'What did Franca say?' The questions from Harrison blurted at the centre of the shadow above him.

'Franca told me to kill you. She said they would not release her. She told me to kill you . . .'

A whisper from Harrison. The breached corn sack, from which the essence is lost. 'Franca said that?'

It's a bloody dream, Geoffrey. There's no reality here. It's fantasy.'

'I'm not your enemy, Giancarlo. I've done nothing to hurt you.' And where was the bastard's face, moulded in the blackness? How could you creep before a boy with no face, how did you win him with your fear and your misery? 'I've never tried to harm you . . .'

'Franca said I was to kill you.'

'For Christ's sake, Giancarlo. I'm no enemy of the Italian proletariat, I'm not in the way of your revolution.'

'You are a symbol of oppression and exploitation.'

'It's like you're reading out of the telephone book, they don't mean anything, those words. You can't take a life for a slogan.'

The same dripping voice, the same cruelty in the unseen eyes. 'There can be no revolution without blood. Not just your blood, 'Arrison. We die in the streets for what we believe is a just struggle. We face the living death in the concentration camps of the regime. Twenty years she will exist in Messina . . .'

'Don't talk to me about other people.' The dream clearing, the nightmare fading. 'It helps you not at all if you kill me. You must see that, Giancarlo, please say you can see that . . .'

'You are pathetic, 'Arrison. You are of the middle class, you are of the multinational, you have a flat on a hill . . . should you not defend that way? Should you not defend that exploitation? I despise you.'

The silence fell fast because the killing words of the boy struck far. Harrison abandoned his efforts, lay still and heard the sounds of

Giancarlo dropping to sit on the ground a dozen feet from the bunker. Man and boy they drifted to their own thoughts.

Crawl to him, Geoffrey. It's not the Golf Club's life, forget the humiliation, screw the dignity lapse. That he couldn't grovel, what a thing for a man to die over.

Shrill little words and a voice he did not recognize as his own. 'What do I have to do, Giancarlo? What do I have to do for you not to kill me?'

The Judas moment, Geoffrey. The betrayal of his society. The boy had read him, that he belonged nowhere, was a part of nothing. 'Answer me, please.'

Endlessly the boy waited. The wave rolled back from the beach, then gathered itself in white-crested accumulation, burst again, shattering with force on the sand. The reply of Giancarlo.

'You cannot do anything.'

'Afterwards I will say what you have told me to say.'

'Franca has ordered it, you cannot do anything.'

'I will go to the newspapers and the radio and the television, I will say what you want me to . . .'

The boy seemed bored, as if wishing the conversation terminated. Could the man not understand what he was told? 'You chose a way for your life, I have chosen mine. I will fight against what is rotten, you will prop it. I do not recognize the white flag, that is not the way of our combat.'

Harrison was crying, convulsing, the great tears welling in his eyes, dribbling on his cheeks, wetting his mouth. 'You take a pleasure in it . . . ?'

There was a sternness in the boy. 'We are at war, and you should behave like a soldier. Because you do not I despise you. It will be at nine o'clock in the morning. You have till then to become a soldier.'

'You horrid, repulsive little bastard . . . they'll give you no mercy . . . you'll die in the fucking gutter.'

'We ask for no mercy, 'Arrison. We offer none.'

Quiet again in the forest. Giancarlo spread himself on the leaves. He pushed with his hands to make the surface more even, wriggled on to his side so that his back was turned on Geoffrey Harrison and beneath a ceiling of moonlight flecked by the high branches, settled himself. For a few minutes he would hear the foreign sounds of his prisoner's choking sobs. Then he found sleep and they were lost to him.

The sun of the day and the food of the evening ensured the farmer's sleep, and the comatose rest was escape from the worries that burdened his life. The price of fodder, the price of fertilizer, the price of diesel oil for the tractor could be shut out only when his mind was at peace. His child stayed silent, close to the rise and fall of his father's chest and waited with a concentrated patience, fighting off his own tiredness. Beyond the doorway the child heard the sounds of his mother's movements, and they encouraged his stillness as he lay fearful that any stirring on the damaged springs of the sofa would alert and remind her that he was not yet in his small narrow bed.

Mingled with the music were the mind pictures that the child drew for himself. Pictures that were alien and hostile.

'Come on in, Archie.'

'Thank you, Michael.' Didn't slip off the tongue that easily, not the Christian name bit, not after the hard words. Charlesworth stood in the doorway with a loose shirt on him, no tie, and slacks and sandals. Carpenter fidgeted at the door in his suit.

'Come on into the den.'

Carpenter was led through the hall. Delicate furniture, a case of hardback books, oil paintings on the wall, a vase of tall irises. Do all right, these people . . . Stop the bitching, Archie, drop the chip off your shoulder. You can't blame people for not living in Motspur Park, not if they've the choice.

'Darling, this is Archie Carpenter, from Harrison's head office. My wife Caroline.'

Carpenter shook hands with the tall, tanned girl presented to him. The sort they bred down in Cheltenham, along with fox-hunters and barley fields. She wore a straight dress held at the shoulders by vague straps. The wife back in the semi would have had a fit, blushed like an August rose, no bra and entertaining.

'I'm sorry I'm late, Mrs Charlesworth. I've been at the Questura.'

'You poor thing, you'd like a wash.'

Well, he wouldn't have asked for it himself, but he'd worn a jacket all day and the same socks, and he stank like a hung duck.

'I'll take him, darling.'

An older man was rising heavily from a sofa. Washing could wait, introductions first. Charlesworth resumed the formalities. 'This is Colonel Henderson, our military attaché.'

'Pleased to meet you, Colonel.'

'They call me "Buster", Archie. I've heard about you. I hear you've a straight tongue in your head, and a damned good thing too.'

Carpenter was led to the peace of an outer bathroom. Time for him as he stood in front of the pan to examine the sentry row of deodorant sprays on the window-sill, enough to keep the Embassy smelling sweet for a month. And books too. Who was going to read classical Greek history and contemporary American politics while having a quick squat? Extraordinary people. The reek of public school and private means. He washed his hands, let the day's grime dribble away, pushed a flannel round the back of his neck. Long live the creature comforts. Soap and water and a waiting gin.

They sat around in the lounge, the four of them, separated by rugs and marble flooring and sprouting coffee tables. Carpenter didn't resist the demand that he shed his jacket, loosen his tie.

'Well, tell us, Archie, what's the scene at the Questura?' Charlesworth setting the ball rolling.

'I think they've screwed it . . .'

'For that poor Mr Harrison . . . ?'

Carpenter ignored Caroline Charlesworth. What did they want, a coffee-morning chat with the neighbours, or something from the bloody horse's mouth?

'Tantardini got her hands on the telephone too early in the game for the trace people. Told her boy to chop Harrison, then pulled the connection. The call was still at switchboard but the boy had the message. He rang off, and that's about it.'

Charlesworth was leaning forward in his seat, glass held between his hands. The honest, earnest young man, he seemed to Carpenter. 'She gave a specific instruction for the boy to kill Harrison?'

'That's the way Carboni put it. "I have failed your man", those were his words. Biggest bloody understatement of the day.'

'He's a good man, Giuseppe Carboni.' Charlesworth spoke with enough compassion for Carpenter momentarily to squirm. 'It's not easy, not in a country like this. Right, Buster?'

The Colonel swirled his whisky round the glass. 'We had full powers in many places, what you'd call nowadays totalitarian powers, in Palestine and Malaya and Kenya and Cyprus. Here the legacy of pre-war fascism is that the security forces are kept weak. But for all we had, it didn't do us a great deal of good.'

'But that was far from the great Mother Britain,' Carpenter interjected impatiently. 'This is different, it's on their own doorstep that they're being whipped. Carboni excepted, they're ambling about like bloody zombies . . .'

'They're trying, Archie,' Charlesworth intervened gently.

'I wouldn't care to make a judgement on their efficiency if I'd been here just a few hours.' The Colonel cut at the air, the swinging of the old cavalry sabre.

Carpenter put his hands above his head, grinned for a moment, dissolved the temper. 'I'm outnumbered, out-flanked, whatever . . . So what I want to know is this: when they say they'll chop him, when Battestini says it, do we take that at face, is it gospel?'

Caroline Charlesworth started from her chair. The plea to be excused

708

from the blunt assessments. 'The dinner won't be more than a few minutes.'

'You answer that, Buster,' Charlesworth said. 'It's the pertinent question of the evening.'

The hard, clean eyes of the veteran fixed on Carpenter. 'The answer is affirmative. When they say they'll kill, they're as good as their word.'

'Black tie job?'

'I repeat, Mr Carpenter, they're as good as their word.'

Caroline Charlesworth appeared from the kitchen doorway. The food was ready. She led, the men followed. In the dining-room Carpenter saw the wine on the table, the port and brandy on the sideboard. There was solace to be found here, escape from a hideous and crippling mess.

Late into the evening, the child's mother came at last for him. With a sweep of her hand she hushed his protest, and swept him up so that he sat on her hip as she took him from the side of his father. It was done quickly and expertly and the farmer seemed as unaware of the child's going as he had been of his presence. She nuzzled her nose against her son's neck, saw the fight that he made to keep his eyes open and chided herself that she had left him for so long. She carried him to his room.

'Mama.'

'Yes, my sweet.' She lowered him into the bed.

'Mama, if Papa wakes soon, will he come to see me?'

'You will be asleep, in the morning you will see him.' She pulled the coarse sheet to his chin.

'I have to tell him what I saw . . .'

'What was it, a wild pig, the big dog fox . . . ?' She watched the yawn break on the child's face.

'Mama, I saw . . .'

Her kiss stifled his words, and she tiptoed from the room.

It was the work of the Agente to check finally the cell doors after the prisoners held in maximum security had finished communal recreation and were consigned for the night to their individual cells. His practice was to take a quick glance through the spyhole and then slide the greased bolt. Others would come after him when the lights were dimmed to make the last muster call of the night.

The Agente had found the paper, folded once, on the mat at the front door of his house. A small piece, ragged at an edge where it had been torn from a notepad. There was a pencil-written number on the outside flap that was immediately relevant to the Agent. Three digits, the number of the cell of the Chief of Staff of the Nappisti.

When he reached that door, the Agente pushed it a few inches, tossed the paper inside, crashed the bolt home, and was on his way. Any colleague who might have seen him would not have been aware of the passing of the message.

The capo abandoned his weekly letter to his mother in the hill city of Siena, saw the paper and slipped from his chair to gather it.

L'amministrazione dice non per Tantardini.

No freedom for Tantardini. It was as he had said. What he had anticipated, because the Englishman was of insufficient importance. Inevitable, but better that way, better if the ultimatum were to expire, the gun were to be fired. The strategy of tension they called it in the Roman newspapers, the creation of intolerable fear. The death of the enemy created fear, something not achieved by negotiation and the making of deals. Better if the Englishman were killed.

But who was the boy, Battestini? Why had he not heard of a youth who could implement so much? The radio in his cell had told him the police held the opinion that the boy worked alone . . . remarkable, outstanding . . . and the commentator called him the lover of Franca Tantardini and expounded that this was the reason for the boy's action. Who in the movement had not been the lover of Franca Tantardini? How many of the Nappisti in this same cell block had not taken comfort from hours spent strangled by the arms and legs of Tantardini, taken pleasure from the flesh and fingers of the woman? His table lamp lit a mirthless smile. Perhaps it was the boy's first time, and he believed he had made a conquest. If it was the first time the boy would climb a mountain for that woman, perhaps he'd die for Tantardini. Certainly he would kill for her. When the ultimatum was met he would issue a communiqué in his own name from inside the walls of Asinara. Courage, my child. We love you, we are with you. But why had he not been told of this boy?

Like sharks homing for offal, the mosquitoes slipped through the opened window of the farmhouse parlour and turned their incisive attention to the arms and neck of the resting man. Instinctively he slapped the side of his face in irritation, and in his growing consciousness there was the drone of their wings, the rising surge of their attacks. He started up, blinked in the flickering light of the television and heard the sounds of the kitchen through the closed door, water running, the quiet clatter of dishes and tins. He scratched savagely at the bitten skin where the bite mark had grown enough for him to gouge a sharp trickle of blood, he rubbed the back of his hand into his eyes, then headed for the kitchen. Time for him to be going to his bed, time for him to encourage her to follow.

710

His wife put her finger across her mouth, the call for quiet, and pointed to the half-open door that led to their son's room. A tall, broad-shouldered woman, red-faced, dark hair pulled back in an elastic band, thick bare arms and a faded apron. She had been his woman since he was seventeen and had shyly courted her with the encouragement of her parents, who knew of the farm he would inherit.

'The little one is sleeping?'

She worked at the final flurry of the day's sink work. 'It's taken him long enough, but he's nearly there.'

'Did he tell you where he'd been?'

She slopped warm water from a kettle into the bright plastic sink bowl. 'In the woods, where else?'

'What kept him there?' He was tired, yearning for his bed, and there was much hay to be moved by trailer in the morning. Perfunctory conversation, made only because she was not ready to follow him to their cumbersome, heavy oak wedding bed.

'He saw something, he said.'

'What did he see?'

'I don't know – something. He wanted to tell you about it. I said it would keep till morning. Perhaps it was a pig?'

'Not this far down the hillside,' he said softly.

She sluiced the pan in which she had made the sauce for the pasta.

'You have much more to do?' he asked.

'I have to wash some socks through, then it is finished.' She smiled at him, kind and dark-eyed.

'I'll say good night to the boy.'

The frown crossed her face. 'Don't wake him, not now. He's dead to the world, don't wake him now.'

'I'll see his bedclothes aren't on the floor.'

When he had gone, she could muse as she doused the socks in water that her man loved his child as the most precious thing in his life. God be thanked, she thought, that if we were to have but one child it should have been a boy. Someone for him to work for, someone for him to dream would one day take over the running of the farm. She worked quickly, the soap lathering in a sea of bubbles among the wool, some whole and some darned. Shirts she would do in the morning, after the chickens had been fed.

'Mama.'

She turned abruptly in response to the strained voice of her man. He stood at the kitchen door, his face dazed and in shock, his hand resting loosely on the shoulder of his son.

'You've woken him.' The petulance rose in her voice.

'You never asked him what he had seen?' The farmer spoke hoarsely.

'A fox, a rabbit, perhaps a heron, what difference does it make, what difference at his age?' She bridled, before her senses responded to the mood her man set. 'What did he see?'

'He found a red car hidden in the bushes beside the small field and the wood. He has a toy, a toy car that your mother gave him last Easter, the one he plays in his bed with. He said to me that the toy was the same as the car that he had found. His toy is a red Fiat Uno Vente Sette. They showed a car on the television, the car for the foreigner who was kidnapped. Fiat Uno Vente Sette, and red . . .'

'A red 127, there would be half a million . . .' Her hands were drawn from the water, wiped nervously at her apron. There should be no involvement, not with something hostile.

'He found a man who was tied.'

'The boy dreams. It is a world of his own.'

'He saw a youth come, with a gun.'

She stammered, 'It's not our business.'

'Dress him.'

Her eyes wide, her lips moving in fear, she attacked in defence of her child. 'You cannot take him there, not in the darkness, not if you believe that he has seen these things.'

'Get his clothes and dress him.' It was an instruction, a command. She did not resist and scurried to the child's room for his day clothes.

From the hallway the farmer took a thick sweater and the small-bore shotgun that he used for pigeon and rabbit when he went with his neighbours to shoot on a Sunday morning. From a nail high in the back door to the yard he unhooked a rubber-coated torch.

Together they dressed their son.

'You remember, Mama, what Father Alberti said at the Mass after Moro. He said these people were the anti-Christ. Even Paolo Sesto they rejected, even the appeal by him that Moro should be spared. They are the enemies of the Church, these people, they are the enemies of all of us. You remember what Father Alberti said? On the television it was said they would kill the foreigner tomorrow morning. We have to go, Mama, we have to know what the boy has seen.'

They slipped the child's shirt and coat and trousers over his pyjamas, drew on his boots over his bare feet. The mother's hands fumbled and were slower than her man's.

'Be careful, Papa, be careful with him.'

The father and his son walked out of the door and into the night. She followed the passage of the torch before the bend in the lane obscured its light, and then she sat at the kitchen table, very still, very quiet.

*

712

The wine had gone and the port after it and Caroline Charlesworth had fled the scene for her bed. The three men sat around the table and the ash and cigarette ends made their molehills in the coffee saucers. They'd been over all the ground, all the old and trampled paths. The issues of principle and pragmatism were digested and spat back. The debate on negotiation had been fought with anger and spite. And then the brandy had taken its toll and soaked and destroyed the attack of Carpenter and the defence of Charlesworth and the attaché. They were resting now and the talk was sporadic. Geoffrey Harrison was no longer the principal subject, replaced by the rate of income tax, Church aid to the Patriotic Front of Rhodesia, decadence on the streets of London. The familiar fodder for Britons abroad.

Michael Charlesworth stood up from the table, murmured something about checking with the Embassy, and moved unhappily away from the safety of the chairs.

'He's a damn good man.' Carpenter had problems with the words.

'Damn good,' growled Buster Henderson. 'You're right, you know, a damned good man.'

'I've given him some stick since I've been here.'

'Wouldn't give a hoot. Knows you've a job to be getting on with. A damn good man.'

'I've never felt so bloody useless, not in anything before.'

'I once did a stint at G2 Ops. Shut up in a bloody office, out in Aden. We had a couple of Brigades in the Radfan, tribesman-bashing. Damn good shots they were, gave our chaps a hell of a run for their money. I couldn't get clear of my desk, and m'brother-in-law was up there with a battalion. Used to rub it in with his signals, wicked devil. Used to get me damned cross, just talking and not doing. I know how you feel, Carpenter.' The weathered hand reached again for the bottleneck.

Neither man looked up as Michael Charlesworth came back into the room. He paused, and watched Henderson refilling the glasses, slopping brandy on the polished wood surface.

'You'll be needing that, Buster, I've just heard something awful . . .' His voice attracted, mothlike, the eyes of his guests.

'. . . it's Harrison's wife. Violet Harrison, she's just hit a lorry on the Raccordo. She's dead. Ran slap into a lorry. Killed outright, head-on collision.'

The bottle base crashed down on to the table and trembled there together with the hand that held it. Carpenter's fist shot out for his glass and dashed a saucer sideways, spewing ash on the white crocheted mats.

'Not bloody fair.' The Colonel spoke into the hand that masked his face.

'I made them repeat it twice, I couldn't believe it.' Charlesworth was still standing.

Carpenter swayed to his feet. 'Could you get me a taxi, Michael? I'll

713

wait for it downstairs.' He didn't look back, headed for the front door. No farewells, no thanks for hospitality. Going, getting out, and running.

He didn't call the lift, kept to the stairs, hand on the support rail, the fresh air freezing the alcohol.

God, Archie, you've screwed it now. Throwing the shit at everyone else but not yourself. Laying down the law on how everyone else should behave. Ran out on the poor bitch, Archie, hid behind the prim chintz curtain and clucked your tongue and disapproved. Bloody little pharisee with as much charity as a weasel up a rabbit burrow. Preaching all day about getting Geoffrey Harrison back to his family, but he hadn't shut the door and seen there was a family for the bastard to come home to. What had Carboni said? 'I've failed your man.' Join the club, Giuseppe, meet the other founder member.

He fell into the back of the taxi. Gave the name of his hotel and blew his nose noisily.

The dog fox crept close to the two sleeping men. With a front paw it scratched the P38 a little further from Giancarlo and its nose worked with interest at the barrel and the handle before fascination was lost.

Four times the fox went over the ground between Giancarlo and the pit as if unwilling to believe there was no food remnant to be rifled. Disappointed, the animal moved on its way, along the path that led to the fields and hedgerows where mice and rabbits and chickens and cats could be found. Abruptly the fox stopped. Ears straight, nostrils dilating. The noise that it heard was faint and distant, would not be felt by the men who slept, but for a creature of stealth and secrecy it was adequate warning.

A dark shadow, flitting comfortably on the path, the fox retraced its steps.

The farmer had laid the shotgun on the ground and knelt at the front of the car. The torch was in the boy's hands, and the farmer cupped his hands around it to minimize the flare of the light as he studied and memorized the number plate. Not that it was necessary after he had seen the prefix letters before the five numbers. RC, and the television had said that the car had been stolen from Reggio Calabria. Cunningly hidden too, a good place, well shielded by the bank and the bushes and the trees. He rose to his feet, trying to control his breathing, feeling his heart battering at his chest. He switched off the torch in the boy's hand and retrieved his gun. Better with that in his hands as the wood threw out its death hush. The farmer reached for his son's hand, gripping it tightly, as if to provide protection from a great and imminent evil.

'Two men were in the wood?'

He sensed the nodded response.

'Where was the path to their place?'

The boy pointed across the car's bonnet into the black void of the trees. By touch the farmer collected with his fingers three short fallen branches, and made an arrow of them that followed his son's arm. He put his hand on the boy's shoulder and they hurried together from the place, back across the fields, back to the safety of their home.

19

Giuseppe Carboni was dozing at his desk, head pillowed lopsided on his folded arms.

'Dottore . . .' The shout of excitement and pounding feet boomed in the outer corridor.

Carboni flicked his head up, the attention of the owl, his eyes large in expectation. The subordinate surged through the open door, and there was a gleam and an excitement on his face.

'We have the car, Dottore . . .' Stuttered out, because the thrill was great.

Chairs were heaved back, files discarded, telephones dropped, men hurrying in the wake of the messenger gathered at Carboni's desk.

'Where?' Carboni snapped, the sleep shed fast.

'On the hill below Bracciano, between the town and the lake.'

'Excellent,' Carboni sighed, as if the burden of Atlas were shifted.

'Better than excellent, Dottore. A farmer found the car . . . his son, a small boy, took him to the place, and he thinks the boy watched Battestini and Harrison in the wood in the day . . .'

'Excellent, excellent . . .' Carboni gulped at the foetid air of the room which had taken on a new freshness, a new quality. He felt a weakness in his hands, a trembling at his fingers. 'Where is Vellosi?'

'At the communications centre. He said he would not return to the Viminale tonight.'

'Get him.'

The room had been darkened, and now Carboni moved to the door and rammed down the wall switch. The response was blinding light in the room, all bulbs on the chandelier illuminated, sweeping away the shadows and depressions.

'The liaison officers of carabinieri and SISDE, get them here too . . . within ten minutes.'

715

Back at his desk, moving with uncommon speed, he pulled from a drawer a large-scale map of the Lazio region. His aide's pencil raked to the green plot of woodland dividing the built-up grey shades of the town of Bracciano from the blue tint of the Lago di Bracciano. Carboni without ceremony relieved him of the pencil and scratched the crosses on the yellow road ribbons for the perimeter that he would throw around the boy and his prisoner. Seal the road to Trevignano, the road to Anguillara, the road to La Storta, the road to Castel Giuliano, to Cerveteri, to Sasso, to Manziano. Seal them tight, block all movement.

'Has the farmer alerted them at all . . . is there that risk?'

'He was asked that, Dottore. He says not. He went with his son to the car, identified it, and then returned home. He left the child there and then he walked to the home of a neighbour who has a telephone. He was careful to walk because he feared the noise of a car would startle the people in the wood, though his farm is at least a kilometre away. From the house of his neighbour he telephoned the carabinieri in Bracciano . . .'

'The carabinieri . . . they will not blunder . . .' Carboni exploded, as if success was so fragile, could be snatched from him.

'Be calm, Dottore. The carabinieri have not moved.' The aide was anxious to pacify.

'You have them, Carboni?'

The direct shout, Vellosi striding into the office, hands clapping together in anticipation. More followed. A carabinieri colonel in pressed biscuit-brown uniform, the man from the secret service in grey suit with sweat stains at the armpit, another in shirtsleeves who was the representative of the examining magistrate.

'Is it confirmed, the sighting . . . ?'

'What has already been done . . . ?'

'Where do you have them . . . ?'

The voices droned around his desk, a gabble of contradiction and request.

'Shut up!' Carboni shouted. His voice carried over them and silenced the press around his desk. He had only to say it once, and had never been known to raise his voice before to equals and superiors. He sketched in his knowledge and in a hushed and hasty tone outlined the locations he required for the block forces, the positioning of the inner cordon, and his demand that there should be no advance into the trees without his personal sanction.

'The men best trained to comb the woods are mine . . .' Vellosi said decisively.

'A boast, but not backed by fact. The carabinieri are the men for an assault.' A defiant response from the carabinieri officer.

'My men have the skills for close quarters.'

'We can get five times as many into the area in half the time . . .'

716

Carboni looked around him, disbelieving, as if he had not seen it all before, heard it many times in his years of police work. His head shook in anger.

'It is, of course, for you to decide, Giuseppe.' Vellosi smiled, confident. 'But my men –'

'Do not have the qualities of the carabinieri,' the colonel chipped in his retort.

'Gentlemen, you shame us all, we discredit ourselves.' There was that in Carboni's voice that withered them, and the men in the room looked away, did not meet his gaze. 'I want the help of all of you. I am not administering prizes but seeking to save the life of Geoffrey Harrison.'

And then the work began. The division of labour. The planning and tactics of approach. There should be no helicopters, no sirens, a minimum of open radio traffic. There should be concentrations before the men moved off on foot across the fields for the inner line. Advance from three directions; one force congregating at Trevignano and approaching from the north-east, a second taking the southern lakeside road from Anguillara, a third from the town of Bracciano to the west to sweep down the hillside.

'It is as if you thought an army were bivouacked in the trees,' Vellosi said quietly as the meeting broke.

'It is a war I know little of,' Carboni replied as he hitched his coat from the chair on to his wide shoulders. They walked together to the door, abandoning the room to confusion and shouted orders and ringing telephones. Activity again and welcome after the long night hours of idleness. Carboni hesitated and leaned back through the doorway. 'The Englishman who was here in the day. I will take him with me, call him at his hotel.' He hurried to catch Vellosi. He should have felt that at last the tide had turned, the wind had slackened, yet the doubt still gnawed at him. How to approach by stealth, through trees, through undergrowth, and the danger if they did not achieve surprise. The thing could be plucked from him yet, even at the last, even at the closest time.

'We can still lose everything,' Carboni said to Vellosi.

'Not everything, we will have the boy.'

'And that is important?'

'It is the trophy for my wall.'

They destroy us, these bastards. They make the calluses in our minds, they coarsen our sensitivities, until a good man, a man of the quality of Francesco Vellosi believes only in vengeance and is blinded to the value of the life of an innocent.

'When you were in church, Francesco, last night . . .'

'I prayed that I myself, with my own hand, might have the chance to shoot the boy.'

Carboni held his arm. They emerged together into the warm night air. The convoy stood ready, car doors open, engines pulsing.

The damp of the earth, rising through the leaf mattress, crawled and nagged at the bones of Giancarlo, till he writhed in irritation and the refuge of sleep fell from him. The hunger bit and the chill was deep at his body. He groped across the ground for his pistol and his hand brushed against the metal of the barrel. P38, I love you, my P38, present to the little fox from Franca. Sometimes when he awoke in a strange place, and suddenly, he needed moments to assimilate the atmosphere around him. Not at this awakening. His mind was sharp in an instant.

He glanced at the luminous face of his watch. Close to three. Six hours to the time that Franca ordered for the retribution on Geoffrey Harrison. Six hours more and then the sun would be high, and the scorch patterns of the heat would have flung back the cold of darkness, and the wood would be dying and thirsting for moisture. There would have been two or three of them with Aldo Moro on this night. Two or three of them to share the desperate isolation of the executioner as he made ready his equipment. Two or three of them to pump home the bullets, so that the blame was spread . . . Blame, Giancarlo? Blame is for the middle classes, blame is for the guilty. There is no blame for the work of the revolution, for the struggle of the proletariat. Two or three of them to take him to the beach by the airport fence of Fiumicino. And they had had their escape route.

What escape route for Giancarlo?

No planning, no preparation, no safe house, no car switch, no accomplice.

Did Franca think of that?

It is not important to the movement. Attack is the factor of importance, not retreat.

They will hunt you, Giancarlo, hunt you for your life. The minds of their ablest men, hunting you to eternity, hunting you till you cannot run further. The enemy has the machines that are invulnerable and perpetual, that invoke a memory that cannot weary.

It was an order. Orders can never be bent to accommodate circumstance. In the movement there has been great sacrifice.

And there is advantage in the killing of 'Arrison . . . ?

Not for your mind to evaluate. A soldier does not question his order. He acts, he obeys.

The insects played at his face, nipping and needling at his cheeks, finding the cavities of his nostrils, the softness of his ear lobes. He swatted them away.

Why should the bastard 'Arrison sleep? When he was about to die, how could be? A man with no belief beyond his own selfish survival, how could he find sleep?

For the first time in many hours Giancarlo summoned the image of his room in the flat at seaside Pescara. Bright on the walls of Alitalia posters, the hanging figure of the wooden Christ, the thin-framed portrait from a colour magazine of Paul VI, the desk for his schoolbooks where he had worked in the afternoons after classes, the wardrobe for his clothes where the white shirts for Sundays hung ironed. Insidious and compelling, a world that was lit and conventional and normal. Giancarlo, one-time stereotype, who sat beside his mother at meals, and wanted in the evenings to be allowed to help his father at the shop. A long time ago, an age ago, when Giancarlo was on the production line, held in the same precision mould as the other boys of the street. 'Arrison had been like that.

The ways had parted, different signposts, different destinations. God . . . and it was a lonely way . . . terrifying and hostile. Your choice, Giancarlo.

He slapped his face again to rid himself of the insects and the dream collapsed. Gone were the savours of home, replaced by a boy whose photograph was stuck with adhesive tape to the dashboards of a thousand police cars, whose features would appear in a million newspapers, whose name grew fear, whose hand held a gun. He would never see Franca again. He knew that and the thought ripped and wrenched at him. Never in his life again. Never again would he touch her hair, and hold her fingers. Just a memory, a recollection to be set beside the room in Pescara.

Giancarlo lay again on the ground and closed his eyes.

Up the Cassia northwards from the city headed the convoys.

The riot wagons of the Primo Celere, the Fiat lorries of the carabinieri, the blue and white and prettily painted cars of the polizia, the unmarked vehicles of the special squads. There were many who came in nightclothes to the balconies of the high-rise flats and watched the stream of the participants and felt the thrill of the circus cavalcade. More than a thousand men on the move. All armed, all tensed, all drugged in the belief that at last they could assuage their frustration and beat and kick the irritant that plagued them. At the village of La Storta, where the road narrowed and was choked, the drivers hooted and blasphemed at the traffic police, and demanded clearance of the chaos, because all were anxious to be in Bracciano when dawn came.

Past La Storta, on the narrower Via Claudia with its sharp bends between the tree lines, Giuseppe Carboni's car was locked into a column of lorries. It was a quieter, more sedate progress because now the sirens were forbidden, the rotating lights were doused, the horns unused. Archie Carpenter shared the front seat with the driver. Vellosi and Carboni were behind among the bullet-proof waistcoats and the submachine-guns, taken as if by a careful virgin from the boot before the departure from the Questura.

Water dripped from Carpenter's hair on to the collar of his shirt and down the back of his jacket, the remnant of his shower after the telephone had broken the total, drink-induced sleep that he had stumbled to. Now that he was awake, the pain between his temples was huge.

A boring bastard, she'd called him. A proper little bore. Violet Harrison on Archie Carpenter.

Well, what was he supposed to do? Get her on to the mattress in the interests of ICH, take her on the living-room carpet . . . ?

Not what it was about, Archie. Not cut and dried like that. Just needed someone to talk to.

Someone to talk to? Wearing a dress like that, hanging out like it was going out of fashion?

Wrong, Archie. A girl broken up and falling down, who needed someone to share it with. And you were out of your depth, Archie, lost your lifebelt and splashing like an idiot. You ran away, you ran out on her, and had a joke with Charlesworth, had your giggle. You ran because they don't teach you about people under high stress in safe old Motspur Park. All cosy and neat there in the mortgaged semis, where nobody shouts because the neighbours will hear, nobody has a bit on the side because the neighbours will know, where nobody does anything but sit on their arses and wait for the day when they're pushing up daisies and it's too late and they've gone, silent fools and unremembered. She needed help, Archie. You galloped out of that flat as fast as your bloody legs would take you.

A proper little bore, and no one had ever called him that before, not to his face.

'Did you hear about Harrison's wife, Mr Carboni?' Spoken offhand, as if he wasn't concerned, wasn't involved.

'What about her?'

'She was killed in a car crash, late last night.'

'Where was she?' Puzzlement rang through Carboni's preoccupation with the procedures of the coming hours.

'Out on what's called the Raccordo.'

'It is many kilometres from where she lives.'

'She was driving home, she was alone.' Carpenter spewing it out.

'No one with her, no friends with her . . . ?'

'So, if we get the man out, that is what we have to confront him with.' A light, chilled laugh from Vellosi. 'Incredible, Carboni, when a man's cup is overfilled . . .'

720

'It is criminal that at this time a woman should be alone.' A distaste hung in Carboni's words.

'I suppose no one thought about it,' said Carpenter dully.

At the junction to the lake road they saw the stationary rows of lorries and vans parked on the grass verge. They passed queues of walking men in uniform, the headlights glinted on the metal of firearms, and there were glimpses of cordons forming in the fields. The car winged on down the steep hillside before turning hard to the right along a weeded driveway with a military barrier and a concentration of elderly brick buildings awaiting them. Carpenter tried to loose the load of self-pity and stared about him as the car stopped.

The doors snapped open, Carboni was out quickly, and mopped himself and turned to Carpenter. 'It used to be a flying-boat station, long before the war, with its lake frontage. It is a place now just for dumping the conscripts. They maintain a museum, but nothing flies. But we are close to the wood here and we have communications.' He took Carpenter's arm. 'Stay near to me, now is the time for you to wish me well.'

They were swept through the ill-lit door of the administration block, Carpenter elbowing to keep contact with the bustling Carboni, and on into a briefing room. Hands out to greet Carboni, hugging and rubbed cheeks, a clutch of bodies around him, and Carpenter relegated to a chair at the back while the policeman found sufficient yet reluctant silence to make a short address on his plan. Another surge of the men in suits and uniforms and battledress, and Carboni, the emperor of the moment, was speeding for the doorway. They won't stop for you, Archie. They won't hang about for that bloody Englishman. Carpenter shoved and pushed, winced as a Beretta holster dug at his stomach and won his way to Carboni's side. In the wedge at the door Carboni smiled at him, looking up, perspiring.

'I have made a great decision. The anti-terrorist unit demanded the right to lead, so did the carabinieri. Both thought they were best fitted. I have satisfied everybody. The carabinieri will come from the north, Vellosi's men from the south. I am an Italian Solomon. I have sliced Battestini in two.'

Carpenter stared coldly at him.

'Allow me one levity, I have nothing else to laugh at. At any moment Battestini may kill your man, he may already have done so. We are going forward in the dark, we are going to stumble in the dark through the wood.'

'You're not waiting for daylight?'

'To wait is to take too great a risk. If you pray, Carpenter, now is the moment.'

They were out of the building.

Muffled, subdued orders. Men in the grey half light hitching over

721

their heads the heavy, protective clothing that would halt all rounds other than high velocity. The cocking and arming of weapons. Ripples of laughter. Tramping feet away into the last remnants of the night. Should have a bloody stirrup cup, Archie, and a red coat, and a man to shout 'Tally Ho'.

The group with Carboni at its heart set off towards the road, and walking beside him was a short, firm-bodied man who wore torn trousers and boots and a thick sweater and carried an old shotgun broken and crooked, farmer's style, across his inner elbow.

From the hard bare mattress of her cell bed, Franca Tantardini heard the soft-soled footsteps in the outside corridor. A bolt was drawn back, a key inserted and turned, and the man who had been her interrogator let himself in.

He smiled at the woman as she lay with her head propped on her clasped hands, with the golden hair spilling on the one pillow.

'I have some news for you, Franca. Something that you would wish to know.'

Her eyes lit at first, then dulled, as if her interest betrayed her before the discipline triumphed.

'I should not be telling you, Franca, but I thought that you would wish to hear of our success.'

Involuntarily she half rose on the bed, her hands forsaking her neck, propping her up now.

'We know where he is. Your little fox, Franca. We know where he hides, in what wood, close to which village. They are surrounding the place now. At first light they will move in on your little fox.'

The light from the single bulb behind its casing of close-mesh wire bit down at the age lines of her face. The muscles at her mouth flickered.

'He'll kill the pig first.'

The interrogator laughed softly. 'If he has the courage, when the guns are around him.'

'He'll kill him.'

'Because Franca told him to. Because Franca from the safety of her cell ordered it. His pants will be wetted, his hand shaking, guns round him, aimed on him, and he is dead if he does what his Franca has told him.'

'He will do as he was ordered.'

'You are certain you can make a soldier from a bed-wetter, that was what you called him, Franca.'

'Get out.' She spat her hatred.

The interrogator smiled again. 'Let the dream be of the failure,

722

Franca. Good night, and when you are alone think of the boy, and think of how you have destroyed him . . .'

She reached down beside her bed for the canvas shoes, snatched at one and hurled it at the man in the open doorway. Wide and high, and bouncing back from the wall. He chuckled to her and grinned.

She heard the key in place, the bolt thrust across.

The noise of Giancarlo twisting from his side to his back was the agent that roused Geoffrey Harrison from sleep. As soon as he woke the bite of the wire at his wrists and ankles was sharp. The first, instinctive stretch of his limbs tautened the flex, dug the knots into the underflesh of his wrists and ankles. A man who awakens in hell, who has purchased a great vengeance. Nothing but the bloody pain, first sensation, first thought, first recollection.

God, the morning that I die.

The mental process that became a physical happening, and his body cowed to a foetal position of fear. No protection, nothing to hide behind, nothing to squirm to. The morning that I die. He felt the tremble and the shudder take him, and the awareness was overwhelming. God, the morning that I die.

The first precious beginnings of the day were seeping into the wood. Not the sunlight, but its outriders in the grey pastel that permitted him to detect the lines of the nearest tree-trunks. This morning, with the birds singing, at nine o'clock. Another shape, suffused and vague and hard to alert himself to, as Giancarlo rose and stood above him and looked down. Giancarlo, called by Harrison's movements and inspecting the fatted goose of the feast.

'What time is it, Giancarlo?' He could hear the watch ticking on his wrist, could not see it.

'A little past four . . .'

The little bastard had learned the role of gaoler, thought Harrison, had taken on the courtesy of the death cell attendant. The hushed tone, and 'Don't you worry, lad, it doesn't hurt and it's quick'. The warm eyes of sympathy. Well, that never helped a poor lad who was going to swing at nine. What do you know about that, Geoffrey? I read it. That was other people, Geoffrey, and half the fucking population saying 'And a damn good thing too'. That's for a criminal. 'No sympathy' and 'Deserves all he's getting'. That's for men who've shot policemen and raped kids. That's not for bloody Geoffrey Harrison.

'Did you sleep?'

'Only a little.' Giancarlo spoke simply. 'It was very cold on the ground.'

'I slept very well. I didn't dream.'

Giancarlo peered down at him, the definition of his face growing with the slow coming light.

'That is good.'

'Are you going to get some food?' He could have kicked himself when he'd said it, could have spat on himself.

'I am not going for any food . . . not now . . . later, later I will eat.'

Cheaper to feed one. More economic to sustain the single person family. Silly man, Geoffrey. Should have your calculator there, the one beside the desk in the office, the one you use for all the arithmetic of ICH, then you'd know the boy would be only shopping for one, and how many lire he would save that way. Only for one, because there will only be one mouth. Not on the bloody bread list, Geoffrey, because you'll be past food, past caring about the ache in your guts.

Geoffrey Harrison's voice rose in crescendo, down the paths of the wood, high with the branches, fluttered the thrushes and blackbirds.

'Don't hurt me, Giancarlo. Please, please, don't hurt me . . .'

He was answered far back, from the shadows among the trees, distant and beyond sight, by the rampage of a dog's bark.

And in the wake of the bark was the drumming of running feet and the crash of branches swept aside.

An avalanche, circling and nearing.

Giancarlo had crouched, bent double, at the sound of the dog. At the noise of the approach of men he surged towards Harrison, pulled him to the limit of the wire and flung himself into the gap between his prisoner and the earth roof where the roots had taken the ground high out of the pit. He panted for breath, wriggled to get lower, held the gun at the lower hairs of Harrison's head.

'If you shout now you are dead.'

The gun squirming against his neck, Harrison played his part, the one he was familiar with. 'Run, you little fool. Run now.'

He could sense the boy's shock of terror imparted through their clothes, body to body, flesh warmth, through the quivering and pulsing of the blood veins. He didn't know why he called, only that this is what he would have done. This was his way. Avoid contact, avoid impact, stall the moment, the lifestyle of Geoffrey Harrison.

'If you go now you have a chance.'

He felt the boy drive deeper into the pit, and then the voice, small and reeded.

'I need you, 'Arrison.'

'Now, you have to go now.' Father and mother, didn't the little bugger understand? Time for running, time for ducking, time for weaving.

'If I go now, they will kill me.'

What was he supposed to do? Feel sorry for the little pig? Wipe his bottom for him, clean his pants out?

'We stay together, 'Arrison. That is what Franca would have done.'

724

The man and the boy, ears up, lying in the shallow hole and listening.

Around them, unseen, among the trees an army advanced, clumsy and intimidating in its approach, breaking aside the wood that impeded its progress. Closing on them, sealing them, the net tightening. Fractured and splintered branches in front and behind them, stamped leaves and curses of discomfort to right and left. And the baying of dogs.

Harrison turned his body from his side, a ponderous movement, then twisted his neck further until he could see the face of the boy. 'It is too late, Giancarlo.' He spoke with a kind of wonderment, astonished because the table was turned and the fear exchanged. 'You had to go when I said.'

'Shut up,' the boy spat back at him, but there was a shiver in his voice. And then more slowly as if the control were won with great effort, 'That is not our way.'

Carboni with his pistol drawn, Vellosi trailing in one hand a submachine-gun, Carpenter keeping with them, all were running in their own fashion down the narrow path, spurred on by the shouts of the advance, and the roars, fierce and aggressive, full and deep-throated, of the police attack dogs. They sprinted on the shadowed surface, buried in the surrealism of the dawn mist that ebbed between the tree towers.

Carpenter saw the shape of the polizia vice brigadiere materialize from the foliage at the pathside, rising to block Carboni and Vellosi. The stampede stopped, men crouched about them and struggled to control the heaving of their lungs that they might be quieter. The trees were infested, the undergrowth alive. Static from the portable radios, whispered voices, distorted replies. A council of war. Grown and elderly men on their knees, huddled to hear, the weapons in their hands.

'Carpenter, come close,' Carboni called, his voice blanket-shrouded. 'The dogs heard voices and barked. They are about a hundred metres from us. We are all around them but I do not wish to move further till there is light. We wait here for the sun.'

'Battestini, will he pack it in, will he give himself up?'

The big sad eyes rolled at Carpenter, the shoulders heaved their gesture. 'We have to try. If the spell of Tantardini is still on him . . .'

Left unsaid because Carpenter mouthed his obscenity and understood.

'But he can kill him now, while we are here.'

'We wait for the sun.' Carboni turned away, resumed the hush of conference.

This was where it all ended. In a damp wood with mud on your shoes and dirt on the knees of your trousers. Right, Archie. Where the family picnickers might have been, or boys with tents, or a kid with his condom and his girl. Only the method and the style to be decided. To be determined only whether it was champagne or a mahogany box. You're within rock-throwing distance of him, Archie. You could stand up and shout and he'd hear you. A few seconds running, you're that close. God, the bastard can't shoot him now. Not now, not after all this. Not after Violet.

The dawn came steadily, imperceptibly, winnowing behind the trees and across the leaves, cloaking the men who peered forward and fingered the mechanisms of their firearms. Drawn-out, lethargic, mocking their impatience, the light filtered into the wood.

20

Horizontal and thrusting with its brilliance, the dart of a lance, the first sunray pierced the wall of trees. The shaft picked at the ground in front of the fallen trunk, faded in the eddy of the branches, then returned. The sharpness held sway over the grey shadowed light.

It was the moment of ultimate decision for Giancarlo Battestini. Move now or be damned and finished, vulnerable to the sniper's aim, naked to the gas and nausea cartridges, open to the bone-splintering bullets of the marksmen. His hands furtive, he reached for the flex at Geoffrey Harrison's ankles, swore at the skill of his own knot, and with difficulty loosened it. By the collar of the shirt he pulled his prisoner close to him and back down into the pit, so that the wire tied to the wrists and the roots would have more play. That was easier to unfasten, the work of a few seconds.

'What are we doing, Giancarlo?'

A grim, set smile. 'We go on another journey, 'Arrison.'

'Where are we going?'

Busy with his work, scraping together the strands of wire, Giancarlo muttered, 'You will know.'

The boy bound together the length of wire that he had used on Harrison's legs to the piece now trailing from his wrists.

'Kneel upright.'

Harrison stretched himself to the extent of the pit, wriggled and turned his ankles to restore the circulation and slowly raised his head above the rim. He lifted his shoulders, tautened his spine, and grimaced at the stiffness carried by his trapped night's sleep. Giancarlo looped the wire around the front of his chest, then snuggled it behind his own back, drew it beneath his armpits and then again to Harrison's wrists.

Pressed hard against his man, the boy entwined the knot that closed them together, linked them as one. With a hand he pulled Harrison's shirt from the waist of his trousers and the metal pistol barrel was formidable against the skin in the small of Harrison's back. The front gun-sight carved a scratch line in the flesh as Giancarlo armed the weapon.

'It is a light trigger, 'Arrison. When we start you should not talk, you should not slip. My finger will barely have to move, you understand?'

Harrison nodded, the questions stifled in his throat, choked on his tongue. No more compulsion to ask questions. Just a new horror, and what use explanation? Just a new abyss, and he was plunging.

'We stand up, and carefully.'

They straightened as one, the vibrations mingled, and Giancarlo pressed his head against Harrison's collar-bone.

But your legs don't work, Geoffrey, been tied too long. You'll slip, you'll bloody stumble . . . and then the bloody trigger goes. How far does the finger move, how far . . . quarter of an inch, eighth of an inch? Concentrate, you bloody fool. One leg forward, put it down slowly, case the weight on to it, stop, put the other foot forward, test the balance, stop again, put the next foot forward . . .

Harrison looked around him, blinked in the air, drank in its freshness, felt the erosion of Giancarlo's stale breath. It was a certain sort of freedom, a certain sort of release. Breathing something other than the odour of the earth. Nothing moved at the front, but there would be an army there, concealed, close and waiting. The voice bellowed behind his ear.

'Is Carboni there?'

Ahead of them was the path that they had walked down the previous morning, long ago, separated by infinite time. The route that Giancarlo had used to get his food and to drift away down when he went to the telephone in the darkness, and it was the way the child had come.

The stream of the sun caught the three men square as they came forward on the path. They wore their badges of nationality, their flags for recognition. A short, rolling man at the front, balding, sallow. One behind him who held a submachine-gun diagonally across his waist, hair combed, the trace of a clipped moustache at his upper lip, his tie sombre and silk. The last was a stranger, clothes of a different cut, hair of a different trim, rounded shoulders and a pallor denied the Mediterranean. Two Italians and an Englishman. Harrison felt the weakness at his knees, the shake at his thighs and shins that was irresistible. The bastards had come. Long enough about it.

Harrison and Giancarlo were fused as one, responsive to each other's tremors, pliant to each other's movements. Three men facing them.

'I am Carboni.'

The words echoed in the trees, bounced from the moss-coated trunks.

Harrison felt the boy stiffen, readying himself. The last great battle, striving for strength and steel stamina.

'Listen, Carboni. This is your 'Arrison, this is your foreign dirt. I have tied him to me, and against his back, behind his heart, I have the P38. It is a hair-trigger, Carboni, tell your criminals, tell your gunmen that. If they shoot, my finger will move on the trigger . . . you are listening, Carboni? If you hit me, 'Arrison is dead. I am going to walk down the path, I am going to walk to my car. If you want 'Arrison alive, you do not impede me.'

Harrison was aware that the pressure of the circled barrel grew in his back, the impetus growing for movement.

'I am going to move forward. If you want 'Arrison, stay back.'

'What does he say?'

Carboni did not turn towards Carpenter and his sharp anxiety. He gazed on down the path at Harrison and Giancarlo. 'The boy has the gun at Harrison's back. He says it is hair-triggered. He wants to drive away from here . . .'

Vellosi, in English, because that was the language of the moment.

'Giuseppe, he doesn't walk out of here.'

'Then Harrison dies.'

'The boy cannot leave here.' The spitting whisper of the cobra.

'I am here to save Harrison.' Confusion, catastrophe ravaging at Carboni.

'If Battestini walks out of here, if he leaves the wood, he has ridiculed us. One boy and he has beaten us . . .'

'I have to save Harrison.' Carboni wavering, torn and pulled and tossed.

'We have to save Italy . . . Think, Carboni, of the implications if the boy walks clear. One against so many, and he wins because we have no courage.'

Violet Harrison dead and mangled on her back in a plastic sack on the morgue slab, incised for autopsy, viewed by pathologists. And Geoffrey Harrison to lie beside her with a pencil hole in his back and a cavity large enough to fit a lemon into at his chest. Get off your arse, Archie Carpenter. Get into the big boys' league. It's your man out there, Archie, so get off your bloody arse and get walking.

A short jab of his elbow and Archie Carpenter was past Carboni and Vellosi. Three quick strides and he was clear of them . . . and who was going to run forward to pull him back?

'Watch the boy, Carboni, watch the boy and be ready.'

*

728

Giancarlo watched him come. Saw the purposeful clean steps eat into the dividing distance. Nothing to be read from the face of the man, nothing that spoke of danger and risk, nothing from which to recognize his emotions. The command to halt, the shout, was beyond the boy. Fascinated, spellbound. And the light caught at the man's face as he passed between two trees and there was no shop window of fear. A man with a job to do, and getting it over with, and wearing a crumpled suit.

Giancarlo felt his hand on the pistol butt cavort with the weapon. He could not hold it still and motionless.

Francesco Vellosi spun on his heel, raking the trees and bushes behind him till he saw the carabinieri sergeant with the rifle, kneeling and in cover. His fingers snapped for the man's attention and he tossed the submachine-gun towards him, gestured for the rifle and caught it as it was thrown to him. The rifle slipped to his shoulder. Rock steady, unwavering, and the needle of the front sight rested centrally in the V of the rear attachment by his right eye. The line was on the small part of Giancarlo Battestini's head that was visible to him.

The void cut, the gap halved, Archie Carpenter spoke. Almost surprised to hear his own voice. Brisk and full of business.

'Geoffrey Harrison. I'm Archie Carpenter . . . does this Battestini speak English?'

No preamble, dominate from the start, the way they taught them far back, the Metropolitan Police drill on approaching an armed man.

He saw the half head on Harrison's shoulder, an unfinished ventriloquist's dummy, dumped on a perch, lacking a body. Harrison's lips moved and then his tongue brushed against them, the moisture glistening. Poor blighter's at the limit.

'He does.'

Still moving, still hacking and cutting at the intervening space, Carpenter called, 'Giancarlo . . . your name, right? . . . I've come for the gun.'

Edging his way forward, slower steps as the distance telescoped, and the spots and the beard growth on Giancarlo's face were sharp and visible, and the colour at his eyes was dark and haunted. Ten yards short and the scream from the boy.

'Stop, no closer.'

'Just the gun, Giancarlo, just give it to me.' But Carpenter obeyed and now stood his ground, fair and square across the path. Saw the sweat on the boy's forehead and the tangled skeins of his hair and the yellowed teeth.

'You move aside, you give us room . . .'

'I'm not moving. I'm here and I want the gun from you.'

Where did you get it from, Archie, which silk hat? Out of the hallway of a flat, out of the staircase of a high building, out of a woman past her break-point. Ran once, not again. Once was enough to turn the shoulder, not ever again.

'If you do not move, I shoot . . .'

'Empty threat. I don't move, you don't shoot.'

Who'd know you, Archie? The girls in the office, in the typists' pool? The men in the pub off the evening train from the City? The neighbour who borrowed the push-mower alternate Saturday mornings? Who'd know Archie Carpenter in a wood at Bracciano?

'I have the gun at his back . . .'

'I don't care where you've put the bloody thing. I don't move, you don't shoot. It's easy, a ten-year-old knows that.'

Stretching the boy. Out into the risk area, out into the storm. Watch the eyes, Archie, watch the blinking and the uncertainty and the fidget. Traversing and hesitant, and the fear's building. The bully when he's outnumbered, when the other kids come back to the playground. Careful, Archie . . . Gone past that place, off Mum's knee, playing it the grown-up way.

'You do not believe that I will shoot . . .'

'Right, Giancarlo. I don't believe it. I tell you why. You're thinking what happens if you do. I'll help you, I'll tell you. I strangle you, boy. With my hands I strangle you. There's a hundred men out there behind me that want to do it. They won't get near you. You'll be done by the time they reach you.'

Carpenter held him unswervingly. Never left the eyes of the boy. Always there when he turned back, always present. Lowering over him, heavy as a snowcloud, absorbing the hatred.

'I've no gun, but if you fire on Harrison, I'm on you. You've trussed yourself, silly boy, that's why I'll get you. I used to be a policeman, I've seen people that have been strangled. Their eyes come half out of their head, they shit themselves, they wet their legs. That's for you, so give me the gun.'

You never saw anyone strangled in your bloody life, not ever. Steady it, Archie. Turn it over, could be possible that the physical isn't the soft belly of the boy. Don't make him play the martyr, don't put coal on that fire. What else gets to a psychopath?

'I'm going to start walking, you cannot take him from me . . .' Giancarlo holding his defensive line. The rout not accomplished. 'Get out of our way.'

Harrison gazing at Carpenter, like he doesn't know what's happening, like he's out on his feet. Best bloody way. Who's going to tell Geoffrey Harrison? Who's that one down to? Archie Carpenter going to do it? Well done, Geoffrey, we're very pleased you've come out of this safely . . . excellent show . . . but there's been a bit of bother while you've been away . . . well, the missus actually . . . but you understand that, Geoffrey, good lad, thought you would . . .

Throw in the big one, Archie. Go for broke. All the chips on the green cloth, into the centre of the table.

'I saw your woman last night, Giancarlo. Raddled old bitch. Bit old for a boy, wasn't she?'

He saw the short-worn composure break on the boy's face, saw the anger lines form and then knit on his forehead.

'I wouldn't have thought a boy would be interested in a workhorse likc that.'

The blood was running fast to the boy's cheeks, the flush dispersing under his skin, the eyes slitted in loathing.

'Do you know what she called you when they interrogated her? You want to know? A little bed-wetter. Franca Tantardini's opinion on lover boy . . .'

'Get out of my way.' The words came fast and weighted by the boy's fury.

Carpenter could see the nausea rising in Geoffrey Harrison's face, the eroded self-control. Wouldn't last much longer, wouldn't sustain the supreme effort. Batter on, Archie, belt the little bastard.

The sound of the voices carried easily among the trees. Carboni had eased his pistol from the jacket pocket and it hung from his fingers as a token of participation. Beside him Francesco Vellosi still stood, eye at the gun-sight, tight in anticipation, ignoring the fly that played at his nose.

'Why does he say these things?'

Vellosi never wavered from his aim. 'Quiet, Giuseppe, quiet.'

'How many others have there been, boy, do you know? I mean, you weren't the first, were you?'

'Get out of my way . . .'

Not much longer, Archie. Hold your ground and it's disintegration time, spitting collapse. Forgetting where he is, and what he's here for, like we want him to be. Don't run now, Archie, just round the corner is Shangri-La that you came for. Almost at the fingertips, almost there to touch.

731

'They'd all been there, boy, every grubby finger, every sweaty armpit in the movement, did you know that . . . ?'

He's rising, Archie. The slimed creature forced out of the deep water. Coming for you, Archie. Hold the line, sunshine. Come on, Archie bloody Carpenter from Motspur bloody Park, don't let old Harrison down now, not when he's flaking, not when Violet's on her back and cold. Watch him, watch the struggle in the shirt. The gun comes next. You'll see the barrel, you'll see the fist on it, and the finger that's lost behind the trigger guard. Hold the bloody line, Archie.

'I wouldn't have done what you've done, not for a cow like that. You know, Giancarlo, you might even have got the scabs from her . . .'

Carpenter laughed out loud, shaking in his merriment, confronting his fear. Was laughing as he saw the pistol emerge from behind Harrison and be raised at him as fast as a snake strikes. He looked into the torture of Giancarlo's face, sucked at the agony. Well done, Archie, you made it, sunshine. First time in your bloody life, across the finish line and in front. Ludicrous, the look on the kid's face.

The gun was coming, something bright with menace from beneath a winter sea. The pistol showing, sharp and tooled, and aiming.

The one shot, the whiplash crack.

Carpenter was on the ground, thrown backwards, the involuntary reflex. Cemented and imprinted high on his face was a splitting smile.

Harrison staggered, legs weak and resisting his efforts to withstand the weight of the smitten Giancarlo dragging down the wire that wrapped their waists. Blood on Harrison's face, loose and dripping, and a mess of brain matter and no hands free to clear the sheen of destruction from his eyes.

Carboni recoiled from the explosion beside his ear. He pivoted towards Vellosi, gazed at him and saw the grim pleasure spreading like an opening flower on his companion's face.

And then the running.

Men rising from their hidden places, careering over fallen branches, bullocking through undergrowth. Carboni joined the herd as if time now were at last special. Francesco Vellosi dropped the rifle barrel with deliberation, bent down and picked up the single brass cartridge case and pocketed it. He turned and with an easy movement tossed the gun back to its owner, the carabinieri sergeant. Revenge exacted. He walked, tall and erect, towards the huddle that was gathering around Geoffrey Harrison.

With a knife a policeman sliced through the flex that held Harrison to Giancarlo Battestini. The body of the boy, shorn of its support, slumped to the ground. One half of his face was intact, unblemished and waxen; the other was obliterated, removed as if in tribute to the marksmanship and the brutal power of the high velocity bullet. Freed, rubbing hard at his wrists, Harrison dived away from his helpers, turned his back on them and vomited into the dried grass at the edge of the clearing. They gave him room, respected him.

Archie Carpenter pulled himself to his knees, rose unsteadily to his feet, and clamped his fingers together to hide the tumult and the shaking that gripped them. He stood aside, a stranger at a party.

When Harrison came back to the group, he spoke simply, without idiocy. 'What happened . . . I don't know what happened?'

Vellosi pointed across the clearing to Carpenter. 'This man was prepared to offer his life for yours.' He spoke gruffly, and then his hand slipped in support to Harrison's armpit. 'He gave himself to Battestini that you should be saved.'

Their eyes met in a fleeting moment, then Carpenter turned his head from the deep puzzlement of Harrison's gaze, and seemed to those who watched him to shrug his shoulders as if an episode had ended, a man had done his work and needed no praise nor thanks. Studiously Carpenter began to wipe the clinging leaves and sticks from his back and his trousers.

They moved from the clearing. Vellosi and Harrison setting the slow pace at the front, Carboni busy and bustling behind them, Carpenter trailing. Harrison did not look round for a final glimpse of Giancarlo's body, stumbled away, reliant on the help of the hand that helped him. They moved at cortège speed and the route along the path was lined with the unsmiling faces of men in uniform who held rifles and submachine-guns and did not flinch from the hurt daubed on Harrison's face. They masked their feelings, those who stared, because death was recent among the trees and the devastating speed of the violence had stripped from them the elation of victory.

'I didn't understand what he was doing, this man Carpenter.'

From behind Harrison's shoulder, Carboni spoke. 'He had to get the pistol from your back, he had to produce the pistol against himself if your danger were to be taken. That was why he taunted the boy. He gave the opportunity to Francesco. Francesco had a half face to shoot for. That there was the chance was because of Carpenter.'

Carboni, still walking, swung his head towards Carpenter, saw only a shaded half smile, a tint of sadness.

'My God . . . God help us.' Harrison walked with his eyes closed, led as a blind man on a street pavement. He struggled for his words,

733

confronting the shock and exhaustion. 'Why was another life . . . why was another man's life, less important than mine?'

'I don't know,' said Carboni.

'Get me home, please, get me to my wife.'

The quick light of warning flashed between the policeman and the head of the anti-terrorist squad. Carboni stopped and grabbed surely for Carpenter's sleeve and drew him forward. The procession had stopped. The four men were in a group, a huddle of shoulders, and those in uniform faded back, abandoning them.

'You have something to tell your man, Archie,' Carboni spoke in a whisper.

'Charlesworth can . . .'

'No, Archie, for you, it is your work.'

'Not here . . .'

Archie wriggling, sliding in the mud stream, seeking to extricate himself, and Harrison peering into him, unshaven face close, bad breath reeking. Come on, Archie, this is what you saved him for, this is the moment you preserved him for. Can't slip the buck to Charlesworth, can't push it further away. It's now it has to be said, and it's you who have to say it.

'It's about Violet, Geoffrey . . .' Carboni and Vellosi watched the shame driving up on Carpenter's face, realized the bewilderment creeping again into the man whose arms they held.

'What about her?'

'Violet . . . I'm sorry.'

'Where is she?' The shriek coming from Harrison, the embarrassment flowing into Vellosi and Carboni.

A sudden coldness from Carpenter, as if from this came his protection, as if his face could be hidden by chilled words. 'She's dead, Harrison. She piled into a lorry last night. She was alone.'

Vellosi and Carboni hurried forward, half carrying, half dragging the weight of Harrison between them. Carpenter detached himself and hung back. Nothing more to be said, nothing more to be done. The speed of the group quickened, past the man who stood with the broken shotgun and the small boy, past the field hedgerows, on down to the road. They slid Harrison into the back of Carboni's car, Carboni followed him, clapped his hands and the driver accelerated away.

His arm hanging from Carpenter's shoulder, Vellosi watched the car spin round the first curve.

'You did well, my friend.'

'Thank you,' said Carpenter.